Slough
COUNCIL

Community ...me

LIBRAR

SLOUGH CENTRE
STREET

RESERVE

D1420369

38067002593171

Edith Pargeter

THE
HEAVEN
TREE
TRILOGY

THE HEAVEN TREE
THE GREEN BRANCH
THE SCARLET SEED

WARNER FUTURA

A *Warner Futura* Book
First published in this omnibus edition in 1994 by
Warner Futura
THE HEAVEN TREE first published by William Heinemann in 1960
Published by Futura in 1986
Reprinted 1986, 1987, 1988, 1989
Published by Warner Futura in 1993

Copyright © Edith Pargeter 1960

THE GREEN BRANCH first published by William Heinemann in 1962
Published by Futura in 1987
Reprinted 1987, 1989
Published by Warner Futura in 1993

Copyright © Edith Pargeter in 1962

THE SCARLET SEED first published by William Heinemann in 1963
Published by Futura in 1987
Reprinted 1987, 1989
Published by Warner Futura in 1992

Copyright © Edith Pargeter in 1963

This omnibus edition copyright © Edith Pargeter 1994

The moral right of the author has been asserted

*All characters in this publication are fictitious and
any resemblance to real persons, living or dead,
is purely coincidental*

All rights reserved
No part of this publication may be reproduced,
stored in a retrieval system, or transmitted, in
any form or by any means without the prior permission
in writing of the publisher, nor be otherwise circulated
in any form of binding or cover other than that in which
it is published and without a similar condition including
this condition being imposed on the subsequent purchaser

A CIP catalogue for this book
is available from the British Library

ISBN 0 7515 0852 7

Printed in England by Clays Ltd, St Ives plc

Warner Books
A Division of
Little, Brown and Company (UK) Limited
Brettenham House
Lancaster Place
London WC2E 7EN

Contents

Introduction

The Heaven Tree, the first volume of this trilogy, came to birth as the incidental offspring of a course of lectures on the nature of art. Discussion set me thinking of large questions. What is an artist? And beyond that: What is a great artist? And what must it be like to be a great artist, with that special perception of harmony, proportion and balance which identifies greatness, in a world which has never so far distinguished itself by conspicuous display of any of these qualities? So I set out to discover whether I could create a truly great artist, make him convincing, and set him firmly in his own society, whenever and wherever that might turn out to be.

Since I wanted greatness, I went for the highest achievement I could think of, and found it in the exquisite churches of the purest period of Early English architecture, around 1200 to 1250, the relatively brief period of the peculiarly English style of carving referred to as "stiff leaf." So England had to be the scene, round about 1220 the time, my own county and the Welsh border the place.

In a world arbitrarily organized into hierarchies, whether determined by feudal blood, commercial wealth, land-holding or force of arms, I suspected and found that the artist must always be to some degree a displaced person, outlawed by and contemptuous of the flawed system that makes artificial differences between men. Conflict began early for my artist, and stayed with him lifelong, as I had always suspected it must. Whether great work is achieved in spite of this, or is molten into resplendent and indignant shape because of it, I am not a great enough artist to determine.

One book only was intended, but time and place had drawn into the story a number of figures, some historical, some my own, whom I could not dismiss from my mind. It was a year or more before I began work on the remaining two books, which were originally conceived as one but outgrew the conception. The truth was, I could not leave my remaining characters dispersed and uncompleted. I had to find out what became of them. They mattered to me far too much to be abandoned.

So here they are, the artist who creates, the turbulent world that destroys, and the communicable passion that proves indestructible.

It is my own personal conviction that this trilogy is the best thing I have done. The best piece of writing, the story best worth telling, the characters most formidably alive, the theme best worth pursuing to the end: The work that came nearest what I wanted it to be.

THE
HEAVEN
TREE

PART ONE

THE WELSH MARCHES

1200

Chapter One

*T*he angel, eternally alighting with arched wings and delicate, stretched feet, spread his hands palms outwards towards the radiance, and bowed in ceremonious humility the youthful, narrow head, with its long gold hair still erect and quivering from his flight. The shuddering hum of his great wings hung perpetually upon the astonished air, for ever stilling and never stilled. His eyes, half-averted from the unbearable brightness, had themselves a brilliance not to be borne, and his face was as taut and fierce as the body arrested for ever in the instant of alighting, straining downwards from breast to loin to thigh to instep, silver sinews braced and quivering under the frozen turmoil of the gilded robe. He touched the earth with long, naked, shapely feet, and the earth gave forth a brazen cry, and the tremulous air vibrated like a bowstring along the descending arc of his passage from heaven.

In the shadowy spaces above him the creator bent his head to look upon his work, and saw that it was good.

Ebrard came to fetch them home from Shrewsbury on a green morning some days after Easter, with his fledgling knighthood glossy and stiff upon him like new clothes, and three armed grooms at his back to keep him in good conceit of himself. They waited at the gatehouse to salute him dutifully as he dismounted, Harry with a brotherly kiss, Adam with a deep reverence. And Abbot Hugh de Lacy came limping through the bustle of the great court to bless their departing. He was lame of the left leg from a certain hunting affray in his youth, when a wounded boar had brought down both him and his horse, and the moist spring season always gnawed hard at the place where his bones had knit awry. He had taken boar and wolf and deer in his time, and not always with license; but that was before he donned the cowl and fixed his sights upon the mitre.

He held them before him by the shoulders, and: "Well, boys," said he, "you are in a fair way to be men. Keep fast what you have learned here among us, and make good use of it in the stations to which you are called, and you will do well. You have both Latin and French, have you not?"

"Yes, Father."

"And some knowledge and skill in music?"

"Yes, Father."

"And of your gifts in the carving of wood and stone we have good reason to be glad, for they have enriched our house." Better, perhaps, not to dwell on that. Harry was going to miss his chisels and punches all too sorely, he needed no reminders. And yet Hugh de Lacy could not forbear from smiling with pleasure at the thought of the little wooden angel on the Virgin's altar, fifteen inches tall and browed like his creator, with the same deep-arched eyelids, the same half-hidden glitter of brilliant eyes, the same narrow, fiery face. Every maker, when he first sets his hands to work, makes an image of himself, whether he will or no. God made man in his own image; Harry was in good company. Plagued by the likeness without recognising the source of his unease, the subprior had never liked that angel. To his orderly mind it seemed proper, no doubt, that only demons, not ministers of grace, should be thus abrupt and terrible.

"All these are of God's giving, and faithfully to be used and valued. And I trust you have as good a grounding in the courses of the spirit, and will hold fast to that learning above all."

"Yes, Father," piped the dark boy and the fair boy in amiable unison. They were listening to him with no more than one ear between them, and he knew it. What boy of fifteen can be bothered with homilies on the day of his escape from school?

They stood before him side by side, Harry swart and wiry and small, with the bold chin and jutting bones and straight, adventurous mouth of his line, Adam gay and fair, half a head taller than his lord, with blue, merry eyes in a face like a wide-open flower. He saw their hands linked in the shelter of their bodies, and the swift exchange of their glances, so eloquent that they had little need of words between them. Separating them, even for an hour, was like wrenching apart one flesh. Yet the one was son to a villein craftsman, and the other distant kin to the great earl himself, the founder of the house, who lay under his massy stone in the Lady Chapel, mouldering in the kirtle of Saint Hugh.

The Talvaces of Sleapford were descended from a bastard half-brother of Earl Roger's first countess, who had attached himself to the earl's fortunes at the invasion of England, and established him-self in a comfortable manor within the honour of Montgomery, with the status of a knight, rights of warren over the forest land he held, and a Saxon wife who commanded the allegiance of two villages, and gave him a measure of security. The family were still proud of reproducing in every generation his face, as well as his name, and traced with care every stage of their relationship with the lords of Belesme, Ponthieu and Alençon.

Ebrard had the name, but Harry had the face. Only his eyes, so often veiled under heavily-lashed lids, and so startling when he raised them, set him apart. The lashes and brows were almost black, but the eyes, when they looked up, were between blue and green like the mid sea, flecked with grey and golden lights, restless and changing, the eyes of the dowerless girl from Brittany who had given birth to the founder of his line.

"Be obedient to your elder, Harry, as is due, deal faithfully for him when you come into your office, and you will do well."

"Yes, Father," said the meek voice patiently.

The spring and the century were new, and the sparkling morning was made for new beginnings; and Harry, to do him justice, had shown some sense of the occasion, for his best cotte was well brushed, and his person so combed and washed that Ebrard might justifiably have failed to recognise the reluctant urchin who had been despatched to the abbey of Shrewsbury five years ago, with a smarting tail but with his foster-brother by the hand as the dual reward of his tears and obstinacy. And the more fool Eudo for letting him have his way, but how many wiser men, before and since, had fallen exhausted into the same error?

"And you, Adam, work diligently at your trade, and doubt not that God values the honest mason as he values the honourable knight and the learned clerk, for his offices are legion."

Better not to have made so pointed a distinction between them; what did it achieve but to make Harry cling ever more stubbornly to his breast-brother? The abbot smoothed his lean, patrician cheek, and wished from his heart that the boy had never been allowed to run wild in Boteler's yard, and discover the dexterity of his hands and the audacity of his imagination. From this day he was to make his future in keeping the manor rolls of Sleapford, exacting from his father's free tenants their due rents, and from his villeins their three days of labour weekly, and their five days in the harvest, and their merchets and heriots and tallages. What better could be done for him, younger son as he was, and born to an estate too circumscribed to be worth dividing? At least he had gained by an education which was thought unnecessary for his father's heir, who could barely write his aristocratic name. If there was to be no knighthood for Harry, neither was there Latin for Ebrard.

"There, I have done! I know you have good sense in you. Only bear it in mind that you have here a friend to whom you may come in your need, at whatever time. Be gentle and patient with your charges, Ebrard, authority has its obligations, too."

Ebrard stooped to the extended hand a head fair as flax. At nineteen he was already touching six feet, with his pretty mother's blooming rose-and-white complexion and long, fine bones. His knighthood was only a few months old, and still fitted uneasily. Hugh de Lacy still remembered the solemnities in the hall of Shrewsbury castle at the Christmas feast, and the loud guffaw which had risen from the rear ranks of the young gentlemen attendant when Ebrard, pale and exalted, had stepped on the hem of his robe in rising, and almost fallen on his face before the king's castellan. Sir Eudo Talvace, luckily, had not identified the voice of his younger

son, but the abbot had, and so had poor Ebrard, withdrawing from
the hall with a face like a peony. Rumour had it that the first act of
his knighthood had been to beat his brother soundly for it, and small
blame to him. Those two were eternally at odds. The abbot had not
failed to remark the hard blue glance that swept Harry from crown
to shoe when they met, expecting defiance, or the aggressive way
the boy instantly jutted his chin at his elder. He wondered which
had come first, the defiance or the expectation. There was no dislike
in it; they would both have been astonished had anyone ventured
to doubt that they loved each other as brothers should. Oil and
water bear each other no ill-will. Nevertheless, it was touch and go
whether they would get as far as Sleapford without coming to blows.

"God be with you, children. I wish you the pleasantest of journeys. When next you come to Shrewsbury, I look to see you at my
table."

Harry rode without any of his brother's graces, but his loose,
inattentive ease would outlast Ebrard's erect, self-conscious gallantry. That comes of not being apprenticed to the trade of arms,
thought the abbot, looking them over. To Harry a horse is a convenient means of moving from place to place, and he feels no more
exalted in mounting it, and no more disgraced should he fall off it,
than does a travelling journeyman. To Ebrard a horse is the symbol
of his status. Fall off that, and he falls off his own self-esteem;
which would be a dangerous fall.

He watched them file through the gateway, Ebrard in the lead,
Harry and Adam already jostling and laughing behind him. The
villein's boy was the handsomest of the three, with his ready smile,
and the hood of his capuchon pushed back to uncover his yellow
hair and sturdy brown neck. And a nature, into the bargain, as
sunny and candid as his face. No wonder Harry clung to him.

Time will take care of all, the abbot told himself; and yet he was
not comforted. Time had had long enough to ease them apart without pain, and had but bound them more stubbornly into one. Why,
he thought with exasperation, as he turned back towards the cloister,
could not Eudo's wife have been a lusty creature like Boteler's, able
to suckle her own child? Or why must Eudo be such a fool with him
afterwards? The time to coax them away from each other was long
ago, as soon as they could ride or run, and that old dotard was too

engrossed in his heir to see the need for care with this one. Had he but cast a father's eye on Harry in time, and sent some other body-servant here with him in Adam's place, maugre his tears and tantrums, he might have spared both himself and the boy God knows what of trouble to come.

Or why, since they were so made as to love each other out of all reason, could not those two young creatures have been born true brothers, predestined alike to the mason's bench? What, and both unfree?

What is freedom? thought the abbot, turning to cast a last look after the twins who were no twins. Tell me, if you know, which of those two is bond, and which is free?

They passed by the mill, where the outlet of the abbey pool fell back into the brook, and the brook curved and leaped the last few paces to the river. The heavy wains passed in and out, lumbering down from the town over the stone bridge. The abbey mills had a monopoly of the multure for the whole town, and the prior saw to it that their rights were not infringed, for they brought in more money than all the rents on this side of the river.

Severn's flood was high but placid, pale, silvery blue under the open sky, grey-brown beneath the bushy banks. Its level had dropped a yard within the last day, and the time of the spring spate was already passing. Beyond the bridge the hill of Shrewsbury rose, double-girdled with rolling water and towered wall, and to the right, where the river left a neck of land unprotected, the broad, squat shape of Earl Roger's castle straddled the promontory, its crenellated towers gnawing at the sky. Between the castle and the bridge all the slope outside the wall nursed the terraces of the abbot's vineyard. Gnarled and black, as yet hardly budding, the vines showed like thorns.

"You and your angel!" Adam said cheerfully, as they turned south on the near side of the bridge, and crossed the brook. "What is there so wonderful about it? I believe you'd steal it back if you could. All the angel, and not a word of the rest of the work. Don't you like the capitals you carved?"

"They're well enough, I suppose, but they're only copies. No, not copies, exactly. You remember Master Robert's drawings from

Canterbury? I had those in mind when I made my designs. I didn't copy, but I made nothing new. Myself I knew it only when they were lifted into place. Anyone could have made them."

"Oh, you're too nice! Don't you think every man who carves makes use of what other men have carved before him? Must everything *you* do be the first of its kind? Though it's true," said Adam wickedly, "that you found quite a new way with the quintain last Shrove Tuesday. Man, that was alone of its kind, if you like! I never saw a fellow clouted so far across the green—"

It had not been the first and would not be the last of Harry's spectacular failures in the field of manly exercise, and he had no strong feelings about his downfall, but he felt obliged to lean across and take Adam round the neck at this, and haul him sidelong off-balance. Adam clawed one-handed at the pommel of his saddle to keep his seat, and with the other arm clipped Harry about the body. They wrestled together precariously, panting and giggling, and the horses, accustomed to this kind of foolery, sidled to a stop, and stood gently nuzzling. Like Adam, they accepted without comprehending. Adam threw his weight back in the saddle, and tried to heave his lighter opponent bodily from his mount, but Harry dug the fingers of his free hand into the brown tunic and the straining ribs under it, and tickled him until he was writhing in a helpless agony of laughter and distress.

"No! Stop! Harry, you'll have me down!"

"I will have you down, and no mercy! Beg my pardon! Do you ask pardon? Do you?"

Ebrard had turned in the saddle, and cried to them peremptorily to come on and stop their antics. His voice had such a ring of displeasure that it split them apart sharply. Even at that distance they could see how blackly he frowned. They shook themselves hastily into some semblance of order, and spurred forward to overtake him, still muttering breathless recriminations, still giggling.

"For God's sake, must you always be fooling? Have you not had long enough time for play?" Ebrard waited for them with a curling lip and an irascible eye. "Before I was fifteen I was in my second year of service with FitzAlan, and expected to behave like a man, and not like a brawling brat of seven or eight years. And you had better learn the trick of it, young Harry, for your soft years among the good brothers are over. I wonder Father kept you there so long, frolicking away your time to so little purpose. I've heard of your stone-cutting and your wood-carving, and your other antics, and even something of your verses, but little enough of any sensible accomplishments. Do you think Father put you to school, and spared you the rigours of a man's life, so that you could tussle like a mongrel puppy, and whittle wood?"

"Here's a sermon over a few minutes' fooling!" said Harry, with a mild face and a conciliatory voice, falling in meekly at his brother's elbow. "I promise you my Latin will be a match for old Edric's, and I can reckon well enough to keep abreast of all your debtors. I haven't wasted all my time."

"It's hard to believe you've hoarded much of it, or you'd have outgrown your childish ways by now. Does it speak well for your masters or you when a son of the Talvaces is seen romping on the high road like a village hind? And you, Master Adam, let me counsel you not to abet him so readily. You are too free with these hands of yours."

As he spoke he flicked the short riding-whip he carried so that the tip of it slapped lightly across the back of Adam's bridle-hand. It was a gesture rather than a blow, and only sheer surprise caused Adam to clap the palm of his other hand to the sting. Harry was the one who started and caught his breath, Harry was the one who blanched with rage and lunged forward in the saddle as though he would fly at his brother's throat. Ebrard was between his two charges, and Adam could not even reach to pluck at the raised arm, or kick exasperatedly at an ankle to recall Harry to sense. He leaned forward, frowning and shaking his head vehemently to silence the threatened outburst. For a moment they hung close together all three, in a tension which made the horses toss and quiver uneasily; then it was all over.

Harry dropped his hands, and sat back in the saddle. The flesh round his mouth and nostrils was lividly pale; the line of his jaw stood out whitely, and for a moment he dared not unclench it for fear of what would burst forth. Then he swallowed the bitter residue of his rage, and said with arduous calm: "That's unfair! It was I first laid hands on him, he did no more than take hold of me to keep his balance."

"I can well believe it was you began it. But it's high time he showed some sense of his own, since you have none. You allow him too much familiarity with you, and he takes it too easily for granted. You had better not let father see how little you prize yourself, to play the fool with him in this fashion." Ebrard spurred from between them and rode ahead, looking back for a moment over his shoulder. "Now come on! We're losing time."

Adam, who had long ago learned to bend before these passing storms, waited resignedly for Harry to provoke fate by shouting some furious last word after his elder, and marvelled that no words came. It was something new if Harry was learning sense enough to hold his tongue. They drew together in silence for comfort, and rode side by side, subdued by a chagrin which seemed to them both far too great for the occasion. Adam felt Harry's angry grief heavy upon his heart. Why must he always make so much of such slight things?

A year ago Adam would have shaken him by the shoulder without a second thought, and told him roundly not to be a fool. Even now, though with an unaccustomed timidity, he reached out a hand to touch Harry's arm, and then, hesitating with his eyes on Ebrard's irate back, withdrew again wretchedly before his fingers brushed the green homespun sleeve. He had already been warned that he took too many liberties, the last thing he wanted was to give Ebrard even the slenderest of reasons to elaborate on the same text.

Harry glimpsed the uncompleted gesture out of the tail of his eye, and turning violently but silently, caught at the hand as it drew away, and held it hard, all the harder when Adam, jerking his head warningly towards Ebrard, sought to free himself from the convulsive grip. The print of the whip, a mere snake-tongue of red, had already almost faded from sight, but Harry stared at it as at a mortal wound, and would not let him go.

By the quarry of Rotesay, in mid-afternoon, a dray with a team of horses was slowly straining out of the cutting on to the road, laden with the dove-grey stone. Almost axle-deep in the mud which peeled away from the iron shoes coloured smoothly grey as the rock, it groaned round the difficult curve with a shoving shoulder at every wheel, and came up on to sounder ground with a great sucking sigh.

Ebrard slowed up to pass by, and just as the boys drew alongside the dray it pulled slowly out of the shadow of trees into the sunlight. The stone flushed and fired into an overglow of pale, creamy gold, like a halo round its soft greyness.

Harry's face took fire with it. He reached for Adam's sleeve, forgetting all resolutions of discretion. "Look at it! Did you ever see such a beautiful colour? Oh, this is what I should like to build in! Think of a church built in a stone like that, think of it on a spring day, half sunshine and half cloudy—a face changing like a woman's, every moment new. It would come to life afresh every morning."

"It's a good stone," allowed Adam, studying it with a craftsman's eye as his father would have done. "It works well, too. Not too hard for carving, but hard; they say it weathers like granite. There's another quarry that has a like stone, and freer working, but it's too near the Welsh border to be safe. I was there once with father, I remember the play of light on the cut face, it was like a mine of sunshine."

"As big a quarry as this?"

"Three times as big!"

"Keep it in mind for when we build our church. I shall need an assured supply." He clenched his fingers on Adam's arm, and shook it in his excitement. "I know now—I'm just beginning to know— how I would have a church look." Not like the abbey church, he thought, for the first time consciously rejecting that heavy, impregnable splendour. Those great round arches led his eyes upwards only to turn them downwards again like the trajectory of a stone. A church ought not to feel like a sealed grave, or look like the motionless leaden landscape of an eternal frost.

"Do you know, Adam, what I was thinking in the Lady Chapel this morning? I was thinking that if I had my way I would have Earl Roger's tomb out of there. I stood looking at it, and it made me so angry. There it stands where space should be, so that the lines of the aisle could bring a man straight to the altar—"

"—and to your angel," said Adam gaily.

"Leave my angel be, I'm serious!—and the lines of the arches could enclose a body of light. And instead, there's that ugly thing that breaks up all the planes and puts an encumbrance where space should be, and darkness where light should be. I would throw it out, and never hesitate."

"As well you didn't say so. Even Father Hugh would have been shocked." Adam picked his way past the slow-moving team, and kept his voice low, for Ebrard, so much more susceptible to shock from such sacrilege than the abbot, was only a few yards ahead. "Remember you once told Father Subprior as much about the crucifix above the rood-screen? You said it spoiled the lines of the roof, and ought to come down. My soul, but he did his best to spoil the lines of you!"

"I was too honest, but I was right. And I never took it back, either." He looked back lovingly over his shoulder, caressing the smooth, honey-coloured faces of the stone with his eyes.

"Oh, Adam, I tell you, stone is the thing! Wood is beautiful, but stone is better! Stone is best of all!"

Chapter Two

*A*fter the long, parched day in the harvest fields it was warm and drowsy in the corner of the hall next to the staircase, and Harry's head nodded over the manor survey.

"In the village of Sleapford there are 28 full villeins, and in the hamlet of Teyne 13, each holding one yardland. Sleapford has 12 half villeins, and Teyne has 5, each holding one half yardland. The full villeins work 3 days a week until the feast of Saint Peter, and 5 days thence until Michaelmas, the half villeins in proportion with their tenures. Sleapford has 14 cottagers, and Teyne has 5—"

He knew it almost by heart, down to the number of pigs and sheep and draught oxen on the manor farm, and the smallest penny rents from the hill intakes, hewn out of the waste above Teyne by enterprising younger sons, who, like Harry himself, had no inheritance to look forward to. He thought it a waste of time to copy it out afresh, for it was some years old, and he could as easily have been writing down for them a new and up-to-date survey. But it was not policy to reveal just how well he knew his father's business, or his father's tenants and villeins. So he copied laboriously but good-humouredly, and let them congratulate themselves that he was learning his trade. Soon the light would fail, and he would be let off for the evening. And the day had been beautiful. He had only to close his eyes to see again the bright gold, shimmering selions of still standing corn, curving gently in their S-bends over the vast sunlit field, and the dusty, trampled green headlands between, and the bristling pallor of the stubble where the grain had already been reaped and carted. And Adam, doing day-labour on his father's behalf, brown and ruddy and bare-legged, laughing and whistling as he swung his sickle. He could still feel the dry prickling of the new stubble against his ankles, and see the languid flight of butterflies low among the straw, and in the baked headlands the tiny scarlet and black harvest moths fluttering in colonies, like flowers in a fresh wind, and the vetches and the pimpernels dimmed with the golden dust of summer. The taste of the field ale was still in his mouth, and the ticklish, warm grain-scent in his nostrils.

Old Edric, his father's clerk for thirty years, peered and grimaced and shook his head over his pupil's round, boyish hand. It was the end of Harry's first week of keeping the rolls, and it was the master, not the apprentice, who would be answerable to his lord for the accuracy of the records.

"Here is an error, Harry. You have written Lambert among the villeins at work today in the gore by the meadows. He was not there. I remarked his absence."

The devil! thought Harry, who knew very well where Lambert had spent his day, with his two dun greyhounds and his bow, while every other man in the shire was absorbed in the harvest. There was no better poaching month than August. "But surely he was there? Did we not meet him with the ox-wain on his way back to the field? Surely you remember?"

"It was Leofric leading the oxen," said the old man, but somewhat shaken by the boy's conviction.

"There were two men with the wain, sir. Lambert was walking behind with the goad. He was singing. You can't have forgotten!" He saw, with some astonishment, that he had the advantage. Was it possible that the old fool was beginning to doubt his own memory? "Let it stand," he said quickly, seeing his father's bulky body rolling ponderously down the staircase from the solar, "and in the morning I'll ask the reeve to confirm what I've written, and correct it if it need correction. But you will find I am not mistaken." That was a prevarication of which he felt ashamed, but he could not have Lambert betrayed to the foresters. He would have to be out early in the morning, and warn both Lambert and the reeve what their story was to be; and not without extracting a promise that the truant would put in his day-labour faithfully for the rest of the harvest. If he had salted away the venison from even one beast, he owed that much thanks for it.

"Well, well, let it stand, then, and do you see to it in the morning. You have made very few errors, child, that I will allow." And mercifully he closed the roll, as Sir Eudo lumbered down the last steps of the stairs, and rustled through the rushes to their corner. Ebrard was with him, flushed with fresh sunburn to the cap-mark on his brow, his fair hair bleached still whiter by the sun. He had been out all the afternoon flying a half-trained merlin on a creance, and the reel of cord was still in his gloved hand. A warmth of content came into the hall with him, and a smell of the stable and the mews.

Sir Eudo hooked a stool rustling through the rushes with one booted foot, and sat down with the vast, satisfied sigh of a fat, ageing but healthy man. "Well, how is our clerk shaping?"

"He has made strides, Sir Eudo, strides. This week past he has kept the rolls himself, unaided, and I have but very little fault to find with him, unless it be in his hand, and time and practice will mend that."

"So he gets his accounts right," said Sir Eudo bluntly, scrubbing in his thick, grizzled beard with hard fingers, with a sound that reminded Harry of the stubble in the fields whispering against his shoes. "I care not if he write the crabbedest fist that ever marred vellum." He looked at his younger son over the bristling hairiness of his cheeks with twinkling brown eyes, a little reddened about the rims with old ale and sack, a little shrunken with the enclosing fat of age and good living, but very bright and shrewd.

"Speak up, Harry, what is there needing my attention about the place? Did Walter Wace send me his idiot son again to do his day-labour for him? I'll have his hide if he try it but once more, and he with four great lads in their wits."

"No, sir, he sent Michael, and I think you had the best of the

four. He could not in any case send you Nicholas, for the poor
fellow's sick. You know he was always a weakly soul—"

"I know he would not work," said Sir Eudo smartly; "not reeve
nor bailiff nor steward could make him stir his stumps."

"To my mind, sir, Nicholas has ailed since he was born, and it
was shame that Walter should send him to the fields at all." Harry
reached for the roll and opened it before him, to give himself time
to quench the jealous tremor in his voice when he spoke of the
gentle, uncomplaining imbecile. Wace would be glad if Nicholas
died, and so removed from his household one hungry mouth and
two unprofitable hands. But Harry, when he was a four-year-old
tumbling about the meadows with Adam, had learned the names of
the flowers in the grass from that same mouth, and been tenderly
restrained from the brook and the marlhole by those same hands.
He frowned over the tally, and said slowly, because this was an
opportunity and he must make a quick assessment of how best to
use it: "There are only a few matters needing your eye, Father.
First, in the matter of Thomas Harnett's rent, which is still overdue.
You remember he had an accident, and has been unable to tend to
his craft, and you allowed him extra time to pay his debt. It is still
unpaid, but if—"

"But if!" said Ebrard lazily, making fast the end of his reel.
"Where's the need of 'but ifs'? If he does not pay, he has a fine
horse that would pay the score for him handsomely. What does a
wheelwright want with a beast like that?"

"If I may speak, sir—I would not distrain on him. If you would
extend his time by two months, I think you would gain by it, for
his wife and the girl have near killed themselves ploughing and
sowing and harrowing his few acres, and have brought him in the
best crop for years. It is still standing. If you distrain," said Harry
trying not to sound triumphant too soon, "they will be slower
getting in the grain, and who knows how long this weather will
hold? They may lose all, and you the full payment—for he'll be a
less profitable tenant if he lacks a horse."

The old knight peered hard at him, but he kept his eyes on the
roll, and his face impartial. Sir Eudo grunted, and eased up the sleeve
of his cotte above a massy arm. "Well, well, I'll not close on him
until the harvest's in. Let him have his two months. What next?"

"There is a debt outstanding from Giles of Teyne, who has not paid his Easter tribute of eggs this year, nor his two shillings at St. Peter's feast."

"Nor ever will," said Ebrard, "if you distrain on every poor pot in his hovel. He does nothing but drink and fish. The whole of his yardland would not bring him in a penny if it rested with him to work it, it's the boy who makes shift to get a crop from it. Has he presented himself for the harvest?"

"Giles? Not he! He sent poor Wat to do that for him, too. He was dropping on his feet with weariness, for he'd worked as long as the light held last night on his father's land, after leaving ours. And so he will tonight, I know. Father, may I speak to the reeve, and have him send the boy back if he come tomorrow? He is not yet fourteen; we have a good legal case to refuse him as not fulfilling the terms, not being of age."

"And let Giles off his dues? No, not for all Salop, boy! What sort of fool's talk is that?"

"No, sir, I never meant it so. Giles would then be legally responsible for his own default. Charge him with it, take it from him in whatever goods he has—"

"He has nothing worth the taking, and you know it. As shiftless a lout as ever tickled trout in the brook yonder. I should never get my dues."

"He has a big body and a rogue's smile," said Ebrard, "plausible properties. Sell him. Or give him to the oratory, if no buyer offers. It would be worth it to get rid of him."

"And his yardland with him? They would not thank me for him without it, I promise you."

"If I may venture, Sir Eudo," said old Edric, "I would advise rather that you sell the boy Wat. He is a bright, well-grown lad, and the abbey at Shrewsbury would have him gladly to train for their company of archers, without any question of land, since he holds none. As soon as he turns fourteen the sale may be made. You would get a fair price for him, and they a fair property for their price. And as for the boy, it would be the making of him. Then you may hale up Giles for labour, and if he do not come you may have justice on him, for he'll have no other to send in his place."

Sir Eudo threw back his grizzled head, as round as a horse-chestnut, and sent a bellowing laugh up into the smoke-stained roof of the hall. "That's well thought of, old fellow. I'll do it! Make a note of it, Harry, make a note of it!"

Harry sat staring at him with eyes very wide in a startled face. "Sell him? Sell Wat? But his mother—! Father, you'll not do it! He'll break his heart." This had gone hideously wrong where he had thought there was nothing to go wrong. What did he care, what would the boy and his mother care, if their lord tossed that profitless husband and father into prison for his defaults? He had thought nothing worse than that could happen, and now Edric, of all people, had launched this dreadful alternative upon him. "Sell—!" The word stuck in his throat. He saw the sleepy boy rubbing his eyes with the back of the hand in which he held the sickle, and again, in his memory, reached over the naked shoulder and took the blade from him. "Go into the rickyard and find a quiet corner, and sleep. You hear me? I'll call you at noon for your dinner, never fear!" The hay made him a better bed than he enjoyed at home, and the bread and pork and ale was such plenty as he seldom tasted. "Sell Wat!" How often had he known this happen, and thought nothing of it!

"God's life, boy, what are you babbling about now? If I choose to transfer one of my villeins to the abbey, why should I not? Have I the right to do it, or have I not?"

"Yes, Father, I know you have, and I know you mean it kindly for Wat, too. But—"

But *sell* him! Like a bolt of cloth, or a bushel of flour, or a side of flesh in a butcher's shop. The same transaction, the money passes and the goods pass.

"But, but, but—" Sir Eudo's colour was rising, and he had begun to bawl. "What's amiss with you, Harry? Will the child be the better off, or not? Will he eat better and more regularly than ever in his life, and get a good coat to his back, and more kindness than ever he knew at home? Tell me that!"

"Yes, Father, I know he will. But what will his mother do without him?"

"Thank God and me for putting him out of his father's reach, if she has a fondness for him."

And that was probably true, too, for indeed she had a fondness, and she would think first of that safe, well-fed, well-clothed, justly

used life opening before him, and the word "sell" would not stick
in her throat. But Harry could not get it down, though for the life
of him he could not have said why it so suddenly offended and
repelled him. He said no more. He himself had a notion that he
was being a fool. He looked down at his own hands, folded rather
nervously on the roll. This right one had held the sickle when he
took it from the boy. The two hands on the haft had lain side by
side, like as two blades of grass, browned by the sun, rippling with
the constant motion of life, which even in stillness is never utterly
still. One hand could be sold, the other could not. Free and unfree.
Adam—!

"You are surely right, sir," he said in a low voice. "I am new to
this, I pray you pardon me." All the same, he protested within
himself, food, clean bed, clothes, gentleness and all, he will not want
to go. Before you send him away he'll weep all night. Foolishly, but
has he no right to be foolish, just because he is unfree?

"Well, well, you have much to learn, Harry," said Sir Eudo
gruffly, almost as rapidly mollified as roused. "That matter is settled. What else?"

"Arnulf wants to marry off his daughter." This was the most
ticklish business of all, but now he was too deeply shaken for subtlety, and could only blurt it out baldly and hope for a happy issue.

"Does he so? Well, so he may, if he can pay his merchet for her."

"He is in some difficulty, Father, and he begs that you will remit
a part of the merchet until he can pay it after the harvest. And since
it rests with you to fix the amount, and he has been always a good
man to you, I venture to ask it of you on his behalf that you will
abate the fine as much as may be fair."

"Well, you are forward to bargain for him. I hope you may be as
assiduous for your brother when you come to be in office. But
Arnulf is a good fellow, I grant you that. Which daughter is it he
wants to marry?"

"The elder, Father. Hawis."

"What, the girl that weaves mother's homespuns?" put in Ebrard,
pushing away with his foot the two greyhound puppies that rolled
and played in the rushes. "You'd better content her, Father, she'll
take out her price in good woollens if need be, and mother would
be pleased to gratify her."

Harry flashed him a look whose startled gratitude he did not bestir himself to understand. "Yes, Hawis is the webster, she wove the cloth you are wearing, sir."

"Why, then, for so useful a lass—Wait a moment, not too fast! Who is the bridegroom? Is he our man?"

No help for it now. If he hoped to maintain any pretence of innocence and detachment he could do no other than answer the question promptly, though it was the very inquiry he had most wished to avoid. As smoothly as he could he replied: "No, sir, he is from Hunyate, Stephen Mortmain by name. Arnulf gives him a good report for a sober, hardworking fellow who will make Hawis a good husband."

"Hunyate?" A spark of calculation kindled in Sir Eudo's small, bright eyes. "So he's le Tourneur's man, is he?"

Harry frowned over the roll and held his breath. Keep silence now, and let him think so, and he'll not stand in their way. He'll even deprive mother of her cloths if he can make a virtual present of an expert webster to Sir Roger le Tourneur. Villein wife goes with villein husband, and he sees Sir Roger's lady sweetened with Hawis's homespuns, and urging her husband to come to terms with his neighbour, and be friends.

Two years Sir Eudo had spent in wooing his old rival and enemy so that they might join forces to palisade their two territories against the growing encroachments of the Welsh of Powis, and two years Sir Roger had fended him off dourly, and avoided discussing the matter. His forest land stood higher and was less vulnerable than the soft valley of Sleapford under its flank, which was the reason Sir Eudo had such need of his goodwill. The transfer of Hawis, valuable property as she was, might well turn the scale. Harry feigned preoccupation with his own scrawled figures, held his peace, and waited in a chilly sweat for his father to rumble on.

"Are you deaf, boy?" roared the old knight irascibly. "Answer my question! Is he le Tourneur's man?"

"I'm sorry, Father, I have been remiss, I made no note of that, and I am not sure—"

"Harry, Harry!" Old Edric leaned forward across the table and shook him kindly by the arm. "Have you forgotten? We spoke of this same matter, and I told you." He looked up placatingly at his

master, and said gently: "He has worked a long day, Sir Eudo, and
he does himself less than justice, for indeed he did take up that
point."

If Harry could have reached him he would have kicked him under
the table, but now it was already too late. The kind old fool had
blurted out the truth: "Stephen Mortmain is a free man."

"Free? Free, is he?" Sir Eudo lumbered to his feet with an ominous
roar, and jerked up Harry's face by the chin. "What are you about,
you rogue? Do you dare try and gull me? You knew, none so
well, that he was free! Did you not, eh?" He released him with a
shake, and by way of admonition fetched him a blow on the ear that
almost swept him from his stool. "Try and deceive me again, and
I'll teach you better sense."

"Father, I wasn't—I can't keep everything clear in my mind yet,
the work's new to me—"

"Very well, let us leave it so. But mind me, Harry, never be
subtle with me, or you'll rue it. In whose interest, for God's sake,
have I set you down to make your surveys and scratch your ci-
phers—mine, or theirs?"

Harry said sullenly: "I conceive, sir, that there should be no
conflict. Master and men should be as one, and have one interest.
If they are content and well-provided, they are of the more value to
you, and serve you with the better will."

"You talk like a priest and a fool rolled in one, boy. Keep a shut
mouth until you have lived a few years more and got a little common
sense. And leave the judgements to me. All I want of you is true
accounting. True, I said! Not this juggling with truth and lies. Well,
so we have it now! This Stephen is a free man, is he? And wants to
take from me one of my best chattels, for nine of your judges out
of ten will swear a free man makes a free wife and free issue. And
Arnulf wants me to abet the theft of my maid by remitting the
merchet for her, does he? No, by God! I would have let her pass
into Tourneur's hands. But give us both the slip? Not unless Arnulf
pay for it handsomely! Thirty shillings is my price and let him be
thankful I set it no higher. You may tell him so!"

"But, Father, he has only two-thirds of a yardland, and no son,
and the two girls and their grandam to feed—where should he get

thirty shillings, or twenty, either? If he sold all the gear he owns he could not raise so much."

"Then the girl remains unmarried. I have named my price for her, it is for him to meet it. I have done!"

"Father, give me leave—and don't be angry!" He himself was so sick with nervous rage that he could hardly speak, and the voice came out of him muffled and breathless round the gall that choked his throat. If I could coax and beg, he thought despairingly, I could win him; he is not so hard, not even wilfully unkind. "Father, if you knew what a great fondness they have for each other—"

Ebrard sprawled out his feet among the rushes with a great shout of laughter. The bellow that came out of the old man might have been of mirth or of rage, or of both together; it startled the pups helter-skelter for the doorway, and made Harry's spirit shrivel in him, but he stood his ground with a pale, mortified, earnest face.

"A great fondness, the brat says! Why, you green babe, what the devil has a fondness to do with marrying? Her duty is to take the husband her father and her lord please to give her, and that's all there is to it. Now let me hear no more of your foolishness."

"But, Father, there is something more—"

"Enough, I said!"

"Hawis is with child!" shouted Harry, scarlet and trembling.

He had succeeded at least in arresting their merriment. They both turned their heads and stared at him in ludicrous astonishment, mouths gaping.

"God's life, child," gasped Sir Eudo, "where do you get your gossip? A man would think they took you to bed with them! There's no such fine, detailed reports ever reach me of what goes on in my own manor. How do you know this?"

"He gets his news in Boteler's yard," said Ebrard scornfully, "where he's for ever hanging about the family and their cronies. Did you not know it, sir? He spends more time there than he does with us, and has a punch in his hand oftener than a pen. He was there this morning before the dew was off the ground."

"Were you so, Harry?"

"I was there but half an hour, and on your business, sir. The wall of the big barn and the gatepost need repair, I pointed out both to you a week ago. I went to bid him come and see to them." He had all this ready, and when there was need of the next excuse he would have another one tucked in his sleeve, ready to palm and produce before them with the same facility. Necessity had forced upon him a cunning of which he was not even aware. "It was Arnulf told me about Hawis. He is in great distress. It was because they knew he was afraid to ask you for leave to marry her—because he could not find the price, and would keep putting them off—that they did what they did."

"Thinking to force my hand, eh? Thinking the old dotard would turn soft and give her to the lad out of pity? They were never more mistaken!"

"No, Father, thinking to compel him to ask you. They had confidence that you would deal generously with them, if he would but speak to you."

"I deal justly. I name my price, and he may pay it or leave it, but it stands. That's the end of it."

"But Hawis will have the child, and everyone will miscall her—"

"She should have thought of that before. Am I to pull her chestnuts out of the fire for her? No, no more! Not a word!"

"Father, you can't mean to be so hard on her—"

"Not a word, I said!" roared his father, thumping the table.

Harry shrank, and was silent. The old man stared him out until he lowered his eyes, and sat mute but not submissive, his black lashes shadowing his cheeks.

"That's better!" He stood over him for a full minute, studying him with diminishing irritation and growing bewilderment, even with some baffled tenderness, though Harry did not feel it. Sir Eudo had contracted a second marriage in middle age to get an heir, and once that was achieved he had settled all his thoughts and affections on Ebrard, and rested content. This one had slipped into the world almost unnoticed, except as the occasion of his mother's long fever and his own banishment to a wet-nurse's care, so that there were times when it surprised and puzzled his father to encounter him in head-on collision, and find himself staring into a fierce face and a stubborn spirit which were strangely familiar to him, though he could never quite recognise them. He looked over the boy's averted head at the clerk, and said in a mollified growl: "Mewed too long, Edric. Let him fly!" And to Harry, in a gruffer tone: "Get you gone, boy! Enough scratching for tonight, and tomorrow you shall have a holiday from your books for once. There, be off with you! Go to your mother."

In the window embrasure of the solar the fading evening light, pale luminous green from the afterglow, shone on Lady Talvace's rounded, youthful face, finding no wrinkles there and leaving no shadows. She had laid aside the embroidery with which she occasionally amused herself when no other entertainment offered. A son fawning upon her, either son, diverted her more agreeably.

"Mother, he would listen to *you*. Dear Mother, you see that we must do something to help them. Stephen wants only Hawis, and she wants to be his wife. I've talked to her, Mother, I know her well. She used to take care of Adam and me sometimes, when we were little. She's so unhappy."

He sat on a stool at her feet, her hand clasped between his, and poured out the whole story into her lap. With her free hand, white and soft and growing plump, she stroked his hair, and his forehead, and his palpitating cheek.

"Harry, your father is a just man, he exacts no more than his due. You must not think yourself wiser than he. Why do you cross him so? You are a froward child!" Her voice, which was mellow and vague as the summer night's quickening wind, turned scolding into a caress, but like the wind she breathed sweetness on him and yet slipped through his fingers. He turned and wound his arms about her waist, nuzzling her breast. Her sensuous pleasure in endearments could always release him from his shyness; only with her was he able to be demonstrative.

"I don't mean to be," he said in muffled tones out of the green brocade of her bliaut. "I try not to be."

"Then why do you vex him so? Is it not froward in you to try to tell him what he must do with his own? Truly, I am sorry for the girl, but she has made her own bed. Sir Eudo does her no wrong in this matter. If the price is paid, she may marry."

"But it cannot be paid! He set it so high that he knows it cannot be paid."

"Harry, mind what you say! This is a bad, rebellious spirit in you. Do you dare accuse your father of unfair dealings?"

"Oh, Mother, I never said unfair. I know he has the right, but it does seem hard on them—on Hawis and Stephen—"

"It is according to law, is it not?"

"Yes, it is, I know it is—" He was not capable of showing her the gulf which was opening before his eyes between law and justice, and he felt his helplessness in argument, and resorted to the blandishments of the body, smoothing his cheek against her breast, kissing the hollow of her neck where the bliaut ended in a narrow stitching of gold thread. "Please, please, Mother, speak to him for them! Think how terrible it will be for her if she has the child, and they can't marry! If she had no skills, father would have let her go for a few shillings. Ten at most—they might manage ten. But thirty! Oh, Mother, you must speak to him! I can't bear it!"

"What a silly child you are! Naturally he sets a high value on her, since she is valuable. How do you think these ordinary affairs of business ought to be conducted? Does one lower the price when the merchandise is better worth? Really, my poor Hal, you have some babyish notions in that head of yours."

"She is not merchandise," said Harry furiously, raising a ruffled head to glare at her, "she is a *woman*. She is *Hawis*. She laughs and weeps and sings, just like you. If I did *that* to her it would hurt—just as it hurts you—"

He pinched her arm, with a sudden impulse of spite more smartly than he had intended, and she gave a tiny scream of surprise and slapped him hard across the cheek.

"You dare! Vicious little wretch! You go too far!"

Her occasional blows, too, had something of sensuous enjoyment about them, and excited and moved him much as her caresses did. Trembling and stammering, he caught at her hand. "Mother, forgive me! I didn't mean to do that—I'm sorry, I'm sorry!" He hid his face in her lap, and shed a few despairing tears of remorse and bewilderment, knowing that he had lost every throw. She put her arm round his shoulders and rocked him serenely, complimented both by his cruelty and his remorse, and contented as a purring cat.

"There, Harry, there! Why should you care so much about

Hawis? What is she to you, that you torment yourself and everyone else like this for her sake?''

She felt him shuddering under her stroking hands, and suddenly she was shaken by the fear that the intensity of suffering to which her palms quivered might not, after all, be on her account. She gripped him by the shoulders, and raised him so that she could look into his face.

"Harry, why are you so anxious that she should marry? What's your concern that her child should be fathered? Harry, look at me!'' He was already gazing at her wide-eyed, in absolute bewilderment, unable even to guess where her thoughts were tending. "Tell me the truth, Harry! You need not be afraid that I shall be angry with you. These matters can be arranged. But I must know the truth.''

"I don't understand,'' he said, staring open-mouthed, and a little frightened now in good earnest. "I have told you the truth, I've told you everything I know.''

"Everything, Harry? Come, I think not. You have had to do with this girl, have you not? Was it you got the child on her? Is that why you are so urgent—''

"Mother! No!'' He burst into a peal of laughter, and then as suddenly his face flamed, and he recoiled from between her hands in indescribable offence. "No! How could you think it?'' Hawis was twenty years old, and had seemed to him, in the days when she used to mind the children for Alison Boteler, already an adult, a generation advanced from him. He had not even liked her very much, because she had carried out her duties in a conscientious fashion which he felt to be tyrannical, though he had long since forgiven her for that. But he had lived in such close proximity to her, and taken her so companionably for granted, that his mother's suggestion outraged him deeply. "I've *never*—'' he said stiffly. "Not Hawis nor anyone.''

"Poor ruffled chick!'' said his mother, and laughed to see him burn crimson to the hair. "Don't be so angry with me, Hal, even if I have misjudged you. Indeed I'm glad if you have not that on your conscience, but you must trust me these things can happen, yes, even to your modest lordship some day. But if I am so clean off the mark, then *why*—why does it mean so much to you that she should marry her Stephen?''

''It is simply that I feel they have rights—a right to marriage, a right to the child, since they cared enough to—to brave all of us—''

''Your father will not rob any man of his rights in law.''

''Oh, in law!'' He laid his cheek, on which the mark of her fingers burned dully, against her knee. ''Mother, help them! If you ask him, he'll let her go.''

''No, Harry, I cannot interfere. It is for your father to do as he thinks fit. And it is unbecoming in you to doubt that he will do right.'' She brushed back the dark hair absently from his forehead, and saw how wearily his eyelids hung. ''They've worked you too hard, no wonder you're tired and fretful. You should go to bed.''

''Yes, Mother,'' he said in a dull voice, and began to straighten up slowly from the low stool.

''And have you not been looking at this matter somewhat inconsiderately?'' she added feelingly, as she held up her face for his goodnight kiss. ''If we part with Hawis, who is to weave wool cloths for me and make up my dresses?''

Sleapford manor had a low, squat stone keep, built on forty years later than the hall, and topped with a slitted watch-turret. In the upper room under the crenellated roof the two brothers had slept together until Ebrard had departed to take service under FitzAlan, and on his return, almost a knight and tenderly alive to his budding dignity, he had asked and obtained permission to take over one of the small rooms opening from the solar. Without recognising the source of his joy, or at least without admitting it, even to himself, Harry had put away that day in his memory as one of the radiant turning-points of his life.

Alone in the stony, six-sided room, with shot-windows all round him, stretching out his toes and his fingers into every corner of the rustling straw bed, he had a kingdom of his own, waiting for his imagination to populate it. In the night he looked towards the hills of Wales, and thought of raids and alarms gone by, and new ones threatening, of Gwenwynwyn harrying the border like a brush fire from end to end of Powis, and the sudden young prince of Gwynedd, Llewelyn, burning up in the north as a comet rises, until he blazed into the castle of Mold and alerted Chester to a new and splendid enemy.

Because of these uneasy neighbours there was always a watchman in the turret on top of the tower, and though he had all the valley spread like a silver bowl in his sight, he spent most of the hours of his watch staring towards Wales. It had taken Harry only a few weeks to discover how simple it was to slip down the staircase with his shoes in his hand, work his way round to the old water-gate in the shelter of the wall, and let himself out on the English side, while the watchman faithfully gazed at the Welsh hills. The tower had an outer staircase to the ground, so no one else in the house was ever likely to hear or see him, and the constant chance that the guard would choose the wrong moment to turn towards that side of the house, and catch him in the act of lifting the wooden bar, only added a particular sweetness to these nocturnal excursions. It had never happened, and he had been sparing in his use of his freedom, to avoid out-running his luck.

In the sleeping village an occasional dog stirred and barked, but he knew them all by name, and they grew quiet at his voice. The stonemason's yard lay at one end of the undulating street, screened at the back by a copse of birch trees. The house was only a low undercroft and one room above, and a loft in the roof, with a shut-tered opening in the gable. There the three boys slept, tangled together in their piled bed of dried bracken and straw. Harry had only to whistle beneath the gable, and Adam put his head out from the window, which was left unshuttered through all the soft summer nights. In a moment he swung himself out by his hands and dropped into the turf.

They went to earth in the copse, and lay on their bellies in the warm, sweet-smelling grass.

"Adam, I'm let off work tomorrow. Can you get Ranald to go to the harvest instead of you, and come with me? There's something I must do."

"I'll come," said Adam without hesitation. "Where are we go-ing?"

"To Hunyate. But roundabout, because no one must know I've gone there. We'll take our bows, and start out through our own woods to the gores beyond the mill. They'll be cutting there, and there'll be plenty of hares and conies breaking cover. We'll take a few, and hide them in the wood to pick up on our way back. That's what they'll expect of us when we have a day's holiday."

"From there to Hunyate we shall have to go through Tourneur land," said Adam dubiously. He had never yet taken a deer, but like all the boys in the village he felt himself identified in loyalty with those who played that risky game, and approached the private chase of the king's verderer only with considerable trepidation.

"That's no crime, we want none of his venison. And we'll keep out of sight. But we must go that way, for I mustn't be seen to set out towards Hunyate."

"Why not? What are you about, Harry?"

Harry hoisted himself nearer in the grass, and told him. Adam, chin on fist, listened large-eyed. "But what do you mean to do?"

"I'm going to tell Stephen Mortmain what my father intends, before word reaches Arnulf. I can do no more. He is my father, and I'll not take active part against him, but what he purposes Stephen has a right to know. Then it's for him to act, and quickly."

"But what can he do? If he can't help Arnulf to raise the mer- chet—and how can he?"

"He has a craft he can carry with him, and no land to leave, for he's still in his father's house. I know what I would do if I were Stephen. I'd take Hawis by night, and have her away to some charter town where a good shoemaker can get more work than he can do, and hire himself journeyman to a decent master, and marry his sweetheart there. And I think him man enough to do it, too, and her woman enough to get up at his call and go with him. No one can pursue him, he's a free man. And for a villein woman my father won't raise the hue and cry he would for a man. If they get safe out of Salop they can set up house where they will. And if they're hard pressed to run far enough before the hunt is up, well, the Welsh wear shoes, too."

"Not all," said Adam contentiously. "Andrew Miller says when they came raiding two years ago, out Wyndhoe way—"

"Who listens to Andrew Miller! To hear him talk he was at every border raid in six shires these last two years, and we all know he runs if a dog barks. I must go, Adam. In the morning I'll come at

eight, but we'll leave the horses with Wilfred at the mill, and go
afoot. And no hounds. I'll not take a dog in the verderer's chase, not
even leashed. But don't forget your bow. We'll make a day of it."

Adam clambered to his feet, and brushed away the ripe dry grass-
seeds from the short drawers of coarse linen which were his only
garment. The hand-cart from his father's yard, braced shafts-
upwards against the door of the undercroft, was his ladder to the
narrow lintel-ledge above, and from there his brothers would be
ready to reach out their arms and draw him back into the garret. It
was a service they had done for him many times, and he for them.
He had already hauled himself up to the front board of the cart when
he turned and scrambled down again.

"Harry—"

Harry halted and looked back. "Well?"

"If your father finds out it was you put this idea into Stephen's
head—"

"Who said I meant to put any idea in his head? He must do as
he thinks best."

"Do you take me for a fool? I know you too well to be cozened.
Harry, if he finds out he'll just about kill you."

"He won't find out. He won't know I've been near Hunyate."

"You don't know that. Something could go wrong. You go and
shoot your hares in the cornfields tomorrow, and I'll go to Hunyate."

"No!" said Harry shortly and arrogantly. "I do my own errands.
I was in two minds even about asking you to go with me, but you
were asked to go and help me pick off the conies, mind that! You
know nothing, if anyone asks you, about Stephen Mortmain or
Hunyate. I have not mentioned them."

"Oh, if you're going to climb on your high horse, I say no more.
But, Harry, have you not thought—could not your mother persuade
him—"

The Talvace brows drew together in a formidable scowl, and the
Talvace nose sniffed the air with quivering nostrils. "My mother
would have her private sympathies, but she could do no other than
support my father. It is her duty." And Harry turned and stalked
away through the birches upon trembling legs, before Adam could

get out a word of either challenge or apology. It might have been either, but for shame Harry dared not wait to hear it; either would have discomfited him to the point of tears.

He hated himself for what he had just said. He wanted to turn back and fling himself into Adam's ready arms, and blurt out: "I'm a liar! I did ask her. She won't help, she doesn't even care." Instead, he walked the faster away from the memory that shamed him; and when he reached the road he broke into a run, but he could not outrun his own desolation.

Chapter Three

*T*he private chase of Sir Roger le Tourneur, the senior member of the four royal verderers for the shire, was enclosed and strictly kept, but several village paths passed through it, and by these it was legal for local folk to move at will, provided they committed no offence against forest law. The Talvaces with their rights of warren might hunt fox, wolf, hare and coney, badger and cat upon their own land, but could not touch the deer without a special dispensation; but le Tourneur's enclosure from the royal forest had been granted to him with all its rights intact. Here in the thick coverts the fallow and the roe belonged not to the king, but to Sir Roger, and he had the same powers to deal with those who encroached on his rights as had the king himself elsewhere. To do him justice, he felt the weight of his office so heavy upon him that he would not be judge in his own cause, and regularly produced whatever charges he had to make at the forest attachment courts, instead of proceeding to summary punishment in his own court. But that said, he insisted on the full penalty at law. He was respected but hated; he might almost have been liked if he had not been the king's verderer. But who could like a verderer?

"Man," said Adam, kicking his heels blithely among the sweet, rustling bed of leaves from many summers, "but he keeps his woods well! These coverts are full of game. Did you see the buck that crashed away from us among the beeches there? Lambert brought in a buck last night, as soon as it was dark. He swears he winged a doe, too, but he lost her." He gave a hitch to the thong of the crossbow that swung behind his shoulder, and reached up to put back a branch from his face.

It had been like one of the summer days of their childhood. They had climbed to the beacon on the Hunyate hills, where the small, lively, short-woolled sheep grazed among the tussocky grass and heather, and the last harebells quivered on their thin green stems. And after they had eaten their bread and bacon and little summer apples, lying in the sun-warmed mosses that smelled of birth and baking, they had bathed and swum in the pool set in the lee of the hill, and then lain naked in the sun upon the grassy shore until the afternoon blaze mellowed into the golden serenity of early evening. Saturated with summer and leisure and content, they made their way homeward without haste to reclaim their horses and their conies from the miller's boy at Teyne.

"Do you think they'll go?" asked Adam suddenly.

"They'll go." He was sure of himself. Stephen's broad, deliberate countenance had cleared magically when the seed was let fall into his mind, and Harry had felt its germination like a bursting of the tension that had confined and restricted him.

"Tonight, do you think?"

"I don't know. It's better we shouldn't know. We have the less to deny. And see here, Adam, we must not let fall a word of where we've been, or they might still be intercepted."

"You need not tell me that." Adam looked along the green ride, dappled with the filigree sun. They had withdrawn from the most frequented path, to reach the fence and Sleapford and their supper by the shortest route; and here the coverts were thick and deep, and the silence and dimness closed over them green and sombre, drawing on the night. The forest was full of sounds, of wings fluttering and feet scurrying, but the sum of the sounds was still silence. Adam began to whistle, but the notes sank into the muffling quietness and were lost.

Then suddenly there was a sound softer than all the rest, but which could not be swallowed up. It touched their ears just audibly, but with so desolate a vibration that they halted instantly, clutching at each other.

"Christ aid, what was that? Did you hear it? Something's hurt— or someone. Listen!"

Faint, distant, inexpressibly sad and forlorn, something between a human moan and the last almost voiceless bellow of a beast too weak to rise or call. It came from the deep woods on their left hand, and Adam was off the path and thrashing through the bushes towards it before the sound died, panting back over his shoulder as he elbowed off thorns: "Something hurt—deer, I think. Was he here? He wouldn't say where he got his buck."

"Don't go!" Harry clutched at him in sudden agitation. "Don't touch it!" But Adam did not even hear him, and he himself did not stop, but blundered headlong after the anguished sound, paying no heed to the noise they made.

They tumbled out into a small clearing, close-turfed and rimmed with densely-growing bushes. One green wall threshed feebly while the rest were still. Adam went forward with steps suddenly piteously soft and gentle, and thrust his arms into the thicket, parting the branches and leaning inward upon darkness. Something pallid and dappled like the filigree sward of the clearing heaved and sighed faintly. A silvery-white face with great eyes of motionless terror and despair stared up at them. Low in the rounded side, towards the silver belly, the head of a crossbow quarrel stood out like a clove from a pasty. Ribbons of blood laced her delicate flanks and folded legs. The smell of blood and the disturbed buzzing of flies turned Harry sick.

"Lambert's doe!" said Adam in a quavering whisper. "Oh, God, there's been something at her—a fox, maybe—she was too feeble—" He stretched a hand backwards without looking round. "Give me your knife! Quick, man, your knife!"

Harry fumbled his hunting knife out of its sheath with shaking fingers, and thrust the haft into the outstretched hand. Adam laid his left palm gently and slowly upon the blood-crusted muzzle, and smoothed it upwards until it covered the anguished eyes. The knife's tip felt for the place. It was something he had never done before, but he had to do it well. He saw nothing but the light shudder that passed along the speckled hide, felt nothing but the one convulsive jerk of the torn body, and then its great quietness, heard nothing at all. Harry, leaning intently over him, was as blind and deaf as he.

Branches thrashed suddenly as though the wind had risen, on this side of them, on that, all round them. A voice among the trees bellowed: "Stand! Come out of that and show yourselves! We have you caged!" And another voice, close, and in the air above them: "In the act, by God, in the act! Lads, lay hold!"

Harry felt the earth shake to the horse's hooves, and flung himself round in confusion and panic, throwing up his arms instinctively to protect his head. The whip curled round head and arms together, and threw him backwards into Adam. He groped for his friend's arm, screaming: "Run!" and caught one glimpse of Adam's face, a pale mask of incredulity, not yet even frightened. He had the knife in his hand. The gush of blood had run down his wrist and was dripping from his sleeve.

"Redhanded, boys!" The man on horseback let the whip hang from his wrist, and swung himself down beside them. The walking foresters, two, three, half a dozen of them, boiled out of the bushes and filled the clearing. Large hands plucked Harry round and dragged his arms behind him. Without consideration, in pure rage and terror, he fought the grip, and tore himself clear. A corner of his mind, still alert, recognised that they could not both get away, and knew only too well which of them was in the more desperate case.

"Run! Get home!" he screamed into Adam's stunned face, and flung himself at the tall horseman. The face for which he reached with frantic fists was nothing but a blur to him, black of beard and brows and white of flesh, without identity. He touched neither face nor throat, though he did his best. The man made a rapid step aside, caught him by one arm as he hurled himself forward and, swinging him about in a circle, flung him face downwards on the grass and pinned him there with a booted foot between his shoulderblades. The whip slashed across his legs.

"Ah, would you! You'll pay dear for that!"

He clenched his arm over his face and set his teeth, trying to strain his head round to console himself that Adam had taken his chance. The next blow left a red weal across his chin and neck, it dragged a moan of pain out of him.

It was that blow that brought Adam out of his daze. He saw Harry pinned to the ground and writhing away from the whip, and with a shout of rage he leaped clear of the hands that clutched at him, and flung himself like a fury at the horseman. The knife was still in his hand, though he had forgotten that he held it. His weight struck the man in shoulder and side, and threw him off-balance, and down they went together in the turf, Adam battering at the bearded face. The knife slashed through surcoat and sleeve into the arm below. Then two of the walking foresters pinned Adam by the arms and hauled him off, and two more pulled Harry to his feet and held him panting and sobbing between them.

As suddenly as the chaos fell the quietness. The tall horseman got to his feet, clutching together the tatters of his sleeve over the knife-slash, and shaking off a thin trickle of blood from his fingertips with a cold deliberation which was terrifying to see. The face he turned upon them, long and weather-beaten and beaked like a hawk, was all too recognisable now that they were compelled to stand and look upon it. Not, as they had supposed, one of the riding foresters; that would have been bad enough in all conscience: but the king's verderer himself, Sir Roger le Tourneur, in all the dreadful majesty of his office.

He squeezed together the lips of his wound, put off with an impatient frown the forester who would have made a move to offer help, and motioned towards the thicket.

"What are you waiting for? Have out the beast, let me see their kill."

Two men dragged forth the mangled carcass of the doe, leaving fresh smears of her blood across the trampled grass.

"A crossbow bolt in her, Sir Roger—and worried by a hound. I heard some beast leave her, I swear, when the lads came near. Her throat newly cut—you need not look far for the knife that did it."

"He's well blooded," said one of the two who held Adam quaking between them, and presented the knife they had wrested out of his hand.

Harry moistened his dry lips with a tongue almost as dry, and croaked hoarsely: "We never hunted her."

"Will you say so? Nor cut her throat, neither? Her fresh blood on you both, and the knife in your fellow's hand, but you did her no harm!"

"We did kill her—"

"*I* killed her," said Adam in a trembling voice.

"—but we never hunted her. We heard her crying, and found her mangled. What could we do but put her out of her pain?"

"So say all poachers taken in the act. And in the same spirit of pure charity you designed to do as much for me? It's no light matter to offer violence to the king's verderer, as you shall find. You may well wish you had no more than a murdered deer to answer for."

"We didn't know!" Harry looked from Adam's fixed face, grey as chalk, to the slow drops Sir Roger wrung from his fingers. "I was at fault—it was my folly. He wanted only to help me."

"With the knife! You may make your pleas to the attachment court, not to me."

"I forgot I had the knife," whispered Adam. "I ask pardon, sir, I didn't know you—"

"What signifies whether you knew me? I'll have no officer of mine, not the meanest, mishandled more lightly than myself. Your names!" They stood mute with misery and despair, unwilling to contemplate the consequences of speaking. "Your names, I said! Speak up!" He had drawn a kerchief from the breast of his cotte, and was knotting it one-handed about his arm over the slit in the sleeve, and now he bent his head and drew the knot tight with great white teeth that bit viciously into the linen. Still unanswered when his attention was again free, he swung the butt of the whip purposefully into his palm. "Will you speak, or have I to cut it out of your hides?"

"By your leave, Sir Roger," said one of the foresters, lugging Harry a step forward. "I fancy this sprig here is Sir Eudo Talvace's boy, from Sleapford. The younger, he that came home from Shrewsbury at Eastertide."

"What? A Talvace?" The thick black brows knit above a terrifying star. "Come here, boy, show yourself!" They thrust him forward, and Sir Roger plucked him round to face the light. "God's life, if you're right! He has the face on him. Speak up, boy, are you a Talvace or no?"

Harry admitted his lineage like a felon confessing to theft and outrage.

"The more shame on you. What says your father to these cantrips of yours?"

"My father knows nothing of it, sir, he—"

"I had not supposed even Talvace would send his own brat poaching in broad daylight in his neighbour's chase."

"We were not poaching, sir, I swear we were not. We were no more than walking through the forest, until we heard the doe crying, and—"

"So, and this you carry with you for the pleasure of its weight?" He dragged the slung crossbow over Harry's shoulder and thrust it in his face. "And these—and this—to pick your teeth with?" The short quiver full of quarrels and the bloody knife were brandished under his nose. "You always take the air armed like this, do you, boy?"

"We spent the morning in the cornfields, shooting at coney and hare—"

"And the afternoon in my woods, harrying my deer."

"No, sir, I swear we did not! Look, she has bled for hours, and lain there in the covert so long the blood is dried black, and, on my head, we have not been in the forest above an hour."

"Where, then? Come, speak! Make account of yourself! If not here on my land, where have you been until this last hour? If you were elsewhere upon honest business, someone will be able to bear you out."

Harry stared into the pit he had dug for himself, and it seemed to him a bottomless blackness. How could they tell where they had spent their day, without causing Sir Eudo to prick up his ears as soon as the name Hunyate came back to him, as most surely it must before night? Then goodbye to Stephen's chance of getting clear away from Sleapford with his Hawis. No, it was unthinkable to risk that betrayal. And even if they could have told a measure of truth without taking that risk, who could have confirmed it but Stephen himself, on whom they could never call? On the hill among the earthworks of their ancestors, with the sheep and the heather, they had seen no one, been seen by no one. Ever since they left the mill they had taken pains to be inconspicuous, because of the secrecy of their errand. And now this gulf opened under their feet, and they had no means of filling in the lost hours of time. Harry opened his mouth, dredging his mind desperately for some other place he might name without treason, some attraction for boys on holiday which might be reached through these woods.

"If you cannot lie faster than that," said Sir Roger grimly, "better not try it at all. You have been here most of the day, and harried and lost her some hours, and found her now in a very ill moment for you. Admit it! Before God, I'd think better of you if you stood to your ventures, lose or win. This is a poor part for a Talvace. I suppose you will tell me next who did course the poor beast, since you are so insistent it was not you?"

That was but one more thing they could not tell, though they knew the answer. Better go to the flayers themselves than give away Lambert. Wherever they turned there was a wall of silence, and they could do nothing but shut their mouths and abide whatever must come.

"Bring them to the hall," said Sir Roger abruptly, reaching for his bridle with his good hand. "I must ride ahead and get this slash dressed. And faith, I must consider what can be done between neighbours to amend this sorry business. I had rather it had been any man's son but Talvace's."

He hoisted himself into the saddle and disposed his left hand and forearm within the breast of his cotte. "Keep them apart on the way, or they'll compound in a lie and be perfect in their story before you get them home to me."

With that he wheeled his horse, and, dipping his head low beneath the branches of the trees, threaded his way into the green gloom towards the open ride, and was lost to sight; and in a moment they heard the soft thudding of hooves as he reached the pathway and spurred into a canter. Too broken to look at each other, they followed between their guards, in the silence of despair.

It was middle evening, and the time of the pale golden calm just before set of sun, when the sorry little cavalcade entered the court-yard at Sleapford. The gateman, gaping to see his lord's younger child come home under escort, crumpled and crestfallen and bearing whip-marks on cheek and neck, sent an archer running to inform

Sir Eudo, while he himself admitted the party cautiously into the courtyard and delayed them there with wary civilities until the master of the house appeared, rolling hastily out from his supper, bundling on his surcoat as he bustled through the doorway from his great hall. Ebrard was at his heels, quivering with curiosity and ready to bristle in defence of his name. Half the household caught the stir of excitement in the air, and crept unobtrusively forth from buttery and stables and kitchen and armoury, to stare and listen as the riding forester dismounted and uncovered.

Behind him two of his subordinates, also mounted, brought the two boys ignominiously before them on their saddle bows, and lighting down, gave them a hand to dismount after, not unkindly. They had been rough-handled enough in the first encounter, and sunk through enough slow torments of suspense and anxiety since, to excite a faint stirring of sympathy even in their captors. Two hours they had spent in the guardroom by Sir Roger's gate-house, constantly watched and held apart, while Sir Roger had debated how best to handle the business, and had his clerk write to his neighbour the letter the forester was now about delivering. No one had told them what was in it, no one had been able to offer them a crumb of comfort about the fate that awaited them; and no one had fed them, which in the state of stunned resignation to which they had been reduced ought to have been a small matter, but which in fact had gradually grown into the greatest grievance of all, for felons or not, they were still fifteen, and had not eaten since noon, and courage and dignity would have come a little easier if they had not been quite so hungry. They stood now side by side, and silently followed the verderer's letter with their eyes as it passed from hand to hand.

The very fact of being thus sent home to their father and master at once encouraged and depressed them. Surely it meant that Sir Roger did not intend to proceed to the attachment court—not out of any love to Sir Eudo, but out of solidarity with his own estate, and reluctance to hold them up to the scorn of the commonalty. If the affair could be compounded in private, Sir Eudo might be less irreconcilable, and in time the storm would blow over. So they were tempted to think, until they remembered the new causes for rage and suspicion likely to confront him before the week was out. And at best, these next hours would be the extreme of discomfort.

They watched the foresters hand over their bows and bolts, and the knife and its sheath. Once, only once, they stole a disconsolate glance at each other, and pledged each other to silence and endurance. Sir Eudo, literate but no scholar, was fingering his way laboriously through Sir Roger's letter, and the lightnings were about to fall.

Harry had thought his heart could sink no farther, but it lurched downwards sickeningly as his father bore down upon him with a suffused face, and the open scroll in his hand.

"So, Master Harry, you have done finely for yourself and for me, and worse yet for this fellow of yours. I hope you know how well you have undone two years of work for me, and by God, I hope you are in good heart to pay for what you have done. Bring my name into common rebuke, would you? Poach my neighbour's deer in my despite and his, would you, and drag this luckless fool to ruin in your wake! You shall answer for all—you hear me?—in full!"

Harry knew the signs too well, the purple cheek-bones, the eyes sunk so far into swollen, angry flesh that he saw them as two sparks in a smothered fire, the great fist clenched so hard on the vellum that the veins swelled and pulsed. He expected to be felled to the ground, and shut his eyes for one instant of terror. He was not afraid, not more than any sensible man must be, of pain or violence, but he was desperately afraid of his father's anger. It lay too near to his own affections, cut too deeply and viciously at the roots of his life. Some day it would sever them.

"Father," he began quaveringly, "I swear to you we did not hunt the doe. By my honour, we did not! If we have done anything foolishly—indeed, I know we did, because we were frightened—I am very sorry. But we did not hunt or wound the doe."

It was a miracle that he was heard out to the end, but perhaps it was only that Sir Eudo could not choke down his fury in time to become articulate and cut him off earlier. He did not really listen; he had never listened.

"Did not hunt her! Did not hunt her! And half a dozen foresters and the king's verderer himself saw your lad cut her throat! Is this blood on your knife? Do you tell me I am blind, or cannot smell? What did you there with bows on your backs? Not hunt her! Do you not know he might have laid a charge against you even for carrying the bow? Two years of peace-making, and you must ruin all with this stupendous folly! Not hunt her! Read, boy, read what he writes to me! Do you talk to me of the doe, as though she were the measure of your roguery? And I suppose you did not offer violence to the king's verderer? Do you know he could have your liberty for that, if he chose to attach you? Read, and see what irretrievable mischief you have made!"

Harry, through his daze, found himself reading stupidly, hardly grasping words or sense. Yet the letter was very much to the point.

To the noble Sir Eudo Talvace, Knight, of Sleapford, with respect, these:

These, taken in arms and in the act of killing a deer in my chase this day, in my presence and in the presence of six of my foresters, all witnesses to the killing of the said deer, namely a doe, before wounded by a crossbow bolt, I find to be yours. And in courtesy, the offences being committed against my game, and not the game of the King's Grace, I return them to you, and desire you will deal with them according to my judgement of what is just, and indeed merciful. To which if you consent, out of consideration to the good name of knight, which dearly concerns us both, I purpose not to proceed to the forest attachment court with the charges to which your son and your villein have laid themselves open, and to which, seeing the nature of the case, they have no defence.

Touching the matter of the deer, since the act was committed, I say, to my injury, and not to the injury of the King's Grace, I can and do remit the severity of the law, which would have submitted your son to a ruinous fine, and his fellow to death by flaying, as you well know. I am content that you should beat into them both that degree of good sense and respect for property that might have been bred into them long since in more able hands.

Touching the assaults made upon my person by both of them, to which six witnesses will stand, and which the culprits, I think, will not deny, as they were affronts to me I can and do excuse them; but as they were affronts to my office I have no right to do so, and in duty to my fellow officers of the King's Grace in his forests I have no choice but to exact justice. The assault made by your boy, as being unarmed and committed in the first astonish-

ment, may be compounded in the severity of his punishment for
the deer. But that of the boy Boteler, being made with a knife
and in despite of my life, though by God's grace the wound was
taken in the upper arm, may not be so compounded. If you so
send word by my man who brings this, my officers shall attend
you tomorrow and execute upon him that penalty which you
know the law demands, he being of age and a villein, namely, the
lopping of his right hand. Until which time I hold you responsible
for the delivery of his person.

If you be not content with this my judgement, I shall proceed
with all charges in due order to the attachment court, and look
to it that you surrender both the accused upon demand to the
court—

He felt his cheeks burn with shame at the tone used to his father
before he could grasp the terrible thing threatened against Adam.
He, being free and noble, might have got clear even in court with a
fine, at the worst with the loss of his liberty. But Adam had no
liberty to lose, and must be deprived of something even the unfree
possess. He had always known these academic items of law, these
niceties of selection between culprit and culprit. How could he have
guessed the terror they would let fall on him when they ceased to
be academic?

He looked up at his father over the trembling hands that held the
scroll, and cried: "No! Father, you can't, you mustn't! Let it go to
the court! Let him charge us! We killed the doe, but only because
she was mortally hurt, and not by us. We'll tell them, they must
believe us. Father, it's the truth! Let it go to the court, I beg you!"

"Let it go to the court, and my name be dragged through the
dust, you fool? Pay a heavy fine for you, and risk his skin as well
as hand? How would that help him? Can you read? Have you his
sense? You know well he is coming off lightly, and you far lighter
than you deserve."

"My hand?" whispered Adam, and blanched to the grey pallor of
clay, staring at them with terrified eyes. He looked round him in
one wild, hunted glance, and the forester who stood beside him laid
hold of his arm and held him hard.

"But I struck him, too! I struck him first! It was only to help me that Adam attacked him."

"With a knife?"

"It was ill-luck that he had the knife in his hand, he never meant to use it. And we did not know it was Sir Roger. I was the first to strike him, I—"

"How will it help him if you lop yourself of a hand to match? Have done! You have made a pretty cauldron of trouble for us all. We must be thankful to get clear of it thus cheaply."

He turned and marched upon the waiting foresters. "You may thank your lord for his courtesy, and tell him I approve his judgement, and will see it faithfully executed. Let his officers wait on me tomorrow at what hour they will." And with a motion of his hand he committed Adam to the staring, whispering archers, who closed in upon him with still faces and blank eyes, and laid hands upon him almost gently. He started at the touch, and began to struggle hopelessly, turning his terrified face wildly round upon them all, though he made not a sound. They held him fast as the foresters withdrew, but they held him as though he might break in their hands.

"Tie him up," said Sir Eudo, "and in God's name let's make an end!"

They had the tunic stripped from Adam's back, and his wrists bound to the iron loops of the whipping-post, before Harry could make his numbed legs move. The brown hands—tomorrow night he would have but one—were strained rather high, because the shackles were set for a man, and for all his handsome growth Adam was not yet a man. He was no longer struggling; what was the use? Even in this there had to be nice differences; even punishment had its hierarchies. Harry could smart in private and without ceremony, but Adam must suffer this violation of his beauty and his humanity in public and with circumstance.

Harry ran blindly, and flung himself on his knees before his father, clutching at his hand and sobbing drily: "No, Father, I beg you! I implore you! I'll make amends, I'll do anything, anything, but don't let them take Adam's hand. Beat me, do what you like to me, but don't maim him! Oh, Father, for God's sake, let us be treated alike—the same fault, the very same! It's unjust!"

"Fool, would you have villeins treated like free men? Is not his presumption more monstrous than yours? It's the law," said Sir Eudo violently, and thrust him off. "Get up, child, you shame me. Go in! You hear me? Go into the house!"

"It's a vile law," shouted Harry, bursting into an uncontrollable storm of weeping. "It ought not to be the law! It's unjust!"

The old man struck him heavily on the side of the head, but Harry clung to him still, and when he would have drawn free and passed on, fell on his face in a frenzy of tears, and wound his arms about his father's ankles, still gasping out inarticulate pleas and reproaches. With a bellow of fury the old man took him by the collar and dragged him to his feet. "Devil take the boy, will you be silent! You make me ashamed of my stock. Ebrard! Ebrard, I say, take this crazed fool out of my sight, he sickens me. Shut him in the mews till we are done with this one."

Ebrard received him willingly, and bundled him out of sight with the same relief, slightly pitying, infinitely scornful and impatient, with which his father saw him go. All this unseemly fuss over a villein, and one who had no more than his due! The roughness of Ebrard's handling of his brother reflected the degree of embarrassment and shame he felt for him. No such distasteful exhibition had ever been made by a Talvace before. Where he got his bad blood, from what distant, dark ancestor, Ebrard could not guess. He bent the boy's arms competently behind his back, and ran him into the mews, where the disturbed hawks were shifting and barking uneasily on their perches; but as soon as he was loosed Harry turned and fought to reach the doorway again and break free. Ebrard had much ado to shut the door on him, and drop the wooden bar into place, and even then the boy beat frenziedly on the door with his fists, and screamed for release like an hysterical girl.

When he was exhausted he slid down the door to his knees, and lay for a while against the boards with his arms clenched over his ears. Even so, he heard Adam cry.

With the first cry it seemed to him that something which had always contained and generally confined him was broken, that he was loosed from it for ever; but whether he came forth into freedom or exile was something he could not determine. Whichever it might be, it was a desolation more extreme than any cold or darkness he had ever known. And in it everything familiar had become his enemy. He thought he would have liked to destroy all that he could see and touch here, everything which had first turned traitor to him and then expelled him. Ebrard's merlin, the new one that was not yet trained, muttered like a spitting cat on her perch above him, and turned her hooded, plumed head to stare blindly. He thought he would kill her, but in his heart he knew he could not do it. But the hoods and the jesses, the perches and leashes, and the fine cage Ebrard was making for his mother's linnets, and all the material things that had been in a sense his, these he would destroy.

In a calm more frenzied than frenzy itself he did what he could to smash and bend and tear all that offered itself to his hands. The birds spat and screamed, but them he let alone. When Ebrard unbarred the door at last, and came to fetch him out of his prison, the floor was littered with shredded gloves, and slashed harness, and Harry, with his dagger in his hand, was cutting the tooled jesses into bits. Peering into the dimness within, Ebrard did not at first distinguish the details of chaos, and waded unawares into the tangle of leather thongs and unravelled creances. He let out a bellow of rage, and seized his brother by the shoulder; and Harry, turning to meet the assault, launched himself like a fury at the angry face looming over him. Adam had struck out with the knife unintentionally; Harry struck wittingly, and with all his weight behind the dagger, utterly reckless of consequences.

"Ah, would you?" Ebrard caught at the thrusting wrist, and twisted it without mercy. "Draw on me, would you, you devil! Draw on your brother! I'll teach you better manners."

The dagger clattered to the floor, and Harry was tossed after it by a swinging blow on the ear. Ebrard taught him nothing, for he was past learning, but he did his best to beat him into a proper appreciation of the enormity of declaring war on his kind. When Harry had given up the unequal struggle, and lay hunched and still under the blows, they ceased at once. To tell the truth, Ebrard, outraged as he was, felt sorry for this creature he did not understand. He stood over him, frowning down at the soiled and crumpled figure that seemed now so small and helpless, and yet contained such a daunting reserve of obstinacy and defiance.

"Get up! I'll not touch you—get up! Father wants you in the

solar. If you have any sense left you'll come quickly and behave yourself meekly. No need to make bad even worse."

Harry picked himself up stiffly, and brushed himself down without a word. He would go to his father, but he had nothing now to say to him and nothing left to ask of him. All that was over.

A hush of curiosity, sympathy and almost pleasurable excitement followed him through the hall. The men-at-arms paused over their dice as he threaded his way through the romping dogs in the rushes, and climbed the stairs to the solar. He looked at no one. Only a little while ago their knowing sympathy would have galled him to the quick, but now it had ceased to be of any importance.

"Wipe your face," whispered Ebrard at the door. "You're no sight for mother's eyes." He thrust his own kerchief into Harry's hand, and waited for him to scrub the filth of dust and tears from his cheeks. That started a quivering nerve of affection and regret, but it did not ache for long.

Sir Eudo was straddling the empty hearth with his hands linked behind him in the wide sleeves of his surcoat. Lady Talvace sat in a straight-backed chair a discreet yard away from him, so that she could pluck gently at his arm if he needed the restraint of her touch.

"Here he is," said Ebrard, and closed the door. He pushed Harry forward to stand before his father, and clattered the dagger down upon the table. "He drew on me! And he's played the merry devil in the mews. I should have stayed with him."

That flourish, in its turn, eased Harry's heart of that one dragging thread of regret. He stood and looked at his judges, still soiled and tear-stained, and a miserable object enough, but stonily calm.

"Drew on you? Drew on his brother? It shall be remembered in the account," the old man promised grimly, and fixed his bloodshot eyes upon his younger son. "Come here, you! Come nearer! You're quiet enough now, are you? Are you in your right senses yet? Drew on your brother, did you?—a thing a very savage would not do. You shall ask his pardon for it here and now, before you pay the rest of your score. On your knees! Do it, I say!"

Harry did not move.

"I ordered you to ask your brother's pardon. Instantly!"

Harry shook his head a little, and maintained his stony regard, not even glancing in Ebrard's direction. The blow his father aimed

at him laid him flat, and he was dragged bodily across the floor and
forced to his knees before his brother, who had contemplated this
flurry of violence with an uneasy and unhappy face. Looking up
through his disordered hair, Harry kept his bruised lips tightly shut,
and would not say one word.

"It was done in a temper," said Ebrard shortly, "he didn't know
what he was doing. Let him be, sir."

Sir Eudo flung him down in a passion of helpless rage, and stamped
away from him. Lady Talvace went and laid her plump, pretty hands
upon the boy's shoulder.

"Come now, Harry, this is no good part," said the soft, caressing
voice in his ear. "It is human to commit a fault, but like a beast to
persist so in one. I know that temper of yours, I know you think we
are all against you, but indeed we're not. You have only to submit
yourself like a dutiful son, take your punishment and purge your
rebellion, and it will all be forgiven."

She raised him tenderly, and kept her arm about him while she
smoothed the hair back from his forehead and wiped a few specks
of blood from a graze beneath his eye. Her demands, it seemed,
were the same as his father's, except that she had a more insinuating
way of presenting them. He listened to her, and was moved to a
distant pleasure and a sharp and agonising pain, but not moved to
submit himself or purge his rebellion.

"There, now you will be my dear boy, and make amends of your
own free will, I know. You have grieved us all very much, and
caused a great deal of trouble, you have need of grace. But you have
only to ask, and it will be granted. Come, now, first to your father,
against whom you have offended most deeply. Go to him, Harry,
tell him you are sorry for your faults, and ask his pardon." She
coaxed him forward in her arm. "It's not so difficult, and I'll help
you. Only a few words, and your peace is made."

And indeed it sounded tempting to him, at this last moment. He
was tired and hungry and sore, and he had still to pay his part of the
doe's price; and it would have been so simple to surrender himself to
the will of his family, and say the few magical words that would
readmit him into its ranks, where at least he knew the worst that could
be done to him, and need only obey, and not think any more.

"Do it, Harry, with a good will, and then you shall have your supper, and—who knows?—perhaps you may even be let off your punishment if you promise amendment."

He had to pluck himself violently away from her, or he would have let her persuade him to his knees, and everything, his honour, his integrity, even his new, bleak freedom, would have been lost.

"I can't!" he cried, and stiffened defiantly, pushing her away. "I am sorry for nothing! I have nothing to be sorry for, except that I haven't the courage to cut off my right hand, too. I'm not sorry I called the law vile and unjust, for so it is."

"You see, my lady," said Sir Eudo grimly, "how you lose your pains with him. There's nothing to be done with one that will not bend, except break him, and by God we'll see if it cannot be done. We have time enough for it."

"Eudo, you'll not be too hard on him!"

"Too hard? Have we not been soft with him long enough, and to no purpose? I swear I don't know the boy for my son. But we'll amend that," said Sir Eudo blackly, halting before Harry and fixing upon him a formidable, glittering stare. "We'll try which of us is to be master and call the tune here. You'll not set foot among us here or in hall again, or eat, either, until you're in your right senses again, and ready to kneel and pray our mercy. Go to your room, and wait there until I come to you. Go, get out of my sight! And strip!" he said through his teeth into Harry's face, and thrust him neck-and-crop out of the door.

She came, as he had hoped and prayed she would. He was no longer afraid of her, she could not drag him back now, he had gone too far away from them all, even from her. She could hurt him still, and delight him still, but she could not influence him to modify any part of his intention. It was for something quite different he needed her now; she was the only one of them all whom he could hope to influence.

He was lying naked on his bed when she lifted the latch of the door and softly drew it open. He knew her touch and her step, and lifted his head from his arms to watch the movements of her shadowy figure as she came in. He turned over and sat up, wincing at every movement, and drew up the skin coverlet to his loins.

"Mother!"

"Harry, my poor, stubborn, wicked boy! Oh, how am I to touch you without hurting you? Harry, why have you brought this on yourself? I tried to help you, indeed I did. But you won't be helped! Did you *want* to be beaten? One might well have thought it, you went so far to invite it, and to drive him to extremes, too. And yet he does love you, Harry, if you would not make him so angry. There, now, I've brought something to ease you a little. Let me look at you. Lie down again—ah, let me help you turn!"

"It's not as bad as that, Mother," he said, feeling on his cheek her easy, sparkling tears that came and passed like spring rain.

"Oh, he was cruel! Poor Harry, poor child! Lie still, now, it's only my herbal lotion, it's cooling and healing. And it would have cost you only a few easy words to spare yourself this! Oh, I could beat you myself for being so stupid! Does that feel good?"

"Wonderful, Mother!" It was cold and fragrant on his smarting shoulders, even the sting of it was good. "Mother!"

"Yes?"

"Is Adam worse than this?"

She was silent for a moment. She drew down the cover to his hips and went on bathing him gently. "I don't know, I was not a witness. Afterwards you must eat something, and then try to sleep. I've brought you some barley cakes and bread, but you must mind that your father doesn't get to know of it."

"Did they give Adam anything to eat? He hasn't eaten since noon."

"Yes," she said, after another momentary hesitation, "I sent one of the scullions with some bread and meat for him." She did not say that Adam had eaten none of it when last the porter had looked in upon him, but was still lying face-down in the straw, half-conscious. "So now, I suppose, you will not refuse to eat something yourself! Oh, Harry, what obstinacy is this? Is it your fault if the law's penalties fall heavier on him than on you?"

"What he did, I did, and did it first. Mother, if you could have seen how he flew to help me—"

"I will do what can be done for him," she said, grieved, but not deeply. "He shall not want for a home afterwards, and some simple work, fit for—" She did not end it, but he heard her thoughts: "—for a one-handed man."

"Has he a bed, Mother?"

"Stop this!" she said, half angry. "I will not play this game with you any longer. Do you want me to go down to the stables and tend him, instead of you? You'd have me carry wine across the bailey, I suppose, all that way in the dark—"

"Oh, is it in the empty stable in the corner of the bailey they've put him?" asked Harry, mumbling out of the pillow to hide the trembling of his voice. Such clues as she had let fall he had put together eagerly: the stables, across the bailey, all that way in the dark. "Isn't father afraid to leave him in a stall with no lock? What, only a six-inch bar of oak between him and liberty? I expect he can still crawl, if he can't walk. But I suppose he has half a dozen men-at-arms to guard him—such a desperate felon!"

"Harry, I shall leave you if you speak so bitterly of your father. I begin to see how you could drive him to use you so. No, of course the boy is not guarded. Nobody is likely to lift the bar, but if they did he would not get far, he's in no case—" She bit off the words guiltily, feeling Harry shrink and gasp. "Ah, I've hurt you!" She had, and shrewdly, but not with her touch. He pressed his face into the pillow, and fought back the tears which might have disarmed his father had he shed them for himself. She stooped and kissed him on the ear, and he turned towards her, and wound one arm about her neck, drawing her down to him.

"There, there, Harry, it will pass! In the morning it will be better."

He turned on his side, and held her tightly with both arms. "Yes, it will! Yes, Mother, it will!" It cost him an effort to hold back the tears. "I think I could sleep now."

"Shall I stay with you a little while?"

"No, Mother, you must rest, too. I shall sleep, I promise you."

"And tomorrow, Harry, you won't provoke your father any more, will you?"

"I won't say a word amiss to him, Mother. Oh, Mother, don't think ill of me!" He was crying now; he wished she would go, and yet he could not bear to let her go. He kissed her warm cheek, and took away his arms almost roughly, dropping into the pillow again with a great sigh. When she stooped over him, peering at him closely, he kept his eyelids half-closed, and breathed long and softly, as though he were already slipping into drowsiness. Satisfied, she kissed his brow, and withdrew with the lamp, closing the door gently after her.

As soon as she was gone he opened his eyes again, and they were dry and bright and wide-awake. He waited a few minutes, lying still, in case she should come back. Then he slid stiffly and awkwardly from his bed, and began to pull on his clothes.

The iron peg which lifted the latch of his door his father had removed and taken away with him, so that the door could be opened only from outside; but it was not the first time he had been thus confined, and he had long ago made provision for such a case. The smith in the village had made him another peg, smaller and lighter, and capable of being drawn out on either side. When he was dressed, an operation which took him longer than usual because every move-ment and every touch of cloth hurt him, he ferreted out his treasure from its hiding-place in the straw of his bed, and inserted it into the hole in the door. The heavy latch lifted, and he pushed the door open gingerly and stood listening. Nothing. The steps of the watchman in the turret never carried so far, and below there was nothing stirring. He was taking with him only the clothes he wore, a cloak, and such money as he had of his own, which was little enough. Long ago he had remembered and kept to himself the blessed chance that the horses were still in the paddock at the mill. They were his, not his father's, both the grey he rode himself and the cob he had provided for Adam, and they would be fresh and ready for exercise.

He pushed the door to after him, and eased the great latch sound-lessly into place. The peg—Matthew Smith had never realised what manner of illicit tool he was providing—he drew out and pocketed, for the sight of it protruding would have been enough to launch the hounds after him, and how did he know the watchman had not been given orders to keep an eye on his room? It would be his father who first came to visit him in exile in the morning, he was quite sure of that; somewhat uneasy in mind after sleeping on his rage, inclined to regret that he had carried execution to such lengths, and firmly resolved this time to be gentle and patient with the obdurate boy, but he would end up by beating him again, of course. Only the boy would not be there to be either cajoled or beaten, on that or any other morning.

He did not know what time it was, but judged it must be after midnight. His mother would not have ventured to come to him until his father was deep asleep; moreover, the early moon was already almost down, and there was only starlight to contend with as he crept down the outer staircase and set foot on the warm, baked soil of the bailey. The shadow of the wall provided him with cover until he reached the extreme corner of the great hall; then there was open ground to cross to the huddle of sheds, armouries, stables and stores built along the lee of the curtain wall. He braced himself, and crossed at a run in the narrowest spot, and dropped under the lean-to roof of the fletcher's store. The night continued silent and indifferent. After a moment, satisfied, he got up and went on, slipping from shelter to shelter along the line, until he reached the remotest corner by the water-gate.

Adam's prison lay not far from the gate, and in deep shadow. By the complete stillness about it he was encouraged to believe that his mother had been right, and the captive was unguarded. No one, least of all Adam himself, had considered the possibility of rescue.

He braced his shoulder under the heavy oak bar that bolted the door, and drew it cautiously back in its socket, and pulling the door open slid inside, and pulled it to again behind him.

"Adam!" he whispered, standing quite still until his eyes should have accustomed themselves to the darkness.

A sharp rustle of straw answered him, and that was all. He groped forward inch by inch along the floor with cautious toes, shaken at every step by the thunderous beating of his heart.

"Adam—it's Harry!"

A square of pallor before him, low towards the floor, stirred slightly, and the straw rustled again. He put down his shoes and the rolled cloak, and went down on his knees, feeling his way forward into the fringes of the heap of straw that filled half the stable. His fingers encountered a foot, and instantly, in a violent recoil, it kicked him away and withdrew, shuffling along the floor. He followed, whispering reassurances and promises, not knowing himself what he said; and he found a naked arm, a body lying breast-down, a head that resolutely buried its face from him. Someone, probably one of the archers, who had hated their task to a man, had wrung out a linen cloth in cold water and spread it over the boy's back; but when Harry touched it now, inadvertently, it steamed warmly, and he felt the flesh through it hot as fever.

"Adam!" He lay down in the straw beside him, shaking him gently by the arm, where at least he was not afraid to touch him, and bending his cheek close to the averted head. "It's me; Harry. Won't you speak to me? How is it with you, Adam? Can you rise and go, if I help you? Oh, Adam, look up! You frighten me! Don't you know me?" He began to tremble, and then to cry, and for the life of him could not stop, but went on straining out the words through the ugly, obliterating sobs that convulsed him, until Adam, turning at last, struck at him viciously with a clenched fist.

"Get away from me!" he spat feebly. "I should have known better than count on friendship with a Talvace."

"Adam, I came to you as soon as I could—"

"Why?" asked Adam harshly. "I'm none of your kin nor kind. Get back to your own!"

He pressed closer, and caught the flailing fist between his hands, and drawing it into his breast held it fast to him and dropped helpless tears over it. "I *have* come back to my own. Don't send me away! I'm not going back there, Adam, I'm going with you, away from here. We must make haste! Can you rise? Lean on me! Try! Put your arm round my neck!"

Adam lifted his head and stared distrustfully through the darkness. "What do you mean? Is this true? You'll let me go?"

"I'm coming with you. We'll go together. No one shall rob you of your hand, Adam, no one who could wish to is any kin of mine. Lean on me, and see if you can stand and go. Only a little way, only safely out of here, then you can rest while I go for the horses. Thanks be to God we left them at the mill, I could never have got them out of here undiscovered, and we couldn't get far afoot."

"My mother," whispered Adam, breaking into tears of relief and hope and regret all desperately mingled, "she'll grieve—"

"Within a day she'll hear that we're gone, and she'll know we're together. Come, your arm round my neck, lean on me—put all your weight on me. She'll know you still have your hand, she'll know why we went, and that we'll always stay together. There, you see, you can do it." Still streaming with tears and stammering with eagerness, he got Adam to his feet and held him up, breast to breast. "Your cotte—is it here? And your capuchon, that I'll roll in my cloak, you won't need it now. Can you bear the cotte?"

The linen cloth was stuck to the bloody weals it covered. Harry eased shirt and cotte down over it, flinching to see how Adam flinched. But he was coming to life again, he was beginning to believe. He took a step away from the supporting arm, and stood alone.

"Where are we going? Where can we go?"

"To Shrewsbury, to Father Hugh. He'll not give us up, we shall find sanctuary there until you're able to travel. Can you ride so far tonight?"

"But Harry, your family," said Adam, shaking.

"What family? My father is a stone-mason, and my mother—" That was too dangerous a line of thought, he turned from it passionately. "You have always been my brother to me, and now you and yours are the only brothers I have. I'm never going back. Even without you I should have to go. Come, stay close to me, cling to me if you like. Only a little way, to the water-gate. We should be seen if we took to the boat, it's a pity."

"Harry, I'm sorry I struck you—I'm bitterly sorry—"

"Don't think of it, I didn't mind it. I knew how it was with you. Now, gently—"

He opened the door and slipped through the narrow space, one hand stretched back ready to hold Adam if he foundered. "Close to me, put your arm over my shoulders, lean on my back."

"I can go, indeed I can. Hush!"

He was fully alive now, even in his weakness and pain. He leaned forward eagerly to the soft coolness of the night, and trod more steadily with every yard of shadow that slid away behind them. In the deep archway of the water-gate they were covered from sight. Harry unbarred the wicket, and they stepped through into the grass of the meadow. From the gate to the copse along the river bank was not far, and the bailey wall screened them. They drew the first breath of freedom warily, knowing how tenuous was their hold upon it; and eagerly, with linked arms, they began to hobble towards the shelter of the trees.

Chapter Four

Towards seven in the morning, when the bell was ringing for Prime, the lay porter at the gate-house of the abbey heard hoofbeats approaching along the dusty road, and marked how oddly they came, sidling and halting as though undirected, until they came to a stop outside the gate. He looked out to see what manner of horsemen these might be, and saw two boys, the one slumped in his saddle as though in a faint, or near it, the other holding him up with one arm while the two horses, long understanding companions, sidled along flank to flank in a patient, delicate walk, shifting and steadying under their precarious load at every change of balance. The second boy was not in much better case than his friend. It seemed he had got his convoy where he wished to bring it, but now he had not the strength to transfer his companion's weight while he dismounted.

The porter, without asking questions, went round to the other side of the anxious horses, and hoisted the unconscious boy gently out of his saddle, gathering him into his arms like a baby. Through the tunic and shirt and the stiffened cloth beneath he felt and knew the harsh encrustations of dried blood.

"Wait but a moment, lad," he said to the other, who was trying with stiff, painful movements to free his feet from the stirrups. "I'll help you down. Sit quiet." And when he had bestowed his burden on his own bed in the gatehouse he stretched up his arms and took Harry, too, beneath the armpits like a child, and lifted him down. When he set him on his feet the boy's numbed legs would not bear him up, and he clung to the porter's large, steady arm for support, and, looking up, showed him a face he knew.

"Master Talvace, what's this? What are you doing here, and in such a case? Here, hold to my arm, and come your ways in." He knew now who the other must be, though he had not yet looked at his face. "What has befallen you? Have you been attacked? Where was your sense to ride that road by night, with all the footpads there are loose along the borders these days?"

"No footpads," said Harry with a crooked grin. "We got our injuries in quite another quarter. Edmund, I must see the abbot. Soon, as soon as he can receive me."

"Well, and so you shall, at his convenience, but it won't be till after chapter, at earliest, and by the look of you you've need of rest, the pair of you. Is young Adam injured—beyond what I know? Or is this only a swoon?" He bent over the limp body, and listened to the lengthening, steadying breath, and smiled, reassured. "What it is to be young! It was a swoon a minute ago, and with the first touch of a bed it's sleep. He'll do well so. Nothing better could be done for him."

"He stood it like a Trojan till beyond the ford," said Harry, his voice quavering with exhaustion. "Then he began to flag, and we had to take it more easily. A walk hurt him less. But the last mile or so I know not how I kept him in the saddle, or myself, either. Edmund, have the horses looked to, would you? I could not unsaddle if my life hung on it, I'm so stiff. Without you I should have had to fall off—no other way."

"They shall be taken care of. First I'm going to find the infirmarer, and have this one carried to bed, and you, too. Time enough when you've had your sleep out to ask you what ailed you to come stravaging through the night like this. Stay with him till I come again."

Harry would not have stirred a step away from the bedside for any lure. Not until safe sanctuary or many more miles of alien land separated Adam from the king's verderer would Harry be willing to let him out of his sight. He sat propping up his sagging eyelids and staring at the soiled, drained face now relaxing into natural sleep, until the infirmarer came hurrying in with two of his nursing brothers, and swept both boys before him into the clean, cool, narrow cubicles of the infirmary. Harry began an arduous explanation to which no one listened, and which soon subsided into incoherent mumbling, and thence into acquiescent silence. He surrendered the responsibility for himself gratefully, and allowed himself to be undressed and washed and filled up with warm milk and bread like a baby. The last half-conscious thought he had as he was settled gently on his breast in a hard but fragrant bed, was that Adam was blessedly too sound asleep to feel the pain as the brothers patiently cut and bathed the linen cloth from his back and dressed his weals. When he awoke it would be to a kind of ease, in an enclave of safety. With tears of gratitude filling his eyelids he fell asleep in his turn, and left his own pain behind, the last sloughed skin of the old life which was over.

In the abbot's parlour in his private lodging the infirmarer reported the arrivals. Hugh de Lacy pushed away pen and inkhorn along the polished table, and sat for a long minute gazing before him into his walled garden, moist and radiant in the fresh morning.

"So soon!" he said. And after a moment, with a sigh: "Poor Harry!" He thrust back his chair, and got to his feet. "I'll come with you and see these truants, Brother Denis."

"They are fast asleep, Father. It was what they most needed. They have been barbarously used." The infirmarer was old and gentle, and disapproved even of the extent to which the subprior used the discipline on his novices and pupils.

"We'll not disturb them. But I must see for myself." If he was to have a difficult mediation on his hands he must have his facts pat. Brother Denis's indignation he discounted; nevertheless there were ugly possibilities. Harry knew only too well how to provoke ferocity, an unlucky characteristic in the young who have so few means of defending themselves.

He limped across the great court beside the infirmarer, and entered the cell where the boys lay sleeping, their two narrow beds drawn close together.

"Harry would have it so," said Brother Denis. "It was all we could do to make him leave go of Adam while we stripped him. I thought it best to humour him. If his fellow lay out of reach of his hand he would be restless, and, poor lad, he has need of rest.''

Flushed and moist-lipped, Harry lay with one smooth naked arm stretched across on to Adam's bed, his curled fingers close to his brother's brown wrist. Brother Denis lifted the coverlet and exposed his back to the thighs, and after a moment as gently replaced the linen.

''The other one is worse.''

Adam's back was covered with a compress steeped in a decoction of snakeweed and centaury to cool and heal the open wounds, and he lay uneasily, brokenly upon his face, but so dead asleep that he never stirred or checked in his deep, heavy breathing when the infirmarer turned back a corner of the cloth and showed the purple-striped corrosion of his flesh. ''How they rode so far in such a case I cannot tell. Motion and weariness and the rubbing of their garments have aggravated their ills, but, praise God they're both strong, healthy boys, and a few days of proper care will mend all.''

''It argues,'' said the abbot, looking down at them with a frowning face and shadowed eyes, ''a degree of desperation in them. Since they were not running to escape this, what else pursues them?''

The infirmarer, smoothing his compress lightly into place, shook his head forebodingly. ''If they had been felons convicted they could not have been used much worse. What more could there be threatening two mere boys? They have not been questioned at all yet, of course, but it is evident the household of Sleapford cannot know they have ridden here to us. I have taken no steps to send them word. As Harry has asked for an audience with you, Father, I thought it best that any action should wait for your considered judgement.''

''You were wise, Denis. We may take it, I suppose, that if they are being sought the search will stay close at home for a day or two. For Eudo will certainly not be unaware,'' he said very drily, ''that they were in no case to travel far.''

''When they begin to look farther afield,'' said Brother Denis candidly, ''we shall be among the first refuges to come to mind. But they will not look for them here until they have combed the valley and their own woods. Surely that should give us two or three days' grace.''

"Good! By then at least I shall know what lies behind this escapade. When Harry is awake and fed and clear in mind, send him to me. If he sleeps till tomorrow, why, let him sleep. We are surely to be left in peace until then; and I cannot well be expected to pass on information which I do not yet possess myself, can I?"

A fly settled for an instant upon Harry's flushed cheek, and Hugh de Lacy stooped to brush it away. The boy shivered and gave a soft, frightened cry in his sleep, and the outflung hand groped distressfully for a moment and touched only the cool, rustling mattress. His lashes fluttered wildly, and his parted lips formed Adam's name, though they uttered only a little animal whimper. Then Hugh de Lacy took the questing hand in his own, and folded the trembling fingers upon Adam's wrist. They fastened eagerly, and clung, and were calm; he sighed away again tranquilly into sleep.

The abbot went back to his own apartments with a heavy heart. On the slender wrist now so lovingly circled he had seen a fading blue bracelet, the bruise left by the iron loop of the whipping-post.

Harry tapped at the door of the abbot's parlour during the hour of the first Mass next morning, while the servants and labourers and lay officials were in the church, and the great court was quiet. He had no fear of the abbot, but he approached this room with a kind of reminiscent trepidation, left over from the days when he had, on rare occasions, been sent here to receive a more than usually solemn reprimand for his casual boyish sins. The feeling discomfited him now, because he felt so strongly that he was innocent of sin. Sometimes in the old days he had entered here in that same conviction, and gone out subdued and near to tears of penitence over faults newly-recognised. And all this Father Hugh had been able to achieve without so much as raising his voice.

Bidden to enter, Harry did so almost timidly. The abbot turned from his table at the window, and smiled at him, though with some anxiety still shadowing his brows.

"Come in, Harry! Have you breakfasted?"

"Yes, Father, I thank you." Harry went forward and kissed the hand Hugh de Lacy held out to him. "I wanted to come to you when I awoke, last night, but Brother Denis said it was too late and you

were busy. I have been remiss, to have enjoyed your grace a whole
day already without waiting upon you, but—"

"Say no more, Harry, I know you were very tired, I was glad that
you should sleep. And how is Adam this morning? He is not up, I
suppose?"

"Not yet, but Brother Denis said that perhaps he may get up
during the morning for a little while. He is wonderfully restored."
He looked doubtfully at the abbot's calm face, and said with some
embarrassment: "I am not sure, Father, if you know—"

"I visited you," said the abbot, "while you were both sleeping. I
know. Come, sit down here by me, and tell me what brings you
here in such a case."

The boy pulled up the low chair the abbot indicated, and sat down
within touch of the long, thin, muscular hand that lay on the crossed
knees.

"Father Hugh, Adam and I are come to throw ourselves on your
mercy. When I left you, you said that I might come to you in my
need, at whatever time, and you would stand my friend. Father, we
are in great need of that friendship now."

"So I had supposed, my child. Tell me the story."

"On the day before yesterday I had a holiday from the rolls, and
Adam and I took our crossbows and went shooting at hares and
conies in the fields that were just being reaped. You know there is
always good sport when they break cover as the reapers close in.
When we had taken several and were tired of that, we rode on to the
mill and left our horses there, and went on afoot into the forest. It is
Sir Roger le Tourneur's chase there. We stayed out all day, and as we
were coming back through the forest in the early evening—"

Thus far he had gone slowly, feeling his way past the need for
mentioning Hunyate and their secret errand there. The record
sounded satisfactorily complete; he went on with growing confidence
to tell all the rest of the story truthfully, even to his own hysterical
fit of temper in the mews, of which he was not proud. His voice
gathered angry way, pouring out the passionate grievance he had
against the injustice of Adam's sentence. The abbot heard him to
the end in courteous silence, and with a grave face. It was worse
than he had feared.

"And so you took Adam from his prison, and brought him here to me. I see."

"I knew that the church could not fail to protect him from injustice."

"Injustice! You are in love with that word, are you not, Harry? Don't be angry with me, my dear child, and don't leap to the conclusion that I am withdrawing the assurance of my friendship if I put some questions to you: the questions you have failed to ask yourself."

Harry looked up sharply, and the sunlight burning in from the walled garden struck gold from his bright, disconcerting eyes. "I shall answer them if I can, Father."

"First, then, imagine yourself to be one of the king's verderers. You, with your foresters, have come upon two young fellows, armed with bows—itself an indictable offence within forest precincts—in the act of cutting the throat of a wounded doe. They deny hunting her, and say they did but find her hurt and put her from her pain. They say in support of this that they have been in the forest only an hour, whereas the doe has clearly bled several hours since she took the bolt in her side. But they will cite no witness to say they have been elsewhere during those hours, nor will they themselves say where they have been. Tell me, verderer, would you believe them or your own eyes?"

"It was a reasonable suspicion, I know it. But I swear to you, as I swore to him, that we did not hunt her."

"And I accept your word without question. But I am in a position to do so, and Sir Roger was not. He is in a situation of trust and responsibility where he must proceed only upon the weight of evidence."

"I have said, Father, that it was a reasonable suspicion. But we have been sentenced and punished without trial!"

"You were taken in a private chase. Though Sir Roger makes it his habit to send all charges to the attachment court—and that is a good and scrupulous quality in him—he is not obliged to do so. He could bring you up at his own manor court and be judge in his own cause, and he would be within his rights. Do you think you would in either case have fared any better?"

"It might at least have given us time to find witnesses who had seen us—'' He broke off just in time, and flashed upwards a brilliant glance of doubt and uncertainty.

"I am not trying to trap you, my child. If you can tell me what you would not tell him, where you had been that day, well; if not—"

"I cannot, Father, because it is not my secret, and it is important to someone else that I should not betray it. But in a little while, even a few days, I might have been free to speak."

"That is unfortunate, but scarcely Sir Roger's fault, or your father's either. Well, so! You deny the charge of hunting the doe, but agree that circumstances made it eminently reasonable you should be thus charged—and certain, Harry, that in a court, upon such evidence as exists up to now, you would have been convicted. Will you go so far with me?"

Reluctantly but honestly, the boy said: "Yes, Father."

"Now as to the second charge, of assaulting Sir Roger's person. Do you deny that?"

"No, Father. I did attack him. I was frightened, I knew we should never be believed. But I didn't know it was he—"

"Folly is no defence. Do you deny that Adam also attacked him?"

"No, Father, but he did it because—"

"He did it. The reason would not, I fear, extenuate the crime. To this charge you both plead guilty. Of what, then, do you complain?"

Harry's head jerked up fiercely: "I don't understand you, Father. They would have cut off Adam's hand!"

"Harry, Harry, when will you learn to accept realities? You know forest law as well as I do. You admit to a crime of the highest gravity, for so the law holds it to be. What does forest law say of the penalties for offering violence to the king's verderer?"

" 'If he be a free man, he shall lose his freedom and all that he has.' "

"And if he be a villein?"

" '—he shall lose his right hand.' Yes, but—"

"No buts! There you read your sentence and Adam's if the charge had gone forward to the attachment court. How would he be helped by your losing your freedom to keep company with his hand? And if the charge referring to the deer had been brought to a verdict— God forbid innocent men should be so beset, but God He knows it must happen sometimes!—you know the penalties for that, too. For you, being free and noble, a heavy fine, but for Adam, being a villein, death under the knife of the flayer. Do you tell me the verderer was not merciful in commuting that to a whipping? He has not exacted his full rights, he has gone out of his way to spare you, as he sees the case. Yet you complain of him."

Harry was on his feet, quivering before the abbot's chair. "Are you telling me that it is right and good that they should take Adam's hand?"

"Whether I think it so or not is beside the point. I am telling you that it is *legal*."

"Legal!" said the boy with an upward jerk of his head and a curl of his lip. "You insist on talking of law. I am talking about justice. It may be legal for him to spare my freedom, if he please, and yet not spare Adam's hand, but it is not *just*, even if you approve the law. And I do not! It is a vile law that makes distinction between hand and hand. You talk of accepting realities! If my hand and Adam's lay severed before you, would you know which was the free, and which the unfree? What respect can I have for a law which pretends there are differences where I *know* there are none?"

"So it comes to this," said the abbot mildly, "that you are venturing to set up your own judgement against the law of this land."

"Father, if I have a mind, if I have that faculty of measuring which you call judgement, is it not the gift of God? Am I to bury it in the ground and let it rot? For God's sake, what can I do with it in conscience and duty but use it as best I can?"

"That is very well said, Harry! And let me tell you this, law is a compromise, a makeshift, a best that can be done with the material at hand, never finished. Human minds, though—forgive me!— older and wiser and greater minds than yours, compounded it, and I think none who had a hand in it will ever claim that it cannot be bettered. And you are right to speak out where you think it fails of its purpose, which is justice, though you must beware of thinking that your criticisms are therefore invariably justified. There are doubtless some laws which are bad—though to be plain with you I do not think this is among them—and in time they will be changed. It is a good part to work for such amendment. But while the law is as it is, you are bound by it, and so am I, and we must conform. It is no cure for a bad law to trample it underfoot."

"Father, what choice had we? In a year, or two years, or ten, this penalty which I find vile may be done away. But Adam would have lost his hand yesterday if I had not taken him and run to you." He stood breathing heavily, staring at the abbot's still and rueful face, and his eyes widened into green ovals of horror. "I see! That's one of the realities you are willing to accept. Well, I am not! Never!" His voice sank to a flat, cold tone that dropped like icy rain on the abbot's listening heart. "What do you purpose to do? Give us up?"

"Sit down again, Harry, and listen to me. You are too hasty."

"I have need to be hasty, I am but one pace ahead of the axe," said Harry in the same bleak voice; but he sat down obediently, and waited with a composed and wary face.

"I shall not give you up, Harry, because you will make it unnecessary. No, let me speak! You were at fault, my poor child, in running away, and a fault, however understandable, must be expiated. I cannot and will not abet a son's revolt against his father, or a villein's flight from his lord. I am bound by the law, and I owe a duty to authority. I can and will intervene on your behalf, and try if I cannot get Sir Roger to stretch his clemency yet again and spare Adam's hand, and your father to forgive your rebellion against him. But if they stand on their full rights I cannot withhold from Sir Eudo either his son or his villein, nor restrain him from exacting the full penalties from you both. I'll stretch every eloquence and every art I know to beg you both off, Harry, but upon one condition—that you submit and deliver yourselves up voluntarily, and throw yourselves on Sir Eudo's mercy."

"I thank you," said Harry, on his feet, "I have experienced my father's mercy. I had thought I was confiding myself to yours."

"You must listen to me, child, and trust me to use all the influence I have in your behalf. But I can do nothing while you are in revolt. The law is the law, and must be respected. Your father's authority is sacred, and I cannot assist you to flout it."

The boy stood drawn back a little from him, the sea-green eyes fixed steadily upon his face. All the warmth which had reached out to him when Harry entered the room had withdrawn into the erect, alert body, and left him shivering with cold in the summer sunlight. He had expected an outburst, but none came. Harry was done with tears and entreaties. Neither law nor church would protect the weak.

It remained only to find some means of ceasing to be weak, and protect himself and his own.

"I cannot argue with you, Father. I only know that I am right and you are wrong, and I will abide by that as long as I live. I will never again ask you for anything. I pray you will not involve yourself for me, I will make shift alone. And now, if you have said all you have to say to me—" He waited for dismissal with his mouth shut tight like a straight sword-cut, and his nostrils quivering, so perfectly a Talvace, so dauntingly a man, that the abbot looked in vain for the boy he had welcomed so short a while ago.

Hugh de Lacy got up from his chair and crossed to the window, turning his back upon the room. He stood for a long moment with his eyes shut against the sun, trying to comprehend the dread and anxiety he felt for this fiery creature who flew his pennant into the teeth of so irresistible a wind. What could be done to control him? What can be done to divert the launched arrow, or turn downward the mounting flame? Not argue with me, he thought, oh child, if you but knew! It is I who am being driven back by the storm, not you.

"Have I your leave to go, sir?" asked the cold voice that had in it all the heritage he was denying, all the steel and arrogance of Belesme and Ponthieu and Alençon.

"Harry, for God's sake and for your own, bend that neck of yours before life bend it for you or tear your head from your shoulders. It is not possible to live as you want to live; every man must give way sooner or later, kings, popes, all who live yield some step backwards on occasion to remain upright and draw breath. Learn humility, while there's yet time, before life teach you with harsher beatings than ever you suffered yet. Bow yourself now, and you will find it less difficult and less shaming than you think. You shall not kneel alone, Harry, I shall be a suppliant with you. And I swear to you that I will find some means to obtain Adam's pardon, though I must follow your father and Tourneur across the shire on my knees—"

He halted there, feeling the room grown cold at his back. He turned and saw the door already closed, and heard the boy's steps receding steadily in the distance along the flagged corridor, until silence washed over his footfalls like the incoming sea.

* * *

In the dimness within doors he went like one dazed from a blow, and felt that the heart in him was broken; and when he came out into the air, and the morning sunshine leaped and clasped him like a warm hand, and the surge of colour and brightness clashed like cymbals and pealed like bells about him in the bustle of the great court, it seemed to him at first that he was only being mocked and tormented with a cruel illusion of summer and life and gaiety. But he walked between the abbey villeins, arguing and laughing over their preparations for the day's field labour, and the beggars sunning themselves under the wall of the almonry, and the merchants waiting to bargain with the prior over pots and cloth and stock and timber before chapter, and the free tenants come to pay dues or air grievances; and in spite of himself he was warmed, and in spite of his conviction of outrage and betrayal his senses reached out hungrily, and fed and enjoyed. The world was busy and beautiful and diverse, no less now that the abbot had failed him; and for the life of him he could not help delighting in it.

Nevertheless, their situation was desperate. They were now utterly forsaken. "Learn humility, while there's yet time—": those were the last of the abbot's words he had waited to hear. All very well, he thought, to be humble in accepting one's own pain and deprivation, perhaps, but what right have I, what right has he, to make a virtue of meekness when it will be Adam who suffers? I call that a cheap humility. And he thought, well, now we have no one to lean on but each other. So much the better, now there will be no one to let us fall.

He stopped for a moment to watch the travellers from the guest-house making ready for the road; two packmen, a ragged jongleur, and a nomad tinsmith with his trade on his back, from the humbler quarters; then a very young knight, probably as new as Ebrard, very pert and pretty in a brocaded cotte trimmed shorter than the fashion to display a fine leg in a well-cut riding boot. He drew in his rein short and tight as he mounted, to make his chestnut horse arch his neck and sidle and dance, so that he might show his skill, and Harry suffered a momentary temptation to slap unexpectedly under the glossy belly as he went by, and start a livelier measure. But he resisted it manfully. He had grown up to some tune, or so he considered, since he had delighted in Ebrard's disaster at the Christmas festivities in Shrewsbury castle. It was beneath his own dignity, now, publicly to upset the dignity of another, even when provoked. Though he would not undertake to guarantee his good behaviour too long where this ineffable lordling was concerned. Now he had wheeled the beast on his hind legs in a quite unnecessary circle, and caused one or two elderly merchants and the jongleur to scuttle hurriedly out of his way. People who used the spur to make a show of their horsemanship in a crowded court should be well rowelled themselves.

A little girl of ten or eleven, who had been tossing a bright needlework ball against the wall of the refectory, dropped her toy and squeezed herself into the angle of a buttress from the dancing hooves. Harry plucked her out of her corner and swept her away in his arm, to put her down well out of range as the horseman cantered out of the court. Her ball had rolled away under a wagon which was drawn up beneath the refectory windows; he retrieved it and tossed it back to her with a smile.

"Fools on horseback need a deal of room," he said.

She clasped the ball to her breast, and looked at him consideringly with large dark eyes, exceedingly grave and intent. She wore a cotte of blue linen, and a flowered bliaut over it, and the toes of little pointed blue cloth shoes, planted formally side by side, peeped from under her skirt. In her two short braids of black hair there was a gilt thread wound. Her mouth was like two tightly folded petals of a red rose.

"I am not afraid of horses," she said loftily. "We have fifteen horses, besides the ones the archers ride."

"You are fortunate," said Harry, impressed. "I have only two."

She turned her head a little, sidewise, and looked at him from beneath her lashes, and arched a foot from under her gown, drawing negligent half-circles in the dust. She was more than halfway to being a woman, and he was not an ill-looking boy.

"But *I* ride in the cart, because all the horses are too big for me. At home I have a little one. Will you show me your horses, if I show you ours?"

"I would, gladly," said Harry, preoccupied with other thoughts, "but I have a friend who is sick, and I must go and see him in the infirmary."

"Afterwards!" said the child, calling after him. "We shall be a long time yet, loading and harnessing. Come back afterwards, boy!"

"Yes, afterwards," he laughed over his shoulder, and passed on, threading his way between the hurrying servants who were carrying bales of cloth from the guesthouse and loading them into the standing cart. A second wain was just being man-handled out of the stableyard, and the lively stamping of horses, fresh from their stalls, followed it across the cobbles. He halted abruptly and turned towards the sound, reminded how brief a time he might have to extricate himself and Adam from this place which had become now so dangerous to them, and how precious were the two mounts which were their only means of escape. He was suddenly desperate to look once again upon the horses and unreasonably afraid that they would no longer be there, and he ran into the yard and began to hunt through it from stall to stall.

They were not there! There was no doubt of it. He searched the stables from end to end, and back again to the gate, but his flecked grey was nowhere to be found, nor the fat brown cob Adam had ridden. As soon as he had assured himself of their loss he turned furiously to rush to the gate-house and demand of Edmund what he had done with them; and then, before he had gone a dozen yards, he checked equally sharply, knowing beyond question in whose private, walled courtyard they were now stabled. He turned to march back to the abbot's lodging and challenge the thief directly. Father Hugh had been wonderfully quick in taking measures to ensure that his truants should not get away again. The last and logical treason!

But if he bearded him and demanded his property, how would they be helped? It would most surely be withheld, and what means had he of forcing its return? No, that was not the way. One angry word to the abbot, and he would be watched narrowly at every move, and goodbye to all chance of getting Adam away. No, he must not approach either the abbot or the gate-house, or do anything to warn them that he was making new plans for escape. The need was to go, without warning, without detection; and how was it to be done?

His rapid walk had slowed, and he was again beside the guest-house. Three carts stood waiting now, the first already loaded and tied down with a coarse cloth coated with pitch for protection against rain. The third was covered with an awning of the same cloth, and had at the front a cushioned seat prepared. The awning was merely a span from side to side of the wain, stretched upon wooden struts, open at front and back. The cart was agreeably deep, and if the load was cloth it would be reasonably soft lying. His eyes began to brighten, and shone with flecks of gold.

"Those are our carts," said an insinuating voice at his shoulder. The child with the ball had a doll, too, now, a small wooden copy of herself, down to the blue shoes. She looked up at him speculatingly through her long lashes, and when he smiled she smiled also. "And our horses," she said.

"You must be very rich," said Harry respectfully, "to have all those horses, and all those bales of cloth. Where are they all going?"

"Home," she said practically, as if that should have been self-evident.

"And where is home?"

"London. My father has a shop there, and he comes to Shrewsbury once a year to buy wool cloths from all the border websters, and the Welsh ones, too, and now we're taking what we've bought back to London, except we shall sell some bolts of it on the way. My father says it is as good cloth as any comes from the north. My father says the merchants of the Staple can preen themselves as much as they please, but finished goods, piece goods, is the coming trade. We deal only in piece goods. What do you deal in?"

"Nothing as yet," said Harry. "How soon are you leaving with the carts? Do you travel far in one day?"

"We shall be ready within the hour. Sometimes we can do more than twenty miles a day in the summer. We shall today, because from here there is a good road. What does your father do?"

No need to publish his name or estate, where they were already too well-known. "He is a stone-mason," said Harry.

"And shall you become one, too?"

She had the freshest and most honest of voices, for all her sidelong glances, and the artful, artless movements with which she sought to engage his attention; and if her lips were the firm, folded convolutions of the budding rose, her cheeks were the round, smooth fullness of the ripe bloom. He looked down at her, and broke into a dazzled smile.

"Yes," he said, "surely I shall! That's very well thought of, and you are a clever lass."

"Would you like to play ball with me?" she offered, encouraged by this success, and made an inviting gesture towards him with the many-coloured ball and a dancing step or two away from him.

"I should like it very much, but there are some duties I have to do before I may play. Perhaps before you leave I shall have completed them."

"Then you'll come back?" she asked, her face clouding slightly, but her eyes hopeful.

"If I'm ready in time, yes, I'll come back."

She watched him go, her brows knit, her small white teeth biting thoughtfully at the end of one of her black braids. She reached up, without taking her eyes from Harry's receding figure, and dropped the doll over the tailboard of the cart, and the ball after it. She had no more interest in them.

Harry went into the infirmary and sought out Brother Denis, who was preparing to attend the second Mass and the chapter which would follow it. He accosted him with a drooping head and a disconsolate face.

"Father Infirmarer, if Adam may get up and dress, I should like him to come with me into the church after Mass. You won't mind? While it's very quiet, during chapter, I want to pray—" he cast down his eyes and compressed his lips for a moment "—for a happy issue out of our trouble." If it would give them a moment's pleasure to see him submissive, that satisfaction at any rate they might have, and welcome. They would be the more likely to let him alone during that vital half-hour of chapter, while every one of the brothers was safely accounted for, and only the lay servants were left to notice his movements.

He felt a tremor of shame, none the less, when Brother Denis, instead of giving him a hurried glance and a word of commendation, took him gently by the shoulders and embraced him, kissing his forehead. "God bless you, Harry! I have prayed, too. Never fear but you shall find grace. But will it not suffice if you make use of the infirmary chapel?"

"No, I have a desire to ask specially for Our Lady's intercession. Since I gave her my angel I have a fondness for that altar most of all."

"Very well, you shall not be disturbed. I will mention it to Father Prior, it will rejoice his heart. Be gentle with Adam, don't let him kneel too long. Afterwards he may sit in the sun in the garden."

Gentle, solicitous and happy, the father of great numbers of adopted sons, from the youngest schoolboy tearful with toothache to the aged and dying turned children again, he looked round his clean, bare kingdom with one loving glance, and bustled away to Mass. No wonder the novices had many times been known to feign illness in order to creep into the haven of his care for a little while, as a respite from the subprior's iron rule. One youngster, homesick and lonely, had even eaten noxious berries once to ensure for himself a long stay in the infirmarer's beneficent shadow, and never grudged the sickness and misery it cost him at the outset. And Brother Denis had seen to it that he was not disciplined for his act when he was well again, though everyone knew that the kind old man's story of an honest mistake was a gracious fiction. They said he missed every one of his patients sorely when they left him. Looking after him with rueful eyes, Harry wondered if even he, unworthy though not ungrateful, would cost Brother Denis another small pang of loss.

Adam, with his scars newly dressed and his stomach comfortably filled, was whistling as he lay on his bed, his chin propped on his fists to lift his face into the small patch of sunlight that found its way in through the window of the cell. His bare toes drummed the mattress in time to the tune. His eyes were closed against the radiance, and his easy eyelids and every line of his face smiled contentedly. He was quite without fear, and did not mind what was left of the pain. His confidence in the abbot was as implicit as Harry's had been an hour ago.

Harry sat down on the edge of the bed. "Get up and dress. You have Brother Denis's permission to come into the church with me after Mass and pray for safe deliverance."

Adam opened one astonished blue eye at him, and pondered a flippant reply; and then very rapidly opened the second eye to look more attentively, and was confirmed in his impression that this was no time for fooling. He raised himself stiffly and swung his feet to the floor, searching Harry's face with eyes alert and anxious. "What has happened? What did he say to you?" He kept his voice very low, in case one of the nursing brothers should be passing within earshot.

"You shall hear later. Hurry! I'll help you dress. How do you feel? Can you walk without pain?"

"I'm well enough, only stiff as an old man. I need exercise." Adam stood stamping his feet experimentally as he drew his shirt over his head. Harry eased it down gingerly over the laced and puckered scars already beginning to fade into livid blue from their blackened crimson. The open wounds had healed over already, for his flesh was as clean as a flower, but the worst among them were covered only by a thin film, and would break again only too easily.

"It hurts you! Badly? Can you bear it so?"

"Bear it, yes, and well! I've nursed myself a whole day and a night, what more could I ask? And if we're going far," said Adam in a very low voice, "you had better remember your cloak."

"Yes, well thought of!" He was wildly grateful for the under-standing they had between them, which rendered words so signifi-cant and enabled them to be spent so sparingly.

"I can't stand the touch of homespun yet," said Adam, smiling at him, "and it's cold in the church after this sunshine. Will you lend me your cloak to put round my shoulders?"

Harry rolled up their capuchons and Adam's discarded tunic into a tight bundle, and thrust it within his own more ample cotte, under his armpit and clasped against his side. Upon that arm Adam leaned to steady himself as they went slowly out and crossed the great court to the church. The cloak, which would have been too bulky to be hidden so, hung loosely from Adam's shoulders by its neck-chain, and in the porch he drew a fold of it round him.

"Where are we really going?" he asked in a whisper, beneath the last chanting of the Mass.

"Out of here. They intend to force us to give ourselves up."

"Father Hugh?" asked Adam, drawing an incredulous breath.

"Himself he gave it to me. I am to kneel and submit to my father, for you and for me. If I will abase myself and pray mercy, he will graciously intercede for us."

"Waste of breath!" muttered Adam, large-eyed in the dimness of the nave, and shivered.

"So I think!"

Mass was ending. From the parochial part of the church, at their backs, a few townsfolk withdrew quietly. The brethren filed away into the cloister on their way to chapter. The two boys kept their places, kneeling side by side, until they were alone and the door to the cloister had clashed to softly for the last time.

"Watch the parish door for me," said Harry, leaping up.

"What are you going to do?" But Adam rose hastily and took station beside one of the great round columns close to the porch. Harry was at the almsboxes; Adam heard wood part with a splintering crack, and stared horrified. "For God's sake, what are you about?"

"I'm about getting what I can for my property." Harry's dagger, fellow to the one Ebrard had taken from him two nights ago, prised up the lid of the box and raised it intact. Pence rattled hurriedly through his fingers. "Nothing near their value. Let's see if the other can do better."

"Harry, it's sacrilege!" Adam was shivering.

"Let him pursue me for it if he choose, and I will charge him with the theft of my horses. What right had he to impound them? I owe him nothing." He thrust the blade beneath the lid of the second box, and levered upwards viciously, and the joints parted. He emptied that box, too, carefully counting the coins he had taken, and then set the lids back into position so that to the passing view they looked undisturbed. "Eleven shillings and seven pence—I'm leaving him still in my debt."

"Harry, some poor devil will be thrown into prison for suspicion of this."

"No, by God, he shall not!" said Harry, brought up short against this idea. "I'll leave his lordship a message that shall let him know to whom he must come if he wants to recover his alms. I'll not let anyone else suffer for what I've done."

He took Adam by the arm, and drew him into the western cloister. In one of the alcoves flanking the garth, which had the sun on this side through the morning, there would surely be someone's copying left, complete with pens and inkhorn, waiting for the labourer's return from chapter. In fact there were three desks thus left vacant. Harry helped himself to the most insignificant piece of parchment he could find, already imperfectly cleaned at least once of a previous text, and wrote hurriedly:

To the Lord Abbot Hugh de Lacy, with respect, these:

Since it has pleased your lordship to impound my horses, thereby denying me their use who alone have the right to it, I have been compelled to avail myself of your lordship's loan of eleven shillings and seven pence, hereby acknowledged. The sum is less than the value of my beasts, but perforce I leave them as security. And I charge your lordship look well to them, for the time shall come when the money shall be repaid in full, and the horses shall again be required of you.

Touching the nice question of ownership, let your lordship take note that the horses are undoubtedly mine, and not the property of my father or my brother, or any other soever, and should they be given up to any man but me I will require of you their price in full.

That your lordship may continue in health until my debt and your undertaking be discharged, is the prayer of your lordship's most humble servant

Henry Talvace.

"He'll be struck dumb by your impudence," said Adam, torn between horror and admiration as he read over the writer's shoulder.

"I think not," said Harry, remembering the scene which had already passed between them that morning. "Sit here in the sun, Adam, and wait for me, I'll be but a moment. And let me take back my cloak." He bundled it under his arm, and ran back into the church. The rolled-up parchment he thrust into one of the empty almsboxes. Then he went into the Lady Chapel.

On the altar the lamp with its small red flame flushed to the warmth of life the vivid face of the angel. Harry knelt upon the steps, looking up at the ancient stone Virgin whose worn features and thick body yet seemed to him to possess so much monumental beauty, and into whose capacious lap he had sometimes made believe he could climb for comfort when he was wretched.

"Holy Virgin, forgive me for taking back a gift once given, and trust me it shall be restored some day. But you know how much I need it, since I have no other work of my own to show. I do but borrow it back until I come again. Holy Virgin, don't be angry with me! Help me to turn it to good account."

There was no time for more. He climbed the steps and caught up the angel, and the bright being turned impetuously in his grasp and embraced him with slender, outstretched arms. He wrapped the cloak about it, and ran, clasping it tenderly under his arm. As soon as he emerged into the cloister Adam rose from his place on the stone bench, large-eyed and nervous.

"What is it? What have you done? Harry, this will end badly!"

"Hush! Come, now, quickly! Afterwards I'll tell you."

Adam, at least, had done nothing this time. If the worst befell, and the carts were already gone, if they were recaptured before they could get clear, at least he could ensure that the penalties fell where they were due. As well be flayed for a buck as a fawn. This time he understood fully his relationship with law; this time he would not lament if it exacted from him every last farthing of his debt, since he had incurred it with open eyes.

But the three carts were still there when they crept out from the cloister into the great court, and the horses were just being put to the foremost one. Harry slipped into the deep doorway of the refectory, drawing Adam after him, and watched from the shadow as the team were backed into place with encouraging words and a busy clicking of tongues. All eyes were on them, even the lay servants and the dogs had gathered to watch. A tall, portly fellow, large-voiced and merry and brisk, marshalled his men to the task with the easy good-humour of long custom. The third cart, a coarse cover thrown loosely over its bales of cloth, stood close to the doorway, its open back not three yards from where the boys stood, its bulk sheltering them from sight.

"Quickly!" said Harry. "Into the cart, and cover yourself!"

Adam hauled himself up without one questioning look, and vanished with a convulsive heave beneath the loose cloth. Harry stood quite still in the shadow until the ripple of movement had ceased, and then lifted the swathed angel and dropped him over one rear corner of the cart. The team of four horses was already coupled; they thrust forward into the harness and drew the first cart away towards the gate-house, there to wait for its fellows. The cluster of archers and grooms stood back placidly while the second team was brought forth from the stable-yard; and in the moment when the horses were again the centre of attention Harry made a leap, and hauled himself aboard the cart.

Beneath the sackcloth it was hot, and smelled of hairy fibres and woven wool. He drew the angel into cover with him, and parting the bales of cloth with his arms, dug a place for it beneath them, and bestowed it there out of sight. Close beside him Adam, breathing heavily and painfully, was hoisting up bales to make a hollow for himself. Harry dragged aside the bolt that lay heavy against his brother's shoulders, and eased him down gently on his side. They lay together, quivering, between the hot stuffs, and Harry tugged at the bales above until they leaned together and touched over their panting bodies. Then they lay still, sweating with the weight of their covering and the want of air, but utterly buried from sight.

Some three minutes later Sir Eudo Talvace himself rode in at the gate, with Ebrard beside him and four archers of Sleapford at his back, and bawled for immediate audience with my lord abbot.

Chapter was not yet over when a lay servant brought word to the abbot. He closed his book, and pushed back his chair, and sat for a moment pondering. He had not expected them quite so soon; it was lucky he had already talked with the boy.

"Very well," he said, "admit them. And find Harry and bring him here to me. Mark me, Harry only! Keep the other one out of sight until I send for him. Tell Brother Infirmarer I wish it so. And Harry is to come straight to me, you understand? No one is to lay hand on him."

"Yes, Father!" And the messenger went tranquilly to the infirmary to find his charge, and from there no less placidly to the church. Even when he failed to find them there he thought no wrong, but inquired yet again at the infirmary, in case they had gone back through the cloisters. They could not be far away. He knew, as everyone knew by now, that earlier this morning the gatekeeper had received orders to set watch for them at the gate, and have a servant ready outside the parochial door of the church, and to turn them back if they attempted to leave. It was only a matter of finding them. He went from gate-house to garden, from

the pool to the stables, from the meadows to the guest-house, and
back to the infirmary again, hurrying now, and in a sweat, for the
abbot did not like to be kept waiting. Brother Denis met him at the
door with an anxious, almost an accusing face.

"His cloak is gone. Why should he need his cloak? What can have
become of them?"

It was high time to report the disappearance. Brother Denis dismissed the servant and undertook the embassage himself. The face
he brought into the abbot's parlour, silencing voices which had been
raised in some choler a moment before, was a reproach to them all.
"Between you," it said indignantly, "you have driven them to the
end of their tether, and you must answer for the consequences."

What he said was: "I am sorry to say it, Father, but Harry is
vanished, and cannot be found. We have looked for them everywhere, but both the boys are gone."

"Gone? How can they be gone? The gates are guarded." The
abbot's temper was ruffled, for Sir Eudo was in no mood to defer to
any man, or to deal leniently with a son who had cost him so much
trouble and annoyance.

"Nevertheless, gone they are. I have sent half a dozen men to
search along the brook and in the pool," said Brother Denis, as near
to malice as he had ever been in his gentle life, "and have ordered
the millers to keep watch at the mill-race."

"Spare your trouble," said Sir Eudo, purple in the face, "that lad
of mine was never born to drown." But his very fury was a measure
of his uneasiness, and Ebrard looked far from happy. "They're
hiding somewhere, the rogues. Give me leave, Hugh, and I'll have
them out of their holes in no time. If the gates are watched, they
must be somewhere close. And whether you are in the right of it or
I, found they must be."

"They shall be," said the abbot grimly. "Understand me, Eudo,
while they are within our precincts they are in my charge, and to
me they must be delivered when they are found, until we have taken
counsel with cooler heads what is to be done with them. Agreed?
Then lend me your four archers, and, Brother Denis, have Edmund
find us half a dozen reliable men, and we'll comb this household,
every building in it, from attic to cellar."

"And first," roared Sir Eudo after Brother Denis's ruffled tonsure and irate back, "close the gate on any who may be about leaving. I'll not lose my rascal for want of looking under a hood." And he billowed forth from the abbot's lodging like a purple thunder-cloud swollen to bursting with lightnings, and himself rolled away to the gate to ensure its efficient sealing.

The abbot followed, limping more noticeably than usual, as always when he was angry. The boy was really impossible, he would not be helped. Talk of the brook and the mill-race did not fool Hugh de Lacy; Harry's bent was for life at all costs. But short of dying there was not much he would not do to win his battle, and who could tell what folly he might not have committed by now?

The hubbub at the gate penetrated beneath the smothering weight of cloth in the covered cart. Harry lay straining his ears, in a scalding sweat of dread, but he could see nothing except a faint filtering of air and light from the front of the carts, between the ends of the rolls of cloth. If he tilted back his head as far as he could, he could see through this aperture an irregular star of blue sky and a corner of the almonry roof; and occasionally the dark passing of some nearer bulk cut off for a moment the clear gold light. Someone was riding in the cushioned nest in the front of the cart.

All the rest came to him merely as sound, and the dominant sound was the bellowing voice of his father, demanding that the gates be shut. On hearing that overbearing roar again his inside liquefied into such molten terror and desperation that he could hardly notice or recognise anything else. A new kind of terror, not of punishment for himself, not even chiefly for Adam's hand any longer, but simply of being dragged back and confined again into the stone circle which had broken and let him go. Tears burst out of his eyes because of his helplessness.

"Boys?" cried the great voice that had coaxed the horses merrily into their traces. "You'll find no boys with us but the ones you see honestly mounted here. And hark you, my masters, mind you ruffle not my little lass, back there, or I'll give you boys! Make haste and look, if look you must. Waste your own time as you will, but forbear from wasting mine. I have a long journey ahead of me."

Sir Eudo was not accustomed to being addressed in such a tone, and roared the expected challenge: "Fellow, I think you do not know who I am!"

"Why, by all I hear you must be Sir Eudo Talvace. Never fear, the tale's gone round ahead of you. I'm on reputable business, I have no need to mind who you are. Come, look in the cart and have done. And take care how you prod among my bolts of cloth, or I'll have the worth of it out of you at law." And all this with so much good-humour that in effect it was all the more formidable. None the less, this independent cloth merchant in his innocence was casting them back into the fire from which they had tried desperately to escape. It could be only a matter of moments now, and they would be dragged forth like dug badgers.

The shadow passed across the little space of light, again and again, seeming to cut off sound as well as sight, so that the strident voices, the stamping of the horses, the clambering of the archers mounting the hubs of the first cart, were all cut off by fits and snatches. Harry craned his head back and saw something round and brightly-coloured that danced in the air; and then two small hands that came up and caught it as it fell, and tossed it again.

"Not here, Sir Eudo—"

"Did I not tell you you were losing your labour? I've no runaways aboard, we've been loading this hour past, we should have seen them."

"The other carts, too! I don't doubt you, fellow. Nevertheless, by your leave—"

Harry strained his shaking lips as near as he could to the opening, and whispered hoarsely: "Mistress!"

She started and tossed the ball awry, and it fell over the back of her nest and rolled between the bales of cloth. Reaching for it, she knocked it farther from her, and it slipped into the hollow and lay close to Harry's face. She touched a hot, quivering cheek, and uttered a barely audible cry, and would have snatched her hand back, but Harry caught at it and clung. Startled and wild, with great black eyes round as moons, and soft, bold mouth fallen open, he saw her face flower against his stifling darkness; and she, leaning to look more closely, caught a glimpse of flushed cheeks, lips dewed with sweat, agitated blue-green eyes that implored her silence and her pity. She knew him. She hung over him for a second, holding her breath, and with an instinct more cruelly cunning than he knew he pressed her hand to his lips.

For an instant she was quite still, then she drew away her hand, and with a finger to her mouth motioned them to lie quiet. Her eyes were sparkling, the startled lips had folded into a single resolute bud. One more conspiratorial glance, wild with excitement, then she propped up her cushions over the gap that let in light upon them, and leaned over them to straighten the cloth that covered them. Over it she spread the skin rug on which she had been sitting, to make a bed for her doll, and whipped off the square of white linen she wore as a wimple, to make a coverlet. By the time the archers reached the third cart she was perched up on the bales of cloth, her skirts spread out about her as widely as they would go, rocking the doll with a plump little hand, and singing a nursery lullaby in a gusty undertone.

"By your leave, little mistress," said one of the archers, smiling at her, and set foot on the hub of the wheel and reached in between the rolls at the rear of the cart.

She stopped singing and stared at him wide-eyed, keeping her place like an outraged princess and spreading a protective arm above her doll. "What do you want? You mustn't come here, you'll make a noise."

"Have you been long in your place, sweetheart?" asked the archer gently. "Have you seen ought of a pair of lads we're looking for? You'd speak out to your father, would you not, if any stranger tried to climb into the cart?"

"I would so," she said, eyeing him distrustfully and sitting up very straight, "and I will, if you don't go away. I've seen no boys. No one has bothered me until now, or I should have called my father. I don't let anyone touch my father's goods. I am in charge of this cart."

She jutted an uncertain underlip, and when the second archer swung a leg over into the cart and prodded farther between the bales she opened her dewy mouth and let out an indignant shriek: "Father, they're trying to steal our cloth! *Father!*"

The probing hand touched Harry's sleeve, but touched only cloth where cloth was in any case to be expected; and the next moment the man had withdrawn hastily before the child's possessive rage, and the merchant was striding purposefully back to see what was offending his daughter.

"Oh, let be!" said the first man, dropping to the ground. "How could they be here, with such a game little lass minding the cart? Sure, she'd bring the whole household down on them if they laid a finger on her bolts of stuff."

The voices receded. They heard the merchant's great, warm laughter: "That's my own bird! And now, master and my lord abbot, if you're satisfied we're not harbouring your runaways, we'll be on our way."

Hugh de Lacy's voice, clear and thin with fastidious irritation said: "Open the gate!"

Hooves stamped the cobbles, and the wheels creaked forward. In a few moments they knew, as the carts swung round in a great turn to the right, that they had passed through the gate and were out on the highroad.

Chapter Five

A shaft of summer sky looked in upon their hot, heavy darkness. "Boy!" whispered the breathless little voice. "You may come out from under the load now. Only keep beneath the cover, in case someone should glance into the cart. *I* will tell you if there's danger."

She had settled herself and her doll in the front of the cart again, as soon as they were well away from the monastery gates. Now even the last corner of the boundary wall was left behind, and the lofty shape of Shrewsbury, a garlanded hill within its silver moat, was dwindling lower and lower into the green bowl of water-meadows.

They hoisted themselves gratefully out of the stifling trough beneath the bales of woollens, and lay panting on the top of them, bathed in sweat and still trembling. Harry raised the canvas sheet upon his arm, and helped Adam to settle himself comfortable before he stretched himself out beside him. Two or three of the scars on his back had broken again and slashed his shirt with thin stains of blood. The little girl's bright, knowing eyes marked their laborious wallowings beneath the sheet, and did not fail to observe Harry's solicitude and trace it to its cause.

"He's hurt!" she said with indignant sympathy. "Who has done that to him?" And with round eyes, not waiting for an answer: "Is that why you were hiding from that cross old man? But I heard them say that he was father to one of you!"

"He's father to me," said Harry, wiping his sticky face and drawing great breaths of the clean, radiant air.

"And lord to me," owned Adam, lying limp with relief beside him.

Through the arched opening of the cart they looked out cautiously upon the heaving rumps of the horses, and the steady, grinding rear wheels of the cart ahead. Two men walked with the team, the long, furled lash of a whip nodding in air above the shoulder of one of them. Four more, well mounted, rode alongside at leisure, ready to spur forward or back as they were needed. The merchant was at the head of the cavalcade, they caught a glimpse of his hat-plume dancing beside the leading cart.

"*I* would not run from *my* father," said the child, studying them as ardently as they studied the opening world of freedom and wonder before them. "You must have done something very bad to anger him so." The great eyes were brilliant with greedy curiosity, but she was unwilling to ask. They owed her their confidence, and she waited for it proudly.

"On my word," said Harry, "we have not done anything that should make you regret helping us to escape capture. And indeed we haven't thanked you yet, and want words enough to do it properly. If you had not been the boldest and quickest-witted lass that ever was born, we should surely have been dragged out of our holes and whipped back to Sleapford, to another judgement worse than the last. Adam here would have lost a hand, and I should have been locked up and beaten and starved until I crawled on my knees and begged for mercy. Lady, my name is Harry Talvace, and I am your devoted servant while I live. And this is my foster-brother, Adam Boteler, and I dare say as much for him. Will you not tell us your name, too?"

"My name is Gilleis Otley. My father is Nicholas Otley, and an alderman of London," she said with conscious pride.

"Well, Mistress Gilleis, you have the best right in the world to know the worst of us and decide for yourself whether you repent of helping us to go free."

He spread his arms comfortably along the bales of woollens, and laid his cheek upon them, and in a soft undertone, in case one of the outriders should pass too near, he told her the whole story, even to the secret meeting with Stephen Mortmain in Hunyate.

"My soul!" said Adam, lifting his head at mention of the name. "I have been all this while so bothered about myself, I had forgotten about them. Harry, if there's one thing sure, it is that we've let Stephen and Hawis safe out of the shire. Lord, with this to-do about us, they could have taken hands and walked out of Sleapford in broad daylight, and no one would have marked them. Every hound in the place has been hard on our trail, there'll be no hunt for them till our scent's lost for good."

"I have been thinking of it, too. There's nothing surer than that they're safely away by now. Maybe we haven't spent our pains for nothing, after all."

"I'd rather it had been done more cheaply," owned Adam, grinning ruefully. "But I don't grudge them a few strips of my skin." The shadow had passed from over him before Shrewsbury was out of sight. He looked at the broad green fringes of the road, on which the hoofmarks were like darker green dapples in the drying dew, and at the Wrekin's bulk stretched along the sky like a sleeping beast in the sun, and he began the soft whistling which was the measure of his wellbeing.

Harry took up the tale where he had left it. Only when he reached the incident of the almsboxes did he hesitate. He was not ashamed of what he had done, but this child might have superstitious scruples about such behaviour, and he did not want either to prejudice his own case or to offend her. It was easy to omit the dangerous confession, and say simply that they had made use of the church to assure themselves an undisturbed passage through the cloisters to the carts. He told it so, not without a chafing sense of humiliation in the deception, and met her bright, intelligent stare at the end of his recital with a heightened colour.

"I should have run away, too!" she said, shivering as she looked down at her own small, childish right hand. "I was frightened of that old man, he shouted so. If he had come to look in my cart I should have cried. He was very cruel to you."

Now that the terror of defeat and recapture had ebbed out of his very bones, however prematurely, Harry felt a fleeting desire to defend his father. Justice, after all, was due to those who kept the law, as well as to those who broke it, however inadvertently.

"He would be aghast if he heard you say so. He never means to be so, but he has a hot temper—and it's been well drummed into me he had the law on his side. Law! On my word, I'm glad we are clear of it."

"And what will you do now?" asked Gilleis practically.

"Why, first, put the length of England between us and Sleapford, and then find work with some mason and go on learning our trade. We're already well grounded, for we've been helping Adam's father ever since we were big enough to handle tools. We shall not be unprofitable workmen. In some charter borough we can work for a year and a day, and then Adam will be free. Then my father could not hale him back home even if he found him."

"The best plan," said the child briskly, tugging at her short, fat black braids of hair, one in either hand, "would be to come with us to London. London is the finest place to hide in, because it is the biggest and the busiest city in the land, and good workmen are always wanted there."

They lay side by side, the cover pushed back to their shoulders, peeping over the cushioned barrier along the straight, dusty ribbon of road. They felt light as air, wanting the weight that had fallen from them with the life they had shaken off. The squat, square tower of Atcham church came in sight, with the low village roofs clustered about it. Looking beyond, into the pale blue sky above the road, they saw other prospects opening to invite them, and like an emanation of dreams at the end, the fabulous city, with King William's great tower at the eastern end of it, and the two strong fortresses of Baynard's Castle and Montfichet's Tower to westward, and London Wall stretching between, with seven double gates in it and towers along the north side. They saw the Thames teeming with ships, and the thriving suburbs spilling over outside the city wall in gardens and pleasances right to the king's royal palace of Westminster, on the river bank. They saw a great and powerful place, rooted like a tree and budding prolifically all the year round with new houses, churches, shops and mansions for its multiplying thousands. Where better could a mason go?

"We have money," said Harry. "Not a great sum, but enough to pay our way. If we should deliver ourselves to your father tonight and ask him to let us travel south with him, do you think he would consent? We could work, if he would have us. We know how to manage horses, and we're strong."

She shook her head emphatically. "No, not tonight, it's too soon, you could still be sent back. I'll tell you what you must do, it will be quite easy. Tonight we shall lie at the hospice of Lilleshall Abbey, at Dunnington. That is too near to Shrewsbury, the abbot may have received word of your flight. But I can bring you food, and you can sleep in the woods for tonight. You *could* sleep here in the cart, for it won't be unloaded, we shall be selling nothing until we reach St. Albans. But if they should send to inquire after you—"

"You are in the right of it, we're still too near home to take risks," said Harry. "The woods will suit us very well."

"But tomorrow you'll join us again, won't you?" She watched his face anxiously. "I shall be looking for you. I'll help you—tonight I'll show you where to wait for the carts, in the wood just beyond Dunnington. And tomorrow night we shall lie at Lichfield, then I think it would be safe for you to come to my father. You need not tell him who you are. You'll come to him during the evening, as though you were boys from the town, and tell him you want to travel to London to hire yourselves to a master there. And it would be better for you to take another name." She drew back a little from them in sudden doubt, seeing how they looked at her sparkling-eyed, and then at each other, their cheeks quivering into uncontrollable mirth. A little of it was the pure hysterical joy of being free and launched upon a new course, but most of it was astonished delight in her shameless cunning. She sat red-cheeked in mortification and offence, her lips trembling. "Why are you laughing? What have I said?"

"Oh, Gilleis, Gilleis, how old are you?" asked Harry in a splutter of laughter.

"Ten years—nearly eleven," she said, stiffening her slender back and jutting her rounded underlip to keep it from drooping.

"And where did you learn to be such a little she-fox in only ten years? Have you had so much practice in conspiracy? Do you deceive your father so frequently?"

"Oh," crowed Adam into his sheltering arms, "I see the city is the place to learn all the tricks of the trade. Here in Salop we're but simpletons to her."

The smallest of muffled sounds brought Harry's head up sharply, and struck the mirth from his face. Gilleis had turned her back on them. Her arms were pressed against the side of the cart, and her forehead upon them, and the two thick, short braids of black hair jutted pathetically, one on either side of the tender, pale hollow of her nape, with its single delicate curl. Under the blue cotte and the flowered over-tunic the small shoulders, hunched against them in outrage, heaved silently.

"Gilleis!" He was suddenly overwhelmed with shame and dismay. "Lady!" She would not turn, even for that. He forgot caution, and scrambled forward to reach over the cushioned partition and take her by the shoulders, trying to draw her round to face him. "I am an unkind, uncivil wretch, and it would serve me right if you boxed my ears. God forbid I should laugh at you, indeed it was not quite such a gross offence as that. Will you not look on me any more? I'm ashamed! Pray pardon me!"

She shrugged him off fiercely, and sobbed out of her muffling arms: "Go away! I don't like you!"

"And you're in the right of it, for I don't like myself. You see how much I have to learn."

"I wanted to help you," she sobbed almost inarticulately. "I don't deceive my father! Never, never, never! All because of you I've told lies, and I shall be damned, and all you can do is make game of me. I never did such things before. It was all for you."

"I don't deserve it. Nor Adam nor I was worth your trouble. But indeed no one would ever have the heart to damn you, though you should tell more lies than there are blades of grass in a meadow. And besides, you never told even one! You said no one had bothered you— well, we were not bothering you, were we? You said you would call your father if you saw someone climb into the cart—and so you would have done, but you did not see us, did you? So where's the lie?'

"Much to learn, have you?" murmured Adam, still shaking with suppressed laughter. "You learn fast!"

Gilleis had stopped crying, and was listening intently, but still she would not look round. Harry tried to turn her about, and she resisted him obstinately, her face still buried from view.

"Come, then, if you won't forgive me, call the archers and have me hauled back to Shrewsbury. Or shall I give myself up, to prove to you how sorry I am for my unkindness?"

"On my soul," remarked Adam admiringly, "when it comes to low cunning there's not a pin to choose between you." He could say what he liked, it was not to him she was listening. Harry's dishonest offer was all she heard, and she turned on him with flashing eyes, her small jaw set in fury, and struck at him with a clenched fist.

"Get down! Hide yourself, quickly! The bridge!"

He let go of her, and dropped back meekly into cover, and she thumped at him vengefully until he had drawn the canvas over his head and vanished from sight. She enjoyed hitting him, because he had wounded her, and she was woman enough to want to make him pay for it; but she would not have him betrayed to any ill-usage but her own.

In his anxiety to placate her he had forgotten the river crossing at Atcham. The leading cart was rattling ponderously on to the unfinished stone arches of the bridge, where the tollman of the abbot of Lilleshall waited to collect his dues. There were always people lingering to talk here, and always there might be disputes over the pence due for the loaded carts, since the abbot's exactions were a standing grievance to the villagers and to many regular travellers. He, for his part, maintained that his rates were unprofitable to him, and would do no more than finance the completion of the bridge; they, for theirs, pointed out that the last arch was still but a make-shift structure of wood, and had been so now for a year or more without a hand's turn being put into it, though every loaded cart during that time had been expected to pay its penny, and every empty one its halfpenny. They said openly that their tolls were building the fine new extensions to the abbey at Lilleshall, instead of their bridge. But what could they expect of those foreigners brought north from Dorchester?

In the darkness of their hiding-place the boys followed with strain-ing ears all the small sounds of the crossing, the new note of the wheels as they ground from solid land on to the first stone arch, the hollow ring beneath them, the lapping of low summer water against the piers; then the halt, which seemed to them, as they held their breath with the last tension of fear, hours long. The horses stamped and twitched off flies, cheerful voices exchanged the casual gossip of Shrewsbury market for news of the traffic on the highroad, and money passed. The grooms chirruped, hooves bit willingly at the dusty road again and clopped hollowly on to wood. They were through and over, and soon the long, straight, impetuous road the Romans had made opened out to receive them.

"Gilleis!" Harry lifted the canvas to put out his head.

"Not yet!" she hissed, and beat him back with one hand, so roughly that he knew she was still angry. But he caught the little fist before it could withdraw, and drew it under the cover with him; and in a moment her fingers relaxed from their tight bunch, and folded and settled confidingly into his. He rolled over on to his back, and lay smiling, cradling her hand against his cheek.

Nicholas Otley had dined well, and was still sitting at table over his ale in the small guest-chamber when they presented themselves before him, cap in hand, with their request. Adam did the talking, for Adam it was who could the more confidently stand up and proclaim his parentage and training in the craft. All he had to do was name a village in this district, and remember that his family name was Lestrange instead of Boteler, and for the rest he had no need even to watch his tongue. Trippingly he told over the accomplishments he had from his father, and the modest works in which he had helped him about the village. Besides, Adam had a winning way with him, stood the taller and looked the elder, though in fact there was but a day between their births. If they were to be brothers, the elder must be the spokesman.

"And my brother Harry here can also carve exceedingly well, both in wood and stone. I can a little myself, but he excels me. We purpose, sir, to travel to London, and go on learning our trade there. If you will agree to our joining your company we shall be greatly obliged. We will gladly work for you on the journey, if you have work for us to do. Or if you have hands enough by you and can make no use of us, we can pay our way on the road, if we may have the protection of going with you. It's a long journey to make alone, and they say none too safe in places, even on the king's highway. We've never yet been so far as London."

The merchant looked them over with gay black eyes very like his daughter's. He was nearing fifty, and in the pride of his life, a tall man so charged with vigour that his every movement had a neat, controlled violence, and every turn of his head or change of expression was quick and pert as a bird's flight. He stroked his well-trimmed brown beard, and spread his long legs amply; and Gilleis, who had already twice been told to go to bed, sidled up to him as he considered them, and slipped her arm round his neck. He smiled, without looking at her, and encircled her waist, drawing her close against his side. She was his only child, and his wife had died in bearing her.

"Sweetheart, did I not bid you go and sleep? We are on men's business, it's time the children were abed." But she pressed close to him, and made no move to go, and his embracing arm hugged her warmly. "Tell me, pigeon, how like you these two lads? Shall they go with us to London?"

"If it please you, Father," she said demurely, and looked at them as if she saw them for the first time, and deeply wise, looked longer at Adam. "It speaks well for their wit," she said very sagely, "that they wish to go to London." He laughed and hugged her again, for she was quoting him, and it was an open secret between them that he liked nothing better.

"I see they don't displease you. Come nearer, boys, let me see you side by side. Brothers, are you? And you the elder, what was your name—Adam?"

Adam said truthfully that he was, but turned his day's advantage into a year.

"And which of you features your mother? For two brothers more unlike in the face I never saw."

"Mother is fair," said Harry, truthfully.

"And father?" The merchant's smile had sharpened, the merry eyes had narrowed a little. Harry should have kept his mouth shut.

"Father is dead," he said, a shade too quickly, and paled at the sound of the words.

"A sudden loss! He sounded very much alive, to my mind—at the abbey of Shrewsbury, yesterday."

They stared him steadily in the eyes with faces of blank incomprehension, and furrowed their brows in pursuit of his meaning, though they trembled inwardly.

"I don't understand you, sir," Adam began slowly.

"You understand me very well, lad. Never lie to me, I have a nose for it. Come here to me!" And when Adam approached dubiously, the merchant reached forward and clapped a hand on his shoulder, and suddenly ground hard fingers into his back. Adam flinched and drew breath sharply, twisting away from the pain. Otley shifted his grip to the boy's arm, and put him off from him by a pace, quite gently. "Your pardon, Adam, that was no fair trick, but you must remember, before you lie to a man with wits in his head, that you bear marks of identification not yet faded. Your tale's too well known this day to any who come from Shrewsbury, they know where to read your name—Master Lestrange!" His voice was hard, but not angry, and he looked at them so thoughtfully that they began to take heart again.

"You should not hurt him," Gilleis said reproachfully. "I don't think they are bad boys."

"I'll not hurt the boy, pigeon, never fear. I wanted only the answer to a question, and I have it. And as for you, my bird, run to bed, and let me deal with the lads my own way. There, I mean it! Trot!" He turned her about and gave her a gentle push towards the door, and a pat to start her on her way; and whether she recognised the third warning which must be obeyed, or whether she heard in his voice a note which reassured her that her presence was no longer necessary, she did indeed trot, with a last flashing smile at the two silent boys out of the corner of her eye before she skipped through the door.

"There, now we are rid of the women, now come and sit by me, and begin to tell me again, from the beginning, who you are and what you want of me. You're newly come into the hospice asking for me. Here I am. Now start fair."

They told him all that they had told his daughter; what else was there to be done with such a man? There was one difficulty to be faced, however; they could do no other than end their story still captive within the closed circle of the abbey wall, since it was impossible to involve the child, and might be impolitic to confess that they had made use of this masterful man to cover their flight, even without the connivance of his daughter. Men of the world, with a healthy opinion of themselves, do not take kindly to being hood-winked.

"We have made shift," said Adam, leaping the gap boldly, "to break out and follow you thus far, as you see. And if you will let us continue of your company from here to London, you shall find for yourself whether we mean honestly."

They waited with held breath for him to probe where he could hardly choose but feel curiosity; but he remained thoughtfully silent for a moment, looking from one to the other of them with a small curl to his mouth within the brown beard, and a quiet gleam in his eye. But he answered gravely enough after his pause for consider-ation.

"I am an alderman of London, and sit every Monday to hear causes in the Husting. As a man of law, I am bound by judgements of court as fast as my lord abbot himself. But no court has made this judgement, not even Tourneur's own manor court, and in my reading it binds no one. It is one man's judgement, and he the complainant, and I doubt not he meant it as a kind of hard mercy, and no malice, yet I call it bad law. There has no charge been laid against you. No one but he that's father to one of you and lord to the other has any right to pursue you, and I am not obliged by law to abet him. Be thankful you are not fallen in with nobility, boys. If I were one of your knights I should pack you back to your fate— the whole estate stands together. But I'm a merchant, born to trade and proud of it, and I know the worth of a hand that can make and do instead of hacking and piercing like a butcher's journeyman. Keep both yours, with all my goodwill, and make good use of them. The world will be the better off."

He had risen from his chair, and was pacing the floor with long vigorous strides. He halted now before Harry, and looked him over steadily from head to foot.

"And you, my young sprig, I like you well for standing by your friend so stoutly. And even better for finding the wit and the courage to take to a trade and stand on your own feet, if you mean in good earnest to do it. Will you stand to it? And can you make it good?"

"Yes, sir, that I can. All that Adam told you earlier is truth, except that I am only his foster-brother. His mother nursed us together, and his father taught us together, and I have had mallet and punch and chisel in my hands since I was eight or nine years old. It's true we had but little training in carving at Sleapford, but we have stood at the banker and cut stone, and helped with the building of walls, gate-posts, all that was needed about the demesne. And at Shrewsbury we made friends with Master Robert, who is at work on the church, and when we had showed him what we could do he let us work under him. We helped in the carving of the rood-screen, and I also carved two capitals for the chapel of the infirmary." He came to his feet in his eagerness, trembling a little in doubt of his own wisdom in committing himself so deeply to this man's discretion; but he could not keep it in. "I brought away with me a work of mine to show what I can do. There was nothing of Adam's we could bring with us, but I pledge you my word he knows his trade as well as I, for we've done everything together. May I show you?"

"Ay, let me see what you can do."

Harry ran out to the stable-yard and tenderly uncovered the wooden angel from its hiding-place. He brought it in and set it upon the table. Two days and a night in the cart had done nothing to dim the angel's wild brightness. With gold hair streaming upwards in the wind of his flight, and radiant wings arched and shimmering with tension, he plunged and lit upon the table-top like a shaft of sourceless light. The air of the chamber cried out about him in one golden chime. It mattered nothing to him that he bent his head and spread his delicate hands now before a merchant of London.

Otley uttered an exclamation of astonishment and pleasure, and put out his hands to the bright being. "This is yours? Verily your own work? No copy of a known masterpiece? Give me leave!" He took it up and turned it in his hands, looking with delight into the narrow, fiery face. "Here's a touch I had not looked to see! There's many a church and abbey would be well pleased to buy this of you, I swear. Are you being honest with me, boy? Your master had no hand in the making?"

"Myself I made it, every bit. I liked it the best of all that ever I did. Will it stand my friend, do you think, with a master? It is only wood, but there was no way of carrying stone, and I had no drawings by me. In stone I have much to learn, but I can learn, and I will. I want to learn."

"That's the best of all teachers, the desire to learn. Hold fast to it. Stand your friend with a master? Ay, will it, with any worth his salt. Why, I have been in Canterbury and seen work set up to praise that was no match for this of yours. Young Talvace, you should get you to one of the great cathedrals and learn your business from the best in their line, for you have the matter in you."

They had both drawn close to him, one at either elbow, tense with eagerness.

"Would they take us? Oh, I would cross Europe to get to a master like that, and to such work! Master Robert showed us some drawings of the new work at Canterbury. And I have heard that at Wells they are doing beautiful things. Father Hugh spoke sometimes of these matters with us."

"And France, sir—do you know anything of what is doing in France? Master Robert talked of the rebuilding at Chartres, after the fire they had there. And in Paris—"

"Ah, France!" Master Otley set down the angel. "You must talk to the master of my ship about France."

"Do you trade to France, too?" asked Adam, large-eyed.

"Ay, do I, and to Cologne on the Rhine, too, and sometimes into the Flemish cities, though they want not for cloth, for indeed they furnish all Europe with fine stuffs. But though your Flemish tapestries and velvets and embroideries be the most sumptuous to be had this side of the East, yet there's nothing like good English and Welsh woollen cloths for gowns to keep out the cold. The lordly lads of the Staple think there's no great trade but in raw wool, but trust me, boys, we shall make our name yet for good English cloth."

"But surely when we are in such hot dispute with the French king," ventured Harry, "there are heavy fines laid on ships that ply there for trade?"

"Why, so there are, when it can be called trading with the enemy. And from day to day, God knows, no master can tell whether he may not be landing a cargo on an enemy shore that was friendly but yesterday. But to levy a fine and to get it is two separate acts, and no king can be everywhere, nor his officers, neither. As for France, we are in no trouble there just now. Since Ascension Day

King John and King Philip and the young Duke of Brittany are all
come to an agreement together. If it hold! Who can tell with kings?
I can compound with a French merchant, and we hold to our bargain
like honourable men, but from a prince I should want heavy security.
And from a baron, cash!''

"And have you been in France yourself?'' they asked him, glowing.

"I have, a dozen times, though now I have a grown nephew who
handles the French trade for me.''

"And have you seen Paris? Have you seen Notre Dame?''

"And St. Denis?''

"And Chartres?''

"Three years ago I was in Paris. Chartres I have seen, too, but
not since the fire. And at Bourges they are building such a great
church as I had never dreamed of. High—ah, you should stand
under the vaults there and see how lofty. Thus—even the aisles as
high as our choirs—'' He sketched the elevation out with his finger
upon the table, while they gazed passionately. "And Normandy is
full of building. Churches grow overnight, like spring grass, like
mushrooms.''

They had forgotten all that had gone before; the young brothers
for whom Adam had shed a few tears secretly in the night, the
mother whose kind, pretty, foolish image had haunted Harry's uneasy dreams, pain, anger and fear, the strange journey they had
made with the child out of the last frontiers of their own childhood,
all were clean swept away out of mind. They sat down with him
round the table, under the angel's burning eyes, and poured out
questions in an ardent flood. By the time Otley marked the fading
light, and remembered the morrow's early start, Harry was already
fallen into an inspired silence, bright and distant of face, his eyes
shining.

"You've kept me talking past sundown! To bed with you, we
make a longer day of it tomorrow, and must rise with the dawn.
There, lads, go join the rest of my rogues in the hall, we'll see you
safe into London. Go ask for my foreman Peter Crowe, and tell him
you are taken on for the journey.'' And he called after them good-
naturedly, as they stammered their thanks from the doorway: "And
if any among my hopefuls get playful with you—for they're a corn-

fed lot, and the boys have a way of playing rough with newcomers—stand to it and give as good as you get. There's no malice in it."

They assured him they would impute none. He had meant the advice for Harry, of course, taking it for granted that the villein's son would drop neatly on his feet in any testing company, by virtue of the toughness, good-humour and resilience bred into him in a hard school. With a knight's son all manner of considerations of privilege, dignity and high temper might be expected to complicate the process of initiation.

They smiled at each other, secure in their mutual knowledge. Harry had stood on his own feet with all the boys of the village from infancy, never even thinking to exact respect or look for quarter. By the time Ebrard had become conscious of his running wild, and tried to hammer into him a right sense of his own estate, it was already far too late.

"Goodnight, my honest masons!"

"Goodnight, sir!"

As they crossed the court to the hall where the commonalty lodged, Harry gripped Adam by the arm. The light, wild shining of his eyes looked yellow in the dusk.

"Adam, I am resolved! I am resolved on France!"

Every summer Nicholas made this journey to buy up the cloths woven during the long winter. From Shrewsbury his men travelled into the hill country to bring back the bales by pack-horse into the town clearing-house; but on this Roman highroad it was simpler, if slower, to concentrate all their goods into carts. The cortège was thereby more compact, the precious cloths safer from the weather and more readily defensible if attacked. Watling Street lay under the king's peace, and crimes committed upon it were the business of the king's officers, but their control was tenuous, and masterless men were everywhere. Nicholas Otley provided his own sturdy army, preferring prevention to reliance upon law.

It was a contented and high-spirited army, from Peter Crowe, the foreman, who was fifty-five, to the youngest of the archers, who was a bumptious sixteen; and it assimilated two new companions without heartburning. The Lestrange brothers, like any untried novices, had to be tested before they could be accepted; but the elder proved to have a temper as sunny as his face, and fists as ready as his laugh, and the younger, though no great man of his hands, took the worst of every rough and tumble with such pugnacious appetite and so little ill-will that both were taken into the confraternity on the night of their arrival, and fell asleep in the rushes of the hall already sworn members, and happy with the few bruises it had cost them.

They had what they wanted. Men among men, they fed and watered and groomed the horses, cleaned harness, ran Master Otley's errands, re-flighted arrows, lent a shoulder to the wheels where the road was bad, and in the evenings crowded in joyously among the grooms and teamsters in hall, listened to Peter's stories, wrestled with the boys, played at draughts and tables with any who needed opponents, and joined in the songs of the archers. A place had been willingly made for them, and they stretched themselves, body and wits and spirit, to fill it to the last corner. They had never been so happy in their lives.

By the fourth day, somewhat timorously, for fear they should be thought to be putting themselves forward too soon, they began to involve each other more deeply in the evening's entertainment. Encouraged by an approving remark of Peter's about the sweetness of Adam's voice in the choruses, Harry piped up that his brother sang well and knew a great number of songs in both Latin and English. Adam, stricken with an unusual shyness, protested his inadequacy and tried to avoid the laurel, and when they pressed him avenged himself by saying that he was used to singing only with his brother's accompaniment, and that Harry could play on both citole and lute, and very well, too. One of the young archers had a citole, though he was no great hand on it, and freely confessed as much. He flung it to Harry across the circle, so directly that he could do no other than catch it, and they were fairly in it.

They conferred in anxious undertones as Harry tuned the citole, reproached each other hotly but very quietly, and were deeply happy. Adam had blushed like a girl, Harry had turned grim and pale. They embarked on one of the decidedly secular songs they had so surprisingly learned, out of class, from Brother Anselm, the young precentor at Shrewsbury; in whom, it is to be feared, the devil of human delight had not yet resigned his claim. Adam sang,

at first tremulously, then captivated by his own gift and confident
as spring:

> *"Suscipe flos florem,*
>   *quia flos designat amorem.*
> *Illo de flore*
>   *nimio sum captus amore.*
> *Hunc florem, Flora*
>   *dulcissima, semper odora—"*

Bent over the citole earnestly, his hair shaken forward upon his
forehead, Harry turned his head away from the company, the better
to concentrate, and so chanced to stare fixedly and sightlessly at one
of the long windows unshuttered on the soft summer dusk. When
he had plucked the last chord, and had leisure to blink away the haze
of absorption, the stone lancet suddenly came into existence for him
as the space of pale green after-light it was, and no empty space,
either. Two rounded arms were folded on the stone sill outside, and
a dimpled chin rested upon the arms. She had the hood of her cloak
drawn over her head, and her braids were unloosed for bed; and in
bed she should have been, at least two hours earlier.

He turned, startled, to shake his head at the praise of his playing,
and back out of the circle hastily, thrusting the citole back upon its
owner. "A moment—I'll come again. I have an errand I forgot to
do." And he slipped away quietly to the door and, tiptoeing along
the wall, pounced upon her before she was aware of him. She was
barefoot in the dewy grass, and as he made his spring she gave a
soft little cry of alarm and slipped through his fingers like an eel
and ran; but he caught her within a few yards, and held her struggling between his hands.

"Gilleis, what are you doing here? And without shoes! What
would your father say if he saw you here running about barefoot
so late? Back to bed, now, quickly!"

She looked up at him from under the shadow of her hood with
great eyes glimmering in the twilight, and her small breast heaved.
"Leave go of me! I need not do what *you* tell me! *You* are not my
father!"

"You may be glad of it," said Harry, putting on the grimmest face he could manage. "If I were, miss, you should go back to bed with a flea in your ear. And if you caught cold from going without shoes, you should have the nastiest medicine I could brew for you. Come now, before someone else sees you."

"I *will* take cold!" she threatened, suddenly in tears. "I *will*! You don't care! You don't play with me now! You never want me to help you. You don't sing to *me*—"

Too taken aback to say anything intelligent, he protested feebly that he had not been singing, but playing, but she rightly brushed that aside as a quibble not worthy of notice, and wept the harder, pushing him away ineffectively and pulling her cloak over her face. He stooped and, slipping an arm under her knees, hoisted her in his arms and sat down in the angle of one of the buttresses with her, on the projecting course of stone.

"Gilleis, how can you say such things? Not care, indeed! You know I care! I don't have time to play, or I would. You know I have to work now, and earn my keep. I gave you my angel to mind for me, didn't I? Would I do that if I didn't love and trust you? But I'm your father's hired hand now, I must do my share. I can't play children's games any longer."

"You don't want to!" she wept inarticulately into his shoulder. "And I'm not a child! You weren't working just now. You always say, presently, when I've finished my work, but when you have finished it you don't come—"

Children! he thought, sighing with exasperated tenderness. A man never knows how to take them. All these last days she's been under my feet. She has no companions of her own age here, and I suppose Adam and I are the nearest she sees. He hugged her closer, rocking her gently and coaxingly on his lap, and whispering comforting noises into her hood.

"Be my good little girl now, and I'll find a fine piece of wood and make a portrait of you before we get to London. And I'll play for you, and Adam shall sing. Don't cry, sweetheart! Hush! You'll have me in trouble for keeping you here in the night."

But the more he crooned over her and soothed her like a baby, the more inconsolably she cried. Her black hair, smoky and soft, tickled his nose and made him sneeze. He was growing weary of his paternal role, and dear though she was and fond though he was of her, if she had really been his child he would have smacked her. Yet he remembered uneasily the halt within the gate at Shrewsbury and her full skirt spread out to cover his hiding-place, and every impulse of impatience in him was drawn in on a golden rein of something more than gratitude.

"Gilleis, my honey-bird, I'm going to carry you back to your own door, and you must run straight to bed, you understand? What shall we do if you make yourself ill? Everyone will be unhappy, I most of all, because I shall feel I am to blame." He rose, steadying his burden carefully. She was small for her age and a light weight, but he was no nobly-grown Adam, and she was as much as he could manage.

"You'll drop me," she said, for the first time unimpeded by tears. Was she not, even, laughing at him a little, or were those only subsiding sobs that shook them both? He could not be sure.

"I shan't. You're not such a big girl yet." With determination he crossed the court and carried her securely to the door of the gentles' staircase. Her body was soft and cool in his arms, naked under the folds of her cloak. Probably he had offended her by catching her at such a disadvantage. That aspect of her complexity did not puzzle him, and he dealt with it with tactful respect, handling her as reverently as if she had been a princess in cloth of gold.

As he set her down gently within the doorway she stirred in his embrace and wound her arms round his neck, laying her soft cheek against his. She smelled of childhood and the after-warmth of the departed sun and the dewy grass.

"Will you make a portrait of me? Truly?"

"Truly, if you'll go to bed this minute."

"Will you begin tomorrow?"

If he must! It would still leave him the last hours of the evening to spend in hall among his fellows. But why had he not ten more years on his back, and a beard on his chin? Then she would pester someone else to play with him in his stead.

"*Only* if you go to bed this minute! Without one more word!" He kissed her on the forehead. "There, goodnight!" He pushed her firmly towards the staircase, and as she gathered her cloak closely about her and climbed the first step he slapped her cheerfully on her neat, round rump to speed her on the upward journey.

It was a sad miscalculation on his part, as she showed him by turning on him like a fury and hitting out at him with all her force. Her hard little fist stung his cheek-bone and sent him a step backwards in sheer amazement.

"Don't dare! Don't *dare!*" Her eyes blazed at him, dry of tears, full of a desperate sadness; he saw a woman staring helplessly out from behind the child's outraged grief, but did not recognise what he saw.

"Gilleis, what have I done? On my soul, I did not intend—"

She whirled away from him and ran up the stairs, and was gone. Rubbing his cheek ruefully, he went slowly back to his friends. He supposed he had trespassed on the field of liberties which belonged only to her father. And of course, like all girls, she wanted to have her cake and eat it, to permit herself whatever familiarities she pleased with him, but resent any he took with her. And yet he would not for the world have offended her so, if only he had known how to avoid the pitfalls; but where girls were concerned there was no rule and no law. A man had to accept the risks, and be prepared to be invited to an act one moment and belaboured for it the next.

Well, he'd make his peace with her in the morning, and seal it by carving the figure he had promised her. And in another week they would be in London. By the time he entered the hall again he was ready to laugh at himself and her, and when the citole was passed to him again with a request for a drinking song he had already forgotten her.

They broached their French project to Master Otley on the last evening of the journey, in the abbey guest-house at St. Albans, over the painting of Gilleis's image. It should, by rights, have waited until they were in London, but the merchant, delighted with the little nine-inch figure of his daughter, could not wait to see it take the bloom of her face and the black of her hair, and had borrowed colours from one of the brothers so that the work could be done on the spot. They had even offered him a table in the corner of the cloister where the light lay longest and clearest, so that he could work in peace, if peace indeed this could be called, with Adam leaning over one shoulder and Master Otley over the other in absorbed admiration. If they crowded him too closely he said nothing, only halted his hand and looked up with the fierce frown and ominous forbearance of a Talvace crossed, and they drew off respectfully and gave him room.

Gilleis had conducted herself, during those sittings, as though she had never in her life shed a tear before him, or aimed a blow at him, or been in his presence upon any but these formal terms. And in that stiff ceremonial dignity he had carved her, a small, erect figure with hands demurely folded and head loftily raised. He found her amusing so, but had the sense not to show it.

"Master Otley, we've been thinking, Adam and I. You remember we were asking you about the church-building in France?" He drew in a delicate, arched black brow, taut as a bow, and frowned thoughtfully as the very look of her face sprang to life in the copy. This haughtiness and distance he had been so intent on reproducing that he had never before stopped to wonder about it. If he looked long enough at the statuette he might begin to understand the original. "We have been thinking that the best thing we could do is to go on into France."

He heard Gilleis stir, and looked up impatiently. She had turned her head and parted her lips, and the trick of the light in her great eyes was lost. "Sit still!" he flashed in annoyance, and got up to take her by the chin and jerk her head into position again, not roughly but quite without gentleness. "Stay like that, and don't fidget."

Without complaint she held her pose. When he managed to remember, with surprise and compunction, that she was not a copy set by a master, but a living child, and one of whom he was very fond, he marvelled that she did not burst into tears a dozen times in an evening. But usually he remembered only when she had already gone to bed and it was too late to appease his conscience by complimenting and making much of her.

"That's a big step to take," said Master Otley. "Do you speak the language?"

"Both of us well enough, Adam better than I. There would be no difficulty there. And you see, sir, there are reasons. London is far from Salop, and a good city to hide in, I know it, but wherever we go in England Adam will always be in some danger. Even in a charter borough, even in London, he would not be free until a year and a day had passed. Runaways have been dragged back when their year was almost run, many a time, some have even been unlawfully seized afterwards, when they were free men, and have been hard put to it to get loose from their masters to have their cases heard in court. In a village there would be no hope of his escaping notice at the next viewing of frankpledge. You know these things better than we. Is it not better to go on into France? We can surely get service there with one of the great master-masons, and learn our trade as well there as in England."

The merchant, watching the features of his child's face spring out like stars under the charged brush and the darting hand, smiled in his beard. "Good reasoning enough, but desire came before reason, I fancy. No need to dress up your longing for me, lad. In your place and at your age I'd be across the sea like an arrow. My ship sails as soon as we have her loaded and provisioned. Are you for taking passage in her? She puts in at le Havre by the longer crossing, a good spot for trafficking into both Paris and Brittany—now the young duke's reconciled with his uncle there's good trade to be had there."

"Do you think we could earn our passage on board ship?" asked Harry, smoothing the curve of a firm, soft mouth, and surprised to find in it so strong a suggestion of sadness.

"You've earned it on dry land. I've no complaints of my bargains. Why not aboard ship, too? Though it's likely you won't feel so spry when you get that ocean swell under you. You're welcome to try, the pair of you."

Harry looked up from his work, and Adam held his tongue and his breath, brilliant-eyed with excitement.

"May we really cross in her? If we are not able to be of use, we could pay something for our passage—"

"You'll do no such thing. Keep your money, lads, to set you on your way over there, and see you keep it well out of sight, and have the other hand on your dagger. And when you have a fair price from me for this little beauty here—"

"No!" said Harry quickly. "This is promised already as my gift to Mistress Gilleis. A most rare woman! For the past hour she has not opened her mouth." And he lifted his head and looked at her teasingly, expecting to see the dimpling quiver of a smile pass over her cheeks and lips and be sternly repressed. But she neither spoke nor moved, not by so much as the tremor of an eyelash. Nor did she lower the great dark eyes that dwelt so faithfully upon him.

"A princely gift," said Nicholas Otley. "When you let her speak she'll thank you for it prettily. Show your master five such days of work as you have shown us, and he'll know how to value you. It's settled then. You shall come home with us, and stay in my employ until the *Rose of Northfleet* sails, and then you shall cross in her, with my very good will and my blessing, and try your fortune abroad."

"Sir, we shall be most happy to take advantage of this, as of all your former kindness. We shall not forget it to you. And if we are to have an opportunity, then," said Harry, straightening his back, "I will finish the painting later. The light is beginning to fail, and I cannot handle the figure so well now until the face is dried. And I think Gilleis is very tired."

It was not the word he had in mind, but the right one would not come. The large eyes, all of her that was eloquent tonight, spoke in an unknown language, disquieting him even in his joy and excitement.

"Rest, Gilleis, we'll go on another day."

"Come and look at your sweet self, my dove," said her father, "see how beautiful you are."

She got up from her place and came to stare at her image with the same unfathomable thoughtfulness she had bestowed upon the artist while she sat silent. And it was beautiful. The newly painted face had changed under the brush and withdrawn all its soft, confiding innocence behind a touching new aloofness. There was something melancholy in it, and something assured, too. She was as he had seen her tonight, and as long as he continued to work on the statuette he would be for ever puzzled and enraged by his inability to understand what he had faithfully recreated.

"What, nothing to say?"

"I see what it is," said Harry. "I'm to blame. I've threatened her into silence so long she's forgotten how to speak."

"Let well alone, then. Tomorrow she'll chatter us all to deafness as usual."

"I could speak," said Gilleis, "if I had anything to say."

"Come, that's better, she still has a tongue. Say a word of thanks for so beautiful a gift, and prettily, mind."

"Only if you like it," said Harry, collecting up brushes and colours. He was sure by her stubborn silence that she did not like it, that to her it meant only a reminder of hours of motionless boredom, of being frowned at and scolded. Even his gift he had managed to spoil for her.

"You should, miss, for he's made you a beauty, funny little squirrel as you are. Give Harry a kiss for it and say goodnight."

Obediently she raised her face, and offered the silent mouth, and when he opened his arms to her and hugged her with goodwill, she slid her hands delicately about his neck and gently laid hold of the thick locks of his hair, where it grew crosswise in curls in his nape. Her mouth was cool and smooth and firm. Kissed, she did not kiss him again, but only permitted the salute in an act of royal condescension; but her fingers, tugging softly in his hair, had no such lofty detachment about them. Looking at her serene face as she disengaged herself, he could hardly believe the hands had belonged to the same person. What she would have liked to do, of course, he reflected, was to pull his hair as hard as she could, in payment for his lack of consideration these many evenings, but before her father this was the worst she could do without being detected.

He watched her regretfully as she went confidingly into Adam's arms and gave him a smacking kiss, kissed her father, and went with unusual docility, and without a backward glance, to seek her bed.

He was sorry now, so far as he could spare a thought for anything but the future and France, that he had dealt so clumsily with her and made her dislike him so much.

In darkness, rolled up in swathes of felt in Harry's bundle, the angel took wing for le Havre. The wrapping was to protect his colours from the salt air, and his slight outstretched hands from the buffeting of the passage. Like the brilliant invisible creature within the chrysalis, he slept and dreamed; and the half-smile on his ardent mouth still made the unseen face beautiful and terrible. There was wonder in it, and wildness, and secret knowledge of everything that had been, everything that was, everything that was to come.

He saw in his dream all that passed about him and thought to escape the piercing intelligence of his hooded eyes: Gilleis clinging with one hand to the side of the little boat that heaved softly under the ship's stern, and with the other to her father's firm hip, the teeming wine-quays of London's foreshore, the needle-sharp gables gnawing the pearly September sky like uneven teeth, the two boys already half-drunk with excitement, half-sick with impatience, turning their backs even on the Tower to strain their eyes down-river, towards the future, towards the sea, towards a fantasy of living, growing rock, a tree, a grove, a forest of stone. He saw the cool, hasty kiss on the child's proffered mouth, the quick embrace, the good-humoured way the boy bent his head low for her while she hung her medal of the Virgin round his neck; and he saw the child waving constantly from the receding boat as she was rowed ashore with her father, waving long after the boys had forgotten her in their curiosity about the ship and its crew and its rigging and all the strange-smelling, salt-coated, strident life within it.

Afterwards, when the tide and the following wind had brought the *Rose of Northfleet* down to open water, and the great estuary had widened and widened into the still greater sea, and the waves had grown bursting rims of snow and plunged like horses, the angel saw his creator brought down to ignominious misery, hanging over the lee rail heaving out his heart in helpless convulsions, while a bewildered Adam, gay as a grasshopper and unable to feel anything but delight in this absurd motion, tenderly held and sensibly exhorted him, torn between laughter and concern.

The angel, tossed ceaselessly in his swathed darkness, still smiled, immune even from pity. The hands feebly wringing away tears of weakness and shakily wiping cold sweat from a clammy forehead and beads of sour vomit from grey lips, were the hands which had made him as he was. They were more and less than he, more vulnerable and immeasurably more wonderful.

Somewhere beyond the water, beyond the misery of sea-sickness and the disillusionment of experience, the golden fantasy grew and flourished immaculately still, a tree of stone tall as the sky, budding miraculously all the year round with new, exuberant leaves of worship and aspiration and knowledge.

PART TWO

PARIS

1209

Chapter Six

The house in the Rue des Psautiers was double-gabled and somewhat broader than its neighbours, and beside it a great studded door
in the wall led through into a stable-yard. Steep-pitched roofs thrust
deep eaves forward over the street like jutting eyebrows, casting the
house door into shadow. In an upper window a light burned, though
a curtain screened it from direct view.

When the house had belonged to Claudien Guiscard, a middle-
aged and wealthy widower who dealt in perfumes, silver, jewels, and
carpets, and other commodities brought in from the Levant by way
of Venice, no one who passed along the quiet street had paused to
give it a second glance; but now that he had died and left it to his
mistress it was a very different story. Traffic along the Rue des
Psautiers was brisk these days. Young men came in their dozens to
try their luck at catching her eye and ear and gaining entry to that
lighted room. Old men who had no such expectation nevertheless
went out of their way to use the quiet thoroughfare, merely in the
hope of catching a glimpse of her at the window, or as she entered
or left with her waiting-maid. Claudien's nearest relative, a second
cousin, was said to be contemplating an appeal to the judiciary to

dispossess the courtesan of her legacy. She, for her part, was rumoured to be quite unmoved by the threat, and had certainly done nothing to abate the scandal which centred upon her person. After her lover's death many people had thought she would sell the property quickly, while it was hers, and go back to Venice, from which city Claudien had brought her. Instead, she had settled herself comfortably in the house and entertained there like a duchess, admitting to her more intimate favours whoever pleased her, even though he were penniless, and declining whoever did not, though he came of the blood royal and brought purses of gold to sponsor his suit. She was the rage. She could sing and play, duel in verses with the poets, and argue philosophy with the schoolmen. Besides her native Italian she spoke Latin and French and even a little English, or so it was said. She kept herself in the modest, dignified state of a noblewoman widowed, but with the freedom and intelligence of an Athenian hetaera. And this curious disregard she had for the charms of money—presumably because she already had enough of it—gave an enchanted hope even to those young creatures who would not otherwise have ventured to fix their eyes upon one so sought after; so that almost nightly the several estates of Paris clashed upon her doorstep.

On this particular evening of late April two parties converged upon the house at the same moment from the two ends of the Rue des Psautiers. From the north, on horseback, followed by a manservant and a little group of attendant musicians carrying their instruments, came a young gentleman of the de Breauté family, dressed in his best and aware of his worth. From the south, strung four abreast across the street, and singing a scandalous parody of Sigebert's hymn to the virgin martyrs, with its catalogue of resounding female names, Adam Lestrange, the English mason, with his three attendant demons from the garret in the Ruelle des Guenilles; in his right arm his brother, in the left the lad Élie from Provence, with his choirboy's face and his street-arab's impudence, and arm-in-arm with him the saturnine baccalaureat Apollon, with his lute slung over his shoulder. They came formidably armed to the lists, with Adam's looks and voice, Harry's new verses, and a tune of Pierre Abelard's dredged up out of Apollon's capacious Breton memory to fit the song. Between the four of them, these last two years, they had produced some notable additions to the street songs of Paris.

Strolling behind them, drawn by the parody, the magnet in the Rue des Psautiers, and the prospect of mischief, came a dozen other students fresh from Nestor's inn and full of wine, come to see fair play.

Apollon first perceived the horseman, his servant and his players, and dropped out of the quartet in the last verse to exclaim: "The enemy are in sight!" His jaw fell at sight of the array of instruments. "God's wounds, they've brought the whole consort! Are they *all* candidates for paradise?"

"A rival!" said Adam, crowing with joy. "The one stimulus I needed! Come on!" And he unlaced his arms nimbly from Harry's neck on the right and Élie's on the left, and led the dash for the doorway, his long legs flashing. They followed willingly, whooped on by the gay rabble behind. The horseman, awaking less readily to the situation, clapped spurs to his horse somewhat belatedly, and reined in in a flurry of sparks at Madonna Benedetta's doorstep just as Adam set foot on it and spread his arms to bar the way.

"Give way, fellow," said de Breauté, secure in his nobility but good-humoured still. "Do you not know your betters?"

Adam planted himself firmly on the second step, and wagged a chiding finger at his rival. "Come, come, sir, do you not know there's no better nor worse here, but only pleasing or displeasing to the lady? It was as close a thing as ever I saw, but I am here before you. Do you give way, like a fair-minded fellow, and take your turn another evening. I stand on my rights."

"I'll see you to the devil first!" said de Breauté heartily, and pressed his horse close, in the hope of intimidating this bold young man into drawing aside; but Élie snapped his fingers loudly under the beast's well-bred nose, and sent it backwards in a startled plunge a yard or two across the cobbles, hooves slithering and clanging hard against the stones. If there was a woman in the lighted room, she could hardly be long unaware of the commotion beneath her window; even if she had been sleeping, she must be wakeful enough now.

The horseman, for a moment thrown off-balance, recovered himself with a rising temper, and swung his whip at Élie's head, but the boy ducked and sprang aside, and Apollon lifted a soothing hand and cried: "Wait, now, not so hot! Do you want to ingratiate yourself with Madonna Benedetta by starting a brawl under her windows? Do you suppose she isn't capable of making her own choice? And is any one of us going to dispute it if she does? Are you afraid to enter the lists fairly, song for song?"

The rabble of students had closed in happily about the two groups, and linked arms to form a semicircle round the doorway. They raised a cheer at this suggestion, foreseeing delicious entertainment, whether the bargain held or broke.

"Song for song! Toss for first place, and give each other fair hearing."

"And if she give either one a sign of her approval, t'other must pack and go, and no hard feelings. Right, boys?"

"Right!" roared the circle delightedly, and swayed inwards to see and hear the better. Such harmless townsfolk as happened to be passing through the Rue des Psautiers first slowed at sight and sound of this noisy assembly, and then halted to await developments, until the circle was three deep and others were craning to look over the shoulders of those in front. Of late it had become the habit with some to stroll by Madonna Benedetta's on uneventful evenings in the hope of diversion.

The musicians grinned with the superiority of professionals at the idea of competing with this shabby handful of students and craftsmen. Their master had nothing to fear. Plainly he thought the same, for he had lowered his whip and was laughing. Like Adam, he had been taking aboard courage and inspiration from a flagon, and as yet it had left him amiable.

"Done! If she signify her favour to you, I'll withdraw and leave you to your happiness. But you must do as much for me."

"Willingly," said Adam. "What's more, I'll give you the precedence. Go first, and you shall be heard fairly."

"Good lad!" whispered Harry in his ear. "There's not a woman breathing could bear to say yes to the first till she's heard the second—and last heard's best remembered."

"Silence, lads, give silence! Play fair by us both!" And in an undertone Adam besought anxiously: "Shall I spring the new song on her direct, or open with some small thing?"

"The new one! Stake everything!" advised Apollon in an answering whisper.

The ring of students, more than commonly disorderly in pursuit of order, exhorted the world to silence, and had much ado to silence one another; but in a moment or two the last ripple of their hubbub sighed away into the shadows, and the consort, assembling in a little group at the foot of the steps, tuned their instruments and broke into a known melody.

> "If I had lilies to bring,
>   or were this the season of roses—"

"We're back with Fortunatus," breathed Élie disgustedly, "picking violets for Radegunde. For God's sake, where are the moderns?"

"Hush, give the man his chance."

He subsided with a sigh of protest, and like his fellows heard the performance out with critical attention, and even some pleasure, for all its antiquity. Having paid for music, de Breauté contributed none himself; no doubt he knew his own capabilities best, and not every man can have a true voice. And if he must purchase his talents, he had got good value enough. The singer had a sure delivery and a sweet tone, and the players knew their business. He sat his horse in mid-street, his eyes fixed on that upper window, where the candle-light flickered a little in the freshening breeze of the night, and the arras stirred languidly, so that at times he stiffened in eagerness, expecting the apparition of a smiling, gracious face. But the violets of Fortunatus reached Radegunde, and still Madonna Benedetta did not show herself.

"Hard luck, friend!" commiserated the students cheerfully. "She-hawks never come to the first lure."

"Let's hear what the other can do."

"She's there," said one, his eyes on the window. "I saw a shadow pass. She marks you, lads, you're not wasting your breath."

"An omen!" piped up a youngster from the third rank, craning his neck and recognising the lutanist. "He has Apollo himself to play for him!"

"Unfair!" cried another. "What chance has the other poor devil against the gods?"

"Without his name be Marsyas," shouted a voice from the back, and there was a howl of laughter.

"Will you hold your din, and let Apollo make himself heard, before he has the knives sharpened for the lot of you?"

They settled good-humouredly into silence, still grinning, and Apollon led softly into Abelard's forgotten air. One listener, catching an echo of something once half-known, drew back his head, and ceased to laugh. Here and there a swaying head picked up the time. They knew a tune when they heard one. They were quiet enough now. De Breauté looked on perforce, frowning to see the visible audience captivated, and fearing for the invisible.

Adam sang, his voice soaring fresh and gay and plaintive between the overhanging walls:

> "Now is the time of maying.
> Beneath thy flowering tree
> I strip my bones with praying,
> And yet thou wilt not see.
>
> The sap of spring is leaping,
> The love-dance takes the deer;
> I cry thy name with weeping.
> And yet thou wilt not hear.
>
> Under thy sheltering blossom
> The coney makes her cave.
> The birds nest in thy bosom,
> But me thou wilt not save.
>
> Yet when the branch is shaken—"

The arras within the window trembled; he saw it, and his voice trembled with it for a moment, and then swept on joyously and steadily to the close:

> "Yet when the branch is shaken
> And summer's pride is past,
> Me, naked and forsaken,
> Receive and love at last,

> And when the autumn dapples
> Thy gilded heaven tree,
> Let fall thy golden apples,
> Bow down thy breasts to me."

There was a moment of stillness and silence, and then a rising murmur and a triumphant cry:

"Look up, lads, the moon rises!"

A hand had appeared from behind the tapestry, and was stretched out over the street. They saw a round white arm from which the fur hem of a loose sleeve fell back to the elbow, as something was let fall from between her fingers and drifted down lightly towards Adam's ready hands. One of the musicians, encouraged by a cry of protest from his lord, leaped to intercept it, but Adam whisked it away and held it high. The circle of students stamped and roared.

"Violets! The ones your fellows tossed in at her window a minute ago! She gives them to me. Are you answered?"

"A judgement, a judgement!" they chorused. "Go home, man, she's made her choice."

The wine de Breauté had drunk was souring in him. He hesitated angrily for a moment, the horse shifting uneasily under him. The hand vanished within, the window was quiet and unrevealing as before.

"She said no word. How do we even know the posy was meant for you and not for me?"

They roared him down indignantly, but now his blood was up and he would not give way. "Song for song till she told us her mind was the bargain!" he cried, and signed furiously to the musicians to strike up again. Insistent above the hubbub rose another melody well-known to every minstrel in Paris.

"Stay by the door," urged Harry, clutching Adam by the arm as he started angrily forward, "for I think she means to open when she has her fill of this."

"Let me alone!" growled Adam, struggling. "I'll have him off his perch though he draw on me, the cheating hound!"

They held him back and thrust him behind them into the coign of the doorway while they shook some sense into him. "What do you want with the man, you fool? The woman's yours, leave the man to us.''

For all their indignation, the audience had stilled to listen. The song was an old favourite, and this was not, after all, their quarrel; they were there to enjoy it, and perhaps to add a little fuel to the fire if it threatened to burn out too soon and too tamely.

"This is dull stuff," said Harry, cocking an ear. "Let's see if we can improve on it. Apollon, lend me the lute!" His eyes were gleaming yellowly, and he had a hungry, cat's smile as he bent over the strings and fingered his way into the air. It was already too late to do anything about the first verse, but he could surely liven up what was left.

> "Now summer comes with splendour,
> The zenith of the year,
> And winter's frosts surrender
> To Phoebus' burning spear,
>
> But I, who dote upon you,
> Your grieving suppliant stand—"

In came Harry with a vicious chord and a drumming of his finger-ends on the wood, and a voice far louder and more penetrating than Adam's, if less melodious:

> "—While my hired gleemen dun you
> For love at secondhand."

A shout of joy went up from the audience. De Breauté's servant darted forward up the steps and lunged with his sheathed dagger at the lute, but Apollon and Élie closed in before Harry, received the attacker into willing arms, and held him a writhing prisoner. De Breauté, black with temper, set spurs to his horse again, but one of the students caught at his bridle and hung upon it with all his weight. The distracted consort, redoubling their efforts, blew and scraped and plucked frenziedly to drown the hubbub. The singer bellowed:

"O fount of pity springing,
Be your sweet mercy shed—"

There his voice cracked grotesquely with strain, and choked him
to silence, leaving Harry's gleeful shout triumphant on the air, sharp
as sour apples:

"—On one more skilled in singing
And better worth your bed."

A howl of delight from those nearest greeted it, and clamouring
complaints from those behind demanded to have it relayed to them,
and so it was, flung back wave by wave to the most remote onlookers
bobbing up and down at the back. The laughter followed it in widen-
ing ripples, echoing from the leaning gables in a riotous thunder.
But high above it floated the loveliest, clearest, most candid peal of
mirth launched in Paris that night. It fell from Madonna Benedetta's
window like a flight of yellow rose-leaves drifting slowly down in a
shaft of sunlight.

Everyone looked up, but the window was empty; and as they
stared upwards, the door was softly unbarred below, and softly
opened. Adam heard it and sprang round to see a girl's face glowing
in the interstice and a girl's hand reaching for his to draw him in.
Overwhelmed now that the heavens stood wide for him, he could
only stare and wonder, until Harry, thrusting the lute back into
Apollon's solicitous hands, took the dazed conquerer by the shoulders and pushed him into the house. The door closed smartly, and
a bolt shot into place with a clang.

Too much occupied with keeping his seat to mark the opening of
the door, de Breauté heard the bolt go home, and casting a frantic
glance in that direction, saw that his rival had vanished. It was more
than his pride could bear. With a yell of rage he lashed out at the
student who clung to his bridle, and the horse, taking the worst of
the blow as the boy ducked under its heaving neck, reared up with
a scream and sent the front rank of spectators leaping back into the
arms of their fellows. The youngster, flung off like a kitten, dropped
as lightly as one, and rolled clear of the clashing hooves, to be hauled
to his feet by his friends. De Breauté, freed of the hampering weight

and no more than half in control of his mount, drove him straight at the steps.

The musicians embraced their instruments and scuttled aside, jostling one another wildly. Élie leaped from the steps in one direction, Apollon, jealously guarding his lute, in the other, and Harry, pinned in the doorway, took the lash of the whip about his upflung forearm to save his head, and clapping the other hand as far up the butt as he could reach, wrenched the horseman's lunging weight towards him. He meant only to disarm his attacker, but the whip had a loop which was fastened securely about de Breauté's gloved wrist, and man and weapon were dragged forward together over the horse's shoulder. Harry went down beneath the flying weight, and rolled upon the steps half-dazed, his enemy sprawling over him and the agitated hooves plunging and clattering on the cobbles not a yard from them, until Élie caught at the bridle and drew the beast away, trembling and snorting. He got it safely clear of the crowd, and then it tossed him off like a flake of foam from the bit, and took to its heels for home; and Élie, ever a practical man, wasted no time on a problem he could not solve, but picked himself up, rubbed his bruises briefly, and hurled himself bodily back into the laughing, bawling, cursing, grunting mass of bodies that filled the Rue des Psautiers from wall to wall.

The wiser citizens made all possible haste away from the battle; the students with whoops of joy poured themselves into it, took whichever side they fancied, and laid about them merrily. It was months since they had seen such a satisfactory affray, and one in which anyone might join. They settled down to enjoy it.

Even the musicians, inextricably tangled into the struggling mass, abandoned all thought of escape, and went to their master's support tooth and nail. There was no hope of withdrawing their instruments intact from such a turmoil, so they turned them into weapons, and trusted in de Breauté to replace them, since they served his pleasure and were being sacrificed in his cause. Élie took a crack over the head from a flute, and sat down hard again on the cobbles. Apollon, shielding his precious lute with his body, since he had no lord to buy him another, was felled by a blow from a viol, and heard its delicate, taut ribs crack and cave in with almost as much pain as if his own darling had suffered injury. Not until his cherishing hands had assured him that it was still intact did he find time to notice the thunderous music in his misused head. The rounded belly of a citole, swung purposefully at Harry's skull as he rolled clear of his antagonist, missed him by a foot and smashed like an egg against the edge of the stone step. He flung himself upon it and seized its slender neck, and planting a foot in the musician's chest from his vantage point on top of the steps, hurled him off to crash into a swaying wall of bodies. He had possessed himself of a weapon only just in time. De Breauté was on his feet and had his sword out.

Someone yelled: "Steel!" and those who could fell back a little from him, for he was in so irresponsible a rage that to be within his range was a risk even these incautious spirits did not care to take. He lunged at Harry, and the shattered citole, cunningly advanced to meet the point instead of battering it aside, was impaled so deeply that the tip of the blade split the sounding-board and grazed Harry's fingers. He twisted the neck of the instrument through a full circle in his hands, and de Breauté screamed and let go his hilt rather than have his wrist broken. Harry uttered a shout of triumph, and swung citole and sword together about his head, intending to hurl both over the surging mass of combatants and out of reach; but at that moment a piercing whistle rang out from the northern end of the Rue des Psautiers, and every student head reared in one abrupt and incredibly brief instant of stillness.

"Scatter!" bellowed Apollon. "The watch!" And the apparently inextricable mass disentangled itself miraculously, and made off like the wind in all directions but the north. The noise of running feet was like a sudden heavy shower of rain.

Élie leaped for the top of the wall which bounded Guiscard's stable-yard, and hauled himself up with a furious scraping of shoe-toes and knees, to straddle the wall and drop out of sight within. Apollon dived into a narrow gullet between the houses, and crept through, holding his nose as he paddled along the noisome gutter into the Rue du Lapin and safety. Harry, dropping the transfixed citole, took a flying leap down the steps to follow him, but the musicians, secure in their master's nobility and seeing a safe and easy way to ingratiate themselves with him now that the odds were so drastically changed, fell upon the fugitive as one man and bore him crashing to the cobbles.

By the time he had regained the breath they had knocked out of him, they had him propped on his feet before the provost and were volubly explaining how the whole riot was his work, how he and his cronies had molested their lord on his entirely innocent occasions, interrupted his serenade with ribald parodies, assaulted his servant, dragged him from his horse, and started a street fight in which all the other riff-raff of the student quarter had rushed to take part.

Harry's eyes grew large with admiration as he listened. "On my soul," he said, "I begin to respect myself! It seems I'm a devil of a fellow."

One of the sergeants clouted him lightly in the mouth with the back of his hand, to teach him to be silent until invited to speak. He shook the slight sting of the blow away without resentment, and looked round upon the empty street, suddenly so quiet. Every soul but himself had got clear away. But for the sad, splintered instruments, and the sword, still stabbing the citole to the heart, no sign of the recent bedlam remained.

The provost, frowning down from his lanky roan horse, was also surveying the battleground, and regretting that he had not delayed entering the street until he could post a second force at the southern end and net a whole shoal of the rowdy students who plagued him so constantly. But half of them, no doubt, would have laid claim to clerical privilege if he had, and been fished out of trouble by masters or canons. Well, at least there were no bodies to be accounted for this time, and no injuries.

"My lord de Breauté, do you bear out all this? You know this fellow for one of the ringleaders, do you?"

"The most impudent of them all," said de Breauté, breathing hard and looking daggers as his servant brushed him down. "It was he pulled me from my horse." But he said nothing of Adam's part in the affair; perhaps out of generosity, but more likely, thought Harry, because the admission of defeat would have made him a laughing-stock.

"Well, rascal, what have you to say? Did you pull my lord from his horse?"

"I did," said Harry, "after he took his whip to me. But indeed it was more of a success than I'd bargained for: it was only the whip I wanted, I got the man as well. I was more surprised than he was. And I was underneath!"

"Wanted the whip, did you!" said the provost with a grim smile. "We may be able to satisfy you there, my lad. What business had you here in the first place, ruffling it and howling gross songs on the public street to the annoyance of an honest gentleman? I mean to have the peace kept in my city, and you and your kind shall learn it."

"Why, I don't deny the fight, but there are two sides to any fight, and I can hardly be supposed to have sustained both sides single-handed. This honest gentleman made a bargain, and refused to abide by it when he lost, and so we came to blows. Take him in, too, and do us both justice. Besides," said Harry cheerfully, "you're more like to get a good fat fine out of him than me, for devil a silver coin have I got to my name since I paid for the supper."

"If you had half the year's minting, you should still cool your heels overnight, young man. It will do you no harm to lie hard for once. Unless you can produce witnesses to speak to your version of this evening's entertainment?"

There were indeed two witnesses almost within call, but to disturb them would have been a kind of blasphemy. The light was quenched in the upper room. Harry smiled, and shook his head. His hard night for Adam's soft one, it was a fair exchange.

"Now you've promised me a bed, how can I be so uncivil as to wish to excuse myself from occupying it? Yours is one guest-house that never turns away even a *vagus*."

"You have a trick of speech that never was bred in Paris," said the provost, frowning over him, and thoughtfully pulling a great nose pitted with pock-marks. "What's your name, fellow? Are you enrolled as a student, or are you indeed *vagus*?"

"I am not enrolled as a student, but I have leave to hear lectures when my duties permit. My name—Master Provost, can you keep a secret? My name is Golias, master of the *Ordo Vagorum*, but I'm in Paris incognito, and you mustn't breathe a word of it."

"Pay him for that," said the provost, but so tolerantly that the sergeants dealt him no more than a couple of buffets on the ears with their heavy leather gloves.

"If you wish to make any claim to being a clerk, make it now," said the provost shortly, "and before witnesses."

Harry shook his thick, disordered brown locks indignantly. "Does this look like a tonsure?"

"I've known tonsures appear mysteriously, even in a cell underground. I'm taking no chances."

"I'll strangle whoever tries to shave this," Harry promised heartily, "even to get me out of jail."

"Bring him along," said the provost, "and we'll see if he has a better will to answer questions in the morning." And with that he shook his reins, gave de Breauté a brusque inclination of his head, and trotted away along the Rue des Psautiers. And Harry, held firmly by both arms and encouraged to speed by an occasional fist thudding into his back, stepped out philosophically after him. It was bad luck to be the scapegoat, but it might have happened to any one of them; and the evening had been worth it. He had no complaints.

The exhilaration of wine and action lasted him half through the night, though he did tell the sergeants, more in sorrow than in anger, what he thought of the narrow, damp, foul cell into which they thrust him. They answered, justly enough, that he had good reason to be thankful they had given him one above ground, with a window, small, high and barred, but undoubtedly a window, and giving on to the outer air. They might just as easily have put him underground in darkness. They rough-handled him a little before they left him, for his impudence, but without malice, almost playfully. Even sergeants have a certain sneaking fellow-feeling with those who are merry with drink, and they did not stop to wonder how much of his gaiety was due to wine and how much to satisfied excitement.

When he was alone he groped his way to the cold stone ledge, and sat down. Through the high window he could see a handful of stars, and the air, though laden with some highly unpleasant smells, was breathable. They were right, he had good reason to think himself lucky. If they had been in a bad humour they would have broken his head for him and pitched him into one of the fetid holes below, where a man could not even stand upright or lie at full length.

Now the worst problem he had was how to pass the time and work off the rest of his animal spirits, for he was too restless to think of sleeping. He eased himself into the most comfortable position he could find, discovering in the process some bruises he had not known he possessed, and began to go through his repertory of disreputable songs, tentatively at first, to see how soon they would feel it necessary to take steps to silence him, then, emboldened by having got through the first unthreatened, at the top of his voice. He was halfway through the ballad of a certain abbess of remarkably irregular private life, with his ears cocked for footsteps and his eye on the door, like an urchin essaying how far he dare go in provocation, when the key turned in the lock and a thread of light split the darkness. He fell silent, half regretting his recklessness and half exulting in it, and waited to see if he had tried his luck too hard; but the turnkey with his lantern brought in only one man, the provost's clerk, a sharp-faced fellow in a scholar's garde-corps and a skull-cap.

"I am come to advise you of the amount at which your fine is fixed," said he, planting the lantern upon a wooden stool in the corner of the cell, and signalling to the jailer to withdraw and close the door until he wished to leave.

"Then you may spare your breath," said Harry, swinging his feet to the floor and sitting up, "for whatever it may be, I cannot pay it."

He looked round his prison with interest, for he had had small opportunity to examine it when they bundled him into it, and this interlude of light and company was welcome to him. He had not, until that moment, realised that he had a stool, and a large, solid stool, too, with a top to it as thick as a refectory table. Nor that he had company of a kind in his solitude, apart from the vermin, for all the walls about him were written and scratched over with complaints, curses and ribaldries left by his predecessors, including some interesting reflections on the provost's parentage, scored deep into the stone above the bench with a knife or a nail.

"Then you may rot where you are, my friend, but it is my duty to acquaint you with the provost's judgement. Your freedom is set at twelve pounds, Paris. If you pay your fine, you may go free in the morning. If not, you may write a letter to someone who can raise the money for you. You must have friends who will bestir themselves for you."

"My friends are all as wealthy as I. You have as much chance of getting twelve pounds out of the lot of us as you have of being taken up to heaven living."

"That is your affair, not mine. But until the fine is paid you will continue to lie here. Have you no money at all?"

Harry turned out his pockets, and unearthed a few small coins, all that the merry party at Nestor's had left him. In the search he found also something which greatly pleased him, for he had forgotten he had it, and if the sergeants had been more thorough with him it would surely have been found and taken from him, along with his dagger. His favourite little pocket-knife in its worn sheath was strapped to the belt of his chausses, under his tunic, and had escaped notice. He took care to keep it out of sight now, for fear the oversight should be remedied. The very feel of it between his fingers, the way the haft settled and fitted into his palm, filled him with confidence and comfort.

"That won't free you," admitted the clerk with a sour smile, "but it would at least buy you a bite of bread and cheese if you're hungry, and a drop of cheap wine. I'm not obliged to offer you these services, nor good advice neither, but out of goodwill I'll get you food if you please to pay for it."

Harry was on the point of closing with this offer, when the feel of the knife against his side, and the sight of the honest dark wood of the stool, filled him with a different hunger and a stronger anticipation. He shook the coins together in his hand, smiling delightedly.

"I'll tell you what I'd rather have, if you'll help me to it. Oh, nothing against your conscience, I swear. A light! A candle—a large one, mind, none of your ends—or the loan of a lantern for the night. What do you say? There's enough here to pay for it, and something over for your kindness."

"It's a queer taste," said the clerk, raising his eyebrows, "to want to see this hole as well as feel and smell it. But if that's your wish, I see no harm in it. Keep this lantern, it's trimmed, and will burn all night. And if you please to send a message somewhere in the morning, I'll see it delivered. Don't thank me for that! How else should we ever see our money for you starved mice from the schools? There's not a one of you ever has the means to pay for his bed."

"Your hostelry charges such high rates," said Harry, grinning, "that it's my belief you owe us that bread and cheese thrown in. And faith, I should only be doing right by my fellows in misfortune if I stood out for it. If they don't send me some food in, I'll go on singing until they do, and nobody shall get any sleep tonight."

"That's one way of looking at the matter," agreed the clerk drily. "On the other hand, the provost lies well out of earshot even of your bellow, and the sergeants are dicing and not yet minded for sleep, otherwise they would have made shift to silence you before now. And my reading of the probabilities is somewhat at variance with yours. I should put it, rather, that if you do not hush your noise, they will soon be in with rods and an iron bridle, to hush it for you."

"Say no more, I'm convinced! Only leave me the light, and I'll be quiet as the grave."

He parted with his last coins upon these terms, without the slightest regret; and when he was left alone again, the jailer having relocked the door upon him and withdrawn with the clerk, he went and set the lantern on the stone bench, and tipped up the stool to examine it more closely.

The top, seven or eight inches thick, projected at either end beyond the roughly carved legs, and made a fine jutting mass of wood. He thumbed it over, and it was shiny and smooth with long handling. To make the most of his light he sat down on the filthy floor with his back braced against the stone ledge, and the lantern shining over his left shoulder, almost on a level with the end of the stool, which he drew close between his knees. When he turned it sidewise to the light he could already see the thick, gross profile leaning out like a devil from a misericord. He drew out his knife, and the haft nestled into his palm like the muzzle of a favourite dog, ready and eager for exercise.

He did not sleep all night, but the provost had never had a quieter or a happier prisoner.

Chapter Seven

*A*dam walked through the early dawn to the Ruelle des Guenilles like one borne on a rosy cloud of delight, and climbed the stairs to the attic, singing softly to himself and unbuckling the belt of the good cotte as he went. At the sound of his step Élie flung open the door and rushed out to meet him.

"I've been waiting for you—Apollon had a six o'clock lecture he couldn't miss. Adam, they took up Harry!"

"They, who?" said Adam, lost in his own surpassing memories, and slow to recognise disaster. "What are you babbling about, man?"

"The provost and his officers. Did you not even hear the alarm? Ah, well, I suppose not! They came soon after you entered the house. We all ran for it. Everyone got clear except Harry; they picked him up for disturbing the peace, and de Breauté and his men swore he was the ringleader. They took him off and tossed him in the provost's prison, and there he is now, and how are we to get him out? We haven't a thing of value to pledge, and if I ask my father for money before my next allowance is due he'll likely bid me come home and render account of myself, and I shall be hauled

out of the schools and put to clerking. The last time he had to bail
me out he swore he'd give me no more indulgences. What are we
to do?"

Adam took him by the arm, and marched him into their room,
and there began hurriedly to strip off the precious cotte and pull on
his working tunic, shooting questions like arrows at the hollow-eyed
and whey-faced Élie.

"How did you learn all this? Has he sent word?"

"I heard them take him away. I was hiding inside Madonna
Benedetta's stable-yard."

"What? You've known ever since it happened? You clown, why
didn't you come and tell me at once?"

Élie clutched his aching head and rolled his eyes heavenwards.
"Talk sense, man. How could I? Can you not see me banging at the
door? 'My most humble apologies to Madonna Benedetta, but I
must borrow my friend back from her, his brother's been taken up
by the watch!' Besides, I didn't know then where they might take
him, I had to follow them to find out."

"Did they mishandle him? And did he manage to hold his fool
tongue?"

"They were in good humour, no more than playful. But you
know him—when the provost asked him his name he told him he
was Golias, and that didn't please!"

"That's like him!" said Adam, savage with anxiety, tugging down
his tunic. "He never could let well or ill alone. Let me get him safe
out of there, and I'll have something to say to him myself. Golias,
indeed! And he knows the trouble they've been making about vaga-
bonds lately! If he must make a joke at the wrong time, does it have
to be the most provocative joke possible? Well, go on, what did you
do?"

"Came back here to Apollon. He makes a better figure than I do
when it comes to bearding officials. He went and argued the toss
with them at the prison, and tried to threaten them with all the
canons of Notre Dame. But they wouldn't turn him loose, and they
wouldn't let Apollon see him. They want twelve pounds Paris before
they'll let go of him. Apollon tried bargaining—you know he can
look as if he has a few pounds about him even when he hasn't a
penny. But he couldn't beat them down. It's twelve pounds or no

Harry. Now what are we going to do? We can't put together two pounds between us until the beginning of the month. Apollon said if we could find some way of making up the rest we could pledge his lute." He offered this extreme sacrifice round-eyed with awe as a child, for he knew its worth. So did Adam, and turned impulsively to fling an arm round his shoulders and hug him briefly.

"We won't cut Apollon's heart out, it's not as bad as all that. No, I'll go and cleanse my bosom to old Bertrand. He'll rave, but he'll pay up rather than leave his best sculptor in jail and have to make do without him, even for a day. I'll get my head in my hands, and so will Harry when he's loosed, but no matter for that. Go and sleep it off," he advised, pushing Élie towards his bed, "you look like a ghost. I suppose you've had no sleep all night."

"Have you?" asked Élie with interest, and a reviving spark in his clouded eye.

Adam shot him a brief, preoccupied grin, and postponed whatever rejoinder he might have had in mind for that. There was no time and he was in no mind for fooling until Harry was free again.

He made all haste to the Ile de la Cité, and in the close of Notre Dame looked for Master Bertrand among the lodges clinging like barnacles to the foot of the new west front. It was early yet, but the old master-mason was often bustling about the site ahead of his men, ready to harry them even if they came before their time. Yet this morning Adam chafed in vain, waiting for him to put in an appearance, and at last had to entrust his vigil to the boy who swept and ran the errands about the masons' lodge. It was an hour before the child whistled up to him on the scaffolding, and fetched him glissading down the ropes from the putlogs embedded in the base of the south-west tower.

"He's just come, and Canon d'Espérance with him. And they have a third one with them. Somebody important. Not a churchman, neither, he looks like a lord. You'll never disturb them while he's there?"

"Needs must," said Adam. "If I'm torn to pieces, sweep up the shreds tenderly and give them to Harry for Christian burial." And he brushed a hasty hand over the corn-coloured hair tousled by the breeze on the scaffolding, beat stone-dust from his sleeves, and approached the three figures gathered in the middle of the close, looking up at the west portals.

"Master Bertrand, by your leave—"

The master-mason was a venerable figure, bearded like a patriarch and aware of his massive dignity. He turned upon his man a frown of reproof, and waved him away irritably. "At a more opportune time! Can you not see I am engaged?"

"I see it, indeed, and I ask your pardon, but this is urgent, and I think you would wish to hear it at once. It touches my brother. You have had no time to remark it, but he is not here this morning, nor like to be until we find twelve pounds to redeem him. To be plain with you, sir, he is in prison, and the provost will not let him go for less."

"He is *where?*" thundered Master Bertrand. Canon d'Espérance and the stranger had withdrawn a few paces and were talking together in low tones, but they could hardly help hearing that bull's bellow.

"In prison," said Adam uncomfortably. "He was taken up after a street fight in the Rue des Psautiers last night, not having committed an act amiss more than the other thirty-odd of us, but being unlucky enough to be the only one caught. I am sorry, the thing was more my doing in the first place than his. But so the case stands. And if you would be generous enough to advance us the money, we could be about getting him out at once."

He drew breath, and waited with interest to see if the explosion would come; but it did not. Master Bertrand swallowed his gall with difficulty, but he swallowed it.

"You and I, Master Lestrange," he said, in a low voice half-choked by the effort at composure, "will discourse further of this hereafter. And I shall have something to say also to that graceless brother of yours when next I see him. He does not deserve that I should advance him a sou, since he has not the wit nor the virtue to keep out of trouble. But he knows I am pressed, and he trades on it—he trades on it! He will do it once too often some day, and find he is left to rue it."

"I cannot call to mind that he ever ended in prison before," said Adam sulkily. "The money shall be regarded as an advance on our pay, sir, and you may dock it from both of us till it be paid off. I am sorry I was the occasion of his ill luck, but I'll take good care not to let him be tripped so again on my account. I can say no more."

"You could hardly for shame say less. How came you to be caught up in a street fight? Have you no discretion in you? Must you frequent the most notorious spots in the city?" And he could not refrain from appealing, with arduous self-control, to Canon d'Espérance. "Your reverence, you hear this fellow? Do you wonder I have difficulty in keeping my times, when my rogues play me such tricks? Master Henry Lestrange, if you please, is taken up by the watch in a brawl, and in some weeks' time you will be asking me why the Calvary is not ready as I promised it. There are no reliable craftsmen to be had these days; the more gifted they are, it seems to me, the bigger rascals they turn out."

Thus invited into conference, the canon bestowed on him a placating smile, and said mildly: "Come, he has not been such an unprofitable servant, I think. He is not the first young man to fall from grace."

The stranger, turning abruptly from his contemplation of the new portals, walked towards them at this moment, and said clearly, in a resonant voice that came rounded on the air like the complex note of a bell: "Lestrange, did I hear? Is this he of whom we were speaking just now?"

Speaking of Harry, thought Adam, turning sharply towards the voice. To what end?

"The same," said the canon. "That is, he who is in prison is the same. This is his brother."

"I have been hearing something of the pair of you," said the ringing voice, "from both your masters here. It seems you are English."

"We are, sir."

"Fellow-countrymen should stand together in a strange land," said the unknown, with a crooked smile. "I am English myself. I should like to hear the full story of your night's amusement, if Master Bertrand can spare you the time it takes to tell it. And if, of course," he added, marking how the hot colour rose in Adam's cheeks at the idea of telling how the evening had ended for him, "it is not too profane for the ears of Canon d'Espérance." The smile drew upwards one corner of a long, embittered, expressive mouth, while the other half of his face remained almost still. "You may omit the improper passages," he said coolly.

It was put as a suggestion, but it was nonetheless an order. This man spoke in commands, and he would not often be disobeyed. Adam found himself telling the tale of Madonna Benedetta's serenade without embarrassment, even with gusto, while he took stock of the stranger.

He was worth looking at, tall and lean and graceful, a man perhaps forty-five years old, richly and sombrely dressed. His head, wonderfully set on a throat like an antique column, was carried very high, and the arrogance which was in every turn and every line of it had been born with him. He wore his hair in the older fashion, squarely cut, with a fringe over his forehead, but it was such a great forehead that it was not dwarfed; and his brows, of a brown darker than the hair, were long and level, and all but met over the long, straight nose. Sunk deep into his head, in great, shadowy sockets, his eyes stared forth restlessly questioning, measuring, assessing, dissecting, fastening with famished intelligence upon everything that came within their sight. Disquieting eyes they were, illusionless yet eager, calm yet full of a smoky secret rage, brilliant yet melancholy; and they were beautiful. His face was clean-shaven, and burned to a deep tan which he had certainly never acquired in France, nor in the England he claimed as his country. Observing it, Adam began to guess from what quarter he was newly come; the dark gold, so startling on the taut, drawn lines of his cheeks and jaw, would soon tarnish and fade in this climate, though the coming summer might preserve it for a while.

He wore a full surcoat of russet cloth, the wide sleeves and capuchon lined with tawny fur; and as he moved, two rings on his lean, bronzed right hand flashed gold and purple. The skirt of his surcoat, slashed to the waist, uncovered as he walked a long, elegant leg in a boot of soft leather, almost knee-high and of a most outlandish cut. Like his tan, he had got those somewhere much farther east than Paris.

Adam debated the wisdom of remembering Harry's improvisations word for word in this company, but when pressed he produced them, adroitly avoiding the canon's eyes. They had a second success.

The canon kept his smile severe and academic, but his eye gleamed for a moment. The sunburned stranger threw back his head and laughed aloud.

"Oh, Master Bertrand, I see you did not tell me the half. You have a man of parts there, it seems. Well, and then?"

"Then the door opened and let me in. And it appears that a free fight broke out in the street, though exactly how it started I'm in no position to argue, for I knew nothing about it until this morning, when I went home and learned that the watch had taken my brother. No one was damaged, God be thanked," said Adam, "and no one was taken in charge except Harry. So I don't see that it would hurt them, or be bad for public order, to let him go. But without the fine they won't do it."

"Irresponsible as children," said Master Bertrand querulously, "the pair of you. I've a mind to let him stew in his own juice for a day or two, and teach him a lesson, but that would hardly be fair unless we could commit you into the bargain. So I suppose we shall have to get him out."

"To visit those in prison is a Christian act," said the stranger with his crooked smile. "I have a fancy to go myself and relieve this gifted young man of yours. Will you lend me his brother for an hour, to bring me to the place? I'll send him back to you as soon as may be."

He used, then as always, the courteous speech of one asking favours, but he used it in the calm manner of one exacting dues so obvious that no man would dare gainsay them.

"You are too condescending, my lord, to two graceless young rogues, but take him, take him if you will." He was relieved to be spared the expense, thought Adam, but otherwise he was none too well pleased about the stranger's interest. Masters may know the worth of their pupils, and to themselves even admit it, but they do not commonly enjoy being excelled by them; and Adam was not alone in holding that Harry had outgrown his instruction. Others, without his understandable partiality, had been known to express the same opinion.

"My lord, this is generous, towards two who are unknown to you. But I do not know how we are to discharge the debt."

"There will be no debt." There was a momentary flash of displea-

sure from the formidable eyes, like a single flicker of lightning out
of an overcast sky. Then he emerged from behind the clouds and
laughed again. "What you mean is that *I* am unknown to *you*. You
are nice in choosing your benefactors, are you? My credentials will
pass muster, I trust. I hear you come from the marches of Wales.
So do I. If you know Mormesnil, or Erington, or Fleace, or Parfois,
you know me. My name is Ralf Isambard. Are you content?"

"My lord!" said Adam, overwhelmed by a name that rang in the
marches as loud and as awfully as FitzAlan or FitzWarin.

"Come, then, we'll not leave your brother any longer in durance.
Master Bertrand, they shall both come back to you within the hour."

With the abruptness which marked all his movements, and the
grace which clothed his naked arrogance and rid it of all offence, he
swept away from them, swerving between men and piled building
materials on the crowded site, the skirts of his surcoat flying, the
barbaric boots spurning the dust of the close. Walking behind him,
Adam could not take his eyes from the uncovered head, with its
short, curled hair blowing back from close-set ears, and the beautiful
subtleties of its modelling showing through the thick locks, as the
slanting morning light touched every salient and the shadow clung
in every hollow. Harry won't be able to set eyes on him, he was
thinking, without wanting to copy that head in stone. He'd make a
terrible fighting saint. Or a magnificent devil!

With the coming of daylight Harry, long accustomed to be sparing
with candles, had put out the lantern in favour of the light from the
small, barred window, lifted the stool on to the stone ledge, and
continued his work kneeling before it on the hard, uneven floor of
the cell. He was completely engrossed in what he was doing, and
incapable of feeling either hunger or weariness.

Had he heard the key grate in the lock during the first hours, he
would have clapped the stool hard against the wall and sat on it, and
the knife would have been slipped out of sight in an instant. Now
he heard it, but as from a great distance, and he did not move or
even look round, but went on paring to his exact delight the curl of
a thick mouth within the bristling beard. He heard footsteps enter
the cell behind him, but paid them no attention. His intent head,
tilted a little on one side to let the light fall full on his work, had

the look of a child's in passionate play, or of a devout man's in prayer. Not until a shadow crossed between him and the window did he acknowledge that he was not alone, and even then he only halted his hand for a second, without turning his head.

"Stand out of my light!" he said imperiously.

The shadow withdrew at once, but a second and a bulkier took its place.

"By God," said the provost warmly, "you have the devil's own impudence!" He came a single menacing step nearer, thus bringing into his view the carved head that leaned out from the overhang of the stool. He gasped, recognising the frowning brows, the great pock-marked nose, the jutting bearded chin. With a bellow of rage he lifted his staff and struck hard at the hand that was so busy with the knife.

The impact of the blow, and Harry's yell of pain and fury, and the clatter of the knife falling, all seemed to come together. Harry whirled round on his knees and flung himself along the floor, reaching for the haft with his left hand, since the right was paralysed. The provost raised his cane to strike again. The tall shadow within the doorway moved faster than either of them, and to better purpose.

Harry's groping fingers touched the haft just as a foot came down hard but silently upon the blade. Through the hot mist of his anger and pain he was aware, with grotesque clarity, of a boot such as he had never seen before except in some drawings at Caen once, made by a mason who had followed Richard to the Crusades, and left two fingers of his left hand in Acre, lopped by a Saracen sword. Leather worked as soft as cloth, and upturned toes drawn to a blunt point, and a small, fine pattern tooled in the upper surface, like Persian diapering. He looked up, by way of a long, muscular leg in dark brown chausses elegantly fitted, to lean hips circled with a gilded belt that supported two jewelled daggers, a spare, energetic body, a shadowed face dark as bronze. A hand as sunburned as the face had gripped the provost's wrist in mid-air, and now flung away wrist and arm and stave in one violent gesture of prohibition.

"If you have broken his hand—!" blazed Isambard, and bit off the threat with a snap of white teeth.

Harry came to his feet in a startled scramble, and stood staring at the lordly stranger in amazement, nursing his numbed right hand tightly in the left to help the pain to pass. Isambard had the advantage of the light. He saw a young fellow of twenty-four or twenty-five, in a shabby tunic of the common drab brown, soiled after his night in this foul cell, bruised and dusty from last night's fighting, a wiry brown lad with untidy hair and a frayed collar. What was there in that to keep him looking so long? The boy might have been any poor little goliard poet, *gyrovagus* from town to town and patron to patron, or a spoiled clerk on the run after his first essays in minor rascality. Just what the provost thought him, in fact. But for that dedicated face, fierce as a sword, single-minded as a hunting beast, insatiable for one thing he desired, into which, for him, the rest of the world crumbled and was swallowed up. Canon d'Espérance, holding up the wooden angel two nights ago, had said: "You will see for yourself where he got the face." At eleven years old, when his childish countenance could have had but the tender foreshadowing of this intensity, he had prophesied what he would become.

"You may pick up the knife now," said Isambard, and withdrew his foot from it. "Put it away. You need no weapon now, and your head, I think, is finished. If you worked over it farther I believe you might regret it."

"I am afraid," said Harry, sheathing the knife, "that even as it stands I am like to regret it." He looked aside with a wry smile at the provost, who was glaring at his portrait and breathing hard.

"Count yourself fortunate, boy, that your fine is already paid, and you out of my hands," he said grimly. "If I had seen this before I accepted the money you should have paid for it with your skin, and handsomely. If ever you come in my charge again you shall lie in irons, and underground, and we shall see what mischief you can get up to then. My lord, I wish you joy of your bad bargain!"

"I am content with it," said Isambard shortly. He stared for some minutes in silence, twice changing his position to have the light on the carved head move. The one-sided smile came suddenly, dazzlingly. "I swear I think you ungrateful. The young man has made you immortal. Why, there is no malice in it, it is not even ill-natured. And touching the workmanship, find me another man who could have produced such a masterpiece by lantern-light, with a pocket-knife only, and I'll give him as warm a welcome as I do to this one. But if you regret parting with him so cheaply, there's more for you. I won't haggle about his price. And a word in your ear—the stool would fetch a price, too, if you show it in the right quarter. We'll not be niggardly over your bill for his night's lodging."

He turned back to Harry, who was watching him in silent wonder and flexing his numbed fingers.

"Has he damaged you?"

"I think not. There's nothing broken. I shall be clumsy for a few days." His eyes, sea-green in the fronting sunlight from the little window, and startlingly bright, questioned and found no answer. "I expected Master Bertrand would send to buy me out. I do not understand, sir, how you can have involved yourself for me, and I am not happy to think I have cost you so much money. Why are you doing this?"

"Call it a whim. I was with Canon d'Espérance and Master Bertrand when your brother came to tell them of your misfortune, so I returned with him to set you free. He is waiting outside for you, and I have promised Master Bertrand he shall have you both back at work within the hour. Make your farewells!" he said, like one speaking to a child, and the crooked smile flashed.

Harry opened his mouth to question farther, and then shut it again helplessly. He looked at the provost, and then at his surly, vigorous effigy, and broke into the impish but sweet smile that belonged only to his moments of achievement and the lovely lassitude that followed them. "Master provost, part friends! I own I did begin it in spite, but I ended honestly, I swear. If you did owe me somewhat for it, you've paid me." He showed a hand already swollen and darkening, and looked a little reproachful through his smile. "No hard feelings?"

"Be off with you!" said the provost gruffly. "And keep out of my hold from this on, you rogue." But Isambard's admiration of the carving, even more than his handful of coins, had disarmed him; it was with something very close to a smile that he let them out into the narrow courtyard and shut the door on them.

Harry looked up joyfully at the sun and drew deep breaths, suddenly aware of hunger and weariness as of luxuries.

"You have neither eaten nor slept," said Isambard then, sharply practical. "Are you fit to go to work? I would not trust you on a scaffolding myself."

"Oh, I shall do very well. I must go and take my tongue-lashing. When he's done with me I daresay he'll tell me to go and get some sleep. Will you not give me another opportunity of thanking you? And tell me to whom I owe my freedom? I fear I was too much confused even to be civil, you came on me so unexpectedly."

"You have not displeased me," said his rescuer sombrely. "My name is Ralf Isambard of Parfois—we are fellow Salopians, so count me as a biblical neighbour, too, and I'll be content. Here I shall leave you. But if you are at liberty tonight, come to me at eight, for there is a matter I wish to break to you. I am lodged at the Maison d'Estivet."

"I will come," said Harry. "And I thank you."

In the street Adam was waiting with an overcast face; he saw Harry, and the sun came out.

"Crusades!" said Isambard, dangling the gold cup between his long hands and staring down into it with a sour smile. "Never run from what disgusts you to look for a clean cause at the other end of the earth, boy. I took the Cross because I had my bellyful of squabbles and compoundings for earthly kingdoms—when King John made peace with Philip at the cost of Evreux and many another good town, and did homage to him for Brittany, that galled me close. And when he took hands with Llewelyn and secured to him all his conquests— to him who burned Fleace on his way to Mold, and left my garrison dead to the last man—that filled my cup. Now, it seemed, the Welshman was to be my king's liege man, and his son-in-law and bosom friend. So I left England and took the Cross, in the hope and certainty of one fight that might hold the ground firm under my feet. I must have been younger than my forty years, Harry! I'm wiser now. We set out for the Holy Sepulchre, but we got no farther than the Rialto."

Harry looked at him without understanding across the width of the table. "But surely, sir, you did take Constantinople—"

"A figure of speech, boy. Where two Venetians are come together, there is the Rialto, and any stranger rash enough to venture there had better keep one hand on his purse and the other on his sword. Yes, we took Constantinople. A Christian city, head of a Christian empire! Strange quarry for Crusaders, if you consider it! We took it from an able prince, who in his turn had taken it from his incompetent brother, and put the old fool in close ward before he could run his land quite to ruin.''

''Is it true,'' asked Harry, ''that he blinded him?''

''True enough,'' said Isambard indifferently, ''but so have others done, and worse, without having holy wars preached against them by other princes of the same faith, and, God knows, no better record. However! We put the doddering old man back on his flimsy throne, and within the year his ungrateful people had had their fill of him, him and that travelling packman son of his. He teamed well with the Venetians, that young man, but the Greeks wouldn't have him. He cost them a second siege of Constantinople, and a second capture, and there was nothing for us to do after that but set up some emperor of our own there, and hold it down by force. That was how near we came to the holy city! They celebrate the Latin rite again in Santa Sophia, but the Greeks still look to their own prelates in exile. Who has profited but Venice? It was markets, not miracles, they set out to achieve, and they at least succeeded. Their grasp is on every city in Romania.

''And do you know, Harry, what sent me home? Another treaty, just like those that drove me away. Our Latin Emperor, the champion of Christendom in the East, feeling himself insecure—as God knows he has good reason!—has allied himself with the Moslem Sultan of Rum against the Christian Greeks of Nicaea! A small thing to turn my stomach, after swallowing down so much. But it makes a neat end, don't you think so?''

''You make me feel,'' said Harry slowly, ''that I have been fortunate in putting all my pains into wood and stone, and not into the affairs of men. And yet men are all the material we have, if the world is ever to be perfected. And I think you must have found, at home and in the East, something better than disgust. If not among doges and princes, among ordinary men.''

Isambard drained the cup with an abrupt toss of his head, and set it empty on the board. ''You think so? Lend me your eyes to look at the England to which I am returning. What am I going to find there? To what sort of household am I come home?"

Thus challenged, Harry cast his mind back in some astonishment, and was shamed to discover how little he had thought or questioned of England in the nine years since he had left it. "A very troubled and much diminished one," he owned ruefully. "You'll have heard that it lies under papal interdict? The quarrel is over who shall be archbishop of Canterbury—the bishops and the monks were in dispute over it, and King John sided with the bishops and would have had Norwich appointed, but the Pope refused to confirm the election and would give us Cardinal Langton or none. And the King will not admit Langton to his see, and there they stick at odds. But you know the circumstances better than I do. And most of what was English here is gone—Maine, Touraine, Normandy—"

"Gone!" said Isambard with a short, hard laugh. "You talk like what I remember of myself at your age—God knows why I should blame you for that! Nothing is gone, boy. Normandy stands where it stood, and Maine and Touraine. All that has happened is that a truth has been acknowledged for true. They are parts of this mainland of France, always were, and always will be, unless God send a miracle to translate them across the sea. Does that make you gape at me? Your willing exile has been better filled than mine, or it would have had you looking back and reconsidering, too. I have done much hard thinking, there in the East, and I have seen that I was wrong to blame the King for letting Evreux go. He would have been wise had he made what terms he could then, to part equably with all he has parted with perforce since that day. Do you know what has been the undoing of my family and many another like it for the past hundred and fifty years? The attempt to ride two horses. It is time and more than time to reconsider whether we want to be Norman or English, for we cannot go on being both. I do not know why I had to go to Constantinople to discover that I was English."

He rose from his high-backed chair, and began to walk the room restlessly, from tapestried wall to tapestried wall, the tremor of his passing making the candles flicker. Harry's eyes followed him steadily, watching and wondering to what end all this tended. What could such a man want of him, that could not be asked outright, without preamble? Why should he be favoured with the confidences of Ralf Isambard, lord of Mormesnil, Erington, Fleace and Parfois in the marches of Wales, a dozen other properties in the north and the south-west of England, and God alone knew how many in Brittany, Gascony, Maine, Poitou and Anjou?

"I am newly come from Brittany," said Isambard, halting abruptly face to face with him, as though he had been reading his thoughts, "where I have been surrendering one of my two horses. I am English, Harry, but my elder son is French to the backbone. Have I surprised you? You did not know that I have sons? Oh, yes, I have sons! The elder is of about your age. I was married at seventeen and widowed at twenty-five. I cannot call to mind that I ever seriously regretted either event. Now Gilles will be lord of every plot of ground I held in France, and do homage to King Philip for it, very willingly. And I shall go home to England and do homage to King John for what I hold there; and that I will hold with my life. One mount at a time is enough for any man. I have resolved my problem. And John would be well advised to cut the knot of his in the same way, sit him down squarely in England, and set his mind and will to work in making it strong and prosperous, and binding it to himself indissolubly against all comers. But he cannot do it. Even if he saw the need and wished to do it, he dare not. Do you know why? Because his people—not even we who are nearest to him, but those ordinary people of whom you were prating just now—would tear him limb from limb!"

He uttered a sharp croak of laughter, and turned away to the open window, drawing aside the arras to look out upon a dove-coloured sky and a rising moon, and floating against the soft, silvery light the lofty outline of Notre Dame above the roofs, quivering like a candle-flame with the reflected radiance from the Seine. "The wine is with you, Harry."

"I thank you," said Harry, and did not touch it.

Isambard turned his head suddenly, and met the young, brilliant eyes full. They neither evaded him nor softened their intent staring.

"You are wondering," he said, "if I am always so talkative. The truth is that I have a desire to be honest with you, Master Lestrange. Before you commit yourself to answering either aye or no to what I have to put to you, I should like you to know something of me, of your own knowledge and not from other men."

"I know you have been courteous and generous to me," said Harry, "and I think that is enough to know."

"The more fool you, for I can be other things."

"And what do you know of me," went on Harry warmly, "but that you took me out of the provost's jail, and that I have a little skill in carving, a very good conceit of my own work, and a nature incurably stubborn and unruly? I'm sure Master Bertrand can have left you in no doubt on that score."

"Do you really believe that is how he speaks of you? You underrate him. Oh, he is jealous of your ability, that's easy to see, and he reports you as self-willed and stubborn, and a hard and arrogant judge of other men's work. He says also that you are the most gifted pupil he ever taught. It was he, not Canon d'Espérance, who told me that you have a daemon."

He smiled, this time almost gaily, seeing Harry crimson to the ears with astonishment and pleasure.

"Did he truly say that of me?"

"That and much more, both bad and good. But as to your ability in every stage of your craft, good. How long have you been with him?"

"Nearly four years now. I did not think he held me so high," said Harry, dazed. "He never let me see it."

"And before?"

"We were rather more than four years at Caen, serving under Master William at the abbey church of St. Étienne. He is a fine master, difficult to please. He would not endure scamped work, he would have from us only the best we had in us."

"And before that? But you can have been only a child before that."

"For a few months after we came from England we were at Lisieux. I will not claim we learned much there, except quickness and obedience to orders. I was glad to get away to Caen within the year."

"I see you must have brought a sound foundation with you from England. Who was your master there? He must have taken you young."

"Adam's father," said Harry without thinking, and could have bitten out his tongue. In nine years he had never made such a slip before, and now it was far too late to take it back. But Isambard, though he lifted one rapid flash of his shrewd eyes to his guest's face, made no sign of wishing to question the relationship. "He was a village mason, with some practice about the lord's demesne," went on Harry, making the best of it. "I was not his own son, but he fostered me along with his own three."

"So you began with practical labour, and not with the drawing-board. It is the right way round, and I am well content with your record." He reached for the wine-jug, and filled both the cups, and taking up his own, began to pace the room again.

"This is the matter, Harry. I purpose to build a church beside my castle of Parfois. I began this work once before, and got nowhere with it. You know Parfois? It was named from the old Parfois which was my family's first seat in Normandy."

"I know it," said Harry, remembering the vast grey curtain wall that rose out of the rocky outcrop and undulated round the hill like a snake in motion, and the twin gate-towers jutting out over a ditch that was a natural fissure in the rock, forty feet deep. He had seen it only twice in his life, on rides to the north-west of the county with Ebrard to buy ponies, but it was not a sight ever to be forgotten.

"Then you know the hazards. In those days we were raided almost daily, either from Powis or Gwynedd, and though they knew better than to attempt Parfois, the site of the church was outside the walls, and they found it sport to steal materials and terrify my masons. I do not know why I happened upon so many timorous men. One after another my master-masons took fright and deserted me. I expended three, and then I razed what they had done to the ground and went off on my Crusade. But now I mean to return to the project, and see it completed. I have been visiting all the great building enterprises round Paris in search of a master to my mind. I think I have found him."

Harry was on his feet, quivering.

"I offer the work to you. I offer you the virgin site, a free hand, and money enough for all you need. Whatever materials, whatever men, whatever engines you want, you shall have. But on one condition: that you will swear to me to stay until the work is completed, in the teeth of Llewelyn and all his men."

In the hungry young face, suddenly grown pale as ash with desire beneath its weathered tan, the eyes glowed like topaz. It was in a husky whisper that he managed to say: "I accept, and I swear!"

Isambard came down the room to him and stood close, searching his face with unsmiling eyes. "You have no doubts at all. You know you can do it." It was not a question; he was reading, and marvelling at what he read. "How soon can you come to Parfois? I have some business here in France which I had better conclude now, while I have the safe-conduct of the Cross, but in three or four weeks I mean to sail from Calais. I should like to take you with me."

"It will depend on Master Bertrand. I must finish the Calvary on which I am working." He had command of his voice now, it came round and ringing with ardour. "That means perhaps a month's work. Then, if he is pleased to release me, as for your lordship I make no doubt he will, I will gladly come. I would only ask you for one thing, that I may take my brother with me."

"Surely you may! I have said that you shall choose whom you will. If you wish to make other conditions, make them now, before you bind yourself."

"Then I dare to ask that you will undertake not to displace me but on one ground—that the work I have done for you is not good enough."

"And on that ground," said Isambard, dazzled by the passion and certainty with which he said this, and the towering pride that blazed at him from the sea-green eyes, "you have no fears."

"No, none! In Chartres, in Caen, in Bourges, I have seen the splendour and energy of other men's creations, and ached for my own. Everything I have learned while I laboured to fulfil other men's designs has been food to what I have in me. I have carried it a long time, and thought of it much, and longed for it to come into the light. If I give it to you, you will not be disappointed."

"With all my heart," said Isambard, "I believe you."

"My lord, there is a certain quarry where I can get the very stone I want and have always wanted." His voice gathered way, rushing joyfully after an entrancing memory. "A warm grey stone in colour, with a pale amber grain in it that flushes to gold in the sunlight. The only difficulty is that the quarry is very close to the Welsh border."

"No matter, you shall have an ample guard and a lease on the quarry for the duration of the work."

"If you should be sending couriers to England before we leave, I should like to send a list of the materials we shall want immediately. It will save time on arrival. Stakes and cords for laying out foundations, leather thongs and wood for scaffolding, hurdles, timber for centring, lead, glass—and carriage for all these. It means the gain of a whole year if we make full use of this summer to assemble them, for we can spend the winter under cover, cutting stone, once we have it on the site. Can you guarantee me carts and teams enough?"

"All you may ask for you shall have. My steward will put forward all the orders you care to send in advance of your coming."

"What manner of foundation shall I find?"

"Rock, and levelled already by those who went before you, though you may, of course, need to level more ground than they did, depending on your design."

"Good, we'll lay the footings of the stonework well into the solid rock. There could be no better foundation, and it means we shall get little or no settling."

"I see you are not afraid of Welsh raids," said Isambard with a smile, "for on that head you have said not a word."

"Oh, I was born in that border country; Welsh raids were the common stuff of our lives there. I would not turn my back on such a commission as you have offered me, not for all King Philip's army, leave alone a handful of wild Welshmen. I pledge you the best work I have in me," he said, suddenly raising his cup with a wild smile, "and my word that I will not leave you until the church be completed. And to that I drink!"

"And I will never deprive you of that I have entrusted to you, until it be finished. That I swear."

Harry had the cup at his lips and Isambard was raising his, when suddenly the ringed hand flashed in a violent gesture.

"Wait!" he said harshly. "This is too easily and too lightly taken up for my taste."

He put down his cup upon the table, and swept away in long, irritable strides to the window, where he stood gripping the arras hard in his long muscular fingers. Without turning his head he said more gently, but with a heavy solemnity: "Harry Lestrange, you should go home and sleep on this. I have taken you in the sails of your longing and blown you away, and God knows that is not as I would have it. I want you, but I want you fairly. It was ill done to spring it on you today, with your foolish gratitude fresh in you and your eyes dropping with sleep. If you give your word to me, you are giving it to a hard master, one who will have no mercy if you break faith. I promise you the full support of my hand while you play me fair, and I promise you the full weight of my fist if you play me false, be it never so venial a default. Such as I am I am, I cannot be other, and if you enter my service you must abide by me as I am. Do not swear tonight! Go home and consider well, and come to me tomorrow."

"No, my lord!" said Harry loudly and joyfully. "I know my mind now. If you were the devil himself I would abide by you for such a prize as this. I pledge you now!"

Isambard had turned from the window, and was staring at him with the faint shadow of astonished displeasure in his drawn brows, for he was not accustomed to hearing the word "no" flung at him so roundly. But the eyes in their deep caverns remained aloof and sombre, as Harry tipped back his head and emptied the cup and set it ringing down upon the board. "I am your man. I swear, on this living heart, that I will remain with you and seek no other service until your church is finished. And if I play you false, you may have this same heart living out of my body."

There was a long moment of silence, then Isambard walked slowly to the table and drained his own goblet and set it gently beside its fellow. "So be it!" he said.

Chapter Eight

*T*he splendours and audacities of Madonna Benedetta Foscari came to Isambard's ears in the common gossip of Paris, and quickened an amused curiosity even in one not greatly given to pursuing fashions.

"I hear she was brought back as booty from the Crusade," he said to Adam one day, as they were rising all three from a long conference over the letters and requisitions to be sent in advance to England. "It pleases me to think that Venice lost something, in the end—a loss to balance all she gained, if report does not lie about the lady. It seems old Guiscard had an eye for more than markets, in those business deals of his in the Adriatic. Is she as wonderful as rumour makes her?"

"Even more wonderful," said Adam, smiling without even a shadow of regret at the memory of his one night in her favour. More than that he had not looked for, and yet he had gained something more, for she still tolerated him about her sometimes in the evenings, for the pleasure of singing with him.

"And you, Harry—are you, too, among her admirers?"

"My lord," said Harry, frowning absently over his lists of materials, "I never saw more of her than a hand and arm. They looked much like any other to me."

"Never saw her, after all you paid for the privilege? This must be remedied! Adam, bring us to meet this nonpareil."

The order was issued idly, perhaps even in jest; but as Adam said afterwards, at home in the garret in the Ruelle des Guenilles, even the jests of a man like Isambard had best be acted upon.

"You might be wise, at that," agreed Apollon, "to humour him. I know him by repute; he has a fief not far from my home. They say he's a man to be feared, very ill to cross, and merciless to his underlings."

"Speak as you find," said Adam, undisturbed. "He's dealt fair enough by us so far, and very surely he knew how to pick a mason for himself." Harry was not present, and so could be freely praised. "Well, we are bound to him, whether it turns out well or no, and if he wants amusement during these weeks while he waits for us, I'll be a serviceable fellow and provide him at least the opportunity."

"I take it very hard," said Élie, looking up reproachfully from his books, "that you'll do for him what you haven't yet offered to do for me, and we bosom friends so near parting."

"My lad, you're never likely to have either the paying of my wages or the flaying of my skin, or I'd oblige you. The way will be clear for you when my lord and I are both out of Paris. And you'll be grown a little, too," said Adam kindly, patting Élie unwisely on the auburn curls dragged every way by nervous fingers as he studied. Élie promptly slammed away his book and closed with his friend happily, swooping to take him about the knees in one arm as he passed, and drop him neatly to the floor. Apollon, without taking his eyes from the lute-string he was carefully fitting, stepped out of their way and let them roll together the length of the room.

Soon, he reflected sadly, he had better be looking round for two congenial spirits to fill the beds of Harry and Adam when they were gone; but they would not be easily replaced.

When next they presented themselves at the Maison d'Estivet Adam bore an invitation with him.

"My lord, Madonna Benedetta Foscari sends her compliments, and begs that you will come and drink wine with her at her house tomorrow evening at eight. She had the whole story out of me," said Adam, grinning, "and she asks that you will bring 'your lively sculptor' to present himself. So she called him. Indeed, I think she missed very little of what passed that night."

Isambard laughed, so carelessly that Harry was persuaded he had never seriously considered that his expressed desire might be taken literally. Nevertheless, his business in France was already completed, and his mind, restless for home, plagued by waiting and idleness. The woman who had diverted the whole of Paris might provide even for him an evening's diversion. "The lady is gracious," he said. "We shall be happy to attend her."

"Why the devil did you have to involve me?" demanded Harry ungratefully, when he was alone with Adam. "I have a drawing for my east window half finished, and now nothing will do for him but I must go along with him and waste an evening."

It was in this temper that they waited upon her, one idly curious, one openly displeased at being kept from his work, which for him was more enchanting than any woman who ever breathed. On Adam's confident heels they stepped into her presence, in that upper room from which she had dropped the violets of her brief but gracious favour. The rich profits of Master Guiscard's Venetian tradings had draped the walls of the apartment with oriental carpets, and covered the floor with rugs of worked skins. The chairs were cushioned, the drapings of the table damask, the winecups of thin and glittering glass. And the woman who rose from her seat in the window and came sweeping across the room to receive them had the assurance of an abbess.

"My lord of Parfois, you are welcome to my poor house."

"Madam, this is kindness in you, for my claim to your notice is small indeed, and my need of your grace is great. I am soon to rob you of this minstrel of yours."

"So he has told me," she said, and gave him her hand.

What had he expected, that his eyes searched her face with so urgent and single an interest? The noblest and most expensive of courtesans must always have been accessible to that bottomless purse of his, but he had chosen rather to buy beautifully-tempered swords, exotic animals, fine carvings, barbaric jewellery, holy relics and fragments of the saints, to judge by the great mass of baggage he

had brought from the East with him. Moreover, he had come here
at her invitation only out of curiosity, and no very profound curiosity at that. Yet his eyes hung heavy upon her now, and his face had
the gravity and passion it wore when he looked upon works of art,
judging hardly, fastidious in criticism, rejecting what was not
unique. Her he did not reject.

"And you," said Benedetta, "are he who wished to improve upon
'*Dum estas inchoatur.*' " Her voice, which Harry had expected to
be rich and sensuous and full of art, was clear and direct as a child's,
and so unselfconscious that it seemed startlingly loud in the quiet
room. It was pitched low, but its ring was of silver, not of gold.
"You ended vilely sharp," she said.

"I know it," he admitted, somewhat taken aback, and uncertain
whether to be a little offended or to laugh at himself. "I was straining
against the odds. And no doubt you noticed that I am no Adam."

"No," she said, "I see you are no Adam."

"Howbeit, you laughed."

What was the power she had to draw to herself even the unwilling
mind that would gladly have kept its reserve in her presence and
gone on considering in happy silence the exact line of an arch instead
of the subtle shape of a face? It seemed that everything about her
was as challenging in its unexpectedness as the candid, unflattering
voice, that made no play with compliments. She should have been
soft and sumptuous. Was it childish to expect a courtesan to be so?
He saw her aloof and erect, impregnable within herself like a man,
open to approach like a man. He had expected to have nothing to do
here but to admire a body which could hardly fail to be beautiful;
and here he found himself withdrawing his attention only with a
kind of agony from the enigma of her mind and spirit, to look at
the famous and resplendent flesh in which she walked.

She was just of a height with him, which was barely medium tall
for a man, but more than common tall for a woman. Their eyes met
on a level, close and searching, mutually intent. She was built like
a tower, broad and noble, and moved with a vigorous grace that
composed itself pliantly to the confined space within these walls,
and yet suggested what breadth and largeness might be hers in
freedom. For the dark red hair Adam had prepared him, and it fell
nothing short of his description, with its crimson shadows and fiery

highlights. But no one had told him how brilliantly white would be the broad brow beneath the coronal, and the throat on which the coiled hair cast reflected colour until it glowed like a clear glass goblet of wine. No one had warned him that her eyes would be set so wide apart, under such a bold line of brows; nor that their shape would be so full and clear, and their colour such a pure grey, with something of violet in it in the shadows. The chin was too generously rounded for beauty, perhaps, the mouth too full, though wonderfully set into that antique shape of rich, resolute curves. The body and face were all woman, yet Harry might have been standing eye to eye with a man, his opposite and his equal. He felt his heart and his mind rise to her; his blood and his body were at peace.

"And your song," she said, turning with a decisive movement to lead the way towards the chairs grouped to receive them, "for Adam tells me it was yours—it has opened other doors than mine, no doubt?"

"Not to my knowledge. When I gave it to Adam I renounced my rights in it."

"And I've sung it but twice," said Adam, "and both times to you. I am not likely to offer it to anyone else." He was at home in this house, as a cousin or a retainer might have been at home, and accepted his status with good humour. He made himself cupbearer for them when they were seated, curiously watching Isambard's face. It pleased him that beauty which had dazzled him should also blind others.

"I have not yet heard this song," said Isambard, his eyes upon her face, and the faint, oblique smile plucking at the corner of his mouth. "He makes none for me."

"He made none for me," she said calmly. "This was made for his brother, and its passion is in the mind only. All the same, a good song. Adam will surely let us hear it again. Take my citole, or the lute if you prefer it."

"He is no hand at it," said Harry, reaching out a hand for the instrument. "Here, let me!"

He bent lovingly to the tuning of the citole, pushing back his chair from the table; and finding its stall-like arms hampered his movements, he got up and crossed to a stool beside the window. The air came back to him tenderly and plaintively, whispering under his fingers. Isambard's imperious profile, sharp against the candle-light and glitter of glass on the table, had a stillness beyond natural, as though he held his breath, as though he had become stone, like the marble mask he had brought back from Greece, a fragment of some broken, beautiful god.

Adam sang as freshly as a lark, without a trace of that poignancy of love-longing the melody suggested. She is right, thought Harry. The passion is in the mind only. All the same, it was a lovely sound.

> "—Yet when the branch is shaken
> And summer's pride is past,
> Me, naked and forsaken,
> Receive and love at last.
>
> And when the autumn dapples
> Thy gilded heaven tree,
> Let fall thy golden apples,
> Bow down thy breasts to me."

Suddenly he felt their summer warmth cupped in his palms, and the closing chords broke false under his hands. Heat swept upwards through his body and stained his face. Not her breasts; he could look at her unmoved, or if not unmoved, untroubled. He did not desire her. Her presence enlarged him, her beauty delighted him, he was at peace with her as with a man who was his match. But she brought with her glimpses of other women, some seen but once, some never yet seen, some known and forsaken and forgotten before he knew what he did. What she was, what she could be to so many men, some woman would be to him. She was the hope of that fulfilment, the promise, almost the certainty; and she was the fore-shadowing of his monstrous loss if he should let the tide of the spring escape him.

He stretched his fingers tremulously along the shoulders of the citole, and the polished wood was cool and smooth to his hot palms. Why was he suddenly possessed by this agonising awareness of his senses, as though desire itself were something to be desired?

"You have a fine touch," said Isambard, "and a nice turn with verses. I see I have found myself a phoenix."

"I'm out of practice," said Harry. "That was not well done. But it's a beautiful air. Since I spoiled '*Dum estas inchoatur*' for you, will you hear it now? Without the improvements?"

Adam sang it, untouched by the disquiet in the room. How pleasant and good a thing it must be to be Adam, and live on such close terms with the present that neither past nor future truly existed!

"The same metre," said Benedetta. "But the Sieur de Breauté was never a very original wooer. And he borrowed not only the song but the rendering, too, and made no acknowledgements to the singers."

"Having paid for the performance," said Isambard, "he felt free to call it his."

"Like Paulus with his poems," she said, and then, seeing his hollow eyes burn up into astonished laughter: "It surprises you that I should be able to follow you into Martial? Why? Because I am a woman? Or because I am the kind of woman I am? I'm right it was of that couplet you were thinking?

> '*Carmina Paulus emit, recitat sua carmina Paulus.*
> *Nam quod emas possis iure vocare tuum.*'

How should we translate it into this English of yours?

> 'Paulus buys verse to read in his own name.
> Why not? What's bought the purchaser may claim.' "

"Martial is a dry study for a woman," said Isambard, "and we are not as generous in having our daughters tutored as we might be. It should not displease you that you show as the exception."

"I was sister to two gifted brothers, and I read with them. It was not so much planned, it happened. I was curious, and I drew in on them before they were aware. Would you rather I sang you something from Catullus—our own Catullus, the stranger from the north? There's a poet for women! I was at his Sirmio once; the olives and the lake and the long arm of land are just as he left them."

She had risen and taken the lute, and carried it with her to the cushioned seat which was built into the window. Her long fingers were rapid and impetuous on the strings, able but inattentive. Harry

heard in their cascading notes here and there a chord that jarred, as
though she had withdrawn her mind from what she did, and left her
hands to fend for themselves.

> " 'Ille mi par esse deo videtur,
>   Ille, si fas est, superare divos,
>   Qui sedens adversus identidem te
>   Spectat et audit
>   Dulce ridentem—'

—though to be sure he took that from Sappho, metre and all. Or
do you know the 'Pervigilium Veneris' written for the night festival
of the goddess at Hybla, in Sicily? It's a beautiful thing, in its
way.

> 'Cras amet qui nunquam amavit, quique
>   amavit cras amet!
>   Illa cantat, nos tacemus. Quando ver
>   venit meum?
>   Quando fiam ceu chelidon ut tacere desinam?—'

" 'She sings, we are mute. When comes my spring? When shall
I become as a swallow, and no longer be silent?' A curious version,
that makes Procne the swallow the sweet singer, and Philomela the
voiceless one. Many critics have speculated on his meaning, but for
my part I think he was human and made a mistake.

> 'Who loves, love on! Who loves not,
>   learn to love!
>   Yesterday's drought tomorrow shall remove.' "

She swept her fingers violently across the strings, and instantly
muted them with her palm.

"I am convinced," said Isambard, smiling at her darkly over his
wine; "no need to dazzle me farther. You are as learned as you are
beautiful. And indeed, if you go any deeper into the classics you
must leave me behind. Tell me rather about yourself, and I'll forgo

Venus. Gladly I'll be a celebrant," he said softly, "at the Pervigilium Benedettae."

Harry sat mute, nursing the citole and longing to be away. What need had they of him or of Adam, to help them to duel with love and Latin across a room, like a couple of arid schoolmen trying to out-pun each other? And yet it could not be true that she was parading her accomplishments seriously; there was that in her voice and manner that mocked her own flourishes as she made them. She seemed to him more like a woman reading over the letters of an old, half-baked girl's love from her past, with satire and tenderness in her voice, before she tore them up and burned them without one look of regret. A little ceremonial pyre to end a phase, a folly, a wasted time. A burning of the weeds from a fallow field which is about to be sown and bear fruit.

They were talking now with quick intelligence of Venice and the East, of the Crusade and its consequences, of courts and markets and the vexed affairs of kings. She left the lute lying in the cushions and came back to the table to pour more wine, but Adam was before her with the crystal jug and the dishes of sweetmeats. Harry let his mind withdraw from them into his own world, where at this moment he should have been busy with his pens and his instruments, adding to the roll of drawings already made.

He knew exactly what he wanted, he had been working over it in his mind for some seven years now, and only in detail would the actual site at Parfois alter his conception. He had yet to see how much ground he had to use, but neither beauty nor splendour have need of great size. What he wanted was light, light and space, and the upward surge of stone like a growing tree from foundations to vault. No oppression, no darkness, no burden of thick, groaning columns and lowering roofs like the stony weight of guilt. He saw the shape clearly. No chevet of chapels, but a square east end, so that he could have a whole wall of invading light pouring in upon the high altar. Short, strong transepts, lofty aisles, and the clerestory tall and fully glazed above a shallow triforium. The west front with a great, deeply-cut doorway and a vast window above, set back in course on course of moulding, where the light could harp all day long on strings of stone, making even that greyer northern air shine lucid and sharp as the dazzling south. Over the west front two minor turrets, tapering to slender fingers of stone. Over the crossing the great tower, as in Normandy, binding all together, rooting all impregnably into the earth, drawing all erect with it towards heaven. In that tension was the significance of life, and next to light, this he wanted above all, the duality of flesh and spirit, manhood and godhead, the tension of man on his way to God. A noble tower, tall and tapered, its long surfaces so subtly fluted and moulded that light and shadow might stroke it into a hundred changing shapes of majesty and beauty as the hours of the daylight passed. Permanence and change, diversity and oneness, in that grey-gold stone that glowed in his memory like—what was Adam's phrase?—a mine of sunshine. There is no growth nor fruitfulness but rises from these paired opposites of darkness and light, earth and heaven. My feet as roots in the earth, my forehead straining into the sun. The tower at once anchoring my church fast to the rock, and translating it into a balanced arrow of light aimed at the sky.

And within, the three-aisled nave; not with austere, unbroken lines from floor to vault, and certainly not with these debased Corinthian capitals that leave me so unsatisfied. Trivial as ornament, and purposeless as halting-places for the eye on its way upwards—no, not those. Capitals that live as flowers live, animals, men, all that comes from the soil and springs towards the sun. They shall shoot strongly from the columns and leap upwards, thrusting the abacus as high as they can reach, straining to sustain the vault like trees growing. Not a single line, but a single unbroken impetus, one surge of energy and faith drawn taut as a bow-string, but as secure as the arch of the rainbow.

There is no beauty where there is doubt or insecurity. A sense of unbalance is the death of art.

That hair of hers, caught up by the wind, could well hold up an arch on its great tresses. Like the leaping flames it so much resembles. Or the breaking wave. Everything that reaches up, everything that stretches and exults, an arm and hand thrusting against the abacus, a squirrel's arched tail, a leaping child, an uncurling frond of fern, a climbing vine, all manner of leaves that lean upwards to the light. And my lord's towering pride, that all-but-visible presence that rears over him like the black shadow he casts above him now, as he leans over the candles.

All his household at the Maison d'Estivet are afraid of him, even his five squires, three of them from blood the equal of his own, go in dread of him. Why? I see nothing so terrifying in him.

Together with all these ascending creatures, angels descending, like my first angel, hair and garments torn upwards in the streaming air of their flight. He could serve for either a demon aspiring or an angel falling. Or for both, perhaps. His head is very beautiful.

The woman made a movement of hand and arm that drew his eyes back to her. What was it in her that dragged so deeply at the chords of his memory, plucking out echoes he had long forgotten? All her motions had a quality of reminiscent beauty about them, as though she comprehended within herself all the women he had ever seen or known. The richness and kindness of her flesh brought his mother back to him. And her voice he had heard before, somewhere long ago and far away from here, clear, candid, direct as her eyes. Across those eyes of hers, temple to temple, her face was as wide as its length from brow to chin. What are the true proportions of beauty? Where, in any case, does beauty reside—in what is seen, or in that which is called to mind by what is seen? And can both be put into stone together?

I must make a drawing of her before we leave, he thought, if she will let me. I wish I knew where I had heard her voice. I wish I knew what is so moving about it, what quality it is that makes it seem remembered rather than heard, as though when she speaks I am listening to someone else, saying to me words she has never said.

"Harry!" said Adam, jogging his elbow good-humouredly. "Have you fallen asleep? Madonna Benedetta is speaking to you."

He started out of his dream and looked up quickly, full into the grey eyes, so wide and limpid that it seemed to him he saw his own image there. It was in that moment, when she had spoken to him and he had not even heard, that he recognised the quality her voice had for him, and knew it for a daunting honesty like that of a child, a fearless and merciless innocence. So had a child spoken with him once. How long a time it was, how long a time, since he had thought of Gilleis!

He opened his mouth to make excuses for his absence of mind, and on the edge of speech was held silent by the apparition of

Isambard's face. While the woman was not regarding him, his eyes glowed upon her from their hollows of shade; through the golden mask of his face the naked blaze of his desire shone molten for an instant, then the heavy eyelids closed upon the fire, and the bronze head was darkened.

The fever of departure had lain long over the Ruelle des Guenilles and the Maison d'Estivet, but into the busy, dusty, populous lodges at Notre Dame it penetrated late, and brought to light a curious accumulation of forgotten belongings. Last of all, neglected in a corner of a chest where it must have lain for over a year, Harry found the frayed cloth scrip in which he had brought his small baggage from England, nine years ago. He picked it out and shook the dust from it, suddenly moved to look back and remember with affection and curiosity the boy who had carried it. From its deepest corner his fingers unearthed what felt like a coin, but when he drew it out he knew it for a small, tarnished medallion, the Virgin and Child on its face worn almost smooth. It was still threaded upon the gold cord by which Gilleis had hung it round his neck in the boat, before he climbed up into the *Rose of Northfleet*. He had not paid sufficient attention to it then to realise what it was, but he knew it now for one of the gilt threads she used to plait into her short black braids of hair.

He stood holding it in his hand, suddenly shaken by such a convulsion of homesickness that tears came into his eyes. How old would she be now? Nineteen! A woman! Did she still travel to the midlands with her father to buy cloth? Hardly likely, he thought; she would be mistress of the household in London now, and have other cares on her hands. She might even be married and ruling another man's house. He tried to see her a woman grown, and could not, his memory brought back so persistently the small, charming child with her great eyes and her flower of a mouth and her stiff little black braids, thick as her wrists. She had cried because he was always too busy to play with her. He remembered holding her awkwardly on his lap, on the stone ledge against the guest-house wall, labouring to comfort her and half-tempted to shake her. He might have made a little time for her, he thought remorsefully, after all she had done for him and for Adam.

And he had not even recognised and appreciated the gold thread from her hair!

He was still clasping the medal in his hand when one of the apprentices came looking for him. "Master Henry, there's one here asking after you."

"After me? What does he want?"

"Not he, but she," said the boy, studiously keeping from his lips the knowing grin that was bright in his eyes. "I thought best not to ask her business—I trust I did right?"

"It's a sound principle," said Harry, making a perfunctory feint at the youngster's ears for his impudence, which the boy as dutifully ducked. "Is she handsome?"

Raised brows and rolling eyes informed him wordlessly that she was; nonetheless, he expected no one more disturbing than the canon's housekeeper, or Master Bertrand's maid-servant, and felt a shock of incredulity when he emerged from the lodge to see Madonna Benedetta moving alone between the stacked stones, splendidly incongruous and utterly composed, with the skirt of her long bliaut over her arm. She saw him and came towards him, and her walk was as direct as her voice.

"Madam, you wish to speak to me? I am at your service."

"I should not be interrupting your work," she said, in that clear voice that came to him now with so significant an echo, "and I must not do so for long. But my opportunities for talking with you will soon be gone, for I hear from my lord Isambard that in two weeks more you will be leaving Paris with him. Is it so?"

"Yes, we are almost ready. Master Bertrand had been good enough to release Adam and me, and the sooner we are in England the better, for I cannot make final plans until I see the site. I am sorry that I cannot offer you here either refreshment or privacy—"

"I need neither," she said simply. "If you will show me your Calvary, I should like that. I have never yet seen anything of yours."

"Willingly! You know it's finished?" He led her to the lodge, and brought her in under the lean-to roof to a solitude and a silence. "My lord has kept you informed? He has—visited you several times, I think."

"He has," she said, something of amusement in her voice, and a certain dryness, too. There was a silence. She had not yet looked at the grouped stone figures. "You," she said, "have not."

He did not know what he ought to reply to that, and for a moment kept a lame silence, at a loss to guess what she wanted here with him, "Was I—expected?" he asked hesitantly at last.

"Expected? No, not that. You owed me nothing. Hoped for, perhaps." She turned from him and walked slowly about the stone group, examining with steady, intelligent eyes the dead Christ, a dragging weight upon the pierced hands, with the Virgin and Saint John on one side, the holy women on the other, motionless figures of grief, terribly self-contained, each one of them a well-shaft of loneliness sealed up from all consolation. They touched each other, but remained irrevocably separate. "So since you did not come to me," she said, still thoughtfully gazing, "I have come to you. Not expressly to see this, but I am glad that I have seen it, all the same. How did you come to understand so much about suffering? Is it something in your experience, or a motion of the will and the imagination? Most Christs have made but a symbolic gesture of dying. Yours has been dragged through the whole process of a cruel execution."

"Have I over-stated?" he asked with real anxiety.

"No, that is how it must have been. I am sure He was spared nothing. And you have let Him keep the wholeness of His spirit. Everything is there to be read, but He does not assault us with it. We are left to choose whether we see or pass by. It was terrible, but He has sustained it. There is no room for pity."

"You are comforting me," he said. "I do not know if you intended that. But it is not true that I understand suffering. Here I have been trying to explain it to myself, how a man could pass through that agony, and still come out of it a man. Dead, perhaps, but not violated."

"That is what He has done," she said.

"If that is true, then so far at least I have succeeded. But I suffered only in the imagination, and still I do not know whether I could undergo the ordeal in the flesh, and remain unbroken. Imagination is not enough. Perhaps those who have never tried to imagine it come best out of the testing of pain."

"It is natural to be afraid of one's own human weakness," said

Benedetta, "but not good to dwell too much upon the question until it arises. If you cannot imagine pain fully, neither can you fully imagine the resources you have in you to meet it and overcome it. Do you suppose you could have put into this figure anything you yourself lacked?"

Harry smiled. "That is a very large artistic question, and I am not prepared to argue it."

She stood considering the group still for several minutes. From the runways of hurdles above their heads the voices of the masons came to them distantly.

"They won't like it," said Benedetta, shaking her head. "They are not invited to take part in it, and that won't please them. To be challenged to think about it is the last thing they want." She turned from it with decision, and stood facing him squarely. "Harry!"

She used his name with a familiarity and authority that came, he supposed, of listening long to Isambard, who had made free with it from the first. "Harry, you must know that I have lived a certain kind of life, spending myself and what was mine as I saw fit, taking a price when I chose, and giving when it pleased me to give. I am not ashamed of it, and I make no defence of what needs none. I see nothing dishonourable in disposing as one will of what is one's own. And hitherto I have owned myself wholly. But it becomes dishonourable to squander the same wealth when it ceases to be one's own. Harry, since that evening when you came to me with your lord my door has been closed at night, and my bed solitary. I will not give to any man but one what is no longer mine to give, but his."

She had drawn a little nearer to him, and stood searching his troubled face candidly and proudly. He did not understand. He thought she must be speaking of Isambard, and wondered what need she could have of such a confidant as himself, if that were so.

"Madam, whatever you may ask of me—" he began haltingly.

"I am asking you for nothing. I am offering you something— myself, myself entire, to be yours without reserve, yours once for all. If you are pleased to take me, I will be faithful to you as long as I live, and never know another man, as I shall never love another. If not, tell me so plainly, as I deserve of you, and I will never trouble you with my love again."

Harry stood stunned and speechless, staring at her open-mouthed. He could think of nothing but that she must be mocking him, and it filled him with a sense of outrage that she should do it in that piercing, spontaneous, child's voice of hers, so wildly sweet in his ears. Closed fast in his left hand, the worn silver medal bit with sharp edges into his palm.

"I cannot believe in this," he burst out, shaking his head in quick and helpless anger. "You have seen me but once, you know nothing of me."

"I know all that I need to know, and more than you think. My life turned from its course when you entered my house. Even before I saw you, your voice had fallen athwart my peace. Adam is Adam," she said, laughter looking out of her eyes for a moment, "and what woman could have the heart to wound him? But it was for you I opened the door."

She could have reached out her hand and touched him, but she would not. It was for him to take her or refrain.

"I know my own mind," she said. "I know there is no returning for me. From the moment that you came into sight my heart fixed on you, and I have been mistress of my heart too long to question or distrust it now. Do you think I am a woman given to self-deceit? Or without experience? I did not choose to love you. Who but a fool ever chooses to love? But truth is truth, and I acknowledge it. This is something not even you can change. Even if you reject me, you cannot deny me the right to love you. Love you I shall, as long as I have breath, whether you will or no, whether I will or no. I know the absolute when I see it, and I am a practical woman, one who wastes no time in fighting God."

She saw the play of doubt and unhappiness in his shadowed face, and even the flicker of a boy's wariness, and her mouth softened in a smile at once tender and ironic.

"Do not be afraid that I am come to plead. I came to give you what is yours, but if you do not want it I can take it away again. You owe me nothing. Unless, perhaps, I might lay claim to the grace of your trust, and ask truth of you as I have told you truth. Look at me, and say what you have to say, and see if I fail of what I have pledged you."

Harry raised his head, and met her glance full. He had indeed considered the kind of evasions any man might have used to extricate himself from so strange a situation, half-protestations of respect and admiration designed to send her away appeased without making her any promises, until such time as he could remove himself thankfully into England. But he put them from him again, for she was worth something better than that. Encountering the proud and fearless eyes, he felt again, and strongly, that first delight of finding himself in her presence and recognising his match. No word or act of his should deface that balance. Truth he owed to himself and to her, and truth she should have.

He said: "I do not love you. God knows I should be a happy man if it had happened so to me, but it did not. From my heart I thank you for the magnificence of the gift you have offered me, but I cannot take it. I will not pretend a passion I do not feel. I neither love nor desire you."

She did not lower her eyes, her face did not change. She stood for a moment in silence, containing the wound, her hands quiet under her breast, and watched his eyes clear and soften from their cloudy frown. In the act of denying himself to her he had given her a fragment at least of his heart; he felt it pass from him, and was eased and glad that all the generosity should not be on her side.

"I was not mistaken in you," she said, after a long moment, in a voice very soft and strangely content. "At least, after so long of being free, I set my mark high. Now be generous in your honesty yet again, and tell me truly whether you are utterly indifferent to me. And if it is so, you are rid of me for ever."

He lifted his head sharply, his eyes flashing as the light caught their startling greenness. A few words only, he thought, hard to say and harder to hear, but we should both be free. She would be rid of me for ever, as I of her, for she has a mind and a heart that cannot go cold through a long life, and in the nature of man there must come a day when she will forget me. I have only to strike her now, and we are both delivered. But when he opened his lips the words would not come. He could not do it. The one lie was as contemptible as the other. Between himself and Benedetta lies were unworthy and unthinkable.

"Only a clod could be indifferent to you," he said deliberately. "I delight in your beauty, your mind I honour, your gallantry I revere. Madonna Benedetta, I like you well and more than well. I'll neither feign what I do not feel, nor deny what I do. If God had pleased to have me love you, I would have accounted myself the happiest of men, and in having your faith and trust I still reckon myself blessed."

Then she did put her hand upon him for an instant, only the touch of her fingers against his breast in an indescribably eloquent gesture of gratitude and acceptance. "With that I am a rich woman," she said. "I shall never speak to you of love again, unless you so will it. Yet this which is yours I swear is yours for ever, and if the day should ever come when you want it, you have only to call to me and I shall come to you—you have only to reach out your hand and I will render you all that is yours. Now I am going. No, let me leave you here and go alone. And do not fear that you have hurt or harmed me or done me any wrong. You are as I would have you, and I delight in loving you."

With that she caught up the skirt of her bliaut again, and flung it over her arm with one of those gloriously large gestures of hers, and would have passed by him with a raised head and a smiling mouth, but he put out his hand to her, and she swung back to lay her own in it for an instant.

"Sweet friend!" she said, and drew her fingers away again before he could kiss them, and so went forth and left him gazing after her.

Now he could never escape her, nor she him. Not even the dear talisman gripped so fiercely in his hand could set them free. Nor could he ever want for her, or take away that morsel of his heart from her.

"The summer can be beautiful at Parfois," said Isambard, caressing the dog's head with his ringed hand and looking down with a faint, remembering smile into the crystal cup of wine. "In spite of our border rains, it can be beautiful. That is good riding country, and full of game. I have taken wolf and boar there sometimes, but they're getting rare these days, even in the marches."

"You are looking forward already to being home," said Benedetta, "I hear it in your voice. I believe you love your England."

"After years of deluding myself that I had many homes, I have at least discovered where my home is. But late," he said, with a melancholy smile, "since it is now a home without a family. Gilles remains here in France, as he always preferred to do, and now he will have the sole care of those honours which used to be mine, and no leisure for visiting me—even if King Philip's policies were not making it hard to pass freely between France and England. And the younger boy, William, is in FitzPeter's service, the Earl of Essex, and comes home only on occasions to refill his pockets. Why not? What's mine in England will be his some day. William is his mother's son, he never liked Parfois, it was too remote for him. The king's court pleased him more than mine. It may be that I shall find nothing but disappointment even there."

"You want too much," she said. "Men, and countries, and causes fail you because you expect too much of them."

"It may be true," he owned indifferently. "I am what I am. Whether it is my fellows who have fallen off from me, or I who have cast them off, I begin to find myself appallingly alone. And sometimes I have a great longing in me for someone who will not fall away."

She turned her head and looked at him across the room. In the great high-backed chair he sat leaning upon one arm, his chin cupped in his palm, the candle-light tremulous upon the tawny golden planes of his temples and cheek-bones and the fine, spare line of his jaw. A man of contrasts, all brilliance and blackness. Out of the caverns of shade the beautiful eyes, reddish brown like dark gilliflowers, burned steadily upon her face. He had a necklet of uncut, polished stones set in gold about his neck. Like his lord and friend King John, he had a liking for jewels and cared fastidiously for his person; and like so many of his fellow Crusaders he had picked up some of the refinements of his Moslem enemies. But luxury could never soften so much restless energy; even his indulgences he used as whetstones for his mind, and his occasional dissipations were only a means of exercising and testing his body when no more violent occupations offered. She could well understand that he wore out his companions as he wore out shoes, and grew angry at finding them inadequate. And his women, too, perhaps, though she doubted if he had turned readily to women. His wife, a bride of policy nine years older than himself, had died early and left him free, young, wealthier than ever, and almost certainly ungrieving, too well-endowed to

want for loves if he needed them, but too youthful, complex and
energetic to devote to them overmuch of his time and vigour.

"Come with me to England," said Isambard.

She was silent so long that he grew impatient, and sat up restlessly, pushing the hound's head from his knee and gripping the
carved arms of the chair with both muscular hands. He had a way
of turning any chair in which he sat into a throne.

"Why don't you answer? I cannot have surprised you. You must
know that I want you, that I have wanted you from the first moment
I saw you. It is not my way to make many words where I know I
am understood in few. Come with me to Parfois, and you shall be
nobly used and honourably attended. All that is mine I will share
with you, and hold you in love and worship. Give me an answer!"

"I am wondering," she said mildly, "if you have really considered
what you are proposing. Now, when you confess to a taste for
permanence, am I the right person to invite to share your life? Does
it seem to you that constancy is what I confer upon my lovers? I
had thought I was more faithfully reported."

"It is not like you to play with words," he said, frowning. "What
you undertake, that you will perform, and well you know it. Where
you have given only a fleeting pleasure you have never promised
more. But I am asking for more. Come with me, and I will never
have any but you, and you shall be my mistress and my peer."

"You tempt me," she said. "I like you well and take pleasure in
your company, my lord, and there is much to attract me in what
you suggest. But there are things about me that you do not know.
If you had come to me like the rest, looking only for a night's
pleasure and ready to pay for it, it would never have become necessary for you to know them."

"Do not attribute to me either coldness or continence," he put in
haughtily, "for holding back until now. I want you body and mind
and heart, or I will have none of you. To hold you in my arms for
a night, and know myself one of a long line of fools who believe
that they have possessed you, that I could not endure. I want a
consort for my days and my nights alike, a partner worthy of my
state."

"You lay the more obligation on me," she said, "to make it clear
what I can give you and what I cannot."

She rose abruptly from the table and crossed the room to draw close the arras over the door, as though the May evening had turned cold suddenly. Her long skirt made a soft rustling like autumn leaves, and shed a faint perfume on the air as she passed by him. He followed her movements, and watched her standing motionless in the doorway, her raised hand still clenched in the tapestry. In the shadows her coronal of hair was darker than garnets.

"My lord, I have loved a man, and love him still. He has never been mine, and in this world I think he never will. I say it to my sorrow, he neither loves nor desires me. Nevertheless, I have given to him that love that cannot be given but once, and if that is what you look for from me, then go away now and think no more of me. The heart of love is gone, and cannot be given again. What remains is the woman you see. I am not of those who die of unrequited passion, though I live the poorer by what I have lost. I have respect for you, and liking, I have a mind that may serve you well, and a body I am free to pledge to you if I choose, and I have a strong appetite for life. If you still want me on those terms, we may be able to strike a bargain. But I will not come to you dishonestly, pretending to be what I am not."

He had risen from his chair, thrusting the hound aside with a brusque movement of his foot. He came towards her slowly, anger and jealousy in the lines of his frowning face, but calculation in his eyes, and something of a hot, unquestioning tenderness, too, that reached for her through the bars of his pride. She loosed her hold on the arras, and went step for step to meet him, a rueful smile on her lips, but her eyes like clear steel mirrors in which he beheld his own insatiable face.

"I cannot believe this! I want you whole!"

"But I am not whole," she said, "the best is gone. And so goodbye, my lord!"

"No! Wait!" He took her by the shoulders, and held her hard between his hands, and she felt him trembling with the force of his pride and rage, that would not have less than all, and yet could not let her go.

She had no mind to influence him; her honour was involved. She stood calmly sustaining his famished stare, and out of her own experience she found a measure of true compassion for him.

"He still lives—this man of whom you speak?" he asked harshly.

"He still lives."

"Here, in France? Or was this beforetime, in Venice?"

"I have told you all that you need to know of him," she said. "I'll tell you no more."

His long fingers tightened tormentedly into her flesh, drawing her close against his breast. She had never been in England, the phantasm could not follow her there, into a new country. And he would be ever beside her, with the persuasions of his body and the graces of his worship for her, flesh and blood and present love for a fading dream. She could not live in memory for long, she was too intelligent, too honest, too keenly alive. With all things new around her, and all in his gift, she could not choose but love him at last.

"Yes, come!" he said hoarsely, suddenly laying his lean cheek against her hair. "Come with me! Even so, come! If you knew my need—"

"Wait! Hear what I undertake, before you bind yourself." She braced her hands against his breast and held him off from her. "If you still desire it, I will come with you. I will bind myself in faith and loyalty to you, and only to you, until one of us two shall openly and fairly pronounce this contract at an end. And then it shall be void, and there shall be no redress. If it is you who cast me off, I will abide it and never complain. And if it is I who abandon you, you must do as much in your turn. But this I swear to you, I will never leave you, except it be to follow that creature I love more than my own life. And if that should befall," she said with a bitter smile, "as God He knows it is unlikely ever to do, you may well say of me, rather than 'God curse her!'—'God help her!', for I shall surely pay in full any debt I owe to you."

"I take you, then," he said, the words strained out of him in a half-suffocated voice. "I take you, on those terms, and will hold you against the world." He caught her to him fiercely, his arms circling her body, his mouth kissing and murmuring against her cheek. The other, the enemy, the man from the past, would never come troubling them. He was a bloodless shadow, a poor thing without the wit to love her then, or the spirit to find her now if he came to his senses. The sea, and silence, and indifference would hold him distant

from her. And even if he came—as he never would come—he was
mortal and could die. So poor a spirit would need little quenching.
"Hold by me!" he whispered into her throat. "Hold fast by me, for
God's sake!"

"Until death or he call me from you," she said, "or you discard
me."

She marvelled at herself a little, that she, born of subtle, sea-
faring merchant stock without pretensions to nobility, should feel
herself bound by the niceties of honour far more inescapably than
by his arms or all the resources of his power.

He twisted one hand in the coils of her hair, and began to pluck
out the bone pins that held it in place, until the heavy sheaves fell
about her shoulders and drifted in a shining darkness between her
uplifted face and his kissing mouth. She embraced him resolutely,
straining to her heart the instrument of her power and means of her
usefulness, and she felt neither fear nor regret for what she had
done.

Harry picked his way across the courtyard of the Maison d'Estivet,
between servants and pack-horses and corded loads, with the din of
departure in his ears. The leaning face of the house, striped with
fitful, watery sunlight and the tenuous shadows of clouds, sheltered
with its overhang the piled furnishings of my lord's bedchamber and
wardrobe, the most precious freight, just in process of being loaded.
Three of the harassed squires were superintending the porters, and
sweating blood for fear a few flecks of dust should be cast upon
Isambard's silks and furs. The heavier and less precious baggage had
already been dispatched to Calais in carts, some days previously, but
these last and most closely guarded goods must travel by pack-horse
to keep pace with my lord and his personal party. The sumpter
column would leave this morning, the riders this afternoon, to make
an easy first stage on the way to the port. Then there remained only
the sea voyage, a brief but abysmal misery as Harry remembered
it, between him and England.

Adam, somewhat below his best after a last boisterous night with
Apollon and Élie at Nestor's, had already ridden ahead with their
instruments, the accumulated mass of Harry's drawings, and the
attendant spirit of their travels together, the wooden angel. The

angel's colours were a little dimmed and mellowed now by many lodgings; he had been the guest of three great churches and won the admiration of many sound critics, not least of them his last host, Canon d'Espérance. Now he, too, was on his way home. He was part of a debt of honour which had been long in the paying.

Half a dozen dogs ran between the stamping horses and bustling men, and were cursed and kicked and tripped over by turns. Most of them would be left here, but the three strange hunting dogs from the East were to be shipped to England after their master, and were intended, so Harry had heard from the youngest of the squires, as a present for King John. They had long bodies like greyhounds, and long, narrow faces, haughty as Saladin himself, and long, shaggy ears and flanks, and according to Walter Langholme they could outrun leopards on their own ground, and pull them down, too. They paced suspiciously through the teeming halls of the Maison d'Estivet, delicate and aloof, nervous but not timid, objects of terror and awe. Only the great wolfhound from Arabia, Isambard's special delight, was more feared. He was trained, so they said, to be one man's beast, and at his command would bring down and kill either man or leopard. He was never seen without Isambard himself holding the leash, or else his handler, a Christian Greek from Romania, bought with the dog. Nobody else could command him, for he knew his rights, and deferred only to his lord and his lord's deputy.

There were falcons in the menagerie, too, and a little green and gold singing bird in a filigree cage for the queen. And there were two caskets of gilt and inlay work containing fragments of the shattered bones of Saint Stephen and a lock of the red hair of Saint Mary Magdalene, which she tore out of her head in the hours of supernatural darkness on Calvary; and most precious of all, an amethyst flask of the water of Jordan, blessed by the last Christian prelate of Jerusalem, before the holy kingdom fell to Saladin, and a second time by the Pope in Rome. It was said to have worked several miracles already, and was intended as a princely gift to the cathedral of Gloucester. It travelled in a bag of worked leather, strapped to the thongs of one of the pack-saddles and watched with anxious care.

As Harry approached the doorway he heard Isambard's voice raised within in a brief but violent outburst of wrath. A servant came scuttling out, his eyes blank with fright, and the mark of a

whip crimson across his cheek and chin. De Guichet, the oldest of
the five squires, followed him with more dignity, but in equal haste
to remove himself from his lord's vicinity. He was scarlet to the
hair, and in a temper he would certainly vent on someone lower in
the hierarchies before the hour was out. Encountering Harry outside
the door, he raised his eyebrows and shook his head at him helplessly, but did not stop to exchange words. It was Langholme who
tilted his head significantly towards the house, and said in an undertone:

"Keep out of his way. The signs mean thunder."

"What ails him?" asked Harry, unable to take the storm too
seriously, since it had never yet blown in his direction.

"Pinpricks. One of the Syrian hawks died, no one knows why.
And now the horse the lady was to ride is gone lame. It wants but
one more thrust and someone will bleed for it."

"The lady? What lady is that?"

"Why, his Venetian beauty, of course, who else?"

"Madonna Benedetta?" cried Harry, staring at him unbelievingly.

"Did you not know? She has been here three days with him
already. Where have you been hiding, not to have heard it? She's
sold old Guiscard's house and is coming to queen it at Parfois."

His first feeling was of alarm for his own peace, but he tossed that
away contemptuously as a vanity on his part. If she had captured
the lord of Parfois she was not likely to waste any thought on his
master-mason, nor to thank him for remembering that she had once
offered herself to him. No, he need not fear any vexation from her,
she would surely play the chatelaine with a particularly forbidding
hauteur towards him, to warn him not to presume on what had
passed between them.

Thus far he pursued these sensible arguments, and then turned
sick with his own shameful stupidity. She was no such person. He
was lying to himself and defaming her. Whatever she did, she did
with open eyes and with her might. What she had said to him stood;
she would not take it back, and she had not repented of it.

It was for him she was coming to England! With what intent he
could not guess, but he knew that it had to do with him.

"I've been out of Paris until last night, on my lord's business,"
he said. "I heard nothing of it. Is she within there now?"

"She is, and he's about choosing another mount for her, and God help the grooms if he fails to find what he wants. If I could, I'd put the width of Paris between myself and him. I've seen his lightnings kill before now."

Harry curled an incredulous lip at what must be an exaggeration. "What, in Paris, with men of law within a stone's throw?"

"Do you think the law cares what Parfois does with his own serfs? Or his free men, for that matter? Or that it dare touch him, if it did care? To those who fall within his honour he *is* law, the high justice, the middle and the low. There was a sheriff once in Flint who did try to move against him," said Langholme simply, "but it ended in the sheriff being thrown out of office and ruined. And law's lost a deal of its force in the marches since those days, let me tell you. Stand away. Here they come, the pair of them!"

The household had not yet grown accustomed to its new mistress; a hush and a tremor went before her as she stepped from the doorway, and covertly all eyes turned upon her. Then, as Isambard appeared at her shoulder, all faces were as quickly averted, and hasty hands, none too steady under that fixed and frowning eye, went on feverishly tightening girths and hoisting the corded loads into place.

He should have known that, however changed and disconcerting the circumstances, she would be their mistress. She moved across the crowded courtyard with that imperial calm of hers, untroubled by the secret assault of so many eyes, and when her glance fell on him she greeted him courteously and composedly, like any other of her lord's more exalted servitors. She wore a plain riding-dress, and her hair was hidden within a white wimple, so that for the first time he saw the pure, strong shape of her face without the distraction of that red splendour; and as the dress had a cloistral austerity, so the face had a power and a confident passion quite without fear of the world.

Isambard, all brown and dull gold from head to foot, had the Arabian hound on its short, thick leash at his hip. Its colour, like his, was tawny, and its hide, like his sun-gilded skin, had a golden lustre. They looked like a group in bronze when they halted for a moment, and in motion they were molten metal. The dog's head, jawed like a mastiff, came level with the man's waist. Its mask was ugly, but its gait was exquisite, the light ripple of controlled power moving that entire great body without a sound or an effort. The sight of every man in the courtyard shrinking furtively aside from his passage moved Isambard to a sour smile, but it was only the ominous flicker of lightning through the cloud that hung upon his face. The whip that had laid open the groom's cheek still dangled from a gloved wrist. By the look of him he would use it again freely on anyone who crossed him, from de Guichet down.

"Ah, you are back," he said, espying Harry. "Are you any judge of a horse?"

"No, my lord, or at best an indifferent one."

"No matter, attend us! I am the worst-served and worst-provided master in Christendom, I think. I hope you have done your errands better than Despard did when he furnished me this stable of mine. Are the accounts all paid?"

"And the receipts are with your clerk, my lord."

"Good, then at least we leave no debts behind us. Are you in mortal fear of this creature, like all the rest?"

"I suppose he was trained with that end in view," said Harry. "Why complain of a success?" But he fell in on the hound's other flank, watching the rippling of the great muscles under the silken hide with a delight which at least balanced his wariness.

The line of stables occupied one long wall of the courtyard. Benedetta sat down on the mounting-block, while Isambard had horse after horse paraded before him, and found fault with all. The two unfortunate squires who had been sent ahead into Paris to rent the house and fill the stables before his arrival sweated and endured humbly, as he pulled their work to pieces. Yet it seemed to Harry that the horses were well enough, if their master's heart had not been set on the Arab mare, now disastrously lame. She was a beautiful creature, but there were others no less fine, if the lady could manage them. He wondered curiously if she rode as well as she did most things. Benedetta on horseback would be a new revelation.

"The black is the best of a poor bunch," said Isambard. "Lead him out, and give him space to show his paces."

"The black?" De Guichet hesitated. "My lord, he'll be a handful for any rider, and if my lady—"

"Lead him out, I say!" snapped Isambard, with a sultry flash of his deep-set eyes. "Am I to mount her on such poor jades as you would choose for her?'' And he strode forward and took the halter himself, and brought the black horse out into the centre of the court, and wheeled him circling about him, with the first glow of pleasure he had shown. Benedetta looked on with a noncommittal face from her seat on the mounting-block, the shadow of a smile on her lips. The beast was too large for her, and far too nervous, Harry thought impatiently, and it was a vicious trick to loose him like this in the middle of the flustered servants and restive pack-ponies. A load was knocked over, and furs spilled across the dusty cobbles. One of the ponies shied. The hound, whose leash Isambard had passed to the Greek handler, lifted his tawny hackles and began to moan with contained excitement, deep in his throat.

"Here, take him, let me see him move.''

De Guichet took the halter from him gingerly, and in that moment the horse, sensing a less confident hand on him, suddenly took offence at the dog, partly in real uneasiness, partly in sheer high spirits, and plunged backwards, rearing and whinnying, and dragging the squire with him. He backed into the file of pack-ponies, and sent them scattering with squeals of alarm, and the liveliest of the line, with ears laid back and eyes rolling, went sideways in a series of stiff-legged leaps from the stamping black hooves, plucking his bridle out of the hand of the servant who held him. The load slid sidelong from his back, and cast a full pannier to the ground, spilling brocades and jewels across the cobbles, and the servant, struggling to avert the disaster, fell with it, his arms still outspread to try and save what could be saved. The pony's plunging feet, tangled in silks, kicked panic-stricken left and right, and stamped flat the leather bag that held the flask of the water of Jordan.

In spite of the clamour of the horses and the shouting of men, the small, terrible sound of the crystal shattering seemed to carry clear through all and reach every ear. De Guichet, cursing and cajoling, brought the black horse to earth again, and led him aside, trembling. The pack-pony, caught and held by one of the grooms, stood shuddering and sweating. Between the cobbles of the courtyard a little, dusty puddle gathered and seeped slowly away, leaving only a damp, dark stain.

There was a single instant of appalling silence. Then Isambard made a strange, soft sound, low in his throat, like a more terrible

echo of the hound's moan of desire; and in the same moment the
servant, sprawling among the ruins, uttered a hoarse croak of terror.

"My lord, mercy! I could not help it!"

The bronze face, fixed in a dreadful stillness, stared upon the
trampled relic and the grovelling man for a moment in silence. Then,
with a flashing movement, Isambard stooped and tore free the heavy
brass clasp from the hound's collar, and setting his hand in the
erected hackles, thrust forward savagely towards the poor wretch on
the ground, and spat into the pricked ear a few barbaric words.
Whether they were Arabic, Greek, or whatever other strange
tongue, they needed no translating.

Harry uttered an almost voiceless cry of protest, and started forward, but Langholme took him by the arms from behind, and
dragged him back, clinging to him obstinately as he struggled to free
himself, and hissing in his ear: "Let be, you fool! Do you want to
be the next?"

Killing was the dog's business, he leaped like an eager craftsman
to the word of command. The great paws bunched under him, and
launched him forward in an easy, beautiful leap. A screaming and
scrambling convulsed the courtyard, men and ponies ran confusedly
for cover, and found none. The man on the ground had dragged
himself up and cast one wild look all round him, and turned to run
desperately but with frantic purpose straight for Madonna Benedetta, who had not moved from her seat on the mounting-block.

He hurled himself at her feet, crouched against her ankles, clutching her shoes against his streaming face; and with a swift movement
she caught up the hem of gown and cloak together and cast them
over him. The weighted corner of her cloak flicked the hound's
gaping muzzle as it loped silently after its quarry, and sent it scrabbling and sliding back a yard or two on the polished stones. The
woman sat quite still, her right arm spread over the servant's heaving
shoulders, her face, composed but watchful, turned steadily towards
the dog. Sensing that he trespassed here at his own peril, but reluctant to quit his victim, he circled her, head lowered, jaws slavering,
and stared at her with baffled amber eyes, dubious of his duty.

In a second he might have made up his mind. But a second was
enough for Isambard, ashen beneath his tan, to leap forward and

slash the weaving jowl aside from her with a vicious swing of his whip. Benedetta looked up at him as he leaned above her, speechless with anger and fear, and said with the faintest of smiles and the mildest of voices: "Yes, call off your dog, my lord, he's trampling my dress."

He could not speak, his throat was constricted with the terror he had felt for her and the fury he had felt against her, an agony of hate and love. He stood towering over her in aching silence, as the Greek crept forward and leashed the dog, and retreating step by step, with held breath, drew it away with him to hide and tremble in the background. Silently Langholme relaxed his grip on Harry's arms, and silently Harry stood off from him, drawing long breaths of the charged air and getting no relief. Until the tension broke between those two facing each other there, no one dared move except softly and stealthily.

The lines of Isambard's mouth, drawn thin and grey, relaxed slowly, and blood flushed again beneath the stretched skin of his cheeks. Under the heavy eyelids the fires burned out to black. She held their hard stare until the anguish passed from it and the breath was even and quiet in his still dilated nostrils.

"My lord," she said then, as naturally as if nothing out of the way had passed, "if you do not want this man, give him to me. I shall have need of a man-servant sometimes."

For a long moment he did not answer. Then with an abrupt movement of his whole body he straightened up from her. "He is yours," he said quietly, and turning from her, strode away into the house, men and dogs and ponies scattering hurriedly from his path.

She waited until he was gone, and then with a lift of her head and a marked glance about her sent the squires and grooms and porters about their business. Then at last she drew aside cloak and skirt from the prostrate man, and looked down at him with a face suddenly grave and thoughtful. His palms were folded about her feet, his face pressed against her insteps; he lay unmoving.

"Get up!" she said gently. "He is gone. No one will touch you now, you are mine."

The man lifted a soiled, drained face. He had bitten his lip so deep that blood had run down into his short brown beard, and with the exhaustion of relief from fear he was almost too weak to move. Harry, who had felt no dismissal in Benedetta's glance, went forward and lent him an arm to help him to rise.

"You were his serf? Are you French?"

"English, my lady." His voice was flat and dazed. "From Fleace, in Flintshire."

"What is your name?"

"John the Fletcher, my lady."

"Well, John the Fletcher, you are no serf now, but my liege man, and free. I do not expect to make any great demands on your skill in fletching arrows, but who knows, some day I may need you."

"I am your man," he said hoarsely, and caught up the corner of her cloak and pressed it to his lips. "Body and soul, mistress, while I live."

"Go now and bathe your face. And keep out of my lord's sight for a while. You are safe enough from him, but I would not have him reminded."

When the man had limped away across the court, Benedetta rose. She encountered Harry's eyes, and smiled, rather ruefully. There was no constraint between them; the freedom he felt with her at once startled and reassured him. How could he have feared, even for a moment, that she would pursue him with the love he had refused? Love with her would be a field of action, not a need. She was complete whether she won or lost the world. She was her own fortress and her own sanctuary.

"We strike these attitudes," she said, "almost by accident. Now I feel more than a little foolish."

"You risked your life," he said, watching her face gravely.

"I think not. I was born with certain disabilities; among other things I am quite unable to feel any fear of dogs, even when I should. It is very disconcerting to the most dangerous of beasts not to be feared. And besides, you saw how fast my lord can move when he pleased. The hound would have had a sword through him before ever he got his teeth through my cloak. Not that I thought of it, either way," she admitted, "at the time. Unless sometimes the act is also the thought. In any case, I could not move aside, he held me by the feet."

"That was not what held you," said Harry; and after a moment, very soberly: "Take good care with such a man!"

"That is good counsel for you, as well as for me," she said, giving him a keen look. Then her eyes softened into a regretful smile: "He has surprised you. I am sorry! As for me, I knew already that there is nothing so bad or so good as to be out of his compass. Except, of course, faith-breaking, the only mortal sin." She brushed a few flecks of dust from her cloak, and turned towards the house. "Ask Bertrand de Guichet to pick out a horse for me, Harry. He need not be a lady's nag. I can ride. I must go in and make my peace."

She went, with that splendid, straight walk of hers, and she did not look behind. But she left with him one more, the last and most touching, of those unbearably lovely memories she seemed to quicken about her at every turn. He saw again the bold hand casting the hem of her skirt over the runaway, and before his eyes the hand dwindled into a child's plump little paw, gallantly spreading out her full skirts to hide two boys from their pursuers. Such a fondness came about his heart that he could not see for tears. This was Benedetta's gift to him, the recognition of the tie that bound him to Gilleis.

He opened his mind to love unresistingly, and it flooded his being, filling him with a sweet and poignant delight more overwhelming than pain. Body and mind, he ached for her. His need was as inordinate as his neglect of her had been innocent and long. Gilleis, I must find you, I will find you, he cried to her silently. Oh, love, Gilleis, wait for me, I'm coming!

It was time and more than time for him to turn homeward.

PART THREE

THE WELSH MARCHES

1209-1215

Chapter Nine

*A*dam awoke with the first sunlight on his face through the narrow east window of the upper chamber, and opened his eyes to see Harry sitting on the edge of the bed, pulling on his hose. He stretched and yawned luxuriously, looking up at him with a dreamy smile, and for a moment lay wondering vaguely and contentedly where he was. Then he remembered riding into Shrewsbury after dark, in the soft summer rain, the drowsy supper downstairs in the inn, and the pleasure of falling half-asleep and bone-tired into this capacious bed beside his brother. They had ridden out of their way to the lead-mines, because Harry would not let even the lead for his roofs wait its time, but must bespeak it from the source now, before he had even set eyes on the site where he was to build.

"Where are we going so early?" he asked sleepily, and groped along the bare floor with one hand for his shoes.

"Not we—I. You can go and look at the town, after all this long time away, and meet me here again in an hour or so."

Then Adam remembered. The mist of sleep cleared from his eyes, they opened wide and blue as cornflowers in his sunburned face. "I could very well come with you. Who's going to remember old scores now?"

"No," said Harry with finality. "You'll not set foot in their gates. I won't be long gone."

"And what if they move against you? You're very tender for me, but foolhardy for yourself, it seems."

"This debt is mine," said Harry shortly, and rose from the bed with a bound that set the wooden frame creaking. Adam lay still and watched him dress, his hands comfortably linked under his fair head. It was characteristic of Harry that he had had to be bullied into buying new clothes in London, seeing no connection between the dignity and authority of a master-mason and the length and amplitude of his cotte. He scoffed at the full-length gown of the selfconscious master as the uniform of infirmity, and could not be induced to interest himself in what he wore, beyond demanding freedom to move as he pleased. It had cost Adam a deal of scheming and cajoling to get him into this trim light-brown cotte and the dark green surcoat with its full sleeves and capuchon elegantly draped. He surveyed his work with contented eyes as Harry combed his hair and buckled on his belt. The gravity, purpose and power of the face had never been in any doubt. He would have no difficulty in commanding respect and obedience, whatever rusty old tunic he put on him. Still, Adam liked to see him doing honour to his role. It was not every man who could set up to be a master-mason at twenty-four.

Harry caught the complacent blue eye, and grinned derisively at the reflection of his own magnificence there. "They'll not know me."

"They'll know you," said Adam positively, with pride and contentment, and closed his eyes and slept again.

Harry went on foot through the town, downhill by the curving streets in the sharp, cool light of the morning. Nine years had not greatly changed Shrewsbury. The narrow shop-fronts between their dark, timbered portals, the leaning gables serrated against the pale, pearly sky were as he remembered them, and the people who rubbed shoulders with him were unfamiliar only in a degree of quietness and reserve, almost of suspicion, as though strangers were no longer so frequent or so welcome as once they had been. A sign of the times, like the silence of the bells. Here in the town which had been his home he felt the want of them again like a gnawing hunger. At this hour of the morning the roofs should have been rocking with sound; but for over a year now all the bells of England had been stilled, all the churches closed, the brides bedded with clandestine ceremonies or none, the dead buried without rites, in pits by the roadside. And the king, acting with as great audacity as the Pope, and as little regard for the effects of his strategy on the innocent and helpless, had appropriated to himself all the lands and rents and properties of the church, on the ground that it was no longer fulfilling those duties in consideration of which it enjoyed such privileges. Without income neither clerics nor monastics could feed themselves, much less provide for the sick and poor around them. It was always on the lowest and least that the weight came down in the end, just as debt found its way down from the king through his barons, through their tenants-in-chief and their sub-tenants, to the free cottagers and the bound villeins on their poor little yardlands of earth. Innocent struck at John, John struck at Innocent, and both blows fell on the poor man in his field. Bishops and abbots could ship themselves abroad until the storm should blow over, but wretched little parish parsons, as poverty-stricken as their own flocks, could not, and now it was the poor who fed the priests and not the priests the poor. All over the appointment of an archbishop!

But no, it was less simple than that, that was the chosen occasion, not the cause. This Pope, able, brilliant and ambitious, was an emperor lost, and saw Christendom as a temporal as well as a spiritual empire; and John, the most stiff-necked of the princes of Christendom, and the one most likely to see his island kingdom as a secular force with an integrity of its own, stood squarely in his way. In their trial of strength, the people of England were the pawns, expendable until the want of them threatened to decide the game.

Isambard talked often of John and of affairs in the world, thinking aloud in front of Harry with a freedom which he felt as a compliment, yet somewhat as a burden, too. Those trenchant monologues, so acidly clear and so unorthodox to come from a man so devout, had opened his eyes to new ideas, and compelled him to look a second time, and more critically, at everything he had been taking for granted. The habit of questioning everything can be dangerous, for sooner or later it will surely bring a man into head-on collision with the unquestionable, and he will not be able in conscience to draw aside.

At the foot of the sloping street the wall shut out the sunlight, and the tunnel of the gateway, between its two towers, was a shaft of golden light piercing the shadowy town like a spear. Harry passed through the gate, and crossed the stone bridge. Beneath him the Severn at its summer level ran quiet and green. He looked back at the buttressed face of the wall and the narrow terraces of the vineyard running down from its foot to the tow-path by the waterside. Had they left Father Hugh his vineyard, or did the king lay claim to that, too?

He looked ahead, and on the other side of the river rose the boundary wall of the abbey grounds, the mill, and the long line of the infirmary roof; and high above that, massive and rosy-grey in the morning light, the silent tower of the church.

They had ridden in from the lead-mines by the Welsh bridge on the far side of the town, so that this was his first sight of the abbey for nine years. He had expected a shock of rediscovery and a surge of memories, for the five years he had spent here seemed now to have been happy and fruitful, and a return after long absence should have moved him deeply; but now that the moment came it astonished him only by its naturalness. It was as if the interval had been no more than a few weeks, and he was returning after a holiday. When he approached the gate-house the shadow of a more piercing memory fell upon him, not of his childish years in this sanctuary, but of the manner of his leaving it.

The fair, dear face swam once again before the eyes of his spirit, half-remembered and soft and sweet in rounded childishness, half-dreamed and remote in daunting womanhood. It had wanted only a glimpse of a little girl by the wayside, or a woman's braided hair, or a child's tossed ball, all the way from London, and she had quickened in him like fire taking hold, and burned unbearably about his heart in a great, sweet pain. At every halting-place on the way he had asked after her, in case someone could call to mind the old journeys with her father, and remember when last she had passed along Watling Street; but no one had been able to give him news of her. He wanted to believe that here there would be a different answer for him, that where he had first found her, failing to recognise gold when he had it in his hands, he would find the way to her again; but now that he set foot in the shadow of the gate-house he was afraid.

He had been so sure that she would be waiting for him in London, that in a world of changes her environment would have stood fast. Even when her cousin's wife had opened the door to him, and husband and wife together had shaken their heads regretfully and answered his questions as best they could, he had scarcely been able to grasp that Nicholas Otley had been two years dead, and Gilleis almost as long withdrawn from London. She had been left well-provided, but had chosen to sell her share in the cloth business to her cousin and attach herself as tirewoman to some noble lady, a wise enough course for a young woman of means left without parents. But with what mistress she had established herself, or in what part of England, they did not know, for she had left London within a few weeks of her father's death, and they had had no word from her since. There had been certain pressing wooers, said the young wife, more pressing still after Nicholas died of his fever and left the girl well-to-do, and that, she thought, was the reason Gilleis had left behind her no word of where she might be found.

He had gone away stunned, telling over the poor facts like beads in his mind, and for a long time unable to grasp their significance. It was the only thing of importance in his life that he had never confided to Adam, and without understanding his own reticence he had been grateful for it. He could not have borne the sharing of this sorrow. So all the way north he had looked for traces of her and failed to find any, and all the way he had ridden in a tension of ardour and despair, delight and despondency, brilliance and blackness, unable to believe that he had lost her, yet day after day refused ground for hope. The world continued beautiful, friendship sweet, the future and the work that waited for him a passion and a wonder. Only she was wanting. The silent anguish she left in her place in his heart was a part of the fury that drove him, a dark source of energy side by side with the bright. But even Adam knew nothing of it.

Edmund came out of the gate-house as Harry entered the courtyard. His shoulders were a little stooped now, and there was more grey in his hair, but otherwise he was hardly changed since the day when he had lifted Adam out of the saddle at these gates, and carried him indoors in his arms. He turned and looked inquiringly at the entering stranger, and at first seemed not to know him, but as Harry drew nearer the peering eyes sharpened and stared hard, and the man's lips opened on a greeting, but hesitated still on the name.

"Say it, Edmund," said Harry, feeling his heart lift with pleasure and hope at being known. "You won't be mistaken."

The porter's face broke into a broad smile of delight.

"Master Talvace! Is it you indeed? After all this time!"

"I would do better to toss my cap in first, maybe, " said Harry, "and see what sort of a welcome it gets." And yet he had no qualms now, the sight of an old friend had made all things simple. All things but one! "And it used to be Harry," he said, reaching out his hand.

"Ay, so it did, when you were a little, sharp thing no higher than my elbow." Edmund gripped the offered hand with pleasure. "But you're come home Master Henry at least, after all your gallivanting about the world. Lad, but it hasn't changed you!"

"Oh, a little, I hope! It was needful! Things are changed here with you, I fear, and not for the better." He looked about the courtyard, and it was a sad and quiet place compared with its old bustle of life. A groom was bringing two riding horses out of the stableyard to the guest-house, and a pack-mule belonging to some small merchant stood awaiting his load. The doors of the church were closed, and the lodges and scaffolding all gone, though the work was uncompleted. Building went on leisurely here, and now the interdict had cut off the funds and made progress impossible. Round the almonry a few beggars and cripples crouched, sunning themselves. "I see you still manage to feed the hungry. But I fear these are hard times for you as for them."

"Why, we have been lucky compared with most. Shrewsbury was always strong for the king, and has found him a mint of money in its time, for charters and the like, so we got off lightly. All the Abbey lands were turned to the king's profit except the main granges, but we've not been interfered with there, and the mills here keep us heads above water, and a little over to give. It's meant parting with all but a handful of the free men who got their livings here, and it's hard on them. But we shall weather it, we shall weather it. It can't go on for ever."

"And travellers still come," said Harry, his eyes on the packman loading his mule.

"We never closed our doors yet. Travellers? It's quiet just now, but sometimes you'd think the whole land was on the move, the roads seethe so with travellers—following the king's example, for, faith, he must know every inch of his own roads by now, he's never still. And the roads of France, too, belike, for indeed he's oftener there than at home, trying to get back his own. And every baron in the realm has half his household out riding courier for news and carrying letters, they're so hot to make alliances and so quick to grow feared of those they have and send out to make more. Harry, lad, there isn't a man here above the hinds who dare trust his neighbour."

"Edmund!" Harry laid a hand upon his arm. "You remember when I left here? It's a long time, but you wouldn't forget that. Do you remember a merchant who was here that day, leaving for London with three carts full of bales of cloth? His name was Nicholas Otley. He came every year in the summer, you may have had him here no more than three years ago. Do you mind the man?"

Edmund scrubbed thoughtfully at his chin, narrowing his eyes to stare back through time. "I mind the day we lost you, well enough— the to-do there was about you, no one could forget it. We ended dragging the pool. Man, I'm right glad we got nothing but fish and weed in the nets! Sir Eudo very nearly had the place down stone from stone after you, and I wouldn't have given much for your skin if he'd found you, abbot or no abbot. But a cloth merchant—and carts—ah, so that was how you got past us, after all! Yes, I call him to mind now. A pretty little lass he had used to ride with him."

Harry's heart turned in him at the mention of her. "His daughter," he said from a dry throat. "She'll be a young woman grown now. Has she been here in the last year or so, Edmund?"

He held his breath and felt the pain of hope take him by the heart, while Edmund cast his mind back yet again, with maddening deliberation. "The last time they came must be three summers ago now. I've seen nothing of man or maid since then."

The fall was harder every time, and yet in his heart he had never expected success. "You've not been away from your duties sometimes? If she'd been here, you'd surely know of it?"

"I'd know. I know every soul that comes through that gate, and those that come regularly I don't forget, you know that. If she'd been here, I should know it. Are you wishful to find her, then, Harry?"

"I have a debt to her father," said Harry, turning his head away as he felt the blood mount in his cheeks. "I looked for him in London and heard he was two years dead. I'd be glad to pay his girl what I owe, if I could light on her."

"Likely she's wed," said Edmund comfortably, innocent of the blow he was delivering, "for I mind me there was a young fellow rode with them the last year or two they came, that seemed to be set on her. And indeed she was a fine lass. Are you for staying with us a day or two, Harry? You'll be more than welcome."

"No, I must ride on to Parfois. But I must see the abbot, if he has time and will to see me. Will you sound him, and I'll be in having a word with Brother Denis while you go."

"Brother Denis, is it?" Edmund took him by the arm gently as he would have turned towards the infirmary. "You'll not find the good old man, Harry, sorry I am to say it. He's five years gone from us."

"Dead?" He had learned to contain the repeated pain of Gilleis's loss, but this blow, which he had never for a moment foreseen, struck him to the heart. Old men die; there was nothing strange in it. Yet no omen had warned him that Brother Denis was no longer in the world; there should have been something changed in this familiar air, a shade of green lost from the river meadows, some kindly warmth gone out of the sun. Now he could never beg pardon for leaving him without a farewell and with a lie on his lips. He had waited nine years to cleanse his breast of that reproach, and now he was five years too late. "I left him unkindly, Edmund—like a thief. Did he blame me? I'd rather it had been any man than him I cozened, but I was pressed hard."

"God love you, lad, you knew him long enough—did he ever blame any child for defending himself as best he could? No more than you'd blame a hunted cat for putting out her claws."

"Did he speak of us—after we ran?"

"Ay, did he, often enough, and always to wish you well. For weeks after, if it rained hard, he'd say: 'I hope the children have a good roof over them tonight.' And as late as the winter, every frost would have him worrying if you were clad warmly enough for the weather. It was your father he had trouble forgiving. Never fret about him, he's with the saints, and knows better what ails you than you can ever tell him. He's the most sorely missed man that ever left this house; the boys have a poor time of it without him to shelter them a little when Brother Martin blows north-easterly."

The memories were coming back on him thick and fast now, crowding in upon him unbearably close. "See if the abbot will admit me, Edmund," he said, flinching from too much remembering. "I'll need to be getting back into the town within the hour."

"I was for telling you, Harry, if we had not got on to Brother Denis—the abbot's a sick man, and has been since Easter, though we think now he'll mend. Oh, likely enough they'll let you see him, most like he'll want it as soon as he knows you're here. He's clear enough now in the head, but it was a long fever, and he's weak and thin as a stray cat."

"I'm sorry to hear it," said Harry. "If he's allowed visitors I should indeed be glad to see him, if only for a few minutes, but I'll not inflict myself on him unless he's fit for it."

"Will you come across with me, or shall I look for you again?"

"I'll be in the church," said Harry, and parted from him so.

He entered the church, as he had left it nine years ago, by the south-west door from the cloisters; all others were closed, and the parochial door locked and barred. The air inside was at once cold and close, and the heavy dimness came down upon his spirit like a threatening cloud. The old oppression of stone and darkness and the chill of the grave made his flesh shrink, even while he acknowledged majesty. He bowed his head before the high altar, and walked round by the ambulatory into the Lady Chapel. The founder's tomb rose like a barricade to block his way, cutting off still more of the precious light. Light, light! How could they bear to seal themselves in from it? How could they teach the soul to soar where there was neither space to unfold a wing nor air to sustain it? He smiled at the old Madonna, blunt-featured and massive, a heavy country-woman, out

of fashion now, but dear to him for the many times when she had
been his comfortress.

"Holy Virgin, I have brought you your own again. Take him back
in your kindness and cherish him. He's no *vagus* at heart, he'll go
wandering no more." He unwrapped the cloth from the roll he
carried under his arm, and set the little angel gently in his place on
the altar, and the delicate wings stiffened and checked on the heavy
air, the thin, frail feet stretched downwards ardently. He lit and
hung motionless, quivering with joy, his hands outspread, his
gleaming eyes averted from the ruby flame of the lamp. Wherever
he went, his hour was eternally fixed in exultant arrival; he knew
no separations and no departures.

"Take my thanks," said Harry to the tired, patient, durable ma-
tron of stone, "for all I have seen and known, and all that I have
made and shall make hereafter. In my church you shall have an altar
all jubilant with gold and amber light, where you shall see all the
colours of the spring and summer, and never be cold."

Her antique smile embraced him indulgently with the rest of
creation, expecting nothing from the promises of children. He said
a prayer for the certain and blessed repose of Brother Denis's soul,
and then knelt thinking of Gilleis, but did not pray for her. And
there Edmund found him when he came from the abbot's lodging.

In the curtained bedchamber a young novice sat reading to the sick
man, but he rose when the stranger entered, and silently withdrew,
closing the door behind him. Harry went forward and stood beside
the great bed, looking down into gaunt eye-sockets in which the
sunken eyes burned brilliantly. They searched his face in silence for
a long moment, while the grey lips quivered into a faint smile.

"You'll have come for your horses," said a voice that rustled
drily, like the wind in dead leaves. "The little cob died. You'll have
to take one of my horses in his place, or keep back his price."

Hugh de Lacy's face was a mask of fine, worn bone on the pillow,
the parchment skin stretched over it tightly. The hand that lay slack
on the covers had the look of alabaster, as though the light could
shine through it. Harry had never noticed in the old days what
beautiful bones he had; now there was hardly anything of him but
bone.

"Sit down, Harry," sighed the autumnal voice, and the emaciated fingers stirred in a gesture towards the stool the reader had vacated.

Harry remained standing, looking down at him with a still face. He drew out from the purse at his belt a little leather bag, and laid it upon the bed beside the lax hand.

"Eleven shillings and seven pence. And something over for the repair of your almsboxes. You will find the amount right, but if you would like someone to check it I can call your lector back again. Let us call the cob's price an alms to the abbey. I have no doubt he was well looked after."

The smiling mouth tightened painfully, but he received the check without complaint. In a moment he said: "Or we might devote it to candles for your father's soul. The Mass, of course, is out of our power."

"My father's soul!" said Harry slowly, and drew off from the bed a little. Father Hugh had taken it for granted that he came from Sleapford; so had Edmund, or he would have told him of the old man's death directly. It must be ancient news, or they would in any case have been quick to offer him condolences as soon as he appeared. So Sir Eudo was gone to his fathers, was he? And Sir Ebrard Talvace was lord of Sleapford in his room.

No doubt it ought to move him, but he contemplated it and felt nothing, neither satisfaction nor sorrow. Old men die, Brother Denises and Sir Eudos alike, it's the common lot of man. He bore no grudges now against his family, and certainly had never wished his father ill. For nine years he had scarcely given him a thought, either vengeful or affectionate. This death seemed now so far distant from him as to be meaningless. When it came to absolute honesty, his father and he had never in their lives been within hailing distance of each other.

"As you will," he said. "It would be better spent on the living, to my mind, but your candles won't hurt the old man's soul, if they don't help it." The words had a more churlish sound than he had intended, but he stiffened at the idea of feigning a grief he did not feel. "I have put the angel back in his place, too," he said.

"Ah, the angel! I've missed him, Harry." Hugh de Lacy moved his hand upon the bed, as though he would have stretched it out to the young man, but his fingers touched the bag of money, and he drew them back with a momentary frown. "Sit down with me," he said again in a low voice. "I ask it of your courtesy. They tell me it is only weakness, but I don't see as clearly as I used to. I cannot talk to you as to an oracle in a cloud."

Harry drew the stool close and seated himself, flushing a little. Were the hollow eyes too weak to see the colour mount in his face?

"And how is your brother?" asked the abbot.

How often in the old days, thought Harry, I fell into this trap through not looking where I was going. It irritated him, I remember. Now I know where I am going, and I am going straight, not round-about.

"I thank you, my brother still has both hands." And after a moment he added mercilessly: "I have not brought him inside your walls this time. I thought it best not to tempt your conscience a second time—he could still not prove free residence of a year and a day in any English borough, and I remember your devotion to the niceties of law, Father."

The corners of the bluish lips drew inward sharply. The face could grow no paler. Motionless in its stony beauty, too drawn to reflect in any tremor or change the moving of the mind within, it stared upwards at the ceiling for a long time. At last he said, so low that Harry had to stoop his head to hear: "Can you not forgive whatever wrong we did you, all those years ago?"

"I can forgive," said Harry, "for what it's worth, because I no longer need anything from you."

"Nor from God?" asked the abbot.

"That is between God and me."

He waited, watching the edge of sunlight creep towards the bed. The silence drew out into a fine-spun thread, like floating gossamer, drifting without tension. He looked again at the man in the bed, and now the transparent blue eyelids were closed, and remained closed, and the face was so still and remote that he thought the abbot had relapsed into a half-sleep. Silently he rose from his place and crossed slowly to the door. There was nothing more for him to do here. He had presented himself and paid his debt, and the debt to him had been acknowledged; what more did he want?

His hand was on the latch of the door when he heard the sick man draw breath in a rending sob, as quickly and fiercely suppressed. It pierced the shell of ice about his heart like a flame, and the molten heat of remorse and tenderness flooded him. He turned and flew to the bedside, falling on his knees and flinging an arm across the abbot's body. He laid his cheek against the bony hand, and then his lips.

"Father, forgive me, forgive me! I had nothing to ask pardon for until now! Arrogant and presumptuous as I am, why should you grieve over me? I never meant to hurt you so." He caught himself up passionately: "Yes! Yes, I did! I did mean to hurt you, I came to hurt you. God forgive me for it!"

The long body, all fallen away to bone, was so insubstantial in his arm that he was afraid to let the slightest weight lie upon it. The ashen mask, broken and contorted for a moment, relaxed into a smiling weariness, and was still. The abbot opened his eyes upon the young, bright face, wild with shame and self-reproach and tenderness. Now indeed he recognised Harry. He had not meant to call him back with pity, yet it was apt enough. Arrogant he was, a very tower of arrogance against every force that opposed itself to him, but one touch of the finger of weakness or suffering could bring him to his knees in a frenzied humility as passionate as the pride that engendered it.

"Even now I am doing you harm," said Harry remorsefully. "You should have quietness and peace, and I've left you none. I'll go, and trouble you no more. Only say that you forgive me my hardness of heart, for indeed I'm sorry and ashamed. I didn't even know I was nursing a grudge all this time. It was easy to forgive those from whom I hoped for nothing, but I put such reliance in you!"

"And I did not mean to fail you," said Hugh de Lacy sadly, "but it is done, and cannot be undone." His thin hand, weightless as a withered leaf, rested on Harry's brown head. His voice, eased of its brittle dryness, said gently: "I forgive, and do you forgive me, my child. My blessing you had with you always. How happy I am to have my peace made with you, and part in kindness, since it may be for the last time."

Harry smiled at him, bending low to the strengthless embrace. "No, Father, you'll live and rule many years yet. You'll maybe see me into my grave before you."

"God forbid, Harry! Sit with me a little while, I'll not hold you long, I soon tire. Tell me how you have fared since the day we lost you, for many a time I have thought of you, and found no comfort."

"Yet, Father, perhaps all was well done, to take me out of a life in which I was unprofitable, and set me on a fruitful path. For I have made offerings of beauty and splendour to God with my own hands, and shall yet make more and better."

He sat beside the bed, holding the wisp of a hand, and talking of Caen and of Paris, of St. Étienne and of Notre Dame, until the dim blue eyelids closed again tranquilly over the assuaged eyes. The knife-sharp outlines of the face had softened, the parchment skin had regained a faint tinge of colour and freshness. And it seemed to him that there was some wound within himself which had healed miraculously when the abbot embraced him, and that the deep scar-tissue was growing lissome and smooth again with every easy breath the sick man drew. He kissed the dry forehead very softly, and went out from him on tiptoe.

Only when he was striding back through the town gate did it occur to him that he had forgotten to collect his horse, but he did not turn back; it was not for the horse he had come.

They came to the crest in the green track at sunset, and rounding the flank of the wood saw from the shoulder of the rolling ridge the river valley beneath them on the left, and before them, overhanging the slope, the sandstone outcrop, seamed with broken folds and shelves in which trees had rooted and grown; and on the summit of the rock, Parfois.

The level site that crowned the hill was not so great that the ambition of the Isambards could not encompass the whole of it. The curtain wall, overtopping the trees and rising sheer out of the stone on which it stood, wound round the hill-top like an enfolding serpent, six towers projecting their rounded sides so that there should be no foothold, even for a raven, that could not be brought under cross-fire. Within the walls the great hexagonal keep, with its three projecting turrets, caught the last rays of the sun and burned into a rose-red glow; the shadows from the valley, heather-purple, were climbing the shelves of rock hand over hand, and groping at the roots of the outer towers.

Three miles away beyond the river Wales slept in shade, only a distant hill-top here and there still golden. Half a dozen villages, down there in the valley, lived their lives perpetually in the darker shadow of that massy pile above them, their shelter and their burden. A dozen more in the folds of the hills on the English side of the castle hid in its lee from the encroachments of the Welsh, but feared their protector scarcely less than their enemies.

The shadow climbed, darkening as it mounted, engulfing one by one the arrow-slits in the rounded towers. The turrets burned like tall candle-flames. Behind the glowing machicolations of the keep the evening sky was a clear bluish-green, the colour of the eyes that stared so eagerly and so warily upon the castle of Parfois from the turn of the road.

The pyramid of the hill and its coronal of stone, shapely and secure, tapered into a burning apex of rosy light, no longer even a beacon lit on the earth, but a star suspended in the pure green heaven. Before they reached it all would be shadow. Already all was silence.

The track wound along the shoulder of the ridge, and then, curving to the right, began to climb the hill by the one easy approach. As they drew nearer to the walls, the keep vanished from their sight, and after it, on both sides, the towers withdrew sidelong out of range, and left them only the upper stages of the gate-house with its turrets. Halfway up the ramp trees closed in upon the track, and suddenly there was no castle, but only a dark woodland about them. Then they emerged again into open planes of grass, and the two outer guard towers came into sight, one on either side the way. The ramp broadened and levelled into a lofty field, a green island in air, for the broken formation of the outcrop severed it from the ground on which the castle itself stood by a fissure forty feet deep. On the far side rose the gate-house with its towers, the drawbridge down, the portcullis raised on the dark archway into the outer ward.

Harry halted on the edge of the green plateau. The track crossed it directly to the bridge, and on either side the rough grass stretched, a neutral grey now in the dusk. On the left lay the greater space, and here he saw dimly spread before him, visible by its own mysterious lambent light, the half-cleared rectangle of rock where three master-masons before him had begun to build. Beyond it confused and shapeless pallors marked where heaps of the old materials lay, and already Isambard's carpenters had thrown up lodges for the new masons soon to assemble here. The evidence of activity moved and excited him, but it was not at these he looked. The uncovered rock, a plan drawn deep through the grass and bushes and soil, held his eyes.

A noble space, and a marvellous setting. The faint luminosity of the rock, the harvest of the day's stored sunlight, seemed to float a foot or two in air over the place, as though the walls had already begun to rise. The north face would be presented to view from the castle, the south from the climbing track. He must consider the whole group, castle and church together, the counterpoise between them here, the unity they would present to those who looked up at them from the valleys on either side, the greater valley of the Severn to the west, the shallow, enclosed valley of the brook to the east. Building is sculpture on a grand scale. A building is as many-sided, as versatile, as complex as a man; it must be as whole and as well integrated as a man, and have regard to its neighbours.

He sat his horse, staring before him in the fading light, and the great reverence he had for form and proportion and the courtesy of shape to shape, his passion for stability and beauty and reticence and harmony, encompassed and transcended the castle and the rock, reached out to the hills of England on one side and the hills of Wales on the other, and found no enmity between them, passed beyond to the horizon, drawn in greenish golden after-light, and the vast profound of the sky, with its faint embroidery of stars. He saw the walls of his church take shape and stand erect towards those hesitant stars, and the tall central tower rear itself high and draw taut, like a worshipping man with his raised forehead tranquil in the radiance of grace. It seemed to him that in order to make it what he wanted it to be, he would have to stretch out the fingers of his senses and the cords of his compassion to the last reaches of the world, and relate every stone of his work to all that moved and breathed and hoped and loved, everything that had form or intelligence. Only so could it be perfect.

That was out of any man's reach. Yet it seemed to him then that he dared hope for it, and that as long as he had the hope he did not need the achievement.

"Let's get in," said Adam, yawning as his horse stirred restively on the edge of the track, "or they'll be raising the bridge on us. I don't know about you, but I'm more than ready to do right by my supper."

Harry turned from his moment of prophecy with a laugh, and they rode forward across the drawbridge and into Parfois.

In this teeming household, where he kept the state of an early palatine, for ever hemmed about with squires and stewards and knights in attendance, and pages and musicians and a multitude of other hangers-on, Isambard yet contrived to live as solitary as a recluse. The great hall that clung to the curtain wall in the angle of the King's Tower was as populous and busy as any market-place, and he conducted the greater part of his day's business there and regularly dined there like any of his peers, presiding over an assembly which sometimes numbered as many as a thousand. But when he withdrew from them into the private part of his life there was not one of them who would have dared to intrude upon him, and not one who would have felt he could follow him there without intrusion. He had trusted servants, but no trusted friends; and that surely not out of fear, like his master the king, who collected family hostages about him as a miser collects money, but out of the long experience he had of disillusionment and disappointment, he who always asked too much.

He had made good use of the situation of Parfois by setting up his private apartments in the Lady's Tower, which overhung the sheerest face of rock and could never come under fire from any point or eminence outside the castle. The narrow shot-windows gave place here to generous lancets, and the heavy gloom within to plentiful air and light. Tapestries draped the stony walls, and the rugs and furs he had brought back from the East with him covered the cold, uneven floors. There he had installed Madonna Benedetta in semi-royal state. But it was a rare occurrence for any other to ask for audience there; and that he should be admitted was an earnest of extraordinary favour. Plainly this master-mason was a man to watch, if he did not over-play his hand.

"I ask your pardon, my lord," said Harry, striding into the candle-lit tower room with a high colour and brilliant eyes, "for interrupting you like this at so late an hour, but this is a matter of some importance. Since supper I have been going through the rolls with your man Richard Knollys, the first opportunity we've had. He is an admirable clerk and a good organiser, and I'm grateful for the work he has done for me here in preparation for my coming. But we are at odds on certain points, and I am obliged to confirm with you at once that there is only one master of the works here, and that is myself. If Knollys will work with me as clerk and executive, well and good, but we shall get nowhere if he is to consider himself joint-master with me."

Isambard turned his chair aside from the chess-board at which he sat with Benedetta. Her hair was loosed from its coils, and hung to her waist in a thick, silken curtain of dusky red. She had a massive repose about her, as though she were so perfectly and so indisputably mistress of Parfois that her position held neither novelty nor gratification for her. She looked, thought Harry, like a wife, and a noble wife at that; and like a noble wife she made no move to withdraw from her husband's councils, but listened alertly and gravely to what passed, and held herself ready to give an opinion if it should be asked, and until then to remain intelligently silent. And any man who had such a wife would be quick to make use of her wit, too, if he were not himself a fool.

"I had no intention of infringing your authority," said Isambard somewhat drily, "and I thought I had made his position clear. He is the most efficient assistant I could give you, but the responsibility for the works is yours. Why, what's amiss between you?"

"My lord, I find that several of the carpenters and masons he has assembled for me are pressed men, some of them brought from as far away as Somerset. Three of them are now imprisoned here for trying to run home. My lord, aside from my own views, surely no one but the king's own purveyor has the right to press men for his works?"

"You're over-hasty with your surelies," said Isambard, "for I enjoy the same right, granted me by the king himself. Within my honour I can hale a craftsman from one end of England to the other if I will, so he be not already engaged upon the king's works. It used to be 'or the works of the Church,' " he added with his crooked smile, "but there's a new dispensation since king and Church fell out. And I can imprison fugitives, too, Harry, and turn them out to work in irons if I please, to keep them from running again. This I knew. Knollys has my sanction."

"He has not mine, my lord." The tone, though he had not intended it, had an arrogance which brought Isambard's head up with a jerk, and caused him to draw his brows together in an ominous frown. "My lord, the right in law I don't dispute, though indeed I did not know of it until now. But for my part, I'll have no pressed men working under me. I think it beneath God's dignity to get his house built by aggrieved souls who hate what they do. A man should be able to sell his labour where he will."

"You intend to teach God his duty, as well as me?" asked Isambard in a steely voice, and spread and closed his hands on the arms of his chair as on the hilts of daggers.

"I intend to make sure I can do my own duty, nothing more. I am here to build you a church, the best I have in me. I must protect my work from influences which would deface it. I'll have no forced men. It is not worthy of you nor of me, nor of the work we are about, to compel unwilling service."

"You are employed to build," said Isambard, suddenly on his feet. "Stick to your banker, and do not meddle with what does not concern you."

"This does concern me. Neither you nor I can get good work out of pressed men. You promised me a free hand in this enterprise, my lord, and I hold you to your bargain!"

They had both raised their voices, the high words clashed in their mouths with the very same sound, and the light eyes and the dark flashed with equal anger.

"Moreover," said Harry, plunging precipitately on, "there is something I like even less than this. I find we are carrying daily a separate roll of some hundred labourers on the site who do not appear among our expenses at all, apart from the cost of their food. Knollys says he had your authority to exact from your villeins two days of extra labour every week for the clearing of the site, and from time to time for fetching and carrying and unskilled work afterwards. I could not believe you ever gave him any such leave, and I am come to you to confirm or deny it."

"I did give it. I maintain it. What offends your tender conscience

in that? Is it beneath your dignity to have unfree hands carry away
the soil from your site?''

"So far from it, my lord, that all I want from you is your leave
to make no distinctions between free and unfree here. I'll welcome
every man of them, so he come of his own will. But to take from
them two full days of labour now, when the harvest will be coming
on, is to take their livelihood from them. You must know, my lord,
that the times come down hard enough on them already. Four days
on your harvests and two on your church, and when are they to
reap their own fields? At night? Even if there are two or three grown
sons in a household, there's work for every one of them, and a small
enough return. If they give their time to you, they deserve to be
paid for it.''

"Paid? My villeins paid for their services?'' He threw back his
head and laughed, full and honestly, but still with rage in the laughter. "Harry Lestrange, you are here to build a new church, not a
new world. Be wise, and stick to your chisels and punches, and let
my dispositions for my people alone. If you turn hedge-priest you'll
come by a hedge-priest's end, and that would be a pity, for you're
an able young man in your own line. I like you, Harry, but I'm the
master of my own estates, and you had better not tell me too often
what I may and what I may not do with my own. I am not always
in so patient a mood as tonight.'' He turned away suddenly to the
table by the wall and poured wine, shrugging off the annoyance
with a toss of his shoulders. "Now abate your fine ardours for an
hour or two, and put down a few quick cups of this, and you'll take
yourself less seriously. You were not so tedious when I found you
in the provost's prison.''

He turned, laughing, to offer the cup, and was amazed and affronted to see how Harry's face had flamed to the forehead, and how
the flesh round mouth and nostrils had whitened in the red.

"It was not necessary, my lord, to remind me of your favours. I
am conscious of them. It is my intention to repay the debt.''

"God's life, boy,'' flashed Isambard, raging again, "I meant no such
reminder. On my soul, only princes can afford a pride like yours.''

There was a moment of thunderous silence, while they stared
upon each other bitterly, like enemies feeling for a killing hold.
Then, with a large, languid movement of hand and arm Benedetta

smothered a yawn, and swept her fingers through the tension as through a cobweb.

"I'm sorry," said Harry, low-voiced, "it was ill done to attribute to you any want of generosity. I know you have never sought any recognition of your kindness to me. Yet I feel my indebtedness, and for my own peace I long to discharge it honestly." His face was pale now, and his lips no longer pinched with anger. "As you found it possible to trust in my ability to do your work, now I ask you to trust in my judgement as to the methods I use."

"We are not talking of building methods, but of administration. Build as you please, but don't meddle with other matters."

"I hold that it is a part of my responsibility, and I have already meddled. I had better tell you what I have done, and then you may tell me if our contract still holds good. It will never be broken by me. I have freed the three men who were imprisoned, and told all the pressed men that they are at liberty to enrol with me or go home, as they choose, and that if they decide to go—as certainly some who are married will do, but I think not a great number— they shall have journey money for the road back. And I have coun- termanded the order to your villeins, and let them know instead that any among them who willingly enrol with me for day-labour will be paid the same rates as the free men who are unskilled. True," he said deliberately, staring full into the deep eyes that blazed at him across the forgotten wine-cup, "I have not the money to make either promise good, unless you grant it to me. But that is for you to decide. If I am the master of your works, as you swore to me I should be, then you will endorse the measures I have taken and give me means to honour my promises. And if you override my decisions, then I am manifestly without authority, and no longer the master of your works. You promised me a free hand and all the resources I need. I am asking you to honour your promises, as I intend to honour mine."

He was within an ace of getting the wine in his face, and most likely the cup after it. He saw the lean brown fingers tighten with deliberation on the stem of the goblet, and the hot red-brown eyes narrow calculatingly on him, debating the manner and measure of the blow and taking pleasure in it before it fell. Benedetta, watching them attentively across the room from the sheltering shadow of her hair, put a hand to the corner of the chess-board; but she found something in Isambard's face that caused her to sit back again and let the moment pass.

The hand that held the cup had relaxed. Harry stood motionless, never taking his eyes from his lord's face, until the flash of Isambard's rings in the light drew his eyes down.

"You had better drink it, after all," said Isambard with the grimmest of smiles, "it will do you more good inside than out. Here, let me pledge you! At least you have more heart in you than most of the fellows I maintain about me. Either that, or you are a plain fool, which I cannot believe. Take it, I say! I seldom play the page to any man, make the most of it. You might well be easier to live with, drunk," he said, turning sharply away. His winged shadow swept across the floor. His hand, as he passed by, touched with a flying caress the smooth curve of Benedetta's shoulder. "Harry," he said peremptorily, turning again in mid-stride, "I do not like having my hand forced. I advise you not to try this strategy again. You have left me no choice but between two extremes. There's nothing to be done with you but toss you into one of the cells under the Warden's Tower and undo everything you have done, or else lend my countenance to all and confirm you in your office. And, by God, I'm sorely tempted to take the first course, but that I should not savour even a masterpiece from the hands of a broken man."

"You would not get one," said Harry. He was glad of the wine, it had warmed the ominous chill out of him. "I do truly believe, my lord, that only free men and willing can create masterpieces. And indeed, in this at least you do me wrong. I did not act first and ask afterwards to present you with an enforced choice. I acted because I believed I had your full authority to act. I am come to you now only because Knollys, in duty to you, I grant him, questioned that authority."

"He will not question it again. I will not shame you before your workmen. Very well, let it be as you have ordained. But mark me, do not try me too far. Keep to your province, and trespass no further on mine."

"My lord, I thank you." He would not say more. What had he to be grateful for? This was no more than keeping to a bargain.

"In the morning I will speak to Knollys. Leave us now."

"Goodnight, my lord! Madonna Benedetta, goodnight!"

He caught one flash of her eyes as he went out, and saw a salute and a smile there, the rueful, amused smile she had turned on him over John the Fletcher's bowed shoulders, that day of their departure from Paris. "We strike these attitudes," he heard her sigh, "almost by chance." Almost, but never quite. She, who knew all about the compulsions of her own nature, could not be astonished by any freak to which his might drive him.

He went out comforted beyond reason. Adam would have backed him cheerfully and wholeheartedly in any undertaking, however outrageous, but without bothering to understand why he acted as he did. She had done no more than slide the chess-board a few inches nearer the edge of the table, ready to overturn it if a diversion became necessary; but it had been enough to show that she understood everything. He was glad that she had been there. He was glad, wonderfully glad, that she had come with them to Parfois.

They made good use of the summer weather, and there was villein labour in plenty, once word had gone round that it was to be paid like the labour of free men and not exacted as manor dues. The site was completely cleared and levelled in a few weeks, since only a scattered, thin grass and a few starveling weeds had been able to find a foothold in the stripped rock, and the setting out of the plan showed that very little extra levelling required to be done. By the time Isambard rode to court at Woodstock in September the footing of the walls and the piers was laid, and the mason-hewers were hard at work at the bankers, and the setters already about the first courses of stonework for the walls. The carpenters were assembling poles and putlogs and hurdles and leather thongs for the scaffolding which would not be needed until the following spring. The master-carpenter, who had once been an assistant at Shrewsbury under Master Robert, was beginning the construction of centring for the great west window and the portal. And there were still six or seven weeks to run, with luck, before the onset of frosts would cause the setters to be laid off for the winter, and the rising walls would be bedded down warmly in heath and bracken.

Harry would have preferred to retain his team through the winter, but for this year that was impossible, since there was no indoor work for the setters. By next winter, if all went well, he would have a part of the fabric under cover, and keep his men on. Security and contentment made for sound work and rapid progress, in his experience. It had given him pleasure that more than half of the pressed men, once released to a free choice, had elected to stay with him.

Word of his straight dealings went round almost too successfully at first. Some of the brightest opportunists in the villages about the Long Mountain took this young master to be a simpleton, and came to hire their labour to him in the expectation of a soft living. Two kindred spirits with an empty hand-barrow between them could put up a very plausible appearance of zealous activity without any great expenditure in actual effort. Unfortunately for them the youngster turned out to have had experience with hard cases. They were marked down within a couple of days; those who were judged to be profitless were flung out without ceremony, and the few who seemed to be merely chancing their arm were picked out and set to work directly under Adam's eye, and kept hard at it until they had sweated out what they owed, with interest. Those who took exception to this treatment took themselves off in haste and were considered well lost; but there were a few who stuck it out in sheer obstinacy, determined to show they could do all and more than was demanded of them if they chose, and these Harry held to be worth the effort. When the driving stopped, they went on working; and they bore him no grudge for being their match, rather they liked him the better for it.

A few came who caused him more trouble. There were two big, bearded, weatherbeaten fellows whose looks he did not like, but he took them on as labourers none the less, and only at the end of the day had them stopped as they would have left the site, and found them swathed in cords and leather thongs from his stores. It seemed an insignificant haul for which to risk their lives, if they were what he deemed them to be, masterless men living wild in the forest. After some thought he made a search under the sheer edges of the plateau in the most secluded places, and found they had dropped a quantity of timber into the grass of a dingle on the English side, whence it could well be fetched away by night.

He turned them over to Sir Peter FitzJohn, Isambard's castellan, and before many hours wished he had not; for one of the two,

recognised as a footpad who had preyed on travellers along the
Roman road for two years and more, was hanged next day, and the
other, almost certainly of his company, fared no better, for when he
tried to break out of hold they loosed Isambard's Arabian hound on
him, and with speed and efficiency it ran him down and tore out his
throat.

Harry saw the beast come padding back docilely when the Greek
called him off, leaving the carcase without reluctance, having done
only what he had been trained to do. The tawny breast was streaked
with blood, the beautiful, rippling body moved proudly and gaily,
glossy with virtue. Harry felt the heat and filth of the blood sticking
to his hands, and he had not the dog's appalling innocence to cleanse
him.

"What are you fretting about?" said Adam impatiently. "They
were thieves, manifestly, and highway robbers by all accounts. What
the devil else could you do with them but turn them over to the
law?"

In spite of these endless echoes of law which left him so uneasy,
Harry could not but agree with that. "But what else could they do
but steal for a living?" he said wretchedly. "The big fellow was a
smith in some village near Caus, they say, until he was laid up with
a broken leg, and Corbett distrained on him. And the other was a
runaway villein, and most likely with good enough reason to run,
too."

"I should be the last man in the world to question that," said
Adam wryly, "but do me this justice, at least I never took to robbery
and murder for a living, and he was not forced to do so, neither."

Harry owned he was right, but could not feel happy about his
part in the affair. And when, somewhat later, he caught the boy
who clerked for him in his tracing-house abstracting cleaned parchments and chalks and other trifles for his own use, the first thing he
did was to bar the door against any intruder, so that no one else
should get wind of it. He could not let it pass, but he took care the
law should have no part in it this time, and all the boy got for his
pilfering was a half-hearted beating that fetched no tears, and a
talking-to that provoked a cloudburst. It ended with his bringing
some of his own tentative drawings to Harry, who commented on
them with hard criticism and sparing praise, but showed him how

to better them, and gave him all the materials he needed to continue his attempts, so that he no longer had any occasion to steal what he could have for the asking. The devoted shadow for ever under Harry's feet became a joke with Adam, but even Adam was never let into the cream of the joke.

That autumn the stone convoys from the quarry in the hills of Bryn came under their first attack from Wales. There was a mile or more to haul the stone down to the River Tanat, and then it was brought in boats down Tanat and Vrnwy and up the Severn, to a temporary quay in the meadows under the ridge of the Long Mountain. The haul of nearly two miles thence up to Parfois was a steep and hard one, but well protected. The trip by water was safe enough and cheap, though in spring, during the floods, they might have trouble. But the vulnerable part of the journey was the first mile to the Tanat, up there in the hills within a stone-throw of Wales, with nothing but the brook Cynllaith to fend off the tribesmen.

For a year now the prince of Powis had been kicking his heels as John's prisoner and living on John's sufferance, but for one incalculable neighbour they had gained another even more to be feared, for Llewelyn had swooped down like one of his own falcons from the peaks of Eryri as soon as Gwenwynwyn was under lock and key, and possessed himself of Powis to add to his northern stronghold of Gwynedd. It would be a marvel if he did not begin to style himself Prince of Wales soon. The unity of his country was clearly his ambition. And given the generous effort of the imagination to feel oneself Welsh instead of English, who could blame him?

He was, however, which was more to the point, at sworn odds with Isambard, and any baiting of his enemy which might be undertaken for sport by the hillmen of Cynllaith would certainly not be displeasing to their prince.

A messenger rode in from the quarry on a blown and foundering horse, with the news that raiders had come down on the wagons half a mile from the Tanat, killed two of the teamsters and scattered the rest, and dumped the loaded stone along the wayside, retiring with the oxen and the wagons. The teams were hired, and there would be compensation to pay, as well as an allowance to the widows of the men who had died. They could not afford constant repetitions of this expenditure in money; and men Harry never held to be expendable, on any terms. He flew to take counsel with FitzJohn, and laid down his demands as briskly as any general planning a campaign.

A company of archers and one of men-at-arms must be stationed permanently at the quarry; it was less open to attack than the wagons in transit, but it was the next idea that would occur to the playful Welshmen. An armed escort must convoy every wagon that passed down to the river, and a small guard must be posted at the place of loading. When the hard frosts began they could draw off all, and still have enough stone in store to work through the winter.

Harry rode for the quarry that same night with a small group of archers and men-at-arms, leaving the main body to follow next day. He was uneasy until he had satisfied himself that no full attack on the quarry itself was planned. However, he found the place quiet as a churchyard, and the quarrymen roused and mounting guard. With the first light he rode over the approaches with William of Beistan, who had charge of the camp, and marked out the best spots to post sentries on the Welsh side, so that the quarry should never be taken by surprise. When the armed companies rode in, about noon, he turned them over to William, and having slept for a couple of hours with the aplomb of a tired puppy, woke no less refreshed, and with three companions convoyed the two dead teamsters sombrely back to Parfois.

One of the dead was a man of forty-two and the father of a family; the other was a young fellow of twenty. Harry went to see the widow and the parents, and slashed out of the building funds a sum of money in gift to them which would almost certainly be questioned by Knollys when they went through the rolls together. There was nothing more he could do, except give them the bodies for burial, and that must be burial without rites. These two had even died unshriven. He rode back up the ridge from the widow's poor hovel with a heavy heart. But at least he'd lose no more men to Welsh arrows if he could help it.

A week later word came that a second tentative attack had been beaten off without loss to the English, and though the raiders had carried away their three wounded successfully, one at least of them was thought to be mortally hurt.

"Well done!" said Isambard. "But I would it were Gwynedd himself!"

Harry wanted neither Welsh nor English dead, but if they came baiting Isambard out of wantonness with little to gain, they could hardly complain of their reception. No doubt in time they would learn to let well alone.

"What fashion of man is this Prince of Gwynedd?" asked Harry, his charcoal sweeping down the long, beautiful line that outlined her cheek and neck and shoulder. "Did you see him in Woodstock?"

"I saw him. Not at court, even Ralf would hesitate to present his mistress to his king," said Benedetta, with the candour which no longer disconcerted him. "I saw them meet in the street once and ride by each other, neither giving way. There was no more than a few inches clearance between their knees as they passed, but they would not rein aside. He has a quick, warm way with him, fierce but gay. He looked at us, and looked curiously, and I think would have spoken, but my lord looked through him as though he had not been there. And once I saw him walking in the garden with his princess on his arm."

"And is he indeed the devil?"

"Only to an Englishman," said Benedetta. "To my alien eyes he is a goodly man. Uncommon tall for a Welshman, as tall as my lord and very dark. He shaves his cheeks and chin, but wears long, soft moustaches. He is all shadow and light, the lines of him are cut so deep. I found it a strong and clever face. But for all its boldness, too good-humoured to belong to a devil. Did you never see him, then? They say he has often met the king in Shrewsbury."

"I've lived all my boyhood on earth that trembled when he stamped his foot, but never set eyes on him. My lord has had manors burned and garrisons killed by more than one honest enemy in his time; why is he so set against this one rather than the rest?"

She considered that thoughtfully for a while, sitting perfectly still as he had posed her, her head thrown back against the high back of the chair. The grey wintry light filtering in through the tracing-house windows, a dead, still, January light that would not last two hours past noon, burned into living warmth in the sheaves of her red hair, that grew from her temples with an upward curve like the curl of a wave.

"I think it is chiefly that he recognises a man who in more than stature is as large as himself. They are not so common, Harry. When he encounters one he cannot be indifferent. He might love, he might hate, but he could not be indifferent. And a little thing then is enough to decide between hate and love. Once in," she said, turning her head suddenly to look directly into Harry's eyes, "you know he knows no half measures. He both loves and hates to the death—his death or the other's. He has told the king to his face that he'll come no more to court while the Prince of Gwynedd is made welcome there."

"Is Llewelyn such another, do you think?"

"Ah, Llewelyn is a man with a cause. He is safe from hates, I judge, for he has an overmastering love. I think he is no more aware of my lord than of any other peer of his who stands between him and the unity of Wales, or advances a foot across the border of her liberty. I think he is the most single-minded man I ever saw. Ralf would sacrifice his life, perhaps, for a cause, but nothing that touched him more nearly." She smiled at the paradox, but let it stand. "Not his faith and truth, not his pride. If John's life hung on Ralf's breaking his word, John would surely die. If Ralf could make England safe for ever by kissing King Philip's shoe, England would have to go in peril still. But—"

"But at Woodstock," Harry took up gravely, "Llewelyn knelt with the other Welsh princes and did homage to King John for his princedom."

"That is something I am glad I did not have to see," she said. "And yet I dare swear that when he knelt to John and put his hands between John's hands, he never lost a whit of his dignity, nor the devotion of one clansman who looks to him as his prince. It seems to me, Harry, that sometimes honour may depend on abasing oneself rather than on guarding one's self-esteem, and faith on breaking one's word rather than on keeping it."

"Not to me," said Harry, curling his lip.

"No, I never supposed it would to you," she conceded, smiling. "You are utterly of Ralf's breed, I know it."

"And you would not lie, nor break faith, nor humble yourself, either," he said forcefully, his eyes flashing between his drawing-board and her face in fiery, absorbed glances. "Not for any cause."

"Would I not?" said Benedetta mildly.

"No more than I would. And as for the Prince of Gwynedd, he is in good odour with the king, and for my part I think he swore fealty in all good faith, and it will not be broken unless this goodwill between them is clean broken, too. It is not the first time the Welsh princes have done homage to the king of England. And he fought for him honestly against the Scots in the summer. After all, he is married to the king's daughter."

"He is. Of all the women in this land, I think she has the most difficult part. If she were not his match I should pity her, but being the woman she is I think she needs no pity. Balancing such a father and such a husband, loving both, preserving either from the enmity of the other, that's no life for any but the greatest of women. Do you suppose she has not abased herself a hundred times, to John for Llewelyn, to Llewelyn for John? Do you suppose she has not lied and deceived to keep them from each other's throats? The pride of women must be a different kind of pride," she said, and shivered a little, for in the tracing-house in the outer ward it was very cold, and she had been sitting still for him until she was chilled even in her furs.

"And their honesty another kind of honesty?" Harry laid down his charcoal, and stood back from his work. "Come and see! Ah, you're cold to the bone! I'm sorry, I did not think. When I'm drawing I forget everything." He had taken her hand with perfect simplicity, and stood chafing it between his palms. She drew it away only to take up the parchment and look at it more closely.

It was the design for a capital, not a portrait. Out of the neck-moulding the long line of her stretched throat grew like a lily-stem whitening into the flower, and her face, simplified and yet most vividly her face still, looked up into the sun from between the uplifted wings of her hair. The blown locks, coiling and twining, held up the abacus as the strong jet of a fountain holds up a rose-leaf.

"It's beautiful," she said, "and I am proud. You must have a hundred such drawn out ready for the stone by now, I've seen you

at it day after day since you put the walls into their winter sleep.
But you'll have to trust many of them to other hands to carve. Are
you not afraid they'll spoil your work?"

"I shall do the marking-out for them all, and see that they're
properly executed. And all the piers of the nave I shall keep for
myself." He could not have borne to part with any one of them. He
saw an aisle in a stone forest, with every slender tree bursting into
matched bud.

"Will you show me your designs?" said Benedetta, turning on
him shining eyes, in which the reflection of his own inward excitement burned generously.

He opened the chest gladly, and spread them on his tracing-tables
for her to see, drawing after drawing; the bay designs of nave and
choir and transepts, the plan of the nave vault, where all the sixfold
buds of the holy forest burst at last into slender sevenfold branches,
sealed together by a roof-rib, and knotted with clusters of starry
flowers; drawings of the many separate mouldings for the west
doorway and the great window above, with its multiple lancets and
tracery of roses, of the elevation of the tower, tapered very subtly
stage by stage and elegantly elongated by delicate free shafts, so that
at any hour of day it would stand outlined in fine vertical lights and
shadows.

"I have heard," said Benedetta, "that towers must be built by
easy stages, not more than perhaps fifteen feet in a year, to allow
for some degree of settling. Is it true?"

"It is, and you are always astonishing me by the things you
know," he said, smiling; "but here we are on solid rock and could
not be better founded, and I shall be able to build faster. And these,
look, these are what I am hoarding up for myself. No one else shall
touch them, except perhaps Adam. No, not even Adam! I can't give
them up."

His hands moved with love even on the drawings, he flushed like
an eager child showing his treasures; and without words she was
suddenly aware that she was honoured with a gift beyond price to
her, though he laid it in her breast unawares.

The capitals of the nave, six to a pier, he set out before her one
by one, tenderly and reverently. She saw everything that had breath
praising God, her own wrists and hands reaching up to sustain the

roof of his abode, the waves of the sea curling strongly upward, Isambard's face with parted lips and pulsing throat like a prophesying angel, his greyhound leaping, his falcon soaring on spread wings, branches blown in the wind, strong, vital flowers, all charmed into those pure, impetuous fountain-shapes, schooled to receive the upward surge of the columns and transmit it in a renewed thrust of exultant energy into the crest of the vault. She saw an entire world met in one impulse of worship, and giving to God the supreme service of its wonderful diversity.

There were many faces, many portraits. She recognised the thin, sharp, dark features of children from the villages in the folds of the uplands, where she often rode, and the misshapen body and derisory legs of a dwarf who begged food sometimes at the gates, weighed down by the great, patient head whose nobility she saw now for the first time. And this one was new, an old woman cradling a dead youth in her lap. At first she took it to be a pietá put into this local shape to bring it nearer home, then she knew it for the mother of the young teamster, nursing her dead. How much he had seen since this vision came upon him, and how much of what he had seen disquieted him! The hapless, wary, intelligent faces of the poor looked out at her from the work of his hands with a direct challenge forbidden to them in the flesh. Did he even know what he was doing, in setting before his lord and his lord's world the revelation that had visited him? Had he himself recognised it for what it was? Not, she thought, consciously yet, not with his mind; but the heart was aware of what moved it, and the hands knew what they did.

"I begin to know these leaves," she said. They were everywhere, the arching, coiling, thrusting leaves, jets of life growing irrepressibly towards the light. Men and beasts and birds looked out from their shelter. "They are like nothing I have ever seen anywhere else. Not in Italy, not in France. Those precise Roman capitals I know, but these are of another world."

"And which do you like better?"

"These," she said at once, and warmly. "They belong to the stem. They grow. Those others are stuck on."

Always, now, she knew when she had pleased him, though he never expressed his pleasure. When he was most glad and satisfied, then he was most silent.

"They live and grow, but they are like no leaves that ever grew in our world. The more's the pity!" She traced the vigorous, curling lines of them with a cold fingertip, and stood looking down with a faint and rather ironical smile. "What are they? You made them, you should know."

"You are right," he said sombrely, gathering the drawings together. "They don't grow in this world. They're the leaves of the heaven tree, this stone tree we're about growing outside the gates."

"And what is the fruit of this tree?" She looked up at him just in time to see the gravity and doubt and wonder in his face, before he turned and smiled at her.

"Kingdoms. Little kingdoms of hope for the villein and the outcast and the landless man. Freedom for the unfree, ease for the overborne, plenty for the hungry, safety for the runaway. All the desire of the heart, for the heart that never yet had its desire."

He fell silent there because of the look in her eyes, suddenly pierced to the very soul by all that she had not said, all that she had sworn never to say to him again. He felt Gilleis knot her small fingers in the roots of his heart, and knew in his own body the anguish Benedetta carried like a monstrous child in hers. He had never been so near to any living creature, not even to Adam, as he was then to her.

"But they never ripen," she said, with the rueful smile that had grown to be one of the flowers of his world. "We're promised that they will in the world to come, if we study to deserve. But they never ripen here. I see you know it, for you have drawn only the leaves, never the fruit."

She shook her shoulders, shrugging off the suddenly falling sadness that came so strangely out of the joy and certainty of the images he had made. "I must go, he will be back from riding soon. But if you will let me I should like to be here sometimes when you are working."

"Come when you will," he said, "you'll be welcome."

She was at the door when he said her name, the first time he had ever called her by it. "Benedetta!" And when she turned, startled and moved, he came to her quickly and took her hand, and kissed it. Wanting words of his own, he found her words in his mouth and they did well enough. "Sweet friend!" he said.

Chapter Ten

*H*arry awoke suddenly in the young summer night, and turned over in his broad bed, and missed something beside him, a warmth, a soft sound of breathing, something without which his peace was gone. He stretched out a hand, feeling for Adam, and the other half of the bed was empty and cold.

It awoke him fully, but did not disturb him. Through the shot-window he could see the brilliance of the moonlight, and the night air was mild and sweet as noon. After the long winter and the slow spring it was delicious to be able to lie naked in the highest room of the Warden's Tower. Vaguely he wondered which of the many possible young women about the outer bailey could be the magnet which had drawn Adam out of his bed. It was past time for the boy to fall in love again. The marvel was that he had continued immune so long. Élie would never have credited that Adam could go a whole year with his eyes fixed only on his work.

He dozed for a while, but woke up again to a nagging uneasiness. Had there not been signs to be read in Adam lately? And not signs of his old spring fever, either. When Adam was in love he did not fall silent, he talked, and every well-disposed person about him soon knew all there was to be known of his condition.

Harry slid out of bed, wrapped himself in his surcoat, and went out to the tower stair, its narrow treads already hollowed slightly by many feet. The mere fretting of a man's feet passing once a day, he thought, can wear out stone in the end. The weather, and the wind, and the rooting of infinitesimal seeds in the crannies wind and weather have made, will fret away my work at last, but I shall be long dead, and my children and grandchildren after me. None the less, he thought of the ages smoothing away the clear lines of his carving, blunting the incisive edges of the leaves of heaven, rounding the sharp, wary features of the villein faces to a worn resignation before it returned them to stones; and a fiery pang of rage and jealousy pricked his heart, to think that even these into whom he had breathed a longer life than his own should die at last. A good stone, a lasting stone; but even the mountains wear away slowly and crumble into dust.

He came out on to the leaded roof of the Warden's Tower, and the upper stages of the keep rose beside him, vast and pale in the moonlight. No sentry was posted here, for the turret on the King's Tower covered the same field of vision, and something beyond in either direction. Between the merlons of the battlements on the Welsh side Adam leaned on his elbows, staring down into the Severn valley, which lay open before him in silver and green, from Pool, up-river, where Wales looked near enough to touch, to the solid grey shape of Strata Marcella, down-river among its level meadows.

He walked across the open space to Adam's side, his bare feet making no sound, and laid an arm about the hunched shoulders. Adam started and turned great eyes on him.

"Oh, it's you!" he said with a faint smile. "What are you doing awake at this hour? I left you snoring." He frowned at the naked feet. "Have you the wit you were born with, to get out of a warm bed and wander about barefoot on the leads?"

"I woke and missed you," said Harry. "What ails you, to get up like this in the night?"

"I couldn't sleep. The moonlight, most likely, it was full on my side of the bed."

"There's more than moonlight making you uneasy," said Harry, settling his arm about his brother's shoulders, and spreading an elbow on the stone beside him. "My mind misgives me that there's been a deal wrong with you for a long time, and I've been too much occupied to take note of it. If it's been my fault for not listening, I'm sorry for it, and I'm listening now. What's amiss?"

Adam hoisted a shoulder against him ill-humouredly, and stared at the coiling ribbon of the river, far below. For a moment he was silent, then he rounded on him abruptly, and burst out: "Harry, I must go home!"

"So that's it!" said Harry. "Well, it's better out than in. What's come over you to turn homesick now, when you've been away from it for ten years, and never given it a thought?" He had not meant to sound that note, but already he felt himself stiffening involuntarily against the idea, and the asperity that spoiled the tone of his voice was the fruit of his own uneasiness.

"I have thought of it," said Adam hotly, "many a time, but it was a long way off, and what was the use of fretting about it when I'd no chance of getting back?"

"You were happy enough!"

"I know I was. Have I said I wasn't? We've seen and done fine things together, and I've enjoyed every day of it. But that doesn't mean I forgot I had a family. I didn't grieve about it when they were out of reach, but they're not out of reach now, they're here in the same shire with me. I want to see them, Harry. I've got to see them! My mother hasn't clapped eyes on me for ten years, and the boys will be men. And my father's getting no younger. I don't even know if he's still alive! I can't stand it any longer, I must go home."

"If you felt so strongly," said Harry, breaking into unreasonable anger, "I take it unfriendly that you've never told me of it. If you want to leave me—"

"Don't be a fool!" cried Adam, outraged. "You know I don't! I only want to see my mother and brothers again and let them know I'm in the land of the living still. And as for telling you of it, I've tried times enough. The minute I speak to you of anything that isn't stone you stop hearing me. I asked you for the time to ride down and visit them once, but I got my nose bitten off for it."

"I didn't know it was for that you wanted your freedom. We

were just cutting the voussoirs for the portal arch, you were needed here."

"You didn't know because you shut your ears, then, for I said it plainly enough. But no, you gave me to understand where my duty lay and I let you have the last word. But now I'll not be put off any more, I'm going."

"You'll go nowhere," said Harry flatly. "You're still Talvace's runaway villein, for all the ten years you've been clear of Sleapford. You'd be hard put to it to prove a year's free residence at law, for it's not yet a year we've been here at Parfois together, and all the rest of the time there's no English witness can answer for us. Even at best, we're in no charter borough here. It would go hard if you had to make your case in a court. Stay here and you're safe enough, no sane man would come and try to take you from Isambard. But once show your face in Sleapford, and Ebrard can clap you in hold whenever he pleases—"

"Ebrard?" said Adam sharply, jerking up his head to stare. He thrust himself off quickly from the parapet, and took Harry by the arms. "What's this of Ebrard? Are we not reckoning with your father any more?"

"He's dead, three years and more ago. Father Hugh let fall the news when I visited him, thinking I was from home then, and knew it already. And afterwards Edmund told me the how and when of it. He had a falling seizure, and lay a month in his bed, and then the second fit carried him off. Likely my mother's married again by now, for she's in Gloucester's gift, and she has some land of her own. And Ebrard would be wanting her out of the house if he's married or thinking of marriage. Think of it he will, for land's land, and there are some heiresses growing up among the neighbours, or there were when we left home, if they're not all taken by now. But there's still Ebrard himself to deal with, and he'll not let go a possession easily, you may lay to that."

"And you never said a word!" said Adam wonderingly. "I tried to get news in the town that day, but I was chary of naming names, and I found folk too uneasy to give even the time of day to a stranger. Oh, I can be cautious, too, when it's a matter of my freedom."

He shook Harry back and forth lightly between his hands, and grinned at him with restored good-humour. "But now I'm resolved, and you won't turn me. I can be in and out of Sleapford unnoticed, before Ebrard even gets wind of it. I mean to see my mother if the devil himself stand in the way."

"You shan't go! I won't let you take such a risk!"

"*You* won't let me?" mocked Adam. "Do you want me to lay you on your back, lad, and trim your ears for you? I can still do it, one-handed, if you want to be shown." He had made up his mind, nothing could put him out of temper now. Only irresolution could cast those shadows of silence and withdrawal upon him.

"Do you know why you don't want me to go?" he said, locking his arms about Harry and holding him fast. "Because if I go, and find all well and the way open, and not a soul holding a grudge against us, you'll have no excuse for not going home yourself any longer. And you don't want to go! Or rather, you want it and you don't want it. You're afraid of what you'll find, afraid of being rebuffed, afraid of losing what kindness you have left for them, and gaining nothing. You're afraid of opening old wounds and starting old hates, when you feel the want of a fixed and quiet mind so that you can do what you have to do, and do it well. Don't you see that the only way to be free of them all is to go back and face them? You could be at rest after that, whether it turned out well or ill. It's the not venturing that undoes you, Harry."

Harry twisted furiously in the prisoning arms, but could not break free. "It isn't true!" he said hotly, turning his head aside to avoid Adam's challenging eyes. "I haven't given them a thought, one way or the other, and I don't suppose they've ever a thought between them to spare for me. Why should they? All that's ten years past and over."

Nonetheless, what Adam had thrown at him was no more than the truth. He had not, indeed, consciously been thinking of his family, but since he had returned to England they had lain secretly in his heart like a heavy burden, a duty on which he had turned his back, or an ordeal he shrank from facing. Adam was right, he would never be free of them until he had encountered them again. At the thought of meeting with his mother his bowels melted into a scalding liquefaction of tenderness and fear and grief. How if she were ne-

glected in her widowhood and lonely, and he did not go to her? How
if he heard of her death, and had to live out his own life in the
certainty that he had shortened hers by his defection?

"It's easy for me," said Adam gently, "everything I left behind
at home was love and kindness, and I want it back, and no buts about
it. I'll bring you word, lad, and ride back with you if all promises
well."

"No!" said Harry fiercely, gulping down his lesson. "I'll go first.
There's still the matter of your freedom. I must talk to Ebrard and
get his word for it he'll not claim you. I'll ride home today," he said
with decision, shutting his hands upon Adam's shoulders, "and in
two days more you shall have your will."

From the head of the long, wandering track through the village he
saw the church tower and the shingled roof that had grown dilapi-
dated in the two years of the interdict. He saw the striped fields
rising on the left, outlined in red because the headlands that divided
the selions were full of poppies, and on the other side the fallow
strips from which a few greedy souls, here and there, were trying
to filch an extra crop. He had often felt it shame, when he was
serving his brief apprenticeship as steward here and taking his new
duties very seriously, that a whole moiety of the village fields should
lie idle every year. Three fields would be better than two; if they
put their minds and resources to work they could cut a third field
out of the waste and bring it under plough.

He had ridden in by the mill through Tourneur land, and the
memories crowded in upon him oppressively. Over there in the
forest Adam had killed the doe. Here in the paddock at the mill they
had left the horses, and from here he had brought them at dead of
night down to the copse by the river. There was a young man
stooping by the overshot wheel of the mill, just raising the sluice
that blocked the head-race; he saw that it must be Wilfred, by the
red hair, but this young giant looked so improbably a development
of the Wilfred he remembered, and gave him such a hard, unre-
cognising look with his greeting, that he was too shy to make himself
known. On his way down through the village no one hailed him by
name, and his tongue stuck to the roof of his dry mouth when he

would have claimed old friends. No, there would be time for that later, when he had faced whatever welcome awaited him at the manor.

He saw the long wall rise into sight, and the squat grey tower looking over it, and his heart turned in him. He did not know what he had expected, but now, as he drew near to the gate-house, he felt at once lost and comforted. The place was unchanged to outward view, and his recollections of it were sharp and clear and curiously ambivalent, charged with burning indignation and wincing guilt. But the porter who came out to ask his business was a stranger to him, and looked at him with the guarded interest he would have given to any unknown traveller. In that impersonal regard he felt all his expectations of pain and high feeling beginning to founder.

"Sir Ebrard's in the armoury," said the porter. "If you'll please to wait, sir, till I tell him who's inquiring?"

"I'll go to him," said Harry, dismounting. "I know my way. Time was when I was at home here. Never fear, Sir Ebrard knows me."

The armoury had a new roof, and so had the dovecote. He was glad to see that Ebrard was keeping the place up properly. In the smithy someone was shaping a hilt for a dagger. It was not the old smith, but a lusty young fellow not above twenty-five. Likely the old man was gone to his rest like his master. One decade can swallow a whole generation of old men.

Ebrard was bending above the anvil, watching the work, his back turned towards the doorway, but he saw the fall of the newcomer's shadow athwart the light, and looked round casually, expecting one of the men-at-arms. He had filled out a great deal between nineteen and twenty-nine. It would take a stouter horse to carry him now. By the time he's fifty, thought Harry with astonishment, for he had somewhat envied his brother his elegance of person, he'll be fatter than father was. But with his height and his finer bones at least he'll carry it better.

The blue eyes narrowed, staring against the light. The tall body straightened, aware of a stranger.

"I trust I see you well, Sir Ebrard," said Harry.

"You!" said Ebrard, and drew a long breath. "Well, well!" he said. "This is something we never looked to see."

"I have been out of England until last summer, this was my first opportunity to visit you. And it is but a visit," he said, to forestall any apprehensions Ebrard might entertain concerning his intentions. "Make no special provision for me, I beg you. I have work going forward at Parfois and cannot leave it for long. I came only to assure myself that all went well with you here, and with my mother."

Ebrard laid down the dagger and walked forth into the court. He took the hand Harry offered, and leaned to kiss his cheek, with so punctilious a civility that it was clear he felt himself to be entertaining a stranger, though with a stranger he would have been less at a loss.

"You'll have heard of father's death?"

The note of bewilderment in his voice was for their brotherhood, which he acknowledged but could no longer feel. The thought that they shared a father set them at an even greater distance from each other.

"I heard it only when I returned to England. It was late then to feel sorrow. I fear I gave him no great satisfaction while he was alive. I hope mother is in good health?"

"In excellent health. I might do well," said Ebrard, checking in his march across the court and casting a frowning side-glance at his visitor, "to send and prepare her before you go in to her. You'll understand, she's not looked for you these many years. First we thought you dead, and then—"

"Gone past returning," said Harry.

"There was little in your going to make us think you would ever come back." The blue eyes searched him again, rapidly and shrewdly. "At least while father was alive," added Ebrard deliberately.

"It wasn't fear of him that kept me away," said Harry, taking this to be his brother's meaning, "nor anger against him, either. Once Adam was safe from him I got over that quickly enough. But we had to keep running until we were clear of pursuit, and we ran ourselves into France before we ventured to stop, and with the novelty of it, and being very busy earning a living, we never had time to cast a thought back to Sleapford. I don't suppose father lost his sleep for long, either."

"He was very bitter against you," said Ebrard. "It's so long ago now I don't remember the exact way of it, but I know he wouldn't have your name mentioned, once he'd fairly accepted you were gone. He came round in his later years, but I wouldn't say he ever really forgave you."

"Then I have the better of him, for I forgive him."

"It's because you had the better of him that you can afford to," said Ebrard drily. "What have you been doing since then? How have you lived? And is that foster-brother of yours still with you?"

This last question Harry chose to ignore, but answered the others readily enough as they climbed the steps to the hall door side by side.

"I marvel you could find any inducement to come back here," said Ebrard at the end of the brief story, "when you've done so well for yourself." The name of Isambard had impressed him; the master-mason who had such a patron was clearly a made man.

"Inducement? After all, I am a son of this house, too, and my name is Talvace, like yours."

Again he caught the narrow, sidelong flash of the blue eyes, and felt the momentary silence sharp as a knife slashing between them; and suddenly he heard his own words as Ebrard was hearing them, and could have laughed aloud.

So that was what worked so uneasily behind the fair forehead and probing glances! Ebrard feared that he was come to claim a share in what Sir Eudo had left, and was at pains to show him that he had forfeited the old man's favour and his own filial rights; and he, with his, 'I am a son of this house' and his 'my name is Talvace, like yours,' had unwittingly caused the ground to tremble under his brother's knightly heels. He opened his lips impatiently to reassure him, and then thought better of it. No, let him sweat! Let him dangle on the hook for an hour or two. He had been on the point of exclaiming scornfully that he wanted nothing from him; but on reflection there was indeed one thing at least he wanted, and Ebrard might be only too pleased to compound with him on those terms. Why stick at demanding only Adam's legal freedom? He could very well bargain for the parents and the young brothers, too. He had a good legal claim to some part of the estate, though it had always been accepted that the land must not be divided. By the time he had taken note of all the evidences of prosperity here, and shown a marked interest in every improvement to the demesne and every handsome beast in stock, Ebrard would think himself lucky to get off at the cost of only one villein family. In the long run he would not even lose by it. He would gain a rent for the toft, and William Boteler and his sons would be able to give all their time to their trade, and make more profit out of it, whereby the whole village would benefit.

Perhaps one of the boys might choose to come and work with Adam at Parfois. But first he had to play Ebrard safely to land, and if he took an impish pleasure in it, at least it was without malice; he had no ill designs on even one square foot of the poor soul's inheritance.

There was a newly-laid stone hearth in the middle of the hall, under the smoke-blacked beams of the lofty roof, and a new carved balustrade to the solar staircase. Harry admired both, and complimented Ebrard on his good management with a bright, appraising face.

"Mother's within," said Ebrard, putting this aside quickly. "I'd better go up first and let her know of your coming."

"No, not for anything! I'll not be broken gently, like bad news. Let me go up to her alone, I promise you the shock won't harm her, I want to be recognised and taken to her heart, not ushered in like a packman trying to sell her pins."

"She may not be alone," said Ebrard with a wary glance. "My young clerk reads to her sometimes of an afternoon. She finds needlework tries her eyes of late."

Harry halted on the stairs to look back for an instant in doubt. "You said she was well!"

"She is well, and blooming, too, you'll see for yourself. My lord of Gloucester wants her to marry again. There's a knight of his he wants to give her to, and I believe the match will be made very soon."

"If the bridegroom doesn't please her—" Harry began with a frowning face.

A brief, cynical and almost lewd smile twitched at Ebrard's handsome mouth for a moment. "He does please her! He's ten years younger than she is, and a nice-looking fellow into the bargain. He's the one will need to have the draught sweetened."

It was the nearest they had ever come to exchanging views on their mother, and Harry did not find it pleasant. Such disillusioning discoveries as he had made about her he had always kept to himself, and always forgiven, though sometimes after a painful struggle. He drew away hastily, and ran up the stairs, and with a sudden tremor of nervousness knocked on the door of the solar before he went in. There was a moment of silence, and then her voice, pitched rather high with surprise, called to him to enter.

She was sitting in the window embrasure, and he saw her first as a clear outline against the light, and thought her miraculously unchanged. She had on a gown of green cloth, and a bliaut of yellow brocade over it; in these, and in the coif of gilt net and the necklet of rough amber, there was more of the bride than of the widow. The young clerk, a boy of about twenty, frocked and tonsured, sat on a stool at her feet, bent attentively over his book, though if he had indeed been reading it must have been in a very subdued voice.

Lady Talvace was peering towards the door with a look of surprise and inquiry on her fair, soft face. Harry closed the door behind him, and came forward a few steps into the room, where the light could shine on him. She blinked at him, and looked again and caught her breath.

"Sir, I had not expected—my eyes are playing me tricks, for a moment I thought—You're very like Harry!"

"I am Harry," he said, very gently.

She clasped and wrung her hands in a gesture of such spontaneous joy that his heart leaped in answer. Then she was on her feet, and had sprung past the tonsured boy, almost thrusting him from his stool in her haste, and in a moment she was in Harry's arms, weeping, laughing, babbling like an excited child, and covering his face with kisses. She wound her arms about his neck, and drew him down cheek to cheek with her, holding him with all her strength.

"Harry, Harry, my dear, dear Hal—!"

The clerk rose, drawing aside to the wall to creep about them as unobtrusively as possible on his way to the door. But over his mother's shoulder Harry saw the extraordinary look the boy gave him, the furtive, grimacing smile, half jealousy and offence, half sniggering collusion, and knew that she had found one more adoring youth to help her pass the time pleasantly, and one who had not been kept at arm's length, either. She could not help it, it was useless to blame her. It was not a vice in her, but only an instinctive appetite, like the earth's need of rain. A son, a baby-faced clerk, a new young husband, they all came alike to her. Deprived of one, she would find another.

He held her in his arms, and was eased of all his fears. He had come here steeled in advance for tragedy and tension, but he should have known the reality would be small and ordinary and confused, the usual sorry condition of man. They were too slight to contain the passion his imagination had bestowed on them; he had better recognise his own inadequacy along with theirs, and resign himself to it.

"Harry, you wicked, cruel boy, how could you stay away so long? How could you forsake me? When you ran away like that you broke my heart."

He held her tenderly and smiled over her shoulder. Surely she had wept bitterly over his flight, but there had been no breakages. His return made her happy, but she had no real need of him, she could get her happiness in a thousand other ways.

When she had cried enough, she held him off and examined him critically, emerging from tears resiliently, without disfigurement. She exclaimed with delight over him, said how well-grown he was and how handsome, which he knew to be false except as her eyes conferred beauty on him; and when he had told her everything that had happened to him since his flight, but for that part of the story which contained Gilleis and was for ever secret and holy because of her, his mother exclaimed over his prowess and his adventures no less generously, and kissed him again, and began to chatter of herself. Did he think she was looking well? She looked like a girl, and so he told her. She was a little plumper, perhaps, a little softer, her fair, pale flesh had slackened very slightly, a few lines marked the corners of her eyes, but her hair was as bright as ever, and her smiling face as charming. Gloucester's young knight would not need much persuasion to the match.

They sat together in the window, and she blushed as she told him of the projected marriage. She was already getting together her wardrobe for the occasion, and jumped up to turn slowly before him and ask if he admired her dress, for it was new.

"I have such a wonderful tirewoman now, Harry, she understands stuffs better than any maid I ever had. Do you remember Hawis, who used to weave cloths for me, the girl who wanted to marry a free man from Hunyate? She ran away with him, the ungrateful hussy, and left me with a gown half-finished."

"Did you ever hear what became of them?" asked Harry innocently.

"Not a word from that day to this. I suppose they must have left the shire. I could never get a girl who knew her business for years after that, but now I have a real treasure. She can cut so beautifully—see the shaping of this sleeve. Her father was in the woollen trade, so she knows how to buy to advantage. She's making me a green pelisse." She brought cuttings of cloth to show him, and drew him to her over them, her arm about his neck. "Harry, must you go away again?"

"I must, Mother, I must go back to my work. But I shall not be far from you now; if you need me you can send word to me."

"At least you must sleep the night here; it's too long a ride to Parfois, and it would be folly to ride these roads at night."

"Gladly and gratefully, Mother. Shall I have my room in the tower again?—do you remember how you came to me there? When I was locked in, that night? You came to comfort me and I knew I was going to leave you. I asked you not to think ill of me."

"I never did, dear Hal!" she said and kissed him. And indeed she had never thought ill of anyone, or never for more than half an hour together. "Wait for me a little while, Harry. I must go and see about making your bed, and set the supper forward. I'll come back very quickly."

When she had left the room he picked up the shreds of cloth idly, and carried them to the window to examine the colours in a good light. All the tension had gone out of him, there were no more ordeals to face, no more pain or joy to be anticipated, he was tired out with relief. He stood looking out across the courtyard, without a thought or an idea in him, too content and too full of lassitude as yet to look even one step ahead. He must and he would talk Adam's full and indisputable freedom out of Ebrard, and deliver all his family with him, but that could wait until after supper, and until then Ebrard could fret jealously over his inheritance in anticipation of the attack which would never be launched. Now he felt nothing but a kind of helpless languor, at once pleasant and disappointing.

He heard the door open, but did not turn until some new lightness and length in the entering step, some different quality in the rustle of the flowing skirt made him aware that this was not his mother. When he turned his head the girl had her back to him, and was just closing the door. He saw the folds of the green pelisse draped carefully over her shoulder and arm, the hood swinging lightly against a waist he could have spanned in his two hands. This must be the wonderful tirewoman. Out of his lassitude he admired the long, smooth movement of her arm and hand in the close-fitting red sleeve, and the black coils of her hair braided high on her head within a narrow gold ribbon. But how truly wonderful was his mother's treasure he did not know until she turned to cross the room and lay out her work upon the table, and for the first time realised that she was not alone.

She made no sound, but she halted, and drew back her head with a start as mettlesome and wild as that of a forest creature recoiling from the touch of a hand. Great black eyes, gay and gallant, opened wide at him above pale cheeks that suddenly flushed radiantly red. A mouth like a budding rose opened and cried "Harry!" loudly and gladly, and curved into a laugh of joy.

He sprang down out of the window embrasure, trembling. "Gilleis!" he said in a shout of delight, and snatched her into his arms.

"How did you get here?" he asked, when he had breath for anything but kissing, and without slackening his greedy hold of her for a moment. The pale prints of his lips on her cheek and chin and throat flushed slowly to rose. She kept her eyes tightly closed, and smiled and smiled on his shoulder with a triumphant delight. When she had her breath again she laughed aloud. "I looked for you in London. They told me about your father. I'm sorry from my heart, love, that I never showed him my gratitude. And they told me you were gone to join the household of some noble lady, out of the city, but could not tell me where. Everywhere along the road I've been asking after you, and nowhere any word. And now I find you here!"

"They didn't tell you," she said breathlessly, "that my uncle wanted me to marry to his liking. The poor creature he threatened me with wasn't the only bidder, either. That's why I took good care not even my cousin, who's a harmless soul enough, should know where to find me. If I'd left a message for you, some other would have taken the advantage of it. And I knew you'd find me in the end."

"But how did you come to know my mother in the first place?"

"It was very easy. You had talked of her a great deal, I knew she liked dresses, and I knew she had lost her special sewing-girl. The next year I persuaded my father to go a little out of his way with some of the Flemish stuffs he took north with him, and visit Sleapford, and she bought some brocades and velvet from us. We used to come here every year after that, and when I was older I began to show her how the stuffs could best be cut and made up, and then to stay with her and sew for her the week or two while my father completed his business in Shrewsbury, until she could hardly get on without me and begged me to stay and be her tirewoman. But I never would, because I could not leave father."

"But all this—I don't understand. To what end?"

"To get news of you, simpleton," she said, and drew his head down to her and kissed the corner of his mouth. "And you have no need to labour so to get such avowals out of me, for I'm ready to shout them from the battlements."

"And I never sent word! If I'd known, if I'd known—!"

"It did not surprise me. I knew you for an unfeeling wretch, with no eyes and no wits for anything but your precious stone. But I knew you'd come in the end. So when father died, and I wanted to escape being pestered—and let me tell you, there were some better bargains than you among my suitors, Master Harry Talvace, if I were not such a fool as to love you!—I came here to your mother, and she received me kindly, and here I've been ever since. And a fine time it's taken you to remember you had a mother!"

"Until last summer I was in France still. And since I came back I've held off because—oh, because I wanted the courage to face it. If I'd known what I stood to gain I'd have been on the doorstep months ago. But how could I guess? How could I dream you'd be here, of all places?"

"Of all places!" she mocked. "Where else should I be? Only here could I be sure that one day I should meet with you again. I knew you'd return to England some day, and then you'd surely come back here to see your mother. Not to stay, I knew that. Not to live in this house again. But you'd come! I could not come to you. I could only take my stand where you must some day come to me."

"And if you had been mistaken?" he asked, tightening his arms about her fearfully. "If I had never come?"

"If I had been mistaken in you," said Gilleis, "no one could have helped me. As well live out my life here as anywhere else. But I was not mistaken."

"You love me!" he said in a hushed voice, not exulting, marvelling.

"Always, ever since I touched your cheek among the bales of cloth, when I reached for my ball." She touched it again, very lightly, and felt him tremble. "Do you remember? You couldn't speak, they were too near us. You caught my hand and kissed it. And I began to love you. You were full of tricks of the kind," she said resentfully. "When I was angry with you for laughing at me, you did it again. Oh, you were a great one for getting your own way with me, but you never gave me anything in return. Even when you made my image, you were so ill-tempered about it I was frightened to blink."

"Is there nothing you've forgotten?" said Harry, aghast.

"Nothing bad. Your good points I forget. Perhaps there weren't any."

"And yet you love me," he said triumphantly.

"Oh, I claim only to be bold and resolute. I never said I was sensible."

"If you scold," he threatened, "I shall beat you, when we're married."

"Who said we should be married? Have you not heard that England's under interdict? There's neither marrying nor giving in marriage—we're one step nearer the kingdom of heaven."

"Isambard's chaplain at Parfois will marry us. He holds that his lord is absolved because he was away following the Cross when the ban was laid. But if there'd been no Crusade he would have thought of another reason why Parfois should be exempt. The Pope is in Rome, and can threaten his soul, but Isambard is close at hand and deals rather with the flesh."

"There'd be nothing surprising in your beating me, in any event," said Gilleis, twisting her fingers into the short, curling hair in the nape of his neck. "I think I was very near it once before, when you caught me peering into the hall where you were showing your paces on the citole, and you ordered me to bed, and I—"

"This I won't bear!" said Harry, roused, and caught her up in his arms and carried her to the window embrasure. She had not grown as tall as his chin, and she was slim as a reed; he had less trouble with her now than on that earlier occasion. All the same, she did not fail to remind him.

"You almost dropped me that time, too."

He sat down in the panelled seat, and settled her on his knee. "Now *I* shall begin remembering things. Thus I held you in my arms, and you cried and miscalled me." He hugged her to his heart, laughing. It seemed that love had no language but laughter. "You had nothing on under your cloak. And your hair was loosed from its braids." He plucked at the ties of the gilt ribbon, and brought the black coils tumbling about them both, over her shoulders, over his cradling arm, heavy and silken and sweet. "So, that's better! And as I remember it, love, it was you beat me, not I you. You hit out at me with your fist like a fury. And not the first time, either!"

"And yet you love me," she exulted.

"I've not said so yet!"

"Too late to draw back. I saw your face when you recognised me. It was touch and go with you whether you shouted with joy or burst into tears on my breast."

"That I may do yet," he said, and set his lips to the opening of her gown, between her firm, small breasts. "I do most truly love you, Gilleis. When I was grown a man I had the wit to know it. Oh, Gilleis, marry me! My lord's away in Ireland now with the king, and will be for a month or more yet, but as soon as he comes home I'll speak to him of our marriage. He'll give us a lodging in the castle, I know, and we can be wed in the chapel there. Oh, my love, how can I bear to ride back without you, tomorrow, now that I've found you? But I must make preparation to receive you at Parfois, and I must get on with my work, and you'll be better here with my mother until all's ready for you there."

"I can wait," she said. "If I've waited until now, and never complained, I can wait a few weeks longer."

"You won't vanish again as soon as I turn my back?"

"And you—you won't forget to come back for me?"

He buried his face in her hair and kissed her through the drifting silken curtain, eyes and cheeks and chin, and the soft round neck, and the eager mouth. With his lips against the delicate cup of shadow at the base of her throat he began to quake with laughter again, and laughed and laughed until it seemed he could not stop. She took his face between her hands and shook him into coherence. "Oh, Gilleis, I'm in for such a scolding! What will my mother say to me when she hears I'm carrying off the treasure who makes her dresses?"

He rode back to Parfois singing, his mother's facile tears still moist on his shoulder, and Gilleis's kiss still warm on his lips. Ebrard had ridden with him to the edge of the demesne, so expansive with relief at receiving Harry's hearty consent in his proprietorship that he embraced and kissed him at parting with more warmth than he had shown since childhood. At this second departure the prodigal son carried everybody's blessing with him, not even excepting the baby-faced clerk, whose nose was clean out of joint as long as the interloper remained at Sleapford.

In Harry's saddle-bag reposed a parchment, drawn up by that same clerk and signed by Ebrard, testifying that William Boteler and Alison his wife, together with all their issue, were hereafter freed and loosed from villeinage, and that all the services by virtue of which the said William Boteler had heretofore held his yardland and his toft were hereby commuted to an annual rent of five shillings.

Adam was up on the scaffolding, watching the master-carpenter direct the striking of the centring from the deeply recessed arch of the west portal. Harry swung himself up behind him, and stealing up unnoticed to his back, stretched an arm over his shoulder and dangled the parchment before his eyes. Adam turned a startled smile on him, at once welcoming and questioning, and read the thing through twice before he could grasp it. He swallowed and stared mutely, his lips quivering. Harry seized him in his arms and hugged him boisterously.

"I wanted to go to them and tell them, but I didn't. You are to do that, and this very day, too. I wish I could come back with you, but we can't both be gone at this moment, and you can tell them I'll come soon, and that I send my duty and love before me. I hope they may be comforted for all the years they've lacked you, now that you come home with this in your hands."

Adam, whose whole being was gaiety, Adam who had hardly ever cried even as a baby, stood trying to speak, and could not. His hands shook on the precious leaf of sheepskin. He put his head down on Harry's shoulder, and wept briefly and hotly, with all his heart.

"Ah, now, I hadn't meant to shake you so!" said Harry, too much excited and moved to be put out of his stride at being tossed into so unusual a role. "It all turned out better than I'd dreamed, and getting this was easy, and on my soul I'm as wild with joy about it as you are. And think what it will be to walk into the yard and give this to your father! Come away with you now, and dress, and be off to get the best of the day. Everything's well at home, I promise you that. I saw the two boys, and heard your mother's voice in the house, and I asked at home about your father, and he's alive and well. So there's nothing to trouble you at all. Ranald's taller than you, I believe, and Dickon not so far short of you. And truth to tell, Adam, I've not been much missed at home, I did them no great wrong, and if they did me any it's long gone by. I'm mortal glad you made me go. Ebrard's concerned only that I shan't lay claim to any part of his manor, and my mother's meditating a second marriage, and happy as a lark, with or without me. Indeed, she has what she holds to be better cause to hate me now than ever in the past, for I'm robbing her of her tirewoman."

Adam raised his head and scrubbed hastily at his eyes with his sleeve, uncovering a face absurdly contorted with laughter, tears and bewilderment. "For God's sake, Harry, either you're out of your wits or I'm so bemused I can't take in a word. Her tirewoman? What can you want with her tirewoman?"

"Ah, but you haven't seen her, Adam!" Harry held him by the shoulders and shook him gaily, his eyes dancing with blue and green lights in the sun. "She's no ordinary tirewoman. Her name is Gilleis Otley. I'm going to marry her."

Isambard came home at the end of August, blazing with vigour and high spirits from the king's triumphal progress through Ireland and South Wales, where he had left his enemies disrupted and scattered. Better still, small seeds of suspicion concerning Llewelyn's loyalty had struck roots in John's mind, and three months of assiduous cherishing had brought the plant to the point of flowering. The charge was never likely to be proved, but then the charge was never likely even to be made; it was within his own walled-in mind that John indicted and judged in silence and without appeal. The execution of sentence was all that the world ever saw of his processes of justice. He moved deviously, even among those who had been most intimate with him, confiding in one only in order to counter the crumb of confidence he had been obliged to place in another; but if he still trusted one man above the rest of the world, the man was Isambard, and throughout that progress from Fishguard across Wales to Bristol, a demonstration of power designed to awe the natives into complete submission, Isambard had been busy pouring into his mind the idea of a final settlement with the Prince of Gwynedd.

The foray into his territories by the Earl of Chester, countenanced though not openly ordered by the king during his Irish expedition, had been useful in encouraging Llewelyn's many minor foes among the Welsh princes themselves. The greatest single blow John could deal at his enemy was to release Gwenwynwyn and set him up again in the southern part of his princedom of Powis, for his hot blood would never rest until he had won back the northern half from Llewelyn. Turn Gwenwynwyn loose this autumn to harry Gwynedd from the south, and by next spring the stage should be well set for a royal expedition to drive westward to the Conway and flush the falcon out of his crags under Snowdon.

Isambard rode home, therefore, well content with his summer's work. He brought his three score knights and his company of archers back to Parfois intact and with despatch, shed his mail for silk, and sat down in his great hall to hear suits and deal justice. At the clamour of his return the countryside, which had sweated to provide him the funds for the expedition, crouched lower between its hills like a hare in a furrow, expecting the next exactions all too soon.

"Marry?" said Isambard, when Harry came to him with his news. "Faith, I thought you were married to your drawing-board!"

He looked from the finished arch of the west portal to the great beams the carpenters were already shaping for the covering in of the aisles, and back to Harry's face, with brilliant eyes that danced with rare pleasure. "It's plain being in love has not sapped your powers, even if you have been racing off to this girl of yours every ten days or so. I never saw a building of its size grow so fast. Ay, bring her to Parfois whenever you will. If you have her here you'll need no time out for the ride. Benedetta will take care of her until the wedding day, and you shall have a chamber in the King's Tower to yourselves, and welcome." He clapped an arm about Harry's shoulders. "And which of your names do you intend to marry in, Master Henry? Lestrange—or Talvace?"

Harry gaped so childishly that Isambard threw back his head and startled the birds with laughter.

"Never stare so, I'm no magician! I've known best part of a year. Do you not remember I told you last autumn that Hugh de Lacy sent you his greetings, when he wrote acknowledging the gift of wine I sent him after his recovery? With what name do you think he named you?"

"True!" said Harry. "I never thought of it. He knew but one name for me, for it never entered my head to mention the other. But why did you never question it?"

"Why should I question it? If you had had anything to tell me, you would have told me. A man's name is his own business—though for my part I'd rather he had but one, and that his true one."

"And so would I," said Harry, "though it never troubled me when I changed it. Talvace I am, and Talvace I'll be from this on."

So Gilleis came to Parfois in the second week of September, and two days later they were married in the chapel in the Lady's Tower, by the good-natured, subtle, pliant old man who was Isambard's chaplain and had served his father before him.

In the great hall that night they sat at the high table between Isambard and Benedetta, too full of their own happiness to eat or drink or speak. On Isambard's left Lady Talvace shone in the most resplendent of the gowns Gilleis had made for her, and basked in the attentions of her exalted neighbour. On Benedetta's right Ebrard wore his finest blue velvet, and drank for two. Below, in the hall, the entire household of Parfois chattered and supped. But in the middle of so many witnesses, those four were alone.

Benedetta looked along the table and saw the three profiles super-imposed one upon another, like three heads on one coin. Isambard, the most distant of the three, flushed with wine beneath his tan, and with some deeper exaltation wine could never have given him, controlled the comings and goings of his underlings with flashing glances and eloquent movements of head and hand. When he laughed and turned his warmth and intelligence outwards on the world, as now, he burned into such lively beauty as could charm the birds from the trees. She understood, with her blood rather than her mind, one reason for his good spirits. It was pleasing to him to see one man about him helplessly in love, and not with her. There was also the pleasure he had from his summer of relentless in-triguing against the Welsh prince. But there was something more, an air of having come to a happy decision, a shining elation for which she could find no sufficient reason.

Against his dark brightness the girl's rose-and-white profile was clear and pale as a pearl. A little creature, slender and beautiful, with great black eyes that observed fearlessly, and a mind behind them that judged with shrewdness and without mercy, after the fashion of children. When I received and kissed her at her coming here, thought Benedetta, those eyes pierced me to the heart, and that mind understood something, at least, of what moves me. I knew she would be young. I thought she would be soft, sweet and timorous; but she is gay and bold and gallant. I thought she would be no match for him, and he might some day look for another; but she is his match and mine, and she will not fail him. She is the death of hope, if that was hope I had and have no longer.

And now, Harry, what remains for me?

On this third face, the most beloved, so close that she could have brushed the flushed cheek with her lips as she turned her head, she dwelt longest, and with the most passionate and wondering atten-tion. His eyes had a light, changeable brilliance, startling as topaz

and aquamarine, and all the impetuous bones of his face stood outlined with the sharp pallor of excitement. He had gone to some pains
to make himself fine for his bride, he who cared not a fig whether
he pleased anyone else, or what old clothes he wore, so he was neat
and covered. The thick brown hair was newly trimmed, the fine-
drawn cheeks and arrogant chin shaven smooth as ivory, and a
necklet of polished brown stones circled his throat within the high
collar of his golden surcoat. Talvace was Talvace again. Ebrard was
a clod to him, for all his graces.

Touch him where you will, she thought, exulting in the fondness
and pride that gathered about her heart like fire, and burned out of
her even the agonising envy she felt towards Gilleis, lean on him as
you will, and he stands firm under your hand. Sound him where
you will, and he rings true. Who but Harry would have stood his
ground with me, never hiding behind coldness, never compounding
with his difficulties by a kind or a cruel lie, never shunning my
company, never shaming me by an evasive compliment or an insin-
cere caress, never in anything that rested between us two taking the
false or the easy way? Who but Harry would have come to me
straight and told me with his own lips of his love and his intent to
marry? Not one of these knights and warriors but would have run
from me as from the plague in the same case, though they think
themselves heroes, and him a mere artisan who has chosen the
poorer part. He came to me not even as an act of courtesy or mercy.
He came as to one having rights in him by virtue of my love, one
who should be encountered fairly, eye to eye, and trusted with the
truth. He has done me more honour in the manner of his rejection
than any other man with the offering of his heart's worship. And I
do not repent me of my love, I exult in it. I gave it where it was
due, and by God, I will never take it back!

I have lost nothing, she reasoned with herself, while some shell
of her mind attended to Ebrard's gallantries. Not Harry, for he never
was mine. Not the hope of some day winning him, for there never
was such a hope. Only, perhaps, the illusion of hope. If she had
been a slighter thing than she is I might have kept that illusion even
now. But she is his true match, and I am glad of it, though it strips
me of the last of my possessions. So noble a creature should mate

nobly. If he had taken an unworthy consort he would have abased me as well as himself. So the delusion is over, and my sense of loss is the greater in measure as I worship and revere him more for his honourable and loving dealings with me.

Now there is nothing to gain. Now, therefore, she thought smiling over her wineglass, we shall see, Benedetta, whether you came after him to England to get, or to give.

In the quiet of the bedchamber Benedetta sat before the polished mirror, combing her long hair. Her eyes looked back at her from the shining surface with a sombre metallic lustre. Her hands, moving in the heavy coils of red, were slow and languid. She had never been so weary.

In the chamber newly prepared for them in the King's Tower bride and bridegroom lay closely folded in each other's arms, between waking and dreaming. They were sealed about with the impregnable armour of their happiness, exalted so far above the world that the world could not reach them. Yet some measure of their joy distilled into the air, and filled the night with a sweet, disturbing awareness, sharpening every desire to anguish.

Isambard, naked beneath the furred robe he kept for wear in his own chamber, came to her back, and buried his hands to the wrists in the masses of her hair. She heard his quickened breath, and the long, fulfilled sigh as he laid his cheek against her neck. Over there in the coign of the inner ward, did Harry twist his fingers so in the black hair, and even so smooth his palm down over the bud of the young, round breast and along the ivory of her side? An unpractised hand, but this skill came by nature; art could only elaborate and perfect it. I wish them well, she said silently within her heart. I wish them this good joy with all the rest. How could I grudge him his pleasure with her, I who would give him the world if I could? Their happiness is my joy, as well as my sorrow. Let him have everything this life has to offer a man, she prayed indomitably, smiling into the mirror at the darkly smiling face that looked over her shoulder.

"Benedetta!" he said in a low voice, and turned his lips into her cheek, kissing and smiling. She raised her hand and held him so, her fingers threading his hair "My lord?"

"This marriage is a strange matter! How often I have seen my friends wedded and bedded, and never been stirred to feel anything but pity for them, that they should have to submit themselves to such tedious embraces with such unpleasing partners, to add a few fields or one more manor to their honours. Only a landless man can afford to plunge into marriage like this boy, without a single furlong to gain. What's to become of our morality if young men are to marry for nothing more substantial than love?"

"And what's to become of women like me?" she said. "One should be properly practical about marriage. Sir Ebrard, they say, is conducting a long, cautious negotiation for his neighbour's daughter. Since Tourneur's son died she stands to bring three manors to her husband. She's thirteen years old, and pockmarked, or she might have been pledged already, even with her smaller dower. Ebrard was contracted once himself, it seems, but the girl died before she was old enough to wed. You'll not catch that Talvace with the bait of a black eye and a rosy mouth. No family can afford more than one fool like your Master Harry."

"No family dare hope for more than one," said Isambard, smiling. "I'm glad I've seen his happiness. Something, it seems, I had to learn from him, how to value this vexed business of love."

His hands gripped her shoulders and held her drawn back against his body. In the mirror their eyes clung.

"Benedetta, I see that I wrong myself and you in denying the name of marriage to this union of ours, that lacks nothing of peace and certainty and permanence. I want none but you, now or ever. I desire with all my heart that you will be my wife."

Her face neither moved nor changed; only it seemed to him that a veil was drawn over the brightness of the eyes. Quiet under his hands, she sat and watched him through the veil, and was silent so long that a coldness came on him.

"What is it? Why don't you speak? Are you angry because I am come only now to this simplicity I might have seen long since? But I am not a simple person. It wanted the directness of children to charm me into simplicity. What was marriage to me while it marched in my mind with haggling and grasping for a few barren manors? This is a new vision of the paradise of the innocent, where the kiss comes from the heart. I should have done you no honour and myself no credit if I had asked you to be my wife in the old dispensation. But enter here with me, and we may be as the children."

He saw tears well in her eyes, the first he had ever seen there, and did not understand that they were for him. They brought him to his knees at her side, his long arms clasping her close. "Ah, have I hurt you? What is it? Best and dearest, what have I done?"

"Nothing!" she said. "Honoured me! Laid me deeper than ever in your debt! Charmed me to the very soul! Nothing but good. But I am not and cannot be as the children, until time goes backwards. And I cannot and will not marry you. Not you nor any!"

The ready fires burned up in his eyes, darkly red with offence. "Why not? What is this? You accepted me; why do you refuse my name and estate? Is it that other? Do you still cling to him? Has he ever shown you such a love as mine?"

Benedetta laid her hands about his neck and held his face before her, eye to eye. "This I promise you, and be content. There never yet was a moment when I drew so close to you in the spirit as now, or was so moved towards you. The vow I made you I repeat and will keep, upon that honour the world would say I have not, but which you will not deny me. If ever I married man, it should be you, but I have that in me that will not let me marry any. Have you not been content with me as I am? Have I not faithfully given you my body, my counsel, whatever wit I have for your service? Let things alone! Let me alone!"

"There is a place in you I cannot come at," he said violently, and plucked his head from between her hands and leaped to his feet, dragging her up with him. "You touch me gently with your hands, you open your breast to me, you give me your body, but I cannot get to your heart."

"You have no need," she said. "A morsel of my heart I gave you long ago. There is nothing left me to give that I have not given you. Be satisfied! If you had means to measure and tell over what I have in my heart, you would surely find yourself there."

"Then give me what I ask! Marry me!" Bending his head in sudden desperate desire, he kissed her from brow to breast, closed her eyes with kisses, and fastened his lips so long upon hers that she struggled to wrench aside from him for breath.

When he withdrew his mouth from hers, the blanched lips flushed slowly back into red, bright as blood. They opened only to repeat, with a vehemence and resolution as inflexible as his: "I will not."

Chapter Eleven

*M*adam, and most honoured lady," wrote Walter Langholme by
a courier from Aber, in the middle of the harvest, "this campaign
having now been brought to a successful conclusion, I am commanded by my lord to write to you that full account for which his
duties about the person of the King's Grace leave him no leisure,
and to convey to you therewith my lord's most faithful greeting and
service. My lord is well, and has taken no hurt in the fighting, in
which, indeed, our losses have been light, though some companies
less well captained than our own have suffered much from the skill
of the Welsh archery.

"As you know, we assembled at Chester in early May, our lord
the King having summoned there all the leaders of the Welshmen
saving the Prince of Gwynedd only, against whom our campaign
was directed. These came in obedience to the summons almost to a
man, even some among them who had hitherto held fast to Prince
Llewelyn, but whether out of duty to our lord the King or envy to
Llewelyn I know not, for in truth there are many who envy him
and would gladly see his downfall. But at this first muster the King's
Grace unwisely paid no heed to my lord's counsel, but would advance

into Tegaingl without delay, though warned that our supplies were
not sufficiently assured for so early a campaign. Howbeit, advance
we did, and the Welshmen after their invariable custom withdrew
before us, making no pitched stand but harrying us from the flanks,
and so retreated before us with all their possessions, cattle and
horses, into the mountains. We came to the Conway at Degannwy,
having consumed the greater part of our supplies by reason of the
season, for that countryside provided no food whereby we might
spare our own, and of beasts it was stripped bare. It was thus clear
that we could not survive a campaign of any length, for already such
trifles of food as could be found commanded their weight in gold
rather than silver, and to go forward was to reckon with famine.
Our lord the King therefore commanded that the army should withdraw to England, and on the march we ate such of our horses as
could be spared, and for the rest went hungry.

"Howbeit the King's Grace was not turned from his intent against
the Prince of Gwynedd, but made new provision to better purpose,
and we were appointed to assemble a second time in the opening
week of July, at Oswestry. And thence, assured of our supply columns, we advanced into Gwynedd and drove fast for the mouth of
the Conway, sweeping Prince Llewelyn before us across that river
and into the mountains of Arllechwedd. The Welshmen fought as
Welshmen ever fight, in flying skirmishes and by means of light-
armed bowmen, the main army dissolving before us so that we could
not come to grips, by which means they avoid heavy losses. But
they could not halt us by such means, and so we came in triumph
to Prince Llewelyn's court of Aber, and there took possession of the
town, the prince having withdrawn into the mountains.

"Now Prince Llewelyn is returned, with his lady, and there is
much haggling over the peace. Our lord the King has an affection
for his daughter, and I make no doubt she will get for her husband
the best terms that are to be had. My lord would have had him
stripped of all he has, but that can never be while the Princess Joan
lives, since his ruin would be hers also. The prince bears himself in
no wise like a defeated man, but very proudly, though I have heard
tell that he is bitter at this invasion of his realm, and myself I have
seen at whose door he lays it. In the presence of the King he turned
to my lord Isambard, and: 'Well I know, my lord,' said he, 'that I

have you to thank for traducing me to the King's Grace. You are he who put it into his mind to believe that I was conspiring with de Breos against him. Here at this time I am but a suitor in my own court, and cannot call you to account for it. But at another time I shall seek a settlement. Until then, keep this for me.' And with that he drew off his glove and let it fall at my lord's feet. Whereupon my lord would have snatched it up, and there would have been swords out, for my lord is, as you know, of no temper to withhold his hand even in the presence of kings. But certain of the barons laid hold on them both, and the King forbade that the gage should be received, and charged them to forgo this quarrel now and hereafter. Nevertheless, neither one of them has promised obedience, though they parted without more words. So the matter stands, and it has been the King's chief charge that they shall not meet again so long as the army remains here. For my part, though in this I speak only for myself, I believe the prince when he swears that he made no compact with de Breos who is broken and fled, though he may well have been approached, and perhaps even tempted.

"It is not yet known what the terms of peace will be, nor when we shall be leaving here, but it is certain that the King's Grace is well satisfied with what he has accomplished, and holds that all Wales may now be held subdued, thus the better freeing his powers for the project which he still has dearly at heart, namely, the recovery of Normandy.

"Believe, most honoured lady, that to my lord's expressed duty and homage I add my own, and at all times pray for your safety and good, and am your most devoted and humble servant

Walter Langholme.

"Given this eighth day of August, the thirteenth year of the King's Grace and the year of Our Lord 1211, at Aber, in Arllechwedd."

"Writ in haste at the courier's departure. Madam, it is now known to what terms the King has consented, and I must acquaint you they are not pleasing to my lord, for he holds that they leave to the Prince of Gwynedd too much scope for mischief hereafter. All four cantrefs of the Middle Country are surrendered to the King, leaving to Prince Llewelyn those parts which lie beyond the Conway. Gwynedd must pay to the King a ruinous tribute also in cattle, horses, hounds and falcons, and surrender hostages from the children of the nobility. I have heard that Prince Llewelyn's natural son is to be among the number, a handsome boy some eleven or twelve years old, who is well liked among the Welsh because his mother was a Welsh lady of note, daughter of a lord of Rhos. But whether it is true that this boy Griffith is expressly named hostage for his father's fealty is not yet certain. Some thirty more noble children will accompany him.

"My lord is greatly angered, none the less, at what he holds to be a victory thrown away, and has said openly that this whole enterprise will be to do again within a year. But I hope he may be proved too cautious a judge. Herewith I salute you reverently, and trust to see you in good health on our return."

"One thing at least goes well," said Isambard, "and one man knows his business. It's rare enough these days. Do you mean to have the nave wholly roofed in before the winter?"

"Yes, my lord, and with your permission I should like to keep on all my hewers and setters this year. The vaulting will more than keep them occupied, we lose nothing by paying them through the frosts, and gain months of time. And we gain in goodwill by the security we give them, believe me. It's much, these days, for a mason to have his work safe and assured before him twelve months in the year, he'll give you value for it."

"See to it, Harry. For it's in my mind that you spoil your workmen." The long mouth snapped at the words, biting them off grimly.

"No, faith, my lord, that's not true. Many of my men must keep a family fed and housed on their few pence a day. The usage they have from you relieves them of anxiety. Never think that matters only to them. It sets their minds free to provide you the whole-hearted service you ask of them. And they respect you for it. Is that nothing?"

"Oh, you are on your old hobby-horse again. Turning artisan in your boyhood has given you an artisan's eyes. But at least I grant you," said Isambard, his eyes fixed on the double lofty arch of portal below and window above, drawn back from light to shadow through eight courses of delicate moulding, "what you have produced is much to my mind. The variation of the colour from dawn to dusk is beyond belief. When the light is slanting on these curves of stone they vibrate like the strings of a harp, such a tension they have. I see them sometimes when I ride out early, and they sing like notes of music." He saw the vivid colour rise in Harry's face, and the pleasure that flamed up in his eyes, and smiled. "Praising you is a luxury, you reflect back so warming a delight. You are like a child who has done his task better than he knew, and gets commendation where he looked for scolding."

"It is not that," said Harry, laughing. "It's the terms of the praise. If you are content with your mason, I am content with my patron. Come and look within."

He led the way between the slender mouldings of the doorway. On a level with Isambard's eyes, as he followed, the delicate columns burst into jubilant leaf. He halted, face to face with himself, startled yet again by the beauty and savagery of that simplified image, with its uplifted hair and passionate bones, and the stony calm of the eyes, staring forth from between the leaves of the holy tree. Angel or man or demon, this creature could have been any or all of the three.

On the other side of the portal the face of Benedetta looked out, bearing up the abacus and the lofty spring of the voussoirs on the erected masses of her hair. It seemed that Isambard would have passed her by without a look, but he could not. His feet lagged in the doorway; he turned about with a sudden helpless motion, and his hand flew to touch the lovely, taut line of the stone throat. The strong fingers lingered with so involuntary and so intense a suggestion of pain and longing that Harry drew off from him and waited with held breath, shaken out of his absorption into wonder and disquiet. Isambard's eyes burned upon the beloved face, searching hungrily and finding no reassurance. He plucked himself away at last with a violent movement, as though it cost him a struggle to release himself, and went on without a word into the lofty, airy shell of the church.

The aisles, not yet vaulted, stood beneath their timber roofs; the nave was still open to the sky, but the transepts were covered, and the base of the tower hung square against the clouds. The aisle windows and the windows of the clerestory printed their empty tracery on the light, laced with the wrought iron windowbars to which the painted panels of glass would some day be affixed.

"You see only the form and proportion," said Harry. "Give me this coming winter, and you shall see all the vaulting in place, at least the ribs. Next spring we'll need to get the heavy hoist installed in the tower, it's bespoke from Shrewsbury, we'll be bringing it up by water. Why build a new one when theirs is sitting idle? For this year I can make do with the two lighter hoists I've got. Richard Smith has a warm winter's work cut out for him, making rods and cramps and dowels for the vaults. Sweating over his tallow-vat proofing iron will be a pleasure through the frosts. He's a good fellow, and knows his trade, none better. I have but to show him the manner of device I want, though the like never was used before, and he'll shape it to the exact pattern. Do you like the line of it? That's what counts. Line, form, proportion, these are the body of beauty, the rest is but the dress."

Isambard stood beneath the western window, gazing before him at the beautiful enclosed shape of air and light. He heard the clangour of hammers on the timbers above, the voices of the mason-setters working on the base of the tower, and shouts of the men bringing up ashlar with the hand-hoist. The whole site hummed with sound and movement like a hive of bees; but it seemed to him that the voice of the builder, leaping with ardour, rang louder than all.

"You are a happy man," he said, in a voice of wonder and envy. "You love what you do. You create, and that which you have made stands. No folly of others unmakes it, it has not to be done again and again, and still to no purpose."

"I am fortunate," said Harry, "I know it."

"The happiest of men in your labours." Isambard turned his face into shadow, leaning his hand upon the pier between them. "And in your love also, Harry?"

"In that also," said Harry in a low voice.

"To have all!" The voice laboured with astonishment and despair. "To have everything there is in life, even that last and greatest of all! What right has one man to so much? Where is God's justice?"

They were suddenly upon ground that trembled beneath their feet, and Harry would gladly have drawn back to the rock, but he could not.

"My lord, I think I have been visited with mercy rather than justice," he said slowly. "I make no claim that I am used according to my deserts."

"Ah, Harry, I should ask your pardon! There's none I would more gladly see happy than you. Yet I cannot choose but envy you, and sooner or later envy will grudge to another the good fortune it cannot share. I think you have your deserts. Indeed, I think so!" He turned about suddenly, and the air between them quaked with the compulsive passion of his vehemence, an inexplicable anguish. "And yet, Harry, how do you know, how can you be sure—"

A quick, light step and a sudden shadow in the doorway cut off the words on his lips, and Gilleis stood silhouetted against the light. In the vigour and rapidity of her movements she was like a bird, and the brilliance and audacity of her glance had something of a bird's knowing wildness about it. She looked quickly from one to the other of them, and stepped forward into the open, sunlit space of the nave.

"My lord, Madonna Benedetta is here with Langholme and the falconer, if you are pleased to be ready."

She spoke to Isambard, but she looked at Harry. Something out of reason flashed between them when they beheld each other. Her lively face seemed to blaze into the proud, piercing image of Harry's countenance, even her great eyes, opened wide at him, reflected the shifting brilliance of the sea. And such a softness and radiance came upon him that it seemed he took her womanliness into his being, and gave her in exchange some part of his steel. Isambard saw the budding rose of her mouth quiver and part, softening without speech, as though she kissed her husband across the space of charged air. "How can you be sure," he had been about to ask, "that you are loved?" Beholding her, he was answered.

"I will come," he said, and turned to the doorway.

"You were about to ask me something," said Harry, following; though if his mind and his eyes had not been upon Gilleis he would have been alert enough to let the question lapse.

"Was I so? No matter! I have forgotten now what I was going to say."

At the edge of the site, where the track crossed the grassy plateau, Benedetta sat waiting on a tall roan mare. Langholme held his own horse and his lord's, and well back from them, in silent attendance, John the Fletcher watched from the saddle of a raw-boned grey. The falconer with his birds had ridden ahead, but Benedetta carried her own little merlin hooded on her wrist. She looked down from her high-pommelled side-saddle, and her smile was warm but weary. Her face had grown a little thinner of late, and a little graver. The spark of laughter that still lit in the limpid grey depths of her eyes had always something of irony in it, though something of tenderness, too.

"I did not mean to interrupt you, Ralf. If you have matters to discuss with Harry I will wait."

"No need, I'm ready," said Isambard, his eyes intent upon her face, where no revelation showed him his own image. He took the bridle from Langholme, and without waiting to be squired made a leap and drew himself up easily and gracefully into the saddle, sending the horse forward with a thrust of his knees before he bothered to feel for the stirrups. Benedetta wheeled and followed him, her close white coif shining in the sun; and after them Langholme cantered at a discreet distance, with John the Fletcher at his back. The deep thudding of hoofbeats descending the grassy track pulsed through the rock and subsided.

Gilleis looked after them thoughtfully. "I marvel," she said, "that she chooses such a surly-looking fellow to attend her. He's always at her heels like a shadow."

"She has good reason to trust in his loyalty, and he has good reason to guard and cherish her. It's thanks to her he's man alive."

Gilleis slanted a quick glance at her husband and bit at her underlip with white teeth. "She rides well," she said judicially.

"She does," he said with unthinking warmth.

"But then, she does so many things well."

Harry caught the significant note in her voice, and looked round with a jerk, searching her face warily.

"She has an admirable intelligence, too," said Gilleis earnestly. "See what an interest she takes in your designs, and how constantly she visits your tracing-house." Sidelong, she watched the shadows of doubt and consternation pursue one another over his face.

"Madonna Benedetta has taken an interest in the church from the beginning," he said. "Why should she not? She has as good a mind as any man, and I value her judgements. Moreover, she is the lady of this castle, whether by right or by custom, and goes where she pleases. She has been always generous and kind to me."

"And how gladly would she be kinder and more generous still," said Gilleis roundly, "if you would but let her!"

The fiery colour mounted in his brown cheeks, and flamed to his hair. "Gilleis, you surely cannot think—Dear, when have I given you cause—?" He reached out his hand to catch at hers, but she snatched them away and turned her back on him, and all he could do was to take her by the shoulders and draw her back against his breast, his cheek against her cheek. She felt the burning heat of that touch, and suddenly repented of her ungentle game.

"Simpleton!" she said, and turning quickly, kissed him at random near the angle of his jaw, and plucking herself clear picked up her skirts and ran like a hare for the rim of the trees, laughing at him over her shoulder as she ran. Between wild relief and real anger, he turned his back on his duties and launched himself in vengeful pursuit. She was surefooted and fleet, but among the trees she stumbled, perhaps of design, and he caught her about the waist and pulled her down into the grass already growing dry and colourless with autumn.

"Tease me, would you? Make a fool of me, would you, miss?"

"Mistress!" spat Gilleis sharply, reaching for her favourite hold in his hair. He freed himself, not without difficulty and pain, and held her down in the rustling grass by the wrists, his weight lying over her; their hurrying breath mingled, in slightly savage laughter.

"What shall I do to you, hussy, for plaguing a good husband like me?"

She fought him for a while with all her strength, then with all her strength wound her arms about him and caught him to her breast. They lay intertwined, kissing and laughing and murmuring until they were spent, and for a moment sank together into the borders of a sweet drowsiness.

"All the same," said Gilleis, "you defended yourself before you were accused." She turned her head, and closed her teeth gently on the lobe of his ear. "I never said you cared for her, I said that *she*—"

Harry silenced her in the most effective way he knew, and

emerged with just enough breath to gasp guiltily: "I must go back
to work! What will they think if they've seen us?"

She lay still for a moment when he had withdrawn his weight,
her hand in his, her face smiling. "Harry!" She drew him down
again, lifting her mouth to his.

"I love you dearly, Gilleis, and only you, and always you. You
know that!"

"I know it! And I love you, too." But he saw by her smile that
she had confirmed to her own satisfaction that this Venetian woman,
who meant nothing to her, loved him no less surely, and that he
was well aware of it. How had he come to betray them both so
easily? It was more than he could do to keep any secret from Gilleis,
she was so much a part of his very flesh and blood. Yet if she was
too perfectly a woman to be compassionate, and perhaps too young
to have room in her as yet for pity, she was also too secure in her
happiness to be jealous. Had she not reason to be secure?

He drew her gently to her feet. The small nest their two clinging
bodies had pressed out in the long grass seemed still to keep the
very print of passion, and a warmth of its own. Surely no snow
could ever lie there, and no frost whiten the grasses. He thought of
Benedetta keeping her promised silence, abstaining from touching
so much as his sleeve. He remembered Isambard's voice in its muted
howl of desire and despair: "To have all! What right has one man
to so much?"

"What is it?" said Gilleis, folding her arms about him in sudden
anxious tenderness. "You're trembling, Harry! Dear love, what's
the matter?"

"Nothing!" he said, shaking off the shadow hastily. "Nothing in
the world! A goose flying over my grave!"

Before the end of the year Isambard's prophecies with regard to
Wales began to show signs of coming true, but it was not at
Llewelyn's hands that the peace was broken. The chieftains who had
willingly joined King John against him had soon awakened to certain
disquieting discoveries. It was understandable that the king should
feel it necessary to build castles in the Middle Country, the better
to hold what he had taken from the Prince of Gwynedd. But hasty
new mottes and timber keeps began to rise also in Powis and in

other parts of Wales, until chief began to whisper to chief that this encroaching power which they had helped to supremacy was aiming its lance not at the throat of the Prince of Gwynedd, but at the heart of Wales itself. Let the English king once establish his castles throughout the countryside, and there would be no safe foothold left for any Welsh prince in his native land. Before the leaves had fallen Rhys Gryg and Maelgwyn, brothers of the line of Deheubarth, had captured and burned the unfinished castle at Aberystwyth, and Cadwallon of Senghenydd was in revolt in Glamorgan. The Prince of Gwynedd had not raised a hand to break the peace enforced upon him in the summer; but many of those who had been the king's allies had become, openly or secretly, his enemies.

"He is throwing away Wales and risking England for the sake of Normandy," said Isambard, thinking aloud before Harry in the tracing-house. "There's still but one man in Wales who can unite the whole country against him, and yet in his haste to make one frontier safe he is playing into that man's hands by offending all the lesser fry. He should have wooed them a little longer. It was too soon to frighten them with a rash of castles."

"Yet you'll not deny," said Harry, "that the Prince of Gwynedd himself has kept the peace loyally. It is not he who has burned Aberystwyth."

"Why should he, when they are willing to do his work for him? But be sure he misses nothing that passes. When he judges the time ripe he will take up the weapon of a Welsh national grievance, and we are the fools who will have forged it for him."

"What, when the king has I know not how many hostages in his hands, and young Griffith among them?"

"Hostages! I'll tell you this, Harry, there are so many hostages in the king's hands, Welsh and English, too, that there's hardly a house in the two countries but stands to lose a son at the least step astray. Years of that, and not so much as knowing how to step to be above reproach, and seeing others, like de Breos, brought to ruin and death for no treasonous act that ever showed—why, those who have sons in hold must begin to despair of knowing how to keep the breath in their children. There comes a time when it seems a lesser risk to act, with some hope of success, than to hold back from action, and still be charged with treachery and pay the same penalty. One

more thing I'll tell you! Of all the boys the king holds in ward, the
only one he dare not touch is Llewelyn's son. It is not fear. It is a
kind of respect for the man, even while he hates him, that holds him
back from abusing what belongs to him. I take it, Harry, that what
I say here to you goes no further?"

"You may so take it, my lord," said Harry haughtily.

"Ah, now I see all the Talvaces stirring in you! There were clues
enough to your line, when I think back, before ever Abbot Hugh
wrote me his charge to you. When we rode to Calais, and in my ill-
humour I told you you rode like a ploughboy, and you laughed, and
said: 'So my father used to tell me'—do you remember?—I should
have known then, by your impudence, as well as by the words,
where to look for your father. Well, be content, for I speak with no
other as I speak with you, Harry."

He moved restlessly away across the room, but in a moment took
up again, without turning his head: "I was much with John when
we were younger, I had some love for him. I tell you, he could have
been a good king and a happy man, who now is neither the one nor
the other. Richard with his recklessness and his empty gallantry,
who saw in England only an asset to be squeezed dry for his holy
wars, him they praised and worshipped. John, if he squeezed them
in his turn, at least began with some knowledge of them and some
thought for them, and might have made them a nation and a power
had he had even moderate fortune. But him they hate. It is too late
now to undo that. As for his own peace, it is gone past recall. He
trusts no one. And he cannot reconcile himself to the loss of any
part of what was his. Normandy will be his death. He still dreams
of recovering it, and for the sake of that delusion he is risking all
that he has. For what purpose do you think he is now levying these
new aids that are causing my stewards so much travail? To equip
his fleet and army for the invasion of Normandy! For what purpose
did he accept the risk of this reckless pressure on the Welsh? So that
his rear might be safe from attack while he sails for Normandy!"

"It seems like to have the opposite effect," said Harry, busy over
his tracing-tables, but listening intently none the less.

"It does, for it has raised the very devil he hoped to bind, and
before the chains were ready for him. But I tell you, Harry, if these
Welsh rebels can make the border so hot as to turn the king from

his enterprise of Normandy—if they can do that, and do it in time—
they will have done England a good service."

"In time! And how soon is 'in time'?"

"By this coming summer," said Isambard, "for that is when the
king purposes to sail. And if he does spend so much energy clutching
hopelessly at what's already lost, not only Wales will slip out of his
hands, but England, too."

Into the groves of Harry's stone forest, now magically coming
into full leaf before the passing of the frosts, these echoes of the
turmoil of the world came strangely and distantly, dulled of most
of their import before they reached the ear. And like the undertow
of a loud and dangerous tide, the long, submerged groan of the
ultimate victims tore at his senses with a far more desperate vehemence. The king's tenants-in-chief complained of the burden they
bore, and indeed if any among them lay under his displeasure he
could readily turn their debts into their death. But the small farmers
and the villeins in their fields could never escape the load. Not the
king's caprice, but the precise operation of social law let fall upon
them, in the end, the full weight of the royal debts. Through baron
and tenant and sub-tenant the burden of extortion came down on
the poorest, and through them upon their labouring soil.

How many more such fittings-out, how many more such expedi-
tions, could they bear? And when would they find the common
sense to condemn the futile fantasy of honour for which they were
wrung, and not the mere act of extortion? They lamented and complained of the tallages that bled them, but they fulminated like
outraged princes in the next breath against King Philip who had
curtailed their majesty, and boasted how his conquest should yet be
wrested from him. If there were other voices, they kept their views
within their own doors. Only the women, struggling to feed their
growing families, sometimes gave vent to their exasperation. Normandy? What was Normandy to them? They had only the haziest
of notions where it lay. They could neither spend Normandy to buy
cloth, nor give honour to their children to eat.

Before Easter the king's courier rode in from Cambridge, with a
letter summoning Isambard to join the court there for the festival.
He entertained his guest lavishly, but made no attempt to prepare
for the journey until he had asked who was to be present, and cut

short the imposing list of names and titles with a dry query touching the Prince of Gwynedd. Yes, Prince Llewelyn and his princess would be there in the king's entourage.

"Then he wastes his time sending for me," said Isambard. "He knows well that I have sworn not to attend on him on any occasion when the Prince of Gwynedd is received at court. Tell him that in all other matters he is assured of my duty and service, but in this I beg he will hold me excused."

"I cannot give him such a message," said the courier, aghast.

"I will have you deliver it under seal. You cannot be answerable for what I write." And he called in a clerk, and dictated a letter of such elaborate courtesy and such inflexible insolence that even the clerk ventured to attempt reasoning with him.

"My lord, would it not be better—may I not write that you are indisposed and cannot come?"

"Do so," said Isambard with a wolfish grin, "and you shall hang for petty treason. After you have been flogged for insubordination, of course. Write what I bid you write, and be sure I shall read it before I seal it, so let it be accurate. You will make it clear to the King's Grace that I *will not* come. Say also that when he sends for me to attend him in arms on a further visit to the Prince of Gwynedd, as I foretell he will do very soon, he will find me as forward as any."

The terrified clerk wrote accordingly, as well as he could for the trembling of his hand, and the reluctant courier took the letter away with him, though Isambard doubted whether he would deliver it.

He did not have to wait long for the echoes of his prophecy. Whatever Llewelyn saw and heard in his Easter visit to his father-in-law, it did not dispose him to fear any very effective counteraction against whatever action the indignant Welsh chiefs might be contemplating, and it did incline him to give serious consideration to joining them. The new castles on which the whole wild, proud population of Wales turned suspicious eyes had not been in the bargain struck at Aber. Who was first breaking the terms of the peace?

But it was another voice, a voice at once infinitely distant and as close and urgent as the well-being of the soul, that sounded the decisive note of revolt. Pope Innocent, that spoiled emperor, took fire with opportunist alacrity from the first mild spark of Welsh insurrection, and hurled his last and most irresistible bolt against his obstinate enemy.

"Did I not tell you?" Isambard erupted in the lodge like a storm-wind, between rage and contempt and pure enjoyment of the complexity and ruthlessness of the pontifical mind. "Did I not tell you, Harry, in Paris, that we had started a dangerous precedent with our Crusade against a Christian monarch? Did I not tell you the weapon would be too alluring to lie neglected for long? The Pope has profited by the example, and been seduced by the temptation. There is not a more subtle or a more able villain in Europe than our Innocent!"

He laughed at the startled face Harry turned from the capital on which he was working, though the astonishment was due rather to the sense of shock he always felt at the world's invasion of his rapturous peace than to any surprise at hearing Isambard so outspoken.

"God's deputy on earth has preached a holy war against the enemy of God, John. He has not only urged the King of France to invade him, but also absolved the Welsh princes from their allegiance and Wales from the interdict. There'll be bells ringing across the border, Harry, and Mass will be sung again. Maids can marry, and old men can be buried in holy ground. If they hesitated before, what is there to hold them now? They're up in arms from Gwynedd to Glamorgan, on God's business. Llewelyn is storming through the Middle Country, sweeping all before him. Everything we were at such pains to take from him has fallen back like a ripe plum into his hand. Rhys has burned Swansea, and the prince of Powis is battering at the gates of Mathrafal. Farewell, Normandy! Now if John can but keep his head we'll have it out with Llewelyn once for all."

"Have you had word yet from the king about his muster?" asked Harry, caught up into this whirlwind of excitement almost against his will.

"Not yet. I've sent a messenger to ask what force he wants of me, and where, and when. Oh, God!" he said, gripping Harry's shoulder with fingers that bit like steel, "bring me face to face with him this time, and no king by! Give me Llewelyn, and whatever the price may be here or in purgatory, I'll pay it laughing!"

The king's summons this time made no reference to the last insolent refusal. The matter was too urgent for remembering such minor scores. He appointed a muster at Chester on the 19th of August, and named the force he required from Isambard; who promptly raised more than the number of knights and archers, and double the men-at-arms, and lashed the husbandmen in all parts of his widely-scattered honour with aids and tallages to pay for the expedition. He was possessed. A trail of distraints, imprisonments, floggings and hangings marked the course by which he advanced upon his enemy. When he marched his levy out of Parfois at the end of July, the villages lay stripped of almost everything that could be commandeered as funds or supplies, their ablest men, their best horses. Even such iron as they possessed had been seized for arms. With the harvest hard upon them they had lost half their means of reaping it.

Harry, who was deaf to the greater voices of the outside world, caught the suppressed whisperings of the helpless little people with an infallible ear. Even if he had not, Adam would have seen to it that they were relayed to him. No one was likely to go to FitzJohn for help. He was my lord's voice in my lord's absence, and dared not stray from his orders, even if he would.

"The want of labour is the worst," said Adam. "That, at least, we have in plenty. And he never touched Richard Smith's supplies of iron. I'm not one for filching from a job, but this is a matter of their living through the winter, and the material and the making for a few new flails and sickles he can better afford than they can, God knows."

They looked at each other speculatively, and began to smile. "We'll have all the masters talk to their men," said Harry, "and spare all they can, all who're willing to go to the fields. Please God he's safely out of Parfois for two months, at least. We'll have everything in by the time he comes home."

But on the 20th of August, long before they were done with the grain, Langholme rode into Parfois with word that the muster was dispersed, the Welsh venture cancelled, and the returning levy only a day away on its march home. He waited only for a change of horses and rode on to the manor of Erington with his news, leaving them to prepare in haste for a homecoming they did not understand, and which could hardly mean anything but disaster.

Harry and Adam were at work in one of the villages on the English side of the Long Mountain, when Gilleis herself rode down to warn them that they had best call home their volunteer harvesters, and be manifestly about their own work before the lord of Parfois arrived. Harry, stripped to the waist and brown and bitten as any villager, stared up at her blankly from the stubble and with a run and a leap scrambled up to join her on the headland. He kissed her almost absently, and: "What, called off?" said he. "Not even delayed? But why? What's gone amiss?"

"I know nothing but that they're coming home. Langholme was not within the ward more than a quarter of an hour, and if FitzJohn knows what's happened he must be the only one, and he's said no word. But it's certain they'll be here by tomorrow."

"Ah, there's time enough, we'll have every man back on the site before morning. It goes hard to leave it unfinished, though," he said reluctantly, looking round with delight on the baked, blonde harvest fields. "It's long since I sweated the mischief out of me this way. They'll have their men back to see it completed, and their horses, too, but I'd have liked to finish what I began. Still, better not give him a holt to take out his spleen on them. I'll come back and put on my gown again, and he'll never be the wiser."

"Never be the wiser, and he has only to cast an eye at the colour of you," said Gilleis maternally, "to see you've been playing truant." She tidied his wild hair with her fingers, teasing out a few blanched husks of oats from the tangled locks. "Show me which girl you've been tumbling in the back of the wagon, to fill this thatch of yours with chaff! I knew I should have come with you."

"You do me great wrong," he said, injured. "Ask Adam if I have not worked like a Trojan. But faith, there's time yet to make up for that, now you've put the idea in my head. You'll be riding back at once, sweetheart, I take it?"

"And so will you," said Gilleis firmly. "Ask Adam, indeed! After all the covering-up you've done for him in your time! I won't stir from here until you put on your tunic and come with me."

They rode back together happily in the decline of the afternoon, now racing like children, now dawdling like lovers. The sky was without a cloud, and their pleasure in each other without a shadow. Only as they climbed the steep track to Parfois did the sudden chill of the troubled world fall upon their hearts again, and wonder and

speculation agitate the surface of their happiness; the inner security
they had between them could never be touched.

Isambard rode in towards noon the next day, with only a handful
of knights in attendance. In the outer ward he dismounted, walking
away from his steaming horse before the grooms could run to take
it from his hand, and shed cloak and gloves on the steps of the Lady's
Tower for Langholme to pick up as he hurried to help him disarm.
The squire was back from Erington only an hour before his master,
and came breathless and nervous into the private apartments, to
unbuckle sword-belt and unlace hauberk and carry away out of sight
all the accoutrements of war. Isambard turned about beneath the
trembling hands with a stony quietness, surrendering to these symbolic rites a body from which the mind seemed to have withdrawn.

When he was stripped of all the useless trappings he stretched
back his long arms for his gown, and wrapped it about him, and made
a single curt motion of dismissal that sent Langholme scurrying
thankfully out of the room. Not one word had yet been said. Benedetta brought wine and offered it, standing squarely before him so
that he could no longer maintain either the assumption or the pretence that he was alone.

"So there's to be no reckoning with Llewelyn," she said.

The eyes which had been staring through her shortened their
range slowly, were aware of the room, of the wine-cup, and at last
of her face. He took the cup from her and walked away to stand at
the window, looking down into the river valley.

"The plans were well-made, for once," he said in a dry, quiet
voice. "This time we need not have halted at Aber, we could have
wrested from him the last corner of Anglesey. The king was to join
us on the 19th, but I left Chester with only de Guichet, and went
to meet him at Nottingham. The Welsh boys were all brought there.
On the day he rode in, before he would break his fast, he had them
dragged out and hanged."

He reached this close with no change of tone, but something in
the look of his back, the rigidity of the broad shoulders, the strained
stillness of his head, made her aware of his detestation. Not the
savagery of the act, but its meanness and irrelevance, revolted him;
there should have been no energy or hate to spare for such petty
revenges while Llewelyn lived, and with Llewelyn dead there would

have been room enough for magnanimity. He saw the death of the
children as a meaningless and contemptible dissipation of the hatred
which belonged all to a more satisfying adversary.

"All?" she asked in a low voice.

A short, hard laugh broke out of him like a cry. "No, not all! Not
Griffith! If he had to kill, I might at least have kept a spark of respect
for him if he had killed Griffith. Did I not say he would never dare?
The father's hand was over him like a canopy, he could not be
touched. And John had just enough wit to realise that if he spared
only one, and *that* one, the meanest must despise him. No, he left
a handful of them to bear Griffith company. I don't know how many
survived—I did not count the wretched little bodies."

"We were not unprepared," said Benedetta sombrely, "for we
have had news from Shrewsbury in your absence that marches with
this. It seems Robert of Vieuxpont held one Welsh prince in the
castle there. He received the king's order to hang him, and it was
done."

"He is the king's lieutenant, he must do the king's bidding or
quit his office. But the end of it all—the cream of the jest! Three
days after this miserable prentice butchery the king countermands
all the preparations for the campaign, dismisses the levies and shuts
himself up from us all. It was two days before he would receive me,
and me he comes as near trusting as any. He had had letters, from
the Princess of Gwynedd among others, and all to the same purport.
He undertook this Welsh campaign, they said, at his own peril, for
there was a conspiracy afoot among his own vassals to take this
opportunity of betraying him to his enemy, or else making him
their prisoner. He believed it, and called off the muster."

"But if his daughter was the source of this," said Benedetta with
a faint and rueful smile, "it is not hard to see her purpose. She has
a husband and a father to save by such an invention."

"So I told him, and begged him to go forward and pay no heed.
There were others to confirm it, he says, but would not tell me who.
And if it were true, what does he gain by this? There will be other
opportunities. The poison is that they should desire to bring him
down. If that be truth, they will not want occasions. What falls not
out of itself they will make. And if he has enemies all round him,
yet he might at least gain by going forward boldly and wiping out

one, the rankest of all. But no, he would not be turned. He could have saved himself. He could have taken the field and dared them to act, met them and outfaced them on their chosen ground. It was the only way to salve anything out of this ruin, with all to gain and nothing to lose. And he would not do it! I prayed him for his own sake, for England's sake, even in mere justice to those poor hanged puppies who were being hurried into the ground, and their sires who had a right to confront him with the sword. I knelt to him!" groaned Isambard, and suddenly laid his arm over his eyes to ward off the remembered image. "I went on my knees and implored him to go forward. And he would not! There'll be no reckoning with Llewelyn, now or ever. It is over."

The autumn and winter passed, and the ribs of the vaulting soared under the timber roof of the church, graceful, impetuous, lofty, until the nave stood like the beautiful, strange skeleton of a fabulous ship sailing keel-uppermost through air, in vindication of its name. Before the frosts ended they had completed the filling in of the cells, and the lovely bones put on spare and shapely flesh.

In his safe, sufficing world Harry scarcely heard the confused rumours from outside the walls. The king's splenetic shufflings to find a champion to fight his Welsh war in his stead, his gift to various cousins of the house of Gwynedd of cantrefs he did not possess, and promises of yet other cantrefs if they could win them, while the Welsh laughed at his promises and threats alike, all these spiteful and ludicrous expedients by which he sought to buy off destiny passed by the builders like withered leaves blown in the wind. They had more important things to think about.

Only when Isambard came out to the church and stood watching them at work, as he did daily, some emanation of unassuageable grief reached out to them from his silence to discomfort and dismay.

Another Easter came and went, and in France King Philip, according to reliable reports, was building up a fleet and an army for his holy war against England, in derisive echo of John's ruined plans for the invasion of Normandy. If John did not move soon England would slip through his fingers like Normandy, like Wales; but there was no move left for him to make.

There was, however, one, it seemed, the last and most irretrievable; and on the 15th of May he made it. And in its immediate effects it was a master-stroke, though it proved in the long run a death-stroke, too. He had received, some two weeks previously, certain Knights of the Temple fresh from France, though not even his household officers knew what had passed between them. After their audience with him they sailed for France again, and in due course returned to Dover escorting the papal legate Pandulf; to whom, as vicar of the vicar of God on earth, the rebellious son of the Church surrendered, in return for the Church's protection, his kingdom of England and Ireland, and at whose hands he received them again as the Church's vassal, and accepted with them the archbishop he had so long refused to recognise.

A stroke of magic passed with the crown from hand to hand. It transformed the crusading Welsh princes into common rebels against the Lord's anointed. It snatched from Philip all claim to the prize he had been promised. It interposed the Church's protecting authority between John and his own discontented vassals. It gave him security, established him firmly in his curtailed rights, confounded all his enemies.

It also dishonoured him and broke his heart.

"But to kneel to him! Harry, to kneel to him and offer him the crown! It was England kneeling. How could he do it? How could he abase himself and us? If he had defied him, we could but have died, and we should have died unshamed. What is there in dying? Every man comes to it, it's nothing to fear. But to unman us all is worse than a death."

After seven days of absence from the church and the world Isambard stood again in the nave, between the stony trees of heaven, in the silence of the twilight. The beautiful serried windows of the clerestory, open upon a soft green sky, looked in upon him like rows of luminous pale eyes in shadowy faces, watching and wondering. They said he had not eaten for four days, nor drunk, nor spoken a word since the one muted cry he uttered when the news was brought to him, before he fell senseless and was carried to his bed. He looked as if it might well be true. All his golden Grecian tan was long since faded; English summers had left him only the dull brown weathering of all men who lead outdoor lives. Now that, too, was blanched to a grey pallor, and the flesh worn away beneath it. His face was a mask of bone, but because his bones were ample and splendidly shaped his beauty was enhanced rather than impaired. The fine eyes, enormous in their cavernous sockets, were windows into a frenzy of pain, and the worst of the pain stemmed from that desolate intelligence of his, that would not let him leave one implication of catastrophe unexplored. His body was fallen away so that the most passionate ascetic of Clairvaux could hardly have matched his emaciation. Seven days of fasting could not account for this dissolution; it came from the spirit.

"Harry, Harry, in the night I see it, I cannot stop seeing it. The crown lay on the ground at his feet, and he spurned it with his shoe. He delayed giving it back, to assert his possession. England! We did not consent to it! Our name was taken in vain. But, oh, Harry, we cannot get clean of it now."

He had reached the midmost point of the nave when he began to speak. It was the quietness and the loneliness that invited speech, here where the coming of night turned all that cheerful, busy, happy turmoil to stillness and peace. The first words came out of him like the first tears of one who has not wept for a lifetime, with spasmodic anguish, rending the tight cords of his throat; and then more freely, and then in flood. He lifted his contorted face to what light remained, and strained for breath as if he could not get enough air to keep life in him; but for the rest he stood very still, his clenched hands pressed together before his breast.

"My lord, it is not for me to accuse or defend him," said Harry, shaken with the intensity of this agony. "And yet I know this, that he also suffers. Out of the many dangers he saw for England, he chose to take this way, and the choice is his, as the burden was his. He sought to deliver England. My heart and my mind cry out in me, like yours, that he was wrong, yet I feel that his intent was not base. It was deliverance he sought, and by an act for my very life I could not match. Remember it to him, and forgive."

"Forgiveness is not mine to give, and England will never give it. I would have spat in Pandulf's face rather than kneel to him."

"And so would I," said Harry, "but who's to say if we should have been right?"

"Everything falls away, Harry! England I loved, and he has so befouled England that I cannot look on it without revulsion. Christendom I revered and trusted, and this is the voice of Christendom, the regent of God, this tortuous schemer who blows now east, now west, as his advantage lies. And thus shamelessly! Last year it was bell, book and candle out, and eternal salvation to all who take arms against God's enemy, John. This year, let all princes restrain their hands on pain of excommunication from the person of our beloved son. Oh, Harry, Harry, is it for the God of such a contemptible brazen weathercock as this that we've built a house fit for archangels?''

He clutched at Harry's arm; the convulsive grip of the bony fingers, so long and able, and now so helpless, the veins standing like blue cords between shrunken skin and starting bone, went to Harry's heart. He felt the shuddering tension of Isambard's body pass into him, and was flooded with so unexpected and uncontrollable an affection that it loosed his tongue from all the restraints of ceremony. He cast an arm about his lord's erect and fleshless shoulders, and clasped him warmly.

"What has Innocent to do with this? Often and often I have caught myself wondering about these same things. But always, when I felt my work growing beneath my hands, I wondered no longer. I build, and I feel no intervention of pope or priest between myself and God, and no doubt in my mind that this act of praise and faith is justified. King John may have failed you, but England has not. Innocent may shuffle his little blessings and bans without scruple, like loaded dice, but I swear God does not. I have not been building for pope or bishop or priest. The house *is* for the archangels.''

"Ah, it's well for you, who have to do with honest stone. But I am for ever bound, not to England, but to John. I am bound to him by oath of fealty, by the lands I hold, by the many times I have laid my hands between his hands. I am his man, whether I will or no. He has degraded and shamed me, but I am his man still. Let him be what manner of worm he will, I am not absolved from my oath, I can never be absolved. My allegiance corrupts and sickens me, but I cannot get free. I am his man till death, and I cannot get free!''

The hoarse, labouring voice, half-suffocated with raging grief, brought forth the words with convulsive effort, like gouts of blood breaking from a wound. He drew back his head, turning tormentedly to right and left, as though he struggled to evade the compulsion that drew him forward along the inescapable path of faithfulness. The arm that held him tightened. He closed his eyes for a moment, and opened the heavy lids again to behold the young, grave, troubled face, heavy with tenderness, regarding him as a loving child regards a parent overwhelmed with incomprehensible sorrow.

"Oh, Harry!" he said in a great sigh, and let his forehead rest for a moment in the hollow of the homespun shoulder. "Oh, Harry, but I'm weary!"

Chapter Twelve

*B*enedetta came down alone to the lodge, where Harry and Adam were inspecting the newly-cut voussoirs for the last of the tower windows. It had been raining, in the fitful April manner, with flashing sunlight between the showers, and the skirt of her green gown was dark from the wet grass. She ran her fingers along the joggled faces of the moulded stones, cut in deep, smooth waves, and asked curiously: "Why do you cut them like that?"

"They key together more securely so. Look, they're matched to bind so close, you'll never see the join when they're raised."

She fingered the mouldings and listened to the grinding hum of the wheel in the tower, hoisting stone, and the snatches of voices that the breeze brought from the scaffolding.

"How much longer now? A year?"

"Maybe a little longer. Call it a year, you won't be far out."

"It seems impossible it can be so nearly finished." The sadness came into her voice against her will. From beneath lowered lids she watched Adam take up mallet and chisel, and return whistling to the corbel on which he was working. "When will the fabric be completed? Before the winter?"

"God willing! We're in the last stage of the tower. But there'll be work enough left for the winter inside. There's the floor tiles to lay, and the screens and stalls to fit, and the altar-stones and sedilia to put up. I doubt the glazier won't get all his windows in until the spring, so the scaffolding will stay up until next year. You should ask him to let you see the panels he has in their cames already, they're a wonder."

"So by next year's summer," said Benedetta, "it will all be over." She looked along the stored stones, fantasies of springing, bur-geoning growth, crockets and mask-mouldings and bosses, and lengths of the prepared brattishing for the cornice of the tower. "What will you do then?"

"I haven't thought of it yet. My lord has hinted at keeping me in his service. So great a landlord must be for ever building some-where or other, there'd be plenty of work for me."

"Yes," she said, leaving the word solitary and lame on the air, though it seemed she must have intended something more; and she listened to Adam's whistling, and waited, he could not guess for what. "You know the king is for France again?"

"So we heard. There's no curing him of this hankering after Normandy. Since his fleet made such short work of the French ships last year off Flanders, he's taken heart again, and no wonder. The churchmen may claim it was a divine judgement on Philip for strik-ing at England sideways, after the Pope had forbidden him to go about it the direct way—but I doubt providence would have had its work cut out but for the king's energy and ability. But he'll find it a harder thing to get the better of Philip on his own soil. And the Emperor Otto isn't the ally I'd have chosen myself. What does my lord say?"

"I should ask you that," she said drily. "It's long since he confided such matters to me. But you know he holds the French possessions well lost, and wills that lost they shall remain, however it may displease his peers to part with half their revenue. He sees the only hope of England in accepting the loss of Normandy. A victory in France could set the king up in popular esteem, I suppose, at least for a time. But I'm sure Ralf prays for a defeat."

"He has not sent for my lord to join him, at any rate," said Harry.

"God be thanked! No, he is too distrustful of the Welsh; he wants

Ralf here to hold the march for him. He puts little faith in this truce the archbishop has patched up between Welsh and English."

She looked round quickly, hearing the light feet of the boy clerk from the tracing-house, running as usual. He bounced eagerly between the stacked stones, saw that Harry was occupied, and applied instead to Adam, in a breathless whisper.

"The devil!" said Adam, cheerfully enough. "He could have chosen a better time. No matter, I'll come." And he laid down his tools and went off briskly, his hand on the boy's shoulder.

As soon as they were well out of earshot Benedetta turned vehemently from her examination of the worked stones. "Harry, send Adam away from here!"

His head came up with a jerk; he stared at her in blank incomprehension. "Send him away? But why?"

"Because he's in danger here, or at any moment he may be. I had thought it might last out the time safely, but I'm no longer sure of it, and he must not be risked. Surely you can make use of him somewhere else? Send him out on your errands to the glasshouses and the pottery where you buy your tiles. But don't let him remain here at Parfois, constantly in my lord's sight."

"My lord?" Harry put down his mallet and chisel among the array of punches laid out on his bench, and stood staring at her in doubt and wonder. "What's awry between him and my lord? I know of nothing. He's taken little note of him all this time, but that little friendly enough. Why should he be dangerous to him now?"

"Because," she said bluntly, "he has begun to brood upon the remembrance that once, for the sake of a song, I received him into my bed. The time will surely come when that recollection will become unbearable. Don't let Adam be within his reach when that happens." It was difficult to say, and ill to hear, and to be harshly practical about it was the only way of keeping it endurable. But his astonishment and reserve drew a smile from her. She had dragged him so abruptly out of the happy glades of his stone forest that he was at a loss with the complexities of a less perfect world. "Have you not seen that he is fallen into a desperate jealousy of me? He talks to you more than to any. Has he never spoken of me in— strange terms?"

"Never!" But he had no sooner said it than he realised how

seldom, in these last years, Isambard had so much as mentioned her name. He remembered, too, occasions when strange things had indeed been said, not of her, and yet closely touching her, now that he considered them more sharply. He had been too much engrossed with his own happiness to have much attention to spare for the dissatisfactions of others. He blamed himself for his blindness. "And in your love, Harry?" the distant echoes mocked him. "To have all, even the last and greatest! What right has one man to so much?"

"I see," said Benedetta, "that you have second thoughts."

He shook his head helplessly. "I've been a fool, I should have seen that there was grave matter in his moods. But indeed there was very little ever said, and nothing of you. And we knew he had always his time of darkness. But I cannot believe in his jealousy. That way it never tended, I swear. He knows well that you are honest in your dealings, he cannot be in doubt of your faithfulness."

"Ah, faithfulness!" she said with a sigh. "You are making my mistake, Harry. He wanted more than faithfulness." She put up her hands and threaded the long fingers into the hair springing so vigorously from her temples; he saw how thin they were, pale among the dark red, and marvelled that he had not seen how she had lost flesh, as though she were being fretted away like her lord by the friction of the dual hopeless passion that at once joined and severed them.

"You'd better know how this thing stands," she said almost roughly. "You will need to regulate your acts accordingly. When he asked me to come to England with him I told him plainly there was one I loved, and in a measure that never comes again. I said that if he was willing to accept what I still had to give, I would be his, and never leave him unless for that one who had my heart's love. And God knows I did not lie, saying that *he* was never likely to beckon me! On those terms he took me, and I have held to my bargain faithfully. The more fool I, to think he could long hold to his! Did ever you know him content with second place? I should have known it could not so continue."

She shook her head wearily between her hands. Harry did not touch her. Often in the past he had laid a hand on her easily, without a thought; now he perceived how terrifying was the power she had conferred on him to give her both pleasure and pain, and held back for fear the pain might prove the greater. And even this constraint between them seemed to him a false quantity, but he did not know how to master it.

"I begin to see," he said in a low voice, "how he has been cozened. Oh, not by you. He compounded for what you agreed to give, but he trusted in time and his own worth to have all at last. He could not know that he was bringing to England with him the very man he hoped to put out of your mind. And this, I misdoubt, you did not tell him."

"You men," she said, suddenly herself again, and looking up at him with a smile half scornful and half tender, "are all the same. You have no more faith than Ralf, I see, in a woman's constancy of purpose. There was no need to tell him. It made no difference to the case whether you were near or far, living or dead. What I gave to you I gave once for all. I told Ralf the truth entire; that to this last sanctuary of my heart he could never come. My sin was not a sin of deceit, only of want of understanding. I should have known that was enough to bind him to the siege for ever. I did not know him so well then as I know him now. But now it is too late to set it right."

"Yet you may yourself be deceived. Benedetta, I am at a loss what to do. Surely if I should go from here, then in time—"

"You cannot go," she said, "until your work is finished. You pledged yourself. But even if you could, it is already too late. He knows he is not—no, I will not say 'is not loved'! How could I not have some love for him, after all that has passed? But he knows that he will never enter the place of his desire. He knows I have not changed towards that other of whom I told him, and that I shall never change. Resignation is impossible to him. The struggle will go on, until one of us is destroyed—one, or both. I am only afraid that it may involve others, and I would not have Adam one of them. Get him away out of sight!"

"Oh, that's the least of the difficulties. I can send him to take charge at the quarry, you'll have heard that we're being raided again from Cynllaith, and we still need stone these next few months. But what of your own safety? If he cannot lay hands on—that other— may he not turn on you in the end?"

"Does it matter?" she said indifferently, not seeking to sting him, but honestly putting aside what seemed to her irrelevant. The consequences of what she had undertaken it was for her to abide.

"You know well it matters," said Harry angrily. "It is in my mind that you must leave him—"

"Then you may put it out of your mind, for I will not."

"No," he agreed, clutching helplessly at his temples, "I see I should be wasting my breath to urge it. You'll hold by your word though it kill you, I know that. But for God's sake, what is to be done for you? I cannot leave it so. I would you might have loved him, for he was worth it, and now what's to become of you both? Oh, Benedetta," he said wretchedly, "if you had been less than you are, life would have been easier for us all."

"I could say as much to you," she said, looking up with that sudden indomitable flash in her eyes, the worn ghost of the old gallant laughter. "Do you think I would have followed a lesser man across Europe? Life is always easy for those who have little mind and less heart. But indeed you need not fear for me. He loves me. He trusts me. He will not harm me unless he come to utter despair, and that I think is a state as impossible to him as resignation. It is not even a matter of pride in keeping faith now," she said gently. "He is mine, even if I cannot love him as he understands love. As for me, I no longer know what love is, it has so many faces. Even if—that other—beckoned me now, I could not go. What I did to Ralf I did unwittingly, but it binds me to him so fast that I can never get loose until death, unless he cut the knot and cast me off. So you see there is no profit in caring what becomes of me. Though I'm glad," she said, with a long, smiling glance of her grey eyes, "that you feel it has some importance. That sets me up again in my own esteem."

"I wish someone would do as much for me," said Harry ruefully, "for indeed I've been but a poor, unprofitable friend to you. At least promise that if you ever have need of one to do you a service, you will send me word before any other."

"Gladly, if you will do as much for me. And it is in my mind, Harry, that I must not approach you so often or so freely as I have done in the past. It would be well if we had some other means of keeping in touch. I have often wished that I might know your wife better. Will you be my advocate to her? Say that I am lonely, that

I earnestly entreat her of her grace to spend some part of her time with me daily."

She laughed at the sudden boyish flush that coloured a face mature, resolute and grave. "It is not all strategy, I give you my word. I could love her, if she will let me. But there is art in it, too, I grant you. Wives and mistresses do not keep company. I would have him in no doubt of your position, and I would have a reliable contact with you, in case of need. Tell her as much as you please of the reason. All, if you will. What you do not tell, I think she will guess."

"I will talk to Gilleis," he said very quietly. "She will come to you. I think she will be glad."

"Ask her to visit me tomorrow while he is about his business with the steward and the rolls. And take care of the matter of Adam. I must go back, I have been longer over my errand than I meant."

"Benedetta," he burst out abruptly, as she made to turn from him, "what was it awakened him?"

She opened her eyes wider upon his face, in quick and wary surprise that he should penetrate so surely into the one corner of her mind she had kept from him. He went on hesitantly: "When we first came here, I swear, he was happy—as happy as it is in his nature to be. I blame myself that I did not mark when he began to change, but I think this was no gradual corruption that came upon him. He knows his worth too well to be lightly persuaded you could hold out against him lifelong. He would be hoping and believing yet, if something had not happened to show him the truth. What was it?"

It was the only moment in which she had ever been tempted to lie to him. He saw the grey eyes veiled and withdrawn for an instant, then they cleared and shone upon him, and he knew she had put the shadow by.

"It was your marriage," she said gently. "It was a novel conception for him that marriage should be the crown of love, instead of a bargain struck as a means to land or wealth or blood alliances. I suppose he had never been so close to such a match before. It went to his heart. That same night he offered me a princely gift. He offered me marriage, a marriage after the new dispensation."

He stood staring at her steadily, while the blood drained from his face. He could not speak, there was nothing to be said to her. He had been always the fool of God blundering about her life without ill intent, innocently smashing all that she valued, breaking down the walls of her peace, complicating all her straight courses into a labyrinth.

"I refused it," said Benedetta simply. "I could do no other. So he could hardly fail to understand."

She turned her head, and saw Adam coming across the trampled, threadbare grass. The gay, light sound of his whistling went before him like a blackbird's rich notes. He had not a care in the world.

"I would I had never set foot in your life," said Harry in a low voice. "I have brought you nothing but sorrow. I pray you pardon me!"

"*Pardon!*" She turned on him suddenly a startled face, bright and fierce as a flame, the eyes enormous with astonishment. She opened unwary lips to pour out to him the spring of molten gold that gushed from her heart. But Adam's foot was already light on the beaten earth under the penthouse roof, and a snatch of laughter, and a voice complaining querulously of the inattention and levity of boys nowadays, followed him in. Benedetta turned and left the lodge without a word.

There were no lives lost in the little war of Cynllaith that spring, though there were a good many knocks exchanged and a few minor arrow wounds to tend and the constant annoyance of losing horses and oxen. It seemed that Llewelyn was doing no more than tease his enemy. Only occasionally did the tribesmen launch an open raid. They sank one cargo of stone in the Tanat, and held up operations for ten days, while the river was cleared again. They made one testing raid on the loaded wagons after Adam's arrival, to see what mettle of man they had to deal with, and drew off with honours even. But for the most part they preferred to thread the picket line by night and filch a horse or two, or drop a tree neatly across the wagon track, or steal the harness. Theft, the most despised and condemned of crimes at home, was an honourable amusement once it crossed the border.

The Prince of Gwynedd had not, apart from these playful activities, laid a finger on the truce which Archbishop Langton, once established, had made it his business to prolong between England

and Wales. Such pinpricks could hardly be regarded as an infringement of the terms; and indeed, why should Llewellyn want to renew hostilities, when he had consolidated all his gains and retained them unchallenged? Innocent had not, after all, quite forgotten the services of the wild hillmen he had never seen.

But at the height of the summer Adam, who had taken to this skirmishing like a duck to water, dealt all too competently with a raiding party by the riverside, and took three prisoners. He sent them under escort to Parfois. Isambard, without hesitation and without even having set eyes on them, had them hanged. After that it was *galanas*, blood-feud, but without the possibility of an atonement price being paid. The clans of the three dead men, all local, began to pick off stragglers from the stone convoys, and any man who unwarily showed himself too near the border was bound to draw an arrow from the thickets beyond the brook. Before July was out it became clear that the Prince of Gwynedd also considered himself to be at feud on his men's account. He had a country at peace, a vigorous little household army of a hundred and fifty men spoiling for work, and many hundreds of his free clansmen willing and ready to provide reserves if they should be needed. Private hate could never have deflected him from the larger affairs of his country; but now he had leisure to indulge it without risk to Wales. The little war of Cynllaith had become more than a game.

Adam held his own through two probing attacks, and sent back information which indicated that Llewelyn's own household troops had come into Cynllaith, and that the prince's captain of the guard, if not the prince himself, was directing them.

"Good!" said Isambard grimly. "There'll be neither king nor court to run between us this time. We'll lead him on so far there'll be no withdrawing."

"Shall I send reinforcements to the quarry?" asked de Guichet. Parfois carried at this time only its normal household companies, but they made a sufficiently formidable array.

"Not a man! No, you take one company by the inland road to Oswestry, and I'll take the second by Careghofa, and we'll lie off until he moves in, and circle him from north and south together."

The quarry continued under increasing pressure, but was not directly attacked, as the two forces closed unobtrusively into position north and south of the outcrop of hills, waiting for the Prince of Gwynedd to ride into the trap. Their scouts filtered towards the border and beyond, and found no Welshmen under arms. Isambard, chafing at Careghofa, devoured his own starving heart and waited.

Two messengers rode into Parfois on the seventh day of August. The first brought the news that at Bouvines King Philip of France had won a resounding victory over the Emperor Otto, scattering the great coalition in fragments about the fields of France, and forcing John to enter into negotiations for a long truce. The second reeled in from the south on a lathered horse, and slid from his saddle in the outer ward to gasp out news that touched Parfois more nearly. While Isambard waited for Llewelyn in the north, Llewelyn had transferred his forces to the south, and struck at the manor of Erington, on the border of Herefordshire.

Every man in the castle who was fit to ride and had any skill in arms was drafted into the motley company FitzJohn flung together within the hour. It had taken him no more than five minutes to send off a courier, on the best horse he had left in the stables, to carry the news to Isambard, but Erington could not wait until the cheated companies rode south. The palisade had been breached before the messenger broke through to ride for help, and the garrison in their timber keep would be only too vulnerable. Harry dropped his tools and offered himself with the rest, a score of his men on his heels. He was no great swordsman, but he could handle a blade in an emergency, and arms they had in plenty.

They rode out from Parfois and galloped south on the ridge road under a cloudless sky faintly shimmering with heat haze.

"August!" said FitzJohn bitterly as they mounted. "No rain for a month, and his reverence preening himself on the success of his prayers for good harvest weather. If he's in his wits he'll be on his knees now praying for a downpour."

The bells were loud in England again; they heard them ringing for vespers from all the churches along the valley as they forded the Clun, hardly slackening speed to find a good footing through the shrunken summer waters.

"And all the brooks dry," fretted FitzJohn, "and the manor well will be low. If they're out of arrows they'll have no choice but to make a sally against odds, or stay and be roasted."

From the crest of the hills, as they climbed out of the river-valley, they saw smoke rising sullenly black against the pale blue sky. Long, drifting plumes of smoke, disseminating very slowly in an almost motionless air, hung like a grey ceiling above the skyline. They fetched a new burst of speed at the sight, though the horses were in a foam of sweat and had been pressed hard all the way.

For all their wild ride they came late. Llewelyn had played his cards well, and he was always a quick worker. Galloping from between the low, rolling hills, they saw the whole broad enclosure of the motte gushing smoke, and heard the crackling of wood as the flames twisted it, and it seemed to them that the whole of the manor was afire. Then, as they rode shouting down the curve of the fields and plunged at the steep sides of the mound, they saw the Welsh tribesmen scatter from the ditch and fling themselves towards their tethered ponies, and marked how one at least dropped and lay kicking with a clothyard shaft through him. The archers within the keep still had arrows, though how they could see to aim them was past guessing.

Under the pall of smoke the Welshmen drew off into the trees, but before many of them could untether and mount the motley muster of English had ridden into them, and they turned to fight. Great tongues of woodland came down here between the hills from Radnor Forest. Such of the Welshmen as broke away and found their mounts could be as elusive as foxes in that covert.

Harry leaned sidelong from the saddle to evade a braced lance, and wheeling his horse, ran his assailant through the upper arm and caused him to drop his weapon. The Welshman promptly sprang within his guard, and clamped his one good arm round his enemy's waist to drag him from the saddle, but Harry reversed his sword and clubbed at the uplifted forehead with the pommel, and as the dazed man relaxed his grip a little, kicked a foot free from the stirrup and hoisted his knee under the bearded chin, to hurl him off like a stone from a sling. He crashed among the roots of an oak, and lay winded. Harry hesitated only a second, looking down doubtfully at the gasping body, and then swung away to look for an undamaged opponent.

In the confusion of that brief battle in the edge of the wood he did no further hurt to anyone. Twice he pursued fugitive shapes that lay upon the necks of their ponies and rode through the coverts as daringly and smoothly as running wolves; but the first outran him easily, and the second he left at the summons of FitzJohn's horn. The English drew together out of the forest and converged upon the blackened shell of Erington, bringing six prisoners with them. The rest of the Welsh were safely away, and without fresh horses they were unlikely to be overtaken now. Far more urgent was the plight of the garrison, or what remained of it.

The gates of the palisade hung charred and glowing on their great hinges, sagging open on the smoky pale within. They hacked their way through into the bailey, and set to work to hew down the timbers that were still burning, and beat out the flames where the fire had taken less firm hold. All the stables and storehouses along the curtain had been plundered and fired, and there was no saving anything there, all they could do was use the axes on them wherever approach was possible, and bring them down. But the keep was still intact, only blackened with smoke and smouldering dully on the windward side. The timbers of the undercroft were hot to the touch, and the archer who threw open the door above and leaned out to hail them was smoked like a herring; but the garrison within were alive. They let down the ladder, and climbed out with their wounded, hoarse and parched and reaching eagerly for the offered flasks of water.

"If we had not been well-found in arrows," said the castellan, "and had four crack shots among us, they could have burned us to the ground long before this. And you come just in time, for we were down to our last dozen shafts. They drove off the stock hours ago, as soon as they had us bottled in here."

They told over their losses, bringing out the wounded and the dead to the open meadow out of the heat and suffocation of the motte. Seven English bodies and four Welsh lay together on the cool turf. There were three English badly wounded, and five with lesser hurts. Two tribesmen were brought out alive to join the six prisoners taken in the fight on the edge of the wood.

"We're here for the night," said FitzJohn, looking round on the falling dusk. He made his dispositions briskly: three parties to make the round of the nearest villages, where no doubt the inhabitants were huddled within barred doors at the rumour of the Welsh raid, to commandeer fresh horses and supplies of food; a line of pickets to cover the Welsh approaches, in case the raiders should be contemplating another visit by night; a lightweight on a fresh horse to ride back along the road to Parfois and intercept Isambard with the news; and half a dozen volunteers to scout through the woods into Radnor and try to get word which way the drovers had passed with the cattle and oxen. Oxen, of all living creatures, will not be hurried. If they could be recovered, so much the better.

Harry undertook this forest patrol gladly. If he was to remain a second day absent from his work, as well get all the freedom and exercise he could out of it.

"Make what use you can of the light that's left," said FitzJohn, "but don't push on after dark. We'll look for you back in an hour or so."

Isambard's land fingered the edge of Wales here, as at Parfois, but with no river between them. Harry rode through the woods alone, in a silence so profound that the blazing turmoil of Erington became a fantasy. Twice he came upon forest hamlets, but the villagers had neither seen nor heard anything of the raiders, or else they made a habit of closing both eyes and ears whenever there was a possibility of such visitors passing close to their solitude. There was a good deal of Welsh blood in some of the veins on this side of the border, too, and even those who were indubitably English had to live at peace with both sides if they wished to make their homes here. And once he found a small, isolated clearing of ploughland with a mean little dwelling upon it, almost certainly an illegal assart, but law limped with both feet these days. How long was it since the king's justices had been on circuit in any of these border shires? A matter of years? And no prospect of much improvement in the future, now that there was open talk of an alliance of barons to put an end to the king's infringements of their rights. When Corbett and FitzAlan and their kind began to talk of defending their rights, there was not likely to be much attention paid to the rights of lesser mortals.

Harry rode silently in the spongy turf, and was deeply content with his loneliness. He did not really want to find any traces of the Welsh. Let them have their spoils, they had lost several men to gain them, and it was Isambard who had first aggravated the rivalry into a blood-feud. He was on the point of turning to make the best of his way back to the manor, when he caught a glimpse of something small and furtive that ran aside among the falling shadows, and vanished into a clump of bushes. The quivering of the branches subsided slowly as he walked his horse past the spot; whoever had dived into cover there was crouching within the thicket.

He drew a yard past the place, and then kicked his feet from the stirrups and vaulted down almost on top of the watcher in the bushes. A shrill cry of fright startled his ears, and a wiry little body, slippery as an eel, fought to elude his grasp and narrowly failed. He caught the sudden narrow gleam of steel darting at his breast, and his parrying hand closed on a wrist so slender that he almost let it go again. A breathless voice bubbled Welsh curses at him, spitting like an angry cat. He had much ado to keep his hold on the furious, frightened little creature, it fought and struggled so; but in a few moments the struggles began to flag and breathless sobs to disrupt the curses. Harry plucked the dagger from a tiring hand and tossed it away into the bushes, and folding his right arm firmly round the boy, hauled him out into the open ride and stood him on his feet.

"Hush, now, hush your noise! I won't hurt you. Do you understand English?"

He got no answer at first. The child stood trembling under his hands, tensed to run like a hare at the first opportunity; a small, dark boy in brown hose and tunic, with a little homespun cloak buckled with gold on his shoulder. The face that stared sidelong up at him looked all eyes in the gathering darkness, a bright, moonlike shining of eyes, wild and wary as a fox's gleaming glance. He could not have been more than nine or ten years old, and small even for his age. Harry saw that the cloak was torn and the left cheek bruised and grazed. He dropped on one knee to bring his face on a level with the child's, and asked again gently: "You understand what I'm saying, don't you? Don't be afraid of me, I don't want to hurt you. But what are you doing here by yourself in the forest? Did you fall from your horse?"

The dark head nodded slowly. "I tried to catch him," said the boy suddenly in English, "but he ran away." He trembled more violently, but he was less frightened now.

"Are you hurt?" But the question was more by way of establishing sympathy than to extract information; to judge by the way he had fought, he had got nothing worse than a shaking. "Well, now, tell me how you came here alone? They surely didn't bring you raiding with them?"

Surprisingly the boy burst into tears at this; plainly there was something here that weighed on his mind even more distressingly than his fears at finding himself alone and benighted on the wrong side of the border. Harry was startled into offering a comfortable shoulder, and held and gentled him while he poured out his trouble in mingled English and Welsh. There was nothing new or surprising in it, after all; disobedient brats grow everywhere.

"Ah, so your father left you safe at Llanbister, did he? And gave you orders to stay there, and never stir a step. And there he'll expect to find you safe and sound when he comes back from his foray, no doubt. And this is how you've obeyed him!"

"I wanted to see," said the child, with a spark of the spirit that had got him into trouble.

"Curiosity killed the cat, did you never hear that? You should have done as you were told, and you'd have missed a fall and a fright. Never mind, we must see about finding you a place to sleep the night, and some food to put inside you."

"My father'll beat me," said the boy, and wept again heartily.

"Very possibly, and well you deserve he should. But not tonight. And who knows? By the time he gets you back he may be so glad to see you, he'll forget about your sins. Come on, now, I'm going to take you back with me. Don't be afraid of anything, I promise you shall be safe with me."

The dark head came up nervously from his shoulder, like a young horse shying. "You're English!"

"So I am, but I'm no monster, all the same. Child, if I left you here what would happen to you? Come along, and trust me to take care of you. I'm better than the wolves, at any rate."

He lifted the child to the saddle-bow, and mounted behind him, and so brought him back to Erington. It was dark by the time they emerged to the acrid smell of smoke and the dull glow of flattened timbers just burning out. Heat still quivered on the air. The boy, whose head had been nodding upon Harry's shoulder during the ride, started awake and looked round fearfully with great eyes and clung tightly to his captor's sleeve as he was lifted down among the strangers.

"God's wounds, Harry!" said FitzJohn, staring. "What have you got there?"

"A venturesome young man who went where he was told not to go, and got himself lost and thrown in the woods. He's shaken and bruised, but nothing worse. I'll share my cloak with him tonight, and see about getting him back where he belongs tomorrow. If you'll feed him you'll have his love for life, I see it in his eyes."

"Welsh?" asked FitzJohn, his eyes sharpening.

"I thank God!" snapped the child, before Harry could answer for him; and he stiffened and drew back his head like a hound raising its hackles.

"And a very proper spirit, too," said Harry, laughing. "Come, we'll find you some food to keep that temper of yours in good heart. Is there news from my lord?"

"He has sent de Guichet from Clun cross-country with most of his force to try and intercept Llewelyn, but it's certain even he expects nothing from it, or he'd have gone himself. They have too great a start of us. The rest he has despatched home, but for his immediate attendants, and they lie at Clun tonight. In the morning he'll be here."

"At least he knows by now that most of his garrison still live," said Harry, and took the boy by the arm to guide him through the camp. He gave him oatcakes, and some of the foraged beef that was already cooking, and watched him eat his fill. Then he cut swathes of the long dry grass from the headlands, and piled it for a bed on the springy turf at the edge of the trees. The child sat hunched, hugging his knees and staring all round him at the alien faces, suspicious and lonely. Harry said nothing to him, but wrapped himself in his cloak and lay down. In a few minutes the dark eyes turned wistfully upon him and the boy edged a little nearer. Harry rose on one elbow, smiling, and opened his cloak without a word. It was invitation enough. The child crept thankfully into the hollow of his arm and curled up against his side; the cloak wrapped them both.

"What's your name, imp? I forgot to ask it."

"Owen ap Ivor ap Madoc," murmured the drowsy mouth into his shoulder, and yawned hugely.

"Then, Owen ap Ivor ap Madoc, goodnight! Don't be afraid when you wake, I shall be here."

* * *

Isambard rode in at dawn, before the sun was up or the camp fully astir. He had shed the weight of his arms at Clun, but for the light hauberk of banded mail, and his sword. Three of his squires rode behind him. He looked upon what was ruined and what was saved of his manor with an equal attentive calm, his motionless face lean and fierce as a haggard's mask. He looked upon the six living prisoners and the two who were half dead, and said: "Hang them!"

"My lord!—all of them? There are two who cannot stand."

"It will be but two yards farther to hoist them," said Isambard in the same flat voice, and looked indifferently along the edge of the woodland. "There are trees enough." The cold glance ended in the piled dry grass, where two slept in one cloak. "What's this? Where did you find the child?"

He went close and stood over them, looking down beneath drawn brows at the boy's flushed face and tousled head, pillowed on Harry's arm. FitzJohn came to his shoulder.

"Harry caught him in the forest, near the border. It seems he must have followed the raiding party out of curiosity, and in the alarm when they withdrew he was thrown, and lost his mount. I think he may be a most profitable capture."

"He's Welsh?"

FitzJohn laughed. "To very good purpose he's Welsh! I asked the same question, and he all but spat in my face. It wasn't till the cockerel crowed that I knew him. Do you not recall that face, my lord?"

Isambard pondered, frowning. "It seems to me that I have seen him before, though I don't know where. Well, speak if you know! Who is he?"

"You must have seen him at Aber. Oh, there was no reason you should mark him there, you had to do with the men and not the children. But when I was there on your lordship's business, after you returned home, I saw this boy very often about the court, in company with the son of Princess Joan. He's heir to Ivor ap Madoc, who was the prince's *penteulu*—the captain of his guard—until he died, some years ago. The boy is Llewelyn's own fosterling."

"Some say he's more," said Langholme, half respectful and half knowing, looking sidelong at his lord.

"What do you mean by that? Ivor ap Madoc I remember well. It was natural enough for Llewelyn to take his child, it would be but a modest extension of their usual custom."

"Yes, my lord, but there's more to it than that."

"I may trust you," said Isambard with a curl of his lip, "to know all the kitchen gossip of Aber after one visit." But he listened, none the less, with a gleam in his sunken eyes.

"Why, there's none bold enough to say it aloud, and I would not claim it's general, even in a whisper. But Ivor had been married nearly seven years to a lady of Lleyn, and was childless, to their great sorrow. He did not want to put her away, being very fond, but he needed an heir to keep his lands intact from three or four quarrelling cousins. I think they came very near parting, when suddenly the lady found herself with child, and all was well for them. The Prince of Gwynedd was dear friend to them both. And it was well for him that there should be a son, too, to keep the land together. Some say they compounded all three. But the usual whisper is that the prince and the lady conspired to make Ivor happy. He died when the boy was rising two years old, but he died content."

"It may be true," said FitzJohn, low-voiced, looking at the child. "He's as black as Llewelyn, and as proud. And it seemed to me in Aber that the prince doted on his fosterling as on his own boy. But the tale of his getting I never heard."

"It may well be true," mused Isambard darkly. "She would not be the first to make shift for an heir with another man's help. Yet Llewelyn acknowledges his known bastard proudly, it would go against the grain with him to hide this one."

"My lord, he could do no other, for Ivor's name and the lady's, even after Ivor's death. The boy inherits handsomely from the father who acknowledged him, he has lands in Arfon and Ardudwy, he has no need of endowment from the prince. And as for any desire he had for the child himself," said Langholme, "you see he has him. On the mother's re-marriage—her clan married her again to a lord of Eifionydd, and she has two children by him now—Llewelyn took the boy into fosterage at his own suggestion, or so they say. It was shortly after young David's birth, they grew up together. Whether the tale's true or not, the prince loves them both alike, by all that I saw at Aber. My lord, I think he would compound an eternal peace with you and pay you indemnity for Erington into the bargain, to recover this boy.''

The rising sun laid long fingers of brightness across the sloping meadows to eastward, and threaded the branches of the trees above the sleepers creeping upwards from Owen's soft, parted lips and round cheeks to stroke his long lashes and smooth eyelids. The touch penetrated his sleep. He stirred within Harry's sheltering arm and stretched and yawned pinkly, like a waking puppy, before he opened his eyes. Then the sharp flash of the sunlight from Isambard's rings made him screw up his eyes and jerk his head aside, starting into wakefulness.

He found strange faces and pale sky and the faintly-stirring branches of trees hanging over him, and felt a man's hard body beside him and the ground under him instead of his own rustling, sweet-smelling bed and his foster-brother's warm softness. He uttered a sharp whimper of fright, and started up, waking Harry, who had the gift of springing immediately into wakefulness and coherence. His reassuring arm tightened round the boy and held him close. His voice, already familiar again where all was unfamiliar, said easily: ''Now, now, Owen ap Ivor ap Madoc, where's the need of a noise like that on such a fine morning?''

He turned his head to smile at the boy, and saw the three men standing silent over them, with a strange and somewhat sinister significance in their hooded stares, or so it seemed to him. Recognising Isambard, he flung off the cloak, smiling, and scrambled to his feet.

''My lord! I did not know you were here. You had me at a disadvantage—I trust my sleep was seemly?''

''As the child's,'' said Isambard without a smile. ''I have been hearing about your prisoner, Harry. It seems you have made a capture of some importance.''

Harry followed the look and the tone together, and came towards the truth by blind leaps. The smile left his face. He put out a hand and drew Owen close against his hip. ''I did not—I do not look upon him as a prisoner, my lord.''

''Then you had better begin, for that is what he is.''

"He was not involved in the attack made on your manor," said Harry. "I found him benighted in the forest, and it is my intent to set him safely on his way home."

"Instead, you may take him back with you to Parfois, suitably escorted. I am not sure, Harry, that you might not lose your way with him if I let the pair of you go alone." He would not be angry; he could even smile on them, though the gaunt face looked strangely cruel, smiling.

"It was never your way," said Harry, matching stare for stare, "to make war on children."

"Not on them, Harry. But with them, perhaps. I think you do not know that what you hold there under your hand is the price of peace along this border. Tell him, boy," he said, looking down at Owen not unkindly, and modulating his voice into a cold gentleness, "what is your relationship with the Prince of Gwynedd?"

Owen, perhaps as a gesture for his people, perhaps in offence at being discussed thus openly, chose to answer in Welsh, and with a defiant sparkle in his eyes.

"Did he not say 'Father'?" asked Isambard, who had but few words of the outlandish tongue.

"No," said Harry. "The word was 'foster-father.' "

"There's little difference to a Welshman. They fight to the death for their foster-brothers, and for their fosterlings, too, if need be. You did not know of the connection?"

"I did not, but it alters nothing. The child is not to blame for this feud, whoever may be. He is not a prisoner of war."

"It is arguable. He was taken on my land, and he was attached, however loosely, to the party that made this havoc here. He is the king's prisoner, since he was taken on land I hold from the king and in infringement of the king's truce. He goes back to Parfois."

"I promised him shelter and safety," said Harry. "Will you do as much, my lord?"

"I need make no promises to my prisoners, and I'll make none to my underlings." By the dryness of the voice and the tight pallor of the lips from which it spoke Isambard was surely drawing near the always abrupt breaking-point of his patience. From no other did he bear so much as from Harry Talvace, but the limit was dangerously close. "If you wish to take him, take him. If not, Langholme shall,

I care not so we have him safe. Llewelyn shall not have him back cheaply. I'll make him sweat for him."

There was no help for it. The boy stood straight, glaring silent defiance, but the small hand gripped Harry's sleeve with a desperate anxiety. "I'll take him back, then, if I must. And give me this, at least, that my wife and I may have the care of him while he remains at Parfois."

"As you please," said Isambard, with a faintly scornful smile. "FitzJohn, find the boy a horse, and have six archers escort them back. Archers, Harry!" he repeated pointedly. "I shall find the pair of you at Parfois when I return—dead or alive."

"I've said I'll take him!"

"That's well! And you had best have him away from here quickly, before we deal with his countrymen."

Harry understood, and felt his heart shrink for the bearded fellow he had wounded. So brief and inimical an encounter, and yet it made them men to each other, as none of his enemies was a man to Isambard. He made haste to feed the boy and get him mounted; they would not delay their grim work out of tenderness to him. Owen, anxious as he was, ate with an appetite that reminded Harry to fill his saddle-bag; small boys are always hungry. The child brightened too, once they were on their way; his lost and frightened condition was not past comforting by a sunny day and a ride and the near presence of someone whom he felt to be friendly. Still silent and nervous as they threaded the low hills, he took heart from Harry's relief as the blackened shell of Erington vanished behind the ridge, and the woodland and its bitterly misused trees disappeared with it.

"Who is that terrible man? Is he the lord of Parfois?"

"Yes, but you'll see little of him, you'll be with me. My wife will make you welcome. Never worry about him."

"Shall I have to stay there long?"

"Not long," said Harry, with more conviction than he felt. "They'll soon come to terms over you and send you home."

"My foster-father won't know I'm gone until he reaches Llanbister. Even then he won't know where I am. No one knows!" He jutted an unsteady underlip, tears not far away. "He'll worry about me."

"Never fret so," said Harry cheerfully, "they'll send him word where you are." But he wished he knew if they would. To leave Llewelyn to his anxiety, scouring Radnor Forest and the border country far and wide for his wayward fosterling, might appeal to Isambard as a sweet first move in the exploiting of his unexpected advantage. "Think that you are come to visit an uncle at Parfois," he said, "and be sure you'll be home soon enough, and forgiven for all your sins. But you'll never disobey again, will you?"

Owen promised, but with markedly less fervour than he would have shown an hour ago. He was beginning to enjoy his ride and almost to look forward to Parfois, and he found Harry's reassurances convincing because he wanted to be convinced. By the time they splashed through the ford he had rebounded into gaiety and was preening himself on his prince's escort of archers, who rode behind at a respectful but watchful distance. Long before they rode up the green track to Parfois he was chattering and singing like a blackbird. The first pair of guard towers on the steep rise awed him into silence again, but when they emerged upon the plateau, to see the castle rising before them, and the church, warmed into gold by the sun, stretching its tall tower skywards in the rigid net of scaffolding, his eyes grew great and round with wonder and excitement. He was too deeply enchanted and too insatiably curious to be afraid. Even Llewelyn's great timber maenol at Aber was never like this. His head began to turn left and right wildly, staring at everything. The questions would come later, in an inexhaustible flood; for the moment he was speechless.

Gilleis was crossing the inner ward towards the King's Tower when they walked in together through the dark passage from the outer ward, Harry's hand on the boy's shoulder. She stood at gaze, astonished and moved as by a moment of prophetic vision.

How often since her marriage, and recently with what insistent and increasing longing, she had thought of the delight of having Harry's son in her arms. They had spoken of it together frequently, always as something that would surely come, but of late she had begun to wonder. After four years of marriage without issue people begin to call a woman barren. Love remains, love always, love without a shadow, but without its crown, too. And suddenly here came Harry, unexpected and without his companions of the muster, bringing her in his hand a straight, sturdy, staring child like a miraculous gift. A bold, black-haired, sweet, striding boy, as dark of eye and as red of mouth as his mother, and as brown and tough and proud as his father. They came straight to her, Harry smiling, the child grave and on his best behaviour.

Gilleis was smiling, too, though she did not know it, a wondering, dazzled smile, as though the sun had shone in her eyes.

"Gilleis," said Harry, his free hand reaching for hers, "I've brought you a guest. Here is Owen ap Ivor, who is going to live with us for a while. Make him welcome!"

The child, anxious to do honour to himself and his blood, made her a bow of such solemnity that only the deep obeisance to a king seemed appropriate in reply, and then redeemed himself by looking up at her as candidly as a flower and holding up his face to be kissed. She took his round cheeks in her palms, and kissed him.

"You are welcome to my heart, Owen. Indeed, indeed, I am happy to see you."

She drew him into her arms, and the stiff little body melted into warmth and softness on her breast. He put his arms round her neck and his grubby cheek against her cheek. She felt the springs of her being rise in flood and spill over in a torrent of silent joy.

In the columns of the south porch, which Harry was carving *in situ*, appeared a small, hilarious angel on one side, and an unruly but engaging imp on the other, both with the face of Owen ap Ivor. A somewhat turbulent and spoiled angel he made, and a warm-hearted and affectionate imp, so that no one could ever be really sure which of the figures was which aspect of him.

By mid-September he was very much at home in Parfois, though his movements were restricted to the two wards of the castle, and he chafed at being turned back every time he followed Harry to the drawbridge. There was scarcely room within the gates for his energy and enterprise, and others, as well as the boy himself, found his confinement hard to bear. The falconers in particular, whom he especially elected to assist, added their heartfelt prayers to Harry's when he begged that the boy should be allowed at least as far as the church. They liked him well enough, and owned that for his years he was knowledgeable about birds, but he was so perilously innocent of fear that he treated even the great gerfalcons like pet merlins for ladies, and they lived in mortal dread that he would lose at least a thumb at any moment, if not an eye.

"He has no notion of running away," said Harry. "But even if he had, there's but one way down from here; you could as well turn him back at the lower guard as here at the gate-house. And he'd be the better for it if you'd let him ride sometimes. If two of the archers rode with him you'd be in no fear of losing him. You could see to it they're better mounted than he is."

"You're mighty solicitous for him," said Isambard, curling his lips in the angry smile that was never far from his countenance.

"I know how I should have felt if I'd been mewed as close at his age, and for as long. I'd have had the towers down round your ears by now."

"I can believe it! Well, let him ride, if it will keep you content. I'll have FitzJohn give him two reliable men as escort, and he shall have his freedom as far as the lower guard."

Harry thanked him, and was at the door, well pleased to be running with such good news, when Isambard called him back. "Does he ask? About when he's to go home?"

"Yes. But not quite so often now. Not every day."

"And what do you tell him?"

"What can I tell him? I say it will be soon." He hesitated, looking down at the bony hand on which the rings hung so slackly. "Does Llewelyn know that he's here?"

The smile flashed from the lips to the deep eyes, and kindled two red flames of bitter amusement that seemed to burn in a waste of hatred. "He'll know by tomorrow. The messenger is on his way at this moment. Did you not know a courier came from him three days ago? Who would have thought it would take him so long to think of inquiring here? It's a long way from Llanbister to Erington, and it seems the pony made the best of its way home before they found it, so there was no way of knowing which way the boy had taken. They've been combing the wilds all this time. There are still wolves in Radnor."

"Not only in Radnor," said Harry bluntly.

Isambard's head went back in a brief shout of laughter, and the feral movement and the savage sound had indeed something of a wolf's howling about them. "You still want to be my conscience, do you, Harry? Did I not tell you once, if you turn hedge-priest you'll come by a hedge-priest's end?"

"There are worse ends," said Harry. "But you will give him his nurseling back, won't you? Since you've let him know that he's here, I take it you've named your terms for handing him back? I tell you honestly, my lord, I'll be happier for you, as well as for Owen, when he's safe home again, though Gilleis will miss him sorely."

"She will have him for a while yet," said Isambard with bitter satisfaction. "It isn't Llewelyn's purse that will buy him back, nor his black cattle, nor an indemnity for Erington, nor his pledge to keep the peace. I have not stated my terms yet, Harry, it's too soon, he has suffered nothing yet. A great many messengers will pass between Aber and Parfois before I talk of terms, and then they'll be terms of delay and doubt. The Prince of Gwynedd shall dance to my tune all the autumn, and then, when we're done with the quarry, I'll make him come here to me in person and beg for his brat on his knees." He waited, watching Harry's face, and there was a silence. "You disappoint me," he said, mockingly, "I had thought you would exclaim: 'He will not do it!' "

"He will do it," said Harry simply. "He has done it for Wales and he'll do it for Owen. And it's not he who will have lost stature when it's done."

He turned on his heel and went out, slowly because he expected to be called back yet again, but no soft, cold voice spoke his name, and no cry of rage halted him. He closed the door of the chamber behind him and went down the stone stairway still listening for the angry summons, even hoping for it; but it did not come.

However, he had the concessions for which he had asked. Owen rode out joyfully with his two guards, esteeming them a fitting tribute to a Welsh princeling; and when he was not scouring the countryside and flying the well-schooled little hawk they had entrusted to him, he was usually under Harry's feet about the church and the lodge, poking his nose happily into everything, misplacing tools, tinkering with the hand-hoists, borrowing drawings to try his own hand on the reverse, all in disarming innocence. The sole way to keep him still was to use him as a model. Harry had only to ask him to sit for one more figure, and he would endure for an hour with cheerfulness and devotion. On the frontal stones for the high altar he appeared as every one of the twelve little angels who played and sang in a seraphic consort. Rebec, harp, citole, shawm, gittern, bugle, cornemuse and organ, he played them all with a rapt solemnity, and four several images of him sang lustily out of one great psalter.

Inevitably he took mallet and chisel to a stone he should not have touched, but hit his own fingers before he did much damage to the stone. Gilleis scolded and comforted him, bathed his bruised hand, and lost him again to Harry as soon as the pain passed.

He was forbidden, under the threat of dire punishment in which he did not really believe, to set foot on the scaffolding except in Harry's company; but that, too, he had to try for himself. They thought nothing of it when they missed him from the lodge, since he came and went freely; but when all the masons had come down from the tower in the evening he was still missing, and the hunt for him ended only when a shrill yell, curiously compounded of bravado and fright, drew their eyes to the highest walk of hurdles that surrounded the half-completed parapet, more than a hundred feet from the ground. The cry came down to them thinly, falling through the clear, still air like a little bird's call; and there sat Owen ap Ivor, clinging to one of the poles very tightly with both arms, and dangling his feet over the void.

Suppressing an instinct to roar his rage and alarm in terms which might well have scared the imp over the edge, Harry called to him firmly and calmly to stay where he was and sit still, and himself went up and brought him down. When he had him safely on the ground, he flew into a temper all the more formidable for being deferred, and bundling the sinner headlong into the tracing-house, faithfully performed everything he had promised him.

Owen would not for the world have cried under punishment, though for less obvious reasons he would have liked to cry. When he was plumped unceremoniously back on his feet, and the hazel switch flung into a corner, he turned his back on Harry and stalked out with his head in the air, like the offended princeling he was, not even deigning to rub his hurts. But in ten minutes he was back again. He peeped in at the door gingerly, first one large, sullen black eye, then both. He put one foot into the room, then the second, and sidled along the wall with elaborate unconcern, as though he had not made up his mind whether he wanted to be noticed or not.

Harry was bending over his tables, assembling the drawings he had made for the altar of the Virgin. He observed the sidelong approach out of the tail of his eye, but made no sign. Owen leaned against the end of the trestle, and drew industriously in the grain of the wood with one finger-tip, and presently prolonged one of his imaginary lines so that it brought him gradually nearer to Harry's hip. Still the fish did not rise. A moment later the boy's shoulder pressed insinuatingly into Harry's side. For the first time he looked down, and beheld the curly head obstinately averted; but as he watched, it turned sidewise, just far enough to bring one reproachful eye to bear on his face. He smiled and dropped his dividers to open his arms, and instantly the child was in them, hugging him passionately. He said not a word, but buried his nose in Harry's cotte, and clung to him, making his peace in silence.

"Owen ap Ivor ap Madoc," said Harry solemnly, hugging him back with goodwill, "you're a terrible fellow! Will you mind me, the next time, and not frighten me out of my wits?"

The dark head nodded contentedly in the hollow of his shoulder.

"I was afraid you were going to hurt yourself—so I hurt you, instead. There's logic for you!"

Owen did not seem to find anything unreasonable in it; the same kind of thing must have happened to him before. Satisfied now, the security of their relationship re-established, he wriggled free and ran off to Gilleis, whistling tunelessly.

Only occasionally now did the anxious thoughtfulness fall upon him, and the familiar question come to his lips again:

"When shall I be going home?"

"Soon," Harry would say quickly, looking round in haste to find a new lure to distract him, "very soon now."

Owen had a bad dream in the night, and started out of it in a panic to the palpitating darkness, out of which it seemed to him the denizens of his nightmare still hunted him. Desirous of company and comfort, but too proud to cry for them, he began to whimper and draw great sighs, as though in a troubled sleep, and presently had the satisfaction of hearing a light footstep in the doorway of his tiny room in the tower wall. The door that separated him from Harry's bed chamber stood always open at night, so that Gilleis could hear if he called to her, but he had never yet done so. At Aber he slept well out of earshot of his foster-parents, but at Aber everything was familiar, and he had David always in the bed beside him, so that he was never afraid of anything.

Gilleis had a small lamp in her hand, and her hair was loose upon her shoulders. She looked down at the restless sleeper, and smiled at the too tightly closed eyelids and the look of sharp, listening consciousness that betrayed him; and stooping, she kissed him on the cheek, so that he could awake and enjoy his success. He opened his eyes gratefully, and stretched up his arms to her, and the denizens of the dream were gone in a moment.

She knelt by the bed and held him half asleep on her breast while he babbled out his confused recollections of pursuit and terror. His trust and warmth and weight filled her with joy, and with that deeper content and fulfilment that made joy seem a slight and ephemeral thing. He lay on her heart, and it seemed to her that the newcomer, the wonderful creature under her heart, already drew breath with him.

"Silly boy, as if we'd let anything hurt you! No one can get in to you here, there's no one but the three of us, and God. So you know you must be safe, don't you? As safe in the darkness as in the day. I'm always close to you, you need only call me. Go to sleep again!"

When he was asleep, she laid him gently down in the bed, where he stirred and stretched, and subsided more deeply into slumber. She watched his sweet, easy breathing for a little while, and marked how all the foreshadowings of manhood, which showed so clearly in his waking face, withdrew from him in sleep and left him as innocent and defenceless as a baby.

She had had him for nine weeks now; one week for every year of his age. She could not hope to have him much longer. Llewelyn's couriers rode persistently between Aber and Parfois, carrying offers of ransom and pledges of peace along the march. When he had tormented the prince long enough, Isambard would surely send him his strayed chick home again. She no longer feared his going; the miraculous bud of promise her spirit had put forth at his coming had flowered triumphantly, and was already rounding into fruit, and

the void he would leave in her heart the child of his heralding was
waiting to fill.

She drew the coverlet closer round Owen's naked shoulders, for
it was more than half way through October, and the nights were
chilly. Feeling the touch, but undisturbed by it, he laughed in his
sleep, a dazzling gift he had, and she felt herself filled to overflowing
with his laughter as with a golden spring of sweet water gushing
out of her heart. She was sorry for everyone in the world who had
not her overwhelming reasons for happiness: for Benedetta who was
childless and loved where she never could possess, for Isambard who
broke every creature on whom he leaned, and then loathed them for
breaking, even for the king, newly landed in the south from one
humiliation to face the threat of another, the wretched king who
was sick and angry and harried, and had lost his last gamble for
Normandy. She was even a little sorry for Harry, because his part
was only to beget and not to bear, and because he did not yet know
how happy he was; and at the same time she envied him because he
had yet to hear it, and that was a joy that could be tasted only once.

The child was deep asleep, the curves of the laughter still on his
mouth. She went back into the chamber where Harry lay, and
shading the tiny flame of the lamp with her hand so that the light
should not fall directly on his face, stood beside the bed and looked
at him earnestly.

Sleep took away years from him, too, but the lines of manhood,
once graven, could not be erased. He had a touching duality, child
and man together. The innocence and tranquillity that spring from
knowledge and experience instead of from childhood and wonder
belong only to the saints, and Harry was no saint; yet in sleep these
were present in his face.

Gilleis set down the lamp, feeling the world shaken by one of
those moments of unbalance and lightness that came on her sometimes now without warning. She was standing with both hands
clasped to her body, her face bright and strange in the small light
from below, when Harry opened his eyes, and sat up in bed with a
soft, startled cry.

"Gilleis, love, what is it? What's the matter?" He reached for her
hands, drawing her down to him. "Little heart, are you ill?"

"Not ill," said Gilleis, smiling. "I've been to Owen, he had a bad

dream, but he's asleep again now. Not ill, no. Indeed, it is very well
with me."

"You frightened me. You looked so strange."

Smiling still, she blew out the lamp, and let fall the cloak she had
wrapped about her to go to the boy. He turned back the covers of
the bed, and she lay down beside him, shaking off the chill of the
night in one tremor before she relaxed in his warmth. He laid his
arm over her, and drew her close.

"I am strange," said Gilleis, her lips against his cheek. "I am a
wonder. I am with child."

"Gilleis!" It began as a shout of joy, but he suppressed it hastily
to a whisper because of the boy. "Is it true? Are you sure? Quite
sure? Oh, Gilleis, when did you know? Why didn't you tell me?"
He was incoherent and trembling with excitement. She laughed and
embraced him, holding him to her heart as she had held Owen, and
talking to him in the selfsame tones.

"Hush, you'll wake him! Yes, I'm quite sure, I waited to be sure.
A month ago I thought it was so, but now I know it. It must have
been in August I conceived, soon after Owen came. Harry, do you
remember how you brought him to me, that day, and I not knowing
who he was or how you came by him? It seemed to me like an omen.
And ever since then it is as if the last secret place in me has opened
and let you in. It always belonged to you, it always wanted you.
But Owen opened the door."

"Oh, Gilleis!" he said in a great sigh of delight. "Oh, my lamb,
my love, my rose!" He laid his hand softly upon her body below
the heart, and lay quiet with it resting there. "I'll be good to him.
I'll make him a cradle fit for a prince. He'll be as beautiful as you."

"And as foolish as you," she said fondly, laying her hand over
his. "And as dear to me." She turned her head upon the pillow and
kissed him tenderly, as she would have kissed the child. "Are you
happy now?"

"Happy? More than happy! I have everything!"

He lay still beside her, their linked hands reverent upon the
marvel, in a touch between adoration and caress. It seemed to him
that all the darkness and cold of the autumn night grew warm and
lambent with the happiness that ran over from his cup. "How grateful I am!" he said. "How grateful!"

Chapter Thirteen

*I*sambard came into the lodge in the bright early afternoon, when the light was at its best, and stood unnoticed for a while, watching the balanced, easy strokes of Harry's mallet as he used the finest of his punches on the wings of the angel of the Annunciation. The slender, kneeling figure lifted to the Madonna a face there was no mistaking, though no man had ever yet borne it; the face that would be Owen ap Ivor's when he came to manhood.

"A pity," said Isambard, "that you'll not be able to finish it from the living model."

Harry cast a surprised glance over his shoulder. "Not be able to finish it—" He found for the words the meaning he would have wished them to bear, and his eyes shone, kindling from sea-green to gold with joy. "You mean you're sending him home? Ah, but I'm glad! I knew you'd give over plaguing them in the end. Why, I know every line of the child's face by now better than his mother does, I don't need his living presence. I shall miss the imp, but for his sake I'll be glad to see him go."

"I do not think you will," said Isambard, "not by the way he is to take. But you may see it if you wish, Harry."

The words effectively stopped Harry's mallet, but it was the tone that brought his head jerking round again, and this time without a smile. "What do you mean? Speak plainly, my lord. What's in your mind for him?" He put down mallet and punch, and came striding out from behind the stone group, wiping his hands on his tunic in the bad boyish habit he had never lost, and for which Gilleis was always scolding him.

"It did not come from my mind," said Isambard, in the same flat, deliberate tone. "I give you my word for that. I have had my orders from the king."

"The king? How does the king know anything of Owen? He has his hands full in the south with Langton, and the rest of the pack who're massing for the kill now he's down. What's this child to him?"

"I hold this march for the king, and whatever happens in it touching the Welsh and him I must submit to him. My messenger went to him as soon as he landed from France, with my full report of all that has befallen in his absence. The boy was merely mentioned along with the rest, and there's but a line in the king's despatch about him, but it's very much to the point." He had the parchment in his hand. Harry had not remarked it until that moment, for the hand that held it was down in the shadow, in the folds of the blue surcoat. "It came but a quarter of an hour ago." He held it so that Harry could see for himself the royal seal.

"Shall I read it to you? 'For the boy ap Ivor, follow your own inclination and my desire and interest. Hang him, and send Llewelyn his body.' "

"Christ aid!" said Harry, and clutched at the wall.

Isambard looked up over the roll, but there was nothing to be read in the look, neither regret nor pleasure, neither disgust nor approval. The cavernous eyes burned, but fire was their natural element; within the great smooth, translucent lids they must burn even when he slept. Harry could neither speak nor move for a moment. The thing came so unexpectedly, he could not grasp it.

"You'll never do it!" he said, dragging a voice out of himself as arduously as though he dragged his heart out by the roots. "The king himself will wish it undone. He'll not thank you if you act on an angry word he surely never meant. God's life, my lord, the child is his grandson's bed-fellow! And think, now that so many of the barons are turned against him, he must look for allies where he can find them. How if he's wooing his son-in-law before the year's out, and you've been too hasty and set the child's murder between them? Do you think he'll be grateful?"

"Since when have I looked for gratitude?" said Isambard, rolling up the parchment. "He is what he is, but he is my sovereign. What he orders I perform. But he will not repent of it. His hate to that man is second only to mine."

"So he'll wreak it on a child of nine years, who has never stood in his way, who is not even Llewelyn's seed, but only his fosterling, and dear to him—"

"Ah, so they never told you the full tale," said Isambard with a hollow smile. "For they say, Harry, that he is Llewelyn's seed, if all was known, got for his friend who needed an heir but could not furnish one for himself. And for my part I think it must be true. Not even for Griffith has Llewelyn so persistently dunned us as for this boy."

"You do but confirm me! This is not policy, it is only spite. He dare not touch Griffith, though he still holds him, because Griffith is acknowledged, and the charm of the father's name is over him. But this poor little creature is vulnerable, the charm does not cover him. The king can slaughter him, and stab Llewelyn to the heart, and yet pretend ignorance of what he does. Owen is to pay for Griffith's immunity. You'll surely not lend yourself to so mean an act?"

"Call it what you please. I have my orders," said Isambard shortly, two hot discs of colour darkening on his cheek-bones.

"You cannot do it, I'll not believe it of you! You are nobody's hired murderer, not even the king has the right to ask it of you." He caught at Isambard's lean wrist, and it felt hard and rigid and cold in his hand, like the hilt of a sword. "My lord, this is a *child*, one who has been in my care, one you've seen yourself often enough, running about the wards. His death serves no purpose—"

"It satisfies a hate," said Isambard, and shook him off, but without anger or impatience. "Where is the boy?"

"Out riding." He passed a hand over his eyes, and said dully: "I wish he might never come back."

"If he does not, the two who guard him shall hang for him. But he'll come. When he does, he shall have a brief while with Father Hubert, and then we'll make an end. I am the king's man, I shall do the king's bidding. To the last letter!"

The voice had not quickened from its sombre quietness, nor the face stirred out of its iron calm, and yet the air between them was suddenly bitter with so intense and incurable an emanation of grief and rage that Harry jerked up his head to stare at the source of it in horror, as though he found himself face to face with a demon. It was Isambard who turned away his eyes, but too late to contain the brief, blinding glare of a hunger that might well devour children.

"Lord God!" said Harry in an appalled whisper. "You are *glad*! This is what you wanted! This is what you planned! It is not the king making use of you, but you making use of the king. You are to have the terrible joy of it, and he the everlasting shame! How many more, how many more have made him the scapegoat?" Isambard would have turned and flung away from him, but he thrust out his arm, and, setting his palm against the wall, barred the way. "Show me his words, or I'll not believe in them. *You* have done this, not he. You are sick to the soul—"

"Sick to the soul!" repeated Isambard in a low voice, halting with his breast against the wiry brown arm. "Sick I am, God knows! There, read! See if you can find some loophole I have failed to find."

The words were there. He had not even read all. "My grandson is too young," the king had written, "to cry for him long." How could a man have the understanding to think of that, and still demand the death? He let his arm fall. There was nothing more to be said, no plea that would be heard, no goad that could sting Isambard into failing in his ghastly duty. His fealty would not stop short of one child's death; and the joy was surely there, whether he knew it or not. Killing the boy would placate for a moment the devil that fed on his heart, the hatred he bore to life, which had disappointed him, to love, which had eluded him, to beauty and innocence, which had abandoned him.

"As God sees me, Harry," said Isambard with weary gentleness, "I'm sorry! I'll have Benedetta keep Gilleis within doors when the time comes. You may tell her he's sent home, if you will."

Harry made no answer. He stood staring unseeingly at the lively head of the unfinished angel; and in a moment he heard the rustle of Isambard's brocade against the timber posts of the lodge, and the rapid, incisive sound of his footsteps receding across the trampled waste towards the gate-house.

Words had lost their potency, and there was no time now for thought, unless, as Benedetta had once said, the act is also the thought. Everything took shape as it must. There was no other way.

He left his work as it stood, the tools lying, and went to his tracing-house in the outer ward, where his clerk was busy cleaning parchments.

"Find John the Fletcher for me, Simon, and ask him to come to me in the lodge, will you?"

The boy ran off willingly. Gilleis was with Benedetta at this hour, they were working together on the altar cloths for the church. To approach them himself would have been simple, but the occasion of surprise and therefore possibly of suspicion. And quite certainly unbearable. John the Fletcher was Benedetta's own man, and had access to her at all times; his comings and goings would excite no comment.

"Get her away out of his reach," wrote Harry at his desk in the lodge, "for I am about to do that for which there is no forgiveness." He did not sign it; she knew the hand. He added nothing; there was neither time nor need for anything more. By the time he had sealed it John the Fletcher was already picking his way between the stacked stones.

"You wanted me, master?"

"Will you take this to Madonna Benedetta, at once?" said Harry. "You need say nothing to her, she will understand. If my lord is there, get it to her nonetheless, but see that it is done so that he knows nothing of it. I'm trusting you with what's more to me than my head."

"She shall have it," said John the Fletcher. "He'll not be there, he's within, in hall, hearing some plea between two of his tenants, and there's another case to be heard after it. He'll be a good hour by the sound of it."

"So much the better! Then, John—if they're alone—say to my wife that I send her my love and service. Will you do that?"

"I'll do it." Out of the brown, bearded face sharp eyes studied him with narrowing attention. "Nothing more?"

"Nothing more."

"If you should be in want of a hand to second yours, master, she'd spare me to you."

"I thank you," said Harry, startled and moved, "but I can make shift alone."

"God be with you, then." said John, unquestioning, and hid the message within his tunic, and so was gone.

Harry made his way to the storehouse which stood nearest to the English edge of the plateau. There was a coil of knotted rope there, formerly one of several used by the young masons as a quick means of descent from the scaffolding, but banished when it showed signs of fraying. He took it on his arm, and slipped unobserved into the fringe of the trees. Below this sheer, rocky face lay the dingle where the two masterless men had dropped their haul of wood, long ago in his first summer here. That was the one occasion when he had paid any attention to this cliff edge, but he remembered it well. There was a drop of perhaps fifty feet, and then some broken shelves where a starved tree or two clung, edging the soft, deep grass of the dingle. Thence the descent to the hamlet was easy. He made fast the rope to the bole of a larch tree close to the rim, and paid the length of it over, leaning out to shake it clear of the stunted trees below. It lay against the rock and vanished, being of much the same straw-pale colour. He debated for a moment whether he should risk leaving by this route and picking up a horse in the village, but speed was more vital than complete concealment. How could he be sure he would get a good mount? He needed a horse on which he could rely. Moreover, he had many valid reasons for leaving and entering Parfois freely, and they would not yet be questioned.

No one but Isambard was likely to find anything suspicious in the fact that Master Talvace was saddling up and riding out at this hour, and he would not see. Harry took the best and fleetest of the horses at his disposal, and rode across the drawbridge and down from the plateau, unchallenged but for the master-carpenter's hail as he passed the lodges.

"Harry, would you cast an eye at the screen with me, now it's in? I've a notion yet the line of it could be bettered."

"When I come back," said Harry. "I'm going down to the quay, with luck they should be landing my last sliptiles before evening.

At the lower guard they passed him through without a glance. Now how far dared he ride, and still be sure of intercepting Owen and his escort? The boy had fallen pliantly into the habit of telling him exactly where he meant to go; today he had said he would ride eastward between the hills to the Roman road, and then south to the great open place where the old earth fort reared its ringed mound. The little hawk would be showing his paces in that bright, still, sunless air above the spongy, blanched turf of autumn. It was long odds they would not turn down into the river valley from there, to give the horses the steep climb at the end of the ride. However they varied their way back, they would stay on this level, and that meant they must use this path between the crests to reach Parfois. He took his station at the edge of the wood, on a grassy mound that commanded a view of the windblown levels over which they must come.

He had not long to wait. They appeared below him, riding in single file along a thin green track, for the tussocky grass was treacherous and full of warrens. He went down to meet them, and Owen saw him, and spurred towards him with a jubilant shout. For the first time he wondered what he was to do if the guards distrusted him, and he without so much as a dagger on him.

"I am sent by my lord to meet you," he said, hushing Owen's chatter peremptorily with a raised hand and keeping his eyes upon the archers. "Something has fallen out which makes it seem to him better you should not go back to the castle with your charge. He bade me say that like Robert of Vieuxpont he has received an order he would liefer not obey." He cast one significant glance down at the child, and they understood him. Why, after all, should they doubt him? He had grown closer to Isambard of late than any other man at Parfois; if their lord wished to evade an unpleasant issue, Talvace was the very person he would choose to be his agent and lift the burden from him.

"It's that way, is it?" said the elder of the two archers, and whistled soundlessly, eyeing the boy. "What's his will now?"

"That I should take the child as far as the quarry in Bryn and start him on his way home."

Owen pricked up his ears at that, and shouted and clapped his gloved hands, startling the little hawk on his wrist so that it ruffled its wings and hissed indignantly.

"Silence, pest!" said Harry, shaking him gently by a handful of curls. "Your elders are talking." And to the guards: "It was always his will that it should end so, and you know he has ways of getting his will."

"Ay, has he, and can go roundabout as well as straight when need be, well I know it. But our orders were plain. He bade us never let the lad out of reach except within the gates."

"Have I asked you to leave him? You are to come with us to Bryn. Understand me, none but my lord and I, and now you, know of this matter. He sent me because the child has been in my care, and will readily trust himself to me. There was no time for writing and sealing of credentials. His name in my mouth should be enough for you." He wheeled his horse. "We'd best be moving. Come, Owen ap Ivor ap Madoc, you've a long ride ahead of you."

In their shoes, he thought, I would believe it; it has the sound of truth so strongly that I wonder if there is not a grain of the real thing at the heart of it. Why did he come straight to me and tell me? Out of rueful courtesy to me as the boy's keeper? Or to torment me because I am too fortunate, and have too much? Or did he tell me in order that I might do exactly what I am doing, and spare him this horrible duty? For all these reasons, it may well be, and which of them was strongest he of all men is not likely to know. God may know. As for me, I do what I must, and that is enough.

They were following. He did not look round, but he felt that the moment of hesitation was over, that they were satisfied of his good faith. He thought of Benedetta talking in paradoxes about honour and faith, of how honour might sometimes depend on abasing oneself and faith on breaking one's word. I am on my way to illustrating her argument for her, he thought wryly, but how it will come out none of us knows yet. Yes, they were following, and they were satisfied. They had fallen into their usual station, six or seven lengths behind their charge. How emphatically he had drummed it into Owen that he must never try to outride or elude them! Thank God the child had never understood why!

"Am I really going home?" asked Owen eagerly, bouncing with excitement on his brown pony.

"You are indeed."

"But I have not said goodbye to anyone. They'll think no one has taught me good manners at Aber." He was seriously worried; the reputation of the Welsh was in his hands. "At least I ought to make my farewells to Mistress Gilleis, when she has been so kind to me."

"Why, it was all arranged in haste, we may waive the niceties for once. I have said goodbye to Mistress Gilleis for you."

And for myself, he thought, feeling the realisation close in on his heart like an iron frost. When I turned back to kiss her once more, there on the stairway on my way to work, and I did not know why it came on me so—that was goodbye.

"His love and service!" said Gilleis, stiff and pale in the window embrasure with the brightly coloured folds of the tapestry fallen round her feet. "And gone! Why? Why? Why could he not send his message to me?"

"Because it's to me that John has ready access. And perhaps because he knew you would need persuading. He did send you," said Benedetta with a wry smile, "the message I would gladly have had. It remains only to do his bidding, and quickly."

"I will not go!" said Gilleis, clenching her hands. "If he is putting himself in danger, so much the more must I be close to him. What's my life to me without him?"

"You will go. You will go because he asks it, and because only he knows what he has done and what he means to do, and therefore none of us can hope to better his plans. You will go because it would be the cruellest blow of all to him if you should stay here to become the instrument of his undoing. You will go not because you are afraid, or do not love him enough, but because you are without fear, and love him more than yourself. Even enough to live without him—except," said Benedetta, folding the parchment and hiding it in her breast, "that you can never be without him now, together or apart."

Gilleis turned her back on the room and looked out from the window into the sheer plunge of air. She kicked the embroidery out of her way with a swirl of her green skirt. "You love him, too," she said.

"God's death!" said Benedetta. "Is that any secret? From the first moment I saw him, and shall do till I die. I would have told you so long ago, if I had thought it needed saying."

"Ah, you mistake me! I meant that—that is a reason for trusting you. If I go—if I must indeed go—you will stand his friend here—"

"His, and yours, too." She saw Gilleis start forward and catch at the stonework of the window, and the marriage ring gleamed on the small hand that pressed hard against the green girdle. Benedetta ran and caught her in her arms, and held her until the faintness passed. Tears were welling slowly from the great eyes and falling heavily upon the trampled needlework.

"That's no secret, neither," said Benedetta, gently, "at least not from me. And that's why you'll go. You have two hostages to save, and one of them a morsel of Harry's very life. Fetch your cloak, quickly, and I'll have John saddle the horses."

At a farm between the rivers they asked for food, and the goodwife found them some oatcakes and apples and eggs, and brought a bowl of warm milk for Owen. Harry gave her three silver pence for the meal, and Owen offered her a kiss of his milky mouth, and she was content. They crossed Vrnwy with Owen still chattering and singing, more often in Welsh than in English, but soon he began to tire, and to nod in the saddle. "Take the poor bird," said Harry, smiling, "and give me up the child, and he can sleep as we go."

"I am not asleep," said Owen indignantly, stiffening as he felt himself lifted from his saddle.

Harry settled him before him in his arm, well wrapped from the chilling wind in his cloak. The boy sighed, and stirred a little until he found the right place to rest easily, his head nestling in the crook of arm and shoulder, his cheek turned comfortably into Harry's breast. "And I am not a child," he said, taking firm hold of the folds of the green cotte that pillowed him. "I am a boy, nearly a man."

"You are an imp, and a sinner, but you have the makings of a man. Don't be in too big a hurry to leave being a child," said Harry. "It's no great blessing to be grown."

Owen slept, flushed of face and moist of lip in the warmth of the cloak, as they rode into the quarry in the October twilight. A voice challenged them out of the dimness where the woods closed in upon the walk.

"It's Talvace," said Harry, tightening his arm reassuringly about the child as he started awake at the cry. "Hush, they're all friends here. Where is Adam?"

"Master Talvace, is it you?" William of Beistan's great beard bristled out of the dusk. "What brings you here at this time? What's the news from Parfois?"

"There is none yet," said Harry. "That's to come. Where's Adam?"

"Within, at the huts. You'll see by the light of the fire as you round the trees."

The rock walls of the quarry stood pale in the flickering light of a fire that burned in an open hearth fenced with stones. Owen awoke fully, and peered out of his nest at the strange faces that gathered from all sides to surround them. Adam came running from the huts to catch at Harry's stirrup.

"Take the boy," said Harry, fending off welcomes, "and let me get down. I must trouble you for fresh horses, Adam, and I could find a good home for a drink and a bite." He dismounted, and a small, anxious hand reached to clutch at his sleeve; he detached it calmly from its hold, and shut it warmly in his own palm. "I'm here, imp, never fear. These are all friends to me and to you."

"Come into the hut," said Adam, "and we'll gladly feed you. Horses we have, too, but why should you want them tonight?"

"I'll tell you while we eat, for there's no time to lose. Owen ap Ivor, now's your chance to be a man. Will you wait here by the fire, and not worry if I stay out of sight for ten minutes? Here, Robin, take care of him while I have a word aside with Adam."

Over the ale and meat and bread that Adam provided he said what he had to say, and briefly.

"This boy is foster-son to the Prince of Gwynedd. I want you to take horse at once—you yourself, Adam, mark me—and carry him to Aber and hand him over to Llewelyn in person. That done, on no account come back here." He looked across the candle-flame at the archers. "I have to ask your pardon for the trick I played on you to get you to come here with me. It was no lie I told you when I said that the king had sent orders to my lord to put the child to death. The lie was that he desired to be spared the duty of obeying. He was and is set to hang the boy. It was I who willed to carry him off and send him home. I could get him from you by no other means than I used, and I could not allow you to go back to Parfois and tell your tale, to set the hounds after us too soon. Now you may choose what you will do. But forget that you carry bows! All in this place will do my will, not Isambard's, and you had best not brave them. If you want my rede, I should throw in your lot with Adam here, and go to Aber with the boy. Llewelyn's gratitude will be assured, he'll receive you like princes." He yawned, and rubbed his hands over his stiff cheeks. "I am sorry I had to lie," he said. "There was no other way."

The three faces stared in upon him in silence. "What is it? What ails you?"

"What ails *us*!" said Adam. "What of *you*, Harry?" By the tone in which he asked and by the look of his face, from which the smile was gone beyond even remembrance, he already knew the answer.

"I am going back."

"No, by God, you're not!" swore Adam, scrambling to his feet. "Not if I have to bind you over a horse to get you into Wales with us. Are you mad? He'll hang you out of hand."

"He will not. He swore to me that he would not deprive me of the work he had entrusted to me—never, he said, until it be finished. And you know he keeps his word. And I swore to him," said Harry, "that I would not leave his service until the work was done. I keep my word, too. I am going back to keep it."

"Your word, man! This is your life! Do you think he'll let you live, when in some sort you've made him traitor? And do you think there's any law left in this country now strong enough to take you out of his hands? Harry!" he begged, groaning helplessly. "Don't throw your life away for a scruple! Come with us!"

"I shall live until the church is finished, some months yet. Indeed, there's only I can fix the term. Who knows, my lord Isambard and King John himself may both be gone before me. I don't think any more," said Harry, emptying his horn and getting to his feet. "Thought's unprofitable. Get me a horse, Adam, and leave

plaguing me. Go I will, and there's no time to lose." He caught
Adam by the shoulder, and held him hard. "No tricks in my defence, mind! I charge you on your soul, get the boy safely home,
or you will have wasted my labour and my head, and for that I'll
never forgive you."

"On my soul be it," said Adam, eye to eye with him. "He shall
be the first charge on me. After he reaches Llewelyn's arms my
actions are my own."

"Very well so. And you two, are you resolved to go on? I hope,"
he said remorsefully, "you have neither of you wives and children
in his hold, but I pledge you my word I'll do my best to hold you
clear of this treason and protect them from his anger."

"My family are all grown and out in the world," said the older
man, "and my wife's dead these seven years. And Harald here has
girls enough about the shire, but no wife. We'll take your counsel,
master, and go the rest of the way with the boy. I don't know but
Llewelyn's service may be more to my mind than Isambard's, and
we'll surely start with a foot in the door of his favour."

"Then I shall have done you no wrong, and for that I thank God.
I thought fast enough for my own," he said, and turned his face
into the shadow and went out from the hut, Adam at his back.

Owen was sitting by the fire still wrapped in Harry's cloak, eating
hungrily, half a dozen of the hewers and men-at-arms gathered
curiously about him. He was already friends with them, and his
strange journey had ceased to be frightening and resumed its charac-
ter of a high adventure. His large eyes shone splendidly in the
firelight.

"It's a wild bird, but a true one," said Harry. "Be good to him."

He thrust through the circle about the boy and dropped to the
grass beside him. "Owen, here I leave you. But here is Adam, who
is foster-brother to me as David is to you. He will take you home
to Aber in my place. Mind, now, his will is my will, and you're to
mark him as you would me. And now give me a kiss, and God be
with you, child. Wipe the grease from your mouth first, I like my
kisses clean. That's better!" He kissed the soft, uplifted mouth and
laughed. "This time tomorrow night you'll be in your own bed.
Carry my greetings to the Prince of Gwynedd and tell him if he gets

as good sons as he fosters there'll be a Prince of Wales from his blood yet." He embraced him briefly and rose. "Where's that horse you have for me?"

His hand was on the bridle when Adam said despairingly in his ear: "Harry, will you not change your mind? Think of Gilleis—"

"For Christ's sake!" said Harry, in a whisper that was like a howl of pain. "Who else do I think of, every moment I sleep or wake?" He kept his face turned close into the horse's chestnut shoulder for a moment, but it passed and the calm came again. "I do what I must, Adam. That makes all easy. I shall trust to see you again, in this world or another." He turned a face now perfectly at his service, and leaned and kissed his brother. "It was a mistake to sit! Squire me, Adam, I'm main stiff."

Adam held his stirrup and helped him into the saddle.

"Get to horse yourself as soon as I'm gone. Goodbye, Adam!" He wheeled the horse and trotted towards the dark space where the rock walls parted.

"Goodbye!" said Adam after him, barely audibly.

Owen, grown anxious because of the disquiet he felt in the air about him, had crept away from the fire and stood looking uncertainly from one to the other of them as they parted. He caught the falling note of Adam's voice and saw the helpless grief in his face, and broke into frightened crying; and in a flash he was off after Harry, calling through his tears: "Master Talvace! Master Talvace!"

Harry swung round at the cry, and the small hands caught at his ankle and clung desperately. He leaned resignedly from the saddle, took the child under the armpits, and hoisted him up to perch before him. Owen clasped him fiercely round the neck and hid his face against him, sobbing desolately. He felt the child's heart pounding as though it would burst out of his body.

"I don't want you to go! Don't go! They'll hurt you, I'm frightened for you!"

"Now, now, Owen ap Ivor ap Madoc, is that a noise for a prince to make? Is this the fellow who told me he was almost a man? No harm will come to me," said Harry firmly, patting the quaking shoulders. "Put it out of your mind. You're overborne with the journey and the strangeness, and you're imagining evil where none is. Look at me! Do I look frightened? Or sad?" He forced a finger under the quivering chin that pressed so desperately into his breast, and hoisted the tear-stained face out of hiding. "Here's a countenance to scare the crows with! Let's see if we can better it." He wiped the round cheeks dry with a corner of his cloak, and smoothed back the rumpled hair.

"He'll be all right once we're started," said Adam, waiting to lift him down.

"He's tired. You'll need to carry him through the night hours, but I'd liefer you got him well into Wales before you take time for rest."

"I'll do that."

"No more tears? That's my true goshawk! Be a good boy, now, and mind what Adam tells you."

He kissed the child once more, and handed him down. The small body lay on Adam's shoulder as horse and horseman dwindled in the shadows and the hoofbeats receded until the wall of rock cut them off sharply. Owen slid an arm resignedly about Adam's neck, and transferred to him faithfully the allegiance that belonged to his brother.

They turned back into the quarry together, and would not look after the vanished rider. For a few shared moments, before the child, childlike, let fall the premature burden of love and loss, and the man, manlike, refused it recognition, each of them knew that he would never see Harry again.

The hunt was up for him, and did not slacken with the night, but he was prepared for that. Most of the searchers would be out along the river valley, expecting him to make directly for Wales with his charge. Not until he was beneath the shadow of the Breiddens did he hear the clatter of riders on the road ahead, and them he eluded by slipping sidelong into the woods. When he returned to the track he took care to use only the grassy verge, where he could ride almost silently; and wherever the shelter of trees offered he took advantage of it gratefully. He was not going to be dragged back like a captured runaway; he was on his way home of his own free will, and of his own free will he would re-enter Parfois and take up the tools he had laid down yesterday.

He had had time to think on that ride, and even time to rebel in his heart against the wanton chance that had cast this inescapable need in his way, and not into another man's arms. Why should God confront him with this cruel choice a second time, and thus freakishly, when his happiness was at its fullest flower? But in a while he perceived that there was nothing wanton in it, and nothing that befell by chance; and that so far from being the second time he had had to choose, it was the hundredth time at least; or, to look at it from another and perhaps a truer viewpoint, it was but the latest reaffirmation of a choice which had been made long ago, and once for all.

From Adam's hand to Owen's head, there was no inconsistency and no chance stroke. The deliberate assumption of responsibility, the affirmation and the challenge, had to be repeated over and over, because the world was still as it had been, and he was still as he had been, and as he would be to his death. Once he had set his own judgement against the world's judgement, the end was implicit in the beginning. Somewhere at the bottom of his heart he had always known that the last choice he made in the teeth of power and privilege and law must be mortal, and that nonetheless he neither could nor would turn aside from making it.

So he had no just complaint against God or man, and he would prefer none. He had what he had chosen, he had never been one to haggle about the price.

Twice on the cautious climb up the flank of the hill he had to draw aside and take to the trees while horsemen passed by; but after that it was quiet enough. They must be seeking him farther afield by now, probably well into Wales. He came without mishap or hindrance to the foot of the grassy ride that led to Parfois, and there dismounted, knotted the reins on the horse's neck, and started him uphill with a slap. The gentle climb round into the dingle under the cliff he made afoot, and found the rope still dangling. The pre-dawn light was just singling out shades of colour, and severing pale from dark, as he hauled himself up hand over hand, and crept over the edge into the long grass, drawing up the rope after him.

Silence hung over Parfois. The drawbridge was raised, and in the quietness he heard the tramp of the guard on the walk between the gate-house towers.

When he had disposed of the rope he went into the lodge, and sat for a while with his forehead against the cold, smooth breast of the Madonna of the Annunciation; he almost slept, but shook himself awake again as often as he found himself drowsing. As soon as there was light enough he took up his tools, but the face of Gilleis smiling on him from the stone was more than he could bear. What was it he had promised to do when he rode out of Parfois? The rood-screen, that was it. The master-carpenter had never been happy about its proportions, its modest height and spare and delicate tracery disappointed his desire to display virtuosity, and he could not reconcile himself to the banishment of the cross. Harry was sure of his judgement; he would not tolerate anything that broke up that great, soaring, shapely space of air and light which was his best achievement, but this fragile and yet strong erection he loved, because it played with the light without opposing it, and its upright, filigree shapes made so many more small, springing fountains reaching towards the vault. Still, he had promised to look critically at it yet again, and at least the looking would be joy. He rose stiffly, and went into the church, mallet and punch still in his hands.

The pre-dawn light was dim but clear in the lofty vault of the nave. The enclosed space filled him with fulfilment and peace; it was like being compassed about by two praying hands. He stood within the west door, filling his eyes and his heart with it, for a long time, while the dove-grey light grew and brightened. He heard, but did not notice, the first horsemen returning empty-handed; they passed by his sanctuary, and the watch let down the drawbridge for them, but he stood untouched, charmed into quietness, no longer even weary. The eastward sky had cleared, and the first long rays of the rising sun, launched clear across the shallow valley of the brook, lit like golden birds upon the rock plateau of Parfois. They threaded the great lancets of the empty east windows, and flying level and radiant from end to end of the church, rang like gold along the western wall. Who would build a barrier in the skyway of the doves of God? Who would shut them behind a lattice of wood and stone, as in an elaborate cage? Suddenly the very vault was full of reflected light that trembled over the slender, braced ribs like fingers among harp-strings, and all the round-cheeked cherubim in the bosses glowed golden and shouted for joy.

The low rood-screen was perfect, delicate, austere. Master Matthew should not touch it again; he should not add one flourish to its spare simplicity. Its springing stems fretted the light into golden ladders across the patterned slip-tiles of the nave. No cross and no figures of mourning should ever cast long, asymmetrical shadows over that field of brilliance, and shatter its unity. He felt for his master-carpenter, but he would not have such beauty marred. He stood and gazed, and he was immeasurably happy, he who had thrown away all the remainder of his life and should have been immeasurably sorrowful.

Presently he climbed up into the triforium and walked along the narrow passage-way to the eastern end. Here he had left a whole range of corbels to be carved on the spot, and had not yet touched them, because this was easy, accessible work which could be tackled at leisure in the winter. He stood in the last of the trefoil openings, just tall enough to hold him upright, close to the east windows and above the high altar, and looked along the flying path of the light. Some of the clerestory windows at this end were already glazed, the rays of the sun slanting through them bordered the vault with burning jewels, emerald and ruby, sapphire and topaz, chrysoberyl and amethyst. He stood in the shadow, but all this light was his.

He was still standing there when the west doorway at which he had entered darkened suddenly with the outline of a man. He came in slowly, his arms hanging wearily, and advancing to where the soft reflected light plucked him out of the anonymity of shadow, lifted to the quivering radiance the ravaged face of Isambard.

He was quite certain that he was alone. How was it that no sensitivity of flesh or spirit warned him? The bitter countenance stared up into the vault filled with the morning, and like a flower in the sun warmed and flushed and opened, clean open to the heart, but upon such a naked anguish of pain and despair that all the air within the church shuddered and ached with it. Love was in it, too, and worship, but love without compassion, and worship without peace. Dark and gaunt with wonder, his eyes adored the beauty and splendour he had caused to be made, and could find no flaw in it and no joy. He bared his teeth and wrenched his head aside, and clenching the fleshless hands that still had such violent strength in them, struck with them hard against his breast.

"Even he!" he cried in the voice of a tormented demon. "Even he! Traitor to me, and forsworn to you!"

The vault was built true, it brought up the suffocating cry magnified but undistorted to where Harry stood, and prolonged it in sad, diminishing echoes from end to end of the roof-rib. He leaned out between the cusps of the trefoil opening, his tools in his hands.

"Who says I am forsworn?"

He had said it quietly enough, but the nearness of the vault took it and turned it into a loud and challenging cry. Isambard's head jerked back, the deep eyes flew to find him, and having found him, there in the trefoil like a stone saint in his niche, hung upon him for a long moment in absolute silence, absolute stillness. Then he flung up his arm and laid it over his eyes, against the light or against what he desired not to see, Harry could not tell which.

"Why did you come back?" he cried.

How was he to understand such a question? Why did you come back to confront me with the necessity of killing you? Why did you come back to force upon me the terrible pleasure and the more terrible pain of revenge? Why could you not lift even this burden from me?

"To finish what I have begun," said Harry, "as I am bound in honour to do, and as I would do even if I were not bound. I well remember my oath. Have I to put you in mind of yours?"

Isambard uncovered his face. Behind the sheltering arm he had composed again the stony mask, beautiful and fierce, that was his public countenance. He looked up fixedly, and smiled.

"You shall finish it," he said. "My memory is also good. All shall be done in accordance with your oath and mine. All! Do you remember the very words, Harry? I hope you do. 'On this living heart,' you said. 'If I play you false,' you said. You have played me false indeed, for you have caused me to play false."

Never once had he asked about the child, never mentioned his name or Llewelyn's. Perhaps even at this moment that disrupted heart was split between gratitude that the boy was got clean away, and rage against the instrument of his escape. The enforced dishonouring of the king's word there was no forgiving, but neither would he ever have forgiven himself for the slaughter of the child. Of all the hatreds that racked him, the sharpest was the hatred he bore to himself.

"Come down!" he said harshly. "I weary of talking to you as to a god."

Harry came down the winding stairway and across the pale, sunlit space of the nave, and stood before him. Now it was he who had to look up. He smiled, acquitting Isambard in his mind of valuing that small advantage. "The boy is safe," he said mildly. "I think you may like to know that. And I remember my oath very well."

"So be it. You shall have all the time you need to finish your work. But when it is completed," said Isambard very softly, "you shall die a traitor's death, you who made me a traitor. I will exact the full forfeit you pledged to me. I'll have that heart of yours living out of your body, and burn it before your eyes."

Chapter Fourteen

The guards who came to fetch him dragged him headlong away over the drawbridge and into the gate-house while the site was still deserted, mortally afraid that some of his workmen might try to rescue him. They need not have worried, and so he told them; labourers and artisans have their own skins to take care of. But they were taking no chances with a charge so precious as Harry Talvace, for their necks would certainly have paid for any miscarriage. They bestowed him in a cell of the guard-house under lock and key, and hobbled with leg-irons into the bargain, and there left him immured most of the day; but they gave him a plank bed and food, and he ate with reasonable appetite and slept as soon as he lay down. Now that it was over, now that he had not to act any longer, but only to sustain what was enacted upon him, he could afford to sleep.

He slept all through the morning and into the late afternoon, while horsemen rode to Fleace and Mormesnil to bring back from among Isambard's other households certain men who would be better qualified for their duties by being strangers to their charge. Too

many at Parfois, officials, armourers, archers, grooms, liked him far
too well to be trusted with him.

The first to come was a smith from Mormesnil, who stood over
the bed and looked at the sleeper in blank astonishment.

"Is that him?" said he. "Why, he's nothing but a bit of a lad.
You could have shut one of your iron neck-collars round his middle
and spared bothering me. I thought we were chaining a wild bull by
the to-do there is about him."

None the less, he settled himself in the armoury, and made them
the harness they demanded. Master Talvace must be free to use his
hands for his work, and free to climb about his scaffolding as he
pleased, and yet be always closely secured. A length of chain joining
two hinged belts of steel, fastening with concealed locks that could
never be picked, was to link him to his perpetual companion, the
thick-set Poitevin man-at-arms, master of sword and dagger,
brought from Fleace in Flintshire.

"Mind you make no mistake in the two girdles," said the smith
when he saw the squat bulk of Guillaume, "or the lad will step out
of his noose and give you the slip."

"And if he does," grunted the Poitevin through his bushy black
beard, "my fellow here can bring him down at anything up to five
hundred paces. I should like to see him get past the pair of us,
without some saint wafts him away in a cloud."

"Saints," said the smith with a grin, "come very seldom to Parfois."

Harry remained in the guard-house all that day, while rumour
upon rumour went the rounds among his men, and hardly a tile was
laid or a stone touched in the church. Parfois shuddered with the
vibration of his treason, and engendered a hundred different versions
of his fate. He was taken. He was dead. He was safely away into
Wales with the boy. The boy was dead, but Harry had escaped. He
had been seized on the very border and taken to Fleace.

John the Fletcher reported back to Benedetta a dozen times that
afternoon, but always to the same purpose. "They say many things,
but they know nothing. He has not been seen since he fled with the
child, or not by anyone who is willing to speak."

"The horse!" said Benedetta, when he came again in the early evening. "Ask in the stables, someone may know which horse he took."

He brought back an answer which he could not get to her until supper in hall, because Isambard was with her in the private apartments. Then he made shift to whisper in her ear as she withdrew from the table: "A horse from the quarry came in without a rider."

"He is here," she said with certainty and clenched a hand under her heart. But she maintained a calm face and a quiet manner, and said not a word of Harry to Isambard. The truth would come out without that, and she would neither betray herself nor beg for him until she must.

In the night they took Harry from his bed, and lodged him unshackled in a cell beneath the Warden's Tower. It was approached through an antechamber, in which for the first time he saw his two guards, the swarthy, squat Poitevin and the long, sad, red-haired crossbowman Fulke. They looked at him with impartial professional eyes, as he would have looked at the plan of a building not his own, which gave him no particular pleasure, but did provide him with problems he would get satisfaction out of solving. He saw that Isambard had been careful to put him in the hands of strangers, and he felt that he had been paid a compliment.

His own cell, the inner one, was small but dry, and, being cut down into the rock, warmer than the draughty precincts of the great hall. It had no window, but a narrow shaft slanting downwards through the thickness of the wall brought in air, and by day at least a feeble shaft of light would find its way down to him. He had a bed and adequate bedding; evidently my lord's master-mason was not to be allowed to die of a chill or grow crippled with rheumatism before he could be half-hanged and ripped open at the brazier by my lord's executioner. For the same reasons there would be food enough, and whatever he needed to keep him active and presentable. He was still master of the works of Parfois, and must continue to command the respect of those who worked under him. He had expected to lie awake, thinking too feverishly, feeling too bitterly, telling over within his mind the steps by which he had destroyed himself. Instead, he slept peacefully and awoke refreshed. There was something dreamlike in the apparition of Fulke at his bedside, with a candle in one hand and a trencher of food in the other. And the coming of Guillaume was even stranger. He brought water and a napkin, and when Harry had washed offered to shave him. Harry stared for a moment and then laughed.

"So I'm not to be trusted with a razor in my own hands! Well, it's an unnecessary precaution, but it's a luxury I never tasted before, to have such a service done for me. What of letting me handle mallet and chisel? Have they thought of that? Am I to be allowed to work today?"

It seemed that he was, for they brought in the harness the smith had made, and locked the smaller of the two belts about his middle.

"Which of us," he asked, plucking experimentally at the chain, "is the hound and which the handler?"

"You have a fine, bell-mouthed bay on you," grunted Guillaume, unimpressed; "we shall see if you'll still be giving tongue so boldly at the end of the day." He had seen a great many jauntily defiant prisoners in his time, but never known their good spirits to last long.

"Well, we'll try the issue," said Harry, stretching and turning to test how freely he could move. "This is well designed. I like to see a man take a pride in his work. My lord promised me a free hand and time to finish mine. That holds good?"

"We are to attend you wherever you go, but so far as the works of the church are concerned you are the master. But mark, no one is to speak to you on any other matter but the work. You'd best warn them of it, for it's they who would pay."

He heard that with the first stab of true terror that had yet touched him. Eagerly he had turned to the doorway, straining towards the one certain and unshakable joy he had left, which was his work, and the one comforting hope, which was for news of Gilleis. Was she safely away? Was she well? Was she with him in what he had done? Did she understand and forgive the enforced abruptness of his farewell? No use asking these two, who were strangers, and in any case surely had orders to carry back to Isambard every word he spoke. But once he was active about the church again, he was certain Benedetta would somehow contrive to send him word. Even if he was to be so closely hedged about from the world, some day his guards must let some whispered word slip through. He would not believe, he refused to believe, that he could be asked to suffer and die without knowing that she was safe—she and the boy, his boy, whom he would never see.

"I see you have second thoughts already," said Guillaume, grinning. "Have you just determined which end of the leash you are?"

"I was debating what I shall need from the tracing-house, so that we need not come back into the wards," he lied firmly, laying his hands for a moment on the cold band of iron about his waist.

The doors opened before him one by one, the layers of stone that walled him in from the world. He stepped out into the grey, sad and yet lovely daylight, chilly and wan after yesterday's splendid sunrise, and passed through the outer ward to the tracing-house with his usual impetuous stride. There was but one thing to be done with chains, and that was to put them out of his mind. He walked as though fetters did not exist, and let Guillaume scurry after him to gather up the slack weight of the chain as best he could. Fulke came behind, his arbalest on his shoulder; he kept the keys of the harness, so that even if Harry disabled or killed the Poitevin he would not be able to rid himself of the incubus of his body.

The reappearance of Master Talvace in the castle of Parfois, and the manner of it, brought the cooks and kitchen-boys from the buttery, the grooms from the stables, the armourers, the waiting-maids, the men-at-arms, the chamberlains, the clerks, the squires and pages, all running from their work to peer and pity. He was not fled to safety, then! He was here, a prisoner and yet stepping out to his own tracing-house with the old authority, in chains and yet neither ashamed nor subdued. He passed among them as if he felt nothing of the dread and awe that shuddered through them at sight of him, and was quite unaware of the two who followed him so close. Word of his return went round like a fire in dry grass, as though his cortège had been a comet casting sparks from its flying tail.

In the tracing-house young Simon was sitting over his accounts with his head in his hands, not attempting to write or reckon. By the look of his swollen eyes he had already cried himself half blind. He saw Harry framed in the doorway, and his face lit up with such an incredulous radiance of joy that the very air brightened round him. He opened his mouth to burst into eager speech, and in the same moment he saw the escort and the chain. The light went out in his eyes. The broad smile of joy froze into a horrified grimace. He groped his way from behind his stool and would have flung himself upon Harry like a stricken child running for comfort, if Guillaume had not thrust himself between and driven the boy back hard against the edge of the tracing tables.

"Hands off! You may say what you need to say to him for the sake of the work, but not a word more. And touch him, if you want a whipping."

"Let him alone!" said Harry sharply. "He is my clerk, I will tell him what he may and may not do." He looked over the Poitevin's shoulder into the boy's tremulous face, and smiled at him. "Never grieve about me, Simon, you see I am still hale, and still master-mason here. We shall go on with our work, and finish it as properly as we began it—both you and I. When that's done it may be time for fretting about other things, but not before. For the present do as he says, speak to me only of the work we have in hand. That you may do, freely. And after all," he said gently, "what need is there to tell me that you feel with me and will be, as you have always been, a good lad and a loyal friend to me? I know it, and am glad of it."

"Watch your own tongue," said Fulke warningly; "it's straying beyond bounds."

Harry laughed aloud. "What bounds? Do you think you can silence me? How, with whippings? Who loses by that? I have only to die once, but if I die too soon my lord will not get his church finished, and if you cripple me with rods or racks he will not get it, either. You dare not lay a hand on me without his word, and you know it. There never was a tongue freer than mine. Don't talk to me of bounds." He turned his back on them coolly, and went to the chest that held his drawings. "Has Knollys been through the rolls yesterday, Simon?"

"Yes, Master Henry, and passed them. The tiles have cost us less than we allowed for." The boy's voice was unsteady, but he controlled it; he had his pride, too. "There was so much uncertainty yesterday, because you were not here, that I think you should make haste to determine what Master Matthew has in his mind. Without you, he conceived it his duty to take charge, but you know he has ideas somewhat different from your own."

"He's a good fellow," said Harry, smiling, "but he would fill the church with fabulous woodwork if he were let. Never fear, I'll guard my rood-screen. He's had full scope in the stalls." He gathered his drawings and turned to the door.

The tremor of excitement and terror and pity passed before him like a fanfare through the gate-house and over the drawbridge, and the labourers, the tilers, the plumbers, the glaziers, the joiners busy on the choir stalls, all stood at gaze, open-mouthed and great-eyed, as he came to the church and entered it, with the alert step and high look he always had. Master Matthew was at that very moment stroking his chin and pondering the rood-screen which was such a disappointment to him; and he had a sympathetic group round him, for it seemed that his star might be in the ascendant now that Master Talvace was fled, or dead, or disgraced, whichever was the true version of his fate. For those slight vertical lines and spare, springing leaves, said Matthew, rubbing his hands, he would have a burgeoning forest of ornament, rich and deep. There was nothing to be done with this but rip it out and replace it entire.

"Over my dead body!" said Harry roundly, appearing unheralded on the borders of this conference. "And that may be possible one day, but not yet, I think."

They swung round in amazement, disconcerted and yet glad, and the apparition of the chain and waist-belt brought the glaze of shock over their eyes and froze the words on their lips. The effect it had on them startled even Harry; he had to clap a hand to his middle to remind himself of the cause of their petrification.

"Oh, never let that deceive you, that's my lord's thorough way of ensuring that he shall not lose my services. You will find I am still the master of the works here, and anyone who questions my authority had best apply to my lord for a judgement. I'm sorry I lost a day's work yesterday—events were out of my control. I make no doubt you used the time faithfully."

Confounded, relieved, dazed, horrified, they found themselves back at work as though nothing had happened, though the very shape of their world had changed. The pointed tone of his voice, the critical glances of his eyes, denied the change, even the hours of the day, passing methodically in the ordinary tasks, conspired to make them doubt it; but the clash of the chain was a continual warning. All day long they heard it at intervals from the triforium, where he had begun the last series of carvings. It made a jarring counterpoint to the measured strokes of his mallet, and the tiny, rustling sound of the falling fragments of stone.

John the Fletcher, who had seen the strange procession cross the outer ward, came out to the site at midday and made to enter the church boldly, as though he had the highest authority. Within the portal two men-at-arms started up. A lance was lowered across his path, and a great hand flattened against his breast.

"Not here, John! None come in here but those who work here."

"That's new," said John equably. "I was here yesterday. Madonna Benedetta wants to have the measurements taken for the cloths for Our Lady's altar, but if you see fit to deny Madonna Benedetta what she wants, on your own head be it. I'll tell her."

It was no small matter to cross the lady of Parfois, but they had their orders, it seemed, for they did not step aside or lower their lances. "If you were here yesterday, why did you not take the measure then?"

"Because the altar's not yet erected and Master Talvace was not here, and only he knows the details she needs. The worked stones they have in store I'd liefer not meddle with. Suppose I should be blamed for a breakage? It's a matter of a minute with him, no more. She sent me down because we heard he was back."

"It's because he's back that no one can go in. With respect to your lady, but we have strict orders. No one, John!"

He shrugged with seeming indifference and went back and told her. If there had to be a struggle for entry, she would be more likely to succeed than any other. Shortly she came herself, sweeping across the trampled waste and in at the west portal with a high, imperious face and a frowning eye. Lances and arms crossed before her, closing the way. In the pale, haggard, lovely face the grey eyes were hard as glass.

"What is this? Who gave you authority to prevent me from going where I will? My lord shall know of this."

"My lady, our orders are from him. We are to admit only those who work within, and else only my lord himself. He made no other exception. Well I understand that he may have had no thought of banning you, my lady, but without his permission we dare not let you in."

"I am coming in," she said, her eyes flashing, "and you will answer for it if you hinder me." And she gathered her skirts in her hands and made two bold paces forward up the steps, her breast to the crossed lances. They quivered before her, almost they were snatched aside from touching her; but the guards were more afraid of disobeying their orders than of offending her. They held their place, though they quaked in their shoes. She leaned hard against the lances, but could go no farther.

Before her the doors stood open. She saw Harry between the choir stalls, the two attendant shadows at his heels. As if her eyes had power to draw his, he turned his head and saw her braced against the barrier. He swung away from the joiners and came striding towards her into the nave, with such forgetful urgency in his step that Guillaume knew, even before he observed the woman at the door, that this was no errand he need countenance. He said not a word, but braced his solid weight, grinning, and let Harry plunge unrestrained to the end of his tether. The chain tightened, jerking him to an abrupt halt. She saw him lay both hands to his waist as the breath was clutched out of him, and marked the gleam of the iron. She heard the Poitevin break into guttural laughter, and her heart was sick with helplessness. They were too far apart even for a look to convey anything of meaning, she could not so much as nod to him that she had done her part. The dimness of the autumn air within the portal clouded their faces, so that they strained their eyes and their hearts to no purpose. And to betray their alliance too clearly was to have no second chance.

She remained for a moment motionless, devouring the very outline of his shoulders, the desperate poise of his head, all that the grey light showed her of him. Then she turned, with one of those wonderful, sweeping movements of hers that caused humiliation to fall aside from her like the dust shaken from the hem of her bliaut, and walked away without a word and without a glance behind.

"It's a long leash," said Guillaume, still guffawing, "but it has its limits. Our lymer hasn't learned about choke collars yet. Give him time, he'll come nicely to heel."

Harry said nothing, though he was white with anger and full to the brim with the scalding realisation of his helplessness. She would try again, a thousand times, she would never give up trying. She would complain magnificently to Isambard of her usage, and he would offer with elaborate courtesy to do all her errands to the church in person. If she pressed the indignity to herself he would have the guards whipped, so that she should feel the injustice to them laid at her own door and never try to pass them again. She would send other messengers, variously, ingeniously, but none of them would ever get to him. Provision had already been made to counter her every move. He was to be incommunicado, to know nothing but the work for which he was being kept alive. But for that, he was already a dead man. He had no wife, no friends, no rights among the living, he had not even nationality or estate, no king, no stake in the happenings in the world. Benedetta would never be allowed to exchange one word with him again, nor could he ask Simon or any other of his subordinates to take the cruel risk of showing pity on him.

So there was one resource left to him, and only one, and that was himself. Come nicely to heel, will he? Not for your training, he thought, nor for my lord of Parfois's whistle. Since I must get my satisfactions where I can, and make shift for myself, let's see how my trainers will take to my element.

The glaziers were at work on one of the tower windows. It was easy to make occasion for climbing to the highest tier of the scaffolding, and his guards had no choice but to go with him. The pace he set them would have terrified even some of his own masons, but they panted after him perforce, sweating horribly in fear of their lives. Once he had to go back and extricate a green-faced Fulke from an exposed corner where he had stuck fast, unable to move either forward or back. When he had got them to the topmost walk and stepped calmly to the edge of the hurdles, they clung desperately to the wall, trembling and sick, not daring to look down. The Poitevin cursed monotonously in a vicious undertone, his bushy beard shaking. Harry stood with his toes over the void, laughing. Parfois was a grey hulk in the fading light, for the evening came on early; the river valley, far below, was a velvet bodice laced with a silver ribbon.

A coldness and a calm smoothed the air before the slow approach of night.

Suddenly he was possessed with such a frenzy of desolation that all his body ached with it. He picked up a tiny stone someone had carried up here on his shoe, and dropped it into the void.

"What's to hinder me from following?" he said, turning upon Guillaume a savage smile. "Unleash your hound, Poitevin, unless you want to go down with him."

Guillaume opened agonized eyes and made a clutch at his arm, but he eluded it and slipped along the hurdles, grinning, and laying both hands to the chain, began to haul his fetter-fellow after him. The black-bearded man locked his arms despairingly about one of the poles and clung there, shaking from head to foot.

"Had you not better unlock him, Fulke? Or are you coming with us? Better that than face my lord without us!"

They cursed him, and then as helplessly pleaded with him.

"Ah," he said at last, sick of the game as of them, "you need not fear, your fool necks are safe enough with me. If I wanted to kill you I could have done for Fulke a while ago, I had only to leave him there to shiver with fright till he shivered himself over the edge. Come down, then, if you still have nerve to stir. Do as I tell you and you're safe as in your beds."

He brought them down safely enough, but Guillaume, as soon as his feet touched earth, went on his knees and was direly sick. Harry dangled the chain at him and laughed, though already he felt a world away from laughter.

When they took him back to his cell that night and brought him food before they left him, all three of them were subdued and silent. Freed of his chains, Harry lay on his back on the bed, his hands linked under his head. His anger was gone, only the desolation remained.

"That was an unfair advantage I took of you," he said, with a sudden grudging smile, "and I'm not proud of it. It's a skill a man gets from long use. No shame to you that you were not born with it, for neither was I. I've no choice but to take you up there again sometimes, in all honesty, but I'll take you at your own speed next time, I give you my word."

Dumbfounded, they stared at him speechlessly. It was the first time any of their charges had asked their pardon for misusing them.

"Is there aught you want?" asked Guillaume gruffly, before they left him to his darkness.

"Only one thing," said Harry, rising on his elbow. "For myself I've no complaint, if I could hear news of my wife. If you could but get me word whether she's in Parfois or safe away from here—"

He saw the closed look that came over their faces, and the side glances they cast at each other, and he understood that it was useless. They were set to spy on each other, no less than to guard him, and neither of them dared offer him comfort, for terror of his own neck.

"No matter!" he said with a sigh, lying down again. "It was too much to ask."

When the door was locked, the great door that was like a stone sealing a tomb, he turned on his face and lay with his head in his folded arms. The lightness and emptiness, the irresponsibility that had clouded his judgement when all possibility of action passed out of his hands, was clean gone now, like the passing of the numbness that follows a wound. The longing and hunger for Gilleis came on him like the throes of poison, gripping his body until he felt that the very heart's blood was being wrung out of him. He lay hugging the agony to him, and biting deep into the hard brown flesh of his forearm, until the paroxysm passed in a brief burst of scalding tears.

Hard on its passing the agony of the mind began, the long anguish of thinking and feeling and fearing, that would never end this side of death.

The last great work of Harry Talvace at Parfois, second only to the capitals of the nave, was the gallery of portrait heads on the corbels of the triforium, the fruit of his captivity.

Because he was still a warm and living man, even though they had banished him into a companionless world not unlike a grave, his energy and passion, dammed up from all channels but one, flowed into that last course as an irresistible flood. One remaining happiness and joy he had, the only one now permitted to him, the exquisite thing he had made. All his virtue flowed into the stone and burst into flower.

By day he moved among his fellows, intent, competent and demanding; and as the weeks and months of the slow, dark winter crept by, what had been strange and terrible became customary and accepted. Men can get used to anything. For days together they forgot about his chains, only to be hustled away from him with reminding blows if they fell into the trap of drawing too near to him or addressing to him some few casual words with no bearing on the work in hand. They pitied him, but even pity flagged with use. They outlived it, as he seemed at last to have outlived fear and regret, and perhaps even longing. The heart can bear only so much and continue to suffer for only so long.

But the stone did not fail him. The stone survived.

He forsook his drawings and made new. All the corbels of the internal wall arcade in the triforium, between the shallow lancet windows, became as chapters in the story of his life. Here, in this most obscure place, away from the public eye, he might justly record his testament. He began drily and with deliberation. As long as one corbel remained uncarved, he would remain alive, he had his judge's word for that. It did not matter that the floorings were laid, the altars raised, the stalls fitted, more than half the windows glazed and the others ready and waiting for the spring; he would not die until the last carving was complete, and complete to his satisfaction. Well, he could make the work last a long, long time, if his life depended on it.

But they sprang to life so readily, they pressed forward under his hands so insistently, that he could not withstand them. There had never been carved heads so sudden, so urgent, or so economical. Guillaume and Fulke rolled dice idly on the flags of the triforium, and took their eyes off him for an hour or two, and when they turned about there was another living face looking down upon them. They came, and he could not maim them by working over them still when he knew they were finished. His father was there, his mother, married now to Gloucester's young knight, thank God, and far away from a death she could not have prevented, his brother Ebrard, and Adam Boteler his foster-brother. Poor Adam, fretting helplessly in Wales, perhaps, and trying to get reliable news in a distracted land where there was precious little of the commodity to be had. Abbot Hugh de Lacy was there, austere and aristocratic, Norman to his finger-ends, and Brother Denis the infirmarer, no doubt busy finding excuses now for the most unruly of the cherubim and seraphim at every celestial chapter; and Nicholas Otley, merchant and alderman of London, who had in him the large nature proper to princes, and which princes so seldom show; and Gilleis the child; and Apollon and Élie, wrapped in the one gown they owned between them. Benedetta was there, and the provost of Paris, and Ralf Isambard, and John the Fletcher, and Owen ap Ivor ap Madoc in his own proper person for once; they crowded out of his memory and sprang into the waiting stone.

The self-portrait that began the sequence, the several faces they recognised, started an unexpected curiosity in Fulke and Guillaume. They followed him from corbel to corbel, waiting to see who would appear, and they asked him many questions concerning those they did not recognise. If he had outlived his anger, they had outlived their indifference. From a leash the chain had become a link. It was late to begin a new relationship, but it was on them before they were aware.

Gilleis the woman came out of the stone with the first flush of spring, like a waking flower.

"That's her that's below on the altar," said Guillaume, watching over Harry's shoulder. He had lost the last of his pay to Fulke and had nothing left to dice for. The winner sat comfortably propped against the wall in a patch of sunlight, at a little distance from them, drowsing within closed eyelids, but how soundly there was no telling.

"It is," said Harry, in a voice that caused Guillaume to turn and give him a keen glance.

"She's a beauty. And by this, then, she's a real woman?"

"She is my wife," said Harry.

Guillaume drew breath sharply and cast a glance at his fellow. Fulke's right hand relaxed slowly, and slid down from his knee; his head nodded gently back against the stone and rested there, and he did not open his eyes.

"I can get no certain word of your lady," said Guillaume in a rapid whisper in Harry's ear. "Some say she's vanished. Some say she's here but kept close. No one's seen her."

Harry turned his head in astonishment to stare at his gaoler, touched to the heart. Even to speak of her, even to hear her spoken of, was like food after long hunger; and to know that his keeper had remembered and tried to do him so much kindness, brought gratefully back to him the world and men and all his faith in them. The touch of humanity came even through the stone walls of his cell.

"Friend," he began, "this was kind—"

Guillaume clapped a hand softly over his mouth, and looked again at Fulke, and leaned closer still. "A word more, while there's time. Every night when you're safe in your nest one of us must report to him on your day. Never a day but he questions if you have not asked to see him. I think he wants it. I think if you begged for your life he might give it back to you yet."

"He would not," said Harry with conviction. "He gave too much of himself to me ever to forgive me my treason against him."

"Then why does he ask? Send word to him, ask him to see you. At least try. If he wants you on your knees to him, isn't your life worth it?"

"He'll wait a long time," said Harry grimly, "before he brings me to my knees."

"But for your life, man! For God's sake, you're as mad as any mad marcher lord of them all."

"What's between him and me won't let either of us kneel. But he'd never forgo the pleasure of killing me, even if I kissed his feet. Trust me, I know."

"Then at least go slowly with your stone-chipping, lad, and live longer. You're bringing the day on yourself."

Harry opened his lips to protest that he had been trying all these weeks to hold his hand; but before he could say a word Guillaume mouthed at him soundlessly: "He's ware!" and stepped back from him to the length of the chain. Fulke had nodded himself clear of the pillar at his back and shaken himself awake. There was no time for Harry to express his thanks even with his eyes. He turned to his work again, and chain and chisel rang together.

"But four more to do," said Guillaume, gruff as ever. "What are they to be?"

"That you will see in good time."

He was smiling as he shaped the beloved rose of a mouth. Two of the four would show them their own faces. Perhaps if Guillaume

had nodded, Fulke would have hissed advice in his ear just as benevo-
lently. Kindness and compassion and liking go right to the edge of
the grave, like the bright gold dandelions that thrust up to the light
even between the sealed stones of tombs. And the third of the
four heads belonged to a man he himself had not yet seen, though
according to his gaolers he was already arrived.

He saw him next day, as he was escorted through the outer ward.
A tall, thin, rather elegant fellow in bright red and black stood with
Isambard a little apart from the tracing-house, leaning on his horse's
shoulder with one long arm. He was there to observe Harry, but in
some degree it disconcerted him when Harry halted to make an
intent and leisurely inspection of him. Even Isambard probably
mistook it for a gesture of bravado, though he should have known
better.

"Is that the man?" asked Harry as they moved on.

"It is."

"French, you say? It's a fine, sinister head. He's never a Norman?"

"From Gascony, I heard. They say he's very skilled."

Harry threw back his head and laughed aloud, without a shadow
of bitterness. There were no double meanings in Guillaume's head,
he meant it in consolation.

"Man, man, if that means he's expert in this new trick of taking
out a man's bowels and still keeping the life in him, I'd rather they
got me an honest English butcher, used only to coarse work like
quick killing." He threw his arm round Guillaume's shoulders.
"Never fret, it's all one. Guillaume, get that fellow to come to the
tracing-house this evening, I need a better look at him. I'd like to
make a drawing."

And the fourth head, the last, he thought of with such secret love
that he was glad no one else would ever realise whom it represented.
They would take it for one more self-portrait to close the story, and
discount the elements in it which did not stem from him. It was
never likely to occur to anyone to match Gilleis's face with his, and
recognise their son.

The need to prolong his life he had forgotten in the more impera-
tive need to perfect his work. He could neither delay nor deface the
issue of his hands, any more than he could have maimed the issue

of his body. Daily his life flowed away into the sacred stone, as the fruit must fall and rot that the seed may germinate and the tree grow, the heaven tree of his achievement. He was the human sacrifice sealed into the walls, he was the ceremonial blood mixed into the mortar. Nothing was left him but the dedicated skill of his hands, the possessed fury of his creative dream. But the day had come when it was enough.

Chapter Fifteen

She came to him in the May evening in his bedchamber, as he was dressing after his ride, and waited motionless by the great bed until his squire had left him. Then she came forward and knelt at his feet. Her hair was unbound and her feet were bare, she had no jewel or ornament upon her. Never until then had she asked him for anything. She laid her hands about his ankles and her face upon her wrists, and the flood of her hair gushed over the skin rugs like an effusion of blood. In the nape of her neck the short tendrils curled small and fine as finger rings.

"I waited long for this," he said, looking down at her with a still face. "It used to be I who knelt to you. That prayer was denied. Well, speak, if you want aught from me."

"Why should I speak," she said, "when you already know what I want? You made me a part of yourself. Now listen to your own prayers, and I will be silent."

"I am doing what I wish to do," he said.

"That I believe. But it is also what you loathe yourself for wishing, and will detest yourself for ever for having done. I ask you to deliver yourself, for no one else can. Send the Gascon away, and set Harry Talvace free.''

''There is no price even you can offer me now,'' said Isambard, smiling into the mirror, ''that could buy his life.''

She lifted her face to him and joined her hands, and said: ''I am not offering to buy. I ask you to give.''

''Go on!'' said Isambard. ''You brought more words than those with you. Let me hear them all.''

She knew then that it was useless. Nevertheless, she embraced his knees and said all that could be said of the six years of his acquaintance with Harry Talvace, of the incomparable work Harry had done for him, of the extenuations of affection and pity that made his crime no crime, and of the unquestionable love there had been between them. She begged for Harry's life in measured words and a low and level voice, without tears or reproaches. Even in abasing herself she matched him in dignity. Perhaps she would have shrieked and wept and loaded him with hysterical entreaties, if she had known how to do it, but it was a skill she lacked. In the end it would surely have been all the same. He was irrevocably set on destruction. Not on Harry's destruction only, but on hers and on his own, on pulling down the whole structure of their life headlong upon them to crush them.

He drew himself out of her arms, not ungently, but with such deliberation that she was confirmed in her despair. She let him go and remained kneeling where he had left her, her hands joined.

''The last scaffolding is down. By the tenth the lodges will be down, too, and the site cleared.''

She neither spoke nor moved.

''On the morning of the eleventh, soon after dawn, we'll make an end.''

Out of the following silence she spoke at last, quite gently. ''You think you will be healed of your hell when you have made hell everywhere about you. But it is your own heart the Gascon will be ravishing. And you will have to live on after it. He will at least be able to die.''

''It will take longer than you might think,'' said Isambard, clasping an amber necklet about his throat. ''De Perronet tells me on one occasion he kept a client alive and conscious for more than half an hour after disembowelling. The heart is more difficult, but he assures me Harry shall live to feel the want of it. Of course, he may be exaggerating his skill—he is a Gascon." He turned his head and looked at her, and she had not moved. Her profile was clear and still. "Of what are you thinking, Benedetta?"

"I am wondering," she said, "what terrible penance you will exact from yourself some day for what you are doing now."

Only silence answered her. She did not look round until she heard the door close after him.

That was over. She had never believed in it, as she had never believed in the letters she had helped Gilleis to write and send to this lord and that along the march, imploring their aid for Harry. It was every man for himself in this distracted England. Who meddled with such as Isambard?

It remained to save what could be saved. She rose and dressed, and before she went down the stone stairway and across the inner ward to the great hall she sent for John the Fletcher. She was sitting before the mirror when he entered; their eyes met in the glass, and they understood each other.

"On the morning of the eleventh," she said, "at dawn. He does not intend Knollys to pay off the men until it is over. There will be a great many people. That should help. Have you considered the ground?"

"The roof of the tower is the only sure place," said John the Fletcher. "It commands the whole field from the gate to the gallows, and the range is easy."

"But it makes withdrawal more difficult. I can have a rope secured for you down the cliff on the Welsh side, and a horse waiting in the woods below. We must look at the place together. But getting down from the tower and out of the church will take a dangerous time."

"There'll be confusion enough," he said, "and the church between them and me, and the trees close. I'll take the risk. It's the one perfect place."

"The light will be on your right hand. Are you sure of your skill? Can you do it clean?"

"Madam, I can."

"Good! I'll see that you have money, and you must get out of the shire as quickly as possible." She twisted the mass of her hair into a great, shining coil, and drew the silken net over it. In the mirror her eyes had a shadowy silver lustre, as though they were great with tears, but her mouth was smiling faintly. "When they lead him out from the gate," she said, "the dawn light will be on his church. I hope there will be sunshine. He will look up to take his farewell of it, and stand still to adore the work of his hands. That is your moment. Promise me, John, that he shall never turn away his eyes from the church to look at the gallows."

"As I hope for the mercy of God," said John the Fletcher, "he never shall."

One more thing she had to do, but it could not be done until the last evening. Father Hubert was old and wily, but in some respects also gullible, a circumstance of which she could make good use, but which she did not intend should be of use to any other. If she prompted him before the event he would have time to betray her design by accident, or, no less disastrously, think it over quietly and think better of having anything to do with it. On the last evening, shortly before they supped in the great hall, that was her time.

The guard was gone from the church now. Harry had looked his last on that prayer-shaped space of air and light between the two folded hands of stone, and there was no longer any need of lances at the portal. She went alone, in the close of the afternoon, to pray at the altar of the Virgin with the face of Gilleis. On the other side of the grassy plateau the gallows stood waiting, the tree of death opposed to the tree of life. She did not avert her eyes from it, she even turned as she was crossing the bridge, and measured it with her glance again, like a soldier measuring his opponent's sword. Then she went in and dressed herself as carefully as a bride, in a cotte of dark blue velvet and a surcoat of gold tissue, and coiled her hair on her head within a golden circlet. The time for despair was over, and the time for mourning was not yet; tonight was a time for triumph, if she played her cards well.

She went down alone to the chapel to find Father Hubert. The old man had been most of his life in service at Parfois, and was treated as a privileged person, a position on which he prided himself not a little.

"Father," she said mildly, turning the rings on her fingers, "I am exercised in my mind about Master Talvace. You know it has been always my lord's custom, as I think it was also his father's, to offer to every condemned man on the eve of his death whatever comfort or entertainment he most desired for his last night. He has not mentioned it in Master Henry's case, and I fear that it has slipped his mind, and that he will be distressed afterwards if he omits it. But I would not myself remind him; it is too like a criticism of him, which I do not intend. But you, Father, can speak of it most fittingly, as a part of your office. You will be visiting the prisoner after supper, will you not?"

"That is my intent," said the old man.

"Then could you not remind my lord at supper, and say that you will, if he so pleased, be the messenger of his gracious clemency? I fear he will feel it as a point of honour that Master Henry should not be excluded from grace, and if he fail in it through forgetfulness it will wound him deeply."

"My lord is always punctilious," agreed Father Hubert, preening himself. "It is my duty to see that all is done as he wishes. Certainly I will speak to him before I go."

"And, Father, for my part you may say to Master Henry that I commend to him my lord's merciful dispensation, and pray that he may use it to his best comfort, God guiding him. I should like him to know that he is prayed for."

"It is right and meet to remember the prisoners and the unfortunate. I will tell him what you say."

"You have greatly comforted me," said Benedetta, and went smiling into the great hall. Now, if I have not over-prized the love we surely have between us, she thought, Harry will know what to ask. And you, Ralf, who perform all your promises, good and evil, you shall have your hand so forced that you cannot withdraw.

He came to table that night in a magnificence as striking as her own, with glittering eyes and high colour, and the oblique smile frozen on his lips. The presence of his entire household never touched his mood; he was so used to them, and so indifferent to them, that he created a solitude about him. Nevertheless, it was well that there should be so great a cloud of witnesses. He ate little, but drank well, he who was usually a sparing drinker. Her sleeve brushed his with stiff whisperings of brocade and velvet, the fine Flemish stuffs he loved, and she felt in every touch the contagion of his dangerous excitement and his appalling unhappiness. She would have pitied him, but she knew he would esteem it the last cruelty.

The chaplain rose from table early and came to his lord's shoulder. He had a good, sounding voice, a dozen or so of the knights and squires could not choose but overhear.

"My lord, I am going to visit the prisoner. All is to be done according to custom? I know the magnanimity of your mind, and I know you would wish me to observe all the forms honoured in Parfois."

"It is a case like any other case," said Isambard. "He has the rights all condemned men have."

"Then I shall ask him, as is customary, what privilege or comfort he most desires on his last night," said Father Hubert.

"Do so, Father!" He smiled, not displeased with the reminder. To offer a crumb to a man starving for life might well be the last refinement of his revenge. "Short of liberty, he shall have whatever he cares to ask."

It was done, that ringing voice of his had committed him too deep to withdraw. Now let Harry do his part, and God give the old fool who brings his reply the courage to speak it aloud, thought Benedetta.

He would be a long time gone, he was invariably long-winded about his office. She could not sit still, nor did she wish to be within touch of Isambard when the answer came, but fronting him and at a distance, that she might see his face full. She rose from his side and came round the high table to the corner of the dais where the musicians sat, and held out her hand for the citole the youngest of them was idly clasping. The boy leaped up and brought a cushioned stool for her, and she sat down calmly and retuned the instrument at leisure. Isambard had turned his head and followed her movements with attentive eyes that revealed nothing of his mind. She let her fingers stray into Abelard's forgotten air deliberately, and watched to see if his mouth tightened or his eyes kindled, but there was no sign. Wait, she thought, there's no hurry, I'll prick you home yet.

It was three-quarters of an hour before Father Hubert reappeared at the end of the high table. What ails him, wondered Benedetta, playing a false note at sight of him. Nervous of his errand he might well be, but this was fear itself. His fingers were scrabbling agitatedly in his venerable tonsure, and his eyes looked sidelong at his lord. Whatever Harry might have said to him, it was more than she had foreseen, and more than the old man had bargained for. He might even lie; she had not thought it needful to take that into consideration, but she questioned if he was as much in awe of hell, in the last estimate, as of Isambard. True, he took his little customary liberties, but he knew where to stop. Yet a dying man's charge is a terrible thing to betray.

"Well?" said Isambard, frowning because the chaplain hung irresolutely silent.

"My lord, the young man is in no proper frame of mind—it is an obdurate soul—"

"He is paying for his obduracy," said Isambard, and his crooked smile was more bitterly twisted than usual. "He has a right to it. He flung my offer back in my teeth, did he?"

No, she thought, her hands rigid on the citole, it is not that, it is something more.

"No, my lord, not precisely so. Though in effect, what he asked being so insolent and malicious—"

"Come to the point! Did he make a request or no?"

"My lord, he did, but—" Father Hubert was more afraid to remain silent than to speak, and too confused to lie fast enough for conviction.

"Then repeat it! In his very words, Father!"

"My lord, he asks—may God forgive him!—he asks for Madonna Benedetta to be his bedfellow."

It carried halfway down the great hall, and in a flurry of frantic whispers that hissed like snakes it was repeated back and back to those who had not heard. The stem of the Venetian glass snapped in Isambard's fingers, the delicate bowl shivered among the silver dishes, and wine gushed across the table like blood. Below the salt the household of Parfois had become a forest of dilated eyes; and in a breath even the whispers died, and silence closed on the hall, and stillness, as though all in it had been turned to stone.

It was better than she had designed, it was a thrust to the heart.

Her own heart was leaping in her with so large and jubilant a pulse that she could hardly contain it. She rose, drawing all eyes to herself, and slowly, slowly she began to cross the hall, the citole in her hand. For a moment none of them, not even Isambard, understood what she intended. But as she passed along the dais and drew abreast of him and still did not halt, he realised her purpose. He leaped to his feet with a scream such as she had never heard or thought to hear from that imperious throat. His great chair went over backwards with a crash upon the floor, and the silver trenchers rang as his fists thudded on the board.

"You shall not go!"

She turned and looked at him with full, mild eyes, sustaining his frenzied stare with the utmost resignation. "I will go, my lord," she said loudly and clearly. "It touches your honour. What am I, beside the sacredness of your word?"

It drove the breath out of his body and froze the words in his mouth. He was taken in the snare of his own inflexible pride; what he had said he could not unsay, what he had given he could not take back. Before the eyes of all his household he was silenced and helpless. Short of killing her, there was no way of stopping her.

She looked him steadily in the face, and suddenly and blindingly she smiled. The dove-grey softness of her eyes darkened and brightened into purple, shining with triumph; the full mouth curled exultantly. She straightened her shoulders, drawing herself up before him in such a transport of defiant joy that the dullest among them could not but understand. She was going not to sacrifice, but to triumph. The unveiling was done deliberately, with a barbaric delight in the opulence of the gesture. If she had cast down her eyes and preserved the pretence of sacrificial devotion she might have gone on living, thought more than one who looked at her. She has just tossed her life away for the pleasure of striking him to the heart.

To Isambard that look of naked joy uncovered a greater mystery. The moment of the dissolution of their compact was come upon him without a word spoken. She had pronounced the contract at an end, and there was no redress. She was abandoning him to follow the creature she loved more than her own life, and he must abide it without complaint. If she had seen the end in the beginning, she could not have found fitter words for it.

"Father," said Benedetta, again veiling her face, "I do not know where his cell is. Will you bring me to the place?"

She went out on the old man's arm, and in stillness and silence all the fixed and fearful eyes followed her withdrawal. Only Isambard stood where she had left him, his hands over his face, and no one dared even approach him to pick up the fallen chair.

In the antechamber of the cell Benedetta paused to look sharply at the two guards, who stood back from her respectfully, as much in awe of her cloth of gold as of her authoritative bearing.

"Wait!" she said. "Before you open the door let me give you a word of warning. When you have turned the key upon us, for your own safety leave this room and lock the outer door also. Sleep across the threshold if you will, but be so far from us that you may be under no suspicion of seeing or hearing anything. Father, tell them what would happen to any man who dared to witness this coupling."

"She is giving you good advice," said the old man, trembling. "He would tear you in pieces."

Afterwards, she thought without astonishment or concern, he will tear me in pieces; but by then it will no longer matter.

"Father, remain with them, and bear them witness if they are called in question."

"Madonna, I will." The hand he held in his was warm and easy; he clung to it to steady his own trembling.

"And pray for us."

Guillaume turned the key in the great sunken lock.

"Mistress, when shall we open to you again?"

"When they come for him," she said, and gathered up her long skirt and went into the cell.

They had left him a great candle for his last night; it burned in an iron candle-stick on the rock ledge beside his pallet, and wavered softly and constantly in the air from the shaft. Harry was lying on his back on the bed, his head pillowed on folded arms, but at the sound of the door opening he turned on his side and rose on his elbow to stare at the glitter of gold in the doorway. He had not believed that they would ever let her come. The flame of the candle shone in his astonished eyes, turning their shadowy blue back to green, and the reflection of her splendour transmuted the green to burnished gold. Between the black lashes, beneath the dark, straight brows, that brilliant, dancing light startled and moved her like the apparition of stars in a night of storm. He swung his legs over the edge of the bed in trembling haste and scrambled to his feet, and the hurried sweep of his arm set the candle rocking. He clutched at it to steady it, and she saw how his hand was shaking.

The door closed behind her. The key turned. The candle-light shuddered up the stony walls in ripples of pallor, and slowly stilled.

He tried to say her name, and his mouth was too dry for speech. She saw him swallow and moisten his trembling lips with a tongue almost as dry. He had not believed she would come, and now that she was here, she who alone could tell him what he ached to know, he was afraid to ask her, for fear the answer should be harder to bear even than the wondering.

"She's safe," said Benedetta, leaping to fill his need. "She's well. She sends you her heart's love."

"Oh, Benedetta!" he said in a long, soft sigh, and the trembling tension ebbed out of him. His cast shadow on the wall seemed to soften and dwindle. "*Nunc dimittis!*" he whispered and suddenly bowed his head forward into his hands and wept, wearily, gratefully, freely, like an exhausted child.

She took him in her arms and drew him down with her on to the bed, and the brief storm spent itself in the shoulder of her magnificent surcoat. She smoothed back the thick brown hair from his forehead and let her hand rest about the back of his head, holding him gently upon her breasts. She had the whole world in her hand. "There, lie still, we have time. We can speak openly, and all night long. No one will disturb us, no one will spy on us. I've seen to that."

"Where is she?" he asked, when he had his voice again.

"Safe with the anchoress sisters at the oratory of Saint Winifrede, in the hills by Stretton. They're kind and loyal, and so holy no one dare meddle with them. And good nurses, you can be easy about her when her time comes. Soon she'll have the child to live for, and neither of them shall ever want for a friend."

"I'd have given my right hand if I could have come to her, that day, but there was no time, if the boy was to live. I was afraid! She's headstrong! I was afraid she would refuse to go."

"She didn't want to leave you, it wasn't in her nature to take cover when you were manifestly putting yourself in peril. But we didn't even know what you intended, and for the child's sake she had no choice but to obey you."

"It was hard for her," he said, and shook in her arms at the memory. "And not even to know for what end I was asking so much of her—"

"She knows now. She's with you heart and soul. What else could he do, she said, being Harry? The hardest for her to bear has been staying there in hiding all this time, knowing what was fallen upon you."

"She knows about me? The whole of it?"

"Not the whole. She knows it's death, but not that it's on us already. God knows I have no right to keep anything from her, and yet I could not tell her, and the child so near. I told her—ah, I hoped it would be truth!—that you would spin out the work you had left and make it last months yet. I hoped there'd be time for his rage to pass, or that the king would call him hence and you be forgotten. For there's a great contention between John and his barons, and Langton has his arms in it to the elbows—some matter of a reaffirmation they want the king to make, securing them all their old rights. Even FitzAlan and FitzWarin are siding against the king, and now it's come to an issue of arms. A few months more, and there might have been no thought to spare for you. Oh, Harry, why didn't you hold your hand and give your friends a little time?"

"I meant to," he owned. "I as good as told Adam I should. But when it came to the point I could not. The work came so quick upon me, I could not turn my hand to abortion. Not even to save my life! Benedetta, does she know—the manner of it?"

"No!" she cried, her arms tightening jealously about him. "Nor shall not! But that none of us knows, Harry. Only God knows it."

"Never tell her! Where's the need? By the time she knows of it I shall be past troubling. I would not have her grieve over what's done. You've seen her since you took her away?"

"Three times. I dared not go oftener. And several times John has been my messenger."

"Did *he* look for her?"

"I know he did, though he never spoke of it to me, beyond asking if I'd seen her that day you took the boy. I said she had been with me in the morning and I had not seen her since. He ransacked Parfois for her, and even after you came back he was still searching for her through the villages below. But it did not continue long."

"Tell me of her!" he begged hungrily. "Tell me everything! Does she speak of me?"

"Speak of you! Oh, my heart's dear," said Benedetta, laying her cheek against his hair, "you are her sun and her moon. You are the spring and the summer to her." She smiled over his head into the candle-flame, and talked to him of Gilleis until she had exhausted every detail of the time they two had spent together loving him. "Only the child has kept her still and silent. When she has put your son from her and placed him in safety, I know, I feel, she means to return and fight for you—"

"Yes," he said, fondly and proudly, "that I can believe." He turned a little in her arms, and rested with his cheek upon her breast. "Now that won't be needful. Benedetta—" He hesitated upon her name, and she looked down to find his eyes searching her face. "When you tell her, carry my undying love to her. And kiss my son for me."

"My best and dearest, you know I will."

"You've eased me of such a load!" he said, and drew a long, weary breath. "Now that I have her blessing and yours, the rest is almost easy. I thank God!" And after a while: "I have been most happy, and most blessed. It was ungrateful to forget."

"How long is it since you slept?" she asked, passing cool fingertips over the blue-stained arches of his eyelids. "Two nights? Three?" He shook his head, faintly smiling; he did not know. "Sleep now, and I'll watch by you."

"Oh, no!" he protested, tightening his arms about her. "I shall be sleeping soon enough." The shadow of the terrible portal of that sleep lay heavy upon his face. Through the breast of his crumpled shirt she felt the strong, indignant beat of his threatened heart. "Let me enjoy you while I have you. I never thought he'd let you come. It was the only bolt I had to loose at him, and I hoped it would find its mark, but I never believed it would win me the prize."

"He'd pledged himself before everyone, he could not evade it. 'It touches your honour,' I said. 'What am I in comparison?' But I laughed in his face, I could not for my life refrain. If you won't sleep, at least lie down and rest."

"If you'll lie beside me. It's but a narrow bed for two, but we're neither of us so great that we need a lot of room."

"True," she said, smiling, "I'd forgotten. You asked for a bed-fellow." She rose and kicked off her shoes, and stripping off her surcoat, let it fall in a corner of the cell. "Take the inner place, Harry, I would be between you and the world."

He lay down close to the wall, and watched her as she lifted the circlet from her head and loosed the flood of her hair. "God knows I should ask your pardon for that," he said shamefacedly. "I am not proud of myself now."

"You did well! I meant you to ask for speech with me, but this was more than I'd hoped for. You pierced him to the heart."

He opened his arms to her, and she lay down beside him in her velvet cotte and clasped him close. He filled his hand with her hair and drew it over them both like a silken coverlet, and she heard and felt a sudden honest crow of laughter go bursting up out of his throat to make the candle flicker again. "It's well seen he lacks experience of my situation, or he'd know I'm in no case to afford you much pleasure or do myself much credit in that kind tonight. But it's a narrow life he's led, when all's said and done."

"Never fear," she said, settling herself warmly in the crook of his arm, "I'll not hold you to your bond."

"Ah, don't mock me! It was a poor joke, I know, but I'm out of practice. If you knew how long it seems since I laughed!"

"You have no debts to me," she said, with the old, large candour. "I want for nothing. I have everything." And indeed she had out-lived, how long ago she could not even guess, the anguish of not being able to be more to him than she was. It had passed unnoticed, some day when it had dawned upon her heart, though not upon her mind, that what Gilleis was to him was not more, but only different. They lay together now marvellously at peace, and not the humble peace of resignation, but the lofty peace of achievement. All that she needed of him she had. It did not matter how small it might seem to others, when it filled her life to overflowing and had been given with a generosity as absolute as love itself.

"Harry, are you afraid of death?"

"Who is not a little afraid of it, if he's in his right wits? We're all in awe of the dark, when it comes to it. But it's not death appals me, it's the dying!" He stiffened angrily against the shudder that convulsed him. "I'm afraid of pain. I'm afraid of that devilish violation of my body. And of being a spectacle, long after I've ceased to be a man. Ah, why did you ask me? I wanted to spare you this."

She laid her hand upon his cheek, and holding him so, said with passionate gravity: "Harry, with all my heart I ask you to trust me. Leave reasoning, leave preparing yourself, leave fearing. You will not be shamed. He'll have no triumph over you. He'll never see you broken. I swear it! Death, we can't avoid, but its coming is in God's gift, not in Isambard's."

"Ah, girl!" he said with a whisper of laughter, "you lift up my spirit. If you could speak so to me at the last, before you leave me, I believe I might not break."

"I shall not leave you. And you will not break. Trust me, and don't be afraid."

"A miracle!" He lay smiling at her with a sudden unquestioning weariness sweet and heavy in his eyes. "You draw out fear with your fingers. I can almost believe that if you have asked it of him God will make the way easy for me and take me to Himself unbroken. The other—ah, the fear of what comes after is a good fear, hardly more terrible than when I had to go before the masters in Paris and submit my master-work. I was sick with fright the night before that, too; Adam had a time with me. But they gave me their approval."

"I am not afraid," she said, stroking him softly, "that you will fail of getting God's." But whether the master-work he was to offer must be his church or his life, or whether indeed the twain were one, she did not trouble to question; they were of one quality both, and God would know how to value them.

"What will you do, Benedetta, afterwards? You have no thought of—of dying? You wouldn't do that!"

"Not while you have a child living for me to love and serve."

He heaved a deep sigh of wonder and content. "What have I done, what have I ever done, to deserve your love?"

"Loved me," she said, smiling, "after your fashion. And it's a good fashion, I wouldn't change it."

He turned his head upon the pillow, and taking her chin in his hand, softly, tenderly kissed her. They lay together a long moment thus, a sweet, cool, tranquil joy possessing them, their mouths married in quietness. When he drew away, as softly as he had come, she lay still with her overwhelming happiness.

"That was no kiss for wife, or love, or mother, or sister, or child," she said at last, marvelling.

"No, it was only for you. For my sweet friend—from the most grateful to the truest and dearest of all sweet friends who ever loved each other well."

She would have spoken, she would have poured out her heart to him like a libation, but his peace was too precious and too fragile a thing to be so shaken. She lay still in his arms, holding him to her heart, and they were silent for a long time; he said at last, in a soft voice already blurred with sleep: "Death is in God's gift! If it might come now!"

In a few moments she knew by the languid weight of the arm over her, and by his gentle, deep breathing against her cheek, that he had fallen asleep.

He slept in her arms through the hours of the night, while she cradled and guarded him as jealously as a mother; and when the first pallid light cast a faint ray through the shaft in the wall she took his face, all softened and flushed with sleep, in her hands and kissed him awake. He opened his eyes and smiled at her brilliantly. Then realisation closed on him, and the smile grew wan.

"Yes!" he said. "How kind you are! Yes, I must be ready."

He sat up and swung his feet to the floor, and shook out the crumpled sleeves of his shirt. "They'll bring me fresh clothes. One must make a good impression. I've told you nothing about my life here, have I? A pity, but it's too late now. It's more interesting than you might think. Guillaume shaves me beautifully every day. I never had so smooth a chin before."

"It's prickly enough now," she said, laying the backs of her fingers against it.

"No matter, you shall kiss me goodbye after he's shaved me. I would his hand might slip," he said candidly, "but there's no hope of that. And look, your beautiful dress thrown down on the floor!

For shame!'' He picked it up and shook out the folds, brushing off
dust with his hands. ''Put it on, I like to see you so fine. Let me be
your tirewoman.'' He held it for her to slip head and arms into it,
and drew it down admiringly over the velvet of her cotte. Thus
having her by the shoulders as he smoothed the shining tissue, he
leaned and kissed her forehead. ''Sweet friend! And now, when they
come to dress me, you must go.''

''As far as the next room,'' she said, ''to wait for you.''

''No, you must go. Somewhere out of sight and out of hearing,
so that you will remember me only as I am now. I will not have
you see me cut down and ripped apart. I will not become a howling
animal and a mess of butcher's offal in front of you.''

''Have you forgotten what I told you? Leave lashing your courage,
it's a shame to treat so fine a horse so cruelly. Leave fearing, it won't
be as you fear. I shall be with you while you live.''

Did he believe, now that the morning was come, and the ordeal
had drawn so close to him? She could not tell. Perhaps even he did
not know. He had a kind of grace and lightness about him, half of
deliberate pride, and half of irresponsible serenity, as if he had drawn
some degree of comfort and reassurance from her certainty. But she
thought it was only the comfort of having eased his heart to someone
who loved him, and talked his fill of someone he loved.

Guillaume and Fulke came in with the dawn and brought him his
best clothes. They took the precaution of turning the key loudly
and then waiting some minutes before they opened the door, and
Benedetta came forth with her hair all about her in a shimmering
crimson cloak. Fulke called her back timidly from the doorway.

''Mistress, you've forgotten this.''

It was the gold circlet she had worn round her coiled and braided
hair; she could not conceive that she would ever need it again. She
looked at it indifferently, and then at them. The two wary faces,
hard enough perforce in a hard world, and constrained in front of
her, looked upon Harry with a rough, regretful kindness. After their
fashion they had been good to him, once prisoner and gaolers came
to know one another. ''Keep it,'' she said, ''and share the worth of
it between you. Drink it to his memory.''

In the antechamber Father Hubert waited, uncombed and rosy
with sleep. He began to babble commiserations and civilities, which

caused her some surprise until she realised that he was hoping for her confidences. She listened to his assiduities with a faint smile she could not repress. He was not sure if she was still worth cultivating or if her star had set, and she was in no mind to help him to a decision.

"My lady, will you not go from this place? My duty is here, but yours is nobly done."

He is still wagering on me, she thought, amused. I ought to warn him how the wind is likely to be blowing from this on.

"No," she said, "I shall wait for Harry. Where is my lord?"

"He has already taken his place."

Close to the gallows and the brazier and the butcher's slab of stone, she thought. She saw the level field of young grass, green and fresh beneath the tree, the great cleared square and the path to it lined with men-at-arms, lances slanted across the curious breasts of the spectators. Outside that armed barrier all the household would be gathered, and all the workmen who had built the church, the plumbers, the glaziers, the masons, the joiners, the clerks and draughtsmen, the labourers. The old man who had coveted Harry's place, though never at this price, he would be there, and that poor boy from the tracing-house, who had smudged Knollys'' accounts with so many bitter tears over his master's fall. On both sides of the cleared square and along the rim of the rocky fissure companies of archers would be spaced out for action in case of trouble. And placed alone within the charmed enclosure, Isambard's great chair, and the man himself enthroned in it. He would have it set where he could command a clear view not only of the executioner's proceedings, but also of the whole of the wide gangway cleared from the drawbridge to the gallows. He would want to see all, every step of the way to death, but whether to exult over his enemy or to crucify himself in his friend not even she would ever know.

"And the Gascon?"

"He is in attendance."

So they would be men of Parfois who escorted him to his death. De Perronet in his black would be waiting by the foot of the ladder. With his pride in his appalling skills he seemed to her an abortion, not a man. Man begets; this thing's function was to destroy, and not only the flesh; to reduce God's best to a jerking, mangled,

mewing horror as long as possible before he let the spirit out of it.
I would I had half a company on the tower, she thought, instead of
one brave man. That creature at least should never go from here
alive.

In a little while the inner door opened, and Harry came out
between his guards. Very neat and trim he looked in his best, washed
and shaven and combed to perfection, hardly Harry at all. He was
as pale as his clean linen shirt, but very calm. Something was left
even of that light, incalculable smile in his disconcerting eyes, the
same look with which he used to meet her flashes of laughter at the
ceremonious life of Parfois.

"Good morning, Father! I hope we have not kept you waiting?"

"We might withdraw into the cell for a few minutes more," said
Father Hubert. "They are not yet here, you have time to ease your
soul."

"My soul is at ease, I thank you, Father. It's my body that feels
itself something less than easy. Come," said Harry, "I made my
confession only last night. I'm fallible, but I don't soil as quickly as
all that."

He knew very well, of course, what the old man had in mind. He
met her eye, and the flash of wicked joy passed between them like
a spark of warmth in a world of frost. If Father Hubert wanted to
shrive him of his supposed grievous sin, he would have to name it
in good round terms; and that was an indiscretion he would not
dream of committing, in case she should miraculously be still in
favour. His dilemma was comic; indeed, she had often found him
so, and was more than grateful for it now.

"Will you kneel with me?" said Harry, the laughter gone. He
held out his hand to her, and they knelt together on the stone floor
while the old man performed his last office. The bright, impetuous
profile beside her was grave; the closed lids and joined hands gave
him the hieratic dignity of a figure on a tomb. When they rose the
escort of men-at-arms was already at the door.

It was Langholme who came for him. He looked sick and unhappy,
she thought, and warmed to him. De Guichet would never have
turned a hair; he had done the same office too often.

"I am ready," said Harry, and turning, held out a hand to either
of his gaolers. "Lads, you've been good company. I've never wished

you ill, and wish you none now. If it had lasted a while longer I'd have made steeple-jacks of you both."

"I wish every man as good a heart as yours," said Guillaume in a grudging growl, and winced at the indiscretion of using the word "heart" on this of all mornings. And Harry laughed and clapped him reassuringly on the shoulder. How much of his remaining strength did every laugh cost him now? He turned to her, and before them all took her by the shoulders and held her to his heart. His cheek was cold against hers, and the steadiness of his breath faltered for a moment. Then he kissed her on the mouth.

"Goodbye, Benedetta."

"Goodbye, Harry. But if I say it now it is only to have it said in quietness. I am coming with you."

He looked at her in wonder and doubt, but half assured now that she had some foreknowledge which he must not and need not question.

"Madam," said Langholme hesitantly. "I have no orders concerning you."

"Then you will not be contravening them in allowing me to walk as far as the field by Harry's side. That is all I am proposing."

She knew she would get her way, because no one could be sure that it was safe to flout her. Evidently Isambard could not yet bear even to speak her name, or they would have known how to use her.

They went out from the cell and climbed the stone stairway to emerge into the outer ward. The purple shadow of the curtain wall lay unbroken across the courtyard, but the sky was pale blue without a cloud, and on the western merlons the sunlight lay sharp and bright. Harry looked up, sniffing the air, and the longing for life shone like flame though his pale face. To be dying in May!

She took his hand, so that no one could thrust between. The outer ward was silent and deserted. Only an old blind man sat on one of the blocks outside the mews, and followed their passing with his tilted, listening head. No point in driving him out to the spectacle, since he could not appreciate it. One column of men-at-arms went before, six men walking in twos, then Father Hubert clasping his breviary, then Harry and she, hand in hand, and after them the remaining six of the escort, and Langholme bringing up the rear. It could have been a marriage procession, and she in her cloth of gold was splendid enough for a bride. She clung to Harry's cold hand and prayed.

They entered the dark passage of the gate-house; at the end of the tunnel the dawn sun was radiant. A bubbling murmur came to them from the crowd on the plateau, and the light before them seemed to shimmer and coruscate with reflections of colours and movements, like a tremor of sick excitement shuddering on the air. They stepped on to the bridge. She checked her pace, so that the interval between the escort and the prisoner might be enlarged. The plateau opened before them as they emerged from between the low towers. From their left the great sighing murmur of pity and horror and anticipation blew upon them like a rough wind; but before them, alone and beautiful and sufficing, the church soared in the dawn.

"Look up!" she said. "The tree is in flower."

She fell back from him a pace, drawing her hand from his. The first ranks of the escort had wheeled to the left, towards the gallows; there was nothing, no one, close enough to separate him from his masterpiece. He halted, looking up from the shadowy ground, up the delicate tapering lines of the buttresses, up the loftly sweep of the wall, to the tower. The light from the east touched the cool grey stone and it blazed into gold. Every pinnacle was an ascending flame. Stage upon stage, the tower drew upwards its gleaming walls, its taut, true, pure brush-strokes of light and shadow, until the golden stem burst into the pale, shining flower of the sky.

He stood with uplifted face, dazzled with delight, worshipping the work of his hands. Death had loosed its hold on him; he withdrew from it by a tower of gold, a staircase of amber, a shaft of crystal filled with the spirit.

Out of the ray of light a ray of darkness, plunging invisibly, cried and shuddered through the air with a note like the vibration of gigantic wings. It struck him true, full in the left breast, and hurled him backwards into her waiting arms. She heard the hard, thudding impact; it seemed to her that she heard even the severing of his flesh as the arrow split the disputed heart; and she gave one cry for the instant of his agony, though he made never a sound. His weight falling against her breast bore her down under him, and she let herself sink to her knees on the grass, breaking his fall so that he came to rest as on a bed, cradled in her arms. The convulsion of pain was already past; she braced herself still, that there might be no second, smiling and weeping over him, and dropping broken words among the tears, though she never knew she had spoken.

"My love, my little one, my heart's dear—!"

The sea-green eyes, gold-flecked with the sun, saluted her with the last fleeting glitter of triumph and laughter, and wandered beyond her, amazed and enchanted, into the radiant spaces of eternity that blossomed from the golden stem. Bending her head, with terrible care not to touch or disturb the arrow, she kissed his brow and cheek, and the smiling, startled mouth. When she drew off and looked at him again the light was fading from his eyes, and the hand that clutched at the shaft protruding from his breast had slackened its hold. Hand and wrist slid down into the grass and lay at ease. She held him dead on her breast.

The arrow, passing through his body, had pierced through her sleeve between arm and side as she sprang to hold him, tearing her gown and grazing her arm. She plucked free the torn shreds of velvet, and her blood and his spattered the grass. Now that he was safe for ever from being hurt she drew him more securely into her arms, and rocked him gently, her cheek against his hair. The world came back to her slowly and grotesquely, its manifestations without meaning for her. The escort closed round her confusedly, at a loss what to do; Father Hubert was dementedly praying, Langholme was shaking her by the shoulder. Across the sunlit field people were running and shrieking, and guards were thrusting them back. There was shouting and confusion and haste as they cast about to see from which quarter the shot had come. Where she crouched in the grass was the heart of the whirlwind, and there all was still and silent and at rest.

Only when the long, single shadow fell across Harry's body, and all the insignificant people who had been battering at the doors of her tower of silence drew off in awe, did she look up. Under the streaming fire of her hair the pale face was fierce and bright with triumph. She looked up over her dead, and demanded in a loud, exultant cry: "Give me his body! It's mine!"

Isambard stood looking down in silence, his eyes lingering upon the dead face, still fixed in the eagerness and wonder of life. He marked the riven breast oozing a thin dark circle of blood about the shaft, and the pale flesh of her arm shining through the tatters of her sleeve.

"You shall have it," he said softly, "since this is what you want. You shall have his body and hold it, hold it fast for the rest of your life."

They cut off the arrow-head, blunted and bloody and fringed with a few tiny splinters of bone, and drew out the shaft. An effusion of blood followed it, and the lips of the slit wound gaped for a moment, and closed again, sealing in the pierced heart.

They handled him gently, as though they went in awe of him, for someone in the crowd had already whispered "miracle." Was it a man who drew the bow? They had found no man in the church or among the trees, and there were not wanting voices to swear that the shaft had been loosed from some vantage-point higher than the tower. Not until they had numbered all the household and determined whether any man was missing would they be sure that God had not reached out a hand and taken his master-mason to him, out of the very noose of his enemies.

They wrapped the body in a cloak and flung it over a horse, and set the woman on another, and so brought them down after Isambard to Severn side. The spring rains had been heavy, and the river was running high and brown, dappled with eddies and full of torn bushes rolled under and over with the stream. On the half-dismantled jetty where the stone had been landed Isambard stood and looked down into the flood. It ran less than a yard below him, tugging at the piles of the stage until the planking quivered. The shrunken green meadows on either hand had the vivid colouring of bog, and sparkled here and there in the hollows with lingering pools. Downstream, where the forest poured down the steep flank of the Long Mountain, all the English bank was hidden beneath overhanging trees.

He turned and came ashore along the tremulous planking, and looked long at the dead man, where they had laid him in the grass. The flesh was at his mercy still, but he had no quarrel with the flesh. He was a bird of prey, perhaps, but not a carrion crow. He had never seen Harry in stillness before; the waking face had been as mobile as light, and only once had he watched his sleep, there at the edge of the wood by Erington, with the boy in the crook of his arm. They had closed his eyes, but still this had not the look of sleep. The recovered childhood was there, the unruffled innocence, but not the helplessness. He was invulnerable now; the face bore the print of it.

"Strip them!" said Isambard.

No one moved. They looked at him with frightened, reluctant faces, unwilling to believe they had heard aright.

"You heard me? Strip this carrion. The woman, too."

They fell on their knees and began to unfasten Harry's cotte, and to slit the bloody shirt from his body, which submitted to their touch with an unmoved face. But they still hesitated to touch Benedetta. She stood waiting, with a slight, mocking smile, and the sun gleamed on her finery, and darkened the tarnish of blood on her breast.

"Are you afraid of her?" said Isambard with a curling lip. He set his hand to the neck of her cotte, and wrenched at it, and the velvet tore with a sound like parting sinews, but the cloth of gold over it was too strong for him. He drew his dagger, and setting the point of it in the cup of her throat, slit all her clothing to the waist, and dragged linen and velvet together down over her shoulders. She stood like a white birch tree shaken and mishandled by the wind, and accepted it with the like indifference. There was nothing he could do to her that could move her now. Sheathing the dagger, he filled his two hands with the slit cloth at her hips, and tore it almost to the hem, and all her garments fell together about her feet. She smiled still, stepping out of the ruins, and herself kicked off her soft leather shoes. It was himself he humiliated. She was clothed magnificently in her triumph and her indifference, and these he could not strip from her.

"Bind them together, face to face. They shall lie in each other's arms till they rot."

Stricken into silence, but afraid to disobey, they lifted Harry's naked body upright, and raised the limp arms to draw them about her neck. Two of them would have taken her by the wrists, too, though they shrank from her whiteness, but she started forward with a wild tenderness in her face, and took into her arms gladly the slender trunk on which last summer's brown was not yet quite faded. Close, close she held him, breast to breast with her and thigh to thigh, and before the cords were drawn tight about them she settled him at ease, his right cheek pillowed on her shoulder. They held up his dead weight from falling all upon her, but he was so slight that she could almost have supported him alone. She spread her hands against his back and pressed him to her, and the two vertical wounds were hidden, the frontal one against her breast, the other beneath her palms. His forearms were drawn together behind her shoulders and bound fast; knee was lashed to knee and ankle to ankle, until they stood like a pillar of marble, held upright by guards as pale as they.

"Throw them in," said Isambard, "let them sink or swim together."

To the end she thought of nothing but Harry. As they were dragged along the stage he saw her, all trussed and helpless as she was, hunch her shoulder and incline her cheek to steady the lolling head from the uncomfortable motion; and when they were held upright for a moment at the end of the quay she turned her head and looked at Isambard with a kind of distant pity, and laughed, before she kissed the curve of the sharp young jawbone that was all her lips could reach.

She did not lift her eyes again. She watched her darling's last sleep, and cared nothing for cold or violence or shame or death or the unassuageable anguish of hate and love that made all the air about her bitter. Neither living nor dead could he ever get her back. If he crawled after her on his knees to the water's edge, and implored her to have pity on him and fear him and weep, and live, she would not do it.

"In with them! Make an end!" he cried in a suffocating voice, and striding along the quay tore them from the hands that clung irresolutely still, and flung them out into the stream.

The rapid water hardly cast up a fringe of spray from their fall, but took them hungrily and sucked them under, and darting eddies followed their submerged passage downstream. Beneath the leaden surface he saw the pallor of their bodies like a great silver fish for a moment, then they broke surface already thirty yards away, and fast being tugged down towards Breidden. The long red hair, streaming about them, coiled round them both as they were rolled over and over in the uneasy currents.

In the shelter of the encroaching forest another pale shape slid unseen down the bank into the water, and stood breast-deep, braced against the impetus of the stream, watching the floating crimson sweep towards the shadow of the trees.

Isambard stood motionless, following their hapless passage, until they were lost to sight. Then he turned and walked slowly back to the shore. His men fell back before him with pale faces and frightened eyes, but he looked at none of them. His face was fixed and grey. He crossed the greensward as though he felt himself to be alone, mounted, and wheeled his horse towards the rising path to Parfois. They followed, but he was not aware of them. He rode in a desolation without limit in space or time; he had depopulated his world.

Chapter Sixteen

*P*ain came back to her first, and in the pain a sense of helplessness that was not all unpleasant. She was taken up in great hands that hurt her sides and forced her to draw in anguished breaths to the inmost deeps of her body, breaths that stabbed like knives and burned like flames. Later there was warmth about her, and a drowsy comfort, and the touch of some rough texture that pricked her body. And after, sleep.

She opened her eyes upon a bearded face that hung over her anxiously, and seeing faint colour in her cheeks and awareness in her wondering stare, shed unexpected tears upon her. There was a warm brown gloom, smelling of wood and smoke and humankind, and the flicker of firelight in the beams of a low wooden ceiling. The hands that had racked her drew up the skin coverings more closely over her naked breast.

"John!" she said.

"Thanks be to God!" said John the Fletcher. "Rest quiet, mistress, till I bring you a drink of milk. I thought we'd never fetch you back." He brought a pitcher of milk warm from the cow, and raised her in his arms to drink from it.

"What is this place?" she asked, looking round the small, bare hut.

"An assart in the wood, close under Parfois."

"You took me out of the river," she said, lying back against his shoulder; and again, in a stronger voice: "Where is he?"

"Here, safe." A pale smile touched her lips at the word, but she found no fault with it. Safe he was, inviolate, inviolable. "He's lying in my cloak, below in the undercroft, and my bow with him, and the horse you gave me. The goodman here helped me to bring the pair of you up from the water, and his wife's about finding some clothes for you when she's done with the cow."

"I can't repay her," said Benedetta.

"I can. I have the money you gave me."

"For your own escape," she said and frowned. Life was flowing back into her mind and will. There were yet things she had to do, since it seemed she must still be doing. "I bade you get out of the shire. Why did you not go?"

"And leave you in his power, and I not knowing how he meant to use you? No, mistress, I am your man as long as I live, I'll go nowhere without I'm sure all's well with you. I made my plans to lie up in the woods here and wait for word of you, but he brought you down to the shore before my very eyes, and did the thing I'll slit his throat for some day if God's good to me. Praise be, I grew up beside a river, and learned to swim as I learned to walk. Lie down and rest now, and keep covered up warm. Her man's off bargaining for another horse for us."

"You'll be as destitute as I am, if you spend on two."

She lay silent for a while, and presently he saw that heavy tears were spilling over from her wide-open eyes and running down her cheeks. He knelt beside her and took her head between his rough hands, and to be held so was a luxury like the return of innocence, and to have him wipe away the tears was a comfort that touched her to the heart.

"Was it well done?" he asked gruffly. He knew how well, for he had seen the body, but he wanted her word to satisfy him.

"Well done, John. Quick and clean. No man could have bettered it." She lay looking up into the smoke-blackened beams, and purpose and will and mastery came back gradually into her face. "It remains to bury him honourably," she said, "before we go seek the living."

* * *

With her own hands she washed him clean of blood and of the stains of the river, and combed out the tangles from his thick brown hair, and with John's help she dressed and composed his body for burial. They laid him in the boat from the mill downstream, and rowed him over to Strata Marcella on the Welsh bank. When the brothers came down at midnight to Matins they found a dead man, closely swathed in a coarse cloak, laid at the foot of the chancel steps, and two in worn homespun clothes who kneeled over him in prayer, one at his head, one at his feet. He at the feet was in the middle years, a bearded countryman. He at the head was young and pale and comely beneath the shadow of his hood. The prior was about to order him sharply to uncover when he saw in the descending light the swell of breasts below the hem of the capuchon.

She joined her hands before him in supplication. "Father, for God's charity give quiet lodging to this child of God, untimely dead, until he can lie in the church which he himself built. And of your grace mark the place where you lay him, that we may find him again even after years. I will not rise from my knees until you receive him from me."

The prior looked long upon the dead, and saw how slight and young he was. The marble serenity of death had not quenched the ardour and energy of the face, but only charmed it into stillness. It seemed that if they raised their voices he might awake and open his eyes.

"Daughter," said the prior, "how may I take in one who died, as I see, by violence, and of whose manner of life I know nothing?"

"He was noble," said Benedetta, "by birth and in the manner of his life. His work was noble, and he died nobly in place of another, whose life he saved. Is it enough?"

It was enough; nevertheless, for his own reasons he asked for a name.

"His name is Harry Talvace, master-mason."

The prior drew a long breath. "Well, well!" he said; and after a moment: "He is welcome to our house. He shall have honourable usage and a worthy grave."

She did not wonder at finding the name known; it would have seemed to her matter for astonishment if she had spoken it aloud

anywhere in Christendom and failed to start golden echoes. He so
filled her world, living or dead, that this recognition seemed only
his due.

She spoke her thanks simply, and bending over the dead tenderly
kissed the cold brow. "Rest tranquilly, my soul," she said, "until
she or I come to bring you home."

When she was gone they took up the body reverently and laid it
upon a bier before the altar; and after Lauds they kept vigil for
Harry Talvace all the night through. At first light a lay servant rode
hotfoot to Aber, to Llewelyn; but he came too late with his news,
for the Prince of Gwynedd was already on the march.

The portress was up with the child at first light, clucking to him
sleepily and walking the tiny round of her cell. The muffled thudding
of hooves on the turf of the valley track came to her sharp old ears
clearly, though it was rather a vibration than a sound. She reared
up her head and froze where she stood.

Who rode this way at such an hour? The recluse sisters of Saint
Winifrede, clustered about their tiny wooden chapel here in the
wilderness, had little to fear even from masterless men at ordinary
times; the virgin martyr was as forward in blasting those who
behaved disrespectfully to her as she was to favour the devout. But
these were no ordinary times. The king was in arms in the south,
and most of his barons compounded in a great alliance against him,
with the archbishop in the van. Shrewsbury, which had profited by
John's want of money in the past to enlarge its civil liberties by
charter after charter, stood by its bargains and declared for John;
but in North Wales the men of Gwynedd were massing to the banner
of Prince Llewelyn, who had joined hands with the rebels. Rumour
had it that the insurgents had entered London. A rider here in the
dawn might be the messenger bringing the alarm of Welsh raiders
already over the border.

Then she heard the knocking at the gate, counted the raps and
marked the intervals and knew who came. She went to the gate in
the wattle fence with the baby on her arm, lifted the pin and let
them into the enclosure.

At sight of two men she drew back in momentary alarm, but the
elder was certainly John the Fletcher, whom she knew well, and the

younger pushed back the capuchon from his head and let fall on his shoulders the red hair of Madonna Benedetta. She had put on chausses and tunic like a countryman, rough, threadbare brown weeds that turned her into a franklin's boy, but for that milkwhite skin of hers on which the sun and the wind seemed to have no power.

She saw the child, and stood with her hands at her heart, the greeting struck from her lips before she could utter it. She reached out her arms and took him gently to her breast, and looked down at him with a pale, wondering smile. He had a fluff of soft black hair like his mother's, and eyes as yet of an indeterminate colour, that might well clear into sea-green flecked with gold.

"When was he born?" she asked, hanging over him like one dazed.

"Four days ago, about Prime."

At much the same hour his father had died.

"And Gilleis?"

"She had a hard time of it, but she came through it well. You'll have news for her—" There she stopped. By the set of the pale face she saw that Benedetta's news would be of little comfort to Gilleis. "He's gone?"

"He's gone. Thank God she has his true-minted coin left!" She looked down at the two tiny fists doubled under the baby's chin; she had never held so new a human creature before, it seemed impossible that he should compress within that infinitesimal measure all the potentialities of a man. They come into the world perfect, she thought. A hand no bigger than a primrose, and as fragile, and yet there are the lines, the joints, the finger-nails, all the marvellous machinery that will raise cathedrals some day, and play on the lute, and handle tools and arms, and write songs to melt the winter ice, and take women by the heart-strings and draw them after him through the world.

"I must talk to Gilleis. We must get her away from here with the boy, somewhere safe, if there is such a place. There's fire and sword out along the borders of Powis already. And I am not easy in my mind while she stays in the same shire with Isambard. Even yet, if he knew there was a child—"

"He'd never touch such an innocent," protested the portress incredulously.

"So some charitable soul must have said of Herod. There is not much he would not do, except break his word. We'll not leave temptation in his way. If I could get her to Shrewsbury we could make shift well enough. But is she fit to ride?"

"Not yet, not alone. John might manage her if you could carry the child. She's not much more than child-size herself. But she ought to rest two or three days longer, even so. Shall I see if she's waking? You'd as well tell her soon as late."

"Ay, do, but if she's sleeping, leave her be. No!" she said jealously when the portress made to take back the child. "Leave him with me! You see he's content, he isn't crying."

She was still carrying him when she was admitted to the cell where Gilleis lay. The great black eyes, dark-circled, stared up at her from the pillow their unspoken question. Benedetta stood beside the bed, and what she had to tell seemed to her to have no possible beginning.

"He's dead, then," said Gilleis, not questioning any longer.

"He's dead," she said, so low that it was difficult to hear the words.

"I was sure," said Gilleis. "I felt him go from me." She turned her head upon the pillow, her face to the wall.

"He sent you his undying love. And bade me kiss his son for him."

The faintest of smiles plucked for a moment at the full, soft mouth. "How like him, to be so sure it would be a son!" Her fingers, spread on the covers of the bed, clenched slowly until the nails dug into her palms. "Was he—cruelly hurt? Was he shamed?" It was not that she cared for herself about that last, but only that it would have wounded him to the very soul to be less than magnificent.

"No, never! He was the victor. He never lowered his head, never bent his knee. He went in God's good time, not in Isambard's, and it was quick and clean and like a bolt from heaven in their faces. One instant, and he was gone. The executioners never laid hand on him."

The averted face was still, faintly flushed, listening and wondering. "Tell me!"

Benedetta told her all, even the full horror of the death he had escaped, since his victory was thereby so much the greater, and the death which had overtaken him so much the easier to bear. Only what had passed between Harry and herself she kept in her heart unspoken. It was enough for Gilleis to know that he had asked for speech with her so that he might send and receive the last messages of love.

"If I might have seen him once more!" whispered Gilleis, voice and heart aching past bearing.

She lay like one dead, her face still turned away. Benedetta leaned over and laid the child in her arm, and by instinct her hands came up and settled him easily against her breast. In a while her drawn brows smoothed a little, feeling his weight and warmth on her heart.

"If you knew," said Benedetta, "how I envy you!"

She sank to her knees beside the bed and laid her head on her arms. In a moment a hand stole across the coverlet and gently touched her cheek, and looking up she saw that the black head on the pillow had turned its face towards her, and that the great eyes were kind and full of tears.

A messenger came on the second day seeking John the Fletcher, who in his turn made haste to Benedetta with the news.

"The lad's from close by Parfois, I made it good with him before I left that if there was rumour of search still being made for Mistress Gilleis he should come and leave word here. For I knew you'd come to fetch her away, her and the child, if it was in your power. He says they've told over the whole household to find who loosed the shot that robbed that Gascon crow of his dinner, and the whole stable to know if a horse is missing. And the upshot is, they know now both the one and the other, and are scouring the countryside for me and the grey. The lad says they've picked up his traces as near as the alehouse at Walkmill, and are bound this way."

Benedetta was on her feet before he had told the half of it. "By Walkmill? Then before they draw near here we could be down into the valley road and head for Shrewsbury, and they'd have to ride clean round Longmynd or clean over it before they'd be able to sight us."

"They would. It should give us a fair start. But the grey will be carrying two."

"No help for it! Saddle up, John, while I warn Gilleis."

"And cover your hair, lady. In this light they'd see it a mile away and more from the top of the ridge."

"They think me dead," she said. "It's not red hair they're looking for, but a grey horse."

"Nevertheless, hide it. They have but to glimpse that and well they'll know you're living, for there's no second such head in Britain."

She hid it within the capuchon she had from the goodman in the assart under Parfois, and pulled on again the coarse chausses and tunic. They had no such concealment for Gilleis, but she took John's dun cloak about her, the same in which Harry had lain shrouded as they rowed him to the abbey. Their farewells were hasty and brief. John mounted first, and Benedetta offered a knee to help Gilleis to the saddle before him. She had protested that she was strong enough to ride pillion and ease him of the burden of holding her, but they mistrusted if her strength was equal yet to her spirit. The baby was handed up to Benedetta and settled securely within the folds of the cloak the sisters had given her. In this fashion they rode out by the green track and wound their way down from between the hills to take the direct road to Shrewsbury.

Benedetta set a fast pace. The valley was open here, and the great ridge of the Longmynd overhung them on the left hand. Several times she cast anxious glances along the smooth slope, straining to see as high as the crest, where ran the old, old road. There was a brisk wind blowing, and when she turned her head it tugged at her capuchon, which was overlarge for her, but she had no hand to spare for clutching at it.

They were almost abreast of the last folds of the ridge when she heard the baying of a dog, high on the crest, and recognising the note only too well, looked up in consternation. The wind filled her hood and tore it backwards from her head, and her hair streamed out in the fitful sunlight. She freed one hand to cover her betraying splendour again, but late. A shout echoed down distantly but clearly from the hill. She saw a tiny dark figure launch itself over the edge of the slope, a second, a third and fourth, six at least, and a tawny thing that flashed before them like an arrow down the green sheep-track.

"Soliman!" she cried, and drove in her heels and put her horse

to a gallop. At least if they were to be ridden down it should be by
the hound only, for he could outrun most horses. She was not afraid
of the beast himself; this great creature had lain with his head in
her lap too often now to be turned against her. But his power to
bring the huntsmen down upon their quarry she did fear.

"A mile to the ford," cried John, close behind her. "We can take
to the water there."

He knew this country as she did not, and she was willing to be
guided. She cast one glance down at the child; he was asleep, as
serenely as in a guarded bed. Who would believe there was so much
resilience in such a tiny creature?

Soliman gave tongue behind them, startlingly close. Over the
rough descent he had had the advantage of the horses, and surely
outstripped them by a long distance. And here the Roman road
plunged into the woodlands, and from men they might be safely
hidden, but not from him. The next time he belled the cry seemed
hard on their heels.

"I'll take him at the ford," cried John, and loosened his dagger in
its sheath.

"No!" She knew which of them would be the more likely to die,
and wished harm to neither. She plunged down to the brook and
swung left-handed from the track into the water as he directed her,
and there she reined in and cried to him to take the child from her.

"He'll not touch me. He's lived familiar with me for six years
and been taught to know me as his mistress. Not even for Isambard
would he harm me. I'll try if I can send him home. Take them
ahead! I'll follow."

"No, it's my part—"

"Take them!" she cried, and thrust the baby into Gilleis' outstretched arms. "I'll come after!" and she wheeled in a shallow
flurry of spray back to the ford. She heard the ripple of hooves
recede downstream until a curve of the bushy bank cut them off
sharply. Then there was silence. She strained her ears for voices or
hoofbeats on the road, but heard nothing. The dog did not give
tongue again. He came out of the filigree shadow and light like a
tremor of the branches, stretched out low to the ground in his long,
smooth gait, his vast head down. She called his name softly, and the
folded ears pricked high and the amber eyes were raised, though he

did not lift his muzzle from the trail he was following. At the waterside he checked, quested a little this way and that, and stood at gaze, waving his tail at her doubtfully.

"No, Soliman! Home!" she said, and lighted down to him, splashing through the water to take the tawny head, broad and heavy as a war-helm, in her hands. "Hear me! Leave it now! Enough!"

The yellow eyes stared back at her dubiously, acknowledging her right to give him orders, but loath to leave a pursuit on which another voice and another authority had launched him. "No more, Soliman, it's finished. Finished! Go home!"

She pointed, not back along the track but due westward, towards Parfois. He turned slowly, looking back at her over a rippling shoulder, and when she motioned to him again turned his head also, and began to lope easily back along the road.

"No, Soliman! Not back! Home!"

The silken ears signalled disappointment and reluctance, but he complied, turning off among the trees; and having made up his mind at last, stretched out into a leisurely run, and laid his nose towards Parfois. When he had vanished she mounted and rode after John the Fletcher down the bed of the Cound brook, picking her way delicately among the stones.

"He's gone. Not back to them, they'd only have set him on again. Straight for home. Unless he falls into confusion now they'll not find him again this side of Parfois. But the creature has a conscience, he hates to give up. We'd best stay in the water a while."

They pushed on as fast as they could, leaving the water only where the brook's complicated windings lost them ground. After two miles of this they thought it better to take to the open track again, and made good speed through Condover.

They had seen and heard no more of the party which had ridden down at them from the Longmynd, but at Bayston they all but rode into them before they were aware. Outside the alehouse a number of people were gathered, looking towards Shrewsbury and making a great clamour with their talk, and Benedetta would have ridden innocently into their council to find out what the excitement was if John had not clutched her suddenly by the arm, and drawn her hastily aside with him into an alley between the houses.

"De Guichet!" she whispered, seeing in the middle of the group the massive shoulders and the tall skewbald horse John had seen, and the Greek, useless now without his hound, turning his narrow, weatherbeaten face from one person to another with the blind look of one who follows speech in a language only half understood.

They were all there, and all between her and Shrewsbury. While the hunted were laboriously covering their traces by keeping to the water, the hunters, abandoned by their guide, must have held to the road and ridden it hard, to reach this point ahead of their quarry, though it seemed they did not realise they were beforehand.

John the Fletcher tightened his arm about Gilleis, and looked down at her with an anxious face as he walked his horse along the beaten earth of the alley. "She's flagging, poor lady. Take the little one again, we'd best be ready to run for it."

Gilleis opened her eyes to say faintly that she was well enough, but she gave up the baby without complaint, and Benedetta made him secure within her cloak and tightened the belt that held the folds of his cradle together. He began a thin wailing, no louder than a blind kitten's cry, but it wrung her heart. He should not fall into Isambard's hands, to be done to death, or more likely raised up in cold blood as Isambard's creature, in ignorance of his father; never, while she lived.

They circled the village by way of the fields, and drew in to the road some way beyond, and there took a gallop again on the grass verge, where the turf was lush and deep. If the crowd outside the alehouse had not been casting such constant and strained glances towards Shrewsbury they would have got clear away; but every moment someone was turning to point that way, and the dappled horse, so pale as to show white against the May greenness, caught the eye all too easily. When Benedetta looked back, she saw the dust of the pursuit rolling purposefully after them along the road.

There was smoke on the skyline, they saw it now as a rising column against the blue, disseminated by the wind in the upper air into a tenuous cloud which lay floating above Shrewsbury. In Meole, too, people were out before their houses, babbling and pointing, and when John the Fletcher would have bellowed his way through them in haste, one of the men ran and caught at his bridle.

"Turn here, master, if you're in your wits. Shrewsbury's afire, do you not see the smoke? The Welsh have fired the mill, and the abbey storehouses are ablaze."

"Better brave a Welsh raid than go back," said Benedetta, kneeing her way forward.

"This is no raid, lad. They're bent on taking the town, and there's no one this side of Gloucester who could stop them. They circled the river to come at the eastern side, where they were not looked for. There was a rider through here half an hour ago who told us the Prince of Gwynedd is on the bridge already and battering at the gate."

"The Prince of Gwynedd?" She cried it aloud in a shout of joy. "Thanks for your warning, friend! Be sure to repeat it to those who come after us." She thrust forward resolutely, and they fell back from her and let her through, though no doubt they thought her mad.

The smoke had thickened over Shrewsbury, she watched it as she galloped. Only once did she look back for a moment, before Meole fell out of sight. De Guichet had ridden past the barrier of excited people, only to halt by the roadside irresolute. They were unwilling to follow him farther; they were six men, and had no orders to ride into a Welsh army. Yet there was more than a mile of road left before the fugitives would reach the bridge, and they might yet be overtaken. He was waving his men on furiously, and they were coming, some of them at least, two more figures, three—that meant all, for the last two would never dare go back to Parfois if they set themselves apart now. She fixed her eyes on the unrolling ribbon of road, and urged the tiring horse with knee and voice and hand.

Down the long slope now towards the great silver coil of the Severn; and already rising into sight beyond, clouded with the hovering pall of smoke, the moated hill, crowned with its turreted wall. The track bore round right-handed to circle with the river, and the town revolved like a wheel on its plateau, slowly bringing into view tower after tower like the terminals of the spokes, and taking tower after tower away. The gate-towers rolled round towards them, first as one, then dual, with the dark inlet between, and on the bridge below a mass of men heaving faintly with movement and flashing fitfully with steel. The smoke had no stem to earth within the wall, it drifted on the wind from the near side of the river, where the abbey and all its attendant buildings lay, and the almshouses, the dwellings of the devout pensioners who had made over all their goods to the abbey in return for this little pittance of board and bed. The church itself stood inviolate, the great boundary wall preserving all within; but the mill was sending up tall flames, and a tower of smoke, and the granaries and the gabled timber houses clustered between abbey and river were all ablaze.

A crossbow quarrel thudded into the grassy verge. Benedetta hunched her body about the child, and drove in her heels and plunged on. If they were shooting now, it was because they were about to draw off. She heard the full, hard impact of a second bolt, fallen short, before the smoke wrapped itself about her, filling her throat and stinging her eyes. She caught the edge of the cloak in her teeth to cover the child's face, and rode on half-blind into the turmoil at the end of the bridge.

There were men all round her, clawing at her bridle, shouting in English and in Welsh. Faces loomed out of the smoke and vanished again, distorted by her streaming tears. She looked round once to be sure John was at her back, and then fought her way forward through the press, kicking off hands that clutched at her, wrenching herself out of their hold. Someone caught at the liripipe of her capuchon, and dragged it backwards from her head, and the tangled masses of her hair gushed down about her shoulders and streamed in the wind of her frantic passage.

"Where is the Prince of Gwynedd? Where is Prince Llewelyn?"

She was on the bridge now. The press of men hemmed her in, dark, darting clansmen, most of them afoot, some on wiry, strong hill ponies. The wind from off the water ripped a clear passage through the murk, and she caught a glimpse of the gate of Shrewsbury between its towers, and a cluster of tall horses and mailed riders, and a young squire clasping a broad war-helm circled with a thin coronet of gold. She tossed back her hair from her eyes and shouted again hoarsely above the clattering of hooves and the babel of voices: "Bring me to the Prince of Gwynedd! Where is Prince Llewelyn?"

"Who's that calls so loudly on Llewelyn?"

The ranks parted before him and she saw him, darkly bright in the flush of his triumph. His head was bared and his sword sheathed, for the town lay open to him with hardly a blow struck. Smoke had soiled the shoulders of the white surcoat that covered his banded mail hauberk, but the outline of the red dragon on his breast stood clear. His black horse was tall and great-boned like the rider, and set him a head above most of those who rode with him. The vivid, falcon's face, all shadow and light about the darting, intelligent eyes, was flushed with exertion and the heat of his helm. He was laughing; laughter, anger, generosity, pity, all that was quick and warm would come readily to this face. He stripped off his mail gauntlets and let them hang from his wrists, and even that small movement had a fiery liveliness about it.

"Who is it cries on Llewelyn?"

"One who has a life's claim on him," she said, reining in at his knee. "His name is Harry Talvace."

The prince's eyes swept over her in astonishment, marking the coarse, countryman's garments, the soiled, weary, lovely woman's face, the long red hair darkened to crimson purple with sweat. By that hair he knew her; it was not difficult to describe Benedetta so that there should be no mistaking her.

"Talvace is here?" He looked beyond her eagerly, searching for one of whom he had heard so much already from two who praised and loved him; but seeing only a grizzled serving-man with a young woman in his arms, looked back bewildered into Benedetta's face. "Where is he? Bring him to me, and more than welcome! We were coming to Parfois to fetch him, but by God's help it seems he's come to us, and I am still his debtor."

She gently loosed the belted folds of the cloak, and held out to him the child, confidently asleep again in the middle of turmoil. He looked down in wonder at the tiny head of black hair and the minute, folded fists, and the shadow of understanding came down upon his face.

"Here is Harry Talvace, son of Harry Talvace," she said, "and this is Gilleis, his mother. They have great need of your protection, and I ask it for them in his name."

Behind the clear grey of her eyes Llewelyn saw an aching emptiness, a void no other, not even the child, would ever be able to fill.

"Dead?" he asked.

"Dead. Seven days gone."

He looked down at the child with a sombre face. "From my heart I am sorry. We counted on having longer, or I would not have waited for FitzWalter to reach London. There's his foster-brother yonder among my men will be sorrier yet, and a gosling at home will cry bitterly when he hears it." He shook his head, and the dark, curling locks, disordered from his helm, fell damply about his forehead. "We counted on having longer," he said again, with angry sorrow. "We meant to have him out of hold by force, or bargain Shrewsbury for his ransom."

From the gate of the town, wide open to receive the conqueror, his knights looked back in wonder and curiosity at the stranger woman with the baby on her arm, and the horses, impatient, stamped and shook their harness. The castellan stood within the shadow of the gateway, the provosts and the keepers of the crown pleas at his back, waiting nervously to deliver up the keys.

"We're keeping the good burgesses waiting," said Llewelyn, looking back over his shoulder with a quick, wild toss of his head. "Come, at least let's get his lady safe to her bed. Follow close after me till we bring her to the castle." He looked with great gentleness at Gilleis, pallid on John's shoulder, her eyes closed. "Talvace's widow is my kinswoman," he said, and putting out his hand, touched with a broad forefinger the child's flushed forehead. "And his son is my son!"

He wheeled his horse, and cried to his men in Welsh, and the ranks drew in about them, and moved slowly forward towards the gate, and there halted to let their prince ride first and alone into the town, but he reached an imperious hand to Benedetta's bridle.

"Ride by me with the boy. For his father's sake he shall make a prince's entry, and lie in a royal bed tonight."

The black horse paced forward with a high, disdainful step over the threshold, beneath the raised portcullis. The confined breeze between the towers lifted Llewelyn's trailing silken moustaches and short dark curls, and fluttered Benedetta's long hair in a cloak of shadowy imperial purple about the child she carried, as prince and fosterling rode together into the captured town.

THE
GREEN
BRANCH

Chapter One

The Commote of Kerry: September 1228
Aber: October 1228

*T*he boy in the beech tree narrowed his eyes, staring due east into the rising sun.

The stabbing points of light scintillating out of the wooded cleft of the brook below him pricked at his vision; the steep knife-cut of the valley lay open to the long rays just piercing the mists, and the light had found the dancing water between the trees. He raised his sights steadily to stare over the glitter, intent upon the blunt promontory where the walls of the half-finished castle rose, and the vast coloured sprawl of the King's camp brocaded the sheepless hill-pastures.

Secure in their numbers, the English could show their bright devices there; but let them stray aside into the woods and a flicker of scarlet or the flash of a crest would cost them dear. More than forty had been pricked out of the reckoning within call of their own camp in the past week alone. Harry himself had put shafts into two of them, as they crept out in the dawn to their rabbit snares, too eager to be cautious. They were hungry men, the justiciar's army. If they had touched meat in the last three weeks it must have been the flesh of their own horses. The villages had been abandoned before them, the cattle and pigs and sheep driven off into the wilderness, even the game in the forests beaten methodically westwards out of reach.

The insistent daggers of reflected light jabbed at his eyes. Shaken by a sudden uneasiness he deflected his attention from the patchwork of tents and pavilions, blinked away the broad receding valley beyond, with its folded bordering hills shadow on shadow, blue on blue against the strengthening sunlight, and peered more sharply at the thread the broken lights were weaving among the trees beneath his perch.

His heart lurched in his breast. The refractions of water had left the water-course; they were winding uphill towards the saddle of the ridge, as though a silver serpent trailed its sinuous length through the woods on the flank of Gwernesgob. Not the play of the stream, but the incautious glitter of helms and arms. They had not even the sense to blacken their lance-heads before they went foraging.

He scrambled headlong down from his tree, barking his knees and palms in his haste, and began to run like a hare through the underbrush, turning his back on the broad valley through which the sunlight was gushing now like bright water, washing the lingering mist before it into the recesses of the hills of Kerry.

His two Welsh foster-brothers were coming side by side down the green ride between the oaks, David tall and slender and grave, like his mother, Owen square and brown and bright. They were wrangling, and as usual about him.

"I told you we should never have brought him," Owen was fuming. "Thirteen is too young, he'd have been better left at home. Why did you ever let him come? You should have known what a pest he'd be."

"He begged so," protested David mildly. "And he's as good a bowman as many a grown man who serves me, that he's proved."

"Ay, if we could but keep him at an archer's distance, but the brat will get to close quarters. The third time I've been put to it to fetch him away from their very lines, and what's his mother going to say to me if I go back without him? If you had to indulge him, why did you make me his keeper? I'd sooner play herd to a young wolf!"

David laughed. He had his mother's laughter, rare and warm and brief, even a little rueful, as though the weight of royalty always silenced the peal too soon. "She'd never have trusted him to anyone but you, as well you know. And wisely! He has but to take one step astray, and you're after him like a hen clucking after her chickens. If you were less anxious for him, you'd abuse him less. You're fretting yourself for nothing, Harry has his wits about him."

"*I'm* fretting! Who was it began turning the camp hind-side-first for him the minute he was missed? Let me once get my hands on him," promised Owen grimly, "and I'll turn him hind-side-first, the imp."

The boy burst out of the bushes on to the path below them at that moment, breathless with running, and flung himself willingly into the brown hands with which Owen had threatened him. They shook him hard, but did him no violence. It was always Owen who threatened, but usually David with his grave sense of duty who performed. They held him between them, both abusing him together.

"Where've you been these two hours, you rogue?"

"Didn't I forbid you to leave camp alone? One more offence and I send you home under escort, you hear me?"

He fended them off sturdily, heaving with breathlessness. "No, but listen! I'll answer for it, I will, only later. The English—I was watching them from the hill, and—"

"Well I knew it!" said David, and cuffed him a time or two by ways of asserting his rights, only to be startled by the sudden passion with which Harry caught at his hand and held him off.

"Will you *listen* to me? There *are* English abroad. I saw them from the hill, a raiding party crossing the saddle yonder, heading for Dolfor."

He had their attention now, they caught him one by either arm, at him with abrupt questions.

"How long since?"

"How strong a company?"

"In whose livery?"

They shook him in their eagerness, but there was no need, he flashed back at them, sparkling, the hasty answers that trod sharp on the heels of the questions.

"Not a quarter of an hour. I made them thirty men at least. I saw them coming up through the trees, and watched the way they took. They kept within cover, but where the sun falls you'll find them by their mail and their lances. They had all their wear bright," he said, quivering with ardour and scorn. "If we go down the river we could take them at the ford."

They exchanged one glance as bright as steel over his head, and dropped him and plunged back by the way they had come. He had to run his hardest to keep up with them, but he held his place at their heels doggedly, clutching at David's arm as he ran, panting out his protests in advance at the prohibition he felt to be hanging over him.

"You'll take me with you?" he cried apprehensively. "It was I saw them!"

"So it was," said David, spreading an arm to slide the boughs away from his face. "That's your part well done, now let us do ours."

"That's unfair! Why did you bring me with you, then? And you wouldn't even have *known*—"

He was pouring out so much of his energy and his attention in indignation that he forgot to mind his step among the underbrush, and came down heavily over a twisted root; but he picked himself up hurriedly and rushed on, hopping and rubbing his scratched shin as he went.

"I'll stay out of sight, I swear I will, only let me come. Why not? What am I here for if I'm not to be allowed to fight?"

They broke out into the clearing three abreast. The boy was still clamouring aggrievedly as David called, and the clansmen came boiling out of the shadowy silences of the forest to their prince's voice, themselves dark and sylvan and silent as trees.

"Ah, let him come," said Owen impatiently, "or he'll deafen us. I'll see him placed well out of harm's way. And I'll see him paid his wages if he stirs a step from where I put him. You hear that?" He turned one formidable flash of his dark eyes on Harry. "Run, then, get your bow."

Harry fled on the instant, in terrible haste and with ears tight shut in case David should call him back and take away what Owen had given him. They had forborne from scolding him for leaving his arms behind when he slipped out of camp before dawn, so he must have been wise in deciding that he would be safer in the guise of a plain country boy in homespun should anyone detect him lingering in the woods near King Henry's camp. But this, his first experience of a real engagement, would be a very different matter. He was in desperate haste for fear they should go without him, but he tugged his way feverishly into the banded-mail hauberk the armourer had cut down for him from one of David's, for he knew he would be sent back to put it on if he appeared without it.

He almost skinned his fingers stringing his bow. John the Fletcher had made it for him and brought it down from the hills at Christmas; it was nicely matched to his weight and reach, and he loved it above all his possessions, except the sword the Prince had provided for him from the royal armoury. The splendour of Llewelyn himself was on the sword, for he had carried it in his first battle, when he was newly of age at fourteen, a dispossessed boy setting out to wrest his princedom from his uncles. Worn it and blooded it, too. Harry might have carried it in this campaign, but he was not yet the master of it as he was of the bow, and though it had cost him a struggle he had elected to stick to what he did best.

They were not in the field for his worship and advancement, after all, but to expel the justiciar from Welsh Kerry where he had no business uninvited, neither he nor that queer young king of his who made such large and sweeping gestures to so little purpose. The whole border raised, Clifford, de Breos, Pembroke, Gloucester and a dozen other lords marchers called together, not all of them too willingly, to bolster still more securely a wealth and power they themselves were already beginning to resent: and what was the result? Not ten miles advanced from the impregnable rock of Montgomery and their supply lines were cut to ribbons, and there they floundered and starved, building frenziedly at a fortress the winter would never let them finish, while a fifth their number of Welsh tribesmen made circles round them and picked them off at will.

He pulled his leather guard over his knuckles and ran from David's rough lean-to hut to overtake the company. They had melted eagerly into the trees along the ridge, leaving only a handful of shadows quiet and watchful about the silent and almost invisible camp. David had no more than twelve of his father's household army here under his command, and as many free tribesmen; the greater part of the host lay securely over the ridge of Kerry with Llewelyn, and from that base encircled and harried the rising castle.

At the edge of the forest they broke cover and plunged in the long, lunging strides of hill-runners down into the cleft of the river, here no more than a dancing stream only a mile old. There was no one to see them but the hawks circling over the rough pastures, and the woods soon began again, shrouding the thread of growing water.

"What if they've passed the ford ahead of us?" Harry asked anxiously, scurrying at David's elbow.

"Then we shall be between them and their camp, to halt them if they turn, and they'll meet their match somewhere along the track to Dolfor."

"Does our father know of them?"

"I've sent him a runner. He'll take his horsemen by the road, and ride round to meet them. But unless they've taken alarm they'll walk their mounts down that slope, and we shall be in time. Hush, now, or we may miss Iorwerth's signal."

An active boy could have leaped the Mule anywhere along this early stretch, but only in one spot did its steep banks level into an easy plane by which horses could be walked across. The track came down the sheer slope by long traverses, the trees crowding close over it almost down to the water. On the near bank there was a narrow level of meadow, and then the semi-circle of the woods. The steep hillside to eastward cut off the morning sun; here it was still dawn twilight, moist with September mist.

The archers and lancers parted the bushes and vanished into the ring of the forest, choosing their positions with deliberation. Somewhere high on the hill a green woodpecker, disturbed, launched its shrill, hard cry of laughter, twice repeated.

"In good time, they're on us," said Owen on a breath of exultation, and dragged Harry well back into the trees. "Here, up with you into the crotch and stay there. You'll have a clear field, and never be seen yourself. No matter what happens below, you stay there. You hear me?"

"But if I'm needed?" argued Harry, hauling himself into the crotch of the oak-tree and glaring down challengingly between the boughs.

"Let me see you set foot to ground until it's over, and I'll take the shaft of a lance to you," promised Owen fiercely, and leaped away to his own post of honour at David's shoulder.

That was no way to address a man who had been accepted into the ranks. If they let him fight at all they should allow him the same rights of judgement as his companions. Harry stood shaking with excitement and indignation in the bowl of the oak, which was broad and solid as one of the outcrops of rock that studded the upper pastures. He shifted his position fretfully, bracing his feet and flexing his drawing arm in an agony of certainty that he would fail of his aim through want of the firm earth under his soles, or find his drawing hampered by the branches. He fidgeted and scuffled, anxious and aggrieved, until the bird that was no bird called again, with a wilder disquiet in its hard laughter.

Then quite suddenly the excitement that had set him trembling with fever froze into a cool, happy competence, his breathing lengthened and quieted, and the head of the arrow he had fitted to his string dipped gently and nosed at the clear space between the branches, fixing its sights at the height of a horseman's breast above the landing of the ford. The line of the shaft drew taut and steady, like a hound pointing game.

Below him in the bushes Meurig from the villein tref at Aber, who was by rights only a packman with the army but could never be restrained from fighting, grinned up at him briefly and kissed the blade of his blackened lance, hefting it lovingly on the flat of his hand. It quivered, true-balanced, as though it would have taken flight of itself if he had not closed his grip and held it back.

Then the English came. Harry saw a flicker of colour moving sidelong down the wooded slope, where a month ago the leaves would have hidden all. Above the first, another showed on a higher traverse. He heard the gentle clashing of harness, then the deliberate pacing and the occasional slither of hooves in the thick mould. They were very quiet and very cautious, threading their way slowly down to the water.

When they broke cover at the edge of the stream the boy saw

with pleasure that they were leading their horses. That made things easier; there was a better chance of killing the man and taking the beast uninjured, and less probability that man and beast together, whole or hurt, might break through the ambush and escape. Harry coveted nothing the English had so much as their horses, tall, great-boned creatures double the size of his shaggy riding pony at Aber. By tonight, with God's blessing, he might well own one.

David withheld his signal until the first half-dozen men were over the stream, and a seventh in mid-crossing. This one rode, disdaining to lead his horse even down the steepest of the descent. A young man in a fine chain-mail hauberk and a buff surcoat, with the visor of his ornamented helm raised to uncover a bright, bold, arrogant face, everything about him a little elaborated and a little insolent, but undeniably handsome. When his chestnut horse trod astray and stumbled in the stones of the stream-bed the knight who had crossed before him darted back into the water to take the bridle and lead him ashore, with a gesture so obsequious that Harry, used to the sturdy independence of free Welshmen, almost laughed aloud. But the rider waved him off imperiously, swaying to the check, and drew in his rein with quick, reassuring gentleness.

One of King Henry's barons, surely, since knights ran to wait on him. A Poitevin, perhaps, one of those foreign lordlings who were exotics even to the English, and such a fruitful source of discontent among them, as he had heard the Prince say gratefully once on calculating the measure of the King's host as they moved in from Montgomery.

The chestnut horse was just heaving himself up the bank when David loosed his bowmen. Cynan's signal shot took the mounted man too high on the shoulder, and clashed and hissed from the rings of his hauberk to bury itself quivering in the bole of a tree beyond. It drove him back hard in the saddle and brought his horse up on its hind feet, pawing the air and bellowing. A rain of arrows followed the first on the instant. Harry loosed with the rest, but never knew whether it was his shaft that found its mark. The first man ashore loosed his bridle and spun round clutching at his middle, to drop and lie kicking. The horse crashed away into the trees.

The mounted man recovered himself gallantly, hunched in the saddle over his bruised shoulder, and rode straight at the bushes.

Two of his fellows mastered their plunging horses and flung themselves after him. Two more were down, dragging themselves frantically into cover and hauling feebly at their swords. Those who were still winding their way down to the water left the path and came crashing dangerously down the steep, to splash through the ford and ride to their leader's aid. Behind them the woodpecker laughed again, and was answered. A handful of David's regulars had crossed the river and worked their way round to cut off the retreat.

The Welsh archers circled invisibly in the thick undergrowth; only Cynan broke cover and ran for the edge of the water to draw off the mounted men from his prince, and when they whirled instinctively to pursue the only visible quarry they presented newly composed targets to the hidden hunters. Whimpering with excitement, Harry reached over his shoulder and fitted a third shaft, and for a few moments saw no clear mark at which he might aim it, the clearing boiled so frantically with a confusion of screaming horses and shouting men.

They were recovering their wits now after the first astonishment. Their commander, deflected for a moment by Cynan's flight, came back vigorously to his first cast, for the thicket from which the archer had broken cover must surely be the one point from which they had wished to distract attention. He set spurs to his horse and hurled himself at it again, driving the beast crashing through the bushes in a rain of leaves and twigs, with three or four knights hard at his heels.

David had drawn back, but no more than a few yards, and the speed of the onslaught took him by surprise. He sprang back, warding off the sword that swung at his head, but went down in the tussocky grass against the bole of a thorn tree; and before Owen could leap to cover him the chestnut horse was reined in and wheeled about beneath Harry's oak-tree, to drive down again upon the fallen man.

Harry shortened his range and shot, too hastily and a little unsteadily, and the arrow thudded harmlessly into the ground. He said afterwards in his own excuse that he had thus betrayed his presence, and made his leap to forestall being pricked out of the branches with a lance; in fact the unfleshed shaft vibrated unnoticed, and the man on the horse never looked up, but Harry's prince and foster-brother was on one knee in the trampled grass, and his assailant with gripping knees and bloody spurs was urging his frenzied mount down upon him to stamp him into the ground, and Harry never stopped to think at all. He flung his bow aside with a yell of rage, and swinging outwards from the crotch of the tree hurled himself down upon the shoulders of the man beneath.

He fell with a shock that drove the breath and the wits out of him, and knocked the rider flat over the pommel of his saddle. The horse reared in terror, lashing out before and behind with frantic hooves, and man and boy together came down in the turf.

Harry lay gulping air in agony for one long moment of thunders and confusions. He heard Owen's voice raised in a cry of alarm, he heard close to him and seemingly all about him a stamping that shook the earth and filled his bones with jets of fear and pain. Then a great hand took him by the upper arm and hauled him clear of the threshing hooves with a jerk that almost started his shoulder out of joint, and a hand, the fellow to the first, swung him another yard out of danger with a box on the ear.

He rolled over and lay with his head in his arms until the earth ceased to rock and heave, and he had recovered a little of his breath, and sense enough to feel gratitude rather than resentment for the blow, which in its casual exasperation marked the continued existence of a world he understood, and in which he could move and act with confidence. His elders, as often as they had been compelled to retrieve him from perilous places, had invariably avenged themselves for the fright by boxing his ears as soon as he was out of danger. He didn't hold it against them; it was another face of the indulgence they showed to him, and the value they set on him.

The ground steadied under him, and dimly he began to feel the shock of his bruises. He opened his ears first, very cautiously, and the clamour of fighting survived only distantly, where the woods threshed still to the pursuit of those who had broken through the cordon. There were voices calling across the wounded and the dead, arguing, cursing, groaning. There was in particular a near, known voice that said with brusque kindness:

"Come, get up, you're not hurt. Not a scratch on you!"

The hand that had been probing gently along his bones stroked its way down his back and slapped him lightly on the rump. He doubled his fists into the grass, hoisting himself up against a steady-ing knee, and opened his eyes upon his foster-father's bearded, weathered falcon's face, with the fierce salient bones of cheek and jaw glossy brown in the brightening light, and the deep lines and hollows dark and quivering with secret laughter.

"We came just in time to see you take wing," said the Prince. "I've seen many a clumsy nestling learning to fly, but never, I swear, so unlikely a bird as you. Were you out of arrows, that you had to fling yourself at him?"

Harry opened his mouth only to ask anxiously: "David?"

"Untouched, never fear. Not a man lost, only a slash or two among us. And seven good horses taken, and one or two more we may pick up in the forest yet."

The mention of horses brought Harry fully to life, sitting up bright-eyed in Llewelyn's arm. He looked eagerly round the clear-ing, now trampled and scored with hoof-marks and littered with debris from the bushes. There were dead men lying still in the grass, and some not yet dead who moaned and twitched. Cynan was back nursing a bloody arm, but grinning well-content, and Meurig was going round the wounded retrieving bloodier lances, not roughly, not gently, as though he plucked them out of trees.

Harry's bruises suddenly burst into a frenzy of aching and throbbing, as though he had newly quickened to the reality of wounds and deaths. He swallowed nausea and held it down, sick with excitement and reaction. But David was there across the sward, slender and lively and whole as ever, kneeling over one of the wounded, and the sight of him was satisfaction enough. And Owen was there, too, gentling a frightened horse that still sweated and shook, and looking across at his young foster-brother with a frown-ing thoughtfulness, between anger and approval; and it was good to be able to meet his eye brazenly and stare him out, secure in the Prince's blessing.

"There's a prize here waiting for you," said Llewelyn, "if you can ride him, saddle and harness and all, and fairly won. The man I can't spare you, but the horse is yours if you will. Come, look at him! He looks better eye to eye than from between his hooves. And he spared to trample you, like the good-natured beast he is."

The chestnut horse shuddered with subsiding violence under

Owen's stroking hands, his gleaming coat creamed with waves of foam like a beach on an ebbing tide. Harry withdrew his eyes from him with difficulty to look wonderingly at the man who lay stretched in the grass.

They had drawn off his helm, and uncovered to the light a thick tangle of black hair, limp and heavy with sweat, and a fine-featured, clean-shaven face now pale and pinched. Even so it had still its arrogance, but an arrogance innocent of offence. Helplessness became him. He lay gracefully, the long black lashes curled on his cheeks as appealingly as a girl's.

"Is he dead?" whispered Harry, for the first time trembling to the possibility of death. It did not seem to him that he was looking at an enemy.

"Not he! He'll live to a ripe old age. He's no more than stunned. And if you'd been in any case to hear the crash he made as he came down on the roots of that oak where you were nesting, you'd not wonder at that. A matter of a couple of ribs broken and a badly bruised shoulder, that's the tale of his hurts. Look well at him, Harry. Do you know what you brought down with him?"

Harry shook his head, marvelling. The still blue eyelids had begun to quiver, the black, straight brows to frown with returning pain.

"When you filled your hands with his person you took seizin of Hay, and Radnor, and Builth and Brecon and I know not what besides. This is he that came into half the baronies of the border only three months ago, when old Reginald died. William de Breos, none other!"

The sound of his own name penetrated the Lord of Brecon's dazed senses. He opened hollow dark eyes, staring blankly at the tall man and the sturdy boy who stood over him. Behind the drawn brows recollection worked slowly.

"William de Breos," he affirmed in a rueful thread of a voice, "none other!"

He remembered the child, though he had seen him only for one flashing instant as a bolt from heaven. The grave face, the large, concerned eyes touched off obstinate laughter in him, but he reigned it in to a courteous and considerate smile. One should be very careful with laughter, it so easily shifts to the other side of one's face.

"I salute you, sir," he said solemnly, tremors of pain contorting

his smile. "You are the only champion who ever engaged me unarmed in single combat and brought me down, and by God, I think
you're the only one who ever will. Will you not tell me the name
of my conqueror?"

The flattery and the irony and the wilful, experienced charm
tangled Harry's senses in a net of gossamer, and he was lost. "Sir,"
he said, stiff with shyness, "my name is Harry Talvace."

"Talvace!" A good Norman name on a wild, brown Welsh boy.
He frowned over it faintly for a moment, but it was too hard for
him. The heavy lids sank again, the flush of reviving colour ebbed
as suddenly back to grey.

Harry broke away abruptly from Llewelyn's arm, snatched up the
unlaced helm from the grass, and ran to fetch water from the river.
He kneeled beside his prisoner, burning with pride and admiration,
tremulously bathing the broad forehead and moistening the bruised
lips, even the horse forgotten.

When de Breos at length opened his eyes again and saw the boy's
face bending over him, tense with solicitude and desperately serious,
it was already a question with them which was the conquest and
which the conqueror.

The escort emerged from the river valley and turned eastwards along
the green coastal plain, between the salt flats and the mountains.
Harry dismounted to walk beside the cart and talk to the sick man
on his rough brychan. For him this was going home, and going
home with glory. He had never tasted what it meant to be a prisoner.
He talked eagerly, pointing out the long, silvery shimmer of water
beyond Lavan Sands, and the soft coast of Ynys Mon beyond, tapering out to the small blue hog-back of Ynys Lanog of the saints. But
it was October, and there was a grievous sadness on the sea, even
at noon, and for all his raillery and his teasing and his brave laughter,
de Breos was sad.

"Aber of the White Shells!" he said, biting into one of the sour
late apples Harry had gathered for him at Nanhwynain, and shivering as its sharpness set his teeth on edge. "What shall I do at this
Aber of yours?" He frowned at the clean pattern his strong white
teeth had left in the hard flesh. "I tell you what, Harry, my friend,
if I loved you but a little less I should wish you to the devil. What

a plague were you doing in the first place, spying on our Babel of a camp from the hill there? What were you looking for? It wasn't glory, for you came unarmed, so much you told me. Then what was it?''

The moment of silence and hesitation surprised him, for the boy had been talkative on every other subject. He had but to touch him, and the confidences came pouring. This time it seemed he had put his finger on a tender spot, and for a moment the issue hung in doubt. He would have drawn back courteously and yielded the point if his curiosity and his vanity had not been pricked. He had had everything he had chosen to ask of the child, and he would have this no less surely. He waited, stubbornly smiling, until the moment of constraint melted in a rush of impulsive words.

"I have an inherited quarrel," said Harry, eyes glittering, "with a certain Englishman. I hoped to catch a glimpse of him, and get to know my enemy."

De Breos kept his countenance admirably straight; it was no great labour, he liked the boy too well to want to make light of the issues that were important to him.

"And have you never seen him, then, this enemy of yours?"

"Not yet," said Harry, and shut his mouth with a snap.

"Who is he? It may be that I know him."

"By name you surely will. Many a time I have been wanting to ask you about him. His name is Ralf Isambard of Parfois."

De Breos stared wide-eyed, the apple gripped between his teeth. "Isambard? Lad, but you're aiming high! What in the name of all the saints can you have against the Lord of Parfois? Why, the man could be grandfather to you! And trust me, he's no mettle to venture lightly, not even for princes."

"It is a matter of *galanas*—a blood-debt," said Harry sternly, suspecting that even the astonished respect he read in the alert face before him covered a shadow of mockery.

"But surely Welsh law will allow you to compound a blood-debt for a price," suggested de Breos delicately. Ralf Isambard! he thought, and could have howled aloud at the incongruity. Life had a way of being out of balance, but to hear the blind puppy gravely declaring his enmity to the old wolf was out of all bounds. These

Welshmen! But the boy was not even Welsh, he bore as uncompromising a Norman name as de Breos himself, and one fully as old.

"Not this," said Harry grimly. "Even if he so desired, I would not forgo it. But he knows nothing of me. The quarrel is my father's."

The pale, hazy air over the sea thickened into heavier cloud on the mountains on their right hand, but already they could see the great shoulder of rock that crowded the fields into the surf beyond Aber. In less than an hour they would be home. Harry watched the unfolding outlines of the hills, and was aware of the eyes that studied him frankly from the cart.

"What did old Ralf do to your father, that you keep so bitter a mind towards him?" The voice was warm and sympathetic and candidly curious. He could ask for things with a child's avid directness when he chose, and there was very little Harry could have denied him, not even the preoccupations that lay at the roots of his life and urged him towards maturity.

"He put my father to death. Long ago, just before I was born. My father was a master-mason in Isambard's service, and there was a matter of a Welsh boy who was taken during a raid and was in my father's care at Parfois. King John gave orders that the boy was to be hanged, and Isambard would have done it, but my father took the child safely away and delivered him back to the Prince of Gwynedd. You saw him by the Mule ford," said Harry. "He is my elder foster-brother, Owen ap Ivor ap Madoc."

"Ay, well I remember him, the one that shepherds you so close every step you take. But if they got clear away into Wales, how did your father fall foul of the Lord of Parfois a second time?"

"He went back," said Harry simply.

"In the devil's name, why? If he'd been in the old wolf's service surely he knew better than to confide in his mercy?"

"No help, he was bound. He was building the church there, and he'd sworn to remain at Parfois until his work was finished. When he'd despatched Owen safely on his way home he went back to keep his word. And there he was done to death. And my mother and I might have fared as ill if there had not been a certain lady there at Parfois who stood our friend to her own hurt, and brought us off safely into the care of the Prince of Gwynedd. And here we've been

ever since. And that's why I'm foster-brother to Prince David and
to Owen, and my mother is waiting-woman to the Princess Joan."

"So that's how a Talvace came to grow up into as wild a fighting
Welshman as the best of them. I own I've wondered. And this good
gentlewoman who befriended you, what became of her?"

"She became a saint," said Harry, as though that solved everything, and needed no amplification.

"Faith. I wish she would teach me the trick of it, if she found it
so easy," said de Breos, ruefully laughing. "What must one do to
become a saint? Alive, I trust? I have no ambition to be a dead saint.
They so often come by uncommonly nasty deaths."

Harry looked sidelong at him in flat incomprehension; the word
was ordinary currency to him, and had no implications of canonisa-
tion about it.

"She went to live in a cell up there," he explained, tossing his
head towards the hills that closed in gently upon the forked cleft of
Aber. "Saint Clydog lives there, and they built her a second cell
close to his. She lives in prayer, away from the world. She's been
there thirteen years now. Sometimes we visit her, and sometimes
she sends John the Fletcher down to us if she wants anything. But
she never comes herself."

"So they pass their days in prayer and meditation, do they, she
and Saint Clydog? And nobody else for a dozen miles round to
trouble their peace!"

"There's John the Fletcher," said Harry punctiliously, the gentle
irony escaping him, since it was not at his expense.

"Oh, by all means let us not forget John the Fletcher!"

"My mother says," confided Harry impulsively, "that she did it
because she did not wish to marry. And yet she was so beautiful!"

"Better and better! I shall have a third cell built there. So she
escaped marriage by embracing sainthood, did she? Not having your
mother's more practical way of escape into the Princess's service."

"But my mother did marry," said Harry promptly. "She married
my father's good friend, the mason who always worked with him.
It was he brought Owen away home, and after that he dared not
venture back into England."

"God's blood, Harry!" cried de Breos, rolling his head back among
the rugs with the first full-hearted shout of laughter he had uttered

in his captivity. "I think you must be the most mothered and fathered of any fellow ever I met. Three mothers and two fathers on the earth, and yet another sire under it! How is it they have not torn you in pieces among them?" And perhaps they would have, he thought, breaking off there sharply, if the boy had not been the bold, tough, self-willed creature he was, if he had not had that audacious Norman jaw to his immature face, and those levelled, challenging sea-green eyes.

Well, at least the dead one must let him alone, he thought, and then caught back even that thought, for perhaps he was taking it too easily for granted. No one can be more demanding than the dead, or the living on behalf of the dead. And no one can be worse traduced than the dead, when the living begin to make demands for him. What did the boy really think of that father of his who could no longer speak for himself?

De Breos stirred painfully, easing his swathed trunk on the rough brychan, and flinching from the stab of the broken ribs. He had been a fool to ride for so many hours earlier in the day, he was stiffening badly now. He looked at the coils of cloud drifting down the mountain, he looked at the darkening silver of the sea beyond Lavan Sands, turning to lead before his eyes, and he shivered. No wonder the English exiles shrank together for solidarity in this barbarous place. No wonder Talvace's widow clung to her own kind, and made haste to barricade herself in behind another man's name, and furnish her son with one more father of his own race.

"And which of your many parents do you mind, Harry? For they can't always speak with one voice."

"I mind the Prince," said Harry very practically, and grinned aside at him wickedly. "Would not you?"

"I would! The stakes would have to be high before I risked displeasing that gentleman, were I in your shoes. And yet it seems to me you have very much your will with him, my friend."

"He is very good to me," acknowledged Harry blithely, "and never angry with me but with reason. But terrible when he's angered." He used the words of fear, but he did not know yet what fear was; there was laughter bright behind the awe in his eyes. "Once I tied old Einion's beard to the strings of his harp when he fell asleep over it in hall, and when he awoke and went to play he got in such a tangle he thought himself bewitched. I never saw the Prince so angry. I got the worst beating I ever had from him, to teach me where respect is due.''

But it had not been severe enough, de Breos saw, to stop him laughing for long, or make him approach either Prince or bard with timidity thereafter.

''I was sorry afterwards, I never thought how he would start awake like that and be frightened to find himself fast. But that was a long time ago,'' he said hastily, recollecting his present dignity as escort to so notable a prisoner, ''nearly three years ago, when I was still a child.''

''I understood it so,'' de Breos assured him gravely.

They were drawing near to the forked cleft of woodland that slashed steeply into the towering hills. He could see in one iron gleam of light the thread of the river pouring down across the track and lacing the flat fields to the salt marshes beyond; and higher, withdrawn into the mouth of the valley, the great wooden wall of Llewelyn's castle half-obscured by the clinging huts of the villein hamlet at its gate. Within the wall the timber keep towered on its high motte, and the squat roofs clustered under its shadow. There was a light haze of wood-smoke over the whole great maenol, withdrawing it from the ebbing day. This neighbour land of his which he had hardly seen in his almost thirty years had never seemed so alien.

''I confess I never tied a bard to his harp,'' he was saying lightly while his heart chilled in him, ''but I once set fire to a chaplain. The old fool was so long-winded, and the devil left a burning candle so near to the skirt of his gown. A passable exploit in my father's son, but unwise in my uncle's nephew. Bishops in the family are a mixed blessing, Harry. But that was long ago, too, of course, when I was still a child.''

William, my friend, he was thinking, with the hot discontent and the cold languor fuming in him like the clouds over Moel Wnion, what are you going to do here, without pastime, without exercise, without women? Oh, for the freedom of that third cell in the hills, with the resolute (and beautiful!) lady who had no use for marriage. Can she really be content with Saint Clydog? And John the Fletcher, of course! It would never do to forget John the Fletcher.

The backs of the riders ahead had straightened as they sighted the walls of home, the horses raised their heads and distended their nostrils to snuff the familiar pastures. The looming barrier that threatened him beckoned to them; there were stables and fodder waiting for the horses and well-warmed beds for the men. And after all, need his own bed be utterly cold? There are women everywhere.

Welsh ladies of rank are virtuous, that's well known. But all? Llewelyn had a bastard son before he married, by a lady with a pedigree nearly as long as his own. The young man proved troublesome, I recall, and is now safe under lock and key at Degannwy to keep him from his brother's throat. As I shall soon be under lock and key here at Aber.

"I hope you lodge your captives above-ground, Harry," he said, eyeing the dark walls. "Light is the last thing a man should willingly surrender. Except breath," he added with a sour smile.

He was instantly sorry for that tone. It was unfair to take out his spleen on the boy, who could so easily be made to pay for an innocent and helpless attachment. He had not missed the way Harry copied even the tricks of his speech, the turn of his head, his seat in the saddle. He had no boy of his own, only a covey of little daughters, and the flattery of being imitated was seductive, he had to watch his every move.

"There are no dungeons here, my lord, we live in daylight. The journey has been hard on you," said Harry anxiously, "but here you'll rest and mend. And the Princess my foster-mother will deal generously and lovingly with you, that I promise you."

"Well, if I never saw her before, at least I have some obscure claims of kinship on her."

The connection was tenuous enough, one of the knots of expediency in the complex net of alliances that made a spider's web of the border country. His father in late middle-age had contracted a second marriage with the darkest and prettiest of the flurry of little girls who had followed David into the world. Young Gladys was no doubt properly glad to be a coltish widow at sixteen—or was it seventeen? Presently they would marry her to someone else, if God was good to her someone nearer her own age.

"But be careful, Harry, how much you promise in someone else's name. If my entertainment is less than generous and loving I shall hold you accountable for what's wanting. I've no doubt I'm going to pay a princely price for it."

Hardly two months set up in his honour, and he had to put it into pawn to ransom his body. But he was resolutely smiling again, and the mouth that was so pleasing even in its drooping weariness had regained its good humour. It was time to gather about him what powers he still had, for they were passing among the huts of the village, and the guard at the gate was already drawing aside to let them in.

Harry fell back for a moment outside the gate, and de Breos well knew why, and considerately refrained from looking round. What boy could resist riding ceremoniously into the maenol on his new horse, fair prize of war? And the plain truth was that he could not reach the stirrup without making use of the shaft of the cart or some convenient stone, and was too proud to get one of his men-at-arms to heft him into the saddle. Better not to see the mounting-block against the timber buttresses of the wall, and the boy's quick dash for it.

In a moment he was alongside again, upright and solemn on top of the tall chestnut horse; and though his men grinned broadly behind his back they kept their faces steady as stone in front of him, only their eyes laughing. He was well liked, none of them would have the heart to spoil his triumph.

The women of the village left their work and came running to catch at stirrup leathers and walk alongside their men into the court-yard. Rhys ap Griffith, who had been in practical command of both the escort and its commander, reined aside unobtrusively and let the boy ride forward alone.

The cart stopped. Out of Llewelyn's great hall came his seneschal, Ednyfed Fychan, with a knot of lesser officials at his heels, and from kitchen and armoury and kennels poured every man who could drop his work and come to welcome his returning fellows. Harry had a worthy audience for his grand entry. But it was not for the elders, not even for his ancient tutor Einion, that he put the nervous horse through a little performance of dancing and sidling before he brought him to a halt.

Two women had appeared from the retired royal apartments in the far corner of the maenol. Harry's two secular mothers, no doubt.

But which of them provoked this touching tribute of pride and ambition, the flourish with which he dismounted, the vivid colour that mantled in his cheeks? Very surely not his own true mother! De Breos examined the two approaching figures with detached and yet gradually quickening interest.

One of them was small, with great dark eyes in a face like a blown rose; not so slender as once she had been, perhaps, and not so young, but her black and white and red was a lasting kind of bloom. The other was half a head taller and a hand-span slimmer, a grave woman with light brown hair dressed in coiled plaits on either side a long, fair-skinned face.

There was no doubt which of the two was Gilleis Boteler and which was the Princess of Gwynedd. This was where Llewelyn's heir had got his fairness and slenderness; and this, surprisingly, was the face that could inflame young Harry's unpractised heart without his knowledge, and make him flush and glow in her presence.

De Breos saw nothing there to start the spring gushing. She had a sombre authority, a too quiet and too indifferent grace in her movements, a certain pale good looks; but she could never have been beautiful, and forty years had worn her thin and weary, brought the bone too near the skin and the mind too close to the fretted surface of the flesh. A little while and she would be old. He took his eyes from her.

A groom had taken Harry's reins from him as he alighted, and the boy turned his shoulder on the seneschal and ran to meet the two women. He bent his knee to the Princess, and then lifted his face to her as he must have been lifting it at every meeting and every separating, all his life long, for the kiss of kinship. She took his head between her hands and kissed him with a simplicity that was old habit to her, and handed him on to his mother to be hugged and made much of. But for one moment, with Joan's hands pressing his cheeks and Joan's lips touching his forehead, he had started and quivered to a tension which was out of his experience and beyond his understanding. De Breos had seen it pass through the braced shoulders and the long, sturdy back like a shudder of bliss. There was no mistaking it, the boy was deep in love with her.

The woman with whom someone else is in love, even a wild green boy, is always worth a second glance.

De Breos raised himself gingerly, holding by the edge of the cart, for Harry was coming running back to him.

"Will you light down, my lord? Will you come to the Princess?"

Yes, he thought, I'll come, and with such arms as I have, too. There must, it seems, be something there worth the finding. The women had joined the group of men, and the Princess was talking to Ednyfed Fychan. She did not look across at the prisoner, perhaps not even to seem to be hastening his clearly difficult and painful descent from the cart.

But you shall look at me, madam, he thought, feeling the old quickening fluid of challenge sparkle through his blood like wine through the heart in drunkenness. You shall look at me, and see me, too, you who have seen almost everything there is to be seen in this realm, but never William de Breos, never until now.

"Lend me your shoulder to alight, Harry, I'm mortal stiff. No, don't leave me so. It was you broke my ribs for me, and you may prop me up until they knit. By rights you owe me a good shirt, too, I would I had one by me this minute. No matter, let me be seen at my worst, and there can be no disappointment after."

She turned her head as they came, the man moving haltingly and wearily with a hand on the boy's shoulder. She had been aware of them all the time, and she turned her head at last because it seemed to her an unkindness to let the sick man come so lamely all the way to her. She was generous, even rashly so; Harry's first promise was fulfilled almost before it cooled on his lips. She left the seneschal, and came to meet them.

Harry walked carefully, matching his step and his breathing with those of his prized captive, proud of the weight on him. She did not miss that. She missed nothing. You see? There's a sign here for you as well as for me. Here's your little falcon, royal by adoption, tamed. Consider the implications and look at me, look well. Does he come to every man's lure?

"You are welcome to Aber, my lord de Breos," she said, in a low-pitched voice which was the greatest beauty she had shown him. "You are not well, and too tired for ceremony. If you are pleased to go to your lodging I will have linen and water brought to you there."

"And if I refuse it?" he said with a rueful smile. "Would you take the sign? And let me go on my way when you had fed and warmed me in your house?"

"I see you know the customs of Welsh hospitality," said Joan, faintly smiling in return. The eyes she raised to his face were grey and clear and very deep. What they saw was not his handsome body and bold, fine features, but the convulsive clinging of his fingers on Harry's shoulder, the drawn lines and the sag of discouragement round his mouth, that so bore down the wilful smile, the crippled beauty of his movements, and above all his youth, so willing to be boisterous and insolent, and so confined and cramped now into helplessness. "All the same," she said dryly, the smile a thought warmer now, "I think in your condition you should not ask to leave tonight."

"No," he agreed, watching her face steadily. "No, I will not ask to leave tonight.

"No, even if you opened the gate to me now I would not go." Generously and lovingly she'll deal with me, will she, Harry? I've seen the generosity, that can walk abroad in courtyards and show itself in front of all men. But the love, that's a different matter. It needs silence and retirement. And time. Time of which, by favour of de Burgh's obstinacy, we may yet have enough.

"Ay, we know, child, we know," said Gilleis good-humouredly, pausing on her way to the linen-press to rap her son lightly on the back of his shock-head with a thimbled finger. "There never was such a paragon. The voice of an angel and the step of a deer-hound, and no bounds gallant and noble. These three days since you brought him home with you you've never stopped singing his praises, we should know the tune by now."

Harry had talked himself out, kneeling on the rug at Joan's feet with his arms spread familiarly on her brocaded knees. He still behaved as one having his child's rights in her bed-chamber. Many a time he had played on Llewelyn's great bed, and many a time she had watched him, the lordly little stranger, and been charmed by his assurance almost into believing that his roots were there.

"But is he not everything I've claimed for him? Didn't I tell you he could hold his own at whatever he touched? Even with as great a bard as ours," said Harry proudly.

Joan sat with her hand loosely clasped between both his, her eyes fixed on her own mirrored face in the polished silver over his shoulder. Her hair was already unbraided, and hung to her waist in heavy brown tresses. She was looking somewhere beyond the mirror, beyond the walls of the room, and there was a sadness about her mouth that made his heart lurch with fondness.

"He's a man like other men," she said. "Voice and face and form, God made him well enough."

"If you cry him up so," warned Gilleis, teasing him, "you'll have folks saying you are but crying up yourself for having the better of him."

"No, truly, I never thought of it!" he protested indignantly. "It's not the fighting well, though he bears as good a report as any man in England. No, it's the way he took it when the luck went against him. And even now—if you could know how sad I've seen him when there was no one by. And he did not deserve it! Do *you* know, do *I* know what it is to be a prisoner? And yet you heard him at supper, how he talked, how he laughed—"

How he laughed! With all of him, the reared head and the broad, young, sinewy shoulders that rocked to the cadences of his mirth, and the unbelievably smooth round throat pulsing above the furred collar of David's cotte. How he talked, between the laughter, with a fiery flow and a heady sparkle, like pouring wine. The pale face in the mirror flushed a little, remembering. She saw herself mute and grave beside him, unable to laugh with him even when he gave her occasion. He had asked punctiliously after his stepmother, letting his civility carry an unmalicious edge of absurdity, too gentle for irony, but she had not smiled. She had been playing the game too long, perhaps, this intricate game of courts and kings and destinies. She had grown used to regarding her daughters as pieces on the board, movable within three generations. Her daughters, yes, but not her son. Never her son.

"And then to-night, when our lord's courier came, you saw how he took that, too, though it was bitter bad news to him. You heard him. How many men could have carried it so well?"

Bad news indeed for an Englishman, that the war in Kerry was over, and the English host retreating ignominiously into their own borders from the winter's early frosts and the threat of starvation.

She heard again the seneschal's voice retailing the news over the trenchers, and de Breos swallowing it manfully. How many men could have carried it so well?

"The terms of peace are already agreed, but for some chaffering over details for form's sake. There'll be a matter of a few head of cattle to pay for the privilege of taking back Kerry intact, but that's a small matter."

"Not to the empty fellows I left behind there! It will be a marvel if the King gets one beast back into England uneaten. And what of Hubert's fortress? I felt in my bones it would never be finished."

"It's to come down. Down to the foundations, my lord."

"God hears everything! His folly, he christened it, and folly it turns out to be. Madam, I hope you never play with words? They have a way of coming full circle into the wind, and hitting in the face the fool who thinks he aimed them. There'll be an indemnity to pay for the work of levelling it, I make no doubt?"

"It's still a matter of argument, my lord, how much."

"It need not exercise you. Whatever it may be, I shall surely be paying it."

And all this while she had not said one word. Words are terrible weapons; even without his warning she would have been chary of using them here. When at last she ventured, the ground quaked under her; she had never known it to be shaken so.

"I am afraid, my lord, you can take no pleasure in this news."

He had lifted to her face one brilliant flash of his dark eyes, for once nakedly unsmiling, and answered in a voice so low and rapid that she barely caught his meaning: "Can you, my lady?"

"Come," said Gilleis, closing the chest upon the gown she had just laid away, "get off to bed, now, and let the lad rest. Do you think women can't see a handsome face for themselves, and value a good heart, too? Say good night to my lady, and be off to your solitary splendour, since you won't come and keep company with Adam and me."

Harry slept with Owen, in the ante-chamber of the apartment David enjoyed as acknowledged heir to his father and though he could very well have gone to his mother's lodging while his brothers were out of Aber, he would not for the world have ceded his rights.

Harry kissed Joan's hand obediently, and offered her his cheek.

He trembled when her lips touched him, and she felt the heat of his rising blood under the smooth skin; but all she saw when she held him off from her was a flushed child, a little fevered perhaps with sleepiness. If she could have heard, he thought, how eloquently he poured out to de Breos those praises of her that stopped short in his throat in her presence, she would have known better how to value him, and found him a man's work to do for her sake. When he brought her all the intoxication and excitement of his first sally in arms, a splendid prize of war to lay at her feet, she only smiled and caressed him with the same serenity as if he had run to show her a new toy. She was too much with his mother, whom he loved dearly, but who never took him quite seriously.

He looked back from the threshold to say earnestly: "Madam, Father Philip says we should remember in our prayers all poor souls hard beset, and all prisoners. Will you pray for my lord de Breos?"

She did not look round, but her eyes in the soft metallic sheen of the mirror sought for his, and the reflected look was at once tender and grim, as though she smiled at him while she fended off another who stood behind him. After a long moment of silence she said in a low voice: "Be content, I will pray for him."

"Such a boy!" sighed Gilleis, kissing his cheek and putting him briskly out of the door. "Did ever you know him so concerned for any of us? The times I've heard him gabble his prayers too fast for sense, if he did not forget them altogether, but for my lord of Brecon he'll have us all on our knees. But there, his geese were always swans. And the young man has a way with him, too," she owned, smiling. "It would be hard to deny him liking."

Joan sat silent and motionless before the glass, watching the long tresses of her hair smoothed and floating from the comb. Fair still, but the honeyed brightness was growing faintly dulled, faintly dry, like grass just beginning to bleach in the height of the summer. Time tarnishes the colours of flesh and hair and eyes with a fine, corroding dust. The cords of this throat had grown a little slack, the delicate white flesh was grained and tired. Dust clouded even the eyes grey as glass, as though all her life had been Lent, and the spring was gone by with no Easter to give it meaning and her devotion respite. She saw that the last May blossom was already withering on the bough, and almost before she could reach her hand to it, it would be gone. Surely she had been a girl once; but the girl had died irrevocably at fifteen, when she had left her dolls behind her to take up the burden of state, and conceived the child for whom she had been busy ever since constructing a kingdom. She had been too much preoccupied, even too well content, manipulating men and thrones and powers to have time to gather the May.

"Well, in a week or so now my lord will be safely home," said Gilleis cheerfully.

"God be thanked!"

She had only to look deeply enough into her own face in the mirror and she saw him there, his darkness flashing through her pallor, his steely metal gleaming through her gentler authority, bone fused into bone and eye matched with eye, an eagle looking through her face from his nest within her mind. She had grown into him flesh to flesh and spirit to spirit long since. If he suffered a wound, she bled. Had there ever since such another burning of two into one? Had there ever been a marriage so absolute as this?

"Go now, Gilleis, I shall sleep directly. Good night!"

"Good night, my lady! I'll leave the lamp burning."

The soft, light footsteps receded hollowly down the wooden stair, for the great bedchamber and its wardrobe were raised upon a tall undercroft so that the windows might look out over the curtain wall and enjoy the prospect of the straits and the distant silvery chain of the coast of Ynys Mon.

When she had heard the outer door below swing heavily into place, Joan rose from her stool and ran quickly down the stairway, and dropped the great wooden bolt into its socket. When had she ever done that before? Why should she do it now? Who would dare to lay a hand to her door? She was her own ramparts, her own armoury, an impregnable fortress. And images cannot be locked out. If the image of a man had ventured to walk through the invisible barrier, how could he be fended off by those meaner safeguards she had never needed? To bolt the door was to admit and acknowledge him. He would be within the room with her, penetrating her sleep with his wakefulness all night long.

Nevertheless she left the bar in place; and going back to her room she prayed passionately for all prisoners, and all poor creatures hard beset.

* * *

Harry started upright in his bed in the chilly darkness of after-midnight, torn out of a disturbed dream that uncoiled from him instantly and left no images behind, but only a sense of tension and fear. His heart was thudding heavily as though he had been running, but it seemed to him that he had been running towards the fear, not away from it, and had been on the point of embracing it when he was jerked awake. He put out a hand instinctively for Owen, but the bed was cold where Owen should have been, and he remembered that he was alone.

He sat hugging the fur coverlet about his nakedness and listening to the silence, and the unfinished dream, formless and furtive now, hung over him waiting in the dark. It was foolish to be afraid. He had only to lie down and pull the covers over his ears, and drift away again without haste into sleep. Broken dreams seldom came back.

But he did not lie down. He crept out of the big bed and felt for his hose, still straining his ears. The dogs had not given tongue. Yet there had been a sound, something soft and rustling and hardly audible, the braced fingers of a hand feeling its way all along the rough timber of the outside wall of his room, as though a blind man had passed by.

Now that he had given it a form he was less afraid, and infinitely more curious. He pulled on his hose hurriedly in the dark, and tugged his cotte over his head, emerging to freeze into quivering stillness again. If he had not been listening with such strained attention he would not have heard the second sound, though it was louder than the first; and when it came he had no idea how long the interval had been. It was a dull, muted fall, somewhere muffled between the buildings towards the corner of the curtain wall. Harry opened his door cautiously, waiting with held breath for the dogs to begin scolding, but the kennels were at the opposite extreme of the maenol, and there was no sudden flurry of baying. Nothing moved in the darkness of the moonless and cloudy night but the boy slipping with the ease of old knowledge between the buildings, running as inquisitively and rashly towards the thing that threatened him as he had run in his dream.

He rounded the corner of the tower and checked for a moment in alarm, for the door at the foot of the staircase was open, he knew it by the hollow sound the cavity gave back to his passing step and his loudly-beating heart. Why should the Princess's door be standing wide at this hour? He wavered, in doubt whether to run in to her and assure himself of her safety, or pursue the sound to its source, but it was no more than ten yards to the angle of the tower and the narrow walk that separated it from the curtain wall, and curiosity drew him on.

A shadow started erect among shadows, close under the wall where he could hardly distinguish one darkness from another. A low voice challenged in an urgent whisper: "Who's there?" And on a quick gasp of recognition and recovery: "Harry! Is that you?"

"Madam, is all well—," he began breathlessly aloud.

She laid a hand over his mouth and hushed him sharply. He felt her palm cool and hard and steady against his lips, and was calmed. She was the mistress of all here, and not by courtesy but by right of will. If she took no alarm he need feel none. He reached his arms to hold her, and stumbled over something heavy and warm that lay at her feet. A man, his arms spread against the foot of the curtain wall, his hands two pallors in the dark just bracing themselves laboriously to thrust him up from the ground. The shock of his hair fallen forward over his face was the darkest centre in the many darks that were beginning to disentangle themselves before Harry's eyes. He was breathing in deep-drawn, laboured breaths, and the first thrust, as he levered himself up, fetched a flinching groan out of him.

"My Lord de Breos!" whispered Harry, and began to shake again with the certainty that filled him. Here in this narrow and private place, at the foot of the wall on the landward extreme of the maenol, the woods not far away, the night moonless—

"But he could not!" he breathed, outraged and incredulous. "He *could* not! He gave his *word*—"

"Hush!" she said peremptorily, gripping him by the arm. "Help me with him, quickly, and be quiet. We must get him back to his bed before anyone else hears."

Bewildered but obedient, he lent his arm, and between them they hoisted the fallen man to his feet. Joan drew the long right arm about her neck, Harry on the other side clasped him about the body.

They moved all three as one flesh, braced and shuddering, and at the first step de Breos straightened himself and lifted his weight from falling upon them. He did not speak, he did not raise his head, but with their aid he walked.

"But how could he?" Harry said in a bitter whisper through his clenched teeth, addressing Joan as though the man between them had been deaf or dead. "He gave his parole!"

She heard the rage and shock in his voice, and smiled wryly in the dark. At thirteen he still lived in a simple world where all bonds were automatically honoured, and all words held good. He had a lot to learn about men, and even more about compassion, but life would teach him soon enough. Let him continue in his delusion, however it galled him; only she need ever know from which wall the climber had fallen.

"Be quiet," she said, but very gently. "Only let us get him home."

Under his breath the boy fretted still at the smart, swallowing indignant tears. "Had we to put leg-irons on him? If we cannot take *Brecon's* word—"

Hurt and ashamed, he leaned an angry shoulder to prop open the door of the prisoner's lodging. Why was he even allowing himself to be drawn into this conspiracy of silence? The shame he felt was for himself, because this man had been a piece of his life, and he had been innocently proud of him, and to have him exposed to scorn was a humiliation Harry himself would have found hard to bear.

"Close the door," said Joan, drawing a sharp breath of relief.

They lowered their burden between them and let him slip down on to the pillow and lie still. Even with the door closed they could distinguish shades of darkness here, their eyes being used to the night by now. They saw de Breos raise an arm with a slow, heavy movement, and lay it over his face. They waited some moments, Harry did not know for what; perhaps for the silence to reassure them that no one else stirred, perhaps for the breath to steady and grow calm in them before they ventured to speak.

"Are you hurt?" Joan asked at last, very quietly. They knew by the tensions of his stretched body that he was conscious and aware.

"No," said the man on the bed in a muffled and bitter voice. "Not as I deserve."

"It was folly to attempt such a climb," she said in the same muted tone. "You should have known you could not bear the strain, half-crippled as you are."

"It was more than folly to attempt it," the moving mouth said from under the sheltering sleeve, "as well you know. It was villainy. And I repent me of it. Now deliver me over and have done."

"My lord, even my prisoner is in some sort my guest, and his honour touches me closely." She turned towards the boy: "Harry," she said with authority, "you will say no word of this to anyone, ever. It is between us three alone."

The man and the boy stiffened as if with the same impulse of recoil. "He broke his bond," burst out the boy, smouldering.

"So has many another, once, under sharp distress, and lived to do honour to his name none the less." He was holding out against her for the sake of his sore heart rather than his sense of justice, and she knew it, though she chose to attribute to him the nobler motive. "Don't be too hard on a single fault, or who will be fit for your acquaintance? Some day you may need a gentle judgement yourself, Harry. It's a long way through the world."

It was easy enough to move him, the proud fondness that had made this betrayal so hard to bear was already fighting on the side of de Breos. "I shall obey you, madam," muttered the boy, grudging but abashed. "I'll never speak of it."

"Good! See you remember. Let God do the judging. Now we had best go back to our beds, and forget we ever left them. The matter is closed. My lord, I shall send to inquire after you in the morning, I trust you will have taken no harm. Are you indeed unhurt? Are you well enough to lie alone?"

The voice from the bed was harsh and right. "I am as well as any man can be who has met himself face to face and is ashamed of what he sees."

"Is there anything you need before we leave you?"

"Nothing," said de Breos, "since you are so merciful as to put this past hour clean out of mind. Nothing but a better heart in me, and that I think you may have given me already." He lowered his arm suddenly from his face, and heaved himself up on one elbow. "Harry! Come here to me!"

The boy drew near the bed with a dragging step, the old compulsion pulling at his senses. Even though the darkness hid the admired face, the voice when it pleased could be so intimate and so winning. And Joan, who was perfection, had warned him against judging too hardly the faults to which he had never yet been tempted.

"Harry, for what I attempted to-night I am heartily sorry. I never shall offend again. Whether you will still take my word I do not know, but for what it is worth to you I give it."

He lay down again abruptly without waiting for an answer, flattening his shoulders into the brychan and turning his head away. Harry stood irresolute for a moment, wanting to find something generous to say, moved towards him and angry with himself for being moved. It was flattering to be asked to forgive, it filled him with the large delight of magnanimity, but his injury was too recent and grave to be so easily adjusted.

"Come," said Joan, taking him by the arm, "let him alone now."

Harry allowed himself to be led mutely from the room. The night air was cold on his cheeks and eyelids. Sleep leaned on him out of the chilly zenith. She laid her arm about his shoulders and led him to his own door, thrusting him gently within.

"Go to bed, and leave fretting. To-morrow will mend all."

"If you knew," he whispered grievously, "how well I thought of him—"

"So you will again, child. One slip doesn't make a man a villain. Go to bed and sleep. This is not the end of the world. And think of him kindly," she said, a sudden desperate appeal shaking the quiet thread of her voice. "Think kindly of all poor sinners. If you think yourself wounded, what must their sufferings be?"

"I will try," he said, almost in tears, and stumbled bemusedly back to his cold bed with the tremor of her distress still vibrating in his ears.

When the door had closed on him she turned and slipped like a silent shadow back to the room where de Breos lay, and let herself in to him without a sound.

He was lying coiled hard into himself on the bed, his face to the wall, his long arms wound round his body tightly as cords. He did not move when she came in, but he knew the moment of her coming by the slight shifting of the darkness and the drift of air that came in in her garments; and by something more that distilled from her presence and set every nerve in him quivering with tension, until his skin was a web of agony constricting him unbearably. She did not speak; it was not to be made so easy for him. In the end he would have to speak for her, but the effort was like a death. Had he not said enough already, and plainly enough?

"Why did you come back?" he said in a voice harsh with anguish. "What more do you want from me? I repent, I shall not offend again. If I could undo what I've done I would but, God help me, that's out of my power. Is it confession you want? Well you know it was to your window I was climbing. What did I want with escape while you were within the wall?"

"I know," she said, and did not move.

"If it had not been for the boy—"

"You need not fear the boy. You have him by the heart still. He'll hold his tongue."

"That you may know the whole of it, I let myself drop of design. I've climbed in at too many chamber windows in my time to fall from one now. The thing was child's play. I could have broken in upon you if I had willed, but when it came to it that was not what I wanted. You must come out to me—of your own will, of your own charity—"

"Yes," she said hopelessly, "you knew how to fetch me forth to you. I am here. Of my own will."

"You were to take me up and pity me—and, by God, you did!"

"Was that pity?" she said. The low, lovely voice was helpless and wondering. "I know only that I had to come to you. And will you not even look at me now that I am here?"

"No!" he said in a great gasp of protest. But in a moment he gathered himself effortfully and turned to face her, and dragging himself erect swung his feet to the beaten earth of the floor. "I played my game too well," he said. "It proved to be no game, or if it was it's I who pay the forfeit, as is only just. I'm taken in my own trap. As God sees me, I love you! I love you, and I cannot touch you!"

He sank his face between his hands and closed his eyes, waiting for the fluctuations of darkness and cold that would mark her going; but there was no lifting and no settling of the blackness within his aching eyelids, and when he looked up again she had drawn a step nearer, and stood within touch of his hands.

"Well?" she said. "Am I to stay or go?"

"Go!" he implored her groaning. "In the name of God! And quickly!"

But still she did not move, and in a moment his arms came out blindly and fastened on her as the dying fasten on the Host, dragging her down into his heart.

Chapter Two

Aber: *January to September* 1229

*T*he price of your liberty," said Llewelyn, spreading one great brown hand to the heat from the brazier, "is two thousand pounds, my lord."

"I have had it in my mind with curious insistence that it might be," said de Breos with a face innocently grave, "ever since it came to my ears that the indemnity for the razing of our good justiciar's new castle in Kerry was fixed at that amount. You will allow me a little time to ponder the odd chance, I hope—and to recover the breath I am going to need sorely before this parley is over."

They had fought a few preliminary bouts already before the Christmas festival, measuring each other with passes and ripostes ever since Llewelyn had ridden back into Aber with his bodyguard in November, and the empty seats below the fire had filled again with the lean, wiry lancers and bowmen of his household army. They came home in high feather, and the bards paid them due tribute. Even to de Breos's English eyes the victory the Prince had won in Kerry showed as greater by far than could be measured by the small ground of the commote for which it had been fought. It was the first setback to de Burgh's steadily advancing personal power, and no doubt it had duly impressed King Henry, who was not altogether whole-hearted in his love for his justiciar. There were profound possibilities of mischief and disunity there.

Delays were always methodical with Llewelyn, whose native impulses were for passion and hate; if he had learned to control both, it was the interests of Wales that had schooled him, and his achievement of patience and subtlety was a prodigy against his nature. Love can do the impossible, even tame barbaric princes to caution, cunning and humility; and Llewelyn, Prince of Aberffraw and Lord of Snowdon, contained within his great, lean, violent body enormous resources and reservoirs of love, for Gwynedd, for that larger vision of Wales which de Breos saw sometimes reflected in his expressive eyes, for his son who was to inherit Gwynedd and complete the creation of Wales, for every oak and whipcord clansman who followed him unquestioningly. And above all, for that grave, quiet woman who sat erect and still at the table, intent on her husband's counsels as other women on their embroidery frames.

Yes, for their sakes, Llewelyn could evade and postpone when he chose. If he had let November and December slip away without formulating his terms, it was only to secure the ground under his feet, to establish his position with the King and ensure that he should be able to press his demands with every prospect of success. Henry had already set up the Princess again in her manors of Condover and Rothley, those two favours he was for ever snatching away and giving back as his mood changed. The indications were hopeful for Llewelyn's plans, and ominous enough for his victim. Yet the King was his only appeal; and of a weapon as double-edged and pliable as Henry not even a master-swordsman could ever be quite sure.

"Two thousand pounds is a deal of money, my lord," said de Breos carefully, playing with the half-empty cup he dangled in his fingers.

"So I said to the King's envoys, but they would not lower their price. And could I ask less for a de Breos than I was paying for a half-built castle?" The hawk-face was solemn, but the far-sighted eyes in their fine nets of wrinkles were laughing.

"But consider, my lord, that whatever terms we agree between us are still subject to the King's sanction. Might it not be better, if only for the form of things, to abate a little and avoid so exact a parallel?"

"Abate?" said Llewelyn, suddenly leaning forward in his chair and flattening both hands with a loud, confident clap upon the table. "When I dance a measure with the King's envoys I can speak their roundabout language as well as any man living, and to them, for the royal record, it may be expedient to use the forms laid down. But here between us two let us have plain truth. His Majesty may take comfort in recording the campaign in Kerry as ended by negotiation, but never doubt for all that he knows, as I know, that Kerry was a war lost and won, and I won it. If I pleased I could extort from you a profit above what I am paying out to him to save his face. If I don't do it you may take it it's because I never set out to make gain out of this issue. The war was none of my seeking, why should I pay for it?"

"By the same token I might complain too, for God knows I never sought it, either."

"And have had nothing but ill-luck out of it, I grant you. But that's the fortune of war, and I did not cast the lots. I might as easily have been in your hold now at Brecon, parleying for my liberty as you for yours."

"Should I ever have that happiness," said de Breos, looking up from his play with a sudden glittering grin, "I promise you I'll exert myself to entertain you as royally as I have been entertained."

"You're very civil. And I should hope to bear my confinement with as good a heart as you have done. And that's no light compliment. I wish every man as high a spirit in captivity. While your father lived I hardly knew you, my lord, but now that we've been thrown together I tell you to your face, I like what I see."

The dangling cup had stopped swinging between the long fingers, it hung still, only the liquor within it trembling. The smiling face froze for an instant, the colour ebbing beneath the fading gold of its summer tan. Joan made a sudden sharp movement of her arm upon the table, and set the quill rocking in the ink-horn. But Llewelyn had continued warmly, his voice riding heedlessly over the moment of constraint.

"I like you, and I'll deal with you honestly. If you have any thought of making use of the King to hold up this agreement by refusing his approval, be wise and put it out of mind. If I extorted twice the sum from you, he would still sanction it. His Majesty received a reverse in Kerry that has made him value my quiescence dearly, and to have good relations with me—at least until he feels his chances of success stand higher—he'll sacrifice you without a qualm.''

"But you, I think,'' said de Breos, recovering his assurance and his sparkle, ''are equally anxious to stand well with him for the time being. De Burgh is still to be reckoned with.''

"He is.'' Llewelyn's voice was grim. "Well I know it. And the best protection I have against him for me and mine is a master who cannot quite love him, if he could but find an alternative to him. I need King Henry and he needs me. He needs me contented, and I need him reassured, and on those terms why should we not do honest business together? But his need is the sharper, as you must know if you know this new design he has of sending one more expedition into France. He is buying my quietness, and he shall have it. No man of mine shall step over the border while his back is turned; I have enough to do here making safe my own borders. You will do well to go along with me and take what terms you can get, the King will not lift a finger for you.''

De Breos took that silently, frowning over his linked hands. The light from the candles glowed in the stones of his rings. His wife had sent him a train of pack-horses laden with clothes and comforts from Brecon as soon as she received word of his captivity, and loving letters with them. He had no need of borrowed clothes now, and his own finery left David's far in the shade. A mistake, perhaps, he thought acidly, to be too magnificent if you are a prisoner, it tends to put up your price. He cast one quick glance at the Princess, erect and regal against the rough dark panelling of the wall. Her hair was dressed in two great coiled plaits springing from above the narrow golden diadem, and ending in a loose, shining tress on either side her fair face. Jewels only made her pallor radiant, sharp and thin as a flame; but no flame ever burned so steadily.

"Well, it appears I have no choice but to pay,'' said de Breos at last.

"Unless you purpose to remain a prisoner here, it seems your only course."

"I hardly think captivity would agree with my lord de Breos for ever," said Joan, turning her head to look at him with the shadow of a smile.

"Madam, in your house I swear I should never complain, but I doubt I should soon outwear my welcome. Very well, I agree. Let it be drawn so."

"There's a matter of an instalment due from me this coming Easter," said Llewelyn. "A mere two hundred and fifty marks. It could very well be discharged without leaving England."

"It shall be. And what more? I see there are more provisions in your draft."

The hand that had drawn it was Joan's. He should have been prepared for that, yet it had confounded him. She was in all her husband's counsels, his right hand wherever he himself could not be, his best envoy and diplomat; he had brought this to her as he brought everything. Perhaps she had even advised; there was no telling from her expression: she sat neutral and withdrawn, only the deep, intelligent eyes moving intently from face to face as they fought out an encounter which was already as surely lost and won as the campaign in Kerry.

"Yes, there are more. I desire, my lord, an undertaking from you that you will never again appear in arms against me."

"It seems to me," said de Breos with a wry smile, "that you are trying to rewrite history. In how many years out of the last fifty has there not been a de Breos in arms against Gwynedd? And what is my answer to be when King Henry summons the march of arms next time?"

"You must answer him as God gives you wit. My demand stands. Moreover, I do not think you are ill-disposed to it, if truth be told. There have been times when de Breos and Gwynedd have been allies."

"There have, for pure respite between the ages of fighting each other. Well, and what else? You have me interested now. What's still to come?"

"A closer alliance between us two. I want to secure my borders,

I want you at least taken out of the tale of my enemies. My lord, I have a son, and you have four daughters. I desire that you will give your daughter Isabella to my son David in marriage—"

"My lord, this is unexpected!" cried de Breos, wide-eyed.

"—with the lordship and castle of Builth as her dowry."

"Ah! Now we have it! Builth is the plum. A good, solid mid-Welsh rock, full in the path of the justiciar's advance northwards."

"There are advantages," said Llewelyn, "for you as for me. And the child would be in good fosterage here. I mean earnestly to enjoy a closer association with you, if you will join me. And I am offering your girl a royal match, and a good, fair, gallant lad to husband. That's but to praise my own, but praise him I must, for he's all I've claimed for him, and so any man in north Wales will tell you."

Any man but one, thought de Breos, glancing from Llewelyn's glowing, eloquent face to the shut countenance of the Princess, in whose deep eyes a sudden unclouded tenderness burned for a moment at mention of her son. That other prisoner, the turbulent young man kicking his angry heels in the castle of Degannwy, would have used very different words to describe his half-brother, though he would find no one else of his opinion, or none openly willing to affirm it. Griffith and David, each of them brought out the devil in the other, oil and water were not more irreconcilable. Between them they might yet destroy everything Llewelyn had built up.

But the builders never recognise the destroyers treading hard on their heels. If they did they would drop their tools and sit down in the sun.

"Well?" said Llewelyn. "What do you say?"

"What can I say? I am as sensible as you of the advantages, and David is very well, I could ask no better for Isabella. But remember I have four of them to set up in marriage, and Builth is a great portion."

"So is Gwynedd, my lord. I take it to be the greater of the two."

"And both will be yours, my lord, if I agree to your terms."

There was no denying that, and Llewelyn did not try. They measured each other eye to eye for a moment, and then they broke into delighted laughter. The woman sat forgotten, watching them with a small, hollow smile. She took up the pen, and delicately reshaped its point with the little knife that lay beside the ink-horn. They would be needing it soon. No doubt Ednyfed Fychan was already waiting for the summons, and wondering what took them so long.

"God He knows, my lord, what trammels we're spreading for our children. Your daughter is my stepmother, and now your son's to become my son-in-law. What does that make us two to each other? But so be it, we'll venture it. She shall bring you Builth, and you shall have your pledge of me. Your terms are accepted, my lord," said de Breos, and held out his hand to seal the bargain.

On a frosty February morning when the fringes of the sea along the salt flats by Aber were laced with snow along the tide-line, an escort of knights from Brecon rode in from the direction of Bangor to convoy their master home in state. They came with ceremony, and were received ceremoniously. Whatever the mean circumstances of de Breos's arrival in Aber, his departure was designed to wipe them out of mind.

The escort lay overnight at Llewelyn's court, and was entertained royally. Old Einion extemporised interminably on the valour, fame and prowess of the distinguished guest, and lamented his going.

"God's life!" said de Breos, listening to Harry's breathless translation, which was but a pale version of the florid original. "One would think it was a great feat of arms to be knocked off a horse by a half-grown boy leaping out of a tree. I wish he had let his imagination soar the first evening I came here, I should have been in a better conceit of myself."

"He's on the Prince now," reported Harry, frantic to keep up with the chronicle. "He's singing Cynddelw's song about the battle on the Alun, when our lord was a boy."

"Ah, I thought we should not be long in reaching Prince Llewelyn. What does he say of him? Translate!"

"He says: 'The Alun ran red with the blood of his foes that day. So perish all who injure or affront the bold darling of fortune, the great Lord Llewelyn.' "

"To which all good Welshmen must cry: 'Amen.' But I am not Welsh, I may hold my peace." And by God, I'd better, he thought, stiffening his throat against the too easily rising words. I've drunk more than enough, it would be folly to blurt out something fatal now, when I'm all but free. If this is freedom to which I go!

"You must be very happy to-night," said Harry, leaning confidently on the arm of his friend's chair.

"Happy?" The note of surprise was so light that it did not strike him how strangely it came from a man just released from prison. "To be going home? Ay, very happy!" And indeed he was laughing, and if there was irony in the laughter it passed the boy by.

And this must be the end of it, he thought, watching that formidable splendour glitter and glow at the centre of the royal table. I must go back to my wife and children and be content to be very happy. In any case, what more can there be now for a man who's known what I've known? It should be possible to live again without it somehow. I have a good reputation for keeping a high heart in deprivation and captivity. Let's see how well I deserve it. And what else I deserve, God spare me! So He may, if this be truly the end, but there is a point beyond which one should not tempt Him.

"And when you come to us again," pursued Harry blithely, "it will be as an honoured guest."

"Ay, so it will. And there'll be no occasion then for you to blush for me, even in secret." It was the first time he had ever made reference to that incident, which seemed to have slipped out of the boy's recollection as lightly, and left as little mark, as the occasional blows he got from his brothers. He half wished the words back even now; one should never ask for forgiveness, but always charm it out of people unawares; very few have the hardihood to wrest it back, once taken. But he need not have troubled, for Harry had not even marked the allusion.

"And you'll be coming to celebrate a match that makes you closer kin to us."

"True, Harry, a match very near to my heart." He heard the double meaning in his own words and was aghast. Was this how he willed that necessary ending? William, my friend, draw in your horns, he warned himself sternly. It was over. But he felt how his own heart stood out against him, and would promise nothing.

"Don't you think, my lord, that there was a purpose behind it when I was the cause of your coming here? For you see how well everything turns out. And later, perhaps in the autumn, the Prince intends to send David to court, and have the King recognise him as heir to Gwynedd. The Welsh lords have acknowledged him, and the Pope, and the King's government, too, but he has to make a state visit and do formal homage for all the lands that will be his—''

"I know it," said de Breos, letting the mead pass him by on this round. "I shall have the honour of being among his sponsors."

"—and Owen will attend him on the visit. And I—I mean to come with them, if I can get my way."

"You?" said de Breos, surprised. He looked sharply at the brown, intent face, caught the green glitter of the eyes, and understood. "Still on that cast! And what would you gain, Harry, even if you found your ancient enemy at court? Under the King's eye you'd be safe from him as he from you, but what folly to parade your name and your face before him and alert him to the threat untimely!"

"Untimely?" said the boy, burning up like a goaded fire. "I'm nearly of age, by then I shall be fully a man."

"You will be fourteen years old, and Welsh law will say you are a man, and may no longer be beaten by any of your many parents, however well you may earn it—ay, I know! But there's more than that to manhood, and not least the learning of a sound and sensible humility. Judgement and wisdom are not come by magically on your fourteenth birthday, and you'll have grave need of both before you match swords or wits with Parfois. It is not brave or noble to provoke formidable men lightly, Harry, it is only rash and presumptuous."

Words, he had once said over this same table, have a way of coming full circle into the wind and hitting in the face the fool who thinks he aimed them. These beat up into his face like spray, stinging his senses. Take them to heart, he warned himself urgently, while there's time. Rash and presumptuous you are, but draw back from this coil now, and leave the Prince of Gwynedd in peace.

"I purpose to do nothing lightly," Harry was protesting, wild to have his encouragement and good-will. "I want only to see the Lord of Parfois in his own place, to watch him and get to know his mind. How else can I ever hope to match him? Do you think I've waited so long and cannot wait a little while now to have my growth and my strength? He need not even know who I am, I shall be no more than one of David's pages, and my name he'll never hear."

"He'll never need to hear it. Your face, they tell me, is close enough to your father's image to sign you his."

Harry received the check with such dismay that it was plain he had not considered this possibility, but he rallied doggedly: "In fourteen years he may have forgotten my father."

"That, Harry, you do not believe. I've lived but distantly with your kin here, but I know this, not one of those who ever had to do with him seems to forget your father. For better or worse he was, it seems, a most memorable man. And his likeness is graven there, as you yourself told me, in the stones of his own church. No, be wise in time, Harry, let the past be. The man is old, death will be reaching for him soon without you to nudge her."

"His death belongs to me," said Harry, suddenly so low and so passionately that the question of how he thought of that lost father of his seemed to be finally and irrevocably answered. "I'll not give him up."

"Harry, Harry, I see you are a Welshman by conviction, after all. You and your *galanas*! How many fine young men have wasted their lives pursuing these endless blood-feuds? You be wiser, and live to do more for the earth than manure it with your blood. Your father would praise you for it, if he was the man I take him to have been. Stand to your rights when you must, and against your fair match. But this man is perilous."

His eyes came back, whether he would or no, to the raised chair at the centre of the royal table. The circlet of red gold in Llewelyn's still dark and lustrous hair burned like a ring of fire in the torchlight, and the face beneath the diadem was molten bronze, quick with movement and passion and energy. He had cast off his light cloak, and unlaced the cotte and shirt from a throat like the strong brown bole of a tree. The short necklace of polished amber stones throbbed and strained to his gigantic laughter.

"Have to do with men if you will, but spare to meddle with demons. Leave the lion and the leopard alone, Harry. They kill!"

In the morning the knights of Brecon rode out from Aber towards the Conway, with William de Breos at their head, and the train of his servants and pack-horses trampling off the hoar-frost for a quarter of a mile behind him.

The women watched them go from the narrow window of the Princess's apartment.

"A happy issue," said Gilleis, glancing contentedly after them along the track between the rimy fields. "Builth gained, and a powerful ally bound to David's cause. Harry fetched home a dear prize in his first battle."

Joan said nothing at all, but she stood gazing until the scarlet and gold of the flying cloak faded into a bright pin-prick against the hazy distance, and even the last infinitesimal point of light vanished in the glitter of the mist-wreathed sun.

The Prince's favourite Cistercian house of Aberconway complained of want of barn-space at its grange of Nanhwynain that autumn, and insufficient sheep-folds in its high pastures under Snowdon. Llewelyn sent his best mason, Adam Boteler, to estimate the need, and promised labour and materials for the work; and within a week Adam came home to report that there was a hard month's work on the barns alone if the brothers were to have all they wanted, and the prior, encouraged by his lord's complacency, had promptly indented for an extension to the living-quarters as well.

"I'll take a dozen or so of my own men down there this coming week," he said, tramping into Llewelyn's presence, steamy from his ride, a fine tall man in his middle forties, flaxen-haired still but for the strands on his forehead that had bleached into white without ever being tarnished with grey. "The rest of the labour I need I can raise there. God knows they'll need but little skill to heft rough-cut stones into place. I wish, my lord, you'd find me something to build with a thought more craft to it than sheep-folds. How's that lad going to learn his trade without practice? He's too easily wearied of work as it is, he'd liefer be off after hounds with Prince David, and small blame to him for that, but learn he must, if he's ever going to earn his way in the world. At Nanhwynain likely I'll be better able to keep my weather eye on him."

"He's young yet," said Llewelyn, stretching lazily with his feet spread out to the fire between the central columns of the hall. He had come in from hunting not an hour previously, well content after a brisk day, and the warmth of the room was on him like a soft, heavy cloud. "Let him run wild a little longer."

"He's young when it's work in the wind," said Adam, grinning, "but he's the first to lay claim to being a man if it's fighting or tilting, or any such play. He's game, that I will say, like his father before him, and better able to fend for himself in a fight. Harry was never any great man of his weapons. But game! I've seen him take such knocks, from lads double his size—and the little one's own son to him there. He got a fall the other day I thought would cool his ardour, but he sneezed it off as though his mother had cuffed him."

He sat back with a sigh and a smile, the big, deft hands that had cut stone for thirty years slack between his thighs. The two Harries elbowed each other in and out of his remembering eyes and dreaming voice. The one had fastened insistent hands on his life the minute the other had loosed it, dying.

"He'll not be best pleased if you take him with you to Nanhwynain," said Llewelyn, yawning. "He's set his heart on going with David to London."

"My lord, you've not promised him anything?" asked Adam, alarmed. The Prince might now and then slide side-wise out of some obligation to the English of which he could not be more directly rid, when a new and urgent heat burned old agreements out of mind; but he would never break his word once given to the boy.

"No, faith, but he may have got round Owen. David was all for refusing him out of hand, but, as fast as David denies, Owen's prone to grant. He growls, but Harry has him round his finger. For my part I shall be glad if you take the child away with you. But it's for you and his mother to fend for him as you think best."

"I think best he should settle to his craft in earnest," said Adam grimly, "and I'll take my oath his mother will think as I do. You know, my lord, why he's so set on going to court? He has that wild-goose mind of his fixed fast on the Lord of Parfois. He was prowling in ambush for him in Kerry—that we got out of him chance-come, one night when he dreamed—and you may wager he's after him now at court, having missed him there."

"Then it shows a proper spirit in him," said Llewelyn approvingly, "though I grant you he's over-young for the venture yet. I never thought of it myself. I thought he was just mad curious to see the world, like all boys."

"So with your leave I'll have him away with me into Nanhwy-nain, and let him sweat the valour out of him cutting stone." Adam rose and hitched at his chausses, stamping off the dust of travel a little stiffly. "Gilleis will sleep more easily, knowing he's with me, than thinking of him strutting in front of Isambard at Westminster with that bodkin of a sword of his."

"And faith, so will I, for I had thought once to have put the old wolf out of his reach long before this, if Wales had not kept my hands full and over-full. But Talvace was his blood, not mine. And mark me, even if you take him with you now," said Llewelyn, prophesying with certainty, "it's but to put off the day, for in the end go he will, I've seen it in him more than a year now. There's not a one of you who knew his father, Adam, not one, loves him as does this child who never knew him. He's had him from our mouths so often and so long, he's lived by him like holy writ, and maybe hated him a little while he was loving him, too, for being so far beyond all matching—I wonder did we do right to make him so fixed and fond?"

"Ah, he's taken no harm. When he thinks it gnaws him hard, but how often does he leave himself energy to think? As healthy a young animal as ever tired himself out running for love of it. He'd rather climb rocks than cut them, that's certain. We shall have enough tantrums before he reconciles himself, but his mother'll sort him. I'll go and find her," said Adam, his blue eyes gentle, and tramped away to his own lodging in search of his wife.

Gilleis heard him out with a flushed face and a hot, indignant stare. The large black eyes in her rose-and-white face dilated and glowed.

"The deceitful rogue! Not one word has he said to me about it. And I suppose he was going to confront me with it the day they mustered, armed with the Prince's promise, was he? I was to have no say in the matter! But we'll have a surprise for Master Harry when he deigns to come home from his gallivantings."

So Harry, bursting in cheerfully an hour later bruised and tumbled from wrestling with his fellows, half a swart early apple in his fist and half in his cheek, walked into a hotter welcome than he had bargained for, and was put to a hasty review of his recent undiscovered sins to account for his mother's irate face and challenging eye. Hopefully he selected the most venial, and advanced contrition like one proffering flowers.

"Is it the big pitcher? I know, Mother, I'm sorry I chipped the lip, it slipped out of my hand against the rim of the well. I meant to tell you, but I forgot." That was no lie, and owning to it now was no indiscretion, whatever the cause of her present frown, for she was bound to see the damage for herself the next time she went to draw water.

"Pitcher? Who's talking of pitchers? I've something else to say to you now, and you'll do well to listen. No, you'll not get round me like that. Let me go!"

He was already an inch or two taller than she, and strong enough to lift her in his arms. He had but to hug her tightly and she could not get free, but this time she warded off his embrace and held him at arm's-length, drawing back her hand to box his ears. He caught it by the wrist and shut a kiss into her palm. It was part of the game to parry her attacks, though they were about as formidable as the pouncings of a kitten earnestly at play.

"Harry, will you leave go of me! I'm not in fun, I tell you." And indeed she was not, she fought him off fiercely and stood confronting him with flashing eyes. "What's this I hear about your going as page to David on his visit to King Henry's court? Yes, you rogue, it's come to my ears, but not from you, dear, no! The last to hear of it from you would be your mother. It was all to be cut and dried before I knew word or hint of it, wasn't it?"

He took his hands from her, suddenly solemn, and stood looking from her to Adam and back again.

"I knew you wouldn't want to let me go," he said honestly. "I hoped I might persuade you, if the Prince gave his blessing. Where was the harm? David's my prince and my brother, why shouldn't I go with him? And think what a chance! David's great triumph, with all the English court to do him honour, and I'm not to be there? Oh, Mother, you wouldn't be so hard!"

"And the Lord of Parfois? He played no part in your plans, I suppose? Ah, you may well draw back, sir! I'm not so easily deceived."

Harry did not argue with that, though he had often found her easy enough. She was very pretty in anger, and looked like a flushed young girl, but this was no time to tell her so. He cast an appealing look at Adam, who had often stood his ally when he had needed a man's support.

"No use, my friend," said Adam, shaking his head. "Even the Prince won't help you to your own way this time. You're coming with me to Nanhwynain to build the brothers their new barns, and that's your Michaelmas jaunt, Hal. Best come to terms with it."

Harry dropped his hands and stood glaring. "I won't go!" he flamed, backing a step to have them both in his eye and share his defiance between them.

"Will you not, sir? We shall see!" Gilleis drew a calming breath. "Harry, it's time we had this out once for all. You've lived all your life with princes, and it's been small help to you in knowing what you are and which way you're to go, though God knows I've been grateful every day for their goodness to us all. But you're no prince, and no Welshman, and the sooner you own it the better for you. It's not for you to waste your time on blood feuds, it's no part of your duty to take vengeance on the Lord of Parfois. You forget these grand notions, and get to your real obligations. It's for you to learn your father's craft and grow up with your father's virtues, if you want to do him honour."

"Honour! While the man who did him to death still lives and goes his gait in peace? There isn't a free man in Wales but would spit at me! And do you say this to me, Mother? Haven't you spoken of vengeance often enough? Haven't you cursed Parfois many a time when you talked to me of my father?"

"God forgive me!" she said, paling. It was many years since she had let her bitterness break out to the child. How long was that memory of his that called her witness now for his own resolute hate? "If I did, I was at fault. Vengeance is God's business, not yours."

"And may it not be both? Doesn't God need instruments to His hand? Oh, Mother, don't keep me back, not you! He was twenty-nine years old, he had marvels still in him—you told me—"

"And so might you have in his stead," urged Adam, "if you would but apply yourself. You have a part of his gift. Use it for him, do his work."

"But I'm not my father! I've work of my own to do, and the first thing I must turn my hand to is Ralf Isambard. If he dies in his bed, I'm no man and never can be. The debt's mine, not yours. Not even yours, Mother—mine! You can't ask me to leave it unpaid."

"There are better ways of honouring your father's memory," said Adam patiently. "Master his art, and try to outdo him if you can, and he'll be prouder of you than of all the fighting men in arms. We're not nobles, lad, to meddle with life and death, we're craftsmen. It's only by long chance and royal charity you grew up in a prince's bed, and it's time you faced your own estate."

"My father was born noble," blazed Harry. "Many a time you've told me so."

"And the sequel, too. He left his nobility and chose to be a craftsman. That's your father himself pointing you your way."

"But my choice need not be his. I'm his son, not his shadow. Do you think I don't remember all you told me of him? He judged and acted like a lord, even when he was denying his birth. He treated his craft as his barony. Yes, and died for it, for his rights and his pledged word, and what prince could do more?"

He was shouting furiously and straddling defiantly as if he stood over his father's body and warned them off from defacing it. They cast one startled glance at each other, acknowledging with honest fear the justice of his argument and the shrewdness of his understanding. It seemed they had reached the point where there was only one answer to make to him, and that satisfying to nobody.

"Be that as it may," said Gilleis, reflecting back her son's glare, "you'll do as you're told, and no more nonsense. You're not going to London, that's the end of it. You'll go with Adam, and you'll work faithfully at whatever he bids you do, or I hope he'll make you rue it."

She melted then, quivering, and reached a hand to stroke away a bead of dried blood from one of the minor grazes he had got in his second fall. "Oh, Harry," she said, laughing through starting tears, "you to go bearding a man like Isambard, and you can't even hold your own yet with Meurig!"

He flung off her hand furiously. "I won't go! I won't!" he shouted, and lunged half-blindly at the door.

Adam moved with large, tolerant strides between, caught him by the arm, and with the other big, hard hand clouted his cheek lightly and turned him back into the room. It was no use struggling; Harry froze into stillness and kept his dignity. Adam could have held him one-handed and beaten him into submission without an effort, yet Harry could not remember a single occasion in his life when those capable hands had struck him anything harder than the lightest of token blows. Talvace's son, like his father before him, was everlastingly safe from any violence at Adam Boteler's hands, whatever the provocation he offered.

"Will you not?" said Adam good-humouredly, and stood him squarely before him and shook him sharply just once. "You'll come, Hal, and you'll work, never doubt it. What more you'll do hereafter we'll wait and see, and I dare say there'll be many a surprise for all of us. But as yet you're not your own master, better make up your mind to that."

Harry cast one brief, measuring look at him, and averted his eyes, but the tensed muscles relaxed a little under Adam's palms.

"And now you'll submit yourself to your mother and kiss her hand, like a good son, and let's have no more shouting and no more: 'I won't!' "

Harry went into her arms stiffly, but at the touch of her he hugged her passionately, and then tore himself loose and ran from the room, as angry with himself as with her.

She looked after him and her face was quick with anxiety and apprehension, but she said nothing more then. Only at night, lying still beside her husband in the September darkness and chill, and feeling him wakeful and aware, she stirred suddenly and said in a whisper: "Adam, he'll go. He will go. Like Harry. He'll leave me and go off after a point of honour, and I shall have no way of stopping him."

"Hush, now!" said Adam, laying his arm over her and drawing her to him. "You know you wouldn't have had the one do any other than the thing he did, and there's a piece of you fighting on the boy's side even now. But at least we'll hold him fast till he's a grown man. And think, Isambard is fully five and sixty years old by this, and his span running out. Leave time alone to take care of him, and he'll be in his grave before the lad escapes us to go looking for him.'

"Yes," she said eagerly, clinging to him, "he's old, that's true, he's old. Oh, Adam, if I lost Harry!"

She used the name as he did, for a single image that was sometimes the father and sometimes the son, and always loved out of all measure.

"You shan't lose him," he said into the cool cascade of her hair. "Never fear! Go to sleep, love, and leave fretting."

He held her until she slept in his arms, the slight weight cradled against his heart. The feel of her littleness moved him achingly, and the clinging of her hands was a painful sweetness, for he knew that what they embraced in him was still the frail image, the residue that Harry Talvace had left there, the print of years of love and brotherhood. Often in the early nights of their marriage she had stirred out of her sleep and reached out to him, calling him by Harry's name. And what right had he to resent that or any other mark of his subservience, he who had taken her to himself to establish his lifelong claim to both the Harries, the living and the dead?

But fourteen years is a long, long time for two people to walk delicately together, trusting and sparing each other and living by the same secret light. And now, holding her gently on his breast and feeling the soft cadences of her breath in the hollow of his throat, he knew that they had something there between them that was more than tenderness and better than forbearance. He felt it to be love; he did not question for whom.

Chapter Three

Aber: *Easter* 1230

Adam wrote from Nanhwynain at the beginning of April, in the clerkly hand he had learned long ago at Shrewsbury Abbey and never forgotten:

"All goes well here and the work well forward, by reason of the early end to the frosts. The walls unbedded of their furze and well set, and the brothers well content with their barns, so your Grace shall be sure of grateful prayers. With the boy I am well pleased since we came back here. He takes well enough to the craft here, where he has not so many sports to be enjoyed. He has not his father's skill in carving, but does moderate well, and has a fine eye for line and proportion, and a will to perfection, and all in all as good a lad as ever stepped when he puts his mind to it, and nothing grudging in him. With your Grace's leave I purpose to remain here through the Easter feast, the weather continuing so fair for building, and the brothers being so urgent for possession of the enlargement to their house. My prayers shall not be wanting for your Grace's health and prosperity, and for the blessing of God on the union so soon to crown your Grace's happiness."

Llewelyn replied, with Easter only a few days away:

433

"Since Harry has satisfied you, as I well knew he could if he had a mind to it, he has surely earned a holiday. Let him come home for the feast, and he'll work with a better heart when we send him back to you. My lord de Breos has forsook the King's court for mine on this occasion, the King being in any case set on proceeding to Portsmouth to embark for France, and his lordship asks particularly after the boy, who is a fixed favourite with him. It is surely a Christian act to content them both, so let him come."

And Harry came, armed for the journey with Adam's reluctant permission and the Prior's blessing. He had been resigned to spending a frugal Easter with the brothers and watching dutifully through the vigils of Good Friday, but all his devout thoughts took wing wildly, like startled birds, when the Prince's welcome command was cast among them. By the time he was three miles up the valley he had pocketed his cap and was galloping like a child let out of school, and singing as he rode. One holiday now, and soon another for David's wedding, and the budding world so beautiful and diverse!

He had only begun to discover its real subtleties when he began to carve them. To have made a leaf is truly to have seen a leaf for the first time. What manifold delights God must know! And to have made man! Such a piece of work, for instance, as my lord de Breos, so express and wonderful in movement, so admirable in proportion and form. He thought again of the smooth, taut action of the muscles round that handsome mouth as it played its dazzling repertoire of smiles, from the first almost imperceptible quivering to the loud, gay, explosive laughter; and of the slow, beautiful raising of the arched eyelids as they opened on stunned dark eyes, that first dawn in the grass by the Mule. Masterly sculpture, far out of his reach; and yet these could be made again in stone, and even the secondary form would carry a deep satisfaction in it. He was beginning to love stone.

But the ride was long, and by the time he was half-way to Aber his fingers had lost the sense of creation, and he thought no more of stone. There were other ways of looking at that admirable engine of flesh and blood and bone, other ways of delighting in it. Better have it articulated and active and aware of itself than fixed and final, however beautiful. The arms to wrestle and embrace, the hands to hold and direct weapons, the legs to dance and grip a horse. Better just once to see de Breos ride at a gallop than make ten stone copies of his and the horse's action; better but once to hear him shout with laughter than to draw, however perfectly, the mechanics of his mirth.

Harry rode in at the gates of Aber enchanted with being and doing, and content to let others make.

The village outside the maenol was busy and populous, and the sunlight quivered over the fresh greens of the hills, uncurling with new bracken like the prodigious carved fronds that hold up the vaults of churches. Within the courtyard there was bustle and colour and energy everywhere, and about the kitchens frenzy. The stables boiled with horses, and there were new pavilions encrusted along the curtain wall to house the train of knights who had ridden in from Brecon. This time de Breos came with ceremony and impressively attended, and everywhere about the kennels and the mews his livery glittered.

It was Maundy Thursday, and they were just coming from Mass, the two magnificent dark men together; de Breos's hand was familiarly on Llewelyn's shoulder, and the matched dozens of their followings streamed after them. The Princess walked on de Breos's other side, silent and tall and slender in blue and white. She looked like an opening flower, she who had raised five children and weathered twenty-five years of care and intrigue and vigilance. She walked with her eyes fixed ahead, faintly smiling as the velvet of her sleeve brushed the brocade of his, and the dew and glow of the spring was on her like a shaft of sunlight on the hills.

Harry's heart liquefied with love at sight of her. He slid hastily from the saddle and ran to meet them, falling on his knee at the Prince's feet.

"Ah, my little archer!" cried de Breos. "I missed you at the gate to see me come."

Llewelyn took him up and kissed him heartily.

"Not so little now. He's grown like a bean in a wet summer, this year and more since you've seen him. Rising fifteen, and a voice on him like a young bull, as you'll find soon enough."

De Breos marked with a secret, sympathetic convulsion of his own vitals the tension of delight that transfixed the slender young body as Joan embraced it in her turn.

"Your mother will be happy, Harry. We've missed you. Well, my lord, do you find him much changed?"

She held him off by the arm to be admired, a tall, slim fifteen-year-old just beginning to put on the proportions and the form of manhood. Large and deft of foot and hand, but not yet sure of his body, he moved with the darting, tentative, unfinished motions of young animals. The brows above the green eyes were level and black, and straight as his wide, resolute mouth. Eyes and mouth smiled together for pleasure in the April world and his holiday, and the presence of people who contained for him much of the charm of living. He coloured easily, but with excitement and delight, not with shyness.

"A long leap nearer what he was always meant to be," said de Breos, throwing about the boy's shoulders the arm that had lain so gracefully upon Llewelyn's only a moment ago. "Not otherwise changed, I thank God! When first I met him he was already too much of a man for me. And what have you been doing, Harry, all this while since last I saw you? Have you brought home prisoner any more crushed adversaries?"

"There have been no wars since Kerry," said Harry practically.

"What, not even between cantrefs?"

"No, my lord. Gwynedd does no raiding now, you're living in the past."

"I wish you would tell my steward, he suffers from a strange dream that certain enterprising Welshmen cross the border now and then and prick out a few head of cattle for themselves. And how have you fared with your prize of war? You have the length of leg for him now."

"Nobly, my lord," cried Harry, glowing, and drew breath to praise his chestnut horse; but Joan laid her hand on his arm and reminded him gently: "Your mother's waiting, Harry."

"Madam, I'll go to her. My lord, with your leave! Will you not come to the stables afterwards, and see for yourself how I have used him? I groom him myself, he stands like stone for me, but he plays the devil with the stable-boys."

"I'll come, gladly," said de Breos, laughing to see the boy with-draw with first an eager leap towards his mother, and then a reluctant moment of walking backwards, still with his eyes on them. He turned at last, with a final inclination of his head, and fled at a headlong run towards the Princess's apartments, where at this hour Gilleis was sure to be.

He burst in upon her at her trestle table, busy cutting out the narrow, intricate sleeves of a new gown for the Princess, and flung himself into her arms so impetuously that he all but impaled himself on her long scissors. She held them away from him and let them clatter from her hand upon the table, and hugged him and laughed and wept over him. He took that as no more than his due, and stayed only long enough to pour out for her all the news of himself and Adam before he was off again to the buttery to coax food out of the maids for his perpetual hunger, and then to the stables to see his favourite properly cared for. There de Breos came to him as he had promised, and leaned in the doorway to watch the grooming, careless of his scarlet and gold finery.

"You have him in fine fettle. I see he fell into good hands." He patted the glossy neck, and stroked with the tips of long, sensitive fingers the white diamond on the dark red brow.

"Harry," he said, low-voiced, "I have an errand for you, if you are pleased to be my confidant in a particular secret."

"Gladly!" said Harry, flattered. "What is it you want me to do?"

"A small thing and easy for you. I have a design to make a present to the Prince when David marries my girl. I want to give him two good litters of my own hounds, five couple that I bred out of my best deerhound bitches by an Arabian sire Gloucester has from the East. They make the best and swiftest van chasseours that ever I met with. I've known them bring down the hart themselves, and leave no work for the parfytours. But I have a childish fancy to keep my gift a secret, and bring the hounds here privily to astonish the Prince when the wedding-day comes. And that's impossible unless I have the Princess's help."

"She'll give it gladly," said Harry, straightening up for a moment to wriggle out of his cotte. He emerged ruffled and flushed to ask: "Does she know what you intend?"

"Not yet. For I never see her but the Prince is with us. I would have you tell her for me, Harry, some time when there's no one else by, for you're privileged. Ask her of her grace to make some occasion when we can speak of this together, and see how it is to be done. If she'll give me the word when the time is right we can whip the hounds into the kennels and have them ready for him, and no one the wiser."

"I'll speak to her this very evening," said Harry willingly. "I never miss going to say good night to her after she leaves the hall."

"That's my true heart! But mind, not a word to any other. One whisper is enough in such a warren as this, and every kitchen-boy knows it within a day."

"Trust me! If it reaches any but the three of us until the day comes you may take my Barbarossa back again."

"That's a pledge indeed! And you'll be her messenger back to me? It will need but half an hour together, and the plot is laid."

"I'll be her messenger."

"You shall have a puppy for yourself from the next litter," said de Breos warmly, and reached an imperious hand over the chestnut's arched neck. "Give me a cloth, Harry, I can keep my hands from him no longer."

They finished the grooming together, in strong content with each other, and boy-like dismayed at the powerful scent of the stables that clung to de Breos's brocade by the end of it. "No matter," said he, shrugging it off with bravado, "my wife's not here to scold."

In the clamour and brilliance of the hall that night de Breos leaned on Llewelyn's arm, and they drank cup for cup, laughing together, as that day they did all things together, every word and gesture an earnest of their new amity.

"I'd give this ring," said de Breos, "to have de Burgh walk in at that door now and see us so fond."

"I doubt the sight would give him no pleasure," said Llewelyn.

"But his face would afford me entertainment for a month after. I wish our good justiciar no harm, but one reverse will do him none, and it's not only among the Welsh that this union will be seen as a check to a power that was growing too insolent. It was no part of my designs to fall into your hands and set this arrow flying, my lord, but I'm as willing as you now to see it close its course with a hit. It's the mead, no doubt," he said, laughing, "but I begin to be glad your little archer brought me down at the ford of the Mule.

Faith, I'm in such spirits I begin to feel I've got the best of the bargain."

The faint sounds of music from the hall drifted on the darkness, curling past the windows of the tower upon a wandering wind. Joan stood with her back to the room, the cloak of her brown hair about her, listening to the light footsteps moving about the bed.

"You need not wait, Gilleis," she said without turning her head. "I'm tired, I shall sleep early. You go to your bed, too."

"After so many late nights," owned Gilleis, smiling as she turned down the covers, "I shan't be sorry to lie longer, and nor will you, madam, I dare say. Though I won't say we're so pleased to lie alone. I miss Adam when he stays so long away. Where will the Prince sleep to-night? He won't remain at Degannwy?"

"No, he'll ride back to Aberconway and spend the night there, he has business with the Prior."

She was taciturn to-night, her voice cool and distant even when she spoke. It still displeased her when Llewelyn turned in his abrupt way to show some tenderness to his elder son who was none of hers, and no doubt she resented it that he should steal one whole day and night from the feast to visit Griffith in his enforced retirement. Not that the Prince had ever wavered in his fixed determination that David alone should succeed him. No, it was a more irrational fear that made her so implacable against any acknowledgement of the relationship; fear of Welsh law that gave the bastard rights equal to his brother's, and of Welsh perversity that veered obstinately to him because his mother was a lady of Rhos and not the daughter of an English king, and because he had their own impetuous and insubordinate temperament, and such a grievance as they loved.

"You should not mind that he is fond even of this stranger child of his," said Gilleis in her gay and gentle voice, that could venture so far into territory forbidden to other women. "It would be shame if he did not cherish his own. And well you know David has no rival with him. Hasn't he made sure and doubly sure David shall be his only heir?"

"He gave Griffith Meirionydd and Ardudwy once," said Joan.

"And took them back from him fast enough when he found he plundered his own territories like an alien raider. And hasn't he kept him fast under lock and key since his threats against David grew too bold? You know he'll never suffer Gwynedd to fall into any hands but David's.''

Yes, she knew it. No one but David, close kin to the English king and strong in a title legitimate by English law as well as Welsh, could have any chance of holding the principality together and perpetuating what his father had created. Even if the Prince had loved the two half-brothers equally—and the wild, defiant elder, by his very likeness to his sire, alienated love as often as he attracted it—he would have staked the future on David. Wanting any other inducement, thought Gilleis, watching the tall, slender figure with an affectionate smile, he would have laid all his conquests and achievements in David's lap for his mother's sake.

"Don't grudge him a day," she said, "now David has Gwynedd and Builth and bride and all."

"Did I seem to grudge it when he told me he was going?"

"No, bless you, you gave him your good word to take with him."

And that in itself was remarkable, and Llewelyn had not failed to notice it. Gilleis had seen the quick, piercing look he had cast at his wife. Her only frowns, her only inimical silences, had to do with Griffith.

"Leave me now, Gilleis. But tell Harry to come and say good night to me at once, for I shall be sleeping soon."

Gilleis kissed her hand and her cheek, and went to look for Harry in the hall. It was still early, and with the Prince and his immediate train absent, the knights of Brecon, and the Welsh freemen, and the privileged men of the bodyguard had taken possession, and were dancing to pipe and harp and the clapping of hands. Harry came out to his mother flushed and breathless, to listen to her message where she could make her voice heard.

"And why don't you come and sleep the night with me, Hal, afterwards? With David and Owen both gone as far as Aberconway with the Prince, what merit is there in guarding an empty lodging?''

But she knew he would not; he cherished his privileges dearly. She sighed and laughed, and kissed him. "There, then, run to the Princess." And she twitched her cloak over her head and ran in her turn, for a soft, clinging rain had begun, hanging on the night air like heavy dew.

Joan was sitting at her mirror when Harry entered the room, as many a time lately he had seen her sit and gaze silently into her own face. It seemed to him that there was a special tenderness in her touch that night, and that speech came to her with difficulty, though when she spoke her voice was low and even as he had always known it.

"Harry, I recall that you asked a few days ago for an audience in private for my lord de Breos. In the matter of these marvellous hounds of his."

"I've heard they're all he claims," said Harry eagerly, thinking he caught a faint note of irony in the beloved voice. "I've heard tell of them from others besides my lord himself. It will be a princely gift."

"I never doubted that," she said with a shadowy smile. "Well, it's yet early, and the opportunity offers, my lord de Breos may come to me now, since he's so urgent for secrecy. Let him have his child's pleasure of surprising the Prince, if he wants it so much. Go and bring him to me. But discreetly, remember he's on secret business. Bring him by the passage through the armoury, he will not know that way alone."

"He's still in hall," said Harry, springing up willingly. "I'll go to him at once."

"Then let him say his good nights, and seem to be going to his bed, so that no one will look for him back or wonder where he's bound. Since the game is his we must play it his way."

"He makes all things play his way," said Harry laughing. "It's raining now, there'll be no one stirring."

"That's well. And, Harry!"

"My lady?" He swung about, his hand already outstretched to the door.

"Not a word to anyone. We must keep his secret faithfully."

"On my life!" said the boy fervently, and only half in jest, and ran down the staircase and back through the rain to slip unobserved into the hall.

The weather, the hour, the occasion, all were with him. Some of the elders had already withdrawn, and some of the knights, finding Welsh entertainment tried their endurance too far, had followed the old men's example. The men-at-arms and the servant girls, the brewers and the bakers and the huntsmen and the grooms had taken the music below the fire with them; and they, who had to be up and hard at work by dawn, would never prolong the night too far.

He looked for de Breos, but the lord of Brecon was not at the high table. He had already done his part perfectly in ignorance, and betaken himself to his own room. Harry found him half undressed, lying flat on his belly on his fur-draped bed, his chin on his fists, restlessly awake and fretted by his own company. He welcomed the boy gladly and boisterously, throwing an arm about him and drawing him close.

"My lord, I'm charged with a message to you. From the Princess Joan."

De Breos was up in a moment, the fur coverlet swirling from his vehement spring. "God bless you for a good lad, Harry!" His face was vivid in the lamplight, the eyes brilliant and solemn. "What says the Princess Joan?"

"She says I am to take you to her."

"Now? Ah, you brought me luck as always you bring it!" He was on his feet, light and quick as a cat, smoothing his black hair before the glass, stamping his feet into his soft leather shoes. "Give me my cotte, there, Harry! So, you'll make a good squire yet. There, am I presentable?"

He was far more than that, he glowed in the dim light, smiling into the boy's dazzled eyes, that only once, and for how short a time, had seen in him something less than perfection.

"Well, take me! We mustn't keep my lady waiting."

They let themselves out into the soft, clinging rain, and de Breos surrendered himself to the boy's hands, and followed where he was led, by devious ways beyond the new pavilions to the passage behind the armoury, and so in darkness and blindness in the moonless night to the tower. All night thereafter Harry felt his fingers tingling from the grip of that long, vital hand as his friend trod trustingly on his heels.

They climbed the stairs softly. Joan was sitting in her high-backed chair, and as they entered she rose and came a few paces to meet them. The long braid of her hair hung to her waist, fair against the dark blue of her gown, and her face was pale and bright.

"Madam, here is my lord de Breos."

"My lord," she said, hardly louder than the whisper of the rain, "you asked to see me."

"Madam, that was my desire."

"Come in, cousin, and welcome."

To Harry she said, level and low: "Go to bed now, child. Good night!" She kissed him. He had never felt in her lips such poignant sweetness, her touch had never been so lingeringly fond.

"Madam, good night! Good night, my lord!"

He slipped away down the stairs, his heart swelling with pride and pleasure, the confidant of his lady, the trusted friend of the lord of Brecon. The hall was still flickering with torchlight, but the music had ceased, and one by one the flames were burning down.

He ran through the rain to his own silent, empty room, but he was too excited and alert to want to go to bed, and with Owen and David absent there was no one to order his going. He threw himself down just as he was, and lay hugging the satisfaction of his secret, so content in his solitary wakefulness that he had no idea of the passing of time or the gradual stilling of every sound about him as the maenol sank to sleep; until at length he, too, slept, wandering over the threshold as lightly and innocently as an infant.

It was the barking of a dog that awakened him; one short, wild burst, and then the sound tailed off, appeased, into silence, but for Harry's quick ears it was enough. He started up in a quiver of concentration, alarmed but unafraid. He had no notion how long he had been asleep, and his senses quested out into the stillness and quietness, challenging the thing he had heard. Why had the hound given tongue? They never spoke at night without a reason. And if someone was stirring, and had roused him, why had he suddenly fallen silent, as though satisfied? Someone had answered him, and someone he knew well.

Harry slid off the bed and crossed to the door, looking out into the dark towards the gate. Somewhere in that direction there was a murmur of voices, subdued and brief, the muted pacing of a horse's hooves on the hardened earth, others following. Who could ride into Aber in the night and hush the dogs with a word?

There could be only one answer, but he went shivering out into the night to be sure, his heart beating vehemently now, and the piercing cold of his sudden awakening shaking him from head to foot. From the corner of the armoury he saw a lantern at the gate, and two men of the guard reaching to the bridles of steaming horses. He saw the foremost rider's cloak billow as he dismounted, and he knew the long, light pace that sprang from the earth resilient as a child's though it belonged to a man already growing old. Two steps were enough for him, even in the dark, and by now there was a faint, lambent light softening the blackness, and the clinging rain had ceased.

Through what uncharacteristic change of plan he could not guess, Llewelyn had foresaken Aberconway after all, and ridden home to his own maenol and his own bed.

Harry found himself running almost before he knew why, confused but determined. The secret had been entrusted to him, and he would see it kept. De Breos might well be already fast asleep in his own quarters, but the time that had passed could not be long. Why should the Prince decide to ride home, unless he had found his business with the Prior completed in time to allow him to cover the miles between and still enjoy a night's rest in his own chamber? Had it been very late he would have stayed, as he had intended. For all Harry knew it was not yet half an hour since he had conducted de Breos to the Princess's presence, and their planning not yet completed.

Roundabout in the dark he wound his way to the royal tower. The Prince must not break in upon them now and spoil all, and it was surely in the direction of his own apartments that he had set off at such a pace from the gate-house. He could go directly, but Harry must go deviously and keep out of sight. If de Breos was long gone, and the Princess already asleep, then nothing worse had happened than the waste of a little energy and a little breath, of both of which commodities Harry had plenty, even at midnight.

He ran confidently out from the passage behind the armoury, and plunged into the deep doorway, and into Llewelyn's arms.

A sharp, faint cry was startled out of him, not of fear, only of astonishment. He flung his arms round the hard, lean body to keep his balance, and panted: "My lord!" on a gusty breath, nearer to laughter than alarm. If there were two within, and they needed a warning, then this flurry at the door would surely suffice; now he had only to draw the Prince off for a few minutes, and all was well.

"Harry, you here?" said Llewelyn, and tightened his great hands on him and dragged him in at the door. There were others behind him, three or four as yet unrecognisable in the darkness, but not David, not Owen. Why had he left them behind when he himself rode for home? "What are you doing abroad at this hour?"

For the first time he felt a thin, terrifying doubt rise in him like nausea. The big hands had never held him like this, they hurt his arms and sent sharp cramps tingling down into his fingers. And the full, fiery voice that had often roared at him without frightening him was tight and low now, and chilled his senses, but he would not believe in fear.

He lied valiantly: "My lord, I heard you come, I heard the dogs. Will you not come to the kennels just for a minute? I went to look at Marared, and I'm anxious about her. It's her first litter—and she's restless and whining. I'm feared all's not well with her. If you'd come and look—"

A torch came glowing in at the door, carried by someone he was too agitated to identify. And why were they all so silent? Llewelyn plucked him round to face the light, and now he could see, dark against the brightness and yet sufficiently defined, the loved and revered hawk-face. It stared at him terribly from under drawn brows, the far-sighted eyes piercing him redly, the long mouth a stony line. He hardly recognised it. His heart failed in him. He groped with numbed fingers for a hold on the Prince's sleeves, understanding nothing, only afraid.

"Is that what you were doing, up and dressed in the night? Why lie to me? What end can lying serve now?"

"Why should I lie? She's fevered—if only you'd come to her, you know what's best to do."

The hands that held him jerked him round and drove him towards the staircase. "My lord!" he implored, his voice breaking in a child's whimper. "What is it? What have I done?"

"Ay, what have you done? Come, and let's see!"

He was thrust mercilessly up the stairs, stumbling and panting but silent now like them, astray in such a wilderness of fear that he hardly knew what was happening to him. The Prince stretched a hand forward over the boy's shoulder and hurled open the door of the bedchamber.

In the great bed there was a sudden convulsion of movement that broke in two with a cry, and the naked lovers started upright and apart, staring into the torchlight with dilated eyes of horror.

The breath went out of Harry's body in a gusty, voiceless cry, as though a mailed fist had driven a violent blow into him below the heart. The pain was physical and terrifying, darkening his vision and softening his bones. His knees gave under him, and he fell in a heap of shocked flesh, retching over fists doubled hard into his middle. He was wailing out of his agony: "No! No! No!" over and over in a frenzy of protest, but there was no breath in him to give voice to his cries.

"*This* is what you have done. Look at it! Look well!"

Llewelyn took him by the hair and jerked up his head, dragging him forward until he leaned upon the end of the bed. He could not avert his face, he could not turn aside; but there was nothing there he had not seen already in that first instantaneous revelation, and it was in his eyes now open or closed, it would be in them even when he slept and make his dreams hideous. He crouched helpless under the prisoning hand, feeling the great dull anguish within him grow hot and expand to fill him to the finger-tips, to the end of every hair.

He had adored her, picked his way by her as by a fixed star; and here he saw only a loose woman taken in the act, a poor naked woman stricken and shamed, holding up the covers to hide pallid, weary breasts that drooped with the burden of forty years. Her face was tired and lined. He saw for the first time the grained lines round her mouth, the softness of the pale flesh at her throat, the dry, colourless tint of dust dimming the long hair. An old face, a soiled face, that might have belonged to a dead woman but for the fixed and dreadful stare of the grey eyes. Beside her the man crouched, tensed like a handsome beast hunted to exhaustion, and a long tress of her hair lay over his shoulder and hung down upon his naked breast. His black eyes, stretched wide with desperate bravery, glared back at Llewelyn, but Harry saw his fear as naked as his too admirable body. The print of them both went into him and stamped itself on his vision for ever.

Joan said, and from first to last they were the only words she spoke that night: "Let the boy go." Her voice was unbelievably heavy and slow, as though the words were stones she could hardly lift. "He's blameless, he knew no wrong. Can you not see it? Let him go!"

Harry felt the clutch of the hard fingers in his hair relax, and in a moment relinquish him. He fell against the skirts of the bed, and dragging himself to his feet with crippled, clumsy movements ran dementedly out of the room, blundering past the silent men who stood aside to give him passage. They heard his broken running on the stairs, growing faster and wilder as it faded, and then he was gone into the darkness and quietness of the night outside, and they forgot him; or if any remembered it was the woman, still and mute among the shards of her shattered world.

De Breos stretched a hand out almost stealthily and reached for his cotte.

"No," said Llewelyn harshly, "let it lie. Get up, my lord, let me see what manner of delights you offered her that you got the tree to bow."

Scarlet stained the fine cheek-bones in the pale face. Slowly de Breos put back the covers and rose from the bed. He stood erect and stared straight, refusing acknowledgement to shame, as the Prince looked him over from head to foot and back again to the face.

"I did not think there was the man anywhere on earth, my lord, could do what you have done. Take it for your comfort. Not every baron of England achieves an unparalleled deed before he dies. Well, cover yourself. It cannot be repeated. You do not dazzle me."

De Breos wrapped his cotte about him with hands that were trembling with recovering fear, live fear that would not accept an ending. The first death was over, he mustered to his support all that he was, Brecon and Builth and Hay and all the manifold complexities of his honour. He should have felt a host at his back, but they seemed to him a world away, even the handful who snored in Llewelyn's new pavilions at this moment.

He tried to look at Joan, but he could not bear the sight for long.

She had not moved. The great eyes, grey and void as glass, stared at Llewelyn without change or expression, but somewhere within them there was a deep, disquieting spark coming to birth, and something warned de Breos that he would do well to turn his own eyes away, never to see it, at all costs to avoid understanding it.

Llewelyn wrenched his head aside, and they saw his mouth contorted by one awful convulsion of grief.

"In the name of God," he said in a suffocating voice, "cover yourself, madam!"

She crept from the bed as though infinitely tired, and drew on her gown with blind movements of hands that were past trembling. She was not afraid; fear would have been irrelevant now, when she had already pulled down the roof over her own head. She stood silent still, watching Llewelyn, and the consciousness behind her blank eyes had drawn nearer to the surface; a little while, and it would show through.

"So it was truth they told me," said Llewelyn, uncovering the fierce dark face that would not betray him again. "I laughed at it first. Then I was angry that they should think me fool enough to credit so clumsy an attempt to damage the strength we had between us. I made the assay to prove they lied. And all I have done is prove it true. Well, speak! Have you nothing to say in your own excuse?"

Her lips moved, saying: "Nothing!" but there was no sound.

"Call the guard," said Llewelyn without turning his head. "Have them take into ward all the knights of Brecon who came here with this felon and thief, and see them made fast in irons. Then bid them come for these."

"My lord, my men have no part in this, the crime is mine only." De Breos moistened his dry lips with a tongue that rasped like leather. Two of the men who stood silent behind Llewelyn turned and went from the room.

"My lord, your men pay for being a traitor's fellows, as you for being a traitor, a spoiler of the house where you were a guest."

The pale and desperate face could grow no paler, nor could anything now call back the blood to his cheeks. "I deny nothing of my fault. I take the guilt upon me for what I have done, and beg you to hold her to be as deeply wronged as you. The thing was my doing,

I planned it, I got my way of her. Of your grace, let me stand to it with the sword."

"I would not ask the meanest among my bodyguard to meet you in arms. You have put yourself outside the grace of honourable men. Stand to it with the law, like other felons."

"So be it!" said de Breos, stiffening his back. "But let me tell you this, my lord, I do not repent me of what I've done. No, whatever it cost me! It was worth all I have to have had your lady's love, as she has mine. Dispose of me how you will, yet I did and do love her, and shall until the day I die."

It was said for her, and she did not hear and would not see him. The only last comfort he could have had in this nadir of his fortunes, and she did not grant it. It seemed to him that she did not know he was there. She watched Llewelyn, and counted over the wreckage she had made, and the light behind her eyes had burned into such unimaginable purity of anguish that it illuminated for him his own eternal loss no less than hers. By that light they saw coldly and clearly at last. All the evidence was assembled, everything fell into proportion. There had never been one moment in their association when she would not have sacrificed him and all he meant to her to smooth one line out of Llewelyn's forehead.

She had not always known it, but she knew it now, as she assessed and told over within her husband's face all that she had forfeited, all that she had brought into danger, all that she had broken and destroyed. She would have torn out her own heart and her lover's to restore it.

Heavy feet trod uneasily on the stairs below. A dozen armed men came into the room, muffling their weapons and moving softly for awe of the unbelievable disaster that was fallen upon Aber. They laid hands with implacable gentleness upon de Breos, and looked at Llewelyn for orders, hesitating to touch Joan. She had been flesh of that princely, outraged flesh so long, to ravish her was to assault the sovereignty of Gwynedd, almost to blaspheme against order and God.

"Take them away," said Llewelyn.

De Breos made no resistance when they led him to the door. He passed close to Joan, looking with longing into her fixed countenance, and she moved her head without a glance at him, so that he should not for more than a second blot out for her Llewelyn's face.

"My lord," said de Breos with a crooked smile, "if you but knew it your debt to me is already paid."

Harry lay all night long curled under the covers of his solitary bed, tensed and aching with wakefulness, contorted with complex pains that would not let him lie quiet for a moment. Even there it was not dark enough for him, and even there he found no safety, for with the dawn he would have to emerge and face the light that waited to assault him. He knotted his fists into his eyes, but he could not rub out what he had seen, and the memory of it ate into his brain like some fearful corrosion that could never again be slaked away. He sobbed into his pillow without the alleviation of a single tear, coiled about the burden of his love and hate and shame and rage like a wild beast about its death-wound.

They had betrayed him vilely, taken his worship and trust and turned it to their own hateful uses. Worse, they had caused him to betray his prince and foster-father. Who would ever believe he had acted in innocence? And even if they believed him, how was he helped? To have been such a blind, gullible tool was almost worse than being a traitor. How could she have done it? How could she have destroyed his image of her, that immaculate image of which he had had no doubts at all? Distrust the Princess? Question whatever she chose to do? It would have been like doubting the integrity of God Himself! In all that lifetime of majesty when had she ever failed of being whole and incorruptible?

Deeper than the injury to his pride, though that cut to the heart, deeper than the loss of his honour and the shock to his faith lay the wound to his love for her, not more than half-understood, but felt with every fibre of his flesh and spirit.

That was at the beginning of the interminable night. But by the end of it, when the light began to penetrate within the folds of his bedding and prick his raging sensitivity like knives, his dishonour had taken pride of place in the catalogue of his martyrdoms. At all costs he must clear himself in the Prince's eyes, justify his actions, however foolish, however childishly confiding, and be received back into his old position of trust. It was not that he wanted to avoid blame; he blamed himself. Or punishment, if he was held to have merited punishment more than he already suffered. But he could not bear to be condemned as a mean traitor, the affront to his self-respect was unendurable.

He dragged himself shivering out of the bed, made himself presentable, and went to beg an audience of Llewelyn, steeled to such a pitch of resolution that he had thrust his way past the guards at the foot of the private staircase and was half-way through the knot of agitated officials in the ante-room before the chamberlain noticed him and haled him back by the arm.

"Let me in to him," said Harry fiercely. "I have always free access to him, you can't keep me out."

"Not to-day. And if you're wise you'll not wish for it. Be off and let my lord alone, this is no place for you," said the harassed chamberlain, and thrust him out at the door.

He slipped back again less boldly when no one was watching, and crept along the wall into the darkest corner, with ears stretched for the fearful whispers that were being passed from man to man through the room. David and Owen, it seemed, had been left behind at Aberconway, and knew nothing yet of any disaster. That had been done of design, clearly, to preserve David from the horror of his mother's disgrace and have his good brother at his side to bear him company if the news flew too fast to meet him. Harry's ears burned indignantly, hearing his own name pass. His part was known, though how judged he could not tell from the snatch of words he caught. They were talking of the politics of catastrophe, of David's imperilled match, of King Henry's shadow like a shield over his great tenant's head, of possible war, of the news flying hot-foot through Wales, and the ancient enemies of the de Breos clan taking joyfully to horse and heading for Aber. It would cost William a deal more than one castle, they were saying, to get safe out of this coil.

Harry wormed his way to the inner door, and was making himself small in the shadow behind it when Ednyfed Fychan came out, grim-faced, to despatch a messenger. The boy was in Llewelyn's presence before anyone could reach a hand to halt him, and had slipped round the court judge's slow bulk and flung himself on his knees at Llewelyn's feet.

"My lord, be just to me! Let me speak! Visit it on me as you will, only don't believe me traitor."

The Prince looked down at him with hollow-rimmed eyes burning in a gaunt face drawn by anger and grief to a semblance of starvation. He was expressly handsome and elegantly-appointed that morning, the short silken beard that encircled his lips and outlined the strong bones of his jaw glossily combed, his dark, curling hair carefully groomed. Even the movement of his hand towards Ednyfed as the seneschal re-entered the room was measured and controlled, and apparently without passion, yet they all felt the titanic tremors of the covered fire, and stepped with wincing care, holding back from the limit of its blaze.

"Put him out," said Llewelyn.

"You should not be here, boy," said Ednyfed shortly, vexed but not unkind. "You heard his Grace. Out!"

There were three of them beside Ednyfed, the chaplain-secretary, the judge and the captain of the bodyguard, the highest inner council of Llewelyn's court. All of them looked down at the wild-eyed boy and frowned him away, but he would not take the warning. When Ednyfed with fraying patience took him by the arm, he leaned forward desperately and laid hold on Llewelyn's knees.

"My lord, give me justice! I swear I didn't betray you, I'm not the wretch you think me. I didn't know—"

The Prince's chair screamed upon the boards of the floor as he thrust it back, withdrawing his person abruptly out of reach.

"I bade you go. Have I to give orders twice? Now go!"

The captain of the guard rose and took hold of the boy by the other arm, but Harry fought him off passionately and followed Llewelyn on his knees, sobbing with vehemence.

"My lord, believe me or kill me! I won't be thought traitor. I won't rise from my knees until you hear me. I didn't know that they—that she—They both lied to me!"

Fire blazed at him for one instant from the deep eyes hollowed with the memory of the long night. Llewelyn clenched his fist and drew back his arm, saw the quivering frantic face jerk with apprehension and palely maintain its ground, waiting for the blow. He sprang out of his chair and away to the draped wall beside the narrow window, gripping the tapestry until the murderous lust had left his hands.

And all for this child's little, fledgling honour, that hurt him no more than a toothache, while the world others had spent a lifetime constructing fell to pieces round them and the tendons of their hearts were severed one by one. Some day there would be a time for appeasing him with the justice he wanted, a time for comforting him, but not yet; he was too sharp a reminder of intolerable pain and loss, it was impossible to look at him or speak to him without revulsion.

"Take him away," said Llewelyn hoarsely, without turning his head, "before I forget whose son he is and do him an injury. God's blood, he shames his father's memory!"

The fist could never have dealt him such a killing blow. For a second time he recoiled stunned into his darkened vision and nerveless flesh, feeling the heavy anguish of despair gather ponderous and hot inside him like molten lead. They put him out, not roughly, and shut the door against him, and he could neither resist nor speak. But in any case there was nothing more to be done, nothing more to be asked. He knew the worst of it now.

When he could make his numbed legs serve him again he took refuge in the remotest corner of the kennels, and hid in the straw there to fight out for himself the implications of his utter rejection.

He was disbelieved and dishonoured, cast out of the Prince's favour for ever. Even in his own eyes his status was lost. He shamed his father's memory! That rankled and festered until all his Talvace blood rose to accuse him. He might never be able to restore himself in the Prince's regard, but he must, if he was to live with himself at all, do something prodigious to redeem himself in his own estimation, and wipe out that affront. There was only one way in which he could demonstrate before all the world how he respected his father's memory, and how worthy he was to maintain it.

To stay here longer was impossible; Aber had cast him out. But after all, he was a man now; his father had been just the same age when he fled from home to deliver his foster-brother. It was time for him to take up his father's quarrel, that had been waiting and beckoning and reproaching him so long. They should see if he shamed his memory!

The pain and desperation had turned all to a fury of energy that would not let him be still for a moment. It drove him back to his own deserted room for his cloak, and the few pence he had of his own, and then to the stables, where he saddled Barbarossa with hasty, trembling hands. If he ceased for an instant his feverish activity he would break into helpless tears, but if he continued to drive himself into motion he would keep his dignity yet, and launch himself on the road to atonement and restitution. No good-byes to anyone. Best not think of his little, pretty, loving mother, or Owen, or David.

But to think of David, riding from Aberconway in happy ignorance of the calamity that waited for him, was in any case unbearable, and he turned in extremity to any minor annoyance, the straps of the harness stiff under his hands, a broken buckle, a tangle in the red mane, to ease the burden of his rage and grief.

He had only a dagger by way of arms, but that would have to suffice. He could not take his sword; it was Llewelyn's sword, he could touch nothing belonging to the Prince who had condemned him and cast him out. He sank his face for a moment into Barbarossa's glossy neck and sobbed aloud. The horse at least was his own, fairly won; he need not be left behind.

They did not halt him at the gate. He had always had liberty to go and come as he pleased, and they had more urgent things to do in Aber that day than shepherd him back into the maenol if he strayed.

Gilleis was with Joan in her sealed prison, the only attendant allowed in to her. How could she leave that silent, stunned presence to mind the comings and goings of her own child, until she had got at least a word or a tear or a sound out of her mistress and friend, something to show there was still a live mind in her? Moreover, Gilleis did not know the half of the story of that night until she was let out of the guarded room at noon and walked into Owen's anxious arms on the steps of the great hall.

He had left David alone with his father not ten minutes earlier, and he knew the whole of it. He held Gilleis in his arms as though she had been his own mother, and: "Where's Harry?" he demanded urgently. There were enough minds in Aber breaking their wits on the problems of state; one man at least had time to think of the boy.

"I don't know. I've been with the Princess all the morning. God help us all, Owen, I hardly know what I'm doing or what to believe. If only she'd *speak*!" She saw the special trouble and tenderness in his face, and knew they were for her. "What is it? What is it about Harry? What has he to do with this?"

He told her what he knew of it, and it was enough.

"Dear God!" she said, aghast. "I carried her message to him myself last night. What has happened to her that she could do him such a bitter wrong? And how could they believe it of him?"

"Hush, now, there's not a soul believes Harry knew what he did, not even the Prince himself. And our lady'll never let him be blamed unjustly, no, nor de Breos, come to that. Let him be what he will, he's not so base as to let the boy suffer."

"But even to have been the instrument!" she said, in agony. "Dear lord, he'll break his heart. We must send to Adam and fetch him home."

"We'll do that," said Owen. "But first we'll find Harry. I shan't be easy about him till we do."

They looked for him in the kennels, in the mews, in every corner of the maenol, but they did not find him. The gatekeeper's boy owned to having seen him ride out during the morning, but judged confidently that he had not gone far. Owen, less sure, took horse and combed every haunt of the boys of Aber, the smithy low by the water, the mill and the banks of the leat, the steep tracks that led to the upland rides; but there was no sign of Harry's dark-red horse anywhere on the soft, pale spring green of the hills. He'd come home with the evening, he told Gilleis with better heart than he felt, hunger and darkness would bring him back to forgive and be forgiven. But the night came down on the salt marshes and the flat fields of Aber, and still Harry did not come.

Chapter Four

Aber: *May* 1230

*T*he two huts lay in a fold of ground beside a spring, several miles beyond the highest sheep-fold that penned Llewelyn's flocks. On every side the grey-green uplands of coarse grass extended, broken by out-crop rock and deep, peat-brown patches of bog; but their small dimple in this empty world was sheltered from the winds and open to the sun.

Saint Clydog's cell was a plain beehive of wattle and daub and turf, with a lancet doorway facing east to the Holy Land; but Madonna Benedetta's was a squarely-built box of good cut stone, with two windows looking south, and carving on the lintel of the door, for Adam Boteler had built it for her when she chose to retire into the anchorite life, and kept it in repair. It had an inner and an outer room, and John the Fletcher, who was growing old in her service, slept across Benedetta's threshold at night, and fished and carried and cooked for her during the day.

She had tried to send him away many times, saying that he was, and in her employ had always been, a free man, and it was unfitting for an anchoress to have a servant waiting upon her. But he would not go, and called Saint Clydog to his support, as he always did whenever there was a point on which she must lose the debate. Saint Clydog was cantankerous by nature, and would always take the opposite side to a woman in any argument, and he had settled it once for all that a hermit must of necessity have a boy to run his errands, since he may not leave his cell himself, and since his especial blessedness gives him a clairvoyance which may at any moment need to send warnings and exhortations to other people, often at a distance.

Once he had had a boy of his own for the purpose, but the poor fellow had been subjected to so much running about on his master's supernatural business that he had finally tired of the life and continued running, to what new employment Saint Clydog's clear sight had never yet succeeded in revealing to him. Since then he had claimed a minor share in John the Fletcher, tempering his demands on him to defer to Benedetta's prior claim. On the whole he was more comfortable so; it would have taken him the rest of his dwindling life to get used to a new face.

They were sitting outside on the sun-warmed turf of the hillside, in the bright afternoon of the first of May, Saint Clydog facing east with his beads fumbled beneath linked hands in the lap of his gown, and Benedetta unashamedly facing the sun as she embroidered at an altar cloth for the church of the community at Beddgelert. Often they sat the whole afternoon and said no word, but they had known each other for a long time, and silence was no bar to their communion.

"You've been watching the track from Aber for the past ten days," said the Saint abruptly, "and I know why."

"That I can well believe," agreed Benedetta, threading her needle. She had to narrow her eyes against the sun, but she would not turn her face away. The sun was her fellow-countryman, who visited her all too rarely in this misty northern climate, and its warmth was like an Italian voice saluting her, in an alien land where the swart, wild herdsmen who brought her milk and bread had intractable names it had taken her years to learn to say, and avoided the necessity for attempting hers by calling her simply "the holy woman'.

"After a week of your company I remember I said there's no one so knowing as a saint, and I say it still. And no one so inquisitive, either."

"I must always be about God's business," said Saint Clydog smugly, "even on your behalf. You are anxious because your son has not been to pay you his Easter visit."

"He is not my son," she said quite calmly.

"In the spirit he is the son of many parents, but not least of you. You are afraid there is some reason why he cannot come."

She said nothing to that, but sat steadily stitching. She had sewn nearly fifteen years of her life into such lengths of linen as this, she who had hardly put a stitch into a dress before, and would not willingly have done so even now if it had not been the fair price of the life she had chosen. Along with the tranquillity and safety of her calling she had accepted with good grace the immobility and monotony, and the obligation to perfect this dreary skill. You cannot make a one-sided compact with God.

"I have been wondering," went on the Saint, casting a sharp sidelong glance at her beneath his bushy white brows, "how many more days than ten it will take to make you pack up and go down to seek for news of him, if he continues absent."

"I have taken my place here. I have no other. Have I seemed to you so restless since I took this life upon me?"

"You have taken no vows. And I've always known that you will not live out your life here—you with your saint's face and your devil's hair."

"What do you know of my devil's hair?" She always kept it covered from sight now under her white wimple, and even when she loosed it about her shoulders in her own inner room its crimson was dusty now with silver, and its texture a little dry and harsh, as though the sap in her had reached autumn almost before the summer was over.

"Devil's hair, Judas-hair on as true a head as ever took thought for another," said the old man angrily. "The ways of God are inscrutable."

"I always knew you had seen through me," she said serenely. "And did you blame me for striking a bargain with God?"

"I found no fault in you. Man and woman alike must do the best they can with circumstances. And as for the validity of your holiness, that's for God to judge, not for me. As He will, when the time comes."

"Then why are you concerned with the constancy of my vocation here?"

He said, suddenly with the simplicity of a child, disarming and confounding: "May I not grieve at the thought of losing you?" And before she could draw breath he added in his usual crusty tones: "Look at the track now. How is it you have no sense of time and events after all these years with me?"

She looked, and there were two riders winding their way at a canter along the stone-grey ribbon from Aber. She put down her work in her lap and sat tensed, watching them; and while they were still hardly more than coloured, moving dots in the monotone she said with certainty: "Not Harry."

"There are other men in the world."

She watched unwaveringly until the two riders had drawn close enough to be recognised. The one in front, big and burly and fair, was Adam Boteler, the one behind, dark and young, was Owen ap Ivor. When they were nearer still, she saw how grave they looked and how urgently they rode, and rose to meet them, letting the linen fall from her hands.

"Adam, what brings you this way? I looked to see Harry here before this. He's not ill?"

Adam checked in the act of dismounting. The question he had been ready to toss into her lap from the saddle was already answered.

"So he's not been here? Not since Easter?" He doffed his cap in a reverence to Saint Clydog, and bent to kiss Benedetta's hand. He had known her even before she had met with the boy's father and set her heart on him lifelong, and once he had had her favours, though now it seemed to them both that that must have happened to two other people, long since dead.

"We hoped to get word of him from you, but that's one more hope turned out hollow. I doubt, then, you've not heard what's shattered the festival at Aber. God knows they've had no time for visiting."

"I've heard nothing. No one's been near us till you. What's happened?" Alarm made her voice quieter and her body wonderfully still. She stood looking up at him straightly from those wide-set eyes that still had their full, pure colouring, a grey as rich and positive as the iris-purple to which it darkened in shadow. Her face with its breadth of bone and its resolute, adventurous, challenging mouth still seemed made for courts and camps rather than the cells of a hermitage, though the old man had called it a saint's face. But who could be sure what Saint Clydog understood by a saint?

"It's a sorry tale enough, in all conscience. Owen here is the better man to tell you, he was closer to the storm than I."

"Not close enough to be of any use," said Owen ruefully as he dismounted and made his salutations. "Neither to the Prince nor to Harry. Why, the short of it all is that the Princess has been surprised with William de Breos in her bed. And through no fault of his own Harry's tangled sadly in the bad business, and came out of it with some blame and a deal of grief, and he's taken himself off somewhere with his hurts and can't be found."

"Child, what are you saying?" Benedetta gaped at him aghast, labouring some way behind this galloping conclusion. "I'm too old for such shocks."

"I doubt it did come a thought too roughly," said Owen, abashed, "but Adam and I have done everything in such haste these past days, looking for him, I'm out of the skill of going more softly."

"But the Princess and de Breos! Here, sit down and tell me the whole of it, it will be time saved in the end." And she drew him down with her into the tussocky grass, and he poured out the miserable story gratefully, easing his mind of details that had been festering unexpressed for days. Adam lay down wearily beside him and added here and there a glum word of his own. Saint Clydog, motionless with his hands halted on his beads and his eyes on the eastern sky, listened and was silent.

"God or the devil only knows what alchemy he used to win her. If it had not come out as it did I would not have believed it from any man living. And God alone knows how the Prince got wind of it, though there's some malice in this somewhere. There are those that had good reason to want to break this alliance with Brecon at all costs, de Burgh in England and for that matter Griffith in Degannwy, if he'd had any way of getting hold of so apt a weapon. And as for blaming Harry for trusting them, that's fool's talk, in cold blood nobody blames him. Nobody can, for we should every one of us have taken her word without a tremor, and done her bidding without question. You might as well suspect the Prince's own right hand of designs on his life because it reaches for a sword."

"But the thing happened," said Adam bleakly. "The Princess is in close ward, David's torn in two, and Harry's gone. I wish to God I'd kept him safe in Nanhwynain with me, but what could I do when the Prince sent for him?"

"And here Adam has spent his every waking minute hunting for him ever since, and I've given the chase every hour I could snatch from the Prince's business or David's company and never a word of him anywhere. And where could he go? All his friends are here."

"Perhaps it was not his friends he wanted," said Benedetta half to herself, and sat for a while thoughtfully frowning with her chin in her palms.

"Indeed they've cost him enough of pain to set him running," owned Adam, "though I doubt if even de Breos wished him any."

"I meant more than that," she said. "At Harry's age, and with his high temper, think what a load he has to heave off his heart now. Is it to his friends he'd take it? If I know the boy, he'd rather have someone to fight than someone to comfort him. Oh, he'd have brought you his sorrow, Adam, or run to his mother with it, but he wouldn't come to you with his disgrace. That he'd visit on someone who could be made to pay dear for it first and wipe it out of the record afterwards. The Prince would not listen to him, you said?"

"Think how he was pressed," pleaded Owen, flushing for his foster-father. "The wound was new, and God knows no man ever took a worse thrust, or one less deserved. And into the bargain he had Gwynedd on his heart, David's inheritance, everything he's spent his life serving. Could you have seen Harry's trouble clear, past such a trouble of your own? And indeed that's not the whole nor the best of his excuse, for the real reason he ordered him out was for Harry's own sake. Innocent or not, the boy's been the instrument of all this fearful coil, and he could not so soon look at him or speak to him fairly, and did not wish to be unjust. I pledge you my word, in the evening when he had put by the first and worst of it he sent for Harry to come to him, and was as moved as any of us when he heard he was lost. He's given me men and leave to hunt for him since, and he'd do more, but the balance of peace or war's still hanging over him. And our Welsh princes running to Aber like hounds on a blood-scent, they aimed only to strengthen his hand but, by God, they've forced it. Even if he had the will to draw back, even if he thought it wise, I doubt he could not do it now, not even he."

"I never thought of blaming him" said Benedetta mildly. "With a world toppling on his shoulders small wonder if he couldn't see the boy's injury. But Harry would not be able to see any other, not yet, not till his smarts cool a little. I doubt the affront to his honour would hit him hardest, and be most in need of soothing. And the devil lent the Prince words better left unsaid, if a man had time to look them over before he uttered them. That mention of his father— you did well to get the words so exactly from Ednyfed, for I fear they matter more than Llewelyn ever meant or knew. 'He shames his father's memory.' That was more than enough to sting him into action."

Adam sat up sharply in the grass.

"You think he took it as a reproach to him for failing in his duty as a son? What, has he gone to salve his pride on Isambard? I never thought of it; this bitter business here at home put it clean out of my mind, but he was harping on his vengeance again last autumn, and took it very hard that we wouldn't let him go to court with David at Michaelmas, to take the measure of the Lord of Parfois. You could very well be right!"

"That's where his father's memory draws him. That's the challenge that's always been waiting for him. If he wanted a deed to hurl in the teeth of all who doubt him, that's where he'd turn for it. He'll show you all whether he shames his parentage."

Adam came up from the ground with a spring. "I'll down tools and ride for Severnside to-morrow. If you're right, then he'll surely make first for Strata Marcella, and we may overtake him in time."

He did not add: "His father's buried there," but she knew that was what was in his mind. The dedication of Harry's misery and rage belonged to no other altar than his father's grave. It was there he would go first.

"I'd come with you, gladly," said Owen wistfully, rising after him, "but I can't go so far from Aber yet. The Prince might bid me go, but David—he can ill spare me, the case he's in. But I hate to see you go alone."

"Take John the Fletcher with you," said Benedetta. "He'll be fain to go, and he's not afraid to leave me now. Wait, I'll call him out and we'll ask him."

She ran to the doorway and called him forth from laying the fire on the hearth-stone against the evening chill. He came ambling out with his slightly bowed stride, a massy, ageing countryman, knotty and solid as an oak, wiping his hands on his short homespun cotte. He listened with sharp eyes, darting from face to face as Benedetta told him of the journey Adam had in mind. It wanted only the mention of Parfois or of Isambard, and the old fierce gleam kindled in his glance; he had an ancient score still outstanding against the Lord of Parfois on his own account, and a longer and more deadly one on Benedetta's.

"Master, if you want a companion on that road, I'm your man. She's no great need of me for a while, she's safe and holy here, she can spare me."

"Then come," said Adam, "and more than welcome. If the boy's there, we'll find him. Come down to Aber this evening, and we'll have all ready to leave at dawn."

When the two of them rode away, in better heart for having found at least another credible place in which to search, Benedetta stood for a long time watching them, and her face was quickened and restless, like a lake troubled by a wind from the sea. She took up her embroidery and sat down with it close to the silent Saint, but the light was already declining, and she could not see to work the infinitesimal stitches. She laid it down again and sat very still, with a rare irresolution in her quietness.

"I marvel," said Saint Clydog, pausing in his unwontedly earnest and concentrated prayers, "that you don't follow your heart and ride with them. How if the boy should really have run his head into the lion's mouth? Will you be content then to sit here and pray for him?'

"Who spoke of content?" she said, in a voice as roused and tempted as her face. "I pay my debts, I keep my bargains. What is it to you whether I am content?"

"You might ask the same of God," said Saint Clydog shortly. "Or do you think He does not care, either?"

* * *

In the night she left her door open to the starry darkness, to have at least the feeling of the Saint's nearness filling her loneliness in John's place; and she heard on the stillness the low, monotonous cadences of the old man's voice, praying aloud before the crucifix under its little penthouse roof.

"It's late, friend," she said from the doorway. "Are you not going to bed?"

"Not to-night," said Saint Clydog, easing his weight from knee to ancient knee in the darkness. "I must keep vigil to-night with a dying man."

They brought de Breos out from his prison in the height of the morning, in broadest daylight and publicly, that the statement of the power and audacity of the Prince of Aberffraw and Lord of Snowdon might be more emphatic, and the challenge to all dissenting authorities more deliberate. Nothing was done secretly, nothing in haste. The court of the maenol had convicted him. More than eight hundred people witnessed his end, among them his own captive knights whose imprisonment was to terminate with their attendance at this spectacle, that they might carry a true account back with them.

Llewelyn had set his course straight ahead, where his anger and his injury led him. To turn aside from absolute justice would have left him exposed to the suspicion of weakness and timidity, encouraged the encroachments of the English and confounded and dismayed his own princes, who had gathered to Aber like ravens out of Snowdon, eager for a death. By the time he had peace of mind enough to consider mercy it was in any case too late to consider it; nor did he contemplate it for long. Only to a superficial view was it even expedient. Better by far, and at all costs, to stand firm upon his human and sovereign rights and demonstrate them once for all in the eyes of the world and in the teeth of England, even though they were rights no one else would have dared to assert.

And this was the end of it, this melancholy morning of the second of May in the field above the salt marshes, with the gulls crying along the tide, and a troubled wind ruffling the strait and tumbling the broken clouds above the gallows. It rained in fitful scuds, light

and vicious between the watery gleams of sunlight. The ladder
glistened, and all the trampled grass was trodden into slimy mud
outside the ring of armed men.

The free Welshmen who had travelled many miles to watch him
die sighed with fulfilment when he came riding down the track from
Aber between his guards, the hated scion of a hated stock, whom
they would never in their hearts have seen as an ally. He was bare-
headed, and not even his hands bound, but one of the guards led his
horse in case even at this late hour he should make a hopeless bid
for his liberty. He was carefully and elegantly dressed, and calm
with a remote, almost absent calmness. He had known for several
days that he was going to die, and lived with the thought of it so
closely that he had grown numbly used to it without growing resigned. He did not know how to achieve resignation, but he had
managed exhaustion. He was in his thirtieth year, and even at this
pass, deathly pale and fallen away as he was, good to look upon.
There were not wanting a few women who pitied him.

From the foot of the ladder he looked back towards Aber, and saw
the clouds rolling over Moel Wnion, and the long dark line of the
curtain wall receding into the cleft of the river valley beneath. He
saw the hunched shape of the royal tower peering over the wall, but
the place of his brief triumph and his everlasting fall meant nothing
to him now because she was not in it. Somewhere in the narrow
huddle of prisons hidden from sight, she was walled in with her
memories that were not of him.

There was no gain for anyone, nothing but incurable and unbearable loss; and for him the ignominious death of a thief and a traitor-
ous guest taken in the act.

He climbed the ladder wearily but unfalteringly, because there
was no other way left for him to go. If they had but known, those
irrepressible tribesmen down there muttering and howling for his
blood, all his debts were already paid. What they were taking from
him now was not so much, he was stripped to the bone already.
Who would think a game so lightly begun could have such an
appalling ending?

He tilted his head compliantly to the touch of the hangman's
hands without fully realising what he did, still straining with all his
senses towards the place where Joan was; and mercifully, his eyes

being full of tears, he had no warning of the moment when they jerked the ladder away.

"Why him?" said Joan. "Why him, and not me? Was I less to blame? Am I to be grateful for my life when it's left to me with the stain of his death upon it?"

It was almost dark in the barred room where she was confined; she would still have it so. The two thin candles were all she could bear, and even by their pallid gleam she would not look now at her own face. But at least she spoke at last, sometimes ironically, sometimes practically, sometimes as now with the words of bitterness and passion, but always calmly. The first time she had broken her silence it had been to assert Harry's utter innocence of complicity in her crime, and to dictate the full story of the use that had been made of him. That was something Gilleis would never forget. All the rankling bitterness she had been harbouring against her mistress, even as she pitied her, bled away into the ink that vindicated the boy. If he was lost, he was not dishonoured.

"We were like two who vowed to die together," said the Princess, "and one crept out of the bargain and survived, and now has the other on her conscience lifelong. And worse than that, Gilleis, worse than that is to be glad of life on such terms, and to look back and see how small and faint a thing it was we staked our lives upon. That's the cruellest offence of all."

"Then why?" said Gilleis, the comb stilled in her hand. "Oh, many a time I've wanted to ask you, why did you do it? What was there in him, comely as he was, to bring you to stoop to him? All this waste for everybody—*why*?"

"Do I know why? The thing happened of itself, like a gale, an act of God. He came when the time was ripe for him, and I had no way of standing him off. I could do no other. Do I know why?"

She was past forty years old, at the turning point where the season begins its long decline, and he had appeared at her shoulder, ten years her junior, handsome and gay, like a magical perpetuation of the spring that was leaving her for ever. A year later and he would have meant nothing, she would have set her feet already on the downward path and been absorbed in the harvest. A year earlier and she would not have felt any need of him, or fallen into the anguished error that there was virtue in beauty and youth beyond their temporary and borrowed grace. But he had come prompt to his hour, filling the moment of desperation and uncertainty with the blinding charm of his laughter. And he was dead for it.

"Only when I no longer had a choice," she said, "only then did I understand that there had been a choice, and that I had made it wrongly. For all of us. That was the inmost sin, and it was mine, not his. What do they say of me now? What do they say of Llewelyn's justice? That he dared reach as far as King Henry's vassal but stopped short of King Henry's sister?"

"No," said Gilleis. "No one says he dared not. Not even the English."

"Then what? How do they account for me?"

"They feel no need to account for you." Was it better to say it or leave it unsaid? Either way there was nothing but pain, a piercing pain or a dull pain. "They know all through this land," she said, "how well he loves you."

"Loved," said Joan, accepting the sharper agony without a tremor. From first to last she had done no lamenting for herself; the ruin that had overtaken her was her own work. "I know what I have lost, and of how much I have robbed him. It's late to grieve for that, but at least I would not have him lose more than he need. You must be my eyes and ears, Gilleis, if you will, now that I'm deaf and in darkness."

She had asked no questions until then, but there were things she had to know. She knew, none better, in what a quicksand she had left Llewelyn stranded. She gathered herself erect, the faint, sunken spark of the old alert fire flickering in her eyes for the first time since her fall.

"Did my brother sail for France?"

"Yes, my lady. The fleet left Portsmouth the first of May."

"Did he know what had happened here before he sailed?"

"They say the news reached him ten days before. At least he gave orders for the care of my lord de Breos's estates before the end of April."

"But he did not question the charge against him."

She did not say: "Or against me!" but her lips contracted in the mournfullest of smiles. She knew her brother; it was not his concern for her she had feared might drive him into action against Llewelyn. And after all, perhaps it had been foolish to suppose that he would postpone yet again his long-delayed dream of invading France and sweeping triumphantly through Poitou and Anjou like a warrior-emperor, merely to remonstrate on behalf of a compromised half-sister and a rash border-baron. Henry was not troubled with loyalties; all his affections were capricious.

No doubt he had raved and reviled the long-suffering officials who surrounded him for a matter of hours, though more out of jealous pride for his own dignity and the sanctity of all things that were his than out of any regard for William's freedom or William's life; and then he had pushed the affair into someone else's hands, most probably Ralph Neville's since de Burgh was reluctantly bound for Brittany with him, and had turned back to his glittering toys of ships and engines and men, and his swollen dreams of reconquest.

The faint spark burned more steadily, from somewhere deep within her.

"And what has happened since? Have there been letters passing on behalf of the crown?"

"The Prince wrote to the Chancellor, and there came a letter in reply. I don't know what he wrote, but it seemed to me that Ednyfed was very content with it. And they've made no move. They're being very discreet. You see it's five days since, and still all's quiet."

Five days since the poor, spoiled body had been taken down from the gallows above the marsh and buried without honours. All that energy and arrogance and gaiety smirched and broken, and the world surely the poorer even for that. There had never been malice in him, the mischief that spilled out from his finger-ends was a natural gift, for good or evil. But it seemed that no one was prepared to venture on avenging him. Henry in Brittany could not yet know that his vassal was dead, but Chancellor Neville knew it, and had replied to the blunt notification in apparently cautious and urbane terms; that was a fair indication of the way the scale was declining.

The facts, it seemed, were too clear to dispute. The boldness of the Prince's justice might have startled and alarmed the whole realm of England, but no one could deny that it was justice. Then they would not move for her, either. If they let his death go by without protest they could scarcely charge Llewelyn with any ill-usage of her.

She breathed more easily for that, and the stony coldness within her softened with the first meagre spark of warmth. If anyone could win such a gamble against the power of England it was Llewelyn, with his iron front and his approaches direct as arrows, and the recent daunting memory of Kerry reverberating like an echo to his every word. The warmth burned into a slow, bitter ache within her heart, because he did not need her, he could play the game no less well without her. Yet she embraced the reawakening pain, and was grateful for it.

"Has he sent word to the widow?"

A death was a death, but a marriage was a marriage, and sound business could not wait on personal grudges.

"Yes," said Gilleis heavily, thinking of the four little girls who were left fatherless, "and to her brother, the Earl Marshall, too, for the children and the estates will surely come into his ward."

"What has he said to them? Do you know?"

"I know what's being said about the court. They say the Prince has told them that this offence and this penalty were between none but my lord de Breos and himself, and are settled, that he bears no ill-will against the house of Breos, and still desires for his part that David's marriage shall take place according to the contract."

It rang true. It was what she would have had him do, whether the poor woman in Brecon, doubly bereaved of her husband and of his faithfulness, accepted or refused his offer. The more tremendous the stake and the more dangerous the bid you make for it, the more inflexibly and doggedly you must stand to your throw. Not a step back, not a glance aside.

"And I've heard that he means to send an envoy to the Chancellor and make a formal claim for Builth, as the girl's marriage portion."

Joan smiled; it was a pale, brief thing, but it was a smile. His instinct was always true. Not one item nor one scruple must be abated from the due he exacted, and nothing wanting from the due he paid. And he had paid, he was paying yet, a longer score than the short and horrible agony on the gallows.

"They've made no answer yet?"

"There's been no time, my lady."

"They'll compound with him," said Joan with conviction. "He'll win his game." She hesitated for a moment, longing and fearing to ask, and at last she said in a low and constrained voice: "How does he look? Is it well with him?"

At the naked sound of the words she felt her own incurable mutilation, and shrank, sick with the certainty of his. And all Gilleis could do was turn her face away, and fumble in vain for a lie.

"No, let it be!" said Joan. "God help me, I know!"

She drew the gown closer round her shoulders, shivering, putting the unbearable regrets from her. It could not be undone. There was no going back.

"You've had no word yet from Adam?"

"Not yet," said Gilleis, very low, and her lips quivered. "It's only six days since they set off for the march, it's early yet."

"I marvel," said Joan, "that you can keep from hating me. And still you are so gentle."

Suddenly her face was wrung by a convulsion of uncontrollable pain, and she bent her head and hid between her thin, pale hands.

"Oh, Gilleis," she whispered behind the rigid fingers, "if only I could put right this one wrong! Of all the treasons I committed against my will I most repent the offence against Harry. Oh, Gilleis, to betray a child—and one that loved and trusted me—"

Gilleis opened her arms and took the fair, bowed head to her breast, protesting through tears that Harry would come back, that Adam and John between them would find and bring him home.

"He'll come, and he'll not hold it against you for ever. Things pass, even this will pass." What better was there to promise her? She could not lie to her. "Ah, don't grieve, don't grieve! When King Henry comes home he'll surely intercede for you, and see you delivered out of this sad place."

"Delivered?" said Joan, breaking strongly out of the circling arms, and raising a face fixed in wonder, derision and despair. "What do I want with deliverance? In his palace or in his prison, where Llewelyn is is the only home I have."

Chapter Five

Parfois: *May* 1230

*H*e rode in at the gates of Strata Marcella in the dusk, tired out and ready for his bed. Mist was rising over the level water-meadows that fringed Severn, and there was a vaporous moon afloat over the black ridge of the Long Mountain, on the English side of the river. He would have to wait until morning to see more of the place than that dark lizard-back against the sky, and the drifting bluish mist between.

Here he was not known, and did not intend to make use of his real name, which would mark him out almost anywhere in North Wales as the fosterling of the Prince of Aberffraw.

He lighted down modestly at the gate-house and doffed his cap to the brother who came out to him, inquiring with appropriate humility for a night's lodging; and being directed to the stables, took care of his horse like any other roving journeyman before he looked for his own entertainment. In the light of a hanging lantern in the stable-yard, busy grooming their mounts and whistling over the work, were two servants in the familiar livery of Earl Ranulf of Chester.

Harry withdrew himself into the deepest shadows, his heart

thumping. Old Ranulf had known him from infancy, and often on his visits to Aber brought him small gifts, a fluffy speckled eyas from his own mews, or some finely worked jesses. If once he caught sight of Llewelyn's fledgling roaming here alone so far from home, he was very likely to probe deeper into the matter, and end by leading him back to Aber by the ear.

But it was too late to withdraw now. There could be no surer way of drawing attention to himself than by riding out hurriedly again at this hour of the night. He went gingerly about the business of seeing Barbarossa fed and bedded, averting his face from the lights; and only when he was drawing breath to nerve himself to enter the hall of the commonalty did he remember that he was wasting the worst of his fears. Earl Ranulf could not possibly be here in Strata Marcella; he was away with the King's host, somewhere in Brittany or Poitou.

There were, of course, many among the Earl's household who would also know Llewelyn's foster-son well, but the danger of being haled back like a runaway child was less grave from any of them. On the other hand, they might very well carry word back to Chester, and so in time to Aber. He would still do well to keep out of sight, and spare to let his voice be heard.

He slipped into the hall unobtrusively, and took his place among the lowest, where the packmen and pedlars and the poor journeymen sat. Earl Ranulf's grooms were at the highest table, well away from him, and three more men in the same livery had joined them, but by good fortune Harry knew none of the five, and was certain he could not be known to them.

Voices were rising at the main table. Suddenly he heard the name of the Princess Joan pass, and his heart turned in him with a sharp, vindictive stab of recollection.

"The Princess of Gwynedd?" said a lean Welsh pilgrim hotly. "Ah, get off with you, man! This world's full of gossips who'd take the name of the Blessed Virgin herself in vain if it served their purpose, but is that any call for you to abet them? The Princess is known here in Wales, let me tell you. Whoever bred that tale about her may swallow it himself, he'll find no one else here to do it for him."

He had raised his voice in his partisan indignation, and now every ear was stretched, the whole room listening.

"Spare your anger, friend," said the oldest of the men from Chester. "I'd have said the same myself, on all counts, a month ago, and I'd be saying it yet if I didn't know different, more's the pity. The tale's all over England and Wales already. Where've you been that you haven't heard it?"

"I did better than you when it first came into Chester," added his fellow ruefully, "for I laughed."

"So did the Prince when someone first whispered it in his ear. But he's laughing on the other side of his face now."

Harry drew away from the trestle table very softly, and curled into his cloak in the dimmest corner. The pain he had ridden off into the freakish May wind and the sweet, active aches of his body was back again in full measure, gripping his throat so that it was hard to breathe. The image engraved upon his inward vision blazed into unbearable clarity again.

The pilgrim said slowly and solemnly: "This is no deceit?"

"No deceit, but a certainty."

"God have mercy on us all!" said the Welshman. "And what's become of her?"

"She's in prison there at Aber, and he'll neither see her nor hear her name spoken."

"And the lord of Brecon?"

The youngest groom twirled an imaginary noose round his own throat, and choked in it in horrible mimicry of the gallows-agony.

"*Hanged?*" said one of the journeymen hoarsely. "What, William de Breos? Hang the biggest baron in the march? By God, he'd never dare! Not even Llewelyn!"

Dead! Harry had never thought of death. Imprisonment, reparations, long legal battles back and forth across the border, bishops running hither and thither, the King's envoys galloping to appease and pacify, he had foreseen all these, but never this ultimate simplicity, this direct and resolute despatch. He shrank into his corner, sick and stunned.

"By God, he did dare. The thing's done. Yesterday morning, and we heard it in Chester before night. De Breos is dead and buried, let the King's officers do what they will."

"But to hang him out of hand! A great lord like him! Like a sneak thief or a murderer!"

Harry had seen men hanged once, two outlaws who had preyed on pilgrims using the hill roads to Beddgelert, and killed and robbed three or four times before they were taken. He had been sick and shaken at the sight of their contorted dance on air, and the struggle they put up for their last breaths. Everyone had reassured him that the felons had only their deserts, and he had owned that they were right; but still he had not been comforted.

"God have mercy on his soul!" said the pilgrim, generously enough for a Welshman who felt himself affronted in the person of his prince; and there was a half-grudging and half-awed growl of: "Amen!"

Dead and buried, the handsome, athletic body that stepped so vigorously and rode so well; the laughter strangled in the round, brown throat, the blue-veined lids lowered once for all over the gay and arrogant eyes. He had only his deserts, that was certain. He had stooped to the meanest and most damaging of thefts, violated the laws of hospitality, betrayed friendship. And yet how could they bear to do it to him? How could they bring themselves to spoil a creature so alive and beautiful?

"You're very quiet, young sir," said one of the packmen, edging closer to him along the bench by the wall, and leaning to peer at him with narrow, shrewd eyes that missed nothing of his unwillingness to be seen. Harry had thought himself plain and ordinary enough to pass muster anywhere, but suddenly he was uneasily aware of the silver chasing on the hilt of his dagger, the modest gold clasp that fastened his cloak, and even the good homespun cloth and court cut of his cotte and chausses. The insinuating voice asked civilly: "Are you looking for work in these parts? I know most of the masters in Pool that can do with likely lads. Maybe I can speak a word for you."

"I thought of trying further south," said Harry, feeling cautiously for his purse against his thigh, under cover of the folds of his cloak. It was an effort to keep his voice firm, or his wits alive to his own situation. "Maybe as far as Hereford. Unless there's some patron hereabouts who needs a prentice stonemason."

"They'd want to know how you left your old master," said the packman, showing broken teeth in an ingratiating grin as he edged still closer. He was on the side away from the purse, but Harry kept his hand on his money none the less. The group at the main table had broken up now, its members were making ready for bed, and most of the torches were out.

"I was apprenticed to a good master the past three years, but he died a month ago, and there was no one to carry on his business. There'll be nothing for me to learn in Pool. In Hereford I might get taken on for the works of the cathedral. But I'd as lief have a lay patron if one offers. I've heard this Lord of Parfois, over the Severn, keeps his own masons. Would there be any use in my going there?"

His head was aching with weariness and strain, but he might as well get his information from a willing source, however little truth or trust he was prepared to give in return.

"Ah, you don't want such as my lord Isambard for a patron, lad, God forbid, he's a cruel hard master. You'd far better come with me into Pool to-morrow, and I'll see you well placed with a good mason who knows his trade and treats his men well."

If I went with you, thought Harry, not too exhausted or too wrung to preen himself a little on his knowingness, I should be picked up somewhere in the ditch penniless, with a broken head, and nothing on me but my shirt and chausses—if you left me those.

"Thank you for your offer, sir," he said, "I'm sure you mean it kindly. But I think I'll try there at Parfois before I move on."

"It would be no use now, lad, he's away from England with all his knights. Even his master-mason's not there, for I know he's building down at the manor of Erington."

It was said too confidently to be anything but true, and moreover Harry should have realised the probability for himself. The King had summoned all the knight-service of the country to his muster for France, where else would the Lord of Parfois be? Nevertheless he found himself startled and shocked to be brought up thus against the absence of his enemy, a check he had never foreseen.

Now what was to become of his bid to re-establish himself? There was no guessing how long the army would remain in France. Campaigning was an expensive business, so he had heard Llewelyn complain, and the rapid assaults and resolute marches of the clansmen of Gwynedd were cheap by comparison with the kind of triumphal progress the King had fitted out for France. Could he even afford to winter there? And would the French Queen-mother and her advisers let him? No, surely he would bring his fleet home for the winter with whatever advantages they could gain by then. But even so it meant Harry must keep his courage and resolution screwed to the point of action for months, and provide for himself meantime into the bargain, unless he was prepared to creep home to Aber with his tail between his legs.

It was too much for him. He felt the tears stinging his eyes, and in pure rage with himself made short and effective work of his informant.

"Then I'll head for Hereford," he said, and stood up, giving a suggestive flick forward to the dagger at his belt, so that the sharp eyes that were studying its hilt so lovingly should be left in no doubt that it had a blade, too, and was for use rather than ornament. "Alone!" said Harry, all the more aggressively because his voice was none too steady.

"As you please, young sir, as you please," said the packman hurriedly, and withdrew with a lingering look that ran down the boy's side like chilly water and settled in his groin where the thin little purse was hidden.

The last of the torches went out. Harry lay down, wrapping his cloak about him in the dark, and under its shelter made fast his purse, knotting it into his shirt under the belt of his chausses, so that even with a knife it should be impossible to get it away from him without awakening him. Then, feeling the irresistible tears growing too great to be contained, he drew a fold of cloth over his face and clenched his teeth in it to muffle and suppress the tremors that shook him.

Everything was ill-done, everything! Everything betrayed him, time, chance and men, even the best and most beloved; and now events had conspired to make a fool of him and snatch his enemy away out of his reach, leaving him caught by the heels still in the swamp of his disgrace. But he would not go back. He was a man, with a man's craft, and he would show Adam he could live by his hands as surely as he would show Llewelyn his honour was to be reckoned with on equal terms with his father's. He could very well do what he had pretended he was bent on doing, look for a master and work for his living until Isambard came back to Parfois. Never on any conditions would he go back to Aber until his vengeance was accomplished.

He lay with his muffled face buried in his arms in the piled rushes of the corner of the hall, and wept out of him helplessly the too complicated tensions of his grief; until gradually the complexities fell away and left him abandoned to the sole thought of de Breos dead, the admirable engine broken, the audacious spirit silenced. Then he felt himself in some incomprehensible fashion reconciled with this chief of his betrayers, and quit of all grievance against him; and the tears came more freely for being recognised for what they were, the earnest of his desperate grief for a man he had loved and admired, who was now pitifully and irrecoverably lost.

He awoke from the absolute sleep of the young at first light, refreshed and calmed, and picked his way very quietly out of the close warmth of the hall into the sweet, chill air of the morning. Beneath the flank of the east end of the church there was a grave he must visit.

He had never been to Strata Marcella before, but he knew exactly where to find it, close under the wall. There was no mitre on it, though it lay among the tombs of the abbots; there was no lettering to identify it. There was nothing but a single leaf carved in the edge of the flat stone, one small leaf uncurling strongly as if to hold up an invisible abacus. He traced it with his finger-tip, kneeling in the grass; unless you knew where to look you could easily pass by and never know there was a leaf there. Adam had carved it, long ago. The hollows were outlined delicately in yellowish moss now, as though he had inlaid his work with gold.

Harry said his prayers more solemnly and attentively than he had ever yet said them in his life. When they were done he did not rise, but remained kneeling, staring over his clasped hands at the little symbol in the stone. Nothing was ever put into words, no vow ever made, but when he rose from his knees he had promised that young mysterious, Protean father of his that he would not rest until he had confronted Ralf Isambard and exacted from him a full repayment for untimely death.

The sense of having committed himself filled him with purpose and peace. He looked up from the wide water-meadows, eastwards across the silvery pools the Severn had left in every dimple after the spring floods, across the broad main stream of the river with its faint, drifting wreaths of mist, to the black hog-back of the Long Mountain, indented in half a dozen places along its vast, forested flank by the seamed valleys where brooks flowed down to join the Severn. Behind the ridge the eastern sky was growing pale and clear as primroses, and outlined against that radiance, hard and black among the feathery fringing of trees along the distant crest, showed the towering shape of the castle of Parfois on its rocky outcrop, staring out over Wales.

As he watched, the first rays of the still hidden sun fingered their way out of the east and launched themselves, quivering like a flight of iridescent birds, across the highest point of the crest. The castle remained dark, but close to it a sudden tapering shaft of gold sprang into sight, embracing and refracting the vibrating light, prolonging itself in a splendid, aspiring tension towards the sky.

For the first time in his life he was looking at the tower of Master Harry's church of Parfois. To him, in the astonishment of that apparition, it seemed that for the first time he had caught a glimpse of his father, not through the eyes of Llewelyn, or Owen, or Gilleis, or Benedetta, or Adam, though all of them had loved and honoured him, but in his own fallible and vulnerable flesh and hot and hapless blood, the same he had conferred, for better or worse, upon his only son.

The woods were thick below Parfois, and crowded him down to the riverside, where a narrow path threaded the undergrowth. All the way from Buttington, where he had forded the Severn, the trees had shrouded his movements and covered him from sight, until now, by his reckoning, he was close to the outlet of the stream that came down from the crevices of the castle rock, and somewhere on his left hand, far above him, the ramparts of Isambard's curtain-wall fretted the noon sky.

The river had left the tide-mark of its spring spate on the sodden bushes and flattened grass, and under-cut here and there a crumbling section of the bank, leaving a perpetual swirl of frothy brown water.

He was skirting one of these pools when he caught the rustle of shaken bushes, and knew that he was not alone. He did not make the mistake of halting; that would have been to betray his awareness. He went on slowly leading Barbarossa along the twisting path; and in a moment the tremor of leaves had moved alongside him.

Not an otter, then; an otter, and for that matter any other beast, would have removed itself from him, not kept watchful pace with him. These borders were notorious for the number of their forest outlaws, since the river provided an effective means of retreat if pursued, and the wanted Englishman was apt to be a welcome ally on the fringe of Wales. Harry loosened his dagger warily in its sheath, and paced on with ears stretched for the small sounds that accompanied him.

He waited until his emergence upon a clear view of the river gave him opportunity to halt in apparent innocence and look across the sunlit water, which here moved unimpeded along a cleaner shore, though still overhung with trees. Carefully he fixed the clump of bushes that trembled faintly before it stilled; and dropping Barbarossa's bridle he flung himself into the thicket, plunging low to take the watcher about the knees and bring him down.

He touched smooth naked flesh that slipped through his startled fingers like a fish, and a light body fled from him through the threshing branches. The next moment he heard the neat plash of a dive as the watcher took to the water.

Harry picked himself up scratched but dogged, and plunged after. Near the edge of the bank, tucked under a low bush, he stumbled over a tight little roll of brown homespun and coarse linen, laid neatly in the grass between a pair of shoes of roughly sewn leather. He stooped and snatched up the roll with a muted shout of triumph, and kicked the shoes out into the open; they were so small that he laughed with relief at the sight of them. So he had made all that needless effort to frighten a mere child, an inquisitive boy!

He looked out into the river, still laughing. Ten yards out from the bank a sleek, small head surfaced warily, trailing streaming hair. "Come in with you," he called reassuringly. "I'll not touch you."

The head hovered, apparently untroubled by the current; he knew from the movement of the surface how the boy turned into the

stream with a stroke just strong enough to maintain his ground; by
the ease with which he moved in it he must spend half his young
life in the water.

"I took you for a masterless man, not a child, and I've got a good
horse to lose. Ah, come away in! Do I look as if I mean you any
harm?"

The sleek head and a naked shoulder dipped against the stream,
the boy ventured nearer but still held off dubiously from the shore.
Harry could see the honey-coloured flesh gleaming through the
soiled water, and the large bright eyes in the wary face watching his
every move. The floating hair was the muted brown of the little
leather shoes; when it was dry it would probably be a dark corn-
yellow. He looked about eleven or twelve years old, and as wild as
a hare. When Harry made an incautiously abrupt movement of his
hand the head ducked out of sight instantly, leaving only a quivering
ring upon the water, and broke surface again a dozen yards away.

"You'll have to come in the end," said Harry reasonably, grinning
at him. "I've got your clothes."

"Put them down," said the head sullenly, "and go away and leave
me come in in peace."

"You might run away from me. And I want to talk to you." A
creature who so clearly lived on familiar terms with these woods
and this river was the very ally he needed, and none the worse for
being only a boy.

"I won't run away," said the swimmer, but with an intonation
which inspired no great confidence, any more than it indicated any
in him.

"By your leave, we'll make sure of that. Here are your clothes,
come and take them."

"I can't!" shouted the child in exasperation. "Fool, why don't
you look what you've got there?"

Even then he didn't understand. He let the edge of the bundle
slip out of his hand, and it unrolled to his feet a rough brown gown
and a linen shift instead of the chausses and tunic and shirt he had
expected. He let the hems fall as though he had been burned, and
withdrew hurriedly and a little indignantly into the bushes; but
before he reached the path again he looked back once over his shoulder, very quickly. It was only a broken glimpse between the lattice

of the branches, but he saw her heave herself out of the water shimmering, and shake her hair like whips round her head, and before he hastily averted his eyes he saw that she was laughing.

And that was strange, for when she stepped out on to the path five minutes later she was grave enough. She had wrung out her wet hair and coiled it in a knot on top of her head so that it should not hang down on the shoulder of her gown. The drab homespun had a tear or two in it here and there, and the skirt was kilted nearly to her knees, but she came out of the bushes like a queen emerging from her robing-room. She had her shoes in her hand, and the small bare feet, where they were not still muddy between the toes from the river, were honey-coloured like her arms, and the slender long neck, and the shoulder that had glistened momentarily out of the water. She looked thoughtfully at him, and more thoughtfully still at Barbarossa, and her bright blue glance came back to him again, to look him over shrewdly from head to foot, and make unfathomable guessses about his origin, his estate and his business there in the forest. She had not missed even his heightened colour and somewhat excessive dignity; and she was older than he had supposed, probably within a year of his own age.

"Why were you following me?" she said accusingly, as though she had set out to prove in one utterance her uncompromising femaleness.

"I following you? *You* were following *me*."

"I was only trying to get back to my clothes. And then you attacked me." She eyed him warily still, but she was not really afraid of him; the measurements she had taken had roused her curiosity but allayed any fears she might have been harbouring.

"What were you doing?" he asked, himself no less curious. "It's cold yet for swimming."

"I was putting down eel-traps. They began to run three weeks ago. What are *you* doing here?"

"Do you live here in the forest?" he asked, ignoring her question.

"Yes. A little way up-river yet, and then a little way inland. With my father," she added with emphasis, to warn him that she was not unprotected, and revolved between sharp white teeth the tender end of a long grass she had pulled from its sheath. Her eyes, he saw, were as blue as the zenith, and fringed with long, dark-gold lashes, and when her hair was dry it would be only a shade darker than the smooth forehead beneath it. She examined him steadily, missing nothing. Not even the hopeful packman at Strata Marcella had made so rapid and shrewd an inventory of his dress and person.

"My name is Aelis," she said. "Tell me yours."

"Harry," he said, and choked just in time upon the rest of it. Why make it easier for anyone who came inquiring for him? He did not think they would follow him here into the wilds, but it would be foolish to be too complacent.

He expected her to pounce upon his too obvious change of heart, and demand another name, but she smiled as though he had told her more than he knew.

"Where do you come from, Harry?"

"From Chester," he lied, and felt the need to spread out for her the whole story he had prepared, of his dead master and his broken apprenticeship. He might as well perfect it upon her before trying it upon others of a more sceptical turn of mind. But it seemed he was still underrating her. The bright, deliberate eyes lingered expressively upon his horse and too princely harness, flashed from the texture of his sleeve to the chased hilt of his dagger, then looked him challengingly in the eye. She laughed. It seemed he would have to change his clothes and part with Barbarossa before he could hope to pass muster in his chosen part.

"And what are you seeking here in the forest?" she asked, drawing still nearer to him.

If lies were of no use to her he'd try her with at least a morsel of truth. "A place to hide in," he said. "Only for a little while, a week, two weeks maybe." That would be long enough to explore and map the approaches of Parfois, but after that he must go into Pool and find work, for he could not pay his way much longer on what he had in his purse. He had even thought of going as far as Shrewsbury, which was a charter town, and used to taking in fugitives and asking no questions; but it was too far from this fortress on which his whole heart was now set. Pool would have to find him a living, he did not greatly care what he did to earn it.

This time she did not laugh, nor did she ask for any more from him than he had volunteered of his own will. She gave him a sudden warm smile and said indulgently: "Why didn't you say you were a runaway? When I first caught sight of you not ten yards from me I got such a fright, I thought you were from the castle. I'd never have run from you if I'd known you were an outlaw.''

Bright with curiosity, the blue eyes searched him through and through, but she would not question him further; all those who were running from justice, from villeinage, from debt, from their families, were natural allies to her. She and her father had always lived precariously half within and half without the law, scratching a meagre crop legally out of a couple of fields enclosed in an unprofitable assart years ago, and poaching fish from the river and conies and hares from the woods, even an occasional hart when it could be done without too great a risk.

''Have I said I was an outlaw?'' he protested, uneasy in so unfamiliar a role.

''Ah, you can trust me,'' she said disdainfully. ''You're not the first that's gone to earth with us, and you wouldn't be the first we've put across the river by night, if that's what you want. You've no need to be wary with me, I'm not anxious to be in your secrets. The less we know the less we can let slip. You keep your counsel. There's a boat at the mill, if you daren't show yourself at the ferry or the fords.''

It dawned upon him then, for the first time, that she had taken it for granted he was English, and it astonished him out of all measure. It was as though he had been brought up suddenly against his image in a mirror, and seen himself as a stranger. How did she know? He did not even feel himself to be English, for all his name and his blood, for all his father's Latin education at the comfortable Benedictine abbey of Shrewsbury, and his mother's good mercantile stock from London. He knew the facts of his parentage, but they did not affect his vision of himself as a young Welsh clansman bound by fostering as closely as by kinship to the royal house of Gwynedd. And here this wild girl looked him over, Welsh cloth and all, and knew him for English. It seemed he was owning another attachment now, whether he would or no, being bound into new patterns of loyalty by ties he had never yet recognised as realities. More and more with every step now he belonged to his father. The very soil this side of Severn knew him.

''All I want is a place to lie hidden,'' he said. ''I can pay.''

"Ah, pay!" said Aelis good-humouredly. "What will you cost us? You'll help me with my snares, and we'll be quits. Come away, then, and I'll bring you to my father. Nobody bothers us. We're well away from the track to the mill, and a good mile off the road up to Parfois, and these woods are poor hunting, the other side the Mountain gives better sport. Nobody'll look for you here."

She coiled up again the slipping knot of her hair, that was beginning to glisten at the edges with drying strands of gold, and began to lead the way barefoot along the narrow path. He followed her, leading Barbarossa by the bridle, and it seemed to him suddenly that everything had become strange and new to him, and held a kind of unexpected and tremulous promise. For the first time in his life he had no idea what was to become of him, what unpredictable and daunting creatures were to cross his path. He was frightened and happy. Not for the world, not even the old, familiar and delightful world, would he have turned back now.

The knot of heavy hair slipped from its coils again, and hung loose about her shoulders. For one instant he was transfixed by the memory his mind had been struggling in vain to excise, the bright, coiling gold dried into limp, fair tresses drawn across blue-veined breasts, and the sword-thrust of hate and anger and love split his heart again. Then the balance swung back and held him poised, shaken but resolute, and the pale, unforgettable disfigurement of the immaculate image was dazzled out of his mind's eyes by his stolen glimpse of Aelis, aloof and self-reliant in her young, fresh, virginal nakedness.

"This is the place," said John the Fletcher, throwing a satisfied glance over the narrow, fenced field and the low roof of the hut receding into the twilight of the trees. "Only two false casts, after fifteen years, is not bad remembering. And there's the man, thanks be to God for him, the same that helped me carry the pair of them up from the river, him dead and her with the life just in her. I had the fear in me all this while he might be dead and gone himself before now; it's a long while to leave a man and expect to find him again not much changed."

They had crossed the Severn at Pool and ridden downstream, without over-much hope in them but resolute to try every chance that offered. At Strata Marcella the gate-keeper had remembered the chestnut horse, or they might never have known whether they were on the right trail or no; and when they had combed every village on the Welsh bank, and every street in Pool, John had set his face for the assart where Master Harry had been brought ashore after his death. It had been a fated place for them once, it might be so again.

There lay the hut before them now, the low undercroft and the one small room above, the starved clearing fields, the corner of poor grazing. The man who slipped his rabbit snares so deftly out of sight within the undercroft as they appeared was perhaps forty years old, old enough to be the same taciturn young woodsman of fifteen years ago; but the girl who sat milking the lean cow in the home corner of the pasture was no more than fourteen or fifteen.

"And there's the horse we're looking for," said Adam in a vast sigh, nodding towards the dark recesses of the undercroft, where a lofty red head nuzzled contentedly in the hay-rack. "Who says we've not been guided? He's here!"

The man of the house came towards them with a wary face, his eyes expressionless. The short, crisp beard had two curved streaks of grey in its brown now, but he was not greatly changed.

"Good even, masters," he said flatly. "Are you out of your way? This path leads nowhere past here, you'll do better to keep to the riverside."

"Good even, Robert," said John the Fletcher. "We're not out of our way, by God's grace we've found our way well enough."

"You know me?" said the man, withdrawing a step and casting a glance aside at his daughter, who picked up her milking pail and approached them with a blithe and innocent face, but sharp and watchful eyes.

"Time was when I did, for a passing while, and you knew me, too, but it's fifteen years since, and I doubt I'm changed more than you." He stripped off the capuchon from his head and leaned nearer, but the man looked up at him sturdily and shook his head. "Ah, well, the light's going. But you'll remember the time when I tell you. Do you mind a day about this time of year—but the floods were later that spring, I recall—when you and I took two queer fish out of the Severn?"

He saw the broad shoulders stiffen and the bearded head come up with a start to stare at him again.

"Ay, you remember. A man and a woman tied naked in each other's arms, the man dead and the woman barely living. Thrown in to rot together, from the stage where Isambard unloaded his stone—" He never spoke of it, but the memory of that day was in him intact still, not one molten detail dimmed or cooled. He had been waiting all these years to repay the debt, and he had but to let the words form in his mouth and he was shaken and aflame with the old unassuaged fury.

"For God's sake leave that name alone," said Robert softly. "I know who it was did it, and so do you. That's enough. So it's you, is it, after all these years? I never thought to see you again. How is it with the lady? Is she still living?"

"She is, and well. I've left her but two weeks ago, safe in Wales. And your good wife?"

"Dead these seven years. The autumn fever took her. But here's my girl Aelis helps me in her mother's stead, and a good lass she is."

"I'm sorry for your loss," said John. "She was the gentlest soul, I mind how she nursed my lady all those hours we thought we'd never get the breath back into her. The girl's like her, if I'm remembering well. She had the same yellow hair."

"She had. Well, how it all comes back to me, and I've not thought of it for ten years, I dare say. It was the year before Aelis here was born. Come in with you both, if you'll not mind a poor man's hearth and poor folks' fare."

"We were glad enough of it then," said John, dismounting. "And this is Master Adam Boteler, who was foster-brother to that same Master Harry we brought in here dead that day, and has taken his wife and son for his own ever since. And Robert, it seems you're always to be our salvation, for this time we've lost the boy, and by the look of things you've found him for us."

Robert froze into stillness with Adam's stirrup in his hand. "Boy? What would make you think I know anything of any boy?"

"His horse," said Adam. "That red beast with the white diamond yonder in your undercroft. There's no mistaking him. If you doubt we're honest we can tell you the whole history of that horse, up to the time he galloped out of Aber with Harry on his back. We've been looking high and low for him ever since."

Aelis drew nearer to her father's side, and her fingers sought his sleeve. Robert hesitated, looking narrowly from face to face.

"You're father to him now, you tell me? Then what ailed him to run from you? What's he done amiss?"

"Nothing amiss. He ran because of a grief not of our making, and no shame to him," said Adam. "Nobody's set against him, and there's only a good welcome waiting for him when we take him home. Boys take things hard at his age, you know it yourself. Man, do you think we'd mean him anything but good? He's Talvace's son. For God's sake don't keep us on thorns, but if you've got him here, tell us."

Robert had made up his mind. "He's here," he said. "He's been with us the past fifteen days." He shook off the insistent hand that pulled at his sleeve. "Leave worrying, girl, can't you, you see these are his friends. Well, sirs, that's the truth of it. Ever since he came I've been plaguing my memory to know where I'd seen that face before, and never could get to the bottom of it. It's plain enough, now you tell me whose son he is. Well, come in, come in! Turn your horses into the paddock there. He's off somewhere in the forest now—where was it he was bound, Aelis?"

She would know; she was in all his planning and all his preparations, though she still did not know to what ambitious end all this strange reconnaissance was dedicated. She said in a small and wary voice: "He was going to try to climb the castle rock on the blind side. I told him it couldn't be climbed, but he laughed at me. He said he learned his business on Snowdon, and he'd write his name on the stones of the Lady's Tower before night."

Adam and John exchanged a long, disquieted glance. "Is that what he's been doing all this time he's been here with you?" asked Adam, eyeing the girl anxiously. "Climbing and scheming about Parfois?"

She nodded, beginning to be afraid, though of what she did not understand. She pushed back the tress that fell over her forehead, and stared back at Adam with great solemn blue eyes. "He's there every day. Sometimes in the gully between the castle and the church, sometimes climbing on the sheer face. And he draws things, scratches them on the rocks and sits and frets over them for hours."

She had caught the infection of their uneasiness, and was trembling. "What is he trying to do? What is it he wants?"

Robert looked from Adam to John, and shook his head. "Only too well I see what he wants! If I'd known what was in his mind I'd have made shift to get out of him where he came from, and sent word to you somehow, but hereabout we never ask questions of them that don't want to share their secrets. I never asked the boy so much as his name. Come into the house, then, and wait for him. By the shape of it," he said grimly, leading the way, "you've come just in time."

Harry came down the sandstone cliff below Parfois in the last of the light, in high content with his own performance but no nearer to achieving his main purpose. It seemed to him that the place was impregnable. The one formal way of approach, the long traverse which had been shored up into a ramp when the fortress was built, was guarded half-way up by two watch-towers, and from that point on had a broken sandstone cliff on either side. He could climb it without great difficulty, but even if he did he would have achieved little, for he would merely emerge upon the level plateau on which the church was built, and between that and the wards of the castle there was a forty-foot-deep gully, crossed only by the drawbridge at the gate-towers. The outcrop on which Parfois stood was an island in the air, sheer on all sides, the curtain-wall with its six great towers rose out of the solid rock.

The most precipitous face of rock, beneath the Lady's Tower, was also the blind face, the only side not overlooked from any turrets, short of leaning out from Isambard's insolent lancet windows and looking vertically down the cliff. But when Harry had taken advantage of these factors and mastered the climb on that side, there remained twenty feet of well-built stone wall above him to the nearest loopholes, and not even the clansmen who had nursed him up the crags of Eryri had yet found a way of walking up a smooth wall.

He had scratched his initials on the lowest courses of the masonry, just as he had promised Aelis he would do, and that was achievement enough for one day. The problem of over-leaping the wall would need more thought. Yet he was in good heart as he dropped through the rough scrub-land into the forest, and made for his supper and his bed; and it was a stunning shock to reach the edge of the clearing and see the two strange horses in the paddock. The roan was almost invisible in the deepening dusk until he moved and called softly; the grey was pale and almost lambent, a horse sketched in subdued light. He recognised them both.

He stopped on the instant, drawing back into the trees. The most frightening thing was that now they had found him, a part of him, hitherto in subjection, rose in thankfulness and wanted to run to meet them; but the part of him where his pride resided was more potent, and soon stamped down the relieved and craven child. He was not going back. That was certainty.

He was Harry Talvace, and he had every right to be here about his father's business. It ought to be possible for him to walk in upon them and say so, and firmly hold to it. He ought to be capable of asserting himself and sending them home without him, or even commanding their allegiance in what he was setting out to do. The trouble was that he was not sure of his authority. To be over-ridden and dragged back home unwillingly to Aber would be humiliating enough in any circumstances, unendurable with Aelis looking on.

He stood irresolute, scuffing his feet against the terraced fungus round the bole of a tree. It was manifestly unfair to think of Adam as an oppressive father, Adam who had never in his life lost his patience with son or apprentice, and preserved in himself enough of the boy to feel tenderly for other boys. But the fact remained that whenever he had come into head-on collision with Adam over any issue, whenever they had stared each other out eye to eye in a test of wills, Adam had always won.

No, he couldn't risk facing him. He had everything to lose now, it was no longer merely a question of his honour, no longer a gesture of defiance made in the face of all who doubted him; some part of his own heritage, even of his own identity, lay within the walls of Parfois, and until he possessed himself of it he could not be complete.

Yet it was not so easy to turn and go away through the forest, and leave them there waiting for him. There was Robert to be thought of, and Aelis. They had taken him in like a son, accepting him without question because they thought him hunted and in need of shelter. He owed them what he had no means of repaying, unless they would accept the gold clasp he had unpicked from his cloak to make him less conspicuous; and if they took that, would it be safe for them to try to sell it, even in Shrewsbury? People had been suspected of theft and banditry on less evidence. But they could sell the good, plain clothes he had exchanged for these old patched weeds of Robert's, at least those were not so rich as to provoke suspicion. If only Aelis would come out from the hut!

And come she did, when he had almost given up hope of her, and was withdrawing with many backward glances into the woods. She appeared suddenly against the lighted doorway, and went round to the back of the hut to shut up the pen on her few scrawny fowls; he heard them muttering sleepily on their perch at her step. He dared not whistle to her at that distance, the men in the hut would hear, and he was desperately afraid that she would go in again and close the door against him. But instead of turning back she came quickly along the edge of the open ride and into the trees, at every few paces checking and listening, and he knew that she was straining her ears for sign or sound of him. She had understood him very well; she knew he would not come in.

He waited until she was within a dozen yards of him, and then called to her softly and urgently between the trees.

"Aelis!"

His own voice sounded discomfortingly plaintive and small to him, and alarmingly irresolute, but it reached her. She turned gladly and flew to meet him, and he caught her by the shoulders and held her close to him there in the dark.

"Harry, they're here! They came for you. We wouldn't have told, but they knew Barbarossa."

"I know," he said feverishly. "I know their horses as they know mine. Aelis, I'm not coming in. I can't go back with them."

"But they mean you no wrong, they only want you home. There's nothing to be feared of—"

"I'm not feared," he said, affronted. "But I have things I must do. I can't go home till they're done, I won't."

"Come in," she urged, closing her cool fingers strongly on his arm. "Come and talk to them at least. They've been in dread for you, you can't leave them without a word."

"I must. If I came in they'd get me home, and I can't go home yet. Tell them nothing. You haven't seen me, you don't know where I've gone. Some day, when they've given me up, I'll come back to see you again. And, Aelis—my cloak buckle—it's for you, if you know of a way of turning it to use. And my clothes—"

"I could bring them to you," she said eagerly. "You can't go anywhere in those tatters you've been roaming the woods in. And I could loose Barbarossa to you—"

"No, I'm better without him. I must go into Pool and find work to do there, and what would a prentice mason be doing with a beast like him? And the clothes, too—I'll do better in these. And, Aelis, I'll come back, I promise I will—"

She heard the tremor of tears not far below the level of his voice, and knew how terribly he was tempted. "They'll be main sad for you," she protested, herself in tears.

"I know! I'll make all right one day, but now there's no way for me but to go. Take care of Barbarossa for me till I come again."

"How if they take him away with them?" she said, wiping her eyes on her sleeve.

"Then let them, for he'll be as well with them. But maybe they'll leave him in the hope that I'll come back for him. They'll want you to send a message if I do, but Aelis, you won't do it, you mustn't do it, not unless I bid you—"

"I'll do what I please," she said sullenly, muffling a sob against her forearm. "Someone has to think for you, if you're such a great fool, and don't know your friends. And there's your mother waiting at home for you, and you'd let her go on grieving—"

"Let my mother be!" he flashed, shivering and raging, and pushed her from him roughly in a convulsion of nervous distress, only to snatch her back to him the next moment in a quick, remorseful embrace. "Oh, Aelis—oh, Aelis, I can't help it! I'll send word to her when I can, I will, but not this way. I can't stop now, I must go on. I've no choice—"

The lighted doorway across the clearing darkened with the shape of a man. Robert's voice called: "Aelis!" placidly into the night.

"Good-bye!" breathed Harry, and was gone, slipping away through the trees in shivering haste.

"What are you doing there, girl? What is it?"

"A fox," said Aelis loudly and viciously, "skulking round the pen in the dark, the creature, and off like an arrow when you come out to him. You'd need a trap to take the likes of him."

She hoped her voice would carry to Harry's ears and set them burning. She hoped he'd find no one to employ him, and have to come creeping back here, and he'd see if she'd do as he bade her or as she pleased. Serve him right if they hauled him back home with a flea in his ear instead of treating him like a man and an equal.

All the same, she kept a blank face and a silent tongue, at some cost to herself, when she went back into the house. And in the darkness of her own bed, while they sat out the night with waning hope, she made her pillow damp and comfortless with tears.

Chapter Six

Parfois: *November to December* 1230

*I*t was half a year before she saw him again.

She was kneading bread, her arms flour to the wrists, when the doorway behind her was darkened, and she knew even before she whirled to face him that this was not her father coming home from his snares. He had not entered the room, but stood warily outside it, looking in at her, and before he would step inside he asked: "He's not home, then? You're alone?"

"Dear God!" she said, easily recalling her indignation even after six months. "Is that any way to walk in on a girl, when you haven't shown your face nor sent a word all this time? You should come with your cap in your hand and ask leave before you step in here. I'm not sure if I'll have you over the door-sill." She had him by the hand by then, and was drawing him in to the hearth, for the early November mist was on his shoulders, and his face looked thin and cold.

"You'll not try to keep me?" he said warningly, looking her in the eyes without a smile.

"I'll never try to keep any man who doesn't want to stay, don't think yourself so sorely missed. We've done without you all these months, we can do without you still." She pushed him into a seat on the stone beside the fire, and brushed the moisture from his hair, taking care not to be too gentle about it; and when he made no move to stop her she unfastened his damp cloak and hung it to dry. "Are you hungry? Though why I should care, when you left us like you did, is more than I know."

Once, if addressed in such a tone, he would have denied his hunger stiffly, even while it stared nakedly out of his eyes; but now it seemed he had learned sense enough not to climb on his high horse quite so easily and unprofitably.

"I am," he said almost meekly, "but I'd just as soon not eat you out of home, when I've brought nothing in. I can't stay but a little while. I didn't want your father to know I was back, for fear he'd want to hold me."

"You're your own master," said Aelis tossing her head, and brought him the end of a loaf, and cheese, and milk to drink, and watched him sidelong, not without satisfaction, as he devoured his meal. "By the looks of it," she said, "they haven't been feeding you any too well, where you've been. Did you find that work you were looking for?"

"Yes," said Harry indistinctly round a mouthful of bread. He had found it and endured it, but it had opened his eyes to what apprenticeship meant under another master than Adam. He'd learned from it, too; not, perhaps, very much about masonry, but a great deal about keeping his temper and holding his tongue, even under injustice. It had been a choice between bearing what he had or running back to Aber where he was privileged and protected, and for Harry that had been no choice at all. If he wanted to reach his goal he must come to terms with the stages of the journey, however comfortless.

"Did you bind yourself?"

"No," he said shortly. How could he bind himself, when he did not know the day or the hour when Isambard might come home? It was unthinkable to pledge his word to stay for a fixed term when he might not be able to keep it.

"Then they'd never take you on as better than a labourer." She knew what that could mean, when the labourer was as young and inexperienced as he, and she looked him over again carefully for the signs of his servitude, ignoring the forbidding stare that warned her off from probing.

He was still wearing her father's patched chausses and cotte, the short, rusty brown one she had mended for him; it needed more mending now. He was taller by a good inch than when she had last seen him, or he looked so for being noticeably thinner. His cheeks were hollow, and his hands scarred and soiled.

"I see he starves his boys," she said, "as well as working them hard." Her measuring glance moved to the corner of his mouth, where the line of his lips was prolonged in a short red scar, and then to his cheek-bone, which bore a suggestive blue stain. "And beats them," she said.

"What's that to you?" said Harry haughtily, turning the bruised side of his face away from her. "You said you know no reason why you should care."

"Oh, Harry!" she said suddenly in a child's wail of reproach, and fell on her knees by him, flinging her arms round him. The hunk of bread was knocked out of his hand and dropped on the edge of the hearth-stone. Aelis snatched it back and blew the ashes from it for him, blinking back tears.

"Oh, now, it's not been as bad as that," he said, shamefaced, and laid his arm awkwardly round her shoulders and drew her close to him. "The worst was keeping my hands from my dagger and my mouth shut. The youngest gets the kicks from all the rest, that's nothing new. One of the journeymen was a good fellow, and taught me what he knew, and stood by me all he could. But I missed having you to talk to when I had an hour to myself."

If the tone was a little condescending she did not complain; it was startling enough that he had brought himself to say it at all, and so he must have felt, for he coloured to the brows. He had wanted to give her something to remember him by; the feel of her warm and strange in his arm had surprised the clumsy offering out of him before he knew. Almost he repented it, it seemed to him so inadequate, not to her deserving, but to his weight and worth. But when she looked up at him astonished and unguarded in her pleasure his heart swelled, and he was glad he'd spoken.

"You're not going back there?" she said, fearful and jealous for him.

He shook his head.

"Where, then, if you won't stay here with us? Harry, what is it you're about?"

"There's a thing I must do," he said. If there had ever been a time when it had been a whim and not an obligation, that time was gone now; the thing was there waiting for him, blocking his path, and there was no way round it to his manhood.

"Will you come back here again when it's done?"

"Yes," he said, "when it's done I will. And when it's done I'll tell you."

"I wish you'd take me with you," said Aelis from under the shadow of her tangled golden hair, in a tone he had never heard from her before.

"That I can't do. But I'll come back. And look, I want you to have this. It's very little, all I've managed to save, but it's for you to use until I come back. Did they take Barbarossa away with them?" A new constraint came into his tone when he spoke of "them"; it cost him a giant effort now, as well as a convulsion of remembering pain, to look back towards Aber.

"No, he's below in the undercroft. They left him here for you."

He looked down into the fire, his lashes low on his cheeks. "Did they wait long for me?"

"A week or more. They inquired for you everywhere. In the end they had to go, there was no sense staying. They said you'd come back for your horse, and my father promised to send them word."

"And you?" he said with a pale smile.

"I didn't promise anything." And she was promising nothing to him, either; he knew that was what she meant, but he did not ask for anything. She must judge, too; he thought she would trust him and let him have his way.

"You could put on your own clothes again," said Aelis practically, pleased when she saw his eyes brighten. Yes, where he was going now he could at least appear as himself; the face was avowal enough, his dress should match the face. She went and fetched out the folded garments for him, and went about her business at the clay oven outside while he stripped and dressed himself again in the good Welsh clothes that had been made for him. The sleeves of the cotte were grown a little short on him, but that was no great damage.

"They're dry and clean," said Aelis over her shoulder. "You'll take no hurt from them. And don't forget your good cloak. I'll hide these rags away; father'll never know you've been here."

She turned, hearing the stillness that followed the rustling of his movements, and he was standing in the doorway, looking at her with a strange, soft look of mingled reluctance and resolution.

"I suppose you're off now, now you've got everything out of me you wanted."

"Aelis—," he said.

"Go on with you, then, and see you keep your word and come back afterwards."

He hesitated before her a moment, and then he took her hands and bent his head, and gave her the solemn kiss of kinship; and before she could draw breath and touch her astonished fingers to her lips, he was out of the paddock and away across the clearing into the trees.

All through the hours of dusk he crouched beneath an overhang of bushes under the broken edge of the plateau on which the church stood, and listened to the comings and goings above his head, where the garrison of Parfois boiled with agitated preparations for its lord's home-coming.

The company had moved fast since landing at Portsmouth with King Henry late in October. Word of their approach had hardly reached Pool before they themselves were in Ludlow. To-night, according to the rumours that were running round the streets of Pool, they would camp at Montgomery, and cover the last short stage to Parfois in the morning. In every village round the Long Mountain at this moment the news was blowing like a cold and killing wind. The jackal de Guichet, they said, was bad enough, but there were limits to his powers; but the old lion acknowledged no restrictions within his own honour, his rule was as absolute as plague. Word of his home-coming sent the very wild beasts quaking to their holes.

The climb had been no trouble to Harry, bred as he had been among the crags of Snowdon. This wedge-shaped promontory that led up to the isolated rock on which the castle itself stood was nowhere quite sheer, and stunted trees rooting precariously in its crevices afforded cover for one solitary boy, though they would not have hidden an approach in numbers. But there remained the problem which had been gnawing at his mind for months as he waited for his enemy to come home: how was he to get into the castle itself? There was only one way in, by the drawbridge and the gate-towers; he had racked his brains for an alternative, but there was none, short of procuring an ally within the walls, and that idea he did not entertain for a moment. No, since there was but one way in, by that way he must go.

At an ordinary time it would have been almost impossible to enter undetected, but tomorrow morning, when the Lord of Parfois brought home from France his forty knights and their followings, and the entire population of the castle came out to meet them and bring them in, then one more insignificant boy might very well slip unnoticed into the throng and get by the guard at the gate unchallenged. Once in he could lose himself among the excited household, and never be in one place long enough to be an object of suspicion, until he could find a means of encountering Ralf Isambard alone. Beyond that he did not look. There might be nothing beyond. Yet he could not stop short of that moment, and that was enough for him to know.

The sounds of Parfois were becoming familiar to him. He heard the hollow thudding of hooves and the duller sound of feet constantly tramping the timbers of the drawbridge. He heard many voices as people passed on the pathway from the bridge to the ramp. He heard vespers sung in the deep dusk from his father's church, and his heart stilled and quietened in him with wonder, as though at last he felt himself to be drawing near to the heart of a mystery.

Cramped and cold in his hide, he listened as the sounds of the day fell from him into silence one by one, until he could hear the measured pacing of the watch on the walk between the gate-towers. Then, closing all, the chains of the bridge rattled evenly through their pulleys, and Parfois withdrew for the night into its impregnable walls. He crouched still for a time after that, for there was no haste, and now that it was time he found himself afraid; there might be something to lose there, as well as something to find.

When the silence had been undisturbed for a long, chilly while he crept out of his nest and drew himself gently up the last few yards of broken rock into the long grass and bushes at the edge of the plateau. There were stars but no moon, and the sky had cleared into a frosty blackness. He could distinguish, when he emerged from the fringe of trees, the toothed edge of the curtain wall, its merlons jagged against the stars; but between him and them, breaking the serpent-line that coiled round the entire rock, the dark shape of the church loomed.

When he looked up, the tapering masses drawing his eyes aloft even in the dark, he could see the tall tower prolonging its leaping tension towards the stars. By daylight it had been a sculptured shaft fluted with runnels of light and darkness, withdrawing stage by stage in charmed proportion, shedding weight and gaining impetus as it soared. Now it was a pillar of darkness covering him from the eyes of the watch as he stepped out from the trees and walked steadily across the open space of grass.

There was a small wicket set in the great west door. He laid both hands to the ring and turned it, and it gave to his cautious thrust and let him in.

In the cold darkness within he groped his way to the narrow stair that wound upwards into the triforium, and climbed it, clinging with nervous hands to the stone. Many a time Adam had drawn him plans and elevations of this nave; he knew its proportions and could find his way about it even in the night. It was not only because of its convenient position and its many sheltering solitudes that he had chosen to watch out the night here. In the dawn, before the host came home, he would surely be presented at last with one window into his father's spirit, and add to the many aspects of Master Harry he had borrowed from other people one at least which was his own.

He felt his way along the narrow walk of the triforium to the distant end, close to the east window that showed a shapely pattern of starry lancets against the blackness; and there he wrapped his cloak about him and huddled into the corner with his back against the wall. It was hard lying, but so much the better, he would be in no danger of falling asleep.

There were times during the long hours of dark when he did drop into an uneasy doze, but never for more than a few minutes together. He was cold to the bone, and with the first faint grey of pre-dawn he got up and began to walk the passageway, stamping his chilled feet with an infinitely small, puny sound against the flags of the flooring.

The light came slowly. About him the walls grew out of the dark in gradations of grey, paling and solidifying, put on bulk and proportion and form. Details unfolded like flowers, the carved heads on the corbels along his walk grew features and hair, and smiled and grimaced as he passed; the procession of the capitals of the nave burst into ebullient growth, leaf unfolding from leaf in the vigour of life itself. Colour came later, even in the glass of the great east window; first there was only the shape of comparative light, then gradually the lattice-work of the lead cames, a filigree of shapes that had no meaning until the warmth of approaching dawn conjured into them cloudy reds and blues and greens, and with every minute breathed into them a purer brightness and a sharper clarity. Then almost abruptly there was colour in the stone, too, a warmth of sleeping gold gleaming through the grey. Shadowy and mysterious, the inverted keel above his head floated, half-defined.

His hands, which were apprenticed to the same mystery, arched and spread their fingers before him in air, involuntarily reproducing the tension and precision of the vaulting. They thrust and tensed with delight in their own intricate machinery of bones and sinews, as the ribs that sprang from the piers of the nave seemed to quiver with joy in their own energy. Then the drifting cloud that had massed before the rising sun parted, and a single shaft of direct light leaped through the east window, setting the rose tracery ablaze with glowing colours, and flew like a lance from end to end of the church, calling out of shadow the strong, slender ribs that patterned the vault with great starry flowers, turning the roof-rib to gold, and glittering in the curls of all the singing cherubim on the painted bosses.

He stood quivering to the gradations of light that sang in the roof, and did not know what it was that moved him so, the hour, or the true beauty of the proportions and spaces about him, or the marvellous and frightening sense of having drawn so close to the spring of his own being. He stared and was satisfied. So much of him was drawn into his eyes that he never heard the drumming of hooves cross the plateau from the ramp, or the rattle of the chains as the drawbridge was lowered in haste. Only when the hollow reverberations of the horses' feet on the timber rolled along the rock fissures below did he start out of his trance to the realisation that a company of mounted men was riding into Parfois.

Already? No, it was impossible, they would not march out of Montgomery much before this. Where was the haste? He stood tensed, straining his ears. The cavernous rumblings did not continue long; perhaps a score of riders, no more. Then quietness again. Some advance party with orders in preparation for Isambard's reception. His part was to lie hidden here until the main body arrived, and all the household poured out to meet them. A score of men, and mounted at that, were no use to him; he needed hundreds.

The wicket in the west door opened silently; he did not mark it until its weight carried it gently right back to knock against the wall. The sound, in itself small, was magnified by the lofty roof, and startled him painfully, and he drew back with a bounding heart into the shadows of the triforium as a man stepped into the church.

He was tall and lean, a long dark shape in a sombre cotte of dark brown or black, cut short below the knee for riding. Harry saw the jut of a sword-hilt at his hip, and watched him strip from his hands gauntlets that flashed sullen gleams of light from the iron rings banded into their backs. One of Isambard's advance party, and by the cut of him a man of importance. His dress was austere enough, but rich and ample, and worn with an authority that comes only by birth, and his movements had the unmistakable quality of nobility, the absolute conviction of one who has never had to hesitate or use caution and humility in order to placate his betters. They were also startling in their fierce, fluent grace. He walked forward into the middle of the nave, and stood looking straight before him at some point above the high altar. His face was in shadow, and Harry, fascinated and fearful, ventured to lean out a little from his eyrie to watch what he was at.

The man below could not have seen the movement, but he felt some shifting of the air above him, or heard, perhaps, if he had a wild beast's hearing as he had its gait, the mere rustle of a sleeve against the stone.

"What's that? Who's there?" he cried sharply, and reared his head instantly to stare into the trefoil opening.

Clinging close in the shelter of the stone, Harry looked down into a face suddenly vivid in the quickening light. Short, crisp hair, iron grey and still thick, lay close as a helmet on a head magnificently and subtly shaped, and was cut squarely across a great fleshless forehead. A clean-shaven Norman face, with a long, straight nose and an arrogant jaw, and eyes burning darkly in great hollow sockets. Why, he was old! The hard brown flesh was grown leathery and dried. And yet he was beautiful. The essential beauty showed through everywhere, and gave him a kind of timelessness that matched his movements. Through the stretched yellowish skin of the great forehead every moulding of the bone transmitted its permanent grace; through the thick, clinging hair the skull imposed its noble shape. Out of this splendid, imperishable lantern the deep eyes glared as though a stranger and a savage inhabited the dwelling an angel had abandoned.

Then he knew that he was looking at Ralf Isambard, lord of Mormesnil, Erington, Fleace and Parfois.

The moment had come upon him too soon; he felt his knees soften, and clung with rigid fingers to the pillar behind which he sheltered.

"What, are you there?" said the voice below, full and clear but very low. "In the old place, at the old time? Will you come down to me, or shall I come up to you? Who calls the measure now?"

Harry felt his way backwards to the wall, out of range of the searching eyes, and leaned there a moment to breathe more easily.

"Very well," said Isambard equably, "I'll come to you, since you will not come to me."

The sound his long-toed riding-shoes made on the flags was not clumsy, and yet curiously halting, like the pace of a lame man whose lameness shows only when he forgets to brace himself. The steps approached without haste the bottom of the staircase, and began to climb. On those narrow treads he must go carefully in such gear. Harry withdrew inch by inch along the dim passageway to the end, where he could have the wall on two sides of him, and flattened himself into the last shallow embrasure, beneath the last curved corbel. He hitched his belt round to have the hilt of his dagger readier to his hand, and loosened the blade in the sheath.

His inside was molten but his hands were steady. As well now as after days of hiding and waiting. Better. His bones bore him up again. His heart rose in his breast, not with hope or dread, only with awareness and acceptance. It was here; he had not to wait for it, and he was glad.

The measured step on the stairs had ceased; somewhere below there out of sight Isambard had stopped. Why?

The answer to that was made plain to him with a stab of dread when he ventured to peer out of his embrasure, for the tall figure was already at the top of the staircase and advancing silently and at leisure along the stone corridor. He had stopped to put off his shoes, that was all. The long feet in their well-fitted brown chausses made no sound. He was smiling, if that could be called a smile that drew his long mouth out of line, plucking the left corner obliquely upwards.

He said in the same low, intent voice: "Is this what you expected of me, Harry? Should I rather have brought with me the cross from the altar?"

Harry's heart had begun to beat thunderously. The man had a devil. How else could he know everything, the name, the intent, all? How near should he let him come before stepping out to confront him? He wanted space to move, some yards between them when he closed. He was young and quick, he had surely the advantage provided he kept room to recoil out of range. This man was old, old, by Adam's reckoning five and sixty years.

Now, he thought, stiffening his sinews. He drew breath hard, and stepped out from his shallow niche and stood in the centre of the walk. The last of the stone heads his father had carved looked over his shoulder. He had paid it no attention, for the light still reached it only by reflected glimpses; but Isambard had lived with it on close terms for fifteen years, and knew it line for line and feature for feature. He saw the stone face and the living face unbelievably alike, and checked in his steady advance, himself for a moment still as stone. Then the two faces which had seemed identical showed him as suddenly all their diversities. The likeness was there, Master Harry's divination had been marvellously guided; but he had carved a man, and this, after all, was no more than a boy, not yet grown. The stone face, lively and young as it was, had a certainty about it the boy could not claim as yet. The one was made, the other still making. He knew now who it was who stood before him.

"Well, well!" he said softly. "You are welcome. I've waited a long time for this."

Said Harry: "*So have I!*"

He set a hand to his belt, and drew the hilt of his dagger forward with a gesture there was no mistaking. Braced with feet apart, his eyes steady upon his enemy, he waited for Isambard to draw. The devilish smile, oblique and sharp as a scar, had come back to the gaunt face. When at length Isambard moved his hands to his belt it was not to the hilt of his sword, but to the buckles from which it hung. He unfastened them without haste, still smiling, tossed sword and sheath out from him through the trefoil opening, and let them fall into the presbytery. The clash they made on the stones below jarred Harry from head to heels, and for a moment shook the intensity of his concentration. He touched his hilt significantly.

"We're matched, my lord."

Isambard followed the gesture and laughed, moving his hand slowly towards his own dagger. The crooked smile was fixed and deliberate. Harry waited no longer. All the years of waiting and longing and wondering poured together into his braced hands and poised, quivering feet. He plucked out his dagger and hurled himself with all the weight and skill he had upon his enemy.

The shock of the assault carried them both a yard or two back along the passageway. The blade tore Isambard's cotte not an inch below his heart, but he had caught the lunging wrist in his left hand and jerked it outwards and downwards, and the thrust sliced through cotte and shirt down his ribs, and left only a harmless surface graze behind. He had not attempted to draw; Harry was aware of that even in the heat of his attack, and it enraged him past measure and gave him strength beyond normal. A long right arm as hard as steel took him about the body, prisoning his left arm above the elbow, and the grazed breast leaned violently over him and broke his balance. Feeling himself falling backwards, he drove his heel hard into Isambard's instep, and brought him down with him, heaving and struggling on the stones.

The fall broke their hold on each other, and Harry tore his wrist free and stabbed again, but again his forearm was caught and held, and this time he did not draw blood. Isambard let his weight lie over

him and held him down, and deliberately lifted the boy's right arm
and dashed his elbow hard against the paving.

Pain flashed like fire from shoulder to finger-tips, and all his
shrieking muscles tingled into helplessness. He fought to make his
fingers remain closed on the dagger, but they would not obey him.
He tried to reach across with his left hand and snatch the blade away,
but his hands were held apart, and he was pinned down struggling
and sobbing until the dagger slid slowly out of his fingers and
clattered on the flags. Then, still smiling, Isambard forced the boy's
wrists together, enclosed and held them mercilessly in one lean,
muscular hand, and with the other picked up the dagger and tossed
it after his own sword.

"Well, have you done?"

He held him down one-handed, smiling at his heavings and pant-
ings as he struggled to break free; but as soon as he tossed the
straining wrists away from him and sat back on his heel to rise,
Harry made a furious lunge for the hilt of the dagger Isambard
himself had disdained to draw. He had it half out of its sheath when
a hard knee came down on his forearm and smashed him to the
flagstones again.

"What, have I to strip myself before you'll cry enough?" said the
deliberate, amused voice, not even blown after all this tussling. And
he an old man!

Harry lay still, gathering his breath and tasting his chagrin, and
the hatred he had never truly felt until then congealed about his
heart like heavy fire. To struggle was only to weaken himself; he
could not displace the weight or break the grip that held him down.
They were still only man to man, and there was still quietness as
soon as they were quiet. He drew long, soft, angry breaths, waiting
mute and dangerous inside his helplessness like a beast in its lair.
Sooner or later Isambard would have to loose his hold of him. He
had promised nothing, asked for no quarter, made no submission.
It was not yet over.

"So, that's better!" said Isambard grimly, and drew off from him
and rose to his feet in one quick movement; but he kept his hand
on his dagger this time, and swung that hip away from the boy.

Harry, heaving all his angry energy into action, caught one dazzling glimpse of the lean, clear profile black against the sunlit air,

framed between the cusps of the trefoil, with a drop of thirty feet at least behind him, and the stone flags of the chancel below. The boy rolled over and came on to one knee in a single lunge, and hurling himself at the man, caught him round the thighs with both arms, and swept him with him through the opening.

For one moment Isambard was caught off-guard, but he had lived in and trained and trusted that hard old body of his for sixty years, and in emergencies his very muscles thought for him. His long right arm went round the pillar at his shoulder, his unshod feet stiffened into the stone of the floor to resist the thrust, and gripped it immovably. Harry's weight swung him round but did not tear him from his hold, and it was the boy and not the man who hung for a long, palpitating moment suspended on the edge of the drop. Even then he did not fight to recover his own hold on safety, but strained at his slipping grip on the man, dragging him outwards.

Isambard braced his weight back and held fast. He thrust his free left hand into the back of Harry's collar, took a fistful of him, cotte and shirt and all, and twisted until the boy's cheeks purpled and his eyes began to swim. Choking, he shifted one hand from his enemy to claw at his own throat, and instantly the fist that was strangling him heaved him roughly back from the edge and flung him down in safety at the foot of the wall. This time he was not released. The pressure on his throat ceased at once, but the hand had only transferred its hold to his arm.

"No more of that!" said Isambard grimly, clapping the bruised wrists together again and pinning them fast. He stooped over the gasping boy, and with deliberation and without apparent anger struck him three light, stinging blows on the cheek with his open right hand. Not even hard blows a man could take with dignity, only the manner of measured punishment he might have dealt out to a misbehaving child with whom he had not lost patience.

"That's for despising your own life, fool," he said calmly. "Learn to kill like a reasoning man when you must, not like a woman crazed with spite."

The boy crouched, glaring up at him fiercely, still panting, his suffused face marked now by the lean white stains of the blows, just beginning to flood with angry red. He set his teeth and said nothing, but his eyes were eloquent.

"I see he bred a good hater," said Isambard, looking him over at leisure as he held him, and smiling at what he found. "Well, well, this is a memorable home-coming! For you, as for me, boy, there'll be a warm welcome in Parfois. Let's go and savour it."

He jerked him to his feet, and separating the thin wrists he held, twisted them together again behind the boy's back, and so thrust him painfully before him along the passageway to the staircase. As they went they heard the clatter of feet in the porch of the church, and voices that spoke in reverent undertones, but not from awe of the holy place.

"De Guichet!" called Isambard, in a tone of high content. "Here am I, and with a guest for you. Call the guard, let them take good care of him, he's a desperate firebrand."

Three or four knights had come hastening in at the sound of their lord's voice.

"Do you know this face?" said Isambard, turning Harry about in his hands to display him to them all, and taking him by the chin to jerk up his face to the light when he turned it haughtily aside. The brief martial exercise, however unorthodox, had put the lord of Parfois in the best of humours. "Well? His temper should name him, if his face is something marred."

One of them, a thickset, bearded knight who by his manner might well be the seneschal de Guichet, said after a long, astonished stare: "This is Talvace's kin, surely."

"Talvace's kin, surely! It seems it was a son they carried off into Gwynedd. He's too like, the signs are too many on him to be son to any other man. We know, do we not, how to entertain a Talvace in Parfois? Here, take him! See him safely lodged in the Warden's Tower. And feed him," said Isambard carelessly, after a searching look into the bruised, defiant face. "Never let him say we starve our visitors, expected or unexpected. He'll be better sport, fed. He's puny enough now."

They received him readily, and haled him away across the moist grass just touched in the hollows with rime. And thus, not anonymous among hundreds but the centre and focus of a tight little group of a dozen guards, Harry crossed the drawbridge and made his entry into Parfois.

*　*　*

"And which of them," asked Isambard lazily, stretching out his long legs before him across the bare floor of the stone cell, "sent you to kill me, Harry? That fiery little mother of yours? Or Llewelyn? We used to be good enemies, that great prince and I, but somehow the enmity's grown cool of late. He's had his hands full with other matters, and so have I. No, I doubt it was not Llewelyn. I dare say he's bred you true to a Welshman's bounden duty, and taught you the sacredness of a blood debt, but I think it was not he who sent you here alone on such an errand. Well? Have you nothing to say?"

Nothing. The boy had not spoken since they thrust him into this sandstone cell under the ground and left him with his single candle and his narrow bed. He was neither too sullen nor too frightened to talk; when he had something to say he would speak up loudly enough. The trouble with him was that he was utterly astray here. There was nothing about him he could understand, nothing of which he could be sure.

What did they mean to do with him? Isambard would make little ado about hanging a marauding boy who had attempted his life, especially one who was no business of the county justices or the crown, and had no one in England to take his part. But if they meant to kill him, why delay? Why lodge him here thus roughly but not in any great discomfort? And above all, why should Isambard come down here in person to visit him after supper, splendid and ceremonious in his brown and gold brocade, attended by servants bringing in a gilded chair for him, and a page carrying wine? And why send all the hangers-on out of the cell? If he was merely bent on amusing himself with his prisoner, did it matter who heard?

"Or was it Benedetta?" asked Isambard.

No answer. Harry stared back at him with wild, wary eyes, the lids drooping a little with weariness.

"I see you know that name, Harry. Am I right in calling you Harry? It seemed to me you could have no other name. Come, you can tell me so much without giving away any other man's secrets."

"Harry is my name," said the boy grudgingly, in a voice that creaked a little with distrust and disuse.

"Good, I see you still have your tongue. I began to think you had bitten it out. So you are acquainted with Madonna Benedetta. Then she's still living?" No answer, but perhaps he found something in the watchful face that was not quite mute, for he smiled, and deep within the hollow eyes a spark kindled. "And was it she sent you on your mission to pay me my due? She had a score to settle, I grant her that. But time was when she could have commanded a grown man to do her errands and pay her debts."

Harry's lips tightened angrily at that slur, but he remained silent.

"And Adam Boteler, is he yet living? And that fellow of Benedetta's who helped her away to Shrewsbury when the Welsh took the town? Fifteen years, Harry, and you see I forget nothing. They soon withdrew from it, it was too hot to hold long. Shrewsbury will never be Welsh again for more than a matter of days, and Llewelyn has the wit to recognise it. It's exposed, but it's English to the bone now, nothing can change it back. Just as Poitou and Anjou and Normandy and Gascony, and all those pleasant counties where we've spent so many foolish months and so much good money are French, do what we will, and will continue French from this on. We may hold them again at a price a hundred times their worth to us, for a few months, a few years at a pinch, but French they will still be, and in the end we must leave go of them. Even Brittany, for all Peter de Mauclerc's homage to our lord the King. Let him call it an English fief if he will, it makes no difference to the truth, it's but a word. And that's all we brought back from this expensive jaunt of ours, boy. Thanks be to God, and to our expert shepherding, for failure may have cost us enough, but success would have cost us and our heirs dearer far. Henry's had his royal progress, since have it he would, now perhaps those of us who do the work here at home may find our hands a thought freer."

He looked up over his wine and caught the stunned green eyes, hopelessly puzzled and disquieted, and laughed. "How you stare, Harry! Am I not to think aloud in your presence? Your father grew used to it. Does it confuse you that I should do the talking and you the listening? Talk, then, and I'll be silent."

He waited, the crooked smile twisting his mouth, but Harry had nothing to say.

"So I'm to credit them all with this attempt on me, am I? I have a long reach, remember, and a long memory."

"I came of my own will," said Harry abruptly. "No one sent me. They've been looking for me to take me back."

"Ah!" Isambard leaned back in his chair, smiling. "You can speak to the purpose when you choose. Well, I see they've instructed you in the story of your birth, since you had so thriving a grudge against me. And what else have they taught you about your father? There was more to him than the dying. Have you a grain of his art in you? I've seen you have his curst temper."

It seemed to Harry that there was nothing he could usefully say to this bewildering and terrifying man, and indeed that he was not required to speak. Whatever was to happen to him would happen without any provocation on his part, and nothing he did in conciliation could ward it off. Better to be silent. He was very tired. All he wanted, all he hoped for now was to be left alone to come to terms with his plight. And he had so nearly succeeded! An inch higher and a thought quicker, and he could have climbed back down the rocks vindicated and free, with all his debts paid.

"True," said Isambard, grinning at him, "it's a pity to think I might have been dead by this, and you ten miles away on your road home. But these reverses visit a man now and then in his life, you'll find. No doubt God had his reasons. Come, let's see if you can be made to speak again. How did you pass the lower guard? Have I to hang all the garrison for letting you slip through?"

"I never passed through the guard," said Harry perforce. "I climbed the rocks."

"Well, well, you encourage me. Ten whole words out of you at a stretch! One more question, then." He spread his long, lean hands on the arms of his chair, and the rubies in his two rings took the candle-light and burned into crimson. Deep in his cavernous eyes the same red glowed steadily. "When they took Master Harry out of the river below here, where did they bury him?"

Harry held his breath, catching at that as at the first landmark by which he might hope to get his bearings. The tone had hardly changed, yet he felt at once that this was different; to this Isambard meant to have an answer.

So his enmity followed even the dead. After fifteen years he was still pursuing his feud against his master-mason, unwilling to let even his bones rest. Suddenly Harry felt the narrow cell so filled and overfilled with his own dread and hatred that he could hardly breathe.

"What do you want with my father's burial-place?" he said thickly through the gall that scalded his mouth. "You provided him his death, others have provided him a grave. You let him be."

"To do strict justice," said Isambard equably, "John the Fletcher provided him his death, and Benedetta procured him to do it. But I don't quarrel with your version. Harry, Truth is more than the naked facts. I killed him. Now answer my question. Where does he lie?"

"Where you'll never trouble him, my lord. As safe from you as you are safe now from his vengeance—"

"Ah, that may well be," agreed Isambard with a hollow, dark smile.

"—but not from mine, my lord! While you leave me alive, I shall be waiting to get a weapon into my hand again, and you within my reach." He was trembling now with the intensity of his detestation, his voice precarious with passion. "I always heard tell of you that you were a wolf, but never that you were come so low as to prey on dead men. As you would hunt him to the end, God helping me I'll hunt you, and see you into your grave before ever you lay hand on his."

"Gently, gently!" protested Isambard with galling mildness. "You're wasting your heroics, there's no one to hear. Better leave showing me all the good reasons for hanging you out of hand. I might be tempted to do it, and no one would be less pleased than you if I did. Never use words as gambling counters, Harry, unless you're prepared to pay the score in good coin afterwards. It's well for you I have other uses for you. There's this one thing you have to tell me before you hang. When that's settled, we'll see. Come, now, I mean to have an answer."

"You'll never get one," said Harry, setting his jaw.

"Oh, but I will, Harry, and from you and none other. Never doubt that."

The voice was silk, but it chilled Harry's blood none the less. There was a stony determination there that set him examining his own resolution in a panic, in case there should be weaknesses in it he never suspected. How did he know how far his virgin courage could be stretched? It had never yet been tested. He moistened his dry lips, and held his tongue, his eyes enormous and apprehensive upon Isambard's face.

"We have infinite resources," said the lord of Parfois delicately, "and all the time in the world. We can afford to go gently about our negotiations. These limited comforts we've provided you here, Harry—in what order can you best spare them? We'll take, say, food from you to-morrow. The next day, drink. Then warmth, perhaps, and last of all, light." He saw the long lashes drop for an instant and the lips contract fearfully, and laughed. Had he known it, he had merely started the echo of another man's voice in Harry's over-burdened mind, saying bitterly: "Light is the last thing a man should willingly surrender. Except breath!"

"A week wanting all these, and who can tell what tune you'll be singing? No need to take to cruder means until we must. You'll not change your mind, and tell me what I want to know to-night?"

He had risen from his chair, taking the refusal for granted.

"Not to-night nor any other night," said Harry doggedly.

"Ah, well, sleep on it. Your spirits may be a little duller and your wits a little brighter to-morrow," said Isambard tolerantly, and left him to his uneasy solitude.

"No!" said Harry.

He had been saying it nightly now for three nights. If his voice was less steady this time it was because he was cold, not because he was afraid. They had ceased to bring him food at the end of the first day, taken away his carefully hoarded drop of water at the end of the second, and the third refusal had cost him his coarse blankets and the thin straw palliasse on his plank bed. It was added cruelty that Isambard never asked twice. The boy's contemptuous: "No!" was always accepted without comment, and with no attempt at persuasion; but each night a soft, sidelong, tormenting smile recognised the growing reluctance and diminishing arrogance with which he spat the refusal at his questioner.

"Very well!" sighed Isambard, and reached a hand to take up the candle in its iron holder from the rocky ledge of the wall. The boy sat hunched on the edge of his bed, his slight shoulders rigid; the green eyes followed with an uneasy glitter the deliberate progress of his captor's elegant, muscular hand through a meagre yard of air, and lived through a wilderness of reluctance and temptation during its passage. His folded forearms hugged his cramped belly. Three days without food is a starvation-while to a boy of fifteen. But he minded the passing of the light more. His eyes lingered wistfully on the flame, followed it through air as Isambard lifted it. Shadows quivered in his fallen cheeks. He shrank a little more compactly into himself.

"In three days," said Isambard, "I'll ask you again. Three days this time—not one."

No answer, but the pinched face reflected clearly enough how the boy's heart sank within him. Above the guttering candle-flame Isambard's crooked smile offered him sympathy; voice and face had a devilish gentleness when he pleased.

"Think once more, Harry, before I go. Only a few words, and you can be taken out of this cell, fed, warmed, lodged in a better place," he tempted softly. "No need to condemn yourself to darkness." The light from below conjured into sharp gold and black every subtlety of the great forehead, and made the cajoling mouth piercingly beautiful and kind, but the demon still inhabited the gaunt pits of his eyes. "Tell me, and spare yourself."

Harry swallowed the soft strangulation of tears and clung with desperate hands to the obstinacy that must do duty for his flagging courage. "No!" he said, so relieved when it was out that the recoil made him faint and set him shaking.

The face, the hand and the candle withdrew backwards, still smiling at him, for the smile seemed to embrace all three, as though the withdrawing brightness emanated from the man rather than the flame. The door closed on them slowly; they thinned into a long, faint strand of light and vanished, and everything was dark, dark for three days; except that now there was no way of distinguishing night from day, and time, like hope and pleasure and companionship and all the human things it measured, had stopped.

A hand took him by the shoulder and shook him awake, and he started up with a cry, for a moment not knowing where he was or what was happening to him. There were torches and men in his cell. He clung shivering to the comfortless bed that seemed now the only tenuous security he had, but he was plucked away from it and hustled through the doorway, still bemused with cold and sleep. It could not be three days since he had been left in the dark; was it even three hours?

They thrust him stumbling up a winding stairway cut in the rock, and along another passage into a large, smoky room, blackened and bare but for certain engines and implements that stood against the walls, and a low brazier in the centre. He saw Isambard standing impassive beside the flame, de Guichet at his shoulder. Hazily through his sense of nightmare and unreality Harry knew the long shape of the rack with its ropes and pulleys, and the blackened irons laid by the brazier, and the whips dropped into sconces on the wall. He had always known this would come next. It seemed Isambard could not wait three days.

Now there was nothing left to him but the conflicting passions of his terror and his furious pride, knotted together in inextricable warfare in his bowels. He would not speak, not if they started every joint in his body, not if they beat or burned the flesh off him. Not even for his father's sake or his honour's sake now, only because he would rather die than give Isambard best. He might endure to be forsworn and dishonoured, but he would not endure to be defeated.

"You know, I imagine," said Isambard briskly, "the purpose of these instruments? Look at them, look well! You understand their use?"

Harry said: "Yes." But the croak that came out of his parched throat was hardly recognisable. He understood; his shrinking flesh understood, and had no hope of being spared anything.

"I want certain information from you, and I shall get it. Will you give in now, or later and at greater cost?"

He dragged out of himself somehow a better voice, loud and passably firm from sheer despair, that said: "I'll never give in."

Isambard made a motion of his hand to the men who held the boy pinned by the arms, and he was half-dragged, half-carried between them to the rack. He let go then of every dignity but the dignity of defiance, and fought like a wild-cat, lashing and struggling and biting, wearing himself out uselessly in an effort that could gain him nothing. But in fact he did get something out of it, a confused, exhausted numbness that almost comforted his aching muscles, and

robbed even his overwrought mind of its sharpest awareness as they
over-powered him. He was stretched helplessly on his back, the
smoky ceiling leaned to his face; he felt the straps drawn tight round
his wrists and ankles.

"For the last time, Harry!"

"No!" he said in a hoarse scream; and even then he was still able
to feel that it must be by the grace of God that what felt like the
terror of an animal in extremity should produce a cry of respectable
human rage.

He heaved and strained in his thongs, gasping for breath, trying
to brace himself, creating the agony before it came.

But it did not come. There was a long, strange, dream-like while
without motion or sound, and then Isambard's voice, controlled and
cool still, saying: "Let him up!"

Now he was hopelessly confused and lost, and the fear he had
extended himself to contain shook him from head to foot as they
unstrapped him and stood him on his feet again. He could hardly
stand, he had to cling to one of the arms that helped him up.
He looked at Isambard with great bruised eyes in which tears of
bewilderment were helplessly gathering.

"You should have taken it further, my lord," said de Guichet,
eyeing the trembling boy with a hard, measuring state. "A little
real pain would get more out of him than all the threatening."

"You under-estimate the little fool's curst nature. You might cut
him to pieces and he would not speak," said Isambard, thoughtfully
frowning.

"You could put it to the test in a very few minutes, my lord."
De Guichet had one of the whips from the wall in his hand; he drew
his arm back quickly, and slashed Harry across the face.

The boy gave a faint, startled cry, and fell back a pace, putting up
his hands to his bleeding cheek. What happened then he never saw,
it remained always a confusion and a blank to him, but certainly
there was another cry, louder and more astonished than his, and a
sudden sharp impact like a blow, and the clatter of the whip falling.
When Harry smeared away the blood from his face and opened his
eyes again it was to see Isambard standing with one foot flattening
the whip to the floor, and the bronze lantern of his face blazing with
such an intensity of dangerous, silent fury that even Harry, who was

no longer threatened, shrank with sympathetic dread. De Guichet confronted his lord with a pale face and fixed, fearful eyes.

"My lord, I thought to get you what you wanted, and what you'll never get by patience," he protested defensively, but with resentment thick in his voice.

"You thought! Did I bid you lay hands on the boy?"

"No, my lord, but—"

"Then keep your hands from him until I do so bid you."

The flame died down abruptly, the bronze head cooled into quietness. He turned on the guards who held Harry between them, and looked at his prisoner for a few minutes in silence. Then he said quite calmly, drawing his gown more closely about him as though the scene was finished: "Take him back to his cell."

The boy was led away staring dazedly. The large eyes, dilated with exhaustion, had the lost look of a child frightened among strangers.

"And leave him a light," said Isambard.

In pure reaction from terror he broke down and wept himself into a deep, swooning sleep as soon as he was alone with his blessed candle; but when he awoke strangely refreshed and heartened he had his wits again, and could reason about his escape. If there was one thing sure about it, it was that Isambard had abated nothing of his purpose, and if he had halted his experiment in terrorisation short of the act, it was not from any impulse of pity, but the result of a calculated probability that these methods would not get him what he wanted. It was not compunction that restrained him, but an inherent sense of economy that objected to seeing time and effort and pain squandered uselessly.

This reflection went far to set up Harry again in his own esteem, for it meant that Isambard had been sure of his victim's obstinate silence even under torture; more sure of it, if the truth were told, than Harry himself had been at the worst moment. It also made a pattern of sense out of the minor ordeals through which he had passed, and put him on his mettle for the future. For if he was right, then this lull foreboded some new and less direct assault upon him, and it behoved him to be ready for it.

Nonetheless he was almost gay that morning. He had his light back, and his blankets, they brought him food, and in every movement he was acutely aware of his still resilient sinews, and the smooth round joints that turned and bent in such a beautiful and ingenious fashion. Suddenly every finger was a marvel and a joy to him. All kinds of pleasures became apparent now that they showed as points of brightness in such an overwhelming dark. He trusted nobody and hoped for nothing, but the little delights that fell into his lap by the way had their due in appreciation at last.

He waited with roused senses for what would come next; and what came was so transparent that he had hard work not to laugh, and set out without more ado to take every advantage of a stratagem that would not have fooled a child in arms. Two of the youngest and pleasantest of his guards began to spend their time in his cell with him day and night, watch and watch about. Isambard was taking it for granted, it seemed, that a boy of fifteen could easily be seduced into giving his confidence, or at least some incautious fringes of it, to companions not so far from his own age and under orders to ingratiate themselves with him. Even if he did not allow himself to betray his secret directly he might let slip something that would provide a clue. But he never would! What, when he was already forewarned?

He welcomed them with open arms, talked freely, played draughts with the younger and learned tables from the elder. He revelled in their company, but he told them nothing. When Isambard came down in the evening with his question, delivered with a dry, impersonal smile as though the brief upheaval in the night had never happened, Harry gave his answer with only the slightest convulsion of fear at the pit of his stomach. It was accepted without comment. The lord of Parfois turned and went away.

It was the same the next day, and the next, and still nothing happened. He was uneasy in the face of this unnatural quietness, but he watched his tongue and waited. And in the afternoon of the fourth day his guards suddenly trooped into his cell and ordered him up and out with them.

"Where are you taking me?" asked Harry, feeling the familiar knot contract in his vitals. It seemed the present experiment was being abandoned as ineffective. What came next?

"Up to fresh quarters, lad," they told him, grinning at his suspicious face. "Fine lying, fresh air and the whole place to yourself. You'll think you're in a palace."

His heart sank, perversely convinced that he was to be transferred to some damp hole where he would be able neither to stand upright nor lie at full length, and chained there in darkness. But when they brought him up into the higher reaches of the Warden's Tower and shut him into his new prison he was stupefied to find it all they had claimed. There was a good bed along one side of the small, square room, a bench and a heavy table, even a brazier; and most wonderful of all, there was a high window, narrow and barred and unshuttered, but if it let in the wind, it let in the light and the sun, too. Many a time he had slept in worst quarters when he had attended David on his seasonal progresses in Gwynedd.

He stood in the middle of the room and stared mistrustfully round him, wondering why he should be so favoured. Was Isambard bent on winning him by kindness now? His strategy changed with bewildering suddenness, but everything he did was devoted to the same end, that was certain. When he came in the evening—it was by this time unthinkable that there should be an evening when he did not come—he might let slip something that would make sense of this new move.

It was later than usual when the lord of Parfois came. His face was serene; Harry had never seen him so content. He looked all round the room, checking its appointments with satisfaction.

"Well, Harry, are you comfortable here? Is there anything you need?"

"I need my freedom," said Harry.

"An error, child. You want your freedom, it isn't a necessity. You came here of your own will, I fear you must stay at mine. But at least you may be comfortable in your captivity." He turned from the window, which was on a level with his face, and came to where Harry stood. "Turn to the light. So!" He raised his hand, and with brusque, impersonal fingers which nevertheless had a surprising lightness of touch he felt the edges of the cut de Guichet's whip had left on the smooth cheek. "Closing well. You have clean-healing flesh, there'll be no scar."

"You're concerned for my face," said Harry, curling his lip.

"I'm concerned that no one shall mar it but myself. You're my meat, Harry, no one else's. De Guichet is zealous, but he overdoes things. Proportion is all, as you should have learned in your craft, and excess, as in this case, is so often unnecessary." He smiled, moving away without haste. "Well, if you have any needs you may ask. I'll leave you to your rest. Good night, Harry!"

It was impossible, but it was happening. He was at the door, he was going away without having asked the question. Harry could not bear it.

"My lord—!"

Isambard turned, his brows raised inquiringly. The contentment in his eyes engendered at its heart a faint, malicious spark of amusement. "Well?"

"What is this game you are pleased to play with me? You bury me underground, you threaten me with starvation and torture, you ask and ask always one thing of me, and then suddenly this ease. And no reason for it! And after all this questioning to one end, now you have nothing to ask!"

"Ah, that!" said Isambard, smiling. "That need not trouble you any longer, you'll not be pestered again."

"Not—?" Harry gaped at him, brought up short. "My lord, if you have repented of this pursuit—"

"I never repent, Harry. No need to trouble you farther, I know what I wanted to know."

"You *know*?" It was a trick, it must be a trick. And yet he had that smoothness of satiety about him, in his voice, in his smile, even in the touch of his hands. "I don't believe it!" said Harry violently. "You can't know. Who else could tell you? And well I know you never got it from me."

Isambard laughed, gently, tantalisingly. "Are you so sure?"

"Do you think I've let my tongue slip once with those creatures of yours marking my every word? No, my lord, you'll not fool me. I know what I've said and what I've not said. I'm sure as death."

"Very well, then you're sure. It's well to have so rock-like a certainty. I envy you. Good night, Harry!"

He could not go like that. Harry ran and caught him by the arm, clenching his fingers desperately into the folds of the wide velvet sleeve.

"You're lying! You must be lying. You *can't* know. I've never said a word to betray it. Every waking moment I've been on the watch—"

"And sleeping?" said Isambard, grinning. "None of us knows what he betrays in his sleep, Harry. Did you ever think of that?"

He wanted to cry out scornfully that it was a lie, but the dreadful truth knocked the voice out of him. How could he, how could anyone, be sure of his silence while he slept? With this one issue so heavy on his mind, might he not have muttered some confused reference to it in his dreams? His mind fought off the idea furiously, and yet it came back to fret his certainty again. How could he be sure?

"Did I not say, Harry, that I'd get it from you, and no other?" said Isambard, still laughing at his stricken face. He plucked his sleeve gently out of the boy's hand, and turned unhurriedly and walked out of the room.

The door which had opened hastily to let him through was just swinging heavily to when Harry roused himself out of his daze of doubt and consternation, and flung himself after in a burst of despairing rage.

"Devil! Devil! Damned carrion crow!" He clawed at the edge of the closing door, but the butt of a lance shoved hard under his ribs heaved him back gasping into the room, and the door closed on his convulsed face. They heard him battering furiously at the panels and shouting hoarsely: "What do you want with him? If you affront him, I'll kill you. Do you hear, Isambard? I'll kill you! Leave him alone, you devil! Leave him alone!"

Isambard had halted and turned in the passage, frowning a little, in two minds whether to go back to him, but in the end he did not; he merely waited for a little while, listening until the torrent of defiance had grown strangely shaken and softened with moments of entreaty. He smiled, recognising conviction. The muffled voice behind the door sank at last into hopeless silence.

Chapter Seven

Parfois: *December* 1230 *to* *January* 1231

*T*he boy who brought him food in the morning was a young fellow he had never seen before, and not one of the men-at-arms, but by the look of him one who belonged behind Isambard's chair in his great hall, or about his wardrobe to help him to dress. He was fair and pertly pretty, and not above seventeen, and his manner towards the guards in the ante-room indicated that he was a privileged person in the household. Some page from a knightly family, most likely, thought Harry, eyeing him distantly out of the obscuring mist of his own preoccupations. The youngster addressed him with condescending friendliness, and got a morose answer.

"You could be civil," said he, injured. "I'm sure I've done you no wrong."

"No, I know it. I ask your pardon," said Harry, stirring himself out of his lethargy of despair. He had been wakeful all night, gnawing over and over the tangle of his doubts and fears, and unable to worry his way through them to any certain hope. He would have given anything to believe that Isambard was lying. But why should he lie? Only to torment? There could be no other reason, and yet that did not accord with the placidity of his face and his voice, nor did it match with the image Harry was beginning to form of him. Everything he did had method and purpose. And if he was telling the truth, what terrible damage had been done unwittingly, and what incomprehensible and cruel outrage was to come of it? He was a prisoner here, helpless to act, and already frayed and fretted with too much and too bitter thinking. He stared out of his constricting net of anxieties and fears at this clean, smooth, well-intentioned boy, and wondered why he should be expected to make the effort to answer him at all.

The page came and sat on the bench beside him and spread his arms confidentially across the table, leaning close. The heavy door of the room was fast shut, but he sank his voice to a mere whisper as he said: "And I could do you right, if you had the wit to listen to me. Unless you want to rot here. It's nothing to me, if you don't choose to speak me fair."

Harry's mistrustful face turned to him slowly. The youth grinned at the dubious stare he got, but not unkindly.

"What do you mean?" The voice was grudging, and slow to have any truck with hope after so many bewilderments and frustrations.

"Here, you'd best be eating. It gives me a reason for staying. And you'll need it before to-morrow if you show sense."

It did not sound like a threat; there was even something of a promise about it. Harry pulled the wooden platter towards him, and broke the bread. "You're his man," he said ungraciously.

"Don't listen, then, if you're so curst. I'm my own man. I'm as free as he is, and my father's Gloucester's knight, not his, if you want to know. You're a fool as well as surly," said the boy, and stuck his neat, short nose in the air and bounced up from the table in dudgeon, but Harry caught him by the sleeve.

"No, don't take offence! I'm so low I can't help doubting every man who comes near me. What did you mean? God knows I don't want to rot here if I knew of a way out, surely that's plain."

The page sat down again, readily appeased. The face he leaned so confidentially close to Harry's was glimmering with triumph and self-importance. "He's given me the task of looking after your wants and bearing you company. And you're to be allowed the freedom of the outer ward, to take air and exercise with me sometimes. But don't think you'd ever get past the gate-towers. No one ever has.

There's no way out for you there." His voice sank to the finest whispering thread of sound. "But I know of a way."

Harry held his breath and reined in his heart from hoping. "A way out of Parfois? For me?" He had begun to tremble at the very thought.

The fair boy brought his closed hand out of the breast of his cotte and opened it proudly under the edge of the table. "Do you know what that is?" It was a small bronze seal, deeply cut. "That's his little personal seal, the one he sometimes uses to give authority to his special messengers. He gave it to me so that I could come in and out to you as I like. Whoever has that," he whispered impressively, "can go where he pleases and give what orders he pleases inside Parfois, and he won't be questioned."

"You'd be questioned fast enough at the gate-house, seal or no seal," said Harry gloomily, "if you had me with you."

"I know that, but we're not going near the gate-house. I know a way out of Parfois that hasn't been used for years, but it's still open if you know where to find it. There's a sally port under the rock. And old Ralf doesn't know I know how to get to it." He leaned back, glittering with triumph. "Well, what do you say to that?"

"You'd let me out?" whispered Harry, dry-mouthed. "Why should you? Why are you doing this? And how can you? As soon as they find I'm gone, what will your life be worth?" It was a trick, it must be a trick. Yet if there was the slightest chance of the offer being genuine, how he would leap at it!

"Ah, but I shall be gone, too. I shan't be here to be either questioned or blamed. Whether you choose to come with me or not, I'm leaving Parfois to-night. It was through you I got this chance, why shouldn't I share the benefits with you? But if you're too suspicious to trust me, stay and be damned. What do I care?"

"No, don't be so quick to offence," entreated Harry hastily. "Would you trust easily, in my shoes? Why are you going? How have they misused you here?" His eyes flickered involuntarily over the rich dress and pampered appearance of his visitor. The boy laughed, not at all displeased.

"Nobody's misused me. But I don't like it here, and I've good reason for going. I'll tell you if you like. My father is Sir Humphrey Blount, a knight of Earl Gilbert of Gloucester, who died last month.

There's a girl my elder brother wants to marry, and my family want it, too, but she likes me better, and I like her, and her parents won't force her. So when my father had to leave in the summer he thought fit to send me here to my lord Isambard, to keep me from under my brother's feet until Isabel's safely wed. Old Ralf likes me, and I've made myself very serviceable to him, and behaved myself circumspectly here. They think I'm reconciled, but I've only been biding my time for a chance like this one you've brought me now. I've not been allowed out of the wards, except under escort, that I owe to my father, I know. And to get to the passage I know of isn't easy, but with this little key I can open the doors now. I'm for home tonight, whatever you choose to do."

"But your father'll only send you back again," said Harry, still dubious. "Where's the use of it? Either that, or he'll see you moved somewhere else out of your brother's room."

"He won't, then, for he took the cross in the summer, after he'd placed me here, and went off to join the Bishop of Winchester in the Holy Land," said young Blount delightedly. "And my mother's on my side, and will talk my uncle round to her way of thinking, and in no time I shall be betrothed to Isabel. Her parents would as lief have me as Humphrey, and she'd a good deal rather."

The picture was so circumstantial that it began to be convincing, and Harry's heart hammered in his breast with hope and dread. He gripped the slender hand that dangled Isambard's seal. "You mean it? You'll take me out with you?"

"Why not? I owe old Ralf nothing. If he's trusted me I've never asked him to, and I've never promised him fealty. I can't help you once we're out, though. I'm for Shrewsbury, I know where I can get a horse there—"

"I'll need no help, once I'm out," breathed Harry, thinking with feverish urgency of the grave under the lee of the church at Strata Marcella, and the little curling leaf on the threatened stone. If Isambard was not lying it might be already late. "Get me past the walls and the rest is for me to do, and I'll be grateful to you lifelong."

"Mind," said the page warningly, "it's rough going down the rocks even from the gully. It has to be at night or we'd be seen. The way down on the eastern side, where I'm bound, is not so steep, but on the other it's a hard climb and a risky one. Which way are you bound? Back into Wales?"

"Yes, but I know the climb, I've done it already. Only let me past the walls and I ask no more." He was trembling now, he hated the thought of the long hours of the day dividing him from his hope. "When can we go?"

"After supper, but soon after, or they'd wonder too much at my coming for you. I'll have orders to bring you to old Ralf, they'll believe that. But hush, now, we're getting too loud, and I'm here too long."

He rose, flashing down at Harry the easy, sidelong smile of a born conspirator. "I'll come again at noon, then we'll have all settled. On my life," he said in a quick, light whisper, "I'm glad you've given up thinking I mean to trick you. I'm not used to being so mistrusted. If I don't put you safely on the outer side of Parfois, may I never see Isabel again. There! Could I give you a better pledge?"

At the last moment, when the barred window was already darkened, and the echoes from the outer ward grown scattered and few, Harry suffered an agony of fear that after all this would be like other nights, that Isambard would come with his taunting smile and his small, shrewd ironies that stabbed like knives; but instead came young Thomas Blount, true to his word, with his tilted nose and his provocative swagger, and flung open the door of the room with a flourish. He stood on the threshold dangling two keys in his hand, and did not bother to step within.

"You're to come to my lord Isambard in his own chamber. You may walk with me like a civilised man if you care to, but I warn you there'll be an archer behind to keep us in view, so I wouldn't advise you to try any tricks, they'd do you no good."

He waved the men-at-arms in the ante-room imperiously out of his path, and led the way out without even turning his head to make sure that Harry was following.

"Look blacker, fool," he said out of the corner of his mouth as they stepped into the cold darkness of the outer ward, "and drag your feet. You're not going to your wedding. There's no archer, don't be afraid. That was a flourish for them."

There were still a great many people about in the outer ward, but once they had passed through the archway to the inner ward the night world about them was quiet, troubled by only a few echoing footsteps. Harry had never been here before. He saw it now as a crowding darkness of giant shapes against the merlons of the curtain wall, dominated by the eyeletted walls of the tall hexagonal keep. Spears of light from loopholes stabbed outwards into the night and charmed up in sharp black and white disconnected passages of masonry.

"Where àre we going?" whispered Harry, quivering at his guide's shoulder.

"To old Ralf's tower, just as I told you. Ah, leave fretting, man!" he said impatiently, feeling the fingers that clutched at his sleeve tighten in suspicious anger. "We're not going near him, he won't bother us. We're going there because the door we want is there. There's another in the keep would have done just as well, but seal or no seal, they'd have wanted a better tale than I could think of before they'd have given me the keys of the keep. This one unlocks his private wine cellars under the tower, and this one is of the inner cellar, where the best wines are. I said he wanted some of his favourite French wine—there's an envoy from the Chancellor in with him to-night, so it rang true enough, even though he's never sent me to bring it before."

"That's a mort of doors between the garrison and the postern, if they were pressed," muttered Harry.

"Parfois never has been pressed. They've never yet had to use it. But his lordship's grandfather was a cautious man, and provided himself with a secret way out at need. Hush, here's Langholme coming from my lord. Keep close and look sullen."

He twirled his keys airily for all to see, gave Isambard's body-squire an amiable good night, and giggled like a girl as soon as they were past.

"In here, now, and quickly to the right, where it's dark."

They slipped like shadows through the great doorway of the Lady's Tower, and along a dark stone passage to a low oak door set in the inner wall. Thomas unlocked it with the larger of his two keys, and taking from its sconce the last of the torches that burned along the passage, led the way through to a narrow spiral stairway, and began to descend without hesitation into the depths.

"Are you not going to lock the door again? Suppose someone tried it? They might really want wine from below."

"No. Wait until I let you through into the last cellar, and then I must take the keys back to the steward. He'd be suspicious if I kept them long. It means I must leave the doors unlocked, but that's less risk than having him come looking for me within the quarter-hour, as he surely would."

"And your things? Where are they? You're not leaving Parfois empty-handed?"

"On my soul," sighed Thomas, injured but patient, "I never did see any fellow could find all the devil's arguments like you. When you're away down the mountain you'll still be sure I've laid a trap for you somewhere. If you must know, I dropped my bundle off the wall four hours ago, down into the copse under the eastern end of the gully. How could I come and fetch you away with my belongings under my arm? I know exactly where to lay my hands on them. Here, through here!"

The second key let them into a vaulted stone cellar, and groping torch in hand along the far wall behind the piled casks of wine, Thomas brushed the cobwebs from a low, insignificant door.

"There!" He drew back the groaning bolts and turned the rusty iron ring, and the door opened inwards with a protesting creak. Beyond there was the reddish darkness of sandstone and a breath of earthy coldness. "Now will you wait for me here in the dark till I take back the keys, and not imagine I've locked you in to starve? There's your warranty of a way out. And here, keep my purse if you like, till I come back. You can be sure I'll not leave that."

"I need no pledges," said Harry, shamed. "I'll wait."

He did not have long to wait, though it seemed an age to him. Within a quarter of an hour Thomas was back, hugging himself with pleasure in his own cunning, and they passed together through the little door, and drew it to again after them. From that moment they drew breath more easily, not afraid to talk above a whisper, and undismayed by the echoing sound of their own footsteps. Already Parfois seemed to lie behind them, and Harry had almost lost that tense expectation that at every step someone would reach out and take him by the shoulder to haul him back into captivity.

There were hanging cobwebs at first, but the torch swept a clean way through for them. The passage continued narrow, clearly cut and low-roofed, a safe and secret way out of the castle by which the garrison could retreat towards Shrewsbury, if too hard pressed, and by which it could receive stores and reinforcements in time of siege, or emerge to raid and counterattack by night.

"It comes out in the gully, well to the eastward end. You'll have to pass under the gate-towers to get down to the west. But you'd do better to come down with me and make the long trip round."

"No," said Harry, already in his mind scrambling down the rocks in the dark to Severnside. Should he make for Robert's assart? No, he would lose time rather than gain it, and a horse would be little help to him, for he'd have to go downstream to the ford. No, tomorrow was time enough to reclaim Barbarossa and see his friends again. Tonight he must make the shortest time of it he could to Strata Marcella, reassure himself that his father's grave had not been desecrated, and warn the prior of Isambard's malignant interest in it. There was a boat at the mill, and the current would help him down-river in the crossing and bring him quickly to the water-meadows by the abbey. Or if by any chance the boat was not there, or too securely chained, he could swim across at a pinch. The level would be reasonably low now, for the autumn had been dry; and the cold he could bear in such a cause.

"As you please," said Thomas airily. "I'd rather you risk your neck than me, but if it's a question of time you're justified; it would take you two good hours and more to work your way about."

The passage in which they walked had changed its nature gradually, and Harry had not noticed it until he stumbled in the broken formations of the flooring where all had been smoothly levelled before. He looked up, and the flickering torchlight showed him a vaulted cavern-roof innocent of tooling by men. They were in a deep crevice of the rock, and the faint lightening of the darkness before them was the mouth of a narrow cave opening upon the December night.

"We'd better douse the torch here," said Thomas. "Someone might look over from the gate-towers and catch the gleam of it. And from here on keep your voice down. When we come out in the gully, go to the right and keep close in under the rocks, and you'll be safe enough, for there's a good overhang."

Harry was shaking with relief and joy. To the last moment he had feared a trap, but this was the fresh air before him, the dim air of the ravine he knew, hemmed in with rock on both sides between the church and the castle. He felt for Thomas's hand and wrung it in the momentary blindness after the torch was quenched against the rock.

"What you've done for me I'll never forget. God speed to you, and I hope you get your Isabel."

They emerged into the sharp, clean cold of the open air, and overhead hung a crumpled ribbon of stars. There in the channel of rock they parted, Thomas going to the left, Harry to the right towards Wales. They embraced at the last, but did not speak for fear of the clarity with which even a whisper might carry here. Thomas was quaking with giggles like a girl, but Harry would never again be so easily taken in by that, after this experience.

Their hands parted, they were away into the night.

Harry went slowly and cautiously through the gully, feeling his way at every step until his eyes had accustomed themselves to the darkness, and could judge distances and distinguish the shapes of the weathered planes of rock that leaned over him. He knew when he was beneath the gate towers because he could see how the machicolations projected against the sky rounded shapes of darkness void of stars; but he heard not a sound, not even the tread of the watch on the walk between the towers. He was alone, the whole of the night was his.

The ravine widened and opened upon the sky, the curtain-wall with its vast bulk of darkness curved away from him to the right, and left him. He was on the rocky slope he knew already from more than one climb, and somewhere here on these smoother protected faces of rock were the plans he had scratched and pondered over so many months ago. He began to descend, and in confidence that he was now too far from Parfois to be heard he abandoned his caution and swung his way down the cliff with frantic haste. Several times he tore his hands and barked his shins, and once he missed his footing and came crashing several yards down the slope before he got a desperate grip with fingers and toes and knees, and clung sweating till he recovered his breath.

He could not go fast enough now to satisfy him. Hope and foreboding struggled in him and drove him, and there would be no peace for him until he saw his father's grave immaculate and at peace still, and knew quite certainly that Isambard had lied. And even then he must warn the brothers to be on their guard. The lord of Parfois was a law to himself; if he ever did discover where Master Harry lay buried, the Severn would not stop him from pursuing the dead with his living and virulent hatred, the Welsh border would be no bar to him, even the sanctity of the church would not restrain him.

The rocks gave place to tufted waste grass and bushes; he was down, and with nothing but a graze or two to show for it. He knew these sheep-slopes, he knew the woods below. He made good speed down to the river, and then there was a path to aid him as far as the mill. The boat was there, tied up and rocking gently to the swirl of the dark water inshore. It was not chained; he untied it thankfully, and thrust softly out into the current.

He was in midstream when the clouds that had covered the moon parted and drifted away, and before him on the distant bank he saw the gracious, massive shapes of Strata Marcella pastured like sheep in their silver meadows. He pulled strongly across into the inshore current, and let it carry him down abreast of the church before he grounded the boat and climbed ashore.

Here in the open grass he broke into a headlong run, lurching and recovering as the tussocks turned under him. He homed to the nameless grave like a pigeon, and fell on his knees beside it with a great sob of thankfulness. The ground about it was undisturbed, the stone unviolated. Isambard had lied. He was absolved, neither waking nor sleeping had he betrayed his trust.

All the tension went out of him. He leaned his forehead against the stone, and was suddenly so weary and so content that it seemed to him there was nothing left to be desired in life, and nothing more he need strive for. He had meant to say a prayer of thanks for his escape and for his mercy, but all he did was to spread his arm protectively across the stone, and lie there breathing deeply, embracing his father, and as gratefully at rest as though he had flung himself into Master Harry's living arms.

Behind him the grasses stirred almost silently, but he heard, and raised his head sharply. Cloud was advancing steadily again over the moon's face, and its shadow rolled across the mitred stones of the abbots, and covered the dark inward movement of the men who had followed him up from the water. Six of them, ringing him round, closing in on him from all sides.

He opened his mouth to shout a warning to the brothers in their distant dortoir; if it was not yet much after Lauds they might be waking, and hear him. But a hand was over his lips before he could utter a sound, and an arm took him round shoulders and breast from behind, and pinned him helplessly against a broad chest. They wound him in a cloak to pinion him from struggling, and twisted folds of the cloth hard round his mouth.

Isambard stepped into the dwindling lance of moonlight without haste, and walked the bright shaft of it until he stood face to face with the swaddled and muted figure of the boy. The stretched, polished skin over the lofty cheek-bones and the finely moulded forehead gleamed golden, the pits of the eyes were black but bright. He was smiling like a happy demon, almost tenderly.

"Well done, Harry!" he said softly. "Did I not say I'd get my answer from you, and none other?"

He smiled for a long moment into the raging eyes that would have struck him dead if they could. He looked from the waiting ring of his retainers to the blank and nameless stone, and in the last pale ray of moonlight his eyes caught the small, obscure shape of the carved leaf. He bent to trace its lines with a finger-tip, and lingered over it long.

"Take him back," he said over his shoulder, without turning his head. "He's told me what I wanted to know."

Aelis was out before dawn, in the frosty end of the starlight and the faint gilding of the still unrisen sun, making the rounds of her rabbit snares high on the hillside. She saw the little procession of horsemen climbing the ramp towards Parfois, and crept up through the trees to see more closely, for it seemed to her that the middle figure of the five was bound, and one of those who rode beside him led his horse by the bridle. They passed close to her, where she crouched still in the bushes. Four men in Isambard's livery, and one, slender and smaller than they, wound tightly in a dark cloak, the lower part of his face swathed, and his feet roped together under the horse's belly.

They might muffle his body and cover his face as they would, but they could not hide Harry Talvace from Aelis. She would have known him anywhere by the very set of his head, the mere shape of him, even so cramped and disabled. She slipped through the bushes alongside the sorry procession until they passed in through the lower guard of the castle, and disappeared up the tree-shrouded ramp. Then she turned and snatched up her rabbits, and ran for home with her bad news.

Where had he been all this time, that she should see him now being led prisoner into Parfois? What had he done, where had he slept, who had fed him? This was the first and only certainty, that he had fallen foul of Isambard, and was now in captivity. And even if the Prince of Gwynedd should send an army to set him free, how were they to get him out of that impregnable hold? She remembered his scratched plans and his frowning concentration, and for the first time fully understood that all that persistence had been devoted to the cause of breaking into Parfois. But now what miracle of ingenuity would be needed to get him out?

She should have slammed and barred the door on him while he was changing his clothes that day in November, and kept him there until her father came. She should never have let him slip away silently to Pool in the first place, but clung fast to him there among the trees and called out the men to overpower him. Better that she should suffer his anger and displeasure than that he should fall into the clutches of the lord of Parfois.

For no good reason she suddenly thought of the bruise on his cheek, the slight blue stain he had tried to hide from her, and burst into angry tears as she ran.

Within the hour Robert set out up-river to the ford by Pool, to carry the news across the river to the castellan at Castell Coch; and before the morning was out, a rider was despatched on the long ride to Llewelyn's court at Aber.

Harry lay all day long on his bed without a word to anyone who came in to him, and would not touch food or drink. In the evening

Isambard himself opened the door of the room, and even in his small closed hell of hate and despair and self-disgust, Harry knew who had entered, and drew himself erect before him. He would not even have turned his head for anyone else, but in the presence of his enemy, now truly and irrevocably his, no longer merely the legacy of his father's wrongs, he stiffened his back and reared his head.

"What's this I hear of you?" said Isambard in the formidably courteous voice in which he habitually gave his orders. "Refusing food and turning your back on the world? No man should do that unless he's ashamed of his dealings with it. Are you shamed? I know no reason why you should be."

"And you, my lord?" said Harry through his teeth.

"It's well known of me that I am not subject to shame. But why should you condemn yourself because you were taken in by an elaborate trick and an accomplished liar? Thomas lies as naturally as other men breathe, if he told truth he would be untrue to himself. It may not be a virtue, but there are times when it's an asset. He and I should be hiding our heads perhaps, but not you."

"What do you mean to do," demanded Harry, looking fiercely up at him from under drawn brows, "now that you've tricked me into this betrayal? If you disturb him, if you dishonour him, I swear to God I'll never rest until I've killed you. There's no name vile enough, my lord, for creatures like you who vent their spite even on the dead. Did he so outdo you, living, that you have not the generosity in you to let him rest even now?"

"He so outdid me, living," said Isambard with a dark and hollow smile, "that even now neither one of us can let the other rest. But just now we are concerned with you. You are another matter. If you think I shall allow you to sink into this silly shame of yours and eat out your own heart until you die of despair, you are in a great mistake, boy. Now you will get up and make yourself presentable— I'll see to it that the wardrobe shall provide you with clothes that will fit tolerably—and you will come to supper at my table and take your place among your peers, and behave yourself like a man and a Talvace, instead of a sick and thwarted girl."

"No!" said Harry, startled and stung into what was almost a cry of pain.

"But I say yes. You'll come, boy, because if you do not I shall have you dragged there. And you'll eat, because, by God, if you refuse I'll have food forced into your mouth and stroked down your throat, like medicining a hound. You'll carry your humiliation—since nothing can stop you seeing it so—in quietness and with a good grace, as other men have had to learn to do before you. Yes, and you'll brush sleeves with young Thomas, liar as he is, and restrain yourself from flying at his throat. He's no match for you, and I won't have him abused for being so good at the one thing he does well. You hear me?''

He put out an imperious hand and tapped Harry smartly on the cheek to turn the boy's face to him. Their eyes met in a long, arching stare. Isambard smiled.

''Leave the small game go free, Harry. Save all that fine, lusty hatred for me. I am the only enemy here worth your steel.''

Chapter Eight

Aber, Parfois: *January to April* 1231

*G*od witness," said Llewelyn, drumming his long fingers on the arms of his chair in a hard-driven rhythm that was always a key to the stresses of his mind, "it could not have come at a worse time. Well, we must do what can be done. My obligation to Harry is sacred for his father's sake, even if I did not love him like my own. As God knows I do."

"My lord," said Gilleis in a low voice, "I well know you do."

Yes, she knew, and she had never blamed him. Yet he had been to blame. He had never willed to injure or dismay the boy, but the thing was done and could not be undone. He looked out through the open shutters at the grey January sky over the strait, where the islands had vanished in frosty mist. The sea moaned and cried uneasily across the salt flats between, the incoming tide hissed beneath the field where the tragedy had ended. How many things had been done last spring that could not be undone? The boy's fate was the last and the least reverberation of that disastrous thunder, but not the least pitiful.

"Soon or late he would have gone," said Gilleis. "A little thing could have set him on his way any time these past three years, and it would have had the same ending."

She did not say a word of blame. How could she accuse the traditional education he had received at Welsh hands, when she herself was not entirely innocent? She had wanted him safe and sheltered, but she had wanted vengeance, too. Now she would have given up every lingering resentment, every long and bitter hatred, to have the boy back at Adam's banker, humbly cutting stone.

"The place is impregnable," said David sombrely. "There's no way of bringing up siege engines to the walls."

"If it were not, I cannot assay it. I'm in no case now to make war on any marcher lord. Wales has the first claim on me, and there's grave enough danger threatening Wales now; God forbid I should do anything to add to it. De Burgh is speaking us very fairly and friendly, but both his hands are gathering up the borders round us. He has an appetite for land and castles I would not willingly see in the King himself, but he's a more dangerous man than the King."

"But no soldier," said Owen with a brief grin, remembering Kerry.

Llewelyn's blazing smile showed abstractedly for an instant and was gone. "That's to make our own prowess less. I grant you we put a check on him once, and could again, but never think you saw the true measure of de Burgh in Kerry, there's more to him than that. It isn't the soldier we have to fear. He gets his conquests without fighting for them, and every one moves in upon us more closely. He has his new marcher holding of Cardigan and Carmarthen now, if the grant's confirmed—and confirmed it will be. And only a month ago he won two successes without a blow struck. You know them as well as I. John de Breos in Gower is no longer a tenant of the crown, but of de Burgh's new fief. And since Gilbert de Clare died in Brittany on his way home from this French campaign, the earldom of Gloucester and all its lands go to a child, and boy and barony are handed over to de Burgh. That makes him the master of Glamorgan. What Marshall leaves Welsh in the south, Hubert devours. It's only a matter of time before he begins to move north, and I have an itch in my sword arm says the time's running short."

"It might be well to strike first, before it runs out," said David. "It's coming to that in the end."

"So it might, but not westwards at Parfois. And the time's not ripe yet. When the hour does come I shall need a good, clear cause, every man I have and all the speed I can muster. I cannot touch Parfois. If I sent my army against a border lord on a private quarrel I should be throwing Wales into Hubert's hands. At best it would provide him with the opportunity to strike elsewhere while my back was turned, and at worst—and he'd see it plain enough—with an excuse to raise the whole royal power against me. What Hubert orders, Henry does."

"It's true," said Owen. Not even for young Harry could Llewelyn be asked to throw away Wales, which was David's birthright. And who would be more bitterly indignant if he risked it than young Harry himself, whose pride in his prince and jealousy of his rights had no match even among David's own blood-kin? "But the border's alive with irregulars. If a few more join them, these next few days, who's to blame you for that? Let me go, and if I run my head into a hornet's nest you may disown me."

"And do you think a dozen or so irregulars are going to break a way into Parfois? Nobody's ever done it with arblasts and trebuchets, let alone bows."

"Not by force," admitted Owen. "But there may be other ways in, or ways of bringing the quarry out."

"If he gave his parole he might be let out of the walls," said David with no great conviction.

"He'll never give his parole."

No one said no to that; they knew their Harry.

"Well," said Llewelyn heavily, "we'll manage as best we can. I can do one thing in the light, and that's send and treat for him in open negotiation. It may be that Isambard will let him go for a price. He's an older man and maybe an easier since he had me galloping the best of my horses lame over you, Owen. But even if he refuses, we have something to gain. We can at least bring the case to the light, and make it dangerous for him to harm the boy privily. We stand to England in a different relationship since John's day, and no prisoner for whom I have offered ransom can vanish now without an account being demanded. If he won't deal, we'll send formal notice to King Henry, and see that the law has at least knowledge of the matter."

Adam said unhappily: "But I doubt Harry went there to kill, and his standing at law may not be all we could wish. And the King's writ hardly runs in the march, to take a felon out of the hold of such as Isambard."

"That may be true, but it has vigour enough to ensure that he shall not be hanged out of hand." He saw Gilleis shrink in Adam's arm, and turned his face away into the shadow of his hand, wishing the words back.

Wales was a different matter. The march might be a girdle of lawless palatines, only elusively within reach of the King's justice, but the shadow of royal displeasure was at least a curb there; but Gwynedd, though it formerly owned Henry as suzerain, was a free principality, and could harbour runaways and make short work of captured felons with impunity. That was his achievement. The final and absolute statement of his sovereignty had been the hanging of a felon out of hand.

All our acts, he thought, come back upon us sooner or later. But Henry was not involved with my prisoner; he sailed for France and abandoned him without a tremor. Isambard has there under his hand a piece of my heart, and draws me by it with cords of custom, and indebtedness, and love, and guilt. And still I deny to answer. Like Henry, for a dream of empire; but his dream was a pageant in the sun through a conquered land, over soil alien to him, among people speaking a language he knows, perhaps, but not his own; and mine is of a country preserved and perpetuated, peopled with my own blood, speaking my native tongue, and the work is to be mine, and the fruit for David and for Wales, after I'm gone. Oh, God, does that justify me?

"And one thing I can do in the dark," he said, "behind my own back while I keep the peace. Take your party, Owen, and go to the march. I'll send Philip ap Ivor to Parfois to treat for Harry's release. Whatever the answer, Philip will meet you at Strata Marcella when he comes from Isambard, and if the man will not come to terms, then it's for you to act as you think fit."

"How many men may I have?" asked Owen, brightening into eagerness. It was only just, as well as practical, that the task should be his. He had once been a prisoner in Parfois himself, he knew the

castle and the country round it, and owed his escape from it alive to
Master Harry and none other.

"You'll do well to keep your numbers within bounds. Take a
dozen men, and if more can serve you, send for them."

"Will you take me for one?" asked Adam.

"There's no man I'd rather have. Come and welcome!"

"Send Philip here to me, Owen, as you go down. We'll put him
on his way to-day, and you shall follow at first light. Gilleis!"
Llewelyn caught her by the hand as she rose, with one of those
warm, moving gestures of his that came so suddenly out of the very
centre of his royalty, to join him by the heart with the simplest of
those who moved about him. Touches like that had bound men to
him for life, and their sons after them.

"Girl, never doubt but he'll come back to you whole and hungry,
as he always used to from the butts or the wrestling when you were
fretting over his lateness."

She said: "God grant it!" and clung for a moment to the great,
warm, vital hand that could put heart into her even now. Adam
drew her arm through his and led her away, for she was half-blinded
with tears. She had lost too much already in Parfois to believe easily
that anything of hers could come unmarked out of it.

When father and son were alone David stood warming his hands
at the brazier, and looking down with a clouded face into the red
glow. "Philip is a good man," he said slowly, "and carries weight.
He's dealt with the King too often to want influence, even with
Isambard. But—"

"Well?" said Llewelyn, dark-faced, knowing what was in his
mind.

"There's one who carries more, and could do this office to better
effect." His brows were drawn together in a frown, his face still;
the reflected light from the brazier made his fairness ruddy that was
usually so pale and clear, but even so the likeness was extreme. It
caught and twisted at the heart, and there was no armour against it.
"If you would but use her," said David, and turned his back and
went to stare from the window at the frosty strand and the shifting,
misty sea.

"I have full confidence in Philip ap Ivor," said Llewelyn, his voice harsh and dry. He felt for the words that should follow, the first step that was as hard as a death, or more truly, as hard as being born again. And yet it could have been said so simply. The hour may come within weeks, within days, to-morrow; and then, before I take the field with the fate of Wales in my hands, I have a need of her and a use for her here; and then I shall be loosed from this dumbness that binds my tongue, and I shall be able to say to her what needs to be said, and what as yet I cannot say.

He opened his lips, struggling to put off the pride and bitterness that held him mute; but the slight rustle of the tapestry at the door spoke first, and eloquently, and when he looked up David was gone, leaving still silent on the air between them the name that was not to be spoken.

Isambard was in his bath, washing off the sweat of the hunt, when they brought him word that there was a groom at the lower guard in Llewelyn's livery, asking safe-conduct for an envoy from Aber. He threw his head back and laughed like a young and boisterous man, till the drops flashed from the clustering wet tendrils of his iron-grey hair.

"The gods have no imagination," he said, stepping out of the tub on to the towels spread on the rugs before his glass, and turning himself about beneath Langholme's ministering hands. "They're for ever repeating themselves." He was known for a devout man, the lord of Parfois, a patron of pilgrims and collector of relics, and long ago he had taken the cross; when he wanted to blaspheme he turned to his classical education and its multiple gods, and loosed his barbs at them.

"So the news has leaked out already, has it?" said he. "Now I wonder how did they get word so soon? I'll swear the boy was alone, he told me himself the enterprise was his own. Llewelyn's well served in these parts, it seems. Well, fetch de Guichet here. I'll have him send an escort down to the riverside to fetch in our guest with ceremony. And tell the chamberlains to have an apartment made ready for him in the King's Tower, the best they can offer. Leave me now, Walter, I'll dress myself, there's other work for you. Take young Harry somewhere out of sight—the armoury, if you will, he's spoiling for exercise, he'll make no difficulties. Provide him

with playmates enough to keep him busy until supper, and see no
one tells him we have a visitor from Aber. And Walter!''

Langholme turned again in the doorway. ''My lord?''

''Let him be late in coming to the table. See to it! We'll have
them both off-guard.''

They ran in all directions to do his bidding. He stood flexing the
body he had preserved to himself by hard exercise and the austere
living that wore so deceptive a cloak of luxury. There would not be
a man at his table that night who did not eat more and drink deeper
than he. He examined himself from head to foot, assessing without
vanity the beauty that had once given him an honest pleasure, and
he marked without fear the changes that moved in upon him now
daily. He had seen to it that his spare flesh should not go soft
with time, or lose its springy vigour; but the years had revenged
themselves as best they could. The slender loins and wide shoulders
kept their elegance of shape and movement, the skin was clear of
wrinkles except for the lines of experience that had graved themselves into his face; but the flesh was drying and withering now,
hardening between weathered skin and shapely bone. The straight,
tall thighs grew lean and leathery, the arched rib-cage broke through
the shrinking flesh and etched its pattern in glossy light on the taut
skin. The magnificent engine was strong and skilful still, but the
suppleness and the sap were drying up in the long sinews, the head
was already a death's-head. He smiled; he had been on intimate
terms with death for a long while, it had no terrors for him.

''They might well send a priest to you,'' he said to his own image,
and reached for the clean shirt Langholme had laid ready for him.

Philip ap Ivor rode into Parfois somewhat before the early dusk
of the second of February. In all his discreet and circuitous years as
one of the most trusted of Llewelyn's clerical envoys, he had seldom
had such a royal reception. He wondered, as he dismounted in the
outer ward, precisely what it foreboded. Not, he thought, an easy
success. No one goes to the trouble to dress up compliance so elaborately. He ran a shrewd brown eye over the formidable ramifications
of Isambard's favourite castle, and speculated on which of the stony
holes under it held young Harry.

There was not a word said of business until they came to table in
Isambard's great hall, where the envoy found himself in the place

of honour at his host's right hand. On his own right there was an empty place, no doubt to be filled by some trusted official of the household. Isambard, like Philip, would be concerned with the discreet placing of witnesses to what was said; the contredanse had begun.

Philip looked round the high table in the blaze of torches and candles, and was encouraged. There were knights there not of Isambard's following, there were two English clerics of rank whom he did not know, and a burly young man whom he recognised as a nephew of Hubert de Burgh. The justiciar, he knew, was on excellent terms with Isambard. It would be well, if the opportunity offered, to precipitate the coming encounter there in public, before all these independent witnesses. They might not avail to get Harry out of his prison, but they would make it extremely awkward for Isambard to remove him quietly from the world afterwards.

They were very civil together, and very punctilious. The old wolf had lost neither his looks nor his sparkle.

"And what is troubling my lord the Prince of Aberffraw and Lord of Snowdon?" He managed to turn Llewelyn's imposing new title, compounded of the old sacred name for a reassurance to the Welsh, and the added flourish for English ears that had scarcely heard of Aberffraw, into a satirical comment, but he did it with great delicacy. "In what particular can I be of comfort to Prince Llewelyn?"

He, too, it seemed, wanted the encounter to be public. He had raised his voice so that it carried through the babel of the many conversations at the high table, and even reached the nearest of the lesser knights below.

"In the matter of his foster-son, who is missing from court since last spring. It has come to the Prince's ears, my lord, that the boy was seen some days ago entering Parfois, escorted by four of your men. I come to you to know if it is true that you hold him here in your charge."

"His Grace has, I believe, more than one foster-son," said Isambard, spreading his brocaded elbows comfortably. "Without, of course, numbering the one he himself holds in charge at Degannwy. With which one are we now concerned?"

"With Harry Talvace, my lord."

So he would have names named, would he? There was far more in this than met the eye.

"Yes," said Isambard readily, "Harry Talvace is here."

"As your prisoner, my lord?"

"As my prisoner."

"Taken in trespass on the hither side of Severn?"

"Taken in trespass on the hither side of my own guard, your reverence, if the whole truth be told."

"Ah!" said Philip ap Ivor. "That was not how we heard it at Aber. As the tale came to us, my lord, the boy was seen bound and muffled, being led up the slopes from Severn into Parfois. But not then within your gates."

"Very like. But you are speaking of an occasion some days ago, when we recovered him after an attempt at escape. The boy has been in my custody since November. As for how he first came into my hands, you shall ask him that for yourself."

"Then I may see him?" said Philip, promptly securing at least this concession.

"Very simply, your reverence. You have only to look down the hall at this moment."

Harry had come into the lower doorway at the right time, and was moving up between the tables to take his normal place among the young fellows of knightly family, his peers. Langholme had done nobly. The boy was flushed and gleaming with exercise and haste, his eyes bright, his cheeks freshly scrubbed, his dress a suit in rich Flemish cloth, long ago outgrown by Isambard's younger son, and re-fashioned now for the involuntary guest. If Philip had been looking for a pale, sickly, ragged and possibly fettered prisoner, Harry would be a considerable shock to him.

They saw each other at the same moment. Harry halted sharply at sight of the slender, elderly priest, austere and grey beside Isambard's splendour. The face meant home to him. He paled, and flushed as richly again, and his composure was shaken for a moment; but the small, testing smile in Isambard's eyes straightened his shoulders and stiffened his back. He left his place and came round the high table to kiss Philip's hand, and was himself embraced and kissed. Philip made use of the moment to compose the countenance which he was afraid had almost betrayed his surprise and consternation, and to revise all his ideas about his errand.

Nothing was as it seemed here. The boy was so far from being ill-used or closely confined that he apparently lived a normal life, at least within the walls, going and coming much as he pleased, and eating in hall like a member of the household. Princes enjoyed such easy captivity, but seldom commoners. Did Isambard intend to let him go gracefully, after all? Was he, for some reason, anxious to have good relations with Gwynedd, and using Harry's well-being as an elaborate move in the game?

"For to-night, Harry," said Isambard, "your place is there beside his reverence. You will want to talk to him about home, and he has things to ask you. He would like to know from you how you came to fall into my hands. Tell him."

Philip's thumbs pricked; in the sudden certainty that any further public avowal was designed to serve Isambard's purpose and not his, he made haste to speak before the boy could open his mouth.

"My lord, we should perhaps postpone this discussion until after supper. I had no intention of turning your table into a business conference."

"I could not discuss in Harry's absence what closely concerns him," said Isambard, "and I trust we can all be relied upon to continue our exchanges like civilised men. Speak out, Harry! Where was it I took you, within my own domain or outside it?"

Harry had lost the high, blooming colour he had got from two hours of strenuous play with blunted swords, and was pale now with a bright, wary, aggressive pallor. And it was surely not merely over-confidence of his good usage here that gave his eyes that insolent green blaze, and his voice the sharp, clear edge of defiance.

"Within it," he said firmly. "In the church, where I had climbed and hidden overnight."

"For some lawful purpose, no doubt, Harry?" prompted Isambard, the small, devilish smile growing warmer and fonder.

Harry's palms were slippery with a sudden, chilly sweat. He understood very well how he was being tempted, and for what purpose. Whatever he did would play into the hands of Isambard, whose traps were always dual, and could not be evaded. If he boldly avowed his real purpose thus publicly, he put himself in the wrong, and his cause past any help from the law, which would tamper here in the march only on unassailable grounds. Isambard did not mean to let him go for money, and was ensuring that the crown should not intervene to take him out of his hands perforce. The temptation to evade the truth was suddenly almost more than Harry could bear, so achingly did he want to go home. The first glimpse of Father Philip had made his heart turn and contract in him with the pain of the memories that tugged him back towards Aber, older memories than the bitterness and anger that had driven him away.

But if he lied, saying that he came to Parfois with no felonious intent, and attacked only when he was surprised and frightened, Isambard would have won a better victory. He would not find fault with the falsehood. Harry felt in his blood with what calming delight and fulfilment his enemy would embrace the lie that made him the victor. That was what he wanted. It would even be worth surrendering his prey, to have brought him down to the ignominy of lying to excuse himself. Everything that terrible man laid in the way between them was a test or a trap, and all his will was bent to break the son as he could not break the father.

"According to such law as I know," said Harry loudly and clearly, "it was lawful. By our Welsh code it's legal to kill in repayment of a blood-debt. No, it's an obligation! I came to kill you, my lord, for the killing of my father."

The brief silence seemed to stretch down the long room and hold fast by the pillars of the door, and every eye in the hall fixed greedily on the three at the high table. Isambard broke stillness and tension together, saying with careful serenity, and to the hall in general: "Lucky for us both that intent and act are sometimes so far apart. As you cannot choose but see, he did not kill me."

Even the oblique implication that he had feared to put his purpose into effect seemed to Harry a new pitfall for his integrity of hatred.

"I did my best, my lord," he flashed fiercely. "How many times in your life have you been nearer dying?"

The cavernous eyes, guarding in their depths those distant red flames of intelligence and appraisal, looked back at him laughing. The lord of Parfois pondered for a moment. "Perhaps three," he said mildly at last, as if he were answering the simplest and most natural of questions.

"Then do me justice, my lord!"

"Be quiet, child," said Philip, laying a hand restrainingly on Harry's arm, though he would have preferred to lay it about his ears if he could have had him to himself for a moment. Who could make a success of any embassage with such a turbulent brat at his elbow, over-ready with all the wrong answers?

"I ask your pardon, Father," said Harry, quivering to the touch. "But I was asked, and I must answer truly. I know no reason to be ashamed of it. I did what it was laid on me to do. But not well enough!"

"You are making things difficult for his reverence, Harry. He is here to inquire into your case and treat for your release, and I am prepared to listen. But I fear your position at law is more vulnerable than you suppose. The pity is that your Welsh code does not run here in England, where the offence was committed. But I grant your sense of obligation, and I am willing to overlook your trespass."

"My lord," said Philip warmly, "this is generous in you."

"On conditions, of course," said Isambard. "I will entertain your offer for his ransom, if he will publicly close his blood-feud against me, and pledge himself to think of it no more."

"I will not," said Harry loudly and quickly, before the temptation could lay hold too treacherously on his heart again.

"My lord, the boy is overwrought, he's saying what he does not mean. Can we not talk the matter over later in private? He'll be reasoned with, give him time and quietness."

"No," said Harry. "This is the time, and I am saying what I mean with all my heart. My debt is not discharged, and I cannot and will not forgo it until it is paid. God grant me another chance, and I'll make better use of it!" He could not help it, for an instant the restraint he was arduously imposing on himself slipped like a mask from his face, and the bitter blaze of his hatred flared from dilated eyes, burning ferociously upon Isambard's calmly smiling countenance.

"That could hardly be called a conciliatory speech," said Isambard delicately. "You'll understand that I'm loath to set him at liberty without some guarantee. I have the reasonable man's preference for continuing alive."

There was no sense in expecting any help from the boy, the only thing to be done was to exclude him as an irresponsible minor from the consideration of his own fate. "My lord," said Philip, "you shall have from the Prince the pledge you cannot get from Harry. Let us discuss what his ransom should be, since you are so generous as to entertain the possibility, and I will get for you full assurance that he shall be restrained from ever infringing your territory or your person again. If necessary the Prince will keep him in close ward until he sees reason. You know him, you know he'll hold to his bond."

"I know Harry, too," said Isambard, laughing. "He's no less a man of his word."

"The Prince has an authority over him he'll not deny. I am empowered to offer you five hundred marks as his price, and he may be held until you have the guarantees you want from Prince Llewelyn."

"No. Unless he will forswear this feud of his own will I cannot release him." He said it thoughtfully, as though he might reconsider, but Philip knew then that he had no intention of changing.

However, he tried. "A thousand marks would come nearer the worth of his release, in my own view, considering the circumstances. I will go so far."

"I regret, your reverence, that I cannot come to meet you."

"My lord, you have been forbearing with him, and I dare make an appeal to you to have pity on this headstrong youth, and trust his future good behaviour to us."

"Why, if he would ask me for pity, I believe he might gain it."

Harry believed it, too, and pity from Isambard was something he could not and would not bear; the mere thought of giving his enemy that satisfaction made his jaws set desperately to prevent the emergence of even one word or sound that might be mistaken for an appeal. Philip cast one glance at him, observed the signs, and thought better of making any demands on him.

"I am concerned to find him like this," he said, sliding away from the immovable barrier. "This is not the mood, these are not the spirits, in which I've known him at home. I fear he is not in such sound health as you may think, my lord. I trust he is allowed air and exercise? Perhaps if he might ride—under escort, of course!"

Isambard smiled. "I've lost fledgeling birds like that before," he said, "even under escort."

"You said he was a man of his word. Will you not accept his parole?"

"I would if it should ever be offered. Try him, your reverence."

They were always back to Harry, do what Philip would. On whose side was the young mule supposed to be? He set his teeth against every concession that might have got him his liberty, bent on doing Isambard's work for him, as Isambard had all along intended he should. He had put it on record firmly that he had attempted a sacrilegious felony, and was justly restrained in consequence. He refused to plead his youth or excuse his act or promise amendment. The Welshman in Philip understood and warmed to him, but the thwarted diplomat would willingly have beaten him.

He saved his last throw for the end of the meal, when the wine was flowing freely. Turning again abruptly to Isambard he said: "My lord, to return to the matter of the ransom. You have refused my offers. I ask you now to name your own price, and the guarantees you shall have also."

Isambard's deep eyes flashed to Harry's face and lingered there, untroubled by the naked hate and defiance that stared back at him. He smiled mockingly into the bitter green glare. "How can I put a price on a Talvace?" he said.

Owen and Adam came running to meet the little priest as soon as he rode through the gate and paced wearily into the stable-yard.

"We'd all but given you up, Father," said Owen eagerly, holding his stirrup for him while Adam took the bridle. "We've been looking for you these five days, and never a sign. Have you any good word for us?"

"Good, yes," said Philip ap Ivor sturdily. "The first and best word we could ask, and we must be grateful for it. The boy's alive and well, and in no hardship."

It was indeed the first and most urgent measure of good, and they breathed the more easily for it; but they read in the tone no less the failure of his mission.

"But he won't let him go," said Adam flatly.

"He would on terms, that's the rub. But on terms he knows the boy won't accept himself or let us accept for him. He plays him like a harp. He'll overlook the trespass on his lands and the assault on his person—oh, yes, there was an assault, and by all the signs a bitter one, too—if Harry will renounce his feud henceforward, but Harry will die first. He'll show mercy on him, if he'll plead for it, but Harry'll cut his tongue out rather. He'll give him a greater measure of liberty even so, if Harry'll give his parole, but Harry'll give him nothing short of a dagger. I can get no sense into him nor out of him, though I've been at him without relenting for days."

"You've seen him and talked to him, then? And Isambard let you speak freely?" asked Owen, marvelling.

"Let me? The man's so sure of himself he pressed me, would have me reason it out with the boy until I was satisfied. The only concession I could not get was leave to see him alone, but it's plain I should have got nowhere with him even so. It's been time and breath wasted. And yet," said Philip, shivering as the bleak little wind from Severn ruffled his grey tonsure, "I swear he has received very tolerable usage there, better than I dared expect, and why he keeps such a particular hatred against the lord Isambard is something I cannot fathom. There's some personal thing and deep between them. The father's quarrel was enough to move him to act, but it's some new offence against himself has sharpened his enmity to this extreme. He says no word of what's been done to him, he shows no mark, but the thing is there, and I cannot account for it."

They looked at each other across his furrowed forehead, and saw each his own thought staring back at him.

"But we can, Father," said Owen grimly, "or so I think. Come and see the thing that met us when we rode in here six days ago."

They led him through the great court and round the cloister to the flank of the east end of the church, where the mitred graves of the abbots lay. Close under the grey buttresses of the wall one of the long stones was propped on its side, the grave beside it laid open to the frosty sky.

Open and empty. Nothing remained of Master Harry but the faint dark staining of the stone where he had lain, a slender shadow outlined in rime at the bottom of the coffin.

Philip ap Ivor stood staring down into the blank cavity for a long moment with drawn brows and tight lips.

"This is profanation," he said harshly, looking up at last. "A sacrilegious outrage against a holy place. Men have been excommunicated for less.''

"So they may have, Father, when those responsible could be named. But who's to show who did this? We may know it very well in our hearts, but what is there to prove the offence on him?'' Owen's voice gathered anger from his own helplessness. "Look here, where they've chipped the stone when they raised it. Those marks are no more than a few weeks old, that's certain, but within that time no one knows when they were made. If it had not been for Adam's quick eyes we might never have seen anything amiss. He came running back from the grave the day we reached here, saying someone had been tampering, and we could scarcely believe it. But we looked, and there were flakes of stone in the grass below, and these fresh marks. And when we prevailed on the prior to let us raise the stone, this is what we found.''

"I know every inch of that stone," said Adam jealously, leaning to finger the carved leaf with a gesture of ungovernable tenderness. "You couldn't so much as bruise the mosses on it but I'd know. And I know the scores of an iron crow on stone too well not to know how these frets were made. We've lost him," he said, grieving. "Even his poor bones we couldn't keep safe.''

"None of the brothers ever heard any disturbance in the night," said Owen sombrely, "but in the night it must have been done, between Lauds and Prime. That's time enough for the wicked work, if they knew where to find him, and it seems they did. And if they did, they knew it from Harry. Where else could they have got it? Only a handful of us ever knew.''

"He never would have told them," said Adam stoutly. "I know Harry, he'd die rather.''

"Dying's a hard enough thought for old men, and terrible past bearing, maybe, for a boy. But God knows I don't say Harry told them wittingly, for I know him, too, and know him as stubborn in holding fast as any grown man among us. I say they must have got the knowledge from him somehow, by what manner of deception I know no more than you. And if I'm right, what better reason could he have for being so implacable against Isambard?''

"But if he'd known of this outrage," said Philip, looking from one to the other of them with searching eyes, "the boy would have told me in Isambard's presence. In open hall, I tell you, he spat out his detestation of that man for every page and scullion to hear. He is too full of hate even to be afraid, he would have accused him to his face."

"Isambard would hardly make him privy to what he's done, if this is indeed his work, as I swear I believe with all my soul it is," said Owen. "But Harry may know only too well that through him the secret of this grave's no secret. That's an issue he'd surely hold close between the two of them as long as he thought no absolute harm had come of it. He'll be clinging to the hope that we'll keep his father's bones safe for our part—and Isambard he wants for his own."

"And this is how we've done our share," said Adam bitterly.

Philip considered, gnawing his lip and frowning. "You've found no witnesses? No one heard men abroad at night or saw the river crossed?"

"None on this side Severn. Beyond that we haven't ventured."

"And what has been done in the matter?"

"Nothing as yet. We were loath to prejudice your dealings there, or do anything to rouse tempers until we had Harry back with us. And then, the prior's reluctant to make any accusations against Isambard but on good, solid evidence. Would not you be? The brothers have to live here, and it's but a perilously little way across the river."

"True, we must not put them in more danger than is needful. But this is a matter for the bishop, so sacrilegious an act as it is. We must make the facts known to him, but make no open accusation. Let the proper authorities do that, and in due form of law. I must talk to the prior." He looked round questioningly toward the river. "Was there never sign of a boat having put over from Parfois by night? No trampling of the grass? Nothing?"

"If there was, it escaped notice," said Owen, "and no one was looking for such signs, well it might pass them by. We know he's thorough, and puts such fear into those who serve him that they do his work as he will have it done. And I doubt the night in question was well past before ever Adam called attention to the sacrilege, and what signs there were to be read were long gone."

"Well, now that I am here and can have the tale formally, direct from the prior, it's for me to join him in sending word to the bishop. And you, where have you lodged your men? Not here? If you're to do any service to Harry, you must not appear in this."

"They're in Castell Coch, Father. I thought better not to burden the prior with such dangerous guests. If it should come to their being used, we could be the cause of burning his roof over him. But come in out of the cold," he said, seeing how the little priest hunched himself like a ruffled bird inside his gown. "Let's hear all you have to tell us."

They looked back at the corner of the church, for Adam was not with them. He had wandered away along the narrow trodden path through the grass while they were talking, to the small hollow cove where boats came in to the abbey meadows. He was standing at the edge of the water, looking into the turgid grey-brown eddies that poured down towards Breidden with such force and in so absolute a silence. His face was as bleak as the frost. They called to him twice before he heard, and then he started and came after them at a rapid walk, like a man driven by some urgent pain he could not slough off. Seeing the set of his countenance, Philip looked down the river where he had looked, and paled with apprehensive anger.

"You think he took that way? What, cast the poor remains into the Severn when he took them from the grave?"

"What else?" said Adam, low-voiced. "He threw him in there newly dead, and Benedetta with him living, to sink or swim together. John the Fletcher took them out of the water and out of his power for a while, but do you think a man like Isambard would ever forget or forgive the crossing of his decree? What would he do with Harry's body when he found it at last, but toss it back again to go downstream as he willed it to go, and leave its poor slender bones scattered all along the banks of Severn without a name or a resting-place? And if ever he got his hands upon Benedetta again, he'd send her after. That's the man he is," said Adam abruptly, and strode before them at a furious pace towards the guest-house, pursued by the pain he could not outdistance.

They forgathered again at Castell Coch near Pool, on a day in March, Owen and his twelve picked men. Three of them had kin along this border, and had spent the patient weeks just past in picking the brains of their cousins regarding the habits of the household of Parfois. Two more, with Adam, had been across the river in the villages beneath the Long Mountain, in Leighton and Forden overlooking the river, and even into the hamlets that lay inland, in the high valley of the brook beyond.

There were men and women there who looked narrowly at Adam when they clapped eyes on him, and being alone with him in quiet places called him tentatively by name. They brought him in after dark to their hearths, and answered his questions as well as they could; and soon they spoke of Master Harry Talvace, drawing up the image of him slowly out of the well of memory. They had not thought of him often in the years between, but he had never been very far from the borders of their hard and wary lives. He came back readily when his name was spoken; they saw him not tools-in-hand in his lodge under the church, nor frowning thoughtfully over his tracing tables, but naked to the waist and brown in the harvest-fields, swinging a sickle instead of a mallet, a slender young fellow with grass seeds in his tangle of dark hair, who might have come out of any cottage in the hamlet. That was what they remembered of him best. It was long since Adam had thought of him so, and he gathered the warmth of their recollection to him as gratefully as if he had salved one bleached and solitary bone of the beloved right hand out of the Severn, and laid it back in holy ground.

So Adam at least came back with a grain of comfort, though for the dead Harry, not the living. For the rest, there was little to report. They recounted all that they had learned in their careful reconnaissance, clustered in a corner of the great hall with the dogs round their feet in the rushes.

"So he's kept close within," said Owen at the end of it, "and that's no more than we expected. Never a glimpse of him since that good little lass saw them dragging him back into the wards. And the place is a nut we're hardly likely to crack with an army, let alone this handful of us. Harry won't be let out of it, we can't go in to him. So we must set about it a more roundabout way. If Harry never goes out and in, there are others who do. And hostages can be exchanged."

"Those who go in and out of Parfois," said Adam, "seldom go in ones and twos. This is border country, and Isambard never had any

illusions about the love the country people have for his household.
I've seen it again these last days. They ride out by companies,
whether it's hunting or hawking there are always enough of them
to make for safety. Do him justice, he looks after his own, or at least
he sees to it no one but himself shall flay them or hang them. Then
there's the matter of the hostage. If we took de Guichet himself—
I saw him pass the other day, twice as thick as when I knew him,
and the beard changes a man, but I knew that thwarted, ambitious
face of his—if we took de Guichet himself, would Isambard give us
Harry for him? Not for love! He despises him, and always did. For
the sake of his usefulness he might, or for his own honour he
might, but if I were de Guichet I'd never feel sure of it. Small use
threatening a man with harm to someone who matters not a rap to
him. And who does matter to Isambard?''

Once, he thought, there had been someone who had mattered all
too much, but by the grace of God and Llewelyn she was safe out
of his reach now, calm in her sanctuary above Aber; a refuge as
sacrosanct as the grave and almost as narrow. But for one other
person, perhaps, Isambard had cared in his time, before affection
changed to anger and hate; and not even the last and holiest stone
cell of all had kept Master Harry safe from his insatiable enmity.

"We'll not make do with de Guichet," said Owen. "We can do
better than that."

His dark eyes were shining hotly in the torchlight. He was remembering, too; the air thus near to Parfois was full of memories.
He remembered a homespun breast rough under his sleepy cheek,
and an arm that cradled him, and the steady rocking of the horse
under them on the long ride into the fringes of Wales that day; and
suddenly at parting the terrible knowledge in him that, if he let go
of Master Harry now, he would never get him back again. He
remembered clinging frantically to the stirrup-leather, and being
lifted back to the saddle-bow and comforted. Comforted but not
deceived. And then Adam holding and reassuring him in his turn,
himself utterly without comfort.

"There's one at least," said Owen, "who rides out from Parfois
almost unattended when he pleases. I've been following every move
he's made outside the walls these last ten days. He and his falconer
go out perhaps once in a week along the ridge towards the Roman

road from Shrewsbury. There's good sport over that high pasture, I remember it well from my time there as a boy. And there's a copse I know of, the end of a tongue of woodland that gives good cover for a retreat to the river with a prisoner. He passes through it every time he rides to the old earth fort on the crest. That's the place where we'll pick off our man. We could climb to the church rock, as Harry did, but getting a prisoner down the slope again with us might be too dangerous and too slow. No, we'll wait for the opportunity outside, if we wait here a month and more. And we'll take no seneschal or steward, either. We'll have someone whose liberty others will be glad to buy with Harry's, if he himself will not— we'll have the old wolf himself, Ralf Isambard and no other.''

It was on the fifteenth of April that they waylaid the lord of Parfois on his own ground, in the thick copse of scrub-oak and brushwood threaded by the narrow path that linked the main approach of the castle with the highway to Shrewsbury. They had lived wild in the forests below for nearly three weeks, waiting for their chance; and three sorry weeks they had been, saturated with spiteful April rains that had discouraged even Isambard from his usual activities. Twice Iorwerth's warning signal had fetched them hastily to their pre-arranged places; but on the first occasion Isambard had shunned the dripping copse and ridden away down the softer slopes eastward of Parfois, with his attendants strung out after him like beads on the string of darker green he left in the wet grass; and on the second it had been a full-scale hunt with a dozen or more guests and very nearly fifty retainers, and Owen had held his hand, unwilling to venture against such odds.

They had waited long and patiently for this third call. It came in mid-morning, and brought them all slipping through the branches and the coarse grass to lie hidden on either side the narrowing of the path with their bows strung and their shafts fitted, listening for the soft thudding of hooves that came as a reverberation along the ground rather than a sound.

This time it did not turn aside. This time it wanted the confused, drum-like fullness of great numbers. From the edge of the trees Iorwerth's green woodpecker laughed again.

''Good!'' breathed Owen soundlessly into Cynan's ear, in the bushes close to the path. The leaves were not yet full, but they served for cover, and the undergrowth was thick here. "Put an arrow into the ground in front of him when I give the sign—far enough ahead to be seen in good time."

Iorwerth had three bowmen with him in the rear, to ensure that once the party entered the wood they should not turn and leave it again. Adam was ahead with two more, to halt any who managed to break through. They would do no killing unless they must. They wanted nothing but the person of Isambard, and a sufficient start on their withdrawal to the river.

Ralf Isambard came into sight along the pathway, splendid in black, riding at a gentle trot. His dress was too rich for his usual strenuous hunting, nor were there hounds abroad, or Iorwerth would have known and signalled it long ago. He had no hawk on his wrist and no falconer at his elbow, only a handful of decorous gentlemen of his household, riding as though to welcome guests on the road and bring them courteously homewards. He wore a sword, but it had the light, ceremonious quality of a court decoration rather than a weapon for use in earnest. Owen counted nine riders at his back, three of his squires and six who might be knightly, officials or soldiers of the household, but peacefully disposed, it seemed, this morning of April. It was hard to believe in such luck. Ten swords to be reckoned with, but never an archer among them, and the soft, constant rain dulling all sound.

Owen dropped his hand upon Cynan's shoulder when Isambard was still some twenty yards short of them. The arrow left the string lightly, almost lazily, and struck and quivered in the centre of the path, some yards before the horse's feet.

The hand that held the rein tightened without even a start, the head that had been inclined easily forward in thought came up smoothly and instantly, every muscle in formidable control. Either he was smiling, or the gaunt hollows of his face gave him the daunting appearance of a smile. He was still, tensed and alert on the sidling, startled horse; but he had not been startled.

"Halt there, my lord!" cried Owen from his deep cover. "There are archers all round you. Make a move and we drop you."

Isambard lifted a hand without turning his head, and snapped his fingers at the shifting, uneasy murmur at his back. "Do as he says.

Be still!" The arrow in the path still vibrated faintly and rapidly, humming like a bee. "Well?" said Isambard. "What do you want with me?"

One of the young men at the rear of the little procession tugged at his rein and made to wheel and ride out of the wood. Iorwerth dropped a shaft across his path, and he thought better of it, jostling back nervously into his companions. Isambard had not so much as looked round.

"Walk your horse forward till I bid you halt," ordered Owen. "You only, my lord."

He had half-expected that the response would be a thrust of the long spurs and a head-down gallop for the open, and those ahead had orders to bring down the horse if Isambard tried it; but instead he stirred gently in the saddle and brought his mount edging forward in obedience to the order, dancing restively past the quivering arrow, and almost abreast of Owen's hiding-place.

"Enough! And now dismount."

Very slowly and deliberately Isambard slipped his feet clear of the stirrups and leaned forward as if to swing himself out of the saddle, but in the act he jabbed home hard into the beast's side with his right spur, and drove him not forward, but flinching sidelong into the bushes in a wild leap; and leaning both hands on the pommel of his saddle he vaulted out of it and dropped crashing into the bushes almost on top of Owen. Old he might be, but he sprang to meet whatever situation he encountered with the alacrity of a boy. He fell on his feet, coiled hard into a ball, and used all the weight of his body and the power of his long legs to project him forward again after the enemy who recoiled from his reaching arms. Owen eluded the embrace, but Isambard flung one arm round Cynan, bow and all, before he could either spring back or draw.

The broken twigs flew crackling from the fall they took together. They rolled with the bow whining and humming between them, and the fitted shaft snapped off against the stony ground. The head lay harmlessly flattened into the grass, but the broken shaft pierced through Cynan's tunic and shirt and stabbed and splintered against his ribs. He flung his weight sidewise and rolled away from the stab, and finding firm ground beneath his knees, heaved himself up with all his power and broke the hold on him. He was on his feet in an instant, and leaping back out of range. The string of the bow, snapping at the notch, coiled with a fierce whine about Isambard's arm, like a spring released.

But for that he would have got his sword out of its scabbard, and the fight they could not afford would have been on in earnest. But the momentary paralysis and the matter of seconds it took him to unwind and cast off the incubus cost him his chance. Owen had closed in behind him and flung a cloak over his head and shoulders, and twisted the skirts of it tight round his body and arms. Cynan flew to pin the struggling legs, and Meurig slid sidelong through the trees to help him.

It was all but over, and they had him. Owen drew breath and plunged back to the little group, still hemmed into a few yards of the pathway. There had been some disturbance there, too, when their master launched his attack. Three of the foremost had tried to ride to his aid, and one of them lay now propped against a tree with an arrow through the fleshy part of his right upper arm, clutching it tightly with his left to slow the bleeding. The other two had taken the warning, and reined in in time. Somewhere behind them one of the younger squires had been pulled from his mount, and was sitting dizzily on the grass nursing a shocked head in his hands, too stunned to give any further trouble.

The rest had taken the lesson. They crowded the path, uneasy on their uneasy mounts, looking from tree to tree in search of their assailants; but they kept their hands from their swords.

Owen reached through the branches to the bridle of Isambard's horse, that stood tossing his head and nervously trampling the path. He parted the bushes and drew the beast in to them, and left Cynan and Meurig to hoist the lord of Parfois across his own saddle and hale him away hastily among the trees towards the river. Owen was swinging back to order the rest of the party to dismount in their turn when he heard a voice raised suddenly at a little distance in a long, challenging hail.

All the tensed heads came up hopefully, all the too quiescent bodies braced, all the wary eyes gleamed. The young squire who crouched clutching his head suddenly slid like a snake for the cover of the bushes and lifted his voice in a great shout of: "*Á moi! Á moi*, Isambard!"

Iorwerth reached out of the leaves for him and choked him mute, but the damage was done. Not for nothing had this little procession presented the air of a party setting out to receive guests. Suddenly the earth was drumming and quivering with the beat of hooves, coming at a fast gallop along the grassy verges of the Roman road from Shrewsbury.

There was no time left for anything but withdrawal. Owen bellowed orders, and the bushes threshed as the Welsh circled their enemies and took to the thickest of the woodland on their way to the river valley. No time to stampede the horses and leave the riders unfurnished, and no sense in it, either, for there were other horsemen coming fast and in numbers, and they could not hope to stand off all of them. The only course was to plunge into the close-set thickets where riders could not follow and run for the Severn.

But it was late even for that. The Welshmen, crouching low and running like hares, overtook the two who led the laden horse only a matter of minutes before they were themselves overtaken. Isambard's men were mad to establish their zeal now, and the woodland rides were not yet too steep and overgrown to give them passage. Crashing merrily on their heels came the newcomers, horseman after horseman, knights and squires and grooms, flashing the red and green mascles of the Earl of Kent's livery.

Owen waved Cynan furiously onward, and turned to stand off the assault. The bowmen slipped backwards from tree to tree, fitting and shooting as they could, the lancers aimed for the men rather than the horses, and brought down three in the first onslaught. Then the riders crashed among them as they hugged their covering trees, and it was a chaos of hand to hand fighting and opportunist running, without shape or direction. Some way ahead in the bushes a horse bellowed, and Cynan's angry voice roared defiance. They had reached the muffled prisoner and overrun his guards.

So it had all been for nothing! They could not hold him now, they could only hope to come off with their lives and unidentified. Outlaws from the forests to the south, grown over-bold; let them be taken for that, and they might yet make another and a better attempt.

But to be so near, and then to fail!

Adam ran crashing downhill in a narrow dark ride, almost into the arms of a man who came striding suddenly out of the bushes, sword in hand. The sword was dabbled at the point, and the man was laughing. The short, iron-grey hair, ruffled from his unceremonious usage, stood in tangled locks on the magnificent head Master Harry had loved to copy in stone. The clear, imperious voice, lately gagged by the folds of an archer's cloak, was singing gently to itself, and did not fall silent even when he instinctively took one dancing step back from the collision, and then as readily translated the movement into a forward lunge that almost passed Adam's startled guard. Only then, as they swung in a half-circle with a hiss of blades between them, changing places on the slope like a pair of dancers with only a foot of air separating their faces, did Isambard know his mason again.

They flung each other off and stared for an instant, each of them aware that he was known, each conscious that this recognition made many things plain. Then Adam closed in again furiously, pressing his opponent with a flurry of strokes, and for a moment Isambard gave ground. He parried almost mechanically, his eyes leaving Adam's face only by swift, flickering glances; and suddenly he leaned hard forward and caught Adam's blade on his own, and with a fierce turn of wrist and elbow wrenched the weapon half out of a shocked and bruised hand. Adam recovered it strongly, but there was an instant when Isambard could have killed him, and they both knew it. Instead he lowered his blade and drew back a rapid pace or two, nostrils wide and long lips smiling savagely, and suddenly turning away, vanished into the bushes.

Adam ran on towards the river confounded and astray, to blurt out his concern and incomprehension into Owen's anxious ears. They drew off as best they might to lie in hiding until nightfall and lick their wounds; and in the dark they crossed the river by the ford at Buttington and went to earth with their defeat and their chagrin in the forest under the ridge of Gungrog Fawr.

Owen had a badly gashed forearm, Cynan some splinters of his own shaft lodged deep under his ribs, and all of them minor cuts and bruises; but they had left behind them on the crest several of their enemies wounded by lances and arrows, some probably dead. They had come off lightly. But they were known now, Parfois was alerted, and the thing was to do again, and against infinitely greater odds.

And why, thought Adam, sleepless and sore in his damp cloak under the trees, why am I here to fret at it still? Why did he withhold his hand and leave me yet alive?

Chapter Nine

Parfois: *April to May* 1231

*A*h, they'll show their hand again," said Isambard, shrugging off his escape lightly. "I'm warned now, I know what to look for. They're over the river by this time, and so should I have been if you had not come so prompt to your hour. It hardly suits me to challenge their comings and goings formally. Let them stew, and they'll soon betray themselves. And when they do I shall be ready to move."

His thirst was deeper than usual that night, his colour higher and his eyes brighter. That brief brush had done him good, body and spirit. He had withdrawn early with his guests, for they were bent on leaving next morning, and their business with him was not for the openness of the hall.

"Well, so the Earl Marshall's gone. And half of south Wales to be disposed of in consequence. His brother gets Pembroke, no help for that. But this wardship of his over the de Breos lands, that's a plum indeed, and one the King won't willingly confide to Richard along with his earldom. I don't wonder my lord of Kent is holding out his hands for it. But it seems it's already fallen into other hands." He smiled, watching the smooth, impenetrable diplomatic faces that maintained their benign reasonableness even for him.

That poor rash fool de Breos, who had run his neck into Llewelyn's noose a year ago at this same season, had left a fine bone of contention behind him with his wide lands and his four little daughters. Now that their good uncle of Pembroke and natural guardian was gone there would be more than one pair of noble and greedy eyes turned on their fat marcher holdings. But it was not the earl's death that had sent these influential couriers of de Burgh riding hard across country to Parfois, it was the fall of the coveted prize into the hands of Richard of Cornwall. How had Hubert let Elfael and Brycheiniog slip through his fingers in the first place?

"Hardly the best hands," said Warrenne carefully. "His Grace the Earl of Cornwall is an excellent young man, but very inexperienced to be put in charge of so grave a trust."

"True," agreed Isambard, obliquely smiling. "He has certain claims, of course."

There was no need to labour that, de Burgh knew well enough how delicately the business of displacing him would have to be undertaken. Richard was the King's brother; according to Henry's mood and caprice that might make the young man either indispensable or unthinkable, but even for de Burgh it made it difficult to disparage his stewardship openly. Moreover, he was recently married to Earl William's sister, which gave him a family claim to an interest in the children and their estates. "His marriage is but two weeks old," said Isambard thoughtfully. "He may be somewhat off his guard where other matters are concerned."

They kept their admirable calm at that, permitting no shadow of a smile to answer the wicked look he gave them.

"The justiciar is chiefly concerned," said Warrenne, "that Brecon and Radnor should be in the hands of someone who understands their importance to England. You of all men, my lord, know that at this moment the issue between Wales and England trembles on the verge of war, and that Brecon and Radnor may be vital to us. No one can present that point to the King so well as you. You have kept this march inviolate from the encroachments of the Prince of Gwynedd, and you have seen his inroads on those less wary and less able than yourself. Moreover you think, as does the justiciar himself, in terms of England, and like him you see no advantage in clinging to old and now artificial connections with territories on the mainland of France. The future of England is here in these islands. If this nation is to grow great in establishment it must grow here, my lord. Westwards into Wales."

"And northwards into Scotland," said Isambard softly.

"My lord, no one has ever proposed any threat to the sovereignty of King Alexander—"

"Not yet," said Isambard. "That's still to come. Not in my time, and not in Hubert's, maybe, but come it will." He rose abruptly, and began to walk the wide chamber with his wine cup dangled lightly between his fingers, a habit of his when he was thoughtful. "I am with the Earl of Kent in this, as he well knows. I divested myself of all my own French honours and laid them in my elder son's lap on condition he should be content to be French, as I had discovered I was English. A man cannot be both. And I see, as Hubert does, that the sea must be our frontier, but within that frontier we can and must be a unity. Nevertheless, I should advise him to tread gently as yet in the march. If he gains this custodianship from the Earl of Cornwall, he will be master of a third part of Wales. He should beware of presuming too far on the patience of the Prince of Gwynedd."

"The justiciar has no territorial ambitions for himself," said Piercey quickly. "He is thinking for England."

"He is thinking for England," said Isambard bluntly, "and for Hubert, too. I have no quarrel with that, provided he sets them in that order. But if Hubert provokes Llewelyn into action, it's England that will take the blame and the blow, and let him remember it."

Nevertheless he would hold with Hubert, that he knew. It was this very vision that drew him to a man with whom he had so little in common besides. The rest, even Ranulf of Chester, still saw only their own palatines, and built at them and fought off encroachments on them feverishly, looking no farther. But this low-born de Burgh, this double man despite himself, even while he leaned back greedily, hankering after lands with the ambition of the landless, even while he envied the de Blundevilles and the Marshalls and composed about himself a synthetic replica of their hereditary splendour, yet saw England by glimpses as Isambard saw it, an empire not decomposing and falling to insecure tatters like the Emperor's sprawling hold, but compact as a clenched fist, solvent as a Jew's treasury and self-sufficient as a well-run manor, a power not hemmed in but completed and transmitted by the sea. For the sake of the veritable man of state Isambard, born to dominion, forgave the collector of castles and amasser of manors. Moreover he was perversely drawn to a man so apt to be hated.

"None the less," he said, turning again to face them with a calm and decided countenance, "I think it indeed needful that this march should come into the justiciar's hands rather than Earl Richard's. He shall have my support in seeking to have it transferred to his care. You may tell him I'll do what he wishes."

"And you'll come yourself to the King, my lord? The court is now at Windsor, but with these Welsh raids already infringing the territory of Brecon who knows how long his Majesty will be left in peace there?"

"I'll come," said Isambard, "as soon as I have dealt with these Welsh raids of my own. If my agent can pick up their traces clear of the garrison at Castell Coch I'll have my friends from Gwynedd running for Aber within a week. And if the King leaves Windsor in the meantime, the justiciar may send me word, and I'll come to him at Gloucester or wherever he may be."

"My lord," said Warrenne warmly, "he knew well he could rely on you. Your counsel on all matters concerning the march carries such weight that the King cannot fail to listen to you."

"It will be no hindrance, either," said Isambard dryly, "that as at this time there is, as I hear, a certain animosity between the King and his brother. Between my arguments for him and young Richard's against, I doubt not that Hubert will get his way."

It was fifteen days before Isambard's inconspicuous agents in Pool and about the hospitable courtyard of Strata Marcella picked up traces of the Welsh marauders. Looking for them was in effect looking for Adam Boteler, who alone had been marked and recognised; and Adam had orders to remain out of sight in Castell Coch until the second attempt was ready to be launched. It was no part of Owen's plan to let his whole company lurk there, now that they were compromised; in case of close inquiry that would have been all too clear an indication of Llewelyn's unofficial complicity in the enterprise, and however little doubt Isambard himself might have on that head, it would not do to let it be established and admitted. They were and they must remain irregulars, to be disowned at need.

So Adam sat chafing in Castell Coch while Owen and his men camped in the forest beyond Gungrog Fawr, and waited until they should find a chance to cross the river again. Owen was for trying to get word through to Harry in his prison; there were men in Leighton who had kin within the castle, and for the sake of Master Harry whom they remembered well might be willing to risk the carrying of a message. But April ended, and their daily reconnaissance confirmed that still the fords and the ferry were watched, and the river shore on the English side patrolled day and night. They waited; he would not keep this up for ever, he was not so wary of his life and liberty.

If Adam had not issued from his hiding-place early in May they would not have been discovered; but the messages which had come from Llewelyn were grave enough to warrant a risk which by then appeared so slight. The disturbances on the borders of Brecon, whether officially encouraged or not, had grown to such proportions that the King had despatched his brother the Earl of Cornwall to the march in haste to try and suppress them, and was himself in the act of setting out from Windsor to join him there. A breath on the flames, and there would be fire from end to end of the march; and the Prince was in urgent but still friendly correspondence with King Henry in the effort to settle the dissensions peacefully and without affront to either Welsh or English honour. So wrote Llewelyn from Aber; and between the lines they read plainly that though he might still be arguing for peace he had ceased to believe in it or greatly to desire it. It was only a question of the hour.

So Adam slipped out of Castell Coch at dusk, and himself carried the word to Owen in his camp in the woods overlooking Cegidfa; and a beggar who had hung about the gates for some days and been fed from the kitchens went after him every step of the way. By the next dawn Isambard had the news for which he had been waiting; and the following night he put two parties across the Severn, one upstream from them and one down, and converged upon their hiding-place from either end of the ridge.

The alarm came at about three in the morning, a barn-owl's

screech out of the night from Meurig on top of the ridge to Iorwerth waking and on guard at the camp. They had damped their fire till there was no red, and yet the attackers came fast and unerringly for them, from the north and from the south. Iorwerth shook Owen awake and they stood to their arms rapidly and in silence, but silence and darkness did not cover them.

"Glad am I," said Adam in a hurried whisper into Owen's ear as they deployed among the trees, "that I never went back, to leave you a man short."

The assault from the north came with a flurry of tinder among the trees, and a crackle of sparks on a driving breeze. The full foliage of May did not burn, but the mould of dry, dead leaves and brushwood on the ground caught fiercely, and flared down upon them so fast that they were forced to turn and run, having no time to take the harder way up to the crest. Southwards the long arms of Isambard himself were stretched to receive them; the fire died on their heels after that brief flare, and left them on the points of English swords.

The archers loosed blind in the darkness, but could do so only once without imperilling their friends, for after the shock of meeting it was stark hand to hand work without any daylight art about it, first a hacking and swinging ahead at any flesh that moved, then body to body fumbling where everyone panted out words in his own tongue to be safe from his comrades, and even swords were of little use. They clutched and wrestled, feeling their way to one another's throat with the dagger or the naked hands. They shortened swords and used them like daggers at armpits and neck. Then the wind rose, fanning the few sparks left alive in the brushwood; the fire flared into life again and gave them light to see by, and they broke apart from their terrible embraces and sprang off to blade-length and lance-length.

The capricious blaze, devouring the easiest fuel, hissed between them and drove them apart, and Isambard came leaping through it, grinning like a demon and bringing with him a shower of sparks and the smoky, scorching odour of hell. For a moment he launched himself upon them alone, and Owen closed with him gladly against the glare, though dazzled by the flickering gleams and blinking shadows. Then the fire died down and Isambard's more timorous followers came hurtling after him, and by sheer weight swept their opponents before them down the hillside.

The fire burned out behind them. Darkling they drew off as best they could, dragging their wounded with them, carrying them when they dropped. Three times their number drove them unrelentingly a mile and more through the broken copses and across the brook south of Cegidfa. They fought, and ran, and stood to fight again, tiring, separated, driven now like hunted hares, until Isambard called his men back at the brook and let them rest at last.

Owen had then Adam and three others still marshalled at his back, not one of them whole, though these at least could stand and go. Searching back wearily and wretchedly through what was left of the night they found Iorwerth dragging himself painfully along the grass like a trampled snail in a slime of blood, and two more who crawled and swooned by turns in the fringes of the wood. Three bodies they brought down hacked and clawed from their camping-place, and Meurig, last of all, they found in the dawn on the crest of the hill, pinned to the ground by his own lance. By the time they had brought the dead down into Cegidfa, Iorwerth was also dying, with the priest from the church kneeling by him; and before noon one of the other two worst wounded followed him.

Owen laboured over the living, mending them as best he could, and over the dead, making them ready for burial, until he fell and lay like dead beside the last of them, but still conscious and aware, and Adam and some of those who had come with the priest to their aid carried him away and bedded him in quietness in one of the cottages. When he had strength enough he turned his face into his arms and hid from the light. He had lost half his command, and failed of winning back Harry for whom he had come. He did not know that Isambard, unsure of the numbers with which he had to deal, and always thorough, had brought forty men to sustain the assault against his dozen; and even if he had known it would have brought him no comfort.

Every one of the dead men ached in him like an amputation. Iorwerth had taught him to ride, Morgan had been his idol in boy-hood by reason of his prowess at wrestling, Meurig, unfree but irrepressible, could never be kept out of any fight though his only real duties with the army were as a baggage-servant. Owen fingered them over with his exhausted and beaten mind, and bled and burned without tears. Even when Adam lay down beside him, groaning with the stiffening of his grazes and flesh wounds, Owen did not stir. Even when he laid his hand on him gently, he did not uncover his face.

Harry was so intent on his work that he did not hear the door open. He had moved the table under the direct light from the window, and was bending over the tough, cross-grained wood and the awkward knife with knit brows, breathing heavily. Isambard, putting the door to very softly behind him, was stabbed by yet another of the recollections that fronted him every way where Harry was. If the boy had growled over his shoulder: "Stand out of my light!" the illusion would have been complete. I see, thought Isambard, that all human life moves in inescapable circles, and brings us back to moment after moment we thought past. Why? Is there yet something that can be changed? An imbalance that can be adjusted?

He came silently almost to Harry's shoulder, and still the boy was not aware of him, so perfectly was every sense concentrated on the block of wood before him. He must have picked it up from among the sawn logs in store for fuel. But where did he get the knife?

"I see you *are* his son," said Isambard.

The boy's head came up sharply, the green eyes flashed their invariable challenge, and flew back jealously to the shape of the opening flower that was heaving itself painfully out of the wood. With a violent movement he clenched his fingers hard on the knife and pared the flower cruelly out of the block like a blemish from an apple. The grain was too complex and cross for him, the blade stuck, and in the same instant Isambard stretched both arms over the boy's shoulders and seized his hands, forcing them apart and wringing them until he twisted with pain and let go both the knife and the wood. Isambard caught up both, and stood for a moment staring down with a formidable frown at Harry, who nursed his bruised wrists and glared back, expecting a blow and tensing every muscle to receive it without a tremor.

It did not come. Isambard's quickened breathing stilled again. He looked at the torn flower, his eyes hooded.

"Was it worth so great a violation to do me such a little hurt?" The boy was silent, his mouth set.

"Who gave you this knife?" It was pitiful, the broken blade of a dagger that he had bound with strips of rag to give him a handle, and sharpened as best he could on the edge of the stone under the window; the worn hollow, paler in colour, was there to be seen. If he had been asked where he got it, that obstinate jaw of his would have remained clenched, but Isambard knew how to ask his questions now. He had only to say, with that threat of punishment in his voice: "Who gave you—?"

"No one gave it to me. I found it in the armoury and hid it. It was thrown away for waste."

The poor make-shift clattered on the table under his startled eyes. Why had it never occurred to him to use it for more than carving? And why, if his enemy had the same thought in mind, should he toss it back to him so carelessly?

"Why have you not asked me for tools, instead of breaking your finger-nails and your heart on firewood and trash?"

"It shall go very hard, my lord, before I ask you for anything."

"God's life, you arrogant imp," cried Isambard between laughter and exasperation, "do you presume to be prouder than your father? Or are you simply afraid to show openly what you can do where he's been before you?"

"My lord, I know better than any that I am not his match," said Harry, stung and colouring vividly. "I never meant to challenge him, I was carving only to pass my time—" His voice faded out wretchedly on the disclaimer, for that, too, was spoiled and finished now that Isambard had stripped it bare.

"Not his match! And have you not the heart in you to be anything but best? How many are his match? How many in this world do you think stand in the front rank? Are all the rest of us to give up and sit on our hands rather than serve humbly where we deserve?" He held the mutilated carving close before Harry's face and made him look at it. "There! Dare to tell me that you see nothing there of him, that you have no feeling for the strokes of your hands, that you have no will in you to venture after him! Say it, if it's true, and I've done with you, you may rust unprovoked for me. Only to pass your time! Faith, that's the first lie I ever heard from you!"

Harry sat mute, his lashes lowered, his cheeks burning resentfully. But when he looked up again fleetingly at the spoiled flower he could not keep all the compunction and fondness out of his eyes.

"Get up!" said Isambard abruptly. "Come with me. It's time you looked at your inheritance."

Harry jerked up his head distrustfully, eyes flaring wide. His inheritance? What kind of talk was that from this man? If there was anything here that came to him from his father, it could be nowhere but in the church, and he had never yet been allowed past the gate-towers, and could not believe in any such concession now. Nevertheless his eyes had begun to gleam with an excitement that was unwilling to be lured into hope.

"Ah, no!" said Isambard, discerning his flight and plucking him back to earth. "Not that, not without your pledge. But come and see!"

Hard fingers encircled his arm and haled him out of the room, and he went like one in a dream, unable to resist but ready for some treacherous pitfall to open under his feet at every step. There had always been a trap waiting for him somewhere along the way when Isambard loosed the reins a little, and it would be the same now. But they went together down the narrow stone stairway, and still he was not jerked back again. They crossed the outer ward, followed by covert glances and whispered wonderings that halted for a moment the bustle and business of the day.

"Here, in here!"

The lean hand gripping his arm thrust him in at a door in the long encrustation of buildings that clung to the curtain wall on the sunny side, where the best light fell and the day lingered longest. A large, bare room with big trestle tables in the centre and benches along the walls. There were several chests and one great press, and on the tables were laid out some unfinished drawings and a litter of instruments. There was no one in the room at this moment but themselves. Isambard pushed Harry gently forward and closed the door behind them.

The boy stood looking round him with a wary face and large, intent eyes. Isambard's hand on his shoulder brought him to the bench at the end of the room, where a film of stone-dust coated the floor, and several fragments of carvings and half-cut blocks of stone lay pushed together against the wall, as though discarded long ago. There were drawings, too, rolled aside out of the way, and ranged along the bench a great array of tools, mallets, chisels and punches, from the coarsest to the needle-fine, all their handles polished and worn with use.

He looked round at Isambard; the green eyes questioned frantically.

"Yes," said Isambard, "this was his tracing-house. Those are his tools."

He watched the quivering face that was averted haughtily from his too close perusal. "Twenty-four years old he was when I found him in the provost's prison in Paris, and paid his fine to get him for my own, him and that foster-brother of his whom you know well."

Was he living or dead this day, that same Adam? Last night's lesson had been taught blind, there was no way of knowing how many had survived to get it by heart.

"A part of your father's gift I think you have, if you can learn not to deface it for spite because I am in the same world with you."

Harry drew breath to deny the slur, and then said nothing after all, seeing in his heart that it was true enough. He put out his hands almost against his will, took up one of the mallets and swung it testingly to get the feel of its balance, picked up a punch at random and applied its point, none too deftly because his hands were tremulous, to a half-defined fold of drapery in the nearest block of stone. The mallet tapped with a sweet, small, occupied sound. The boy smiled faintly, and then bit hard on his lips and gnawed the smile away. He looked at the handle of the punch he held, fitting his fingers wonderingly into the shape another hand had worn in it; a good hand, muscular and slender, shaped very much like his own.

"His tools," said Isambard softly. "Your tools, if you want them."

He heard and would not hear. In his extremity he put down the punch he could not hold steadily, and began to handle the half-shaped blocks of stone, dragging them forward and turning them to the light. One of them, small and dusty and obscure in its corner, took the sunlight as he drew it towards him, and showed him the vigorous sketch of a face he knew well, a face he had seen long ago in the triforium, when he had crouched against the wall in the last embrasure of the walk, listening to the approaching footsteps of his enemy. He had not marked it then, but he remembered it now.

"A study for the last head he ever made," said Isambard, watchful and patient at his shoulder.

"His signature at the end," said Harry in a whisper.

"So I used to think, too. When you stepped out of hiding and fronted me, this same face looked over your shoulder. Then I knew better. Look again! This is no signature at the end, Harry, but a prophecy at the beginning. Do you not know yourself?"

Harry stared, and was slow to see his own face, and yet he could not but believe. Love reaching out to him took him by the heart and wrung him. He shut his eyes upon a rush of tears, and painfully contained them, but the springs of fondness in the middle of his being were weeping inconsolably for the stilling of the quick hands and the creative mind. He felt older than his lost father, and desperate with protective love. He wanted to hold him safe from every profaning touch, and fend off every malignant thought from him. He wanted above all to know that he still lay safe and quiet in his nameless grave; he was heavy and burning at heart with his longing to ask, but he would not. It was fear that locked his tongue, but mercifully he mistook it for pride, so its bitterness did not poison him.

He stood there silent beside the bench for a long time, fondling with a wondering hand the unknown contours of his own young head in the stone, thinking himself strangely wonderful suddenly, and a terrible responsibility.

"Your tools, if you want them. Tools can be used as weapons, Harry, but if you'll promise these shall never be put to any purposes but those for which they were intended, you may work here whenever you wish. This bench shall be yours. My mason shall provide you with materials, and if you choose to work under him and learn from him, he shall find you enough to do. The tasks he'd give to any apprentice, until you prove yourself. You'll not be privileged. Well?"

The silence continued long, while Harry picked up and laid down tool after tool, smoothed a fingernail along the chisels, hefted the mallets, turning and twisting like a caged animal with the fury of his longing and the rigidity of his pride.

"Unless, of course, you're afraid to venture where you dread you'll prove less than excellent?"

"I pledge you my word," said Harry with a tearing gasp, "I'll not misuse them."

"That came out of you like drawing a tooth," said Isambard critically, "but the first time's the hardest. Come, let's try you once more. To-morrow I must leave Parfois for a matter of some days. Give me your parole until I return, and you shall be free to go where you choose about Parfois, and free to use this tracing-house. Otherwise I fear you must wait in closer confinement till I come back, for I'll trust no one but myself to keep you safe for me. And you—if it please you to give me your word?"

It did not please him; almost he wished the first pledge back again, so naked did he feel now without his armour of obstinacy. But the giving had begun, and now it was harder than ever to draw back. The feel of Master Harry's mallet in his hand, the way the heel of it swung in his palm, filled him with a fever of ambition and impatience, and he could not wait the threatened few days for the assay. Trembling, he hugged the most worn and shortened of the punches to his heart, thumbing its point, and wrestled with the words of compliance that rose all too readily.

"Well? Will you give me your pledge?"

"Yes!" he said, the word jerked out of him furiously, and twisted away to hide from the malicious smile he dreaded. Such a despair seized him at the sound of his own acceptance that he made a half-hearted attempt even then to deliver himself. "Only until you return! After that I promise nothing—"

But only silence answered him, and when he looked round he was alone in the room. Isambard had accepted his bond on the instant without a word of triumph or mockery, and left him alone to exult and grieve over his father's belated legacy. Suddenly he took the visionary image of his own manhood into his arms, his ruffled hair against the stone curls, and burst into a storm of silent weeping.

Chapter Ten

Aber: *May to early June* 1231

*I*t was late before the members of the council left Llewelyn's chamber. Owen could not bear the emptiness of the anteroom and the abrupt murmurs of the low voices behind the inner door. He went out and sat on the top step of the staircase like a banished child waiting to be admitted. He was still sick and light-headed with the fever that had kept them so long immobilised at Cegidfa, and made the ride home such long-drawn discomfort to him; but the sorry account he had to make of his stewardship weighed more heavily on his spirit than his wounds did on his body. At least two of the five he had brought back with him were in worse case than he; and Adam, who had perhaps come off lightest in actual injuries, was by no means to be envied for that, for the same story Owen had to tell to the Prince, Adam was at this moment telling to Gilleis. Owen thought wretchedly that his own was the lighter task of the two.

The door of the inner room opened. He roused himself wearily to exchange greetings with the elders as they passed him, and went in to his foster-father.

Llewelyn had been in council for several hours, and was no less weary; nevertheless, he saw the labour and pain with which Owen bent his knee to him, and reached to take him up before he could complete his reverence. His kiss was brusque out warm, and his hands transmitted a vital vigour of which no one else had the secret.

"No, no ceremony, boy, we're alone here. There, sit, and take your time. No one will disturb us now. I ask your pardon for leaving you waiting at the door, but I'm pressed, Owen, the days crowd me, and there are things I must set forward while I may. I had your despatch from Meifod." It was his way of saying at once that he knew the worst of what was to come, and had only the details to learn.

"I've lost you six good men," said Owen, "and gained you nothing. I took the best I could, and this is how I've made use of them."

"Did they reproach you?" asked Llewelyn sharply and dryly. He poured wine and brought it across the room to Owen's chair, pressing him back brusquely when he would have risen to receive the cup.

"They had no time," said Owen bitterly.

"They had no will, and well you know it. The like is waiting for us all, when God so designs. Tell me the whole of it, and if you have done ill, you shall hear of it."

Owen eased his stiffened shoulder wound against the cushion, and began the story of his failure. He was not sparing with himself, and yet the tale ran more readily than he had supposed possible, so completely did he trust the listener. From Llewelyn he would get his deserts, and be grateful for them. He had never rested with such absolute confidence in the judgement of any other, excepting once for that brief while in his childhood, when he had been in the care of Master Harry.

"How he found us I still don't know. Adam fears it was through his coming to us from Castell Coch, and indeed it may be so. Yet I cannot feel that Adam was to blame. How could he know the man had his creatures planted even there to watch for him? I should have allowed for it that he was no ordinary man, and could move like a thunderstorm when he willed. He knew straitly where we lay, and all our dispositions. He could not plan for the way of the wind, that was luck, but for the rest he had everything at his finger-ends. And he fights like ten men still, as old as he is. I cannot feel that we had been negligent, had we been dealing with another man. But we were dealing with Isambard, and what I did was not enough."

"Twice luck was with him," said Llewelyn. "Once with a favouring wind, and once with reinforcements when he most needed them. For neither of which favours can you be blamed. The devil has looked well after his own."

"And once we all but had him safe," said Owen, groaning into his hands, for he was very tired. "I ask myself every hour now if we might not have held him and still drawn off well enough if I had but kept a better watch on the road to Shrewsbury. I meant to try again and better, either to get at him, or to find a messenger who would carry word to Harry inside Parfois. For you know he has a measure of liberty—?"

"I know. I have it all from Philip ap Ivor. I know what that man owes to Harry, and what to me, and I have kept the account, and in good time I shall take what is due. A measure of freedom to the son, and the last indignity to the father's bones—what manner of dealing is that?" said Llewelyn, smouldering.

"And I fear him," said Owen feverishly, "truly, sir, I fear him. This forbearance with Harry is too capricious and cruel for me. If he so mortally hated the father, living and dead, how can we trust his indulgence with the boy? If Harry should come to worse harm through me—"

"You take too much to yourself. It is not your blame, and I will not spare to you what is mine."

The Prince's voice was hard and hot. How often in his life had he admitted guilt before anyone but God?

"It was I sent the boy out after his act of vindication. These six lives are all of my spending, and if I were free I would go with any army and take them back with usury. But I am not free. It is no part of my duty now to give any thought to the making of my own soul or the righting of what I have done wrong. God deals as He will, I as I can. I am the servant of the cause I have at heart, and you and I, and Harry if need be, are coin to be spent for it."

"Did they get so bad a reception at Worcester?" asked Owen, dismayed by the tone rather than the content of this speech. The Prince's envoys had returned to Aber from the latest of the long-

drawn conferences with the King's representatives, two days ahead
of the battered remnant from Parfois.

"No, not ill at all. There were civil looks and fair speeches, and
there's another meeting called three days hence, at Shrewsbury. But
it means little now, for the mountain is in motion, and slide it must.
Two ideas over-large for reconciliation are fronting each other now,
and there'll be no peace until there's been—no," he checked himself,
"I won't say a settlement, but at least a temporary losing and winning that shall silence us both until we get our breath for the next
bout. Sometimes I have a fear in me that this is but the first of many
engagements in a struggle which is new, in scope if not in kind."

He crossed to the window to set wide the shutter on the last night
of May, and heave the smokiness of his long closeted hours out of
him in great, assuaging breaths. "You know the crown still holds
back from acknowledging our title to Builth? The act of denying
matters little. So my constable continues to hold the castle, let the
King garrison the title as strongly as he will. Yet the sign is there
to be read. They deny their own law, denying my right, and the
precedent is there to stead them in the next encroachment. They are
ready, as they think, to devour me. But by God, they shall find me
stick in their gullets and rip their bellies open."

"De Burgh is the mover," said Owen, propping up his drooping
eyelids. "My heart misgave me when I saw his livery at Parfois, for
Isambard is close and confidential with him, and sure they had some
business between them that bodes us no good here in Wales."

"They had indeed! Have you not heard it yet? They brought me
the news back from Worcester. Isambard joined the King at Hereford
early in May. He must have left Parfois no more than two days
after his raid across Severn. King Henry respects my lord's views
on all that pertains to the march. And the upshot of it is that he has
taken the custody of the de Breos lands from the Earl of Cornwall,
and bestowed it upon his beloved justiciar. De Burgh hems me in
on every side but where the sea is, save only Chester, where I thank
God for Earl Ranulf. The cause is complete now, I need no more to
show me the time is on me. Now there wants only the occasion,
which, God willing, shall be of my choosing."

"I thought at least to have taken Harry off your mind," said

Owen wretchedly, "so that you might give all your heart to this. And I've done nothing but lose you six good men."

"All my heart is given to this. Harry, poor lad, must wait his turn. The keeping of my vows, the honouring of my obligations, all give way to this. If I live, I will redeem all my pledges, and if I die, I will answer for their going unredeemed in the judgement."

He leaned his great bronzed forehead on his hand, turning his face gratefully to the cool of the night air, and went on talking in the soft, absorbed voice of one alone with his own spirit.

"I tell you, boy, we are engaged with more even than I knew. While I have been busy compounding a kingdom here for my son, I have borrowed from the English as I thought fit. There is no way of standing them off in the old fashion. I have paid for my court and my campaigns by means they showed me, by taxation, and rents, and fees levied on settlers in my townships. I have given lands and privileges to get knight service, and kept my army in the field by contracts my forefathers never countenanced. I have settled the succession by English law and not by Welsh, to make it hold the firmer, and stop their mouths from questioning it. So, while I stood off their changes and challenges with the right hand, I let them in with the left. And I see that by the left or the right, by compact or by conquest, come they will. There is no way of preventing. All we can do is shape the means by which they approach us and the terms on which they will live with us in the time to come, that we may keep our honour and our identity, and be their free neighbours and allies, not their villeins. And I know this, that if we are to gain such a bargain with them we must first know ourselves who and what we are, and set a true value on our blood and our tongue. Not we only of Gwynedd, not the men of Powis, not the gnawed remnant of Deheubarth. But we Welsh. And this is more than the ambition with which I began, and more than my son's inheritance. If I die for it, if David must die for it in his turn, no matter, so the spring survive and the unity grow. And if Harry dies for it, his death be on my head, and I will answer for it to God and to him when my time comes."

When his voice had ceased there was silence in the room. He stirred himself at last and looked round, to find one even more worn out with weariness than himself. Owen had dropped asleep in his chair. The heavy brown head lolled a flushed cheek on the red cushion that supported his bandaged shoulder.

Llewelyn crossed to him, smiling, and gently shook him awake. He started up in alarm, staring dazedly, and then, realising his lapse, paled with mortification.

"My lord, give me your pardon! I've ridden far to-day—and then the wine—"

His long fever had peeled the flesh from his bones and left him half his proper bulk, and the brown of his cheeks was yellow and drawn. When he started to his feet he had to lean hard on the arm of the chair while a moment of dizziness passed.

"Go to bed, boy," said Llewelyn, holding him reassuringly between his hands. "You can, with a quiet mind. What you attempted was not blessed, more's the pity, but none the less it was well done, few could have done better. I find no fault with you. There, go and sleep! Who knows if I may not have need of you by to-morrow?"

In the late afternoon of the second of June a courier rode into Aber on a reeking horse, the last of a chain of messengers who had carried urgent news from Cydewain. Llewelyn was close in his chamber with his chaplain-secretary and Ednyfed Fychan over the dictation of letters, and his seal was already on the credentials of the envoys who were to represent him in Shrewsbury; but David, when he heard what the messenger had to report, on his own authority brought him in to the conference and shattered it.

"What is it?" Llewelyn looked round from the table with a formidable scowl. "Did I not say I was not to be disturbed?"

"My lord and father, blame me for this interruption, not the courier. But this cannot wait."

Llewelyn looked from his son to the rider, who was dusty and streaked with sweat from his gallop. He pushed the papers from him as though he knew already he had done with them.

"Speak out, then. What is it?"

"My lord, I bring word from the march by Montgomery. A week ago the garrison there made a sally against us and surrounded and took a company of our men." The man came up from his knees coughing the dust out of his lungs with the words. "The number I do not know. But they took them into the castle at Montgomery, prisoners.''

"This I know," said Llewelyn, his face dark. "Come to the news."

"My lord, yesterday the Earl of Kent came to Montgomery, and himself saw the prisoners. He ordered them out to execution on the instant, and it was done. Beheaded, every man!"

"*Beheaded?*"

Llewelyn came to his feet with a leap that shook the chair jarring back across the floor-boards, and tumbled the scattered rolls of parchment to the rugs.

"Has he dared? In my face! He spits this in my face!" He whirled away from them to stalk the floor for a few raging paces, and as abruptly rounded on them again. "Is there more?"

"My lord," said the messenger hoarsely, "they are saying the heads are sent to the King of England."

"Two days before the King's envoys were to meet mine!"

"This he could not do in folly, fool though the man can be," said David, white to the lips as he watched his father's face. "This is deliberate."

"It is deliberate. He conceives that he is ready." Llewelyn plucked the pen from his secretary's hand, and swept the remaining letters from before him. "Leave these, they'll not be needed. There'll be no meeting in Shrewsbury. Hubert shall see where to-morrow will find me, and I'll be there before he looks for me. Ednyfed, the writs go out within the hour. See to it!"

"They've been ready this week past," said Ednyfed Fychan, and swung to the door with alacrity.

"And send my captain here, and Rhys with him. It is time," said Llewelyn, drawing a great breath. "He'll choose it for me, will he? So be it! We shall see who'll come best out of it. But was it necessary to kill my men in cold blood? Was there no other gage he could have flung in my teeth? By God, he shall rue it! I'll make him pay dear for every head." He swung on the messenger again, his hawk-face sharp as a sword. "Is the earl still at Montgomery?"

"As I heard it, my lord, he's already gone back to Hereford."

"So much the worse, I would have wished him to see his township burn. But he'll keep. What I owe him shall be paid in full, and I'll make him count the coin over in his ruin. David, see this good fellow fed and housed, and come back to us here. We have yet some planning to do. Before dawn we march."

They ran every one, ablaze at his fire, to do his bidding. The columns for support and supply had been alerted long ago, the clansmen waited only for the signal, and his great seal on the writs his messengers carried would bring them out to join him like bees from a hive disturbed. He had only to call and they would come, eager and hungry.

"I have dealt moderately," said Llewelyn through his teeth, flexing his great, shapely, sinewy hands before his face to take hold on the challenge and the promise in the air. "I have held my hand time and again, and even when they drove me to act I have abated my askings to keep the balance true and save Wales from worse enmity. But now we cannot be so saved. They think their hour is come to close on me, and to deal moderately now would be a thing in their littleness they could not but mistake. Now they shall see that I can do extremes, and by God they shall learn to keep their hands from Gwynedd while I am yet alive."

Owen, when he heard the news, came limping in great haste through the furious bustle of the maenol to claim his rights, afraid in his heart of being rejected.

"I am fit," he persisted, holding Llewelyn fast by the sleeve, for he was apt to flash away from armoury to store and stable to council chamber disconcertingly upon his universal errand of supervision. "David is my prince, and well I know this is not border play this time. Where David goes I must go. You would not leave me behind?"

Llewelyn turned from the harness that was being checked out of the armoury, and looked at his foster-son for a moment from so far away and by so dazzling a light that he seemed hardly to know him. Recognition came with a sudden warm and brilliant smile out of his preoccupied frenzy.

"Ah, you! Leave you I would, if I did not know you'd fret your heart out worse than I'll let you fret your body in the field. Yes, you shall come, if you'll be ruled and do as I bid you. I would not let you from David's side willingly, no more than I'd send him into the battle without a shield."

He saw Owen redden with pleasure, and laughed, flinging an arm about his shoulders so forgetfully that it was a worthy as well as a willing sacrifice Owen made for him, containing the pain of the embrace. "And, Owen, I have yet a use for you here and now. Find Gilleis and Adam for me, and bring them to the chapel. I would have you all three witness a certain vow I have to make before we march."

Owen brought them within a quarter of an hour, grave-faced both, and heavy-eyed from nights broken with too much thinking of Harry. It seemed to Llewelyn, watching Gilleis approach, that she had lost flesh sadly in the year of lacking her son, and her rose and white had faded into the pallor of prisoners. Half at least of her day she spent in the closed and sealed place of her lady's captivity, half of her night imprisoned with the boy. And yet she neither pleaded nor complained. Her great dark eyes questioned and hoped, but without reproach. And even now, he thought, all I have to offer will seem so little to a woman.

It was dark in the wooden chapel even in the early evening; the candles on the plain, linen-covered altar guttered faintly in the draught before the door was closed, and after its closing there was an astonishing silence, all the sounds of the activity without banished to infinite distance.

Llewelyn kneeled and prayed. Even when he raised his face open-eyed to the altar the silence still continued for a while.

"Bear with me," he said. "I am not adept with words without my elders by me, and this is matter for care. A man never thinks, when he undertakes one journey, that he may not return from it to contemplate another. And yet I think my time is not yet, and God wills well to hear me."

He set both hands before him on the crucifix. His touch could be wonderfully gentle, but it was never tentative; he laid hands on holy things with the same direct and innocent fearlessness he used towards men and women.

"So be my witness," he said, "that before the face of God and in your presence I swear this: that when God's good time serves me to do it without injury to my foremost obligations to Him and to my country, I will take and destroy the castle of Parfois for the wrongs of Harry Talvace dead and Harry Talvace living. If my foster-son be still held there, by the grace of heaven I will take him out of his captivity. And if not, yet I will not spare of what I have sworn touching Parfois. So help me God I will not forget nor fail of making good my word on my enemy and Harry's."

Owen said: "Amen!" gladly, but his was the only voice to answer. Adam would have echoed it, but he was intent on his wife's face, and in his anxiety he let the words go by him. She was regarding the Prince with the faintest and saddest of smiles, in which he thought he could read affection and indulgence, and surely also a soft, secret gleam of derision. Llewelyn turned from the altar in time to catch that disconcerting look, but it neither puzzled nor disturbed him. When he was roused to such a peak of experience, confronting the issues of life and death for thousands besides himself, all things became simple to him. Things which had bewildered him were clear as crystal, problems which had daunted and defied him gave like locks opening to the right key. The power of words which he had disclaimed sprang golden in his mouth.

"Well I know it, girl," he said, "this fills neither your arms nor your heart. Yet it is all I have, and, if it does not loose you, yet it binds me. Take it for a pledge of my faith that God will hold Harry safe for us, howsoever we miss him now."

"My lord," she said, "I do believe it."

"So trust, then, as you have spoken, and, if God will, you shall yet stand by the altar of the church of Parfois, when the day comes for me to fulfil my oath, and see Master Harry's bones honourably buried there."

He saw her blanch and veil her eyes, and said no more of that for kindness. He was moved and promising miracles, the recovery of things lost, the wholeness and holiness of things profaned; but the faith she had professed was perhaps no more than a conviction that the star of the Prince of Aberffraw would not fail him, and that God would humour him and not cheat him of the fulfilment of his vow. Yet Llewelyn felt the forces of heaven moving him, and aligned himself with them boldly, going without hesitation where they carried him.

The thing which had seemed so hard was simple now, the gulf that had appeared unbridgable shrank to a child's leap, and vanished as he stepped over it.

"Gilleis, one more thing I must lift from my heart before this hour breaks over me."

She raised her eyes to him quickly, wondering and doubting.

"Go to your lady, and ask her if she will receive me."

She was sitting beneath the narrow, barred window when he entered the room, and the first thing he saw was the light lying ashen in her fair hair; there was more grey than gold in it now. She had grown heavier in her enforced stillness, her body was ripe and full that had been so slender, and moved with something less than the old negligent grace. But her face was not full but fallen, the pale skin stretched over slight bones, the eyes grown enormous and calm like grey glass. They looked upon him and gave no sign. Her hands were spread upon the arms of the chair, as she used to sit beside him on occasions of state, erect and observant, quick to anticipate, deft in manipulation. She was richly dressed. He saw and understood that she had prepared herself for him. She was a king's daughter and the wife of a prince, whether in his palace or his prison.

For a year he had neither seen her nor permitted her name to be spoken in his hearing. He had thought that he must come back to her now as a stranger, learning afresh the shape of her wide forehead and tapering face, and the way she had of opening her eyes wide to take in entire the person to whom she spoke. He had expected to have to batter his way laboriously through the months that had separated them, as through the stockade of a castle into which he must break by force of arms. But at the first sound of her voice even this changed woman became familiar to him, and the veil of estrangement between them broke and drifted like gossamer.

"You are welcome, my lord," she said. "There was no need to ask permission, your prisons are always open to you."

Gilleis had gone, and closed the door quietly behind her. He stood just within the room, looking steadily at the Princess, and went headlong where his genius pointed him. Constraint and ceremony could have nothing to say to her that would not be wearisome to hear as it was costly to say. There was no time. He had always been at his best when he was pressed hardest.

"Joan," he said, "I need you."

In spite of herself she stirred so sharply that he felt her astonishment recoil upon his own flesh and set him trembling. If he had spoken of forgiving, or pitying, or even loving, she would have been ready for him, but to be needed was something she had not looked for.

"That cannot be true," she said. "You have done without me well enough for a year, and so you can now." She said it very mildly, without reproach or complaint, only uttering what she felt to be true. He saw now where Gilleis had learned her patience and endurance.

"I have done without you, but not well. Without you nothing is well. I need you. I am going into the field to-morrow against King Henry's army and against the Earl of Kent in particular, and God knows what the outcome will be. It is a long tale."

"You need not tell it," she said, "I know it already. Do you think I have not been following all that you have done and all that has been done to you all these months?"

"If you know it, you know the need I have of you. Always before when I ran my head, and my country, and my son's inheritance into danger, and stood to it in arms, always I had you by my side, heart in heart with me. I am well served as princes go, and I have wit to know it. But when I go from hence to this testing I must leave affairs here in one pair of hands, the closest and dearest to me. There is no other I can trust," said Llewelyn, "as I trust you."

At that word she raised her head and looked at him again, and long, and behind the clear disillusionment of her eyes a burning darkness had gathered and hung, glowing from deep within her. The pale mask of her face fended him off, incredulous, but the bright creature within, so long coffined and mute, knew that she had heard aright.

He came nearer, and the light of the June evening turned the tanned planes of his hawk-face and the ridge of the bold, importunate nose to copper, and picked out the russet reds in the short, dark beard, scoring deeper the deeply graved lines of audacity and laughter. The laughter had been absent for a while, but it had not withdrawn far from him, the marks of its permanent habitation were still there.

"Don't think this is merely habit," he said, "though habit it has been for twenty-five years. Without you I do well enough? Ay, so

I do, for a man lamed and distracted in mind. Self-maimed and a sinner against the truth, such I am without you, Joan."

"And I," she said, very low, "what am I?"

"You are that part of me that I cut off, and I never have been and never shall be whole without you."

She turned her head a little and put up her hand to shield her face. "The diseased part," she said.

"No, but wounded. And I who should have healed it severed it."

"Dear God!" she said in a shaken whisper. "Be careful what you do with it now. Do you think you can restore it and it will knit again without festering?—"

"By the grace of God, yes," he said, and leaned and took her gently by the wrist, but did not force her hand away. "Do you not feel the two halves closing? Flesh of my flesh, blood of my blood, I want you though you poison me, but well I know you never will. Come back with me to the place that was and is yours, be to me as you were before. Complete me. Make me a whole man before I go out to take the field with Wales in my hands. With one hand only, how shall I carry it safely? The heritage of your son and mine!"

"Have you forgotten," she said harshly, starting and quivering at his touch, "my offence against you?"

"Have you forgotten mine? Even in the right a man can offend past any forgiveness. The measure of my outrage and anger was the measure of my love for you. God witness, at the worst I never ceased to worship you."

He had used another word of power. She looked up, and the prisoned creature within her was bright and burning close within her eyes, frantic for freedom.

"Nor I you," she said, amazed, and let her hand slip into his and be held fast. "God witness!" she said after him. "At the worst, even when I was bound and blind and mad, I swear it never touched you or anything that was yours. If you could take my love in your hands, you would not find one mark upon it, not one. Never a break nor a blemish!" She leaned her head against his sleeve and drew deep breath. "I am in the dark still. It will always be a mystery, a thing that happened to me like the seasons, like floods and lightnings, without question or escape. And yet I would not lay it all on him—"

She broke off there. It was the first time they had mentioned the third who was there in the room with them, though they had both felt his presence, and she, indeed, had lived with it close and uncomforted for a year.

"Yes, speak of him," said Llewelyn, looking down at the heavy ashen head that lay so still upon his arm. "It's meet we should. It's time we should."

"He was blown in the storm as I was, however the thing began. Your rival he never was. You never had a rival." The beautiful voice bled words in short, hard sighs into his arm. "When he came he was weak and in pain. And so young! He needed all those things in me for which you had no use, pity, indulgence, even forgiveness. By his youth he showed me how late it was, and by his admiration that it was not yet too late. He made me know that I was growing old, and that everything he was was slipping out of my hands. And I closed my hands and grasped it while I could. And then I could not loose."

She was silent for a moment. She turned her head a little, and he saw that the calm had come back to her face, but now there was light and colour in it, as if the blood curbed and slowed to solitude and stillness had begun to flow again.

"You it never touched," she said. "Your place it never threatened. The world would not see it so, but I tell you, this is truth. And yet it all but shattered your life and mine and all our work, and killed an unfortunate, rash young man no worse than the most of men, and hardly deserving of death. Night and day, I never can forget him."

"You need not," said Llewelyn, "as I have not forgotten him. Wherever we go, he will go with us, that I know. But he will not go always between us."

He took her by both hands, and drew her up to stand breast to breast with him. His arms he folded round her, and so held her for a moment passive; then with a sudden sharp sigh she embraced him again, quivering, and lifted her mouth to him ravenously.

There was the taste of death in the kiss, but she accepted the price with the prize, and clung to the bitterness and the bliss alike, knowing them for ever inseparable now. Llewelyn felt the chill shudder through her before it died in his heart. He held her face cupped and cradled in his great hand, hard against his cheek, and the beat of his blood passed into her veins and drew her own blood into the same passionate measure.

"Death is waiting for me no less," he said low and gently into her ear, "and for you. When the time comes that we must face William de Breos, we'll face him. What's in store for us then is not for us to ordain. God be thanked! And let God dispose."

She could not speak, but her lips shaped against the pulse in his throat: "Amen!"

After a long while of silence he unlocked his arms from her. He was smiling. His long-sighted eyes reflected gold back to the sunset, and the brightness did not fade as the sun went down. She saw the pale flame she had lit in him burn tall and steady, a miracle of faithfulness out of unfaithfulness. He would be a lantern to his clansmen, and lightning striking at his enemies. And she had thought herself quite spent!

"Put on your robes and your crown, my lady," he said, "and come with me to the hall."

In the court a little groom was crossing from the stables, in haste for his supper. He saw them and halted, standing at gaze for a moment open-mouthed and great-eyed, and then he whooped like a huntsman hot after game, and turned and ran like a hare for the hall, bounding as he ran. The word was before them, the fire ran through the brushwood. Heads came bursting from every doorway to see them pass, and the warm hum of excitement and eagerness span after them in a golden thread, the voice of the brightness that flashed like sparks from face to face. The old formidable unity, that had seemed lost and broken irrecoverably, blazed torch-like through Aber to confound its enemies.

David was coming from his own lodging, pale and grave and preoccupied, with his child-wife by the hand. He smiled as he looked down at her and answered her quick, light speech with conscientious gentleness. Some distance behind them her ladies walked; they were kind, but they oppressed her with their insistence on her royalty, and it was hard to live up to them. She had never fully understood why her life should have changed so suddenly and drastically, though she knew by rote the duties and privileges of married ladies,

and did her best to play her part decorously. So suddenly fatherless, and so abruptly given to a husband, translated from the familiar
company of her sisters at Brecon to this barbarous foreign court
where she was the last and loneliest of the children, Isabella had
looked round her forlornly for an anchorage to which she might ride
in safety. And she had found it. She held to it confidingly, at rest
in David's hand.

He was more than usually serious and thoughtful tonight, he
went with his eyes on the ground and his brows drawn, and smiled
only fleetingly when she poked fun at Ednyfed's wife to amuse him
and get his attention. He had his eyes downcast when they came to
the corner of the great hall, and he did not see the Prince approaching, leading by the hand an unknown lady. A tall lady in dark
blue velvet, with a string of agates round her neck and a golden
diadem in her hair; a lady Isabella had never seen before in her year
at the court of Gwynedd. Child and woman looked at each other
with the same wonder and wariness, attracted and afraid.

Joan saw a little girl of eight or nine years, eyeing her alertly and
clinging—to David's hand. The child wore a soft yellow woollen
cotte and a brocaded surcoat stiff with gilt thread, and smoothed at
her finery with her free hand as she approached, aware of the need
to look her best before this unknown lady. The soft, rounded face
had a fresh, high colour, and was framed between two short braids
of wavy black hair. Innocent and anxious, her father's long-lashed
dark eyes looked up bright as swords.

She tugged furtively at the hand she held, drawing close against
David's hip. He looked sidelong at her with a quick smile, and she
frowned and nodded his attention quickly towards the stranger.
David raised his head, and saw the two who walked towards him
hand in hand.

He checked and stood amazed, half afraid to believe, and the
colour of incredulous joy flushed through his fairness and made him
bright as a rose. The child, watching him hopefully but without
understanding, shone with reflected eagerness. For a long moment
there was silence as they converged upon the steps of the hall, until
David got his voice again.

"Why, here's my mother home at last," he said, and came smiling to meet her, putting forth the child by the hand to her, a little clumsily because he could not see well for the tears in his eyes.

"Madam, here is one I beg you to love and cherish as your own child. Here is Isabella, my wife and your daughter. She has been waiting a long time for your kiss."

Joan drew near and took the dead man's child by the hands, and kissed her. The soft, shy fingers quivered in her palms, the half-formed flower of a mouth tasted of the spring and the sun. The great black eyes were clear without a shadow as Isabella, recognising the bright aspect of love and unaware of its dark face, looked up and smiled.

Chapter Eleven

Parfois, Aber: *June* 1231

*T*he first cluster of strong, uncurling leaves in imitation of Master Harry's capitals in the nave came flawed out of the stone, a little pretentiously conceived from too much ambition and a little clumsily executed from too little practice. But the second, which was more truly his own, fell within his range, and he had the feel of his tools by then, and went at it easily and gently, bullying neither himself nor his material. Once he almost marred it in sheer nervousness when Master Edmund came to his shoulder and watched him for a while; but the old man scolded him first and praised him after, both tersely enough, and he mastered his dislike of being observed at work, and stood to his strokes sturdily from then on, whoever approached him.

He heard the door of the tracing-house open towards evening, when he was alone there and lost in his unfolding leaves, and taking the newcomer to be Master Edmund again, schooled himself to continue steadily. The strokes of the mallet came neat and light and even, an engrossed and happy sound. The hand that poised the punch moved with delicate care, still a little hesitant but gaining confidence. Not until he paused to choose a finer punch did the presence a yard from his elbow speak to him.

"And you did not even know who I was," said Isambard's provokingly amiable and considerate voice. "A month ago your blood would have curdled when I entered the same room with you."

Harry tried too late to suppress the start which had betrayed him, and made his selection from among his father's tools with fierce concentration. Other things also, it seemed, were changing. A month ago he would not have made any reply to the hated voice; but now it seemed to him that his own dignity called for one. He looked round with the fine punch in his hand. Isambard was still in half-harnesss; he could only just have ridden into Parfois, and in his own apartments in the Lady's Tower no doubt Langholme was waiting to disarm him.

"Welcome back, my lord," said Harry, vexed at the lame, false sound it had when it was out.

"Am I indeed welcome? And to you?" Isambard swept aside some of the dusty drawings that lay on the end of the bench against the wall, sat himself sidewise there and made himself comfortable with his back against the stone sill of the window that gave the sculptor light. He laughed again to see how the boy scowled to find this added shadow cramping his vision. There was a reference there of which Harry knew nothing. "That's very civil of you, child, considering my return shuts the gate on you again and pens you within the wards. Unless, of course, you're willing to extend your parole indefinitely? Are you?"

"No, my lord." And then, setting his jaw, he said the words for which Isambard was waiting and listening: "If you'll be so good as to move aside from the window, my lord, I'll go on with my work."

The note of the soft, remembering laugh that answered him was something he could not understand, and it daunted him. He looked sidelong at the man who sat with wide shoulders spread against the light, and folded arms quiet on his breast, lounging at ease.

"No, Harry. This time no. Move for you I would, but the light's too far gone already, and I won't have you spoil your eyes or your work by pushing too hard. Let it lie till the morning. Not at my orders," he said patiently, seeing the mutinous tightening of Harry's lips, "but because your own good sense tells you to. It's a poor craftsman who'll ruin his own work even to spite his worst enemy.'

He watched with a slight smile as Harry turned an abrupt shoulder on him, and with deliberation set his left hand once more to the fine edge of the leaf. The mallet hesitated in air. The light was indeed too far gone, and the smooth curve pleased his eye and dared him to mar it. He wanted finer detail yet, but he knew the evening would not serve for it. After a brief struggle with his own obstinacy he turned back to the bench and quietly laid down his tools, and began to roll down the sleeves of his cotte.

"Well done!" said Isambard. "We shall make a reasonable man of you yet, if we keep you long enough. You still say no to holding by your parole, do you?"

"My lord, I gave it only until your return, and you are returned."

"Returned and made welcome. That was more than I hoped for." He reached to pick up one of the row of chisels, testing its edge against his thumb. "And do you know what news I've brought back with me from Hereford, Harry?"

"No, my lord." He stood frowning down at his work, but the frown was one of concentration and pleasure. He turned the block of stone between his hands to observe in its deeply cut faces the play of what remained of the light.

"Wales is at war," said Isambard carelessly. "Llewelyn burned the town of New Montgomery to the ground three days ago."

He had his satisfaction this time, and in full measure. The caressing hands quitted the stone as though it had burned them, the sullen face came round to him glittering with the green of startled, ardent eyes. "At war?" said Harry's lips, framing the words silently.

"Two days before the date fixed for one more tedious parley at Shrewsbury, our noble justiciar chose to sting him into action by executing certain prisoners at Montgomery. His calculations may have been accurate," said Isambard with a sardonic grin, "but between you and me, Harry, I doubt it. Howbeit, he did it, and your great Prince of Aberffraw and Lord of Snowdon took fire like a pitch-flare, and is busy now setting light to the borders. While my lord King Henry debates and hesitates, and leans on his bishops to bring the fire to heel with a little holy water."

"And Montgomery's burned?" said Harry, himself as bright and fierce as a torch.

"Houses, shops, tofts and all, and the church into the bargain, Harry. And certain unlucky clerics and ladies inside the church, so I've heard, though I doubt if the fire inquired who was within before it caught. They builded close-set under that rock."

"And the castle?"

"Harry, Harry, you're too ambitious! Did you ever see New Montgomery castle? As well begin throwing stones at Parfois. But he's after Radnor, now, castle and all, and the mere climb up a mound won't stop him. Llewelyn's blood is up, he means to scorch his way through de Burgh's lordships and wardships from Powis to Gwent, and for all I can see he'll do it. Did you speak, Harry?"

"No, my lord."

No, he had not spoken, he had only drawn breath deeply into him like a cry of protest. He turned aside to the bench again, but this time his averted eyes hardly saw the pleasant thing he had created. The hand he put out to touch it moved blindly, only to give him an excuse for steadying his fingers against stone. He could not keep still. He walked a few paces furiously, trying to contain his rage and desire. The Prince was in arms, the border was ablaze, and he was penned up here, chipping stone! And they had been so near, as near as Montgomery, and he had known nothing!

"Yes," said Isambard softly, smiling at his hunched back, "your prince is in the field, and you, his faithful foster-brother, not by his side. What a disgrace to a young man bred in the time-honoured ways! You'll never venture to show your face again in Wales, Harry, after such a defection."

"It ill becomes you, my lord," flared Harry, quivering and glaring, "to taunt me with it."

"Ah! I see I've touched a sore spot. And your David, your prince-brother, will he hold you excused?"

He saw the braced shoulders flinch, and the lips caught in and bitten hard. An unbearably sore spot! He fingered it again, gently, experimentally: "How if I should let you go to your bounden duty, Harry? On your parole to return here to captivity as soon as peace is restored between England and Wales? How then? Would you give me your word? And keep it?"

Harry wrung his hands in a sudden convulsive rage of grief, and flung round and stalked to the door with rapid, angry strides, to put himself out of reach of this ignoble baiting. The dignity of his withdrawal was jarred a little by the sharp collision of his hip with the corner of Master Edmund's tracing-table; he had been too angry to look very straitly where he was going.

"We must find a way of bridling that temper of yours," said Isambard critically after the boy's rigid back. "It affects your judgement." This he had uttered in the same mild tone, but he raised his voice to a sudden peremptory crack like a whip-lash as Harry reached the door. "Come back!"

Come or be dragged, thought Harry, reading the tone, and for a moment was inclined to make them drag him; but as soon as he had the door open he heard too many loud, young, boisterous voices raised in the outer ward, and remembered that Isambard's train of attendants had just ridden in from Hereford. To be marched back before so many hardly older than himself was more than he was willing to contemplate. He closed the door again slowly, and turned to look back at Isambard, who sat playing with the chisel and watching him with his crooked smile.

"Come here!"

And when Harry with a grim face had marched himself back obediently to the bench, and stood staring him out eye to eye: "It is neither civil nor gracious to turn your back and walk out when you are asked a straightforward question. If you had been my page instead of my prisoner, that would have cost you a whipping."

"And is it civil and gracious, my lord," burst out Harry furiously, "to taunt me with a default I cannot help, and mock me with offers you never mean to fulfil? Is it not enough that I am mewed up here, without your holding out such promises to torment me?" He was quivering with passion; the hands that had swung the mallet and steadied the punch would have made botched work of it if he had put them to the test now, but they might have cooled capably enough if he could have got them on a sword.

"How do you know I am mocking you? Put it to the test, and see. Answer my question! What if I should let you go to your prince and your duty, on your parole to return here as soon as peace is made again? Would you give me your word? And keep it?"

He held off still, distrustful and in an agony of bewilderment. "My lord, you know this is no real offer. You're tormenting me for your sport. It's unworthy!" he said, twisting.

Isambard tapped the head of the chisel gently against the bench, held him steadily in his eye and smiled. "Well, Harry? Would you swear?"

The boy held his breath for a moment, struggling, and heaved out of him at last in a monstrous gasp: "Yes, surely I would!"

"And keep it faithfully?"

"Yes, and keep it faithfully." He wrenched his head aside, frantic to contain the sudden threat of tears welling in his eyes. Answer and have it over, and be loosed the sooner from this cruel teasing. And answer truthfully, because in the end there's no other way.

"Go, then," said Isambard, laying down the chisel so softly that the metal made no sound as it touched the bench. "I take your word."

"Go?" Knocked clean out of words but for that faint echo, Harry stood helplessly eyeing him through the glitter of his distress.

"Yes. Go to your foster-brother, I accept your word."

It could not be honest, of course, there was some devilish contrivance in it to take him in a worse snare, something that would not merely make him prisoner, but undo him utterly. And yet he could not but seize the offer with both hands, trick though it must be, and fight his way through the complex treacheries as they came. His eyes began to glitter with a very different light, burning away the sheen of tears.

"You mean this, my lord? I may go? I shall be passed through the gates?"

"Put it to the test, Harry. To-night if you will." The oblique smile jerked at the corner of Isambard's mouth. "More, you shall have money for the journey home, if you need it."

"I thank you, my lord, but I need nothing from you but this grace."

"And for nothing but this grace do you intend to have to thank me! Not even a horse, Harry?"

"Nothing, my lord."

The shadows of the deep smile tugged at both hollow cheeks. Isambard's fine chain-mail rang softly as he slid from the bench and stretched his long arms. "Go, then, Harry, you'll find the way will be open. I shall look to see you again when your prince and my king make their peace."

There had never been a plainer dismissal. Harry turned dazedly, so lost in the wild bewilderment of joy and disbelief that he had to grope his way for a few paces before his feet grew wings.

The voice behind him said: "And, Harry—!"

He caught himself back from the delirium of flight with difficulty, and looked back. Isambard was tilting the unfinished block of stone between his hands, and examining with grave attention the springing leaves. "I shall see that this is left untouched for you. You can finish it when you return."

Harry came down from his prison pale and tense, washed, tidied and trim for his journey, though still he did not believe in it. He had begged back his own old clothes, only to find that he could barely get into them, and perforce he was still wearing the suit which had once belonged to William Isambard, the old wolf's second son, the man of affairs, the courtier, who somewhere in comparative obscurity in the royal household awaited his long-delayed inheritance. If he was really allowed to leave the castle, then this enforced endowment should some day return with him. But he did not believe, he did not believe, he told himself so all the way across the outer ward, desperate with the fear he had of believing and being disappointed.

No one paid more attention to him than on other occasions, no one halted him. His passage to the gate-house had the abnormal normality of a dream, where all things, no matter how fantastic, are taken for granted. He stepped into the shadowy passage, where the chill of the night fell first, and his heart rose into his throat protesting, daring him to believe that he would ever reach the other end of the tunnel. The guards stood back and watched him pass. He stepped on to the bridge. This could be the crux of the whole cruel joke, to let him on to it and then begin to raise it and bring him scrambling back. He trod stiffly, his ears strained for the first grinding engagement of the chains. Nothing. He could hear the desultory clash of arms shifting on the gate-towers, and the trees stirring with the rising breeze that came with the cool of the evening.

He stepped on to the trampled grass. The plateau was almost

deserted at this time; a few falconers and huntsmen were coming back into the wards, and Isambard's old chaplain ambled in on his mule. After that Harry was alone, walking the long diagonal path from the bridge to the ramp, with the church on his right hand. He watched it to the last moment before he entered the trees. The colour of the stone by this soft light was like the feathers of doves, bluish-grey with a living lustre, the gold of the day lingering still on the upper stages of the tower. Chin on shoulder, he gazed until the trees took it from him; and that, from one whose whole heart was away on a wild ride to Aber, was the greatest of tributes.

And now he knew in his soul that he did believe, and only his cautious, earthly, suspicious common sense was nagging at him that he did not and must not. If they turned him back at the lower guard, the remnants of his distrust would not be enough to save his heart from breaking. But he clutched jealously at the shreds of scepticism, and went on with a bold front and a pale and frightened face, afraid even to hurry to the testing point in case too noticeable an eagerness should tip the balance against him.

He came to the narrow passage between the towers, halfway down the ramp. Here it would happen. The guards would let him come abreast of them as though they had orders to let him through, and then pluck him back. Half of him believed, half disbelieved. Torn in two, counterpoised against himself, hardly breathing, he came and passed. They eyed him and waved him through.

He was on the outer side of the defences of Parfois. He was walking away down the ramp, stunned to find himself there at all, free and alone and on his way home.

So, if this was a trick, it was a deeper and more subtle one than he had supposed. He fretted at it all the way down to the riverside, and by the time he had turned instinctively towards the forest and Robert's assart he had fumbled his way through the cloud of bewilderment and was beginning to understand. He was to be allowed to go free, having given his word to return voluntarily into captivity; a promise so easy to make now, so hard to keep in cold blood later, when the time came to make it good. He was being tempted to break faith, let out on a long, long line in the deliberate hope that he would gnaw through it and never come back.

So he's sure, thought Harry, his mind suddenly clear and dark with hatred, that I shall fail him, that he can get from me what he never could get from my father. Then he would have triumphed over my father's blood at last. That's what he wants, that's what he's always wanted of me. But I'll not fail him!

He turned his back from the assart to the ford, after all, and waded the Severn in his shirt with his cotte and chausses under his arm, and went a good half of the way to Castell Coch before he dared take to the woods and lie waiting for full darkness; for it had burst on his too eager mind that once already he had been loosed out of Parfois to provide information by his movements, and he could not take the risk of doing as much again. Maybe they suspected that he had friends in the district, maybe his refusing a horse had only served to confirm their speculations, and they were relying on him to lead them, like the simpleton he'd proved himself on the first occasion, straight to Robert and Aelis.

This time they would be disappointed. He lay up in the woods until it was dark, and then with infinite care and many halts to confirm that he had the silence to himself, he worked his way roundabout back to the ford. Naked he waded across in the warm June night, and naked he slipped through the woods until he was dry, and put on his clothes again among the bushes near the silver-gleaming river. With Barbarossa under him he would not need to strip again.

Aelis had shut up the fowls, and was sitting on the bottom step of the wooden ladder that led up into the hut, listening to the night. She heard among its soft, stealthy sounds the small, crisp snap of a dead twig under an unwary foot, and froze into stillness, listening. Her quick senses followed a man's step round the rim of the clearing by the paddock fence. Suddenly and softly Barbarossa in the undercroft began to stir and stamp and whinny. Trembling, Aelis slid from her step and advanced into the open, turning slowly after the invisible visitor.

"Harry?" she said in a whispered call that hardly disturbed the silence.

He was wildly moved by the tone, so tentative and yet so bold, afraid to believe and yet fending off disappointment with so much resolution. It set him quaking with an excitement for which he was not prepared, and he came bursting out of the thickets in haste to satisfy her.

"Aelis! Here I am!"

She spun on her toes and ran, and flung herself into his arms.

"Harry, it *is* you! How did you come here? How did you escape? Are they following you?" The rapid questions fluttered in his face like blown feathers, like the stroking caresses of hands. She embraced him with all her strength, and he felt by the tingling of his body the change in hers. She had been a little, wild, hard, boy-like creature, and suddenly in his absence she had become a woman. Small, high breasts pricked his heart, bringing the blood flooding up through his throat to his cheeks. He held her stiffly, frightened by the translation of so simple a companionship into something so unfamiliar and daunting, while she stroked him still with questions and entreaties.

"Will you stay now? At least over-night! Is it safe for you here? Have they hurt you in that dreadful place?"

"I'm well enough, Aelis, I'm very well. But I can't stay. I must get back over the river. At dawn I should be on my way home. Come in to your father, and I'll tell you everything."

But would he? Everything? Would she understand if he did? Or think him mad for letting his sworn word stand between him and his certain and permanent freedom?

As she drew down her arms from his neck, her fingers brushed his chin, and she felt the fluff of downy beard that told her suddenly he was sixteen and almost a man. She drew back from him a little, from breast to knee shrinking warily into herself, but not so softly that he did not feel the recoil. His risen blood stung in his face. The arms that held her so gingerly tightened instinctively at the threat of withdrawal, jealous of their privileges.

"Now you'll ride home," said Aelis, startled and glad and sad and afraid all in one convulsion of feeling, "and we shan't see you again. Now you're free you'll never come back here."

He drew her with him towards the house, reaching his hand into the undercroft to the warm silken touch of Barbarossa's stretched muzzle.

"Yes," he said, in the voice which had deepened and filled and gained formidably in authority since last she had heard it, "I shall come back."

Did he mean only because of his sworn word to Isambard? He had thought so when he spoke, but once the words were out he heard them in a different sense. And Aelis arched herself away from him like a drawn bow in his arm, and laughed softly and derisively with joy, mocking him and herself as she said: "And even this time you know well you've only come for Barbarossa."

So he himself would have avowed, honestly enough, only an hour ago. Now he knew better. The feel of her body braced against the pull of his arm excited and roused him; he took both arms to her and dragged her back to him, pleased with his own strength and stirred and challenged by hers. She doubled her fists into his chest and fought him off vigorously, and down they came together in the long grass at the edge of the paddock.

Her small, firm breasts heaved under him. He cupped his hands round them, lying over her, and the delight of their shape shuddered through him with as wild a triumph as if he had created them. Her mane of hair lay spread under his cheek, cool and heady as meadow-sweet. He fumbled inexpertly but ardently after her lips, and she turned her head aside from him defiantly so that he encountered only her ear; but when he persisted, laughing and panting, she turned towards him again with a sharp sigh of astonishment and pleasure, and met him mouth to mouth.

"You shan't go back," said Gilleis, straining him to her heart, dusty and tousled and travel-stained as he was. "You shant'! You shan't! No one has the right to extort such a promise, God will absolve you from it."

"He won't, Mother. And if any of his bishops takes so much upon him, I won't listen. I gave my word, and I'll abide by it." He was on his knees at her feet, his arms round her waist, hugging her littleness to him boisterously. She clung round his neck, laughing and crying, holding him off to marvel at his growth and man-nishness, snatching him back to rock him like a small child on her breast. It mattered nothing how foolishly she behaved, there was no one else to see.

"The Prince will never let you," she said, all the more fiercely because she did not believe it.

"The Prince will understand that I must. He'd thunder if I tried to slip out of the obligation. But I shan't. And you—you're a fine one to talk! If my father's son broke his word—why, you'd beat me first and turn me out afterwards."

"I wouldn't. I'd claim you got your good sense from the Otleys, and commend you for it."

She stroked back the tangled dark hair from his forehead that was brown and broad and formed like a man's, with the salients and valleys of thought and reason proudly marked. Who would have thought a single year could make such a transformation? He was grown so big she could hardly embrace him, and so masterful she could not imagine ever again boxing his ears, however well he might deserve it. "And now you're going to rush away again after the army," she said, exasperated. "Stay here awhile with me. Why shouldn't you, when I've lost a whole year of you?"

"Mother, Mother, I was set free to go to my duty. I made it my excuse to come here that I must get the latest news to know where best to report myself, but well you know it was to see you I really came. But I must go to David as quickly as I can. It would be cheating to stay here. To-morrow I must go."

"The day after to-morrow!"

He crushed her little fist in his big one, and mumbled it against his lips and cheek. "To-morrow!" She shook him, and he buried his face in her shoulder and held fast, so that they shook together.

"Unfilial boy, you ought to obey your mother."

"Froward woman, I'm a man now by Welsh law, and you ought to defer to me. And if you weren't the prettiest mother in Aber, you wouldn't get your way with me so easily."

"Then the day after to-morrow?"

He kissed her heartily, but he said with finality: "To-morrow!"

She let him think her persuaded, or at least resigned. Time would weaken the urgency of his vow, and events might yet dispose all. The Prince might forbid him to return, Isambard might die, either with the King's host in the field or of sheer old age at home, Parfois might come within Llewelyn's fiery orbit and be stormed and taken. Or even a wound, a small, mild wound or a light fever, might commit this madcap to his bed and to her eager care. She clung to the comfort and the anxiety of the moment. Only let him go safely and safely return in this war she feared.

"And, Harry—!"

He raised a flushed, merry face. "Yes?"

"You should go and pay your respects as soon as you've made yourself presentable."

"To Ednyfed?" he said carelessly. "Supper's time enough, I shall see him in the hall."

"To the Princess," said Gilleis.

His face sharpened into instant gravity. She saw the old trouble gather very distantly, like a passing cloud-shadow on a bright hill. He rose to his feet, still holding her hands in his. He was already bigger than his father had ever been, and surely he had a year or two of growing to do yet.

"May I go in to her?" he said in a low voice.

"No need. She has come out to us, Harry. You'll find her in her proper place, in the Prince's chamber."

When he heard her voice call him in he felt himself tremble, and his hand upon the latch of the door was stiff and cold. He went in bitter still with wounded pride and the memory of betrayed love. It was hard even to step over the door-sill.

She was sitting at the table over a despatch brought in only ten minutes previously, alone in Llewelyn's room, in Llewelyn's chair, with the circlet of gold in her piled grey hair, that had still certain rich strands of pale brown in it. She turned her head and saw him enter. Very gently and carefully she laid down the pen, and turned her chair away from the table to meet him. Her face was pale and grave as he remembered it, the eyes wide and plaintive and calm, without a shadow; and her brows were drawn a little with thought and care, both princely. She had to make her way through the cloudy mazes of policy and state back to him.

"Harry!" she said. "You are welcome home."

He saw the colour flood her pallor and fade again while she looked at him. The year of his life she had lost was bound up for ever with a lost year of her own. Once, how long ago now, he had said to her: "Do you know, do I know, what it is to be a prisoner?"

"My lady!" he said, and went quickly forward and fell on his knee to her.

The hand she laid in his wore Llewelyn's ring. Harry bent his head and kissed the cool fingers close to the stone. There was a faint scent afloat above her brocaded lap, and close before his eyes he saw the slow, even heave and fall of her breath through the ageing body. He kept her hand long, lost out of time and beset with the rending memories of the end of his childhood. With resignation and humility she watched the struggles that convulsed his averted face, fighting out between pride and resentment and love and grief the prolonged battlefield of his heart. She waited for what he would say, willing to receive it whatever it might be; and she had long minutes to wait.

She had abused and betrayed him, and yet now that he touched her hand and let his own hands rest upon her knees he felt no change in her, nothing wanting in the affection that could still warm him through to the spirit. Had disillusionment itself been no more than an illusion? He was the one who was changed. Something had happened to his eyes and ears. They saw and heard all the events of a year ago from some new place to which he had never aspired or attained, somewhere above the battle but not out of reach of the pain. He remembered the dead man in his living brightness and in his frightened nakedness, and no longer saw them as separate. He heard Joan's voice pleading with sudden terrible urgency: "Think of him kindly. Think kindly of all poor sinners. If you think yourself wounded, what must their sufferings be?"

He was filled with something he did not know how to name, for he had never yet had to identify compassion. Reverence he knew, and that also he felt towards her, but this other and more desperate engagement flooded his whole being, brimming over at his heart, and he was possessed without understanding.

He had writhed and agonised over the offence against himself, seen nothing beyond it, challenged the Prince and importuned God with it, banished himself and abandoned her on the strength and spleen of it. And yet if he had thought himself wounded, what must her sufferings have been?

"Forgive me!" he gasped, quivering, his lashes low on his cheeks. "Forgive me!"

And he had meant in his magnanimity to forgive her! He did not understand, but neither did he question. When the words were out he knew they were the right words, and laid his head on her knee and repeated them again and again in a passion of joy and gratitude.

Joan uttered a brief, sharp sigh, and leaned to him and lifted his head between her hands. His face came up to her wide-eyed and solemn; he held up his mouth for her kiss like the child Harry, but when she had given it gladly and drawn back from him to look into his eyes she saw that the Harry who had come home was far on the way to his manhood.

Chapter Twelve

Brecon, Cardigan,
the Wye Valley:
July to December 1231

*T*he garrison of Brecon castle made a sally as soon as all the fires were embers, and the smoke of the burning town had begun to settle in a sooty pall over their walls and roofs. They were reasonably certain that their defences would hold against anything short of a prolonged siege, and by the rapidity of the Welsh advance it was clear that Llewelyn was not bent on starving out one de Breos castle, but doing as vast and as widespread damage to the justiciar's holdings as he possibly could before his own impetus was spent or King Henry got his slow-moving host into the field; but they were being forced to feed a great press of refugees, their stores were none too plentiful, and if there was anything eatable still to be looted within the borough they wanted to do the looting themselves rather than leave it to the Welsh. Moreover, they were anxious to discover whether Llewelyn was yet withdrawing and by what road, and to be sure that their way to the bridge was clear at need.

Llewelyn was encamped east of the town, on high ground over-looking the valley of the Usk. He had battered the gates of the castle for sport, and made a few feints at the walls, to keep the garrison on tenterhooks, but he had no intention of wasting time and energy

on Brecon. The borough was so much charcoal and ash, and little
left in the rubble worth the taking. The prior and his six shivering
brothers of the Benedictines were on their knees in Saint John's
church, praying for a safe deliverance, mourning the still smouldering timbers of their fine choir roof, and thanking God for their good
stone walls. And David and Owen were patrolling the castle hill,
and standing off hopefully in case the garrison should raise the
courage to come out to them.

It was David who saw them issue from the lower port and sweep
down the steep banks of the Honddu into the town. He held off out
of sight beyond the priory walls until the quarry was well clear, and
then loosed his men joyfully after them down the hill, took them
in the rear before they were aware of him in the foul twilight of
smoke, and swept them before him as far as the bridge. They turned
then and fought, and David, who had outridden his men, found
himself suddenly islanded among his enemies, and engaging four or
five at once. His impetus had carried him well out over the river,
where they could pin him on both sides, while half a dozen of them
sealed the end of the bridge after him. And how often had Owen
abused him and his father warned him for his too light and impetuous valour!

Owen had been caught on the north side of the castle when the
pursuit began, and even when the clamour reached him he had a
long ride round with his company to the fight. David wheeled his
horse in a frenzied circle to beat his enemies to arm's-length, and
for a few confused minutes held them off; but one wrenched at his
bridle while another was crossing swords with him, and two more
closed in flank to flank and dragged him out of the saddle. He kicked
his feet from the stirrups and fell clear, and among the stamping of
the horses braced his sword under the armpit of the first man who
swung his arm back to strike at him, prised for the cloth where the
banded mail was strained apart, and drove home with all the force
he could from one knee.

He brought down over himself a gush of blood and the weight of
a heavily armed body, and was flattened to the ground beneath the
burden, and half-stunned. Vaguely in the distance he heard the clash
and shouting of Owen's men as they drove down the hill at the
guarded bridge, and somewhere from the further side a closer echo

rang back in answer. From the west, where no one kept the narrows, hooves thudded from the solid ground to the hollow-ringing span of the bridge, and suddenly the whole mêlée was swept back towards Brecon by the impact of four horsemen coming at a headlong gallop.

David, heaving at the dead weight that lay over him, saw his own horse rear and recoil before the shock, saw his mounted foemen suddenly closing at disadvantage with the newcomers and being carried with them, locked in a confused mass, back into Owen's arms. He recovered the sword that had been wrenched out of his hand, and hauled himself dizzily to his knees; and someone came plunging down from the saddle with a shout of rage and grief to catch him about the body and hold him in one arm, while the other ringed him with a briskly-circling sword.

"My lord! My lord!"

He got his eyes clear of blood that was not his own, wishing he had had the sense to quit his Welsh habits and helm properly, and blinked unbelievingly at a furious, anxious face that devoured him with blazing greenish eyes and entreated him to be whole and un-wounded.

"Harry!" he cried, and came lurching to his feet, crowing with astonishment and delight.

"My lord! David!" Harry felt at him with a frantic hand, seeking the source of the blood. The fight had left them behind by a few meagre yards only, they shouted and still could hardly make them-selves heard.

"Not mine!" David embraced him for an instant, gasping and laughing, and would have plunged back afoot into the chaos at the bridgehead, but Harry caught jealously at the stirrup of his own horse and held it for his prince, with so absolute a pride in his privileges that David had not the heart to refuse him. He swung back into the fight on Barbarossa, with Harry clinging by the left hand to his stirrup-leather as they charged. Their weight drove the knot of struggling men swaying to the end of the bridge. By the time the survivors from the foray realised how the scales were tipped against them, and turned once more to take on five men rather than fifteen, they had left it too late. The bridge was littered with their casualties by the end of it, and only a handful clawed their way through by luck to take the tale back to the castle.

David dropped to the grassy bank of Usk to wipe his sword, and came bounding back to catch Harry into his arms. He hugged and was hugged again. They were both panting with excitement and pleasure.

"But how do you come to be here? Man, but I was glad to see you! But for you I'd have been hard put to it before Owen could get through. Where did you come from so happily?"

"We crossed Eppynt by the old upland track," said Harry, breathless. "They told us at Builth we'd find you hereabouts. We had to go out of our way to avoid an English party at the end, and forded the river upstream. Glad I am we did! The fright you gave me, with such gouts of blood on you!"

"And not a drop of it mine." He held the boy off to look him over from glowing face streaked with smoke and sweat to dusty stirrup-shoes. "God save you, boy, but you're grown! Such an arm on you, and such a grip! But how did you break out of hold to come to us?"

But he got no answer then, for Owen came plumping down from the saddle beside them and snatched the boy away from him to shake him delightedly between his hands. The hug he got in return made him wince and gasp, and fetched a wail of remorse out of Harry.

"Ah, pardon, Owen, I forgot! They told me at Aber what befell you. Sooth, I'm sorry to have been the cause of it all."

"I'm well enough, Harry, but it's thanks only to God and you if this madhead here can say the same. Keep your best horse-play for a week or two yet before you loose it on me, that's all I ask. God's blood!" he said, eyeing the boy's sturdy shoulders and long, lissom body admiringly, "I wouldn't give much for my chances at a fall with you in a year or so." He patted him happily, still bent on touching to prove him real. "That was a bonny little charge you made there on the bridge, Harry. Wait till we bring you to the Prince and tell him, you'll be a head taller."

"And I shorter by an inch off my nose," said David, grinning as he wiped his grimy face. He looked at Harry's suddenly grave and anxious countenance and leaned impulsively to do the same service for him, guessing at a part of the reason. "Ah, never worry, you've more than made your welcome even if it had needed making, but it never did. He's been waiting for you as hungrily as your own mother. Come and see!''

They drew off in close order, leaving the field to the dead, and to the parties that would steal out of the castle to salvage the living when dusk and quietness came to cover them. They brought Harry between them, sobered and quiet now, up through the black and reeking town and out to the clean hills, to the level grassy plains where the Prince's army was encamped. When they reached it he had still told but half his tale, and that in brief and difficult answers to their eager questioning. Not until he had seen the Prince's face would the words come freely, and then they might all share the flood.

Llewelyn heard the loud, excited voices, and knowing two of them so well, jumped by the tone of their exchanges to the identity of the third, though it had deepened and achieved a new fullness and firmness since he had last heard it shrilling at him for justice. He tensed to listen, sure that his heart was wilfully deceiving him. But when he came striding out of the tent he saw that it was indeed Harry his two brothers were bringing between them, Harry on the chestnut horse he had won from de Breos at the ford of the Mule.

He would have sprung to meet him, if he had not concentrated so much of his affection and understanding into the bright, measuring stare he fixed upon the boy. He would have taken him between his hands and hoisted him bodily out of the saddle, and held him a moment wriggling in mid-air like a small child before he plumped him down on his feet, but for the tender and strange consciousness he had of past failures, and the way the young shoulders squared and the straight back stiffened to approach him with dignity, shy with the same painful recollection of mutual wounds. Instead, he stood before the entrance to his tent, his falcon's face burned dark copper-coloured by long days in the June sun, and let them come to him.

"We've brought you another son, sir," said David, smiling. "He came in time to help us with a company of English down at the bridge of Usk, and well for me he did. No brother ever did better by his brother than he has today by me."

Harry dismounted, cap in hand, with exact and solemn respect

and a high colour, and went on his knee before Llewelyn. The great
brown hand to which he laid his lips felt the fervour they gave to
their kiss as a ceremonious amend for something past; but if they
began matching consciences which of them would be off his knees?

"My dear lord," began Harry, and had to wait a moment to be
sure his voice would serve him. "My dear lord," he tried again
sturdily, "I have been much at fault. I am set free to join you so
long as this war lasts—if you are pleased to forgive me my defection—and to take me back to my place."

Llewelyn took him by the hands and raised him, and only then,
with restraint, drew him into his arms and kissed him. A man can
be treated like a child without damage where there's love, but a
youngster hesitant and awkward between childhood and manhood
needs to be handled like a royal envoy on a mission of moment.
Llewelyn did well by him, muting even the brilliance of his smile
to a reverent gravity.

"Pleased I am indeed, Harry, and you're dearly welcome. There
could not be a more grateful sight to me than you here before me
alive and well. Your place is yours always, and well I know you'll
fill it like a man."

"I've given my word and I shall keep it," said Harry, when all the
tale was told. "Whatever he willed by it, he's made good his part of
the bargain, which is more than ever I had the right to expect. And
I'll make good mine."

He looked up appealingly into Llewelyn's eyes, longing to be
approved. The Prince was smiling at him, not indulgently as to a
valiant child, but thoughtfully and calmly, as he might have smiled
at Ednyfed to seal in silence a point of policy over which they were
at one.

"So you will," he said, "no question. But we have a long way to
go before that debt will fall due, and, by God, we'll enjoy you while
we have you. Take no thought yet for what follows. A little while
now, and King Henry's army of the west will be marshalled there
on the borders to meet us. And Ralf Isambard with them. Bear that
in mind, and keep your quarrel bright, and the account may be
settled before ever you see Parfois again."

He saw the fierce brightness of hope blaze up in the boy's face, kindling his eyes almost to gold. He had never thought of that; Llewelyn had made him a gift on which he closed his hands greedily. He looked round them all with an imperious lift of his head.

"If we ever meet with him in arms, my lord, remember the man is mine."

"Yours he shall be," said Llewelyn, strongly suppressing the gust of loving laughter that filled him like wine. "You have the prior right to him, Harry Talvace, and no one shall rob you."

Down the Usk from Brecon the fire ran blazing into Gwent, and burned and battered Caerleon to the ground; and thence, leaving a minor force to pen the garrison of Newport castle within their walls, Llewelyn swung westwards over the mountains. The princes of Glamorgan rose gleefully to join him, and reinforced his host with the musters of Senghenydd and Miskin and Neath. By the end of June they had taken and razed the castle of Neath, that had been a Norman thorn in the good Welsh flesh of Morgan ap Morgan ap Caradoc and his ancestors for a hundred years.

While King Henry was making feverish provisions for relieving the hard-beset garrison at Newport, Llewelyn was riding westwards again across the neck of Gower for Kidwelly; and before the bishops of the province of Canterbury met at Oxford in solemn conclave on July the thirteenth to consider the Welsh Prince's outrages against the church, Llewelyn's constable was in what remained of Kidwelly castle, and the Prince himself with the main body of his army was across Gwendraeth and Towy, and five miles beyond Carmarthen, and his fiery breath not yet spent.

Messengers from the princes of Cardigan came to meet him a few days later, and a courier from Builth, his clearing-house for intelligence from England, overtook him the same day. He feasted them royally at his own table while he listened to the news from the borders.

"Excommunicated, am I?" he said, and threw back his head and shouted with laughter. He was lodged that night in a grange of Whitland abbey, and the wine that danced in his cup and the pasty disembowelled before him on the board had been sent in to him with the prior's own compliments. Moreover, the young man who had ridden from Builth with the word was himself a clerk, and of good repute in his church. "Well, it's not the first time. And my allies with me, you say?"

"Twelve of the princes, my lord, had the same sentence pronounced against them." He named them.

"But they hope God had his back turned, I suppose, when de Burgh murdered my men," growled the Prince contemptuously. "The sentence is already promulgated, is it?"

"Throughout England, my lord."

Llewelyn laughed again at that; they had little hope of getting much respect for it in Wales. "I hope none of the twelve will lose more sleep over it than I shall this night. Well, at least their bishops move faster than their marshals, and are not so tied hand and foot with law and precedent. I wonder if the Archbishop in Italy knows of it? My heart tells me his prayers will be on the side of whoever shortens the Earl of Kent by a head, communicate or excommunicate. And which of the sees of Wales were represented at Oxford?"

"Bishop Anselm of Saint David's was there, my lord, and Bishop Elias of Llandaff."

"Both Englishmen! But I'll wager they never so much as sent the summons to Martin of Bangor or Abraham of Saint Asaph."

"No, my lord, they left the Welshmen well alone."

"You need not tell me. Where is the King now?"

"On his way to Gloucester, my lord. The muster was summoned there and at Hereford, and must surely be due. And we have heard in Builth that a letter has been sent to the justiciar of Ireland, making offer that any knights of Ireland who wish to come venturing for lands in Wales may keep all they can conquer."

"And so they may," said Llewelyn with a short bark of laughter. "But he's very forward to give away what's mine. Let's see if he'll grant the same rights to Welshmen. We'll present him with a test case. Here are messengers from my good friend Maelgwn Fychan in Cardigan. He's levelled the town, now we'll lay our forces together and finish the work between us. There's time yet to snatch castle and all, before I go back to straddle the roads into Powis and let the Earl of Kent break his head against my forehead."

Harry was down among the bowmen, in one of the loopholed shooting shelters the engineers had thrown up under the walls on the north bank of the river, in the charred and flattened waste Maelgwn and his allies had made of Cardigan town. It was the third day of the onslaught, and he had been crouching all morning at his slit in the timber shed, covering one of the wooden galleries built out from the crest of the curtain wall on the north side of the gatehouse.

On his right hand the long, dim, hot shape of the shelter stretched, and beyond the dozen intent bowmen at their slits of light showed a triangle of blackened ground and a charred stump of hawthorn. Beyond, invisible, the ash-smeared rubble climbed the slope to merge at last into the clean wooded uplands. On his left hand, from the open end of the shed, he could see the thinning smoke drifting away and the gulls wheeling and screaming above the tidal waters of Teifi and the bridge under the castle wall.

There along the river bank the fire had burned more fitfully, leaving streaks of green untouched, and living trees. The wooden houses had blazed like tinder, but the stone walls of store-houses and boat-yards along the tide survived, and within their cover, drawn back from arrow-range of the bastions, the princely pavilions were pitched. The nearest broken wall of stone, no more than a foot high, helped to seal the end of the shed, and red valerian flowered in it, and a great clump of ripe barley grass, not even stained by smoke.

There was no work here yet for a swordsman: Harry had reverted to his old weapon gladly. They had no time for a methodical siege, nor was Llewelyn in any mood to construct vallations round the castle of Cardigan and sit down to starve it into submission. Behind them in the march the King's host of the west was mustering. Cardigan had to be settled and done in a few days, and they on their way back to hold the approaches of Wales. The storming of the justiciar's prized fortress was work for the engineers, for the huge siege engines, mangons and arblasts and trebuchets, that hurled darts and charges of stones at the battered walls, and the iron-beaked rams that their crews ran up by night against the bastions and swung and swung on their chain slings to peck holes through the masonry. But there was still work for the archers, picking off any defenders who showed themselves in the merlons or ventured out on to the wooden galleries to drop stones and iron weights on the attackers below. The knights must loiter in the background, waiting for their *coup de main* until there was a large enough breach in the wall, or an opportunity of mounting one of the scaling-towers against it. Harry preferred to let knighthood take care of itself for the moment, and consider himself a bowman.

David came at a crouching run along the timber shed in the heat of the noon, and dangled his leather water-bottle over Harry's shoulder. Intent upon his watch on the gallery slung like a martin's nest against the parapet, Harry had failed to identify the running feet, and reached for the bottle greedily without a word. His eye fell on the familiar slender hand, the topaz ring and the hem of the dark green sleeve, and he turned his head, frowning. Unhelmed, uncovered, in half-armour only, David smiled at him.

"My lord," said Harry, surprised and disapproving, "you should not be here." He was exact in observance when on duty, but it was the anxious foster-brother, not the dutiful subordinate, who shook his head at his prince.

"Should I not? I saw you reach out of your burrow for a sprig of sorrel to moisten your mouth. There, drink! Why do you suppose I went to the trouble to bring it?"

The sun had been on the steep-pitched roof all the morning, and beneath it the air was hot as in an oven. Harry had sweated rivulets of pallor down his smoke-grimed face, and his shirt was glued to his back. He tilted the bottle and drank gratefully until David pulled down hand and bottle together.

"Take it slowly, lad, and taste it! There, let it pass along to your fellows, it's deadly dry work you have in here. Why should I not be here?"

"Because there's an archer up in yonder gallery who's too good a marksman by half, and if he catches a glimpse of you he may guess who you are. Look! There, you see the loophole at the end? Watch, and you'll see his russet-brown against the black of the timbers when he draws."

Faintly the lighter colour showed, the buff of a leather coat as the archer moved sidelong in search of his aim. A drift of thick smoke from within the wards was ascending steadily into the sky, darkening the upper air. Somewhere among the encrustations of wooden buildings clinging to the curtain wall, the barrels of flaming pitch had found their mark.

"He and I have been shooting it out the past two hours. How near I've come I can't tell, but he's been a deal too close to this slit of mine for my comfort. You mustn't leave cover here, go to the far end, and I'll engage him while you go. If he would but show more than a forearm, just once!" said Harry with bloodthirsty longing, and flattened his cheek against the timbers to squint up at his enemy.

"Take care for yourself," said David warmly. "You are no more proof than I am."

"Never fear, I have too good a respect for this fellow to take risks. Is there no breach yet under the bastions there where they had the rams working all night?"

"There is, and we have three trebuchets battering it wider at this moment. Within the hour we should be able to break through. And faith, we should have reduced the odds by the time we go in, for we've surely thrown half the masonry of Cardigan over the walls. And by the smoke, all that isn't stone within must be afire."

"You'll call me to you before the attack?" cried Harry, turning a soiled face anxiously, and smearing the running sweat out of his eyes with a bare forearm.

"I'll call you."

David reslung the empty water-bottle at his hip, shook Harry briefly by a handful of his hair, and wound his way back behind the kneeling bowmen at their slits, to break cover and run for the shelter of the standing walls. Harry took careful aim at the distant loophole in the timber turret, gashed and splintered now by a partial hit from a charge of stones. His shaft struck quivering across the opening, like a bar across the window of a prison. The answer came with a hissing impact that slit the thick boards of the shed, and a steel-shod tip, blunted and dulled, showed through the splintered edges of the wound in the timbers, close to Harry's cheek. He had flinched aside instinctively to flatten himself against the barrier; he recoiled again as hastily, feeling the heat of the steel scorch his ear. That was too close for comfort, but at least David was clear.

Nettled, he turned in earnest to the duel with his unseen opponent. Shot for shot, they matched skills and waited for the grain of luck that would settle the issue between them. Harry forgot heat and thirst in his single desire to have the better of the battle.

It was a chance shot from one of the mangons that gave him his opportunity. The great stone left the cup awry, and struck the wall somewhat below and to the left of the gallery, and there in its impact hollowed the masonry and flung off two or three sharp fragments that flew at random. The largest thudded among the propping timbers of the gallery and snapped one of them, and all the defenders sprang back from the shaken corner and hugged the solid stone wall behind them.

Harry had a shaft fitted and was in the act of drawing when the shock made the gallery quiver; and his quarry, for once forgetful of the danger of showing himself, leaped away from the impact with the rest, and came full into the open loophole. Harry saw his target at last, not a glimpse of a bow arm this time, but the broad russet of a body.

He shot, and saw clearly the convulsion of the two arms that clawed across the riven breast, and the leaping contortion of pain that seemed to lift the man bodily into air. He sagged into the loophole, and there hung for a moment swaying, to slide slowly outwards in a long, revolving fall, like a spider dropping down a thread. He crashed under the wall with a sickening sound that carried through a sudden comparative silence.

The mangon had not been reloaded, the trebuchets stood unmanned, their great arms swinging in an empty balance. Over Cardigan the smoke drifted faintly, trailing out into an attenuated pennant on a rising breeze; and down there to the left, fronting the breached wall and the battered gate-house, a knot of princes gathered from the river bank, and stepped out into the open sunlight. The last reverberations died along the Teifi like receding thunder, ebbing out to sea.

Harry, standing quivering with the bow still humming in his hands, looked round him for a moment without understanding. Then the man beside him caught at his arm and thumped him on the shoulder joyfully, and pointed him to the gate-house. The wicket in the great gate stood open, he saw the figure of a man form in the darkness as in a frame, and a white cloth lifted and fluttering in the breeze.

The archers were coming out of their steaming shelters to stretch themselves erect in the sunlight. Behind Llewelyn's company of princes the captains gathered, stripping off helms and gloves, uncovering their heads to the coolness; and out of Cardigan castle came the justiciar's castellan behind his flag of truce, to stave off at least the further battering and inevitable assault and sack of his crippled fortress.

Harry could not believe it. He blinked at the distant meeting of magnates and shook his head and stared again, until he got it into his dazed brain that it was over. David would not need him at his elbow in the assault, after all. Cardigan had surrendered. De Burgh, the great Earl of Kent, justiciar of England, the King's master, had lost his proudest castle. Llewelyn could leave it safe in the hands of his subsidiary princes, and take his army back in triumph to confront the royal host as it moved in from Hereford.

Harry crept out stiffly to the edge of the ditch, gulping air and feeling the sweat begin to dry on his soiled face. There at the foot of the wall beneath the gallery he looked for the russet-brown leather coat and found it lying among the debris of stones and rubble. The body was grotesquely broken, the head bent aside at a cruel angle, face upturned. Harry saw that his enemy had been a young fellow no more than a year or two older than himself, fair-haired and well-made. The hands that had nursed such an alarming skill lay sprawled empty in the dirt; the face was empty, too, still contorted into the formal shape of agony, but motionless and indifferent.

And he need not have done it! He had loosed the last shot of the siege, loosed it perhaps after the gate had been opened and the flag of truce displayed. Why had he been so set on this killing? The exultation had not lasted more than a moment. He felt nothing now but the sickness of regret and shock, as though he had wantonly broken something beautiful and admirable. And so he had, the wonderful machine that gauged the distance and fitted the shaft and drew the bow.

He was reminded suddenly of another spoiling. He saw again the young groom in Earl Ranulf's livery pantomiming hideously the obscene outrage of death by hanging.

What difference did it make that the body lying under the wall might as easily have been his own, and this broken boy might have been boasting happily of the shot that brought him down? That did not excuse him. He knew the value of making and the violation of breaking, the marvel of the engines of God which sculptors and artists copied so lamely. By so much he was the guiltier of the two.

David was beckoning him. He saw it and was loath to go, but go he did, stiffly and blindly, the poor, disjointed doll still before his eyes.

"What's the matter?" said David, quick to feel discomfiture in him even when there was no apparent reason for it. "Are you hurt? Did he graze you in the end, after all?" And he laid hold of him anxiously, and handled him with an open concern which Harry felt to be almost an indignity.

"No," he said, short and hard, putting off the solicitous hands with a gesture over which he would grieve helplessly later in secret. "I grazed him. He's down there under the wall with the rest of the wreckage."

At Llandovery a messenger from Builth met them, with word that King Henry's host was on the move westwards from Hereford up the valley of the Wye. From there they made forced marches accordingly, to deploy their forces astride every possible way into the fastnesses of Wales. But they reached the ridgeways of Eppynt without making contact, and David slept two nights peacefully in his own castle of Builth before they got certain news of the King's progress. Scouts came in from the march to report that the English army had left the Wye at Hay and was moving west over the easy upland road towards Painscastle.

"We need not go to them, it seems," said Owen, roused and serious. "They intend to come direct to us."

Builth seemed, indeed, the most likely target for this advance, and with such a force as Henry had collected marching against them they had good reason to provision and garrison the castle for a long and determined siege. But they watched alertly day after day, and their patrols sighted no marching columns on the nearer upland reaches or threading the open, wide valley beyond. Somewhere in the region of Painscastle the English army appeared to have slowed or halted its advance. Llewelyn himself rode out to see why.

From the flanks of the hills he looked down towards the old mound of Painscastle, and the timber fortress another William de Breos, the second of his line, had built there to hold down lower Elfael.

Maud's Castle, the English called it, after William's formidable wife, who had held it tooth and nail against the Welsh, and become a monster they used to frighten their naughty children.

"God's life!" said Llewelyn blankly, staring upon the teeming bowl below. "But this is Kerry over again."

All the broad green floor of the valley was alive with the colour and motion of men, and patterned with the tents and lines of the royal army. Above these the vast mound, several times added to, heaved its multiple levels of green, and the watchers on the hills saw that the grassy planes had now been enlarged and extended with new, raw erections of earth and rubble that glared in arid whitish greys under the sun.

"There's stone there," said Harry eagerly, pointing. "Look where it's stacked. And can you see the lines traced in white there? That's stone, too, they're laying the base of an outer wall."

They stared, and could hardly believe what their eyes told them. So vast a muster, answering so direct a provocation, had seemed to threaten a determined campaign against the whole of Wales. Why, then, sit down here to build a fortress? Castles are a means of attack when advanced far into enemy territory, but this was no outpost among the clans, but the old Breos link between Brecon and Radnor, one in a chain of marcher castles already familiar and long hated. Turning it from timber into stone would threaten nothing new.

Llewelyn shook his reins and turned his shoulder on the scene. "I thought we were blocking his way into Wales," he said. "It seems King Henry's content with blocking my way into England. Well, if he's chary of moving in for a direct assault, so much the better, we'll keep our own ways open all round him, and pick off his strays as fast as they wander."

And so they did, all through the hot weather of August, and it was work after the Welshmen's own hearts. They cut off such parties as foraged too far afield, harried the supply routes back through Hay, and raided the English borders as much for devilment as for gain, behind King Henry's pre-occupied back. When they were hot and dusty they even made time to halt and bathe in the Wye and lie in the sun along its banks, while their sentries kept watch from the uplands. Llewelyn prowled mid-Wales from Brecon to Caersws, and took toll from his English neighbours wherever he could, until some among them, like the prior of Leominster, preferred to pay him handsomely for the privilege of being left alone. And all the while the King's engineers and his immobilised army of labourers continued the rebuilding of Painscastle.

"Do him justice," said Llewelyn, making a passing inspection early in September, "he builds better than he fights, and past question he makes more speed with it. Surely, Harry, you should rather follow his army than mine, you'd make a career there in your own profession."

"My profession is arms," said Harry, so emphatically that he might have been trying to cry down a doubt, couched small and stubborn in a corner of his own mind.

"To understand building may be useful to a soldier also, as you see."

Said Harry, thoughtfully: "My lord, *why* have they done so? Why have they let their chance slip? Is it the King's policy? Or the justiciar's? We've done him harm enough in this summer's campaign, and he seemed to mean grim business when he began. Why have they let it all come down to this? Are they afraid of us?"

"Afraid, no. Beware of ever thinking that of your enemy. They're even more wary of me than I thought, that's true enough. Nevertheless," said Llewelyn, narrowing his eyes upon the distant, feverish activity in the valley, "surely something happened to change their plans since they began their march. You say truly, this was meant to be an expedition to drive me back into my own mountains, if it could not end me altogether. About the end of July something happened to change things."

"What was it?" asked Harry, confident of an answer. They were alone on the little headland in the trees; a quarter of a mile back in a bowl among the hills, a company of the Prince's guard was encamped.

"Do I know? You might look and find a dozen things, and any one might be the worm that ate the heart out of their harvest. But I know one at least that fits well enough. At the end of July the Bishop of Winchester came back from his victorious crusade and returned to his see—and to the King's ear. Ever since he heard that news, I think de Burgh has lost his appetite for this war. True, he's suffered enough by me, from Montgomery to Cardigan, but by Peter of Winchester he stands to lose all. And I think he willed to come no farther into Wales, to risk no more time and energy in fighting me, when he has a more deadly battle on his hands, for his very survival.''

''But could he make the King do what he wills? What, curb him here when he thought to go on a triumph?''

''Ay, could he! The King may chafe and complain, but though he has no love for his justiciar, and I think never did have, he'll do what he urges until there's another stronger will at his other elbow to urge the opposite. And that, I think,'' said Llewelyn with a sombre smile, ''will not be long.''

''Then if he's so little fain, surely you could close the campaign whenever you please. He'd be glad to come to terms and have us off his hands.''

''Softly, softly, boy! He may sweat a little longer, till I'm sure of my ground. I'm in no hurry to make terms. If I came too lightly they'd suspect I was in haste to cover up a weakness, and be encouraged to take up the quarrel again at a better time for them. No, let Bishop Peter prick de Burgh behind, and the King fret under his thumb a little longer, till they tear each other and let Wales alone. Then I'll let them know, in my own good time, that I'm willing to talk terms.''

Harry rode back into the encampment after him at once elated and sad. The Prince's confidence he prized dearly, and these large and venturesome speculations delighted and enslaved him; but, if they were to give up all thought of a major encounter with the English army, then he had lost the hope of meeting Isambard in arms, and settling his feud in the field. The shadow of his return to Parfois fell like a thundercloud over his spirit. He wished the Prince his triumphant peace, but he longed anxiously to achieve his own deliverance while there was time.

To take to himself every chance that offered, he begged David to send him out with every raiding party that wound its way through the hills to the rear of the English host and crossed the Wye after plunder; and David, not without misgivings, sympathised and let him go.

They had been out on one such party late in September, and were recrossing the river upstream from Hay, and because the summer had been dry and the water was low they did not bother to go down to the ford, but splashed through at a level place that gave them easy passage. The bank to which they climbed was meadow and sallows, and they rode out of the silvery willow-groves head-on into a company of English that outnumbered them three times over. By luck the Welsh were all mounted, for speed was their chief stock-in-trade on such forays; the English had perhaps as many knights and double the number of foot-soldiers. They clashed in equal astonishment, and with the slope of the land rolled back in untidy conflict to the water's edge.

It would have been folly to let this clash become a pitched battle; the English could very well be reinforced, the Welsh could not, and had to circumvent the entire English position in order to get back to their own. Along the bank to their left there was cover in the woods; they drew off in that direction and ran for it, Harry and a handful of the best-mounted keeping the rear and standing off attack to give their fellows time to scatter and run among the trees, where the bowmen among them could deploy and turn to help their rearguard. Nevertheless they left three dead behind them, and lost two more wounded into English hands, before they reached cover.

The foot-soldiers were all left out of reckoning now, and the odds had levelled, and had Harry been in command he would have been tempted to turn and fight it out on those terms; but he was under orders, and he obeyed faithfully and drew off with the rest, running and fighting and running again until the pursuers had dwindled to a handful.

They were still among the trees, scattered but within call of one another, when Barbarossa stepped astray in sandy ground honeycombed with rabbit warrens, and pitched Harry over his head into the grass.

Winded and shaken, Harry rolled head over heels and scrambled up in frantic haste to clutch at the bridle, but he was too late; it slipped through his fingers, and Barbarossa, frightened and indignant, thudded away between the trees. Close and threatening behind came the beat of other hooves. Harry turned to dive into cover, but a low halloo of pure mischievous pleasure told him he had been seen; and in a moment a horseman came crashing between the branches, and leaped down from the saddle without hesitation to plunge after him into the bushes.

Until then he had seen no faces he could identify among the English party, and few devices, for they had been moving back light-armed and at leisure into Hay, with no expectation of trouble and no parade of their liveries, and the action had been too confused for thought. Now he was presented with the abrupt and awesome apparition of a long, lean, steely body that closed on him with violent, beautiful movements he knew well, and above the light chain-mail of the hauberk he glimpsed at last the ageless bronze head, polished skin gleaming over fine-metal bones. The last to abandon the pursuit, the first to discard the advantage of a horse as once he had discarded the advantage of a sword, and go to earth after his quarry on equal terms, would inevitably be the old wolf of Parfois.

Spoiled and wasted in the long frustration of Painscastle, he burned bright and hard and happy now in his moment of release in action. Harry sprang away from the arm and the sword that probed for him with such disdainful hardihood, and parted the bushes to leap back into the open. The man whirled after him, responsive to the rustle of the drying leaves, and met him blade to blade. The swords hissed and locked for a moment, hilt against hilt. Isambard's deep eyes, quick with reddish flames of pleasure, blazed up into recognition.

"Well met, Harry!" he said, laughing, as they matched bodies and strongly heaved each other off, and came to a swordsman's distance.

Harry said nothing, he was too full of the exultation and the anxiety that stretched his senses to breaking and impeded his breath. He gathered to his aid every last resource of strength and skill he had, and came in like a fury, poised to meet and break the expected parry; and in mid-stroke he faltered and swerved with a gasp of horrified protest, turning his own blade wide at what should have been the moment of impact. Isambard had not lifted his sword to meet him, but deliberately lowered it and lodged the point in the turf, and stood uncovered to him. Harry had barely diverted his stroke in time, his point had sheered down the white surcoat beneath the left breast, and sent a rag of linen fluttering.

Trembling and raging, he heard a voice thick with passion, hardly recognisable for his own, crying hoarsely: "God damn you, my lord, will you never fight fair? Guard yourself and stand to me! Do me right, and cover yourself, or, by God, I'll kill you uncovered!"

"By God, then, kill me," said Isambard in soft and smiling invitation. "There's no one to see."

Harry heaved up his sword in a fury, and advanced it desperately against the unguarded breast. In his anguish of injury and helplessness and despair he wanted to strike, but when it came to the assay he could not do it. The point wavered and sank; and Isambard laughed, never moving.

"You know well I can't! Not in cold blood—Do me right, my lord! Guard yourself!"

With a long, deliberate movement Isambard sheathed his sword, and reached to the bridle of his grazing horse. Without haste he mounted, and looking back once, flashed a crooked smile at the boy who stood sick and shaking with hatred where he had left him. Then he rode back at a trot by the way he had come, and in a moment Harry heard a voice hailing, and the ringing of harness, and Isambard's voice calling calmly: "All clean away. You'll see no more of them this side of Builth. Let them go!"

That brought a sweat of honest fear out on Harry to cool the sweat of rage. He turned and blundered after his companions in a daze, swallowing down his detestation and gall as best he might, and in a few minutes was shaken back to reality by a voice calling his name low and urgently through the woods; and there was Morgan ap Einon, wild-eyed and uneasy, leading Barbarossa back towards the river to look for him.

There were no more such meetings. The advance parties of the English host were already moving back upon Hereford; by the end of September the entire army had withdrawn, leaving their hasty new castle garrisoned but unfinished. Early in November the Prince of Aberffraw let it be known, by oblique channels and without suing, that he was willing to discuss terms of peace.

Chapter Thirteen

Builth, Parfois: *December* 1231

*T*he envoys came back from London early in December, and rode into Builth in the first flurry of the valley snow, though the hills were already white. What they brought was not a permanent peace, but a year of truce, signed and sealed on the last day of November, a year's breathing-space to be employed in negotiations for a firm and final peace to come. Nothing was to be recovered in the meantime, nothing given up. What Llewelyn had taken, Llewelyn kept.

"Ah!" said the Prince, drawing large, pleasurable breath. "So we go home to Aber to keep Christmas with Cardigan in our baggage, do we? Did I not say if we waited we might have all we wanted? And how did the Earl of Kent stomach the loss of his castle? I warrant he looked sick and sour enough. Or does he think I can be made to give up in a year's time what I made plain I would not restore him now?'

Philip ap Ivor warmed his venerable toes at the fire in the royal chamber, and exchanged a quick glance with his younger fellow.

"My lord, I cannot suppose it gave him any pleasure to part with Cardigan, but I doubt he has other and worse deprivations on his mind. Since September he has lost a liege man from office. His old chaplain Ranulf the Breton is dismissed from his post as treasurer of the chamber, and told to take off himself and his family out of the kingdom. And Peter des Rivaulx holds office in his room."

"What, Winchester's nephew?" said David, looking up sharply from his stool at Llewelyn's knee.

"Winchester's son," said Llewelyn bluntly, and laughed as Philip looked severely down his nose, though he made no protest at such plain speaking.

"And it was rumoured before we left London, my lord, that the King will keep Christmas this year as Bishop Peter's guest at Winchester. The bishop already has the King's ear, and by all we could hear he's forgotten none of his old scores against the justiciar. And there's no Langton now to hold the balance true."

"Small wonder de Burgh's willing to compound with me, even at a price he dislikes paying. He'll have need of all his wits about him if he's to hold his own with Peter des Roches."

"My lord, that's truer now than ever it was," said Philip gravely. "Bishop Peter is come home with honours heavy on him, a crusader fresh from the Holy City, a close friend of the Emperor and deep in Pope Gregory's confidence. And the King's temper is such that he puts a reverent value on such presence as this man has, and such address."

Llewelyn heard the tale out, and said at the end of it: "I doubt we've seen the last time that ever de Burgh will come venturing into Wales in arms. God knows I owe him no quarter, as he gave my men none at Montgomery. Yet I'm almost sorry. I never yet bore him so much ill-will as to wish him made a mounting-block for these Poitevins."

When the two weary clerics had gone yawning to the lodging prepared for them, David came back to his father's presence with a shadowed face.

"My lord, here's Harry asking to speak with you alone. Give me leave to send him in."

"Ah, Harry!" said Llewelyn with a sharp sigh. He partly guessed what the boy had to say, and would liefer not have heard it. But where was the remedy? "Well," he said heavily, "let him come."

Harry came in and closed the door after him in purposeful silence. His face was pale and grave, his jaw set in a way there was no mistaking. Llewelyn beckoned him to the stool David had quitted, that still stood close to his knee, but Harry moved it round to front him squarely, so that they could look each other in the eye.

"My lord, I came to ask you for leave to go from here." He was marshalling his voice and his face as mistrustfully as a general mustering uncertain levies in the field. "The peace is signed, and my term of freedom is ended."

"The truce is signed," corrected Llewelyn gently.

"Within the sense of the promise I made, a truce is peace. I gave my parole to return as soon as peace was restored between England and Wales. It is time for me to make good what I swore." His lips were tight and pale. Isambard had known only too well how this moment would wring him, how easy his promise had been to make, how hard it would be to keep.

"Thus instantly? Need you be so exact in observance, Harry? There's a certain grace allowable, surely, you need not mount and ride the minute you receive the news. I had thought you would wish to bring your prince safely home again to Aber before you'd consider your term of duty finished."

He said no word of Gilleis, or Adam, or the Princess, but he knew by the tightening of every muscle of Harry's face and the hurried way he averted his eyes that he saw only too clearly through this deceptive temptation that was being held out to him. The thing he most wanted in the world now was to go back with them to Aber, though it was no less the thing he most dreaded. From Aber return to captivity would be twice as hard, even though he would take back with him the embraces and the prayers of all who were dear to him.

"David is in his own country and his own castle," said Harry in a low and careful voice, "and the war is over. There is no danger threatening him. I should be making a pretence if I argued that it was my duty to bring him home. I know you will not ask me to lie to myself. I hope you would keep me from it even if—if—I should be tempted."

"God forbid," said Llewelyn, "that I should ever make it harder for you to keep your word. What you must do, that you must, and you shall be the judge. But in all honesty, I think even Isambard would not grudge you the concession of those few days it would take to ride home."

Harry turned his head away, and wrestled with himself in silence for a few minutes; and suddenly he slid forward from the stool and was on his knees at Llewelyn's feet.

"I meant to! Oh, I did mean to go home. But now—My lord, I must not! I dare not! If it were to any other man I could, but to him never." He clung with cold, quivering hands to Llewelyn's knees, and laid his head on them, and poured out everything he carried heavy on his heart, in great gasps that were torn out of him like blood. "He would not fight me fair! He cheated me of the only chance I had to be free of him. But all the more I must not cheat, not even by a day, to make myself fellow to him—"

This time, when the Prince laid a hand on his head and stroked him like one soothing a child, he did not refuse the comfort or even stiffen under it, but took it thankfully for ease and warmth in the great, discomforting coldness that was closing upon him.

"Not one day less than is due, rather more! Every word, every act of his puts me on test. Among his friends a man can fail a little and not be undone, but before his enemy he may not. And I am the keeper of more than my own honour. He wills to break me, to find the weaknesses in me and prise me apart. And could he do it, he would have ruined more than me. My father had the better of him at all points, him he never could move. Could he bring me to break faith, or to fall short by the least grain of what I owe, I think he would be eased of something that poisons and darkens his life. And I would rather die than give him that satisfaction. Owen told me how he has profaned my father's grave and despoiled his body. But I am the keeper of my father's soul, God alone knows how, and I cannot abate one farthing of my debt, for his sake. Oh, my lord, my father, help me to pay my dues! It is hard enough—truly it is hard—"

"Child, child!" said Llewelyn, grieving, and lifted him into his arms and held him on his knees. They were alone, and no one would ever know. And he was so forlorn, and so in need of help to keep his hold on his duty. He let himself be cradled and comforted, grateful for the respite.

"You shall not fail of any scruple by my contrivance, I promise you," said Llewelyn in his ear. "To-morrow you shall ride, with proper provision. No one could ask more than that—one night's sleep on the news, and then the return as due. Never fear, I'll be your advocate at Aber, and hold you excused. You shall not be misunderstood. And shall I not send an escort to bear you company on the way?''

"No! Alone, I must go alone. He'd think I had to be brought back unwilling!''

"As you will, child, as you will. I'll never say the loath word to whatever you need for your own content. There, be easy! This is not for ever, and you shall not be left to carry it alone. Though well I know you'd keep your father's spirit and your own, and come out of it the victor, even had you no friends to be your stay.''

Harry wound his arms round his foster-father's neck and clung to him unashamed. It was like holding fast by a rock, but a living rock that warmed and quickened to his touch. Eased of the solitary weight of his burden, he said in a soft voice: "You'll not let David take it ill that I have to leave him? If I were free, I would not stir from his side.''

"Lad, he knows it.''

"And Madonna Benedetta—I never visited her—I thought to go when we returned—''

"Have I not said I'll be your advocate? There, never grieve for us who love you, we know you too well to mistake you.''

The boy in his arms heaved a great sigh out of him, like a stone of heaviness. Presently he untwined his arms and made to free himself. The Prince let him go gently, and he stood off with a high colour, but resolutely calm.

"My lord, I would ask something of you.''

"Ask, and you shall have it.''

"I know that for a year you are bound by this truce. But even when the year is over, I would ask that you will never venture for my sake anything that may put David's inheritance into danger. I would rather lie in Parfois till I die than be the means of harming him.''

Llewelyn rose and kissed him with respect and tenderness. "I will do nothing that shall trespass on your rights and your desires. Now go to David and Owen for a while, and then get your rest. In the morning we shall set you on your way.''

Harry kissed his hand and went, drained and sleepy. When the last light echo of his foot had receded into silence Llewelyn sent for his constable of Builth.

"Find me a reliable man to do an errand for me, one who can get a message by heart and deliver it like an ambassador. And one who knows the roads even in the dark, for I want him to ride to-night. I have somewhat to say to Ralf Isambard before he receives my foster-son back into captivity."

Rhys ap Tudor rode into Parfois about ten in the morning, when Isambard had just come to table after a morning's riding. There were some dozen noble guests in his company, halted on their way to their own dispersed honours, and the outer ward of the castle was encrusted along the lee wall with the temporary pavilions which had been thrown up to house their retinues. Men-at-arms in nine or ten different exalted liveries gathered in the wards to stare blackly and bitterly at the Welshman who trotted briskly in over the drawbridge, and struck sparks from the frosty cobbles under the gate-house.

The recent campaign rankled, and the truce terms bit deeper still. Rhys, who was well aware of himself as a living provocation in this place at this moment, was blessed also with the temperament to enjoy his irritant value. He spurred between the silent, scowling ranks with a jaunty gait and an arrogant face, not deigning to notice them, and dismounted in the middle of the courtyard, tossing his bridle to the nearest muttering archer, who perforce held it until a groom came to take it from him.

They could do nothing. The lord of Parfois had decreed that Llewelyn's courier should be admitted, and that word alone guaranteed his safety. For that matter, to give the Welsh direct cause to cry that the terms of the truce were already being infringed might have invited penalties even from the law, if the shadow of Isambard had not been deterrent enough. So they kept what they had to say below their breath, and spat after Rhys's deliberately provocative back only when he was well out of range.

A chamberlain brought him into the hall, and through the scurry of servants to the high table. The babel of the household froze suddenly into silence as he passed, and became a low and guarded rustle of excitement after his passing. Isambard, with a countess on his right hand and a bishop on his left, looked across the loaded board at him and measured him from head to foot with a brief flicker of his hollow eyes. The flame of interest came to life within them. He acknowledged the formal salutation courteously. The man Llewelyn had sent to him had a presence, in his barbaric way, and knew how to do justice to the compliments of princes.

"My lord Isambard, the Lord Llewelyn, Prince of Aberffraw and Lord of Snowdon, sends me to you with a message concerning the future of his foster-son, Harry Talvace."

"Ah!" said Isambard, faintly smiling. "Are you Harry's herald, come to assure me of his return?"

"No, my lord. He needs no herald, and of his return you need no assurance. If I am here before him it is because I have ridden through the night, and even so you shall find I am not by many hours ahead of him. He knows nothing of my errand, and it is not the will of the Prince of Aberffraw that he should. I am sent to sue to you yet once more for this boy's ransom. My lord offers you the price of an earl. Two thousand marks for Harry Talvace's freedom."

The nobility at the high table drew respectful breath and watched with curiosity the face of Isambard, which had not stirred from its contemplative and faintly mocking stillness. The corner of his long mouth drew upwards in the oblique grimace that marked his moments of mild amusement.

"I regret I cannot accept the Prince's most generous offer."

"Then, my lord, I am bidden to say to you that the Prince of Aberffraw is willing to consider whatever price you choose to put on Harry Talvace's liberty—and not merely in money. Name what you desire of him, and I shall faithfully convey your message to him."

"I regret exceedingly," said Isambard, "that I must disappoint the Prince, but there is no price in money or any other commodity he has at his command that I would take for Harry Talvace. I will name none, and I will consider none he may name, not in land, nor falcons, nor flesh. I am content to keep what I hold."

Rhys ap Tudor lifted his chin and curled his lip. "You neither disappoint nor astonish my Prince. He bade me, if you refused to treat, as he said you surely would, to deliver to you another message."

"Deliver it, then," said Isambard, tranquilly, "here, before all these fair witnesses. Let us have in form both the embassage and the reply. Unless you would rather we dealt in privacy?"

"No, faith, this is the place I would have chosen of all places. The Prince bids me say to you in your teeth, my lord, that in due time, when he may do so without offence to his sacred obligations or his plighted word, he purposes to come for Harry Talvace in arms. And he has sworn that when that time comes he will take and destroy Parfois for his sake."

The hum of consternation and excitement that went down the hall made the green and gilt hangings shake. De Guichet came to Isambard's elbow and whispered angrily in his ear, and some of the young men were on their feet. Smarting already from the ignominy of their long inaction at Painscastle, stung afresh by the agreement that left the Prince of Aberffraw in possession of all his conquests, they would have welcomed the excuse to tear a Welshman piece-meal. But Isambard lifted his head and swept over them one glance of his formidable eyes, lifted his hand and made one controlled and delicate gesture, and they sank back into their places and shut their mouths. It was a fearful thing how daunting a threat he could put into a flick of his fingers.

"I am indebted to the Prince for his message," said Isambard mildly. "Before I give you my answer, will you sit down with us and eat and drink? We are no longer at war, you need not scruple to accept my hospitality."

"I thank you, my lord, but with your pardon I must excuse myself, not from ill-will, but because I am pledged to be out of Parfois before Harry Talvace enters it, and so far as lies with me, to keep him in ignorance that I have been here. That means I must not meet him by the way. What you do in the matter, my lord, is for you to decide, but as for me, I shall keep to my orders. Give me your answer, and let me be on my way."

"Then say to the Prince, with my most reverent compliments: Come when you will, fetch him away if you can. Till then I'll hold him safe for you."

Rhys ap Tudor hitched at his sword-belt and settled his cloak over his shoulder, drawing a cautious breath of satisfaction, for he might very well have got less to take back with him, and of what he now had he would make the most.

"My lord Isambard," he said, "I'll gladly bear him that answer. For it is well known of you, my lord, even to your enemies, that you are a man of your word."

And with that, loudly and emphatically uttered, he made his ceremonious reverences and stalked out of the hall of Parfois, brushing off the dour stares of the young gentlemen-at-arms as a large-minded man brushes off flies.

The worst moment Harry had was when he came to the place where the path forked, and to the left the narrow track wound away into the woods along Severnside. He set his course straight ahead, and rode past it, but in spite of himself his hand fell slack and irresolute on the rein, and Barbarossa lagged, feeling his rider torn two ways.

Not a mile by that track, and he could be at Robert's assart. All the way from Llanfihangel in Kerry he had been struggling to put away from him the thought of Aelis, and constantly she had come slipping back into his senses like a remembered music, or the taste of ripe fruit from a lost summer, now sweeter than ever in life, unearthly sweet on his tongue. He would not think of her; but she would be thought of. So brief a while he had had with her that summer night, and even that while stolen from the duty for which he had been expressly released. It seemed he had not been too scrupulous to borrow a little of the time he owed to David; why, then, should he hesitate to take just one hour from Isambard?

And yet he could not do it. To take from your friends, in the certain knowledge that they would not grudge you that and much more, is well enough, but to your enemy must be rendered the last penny of his dues. Especially when you are the custodian of two souls and two honours, and are going back to the renewal of an ordeal for which even the least indulgence would be a poor preparation.

He held his head straight, he would not turn and look along the dark thread of track between the trees, where the thin snow had been bruised into black ice by a few passing feet, perhaps hers among them. How very little he had ever had of her! A few short weeks of unheeding companionship, wanting the wit to value it, and since then only crumbs of moments bedevilled by secrets and reticences he could not help. Even that one June evening seemed to him now to be marred by his failure to tell her the truth about his conditional liberty. How lightly he had promised her he would come back, explaining nothing, demanding her continued trust, not realising then how grim and exigent his return would be. He should have told her everything. She might have found it hard to understand, she might have tried to dissuade him from keeping his bargain; but at least she would have known that in his own eyes he was bound, and she would have made the effort to accept and bear with his conception of his duty. Now, because he had failed to speak, she would wait for him to come back as he had promised, and who could guess how long before he would be able to keep his word? She would not know; she would grieve, thinking he had forgotten, or never meant to come. And it was such a little way!

The Prince's stout comfort could not help him here. All the fine cords that bound him by the heart to Builth and Aber had been drawn out mile by mile behind him, until they had nearly dragged the heart clean out of him and left him a hollow-ache; and yet he had the absolute assurance that all those whom he had left behind there would understand him and be constant with him in love, whatever pains the hard present cost him and them.

But who was going to explain him to Aelis? No one knew the need. No one knew of the unforeseen kiss in the long grass at the edge of the paddock, that had excited them into fever and then frightened them apart and driven them speechless and trembling into the house, to the safety and restraint of Robert's presence. No one knew the beauty that was budding in Aelis, or the worth she had for him. He had not known himself how to value her until now, when he could not, for the integrity of his soul could not, go to her.

And he did not go. He shook the reins on Barbarossa's neck, and kicked his heels into the glossy sides and went on, the newest and most sensitive heart-cord of all beginning to lengthen and tear at him in a gradual, quivering refinement and attenuation of pain. Every pace must be the last it would bear without snapping and leaving him to bleed to death from the wound.

But yard by yard he went on, to the foot of the darkening ramp where the path turned, to the place where the trees crowded in, to the towers of the lower guard; and the thread of anguish did not break, and the pain did not become unbearable. He knew that because still he bore it and still he went on, dimly realising, half in dismay and half in consolation, that ultimately there is nothing that cannot be borne.

The guards challenged him from the towers, and he stood meekly at their order, sensible of the fitted shafts nosing at his breast from the loopholes, and walked Barbarossa obediently forward when they bade him. The tension eased in him then without breaking, and he found a kind of rest, because from this point there was no drawing back, and all the heavy weight of choice was lifted from him.

He had half expected that when they knew him they would put him under close escort to go the rest of the way, but it seemed they had their orders concerning him, for they passed him through without question, and let him go to his surrender alone. He paced up the long ramp between the fringes of trees. On the left hand and the right, just beyond these fringes, the ground fell away. He was ascending to the green peninsula in the air, and the stone island beyond, where no one could reach a hand to him, and now he could not turn aside even if he would.

The trees rustled with a dry, frosty tinkling of leaf and twig, the thin coating of snow crumpled and darkened under Barbarossa's hooves, and the chill wind fingered its way in to him through the folds of his cloak as he climbed higher, and set him shivering; and it was apt that he should be returning in winter, when there was neither flower nor shoot nor harvest nor active seed, but only a sleep out of which, when God turned the glass, something might stir and awaken. He could not believe, he would not believe, that any season could be meant to run utterly to waste.

It was getting dark, the early, leaden December twilight that went before the Christmas feast. The bridge was still lowered when he reached the plateau, and the red, leaping light of pitch-flares from within the gate-house archway corrugated the cross-poles of the span and made of it a ladder into hell. But over against it, still faintly lambent against the wintry sky, the assuaging shape of the church rose and soared. Surely he could borrow a few moments of his captor's time now? He was within the territory of the castle, his parole was almost redeemed; and since he was resolved not to renew it, once he entered the gateway this treasury of his father's spirit and refuge of his own would be out of his reach.

He dismounted, and turned Barbarossa loose on the frosty grass to wait for him. He twisted the great ring of the west door, and crept silently within. The light was almost gone, but surely he could touch and sense even what he could no longer see, and for prayer no man needs his eyes.

The noble, shadowy shape of the nave, almost lost in the closing dusk, preserved still a form the mind reached out eagerly to fill. He went forward and fell on his knees before the high altar, and faltered through a prayer for his mother's comfort; and for a moment such a desolation came on him that he could hardly breathe. Then at the core of his being a little intractable flame of delight quickened; he had opened his eyes and traced in the dimness of the altar frontal before his face the boisterous shape of a small, turbulent but devoted angel, clutching a psalter and bawling out his ebullient heart in praise to God. One of the nine several images of Owen, carved here in heavenly consort. And suddenly the church for all its cold and darkness was full of the laughter and love that Master Harry had put into the making of the stone children, and the same love at its apotheosis touched and comforted the child of his own body.

After all, he was not alone. In Parfois he could never be alone, in Parfois of all places, for it was full of his father. His father's integrity made his footing firm there, and his father's works were all round him, a defiant prophecy of his own works some day to be. They were one force. They opposed their unity to Isambard's solitary and monumental hatred, and while they held fast to each other they could not be moved.

He fumbled through his prayers with half his mind and all his heart lost in an astonishment of grace.

"While you're on your knees, Harry," said the voice of Isambard softly and dryly from behind him, echoing hollowly under the vault, "say some prayer for my poor soul. You can hardly do less, seeing the peril I shall be in if you ever win your way with my sinful body."

Had he come there so silently on the stones that not even the rustle of his clothing or the soft tread of his shoe had betrayed him? Or had he been there all the time in the dimness, quiet and motionless in some retired corner, perhaps himself on his knees? He was a devout man, they said, in his terrible way. His voice had pricked like a sword, the feel of his stillness, there in the dark so close and so silent, had made the hair rise in the nape of Harry's neck. He got to his feet with the conscious dignity of one who knows he is watched and measured. From this moment everything he said or did would be inflected by his awareness of those hollow eyes upon him. The malice that had never been able to let his father alone, living or dead, would now never relinquish him.

"I commend you, Harry," said the soft voice. "You come very strictly to your time." He came out of the dark of the north aisle, tall and shadowy, and silent in movement as a shadow.

"My lord, I've made what haste I could. I left Builth on the morning after our envoys returned from London. Are you content that I have kept to terms, my lord?"

"Very content, Harry—very content."

"Then I have now fairly redeemed my parole, from the moment when I pass through the gate. I give you to know, my lord, with all respect, that I do not intend to renew it."

He felt though he could not see the slow, red flames burn up in the bronze lantern of that wonderful head, and the oblique smile tugging at the long lips. The voice of seduction, golden-sweet and rueful, tempted him gently: "This habitation he left you, these marvels of his making, lie outside the wards. And that spring of comfort you were drinking at just now, that will be out of reach, too."

"I do not intend to renew it," said Harry again, himself astonished that he could repeat it so mildly and yet so finally.

"As you will, Harry. Come, then, shall we go in? You must be weary, and supper will be waiting for us."

He laid his hand upon Harry's shoulder, and so brought him out of the church.

"You'll find your lodging prepared, and your work and your tools as you left them. That at least you may have within the wards. And my company, Harry, my company, in which you take such delight, that you shall have daily."

Harry released himself with constraint to go and bring Barbarossa by the bridle. Isambard made no move to follow or press him close, but stood and waited for him in quietness.

"I see you've made provision for a long stay," he said, his eye lingering maliciously on the plump roll strapped behind the saddle. "That delights my heart, Harry. I half feared Parfois might pall on you now, you're grown such a man of the world."

"I would not for shame put you to the trouble and expense of providing for me, my lord. It's imposition enough that you must feed me, I would I might spare you that, too."

"There spoke your father's true son! He would not be beholden even for his life, and neither will you," said Isambard, amused.

"I'm sorry you think so, my lord," said Harry, walking beside him with a set face. "I was about to ask a favour of you, but I should be loath to spoil your image of me."

"Ask it, Harry, ask it! It's good for the soul to venture something new."

"I was about to ask you if you would see my horse properly exercised, since I shall not be able to take care of the matter myself."

"I would have done as much for the poor brute's asking, Harry, you need not strain against your nature. Will you not be as considerate of yourself as of your beast?"

"I thank you, my lord," said Harry. "My own needs are simpler. I shall do very well as I am." The spring of comfort was not out of reach, he felt it quicken in him now at need; just as he was he would do very well.

Side by side they came to the bridge and, treading hollowly over it, reached the outer rim of the torchlight, and there as by consent turned and measured each other. Harry beheld his enemy in splendour of black velvet cotte and surcoat all copper and gold thread, a tall, bright demon coruscating with points of gleaming light. Isambard saw a young, passionate face, a man's face, armed with a glittering green stare that advanced against him as straight and implacable as the sword he had declined to encounter beside the Wye.

"Be pleased to enter Parfois, Harry Talvace. You are welcome home."

Side by side they stepped from the hollow-ringing timbers of the bridge and into the torchlit tunnel of the gate-house. Behind them the chains engaged, and with a long, grinding rattle the drawbridge rose and sealed them in from the world.

THE
SCARLET
SEED

Chapter One

Parfois, Shrewsbury: *August* 1232

*T*he blunted tourney swords clanged in mid-air, shivering the sun-light in sullen blue splinters. The shock jarred Harry from wrist to shoulder, but he held his grip doggedly, and slid his opponent's blade clear of his head by all the inches he could gain. If that stroke had got home he would have been stunned at the least, even if he had escaped being carried from the exercise-ground with a broken head. Old Nicholas Stury never played gently. Sometimes Harry had suspected that he enjoyed bruising and battering the young gentle-men-at-arms who came under his tuition, and certainly there were several among them who were afraid of him.

They circled with the impetus of the swing and the parry, chang-ing ground in two quick steps. The ring of intent faces swung with them, the hushed voices muttered in speculation and excitement. Harry knew them too well to suppose that he had their good will in this bout. They used him tolerantly enough, some among them had even grown to like him in the long months he had spent in their company, but when it came to a passage of arms they could not wish success to the Welshman and the prisoner, not even against Stury whom they heartily detested. Let old Nicholas be what he would, he was of Parfois, and one of them, and they were for him against the stranger.

He was fond of that full, swinging stroke at the head, was Nicholas, perhaps he liked to see it terrify before it got home or was desperately parried. Give him time, and he'd try it again, and Harry knew more than one way of dealing with it. He wove warily to the right, clashed aside a couple of probing strokes that were meant only to mislead, and essayed a few of his own no less guilefully; and then it came, fast and hard, intended to club him into senselessness through the padded exercise helm. Instead of flinching away from it and flinging up his blade to slide it from his head, this time Harry crouched and sprang in under it, and as he darted past his opponent, right side to right side, swung his sword back-handed and thumped Stury in the ribs so heartily that he fetched a great grunt out of him, and then, for good measure, dug his rounded point into the stretched armpit in token that he could have pierced him there at will had this play been earnest.

The young men roared honest acknowledgement. One of the pages perched astride the sill of the nearest armoury window shrilled: "A hit!" with an ungrudging glee that warmed Harry's heart; it seemed he had at least one partisan among them. Walter Langholme, my lord's own body-squire, echoed the cry with authority and, when Stury pressed in again, advanced a tilting spear between them and prodded him in the breast with the three nodules of its blunted end.

"Let be, that's enough. Talvace had the better of you, Nick, you may as well own it."

A hard enough thing for a seasoned master-of-arms to do at any time; harder still when his too apt pupil is an alien prisoner, and a mere stripling of seventeen at that, kept kicking his heels in the household at its lord's whim, and allowed his share in the games of the young men as an act of grace.

"He barely touched me," protested Stury, pushing down the tilting spear from his broad chest with a hand like a projection of the sandstone that held up Parfois. "Call that a hit? If my foot hadn't slipped he'd never have got below my stroke."

Harry turned away into the shadow of the armoury and dropped his sword on the stone ledge that ran beneath the high windows.

He unlaced his padded helm, as squat and plain as the ceremonial tourney helms were lofty and elaborate, and emerged flushed and panting into the air. The page in the window dropped a napkin down to him and he wiped the sweat from his face and neck gratefully, and flung over his shoulder:

"Give me another bout, then, if you dispute my point. It's all one to me, I can do as much again."

That was no wise thing to say in the circumstances; it roused the local loyalty even of those who liked him best, and brought a howl of aggressive acceptance of his offer. And to tell the truth, he was by no means sure that he could make good his boast. To turn the tables once might be all very well, it was merely a matter of patience and caution; but when Stury was forewarned, as now, and his blood well up after one setback, he was no man to be meddled with. But it was too late to think better of it now; he'd said it and he must stand to it. He picked up the pitcher of water that stood on the stone ledge and drank thirstily, while they wrangled loudly over the issue, and Langholme thumped the tilting spear against the ground and bellowed for order.

From the shade of the archway which led into the inner ward of the castle a loud, clear voice said: "It was Talvace's win, no question. Who disputes it?"

The clamour died instantly. How he had made himself heard through the babel of voices Harry could not guess. Perhaps the first words were felt rather than heard, cutting their way to the stretched nerves of awe as a small, sharp sound can set the teeth on edge; but by the end of even so brief an utterance he had created a silence about himself, and every man in the group before the armoury was respectfully on his feet. When their lord came among them they looked only at him, with an attentive anxiety to which Harry had long become accustomed.

He thought now: I am the only man here who is not afraid of him. And then, correcting a too hasty estimate: No, perhaps Langholme has no fear of him any longer, though I'm sure he had once. He's been close about his body so long now that he's outlived his fear, and they've come by a sort of understanding of each other that puts it out of mind. Walter has no ambitions towards knighthood, and wants nothing from him more than he has, and my lord

Isambard knows there's no self-seeking in him, and puts a value on him I doubt if he sets on any of these others.

He watched the tall, lean figure of the lord of Parfois walk towards them at leisure from the shadow of the archway, through the silence he himself had made. He did not hurry for them, as he had never yet checked or hurried for kings. He had cast off surcoat and cotte in the August heat; and unlaced the collar of his loose linen shirt from the gaunt but erect throat in which the cords stood taut as bowstrings from the brown flesh. He loved the sun; he had torn deep lancet windows through his grandsire's tower walls to let it in to his chosen apartments; and it seemed that the sun was a good friend to him in return, for yearly the summer burned him into a dark recollection of beauty, stripping from him with his Flemish brocades fifteen at least of his sixty-eight years. It could not put back the black into his iron-grey hair, that coiled thick as a boy's on his head, but it gilded and polished the shapely, dominant bones of cheek and jaw, and the weathered cliff of his forehead, and warmed the winter stiffness out of him, so that it seemed right he should move like a yearling roe, and glare like the sun in the zenith in a red August.

"As clean a hit as ever I saw," he said. "Man, he could have cut the heart out of you. You've taught him too well, he knows your every move."

"He'd never have touched me, my lord, had we been out on the grass. But the hit I don't dispute."

He could not, thought Harry grimly, with Isambard staring him in the eye and laying down so absolutely what was truth. His own obstinacy stiffened in him against all of them; for essentially they were all his enemies, and he was damned if he'd conciliate any one of them.

"My lord, I've offered him a new match if he's not satisfied. I'll not stand on what he claims to be no more than a stroke of luck. If I can repeat it we may come by a just name for it."

He stood passing the pitcher from hand to hand, pouring a little cold water over his wrists and letting them steam dry in the hot air of mid-morning. He knew he was being foolish, but he was sick and tired of being wise after seven months of going patiently and abiding without offence the constrictions of his isolated position among them. If Stury could prove on his body that he was the better man, then let him do it. Harry would not go back a step for him until he was felled by force. Nor for Isambard himself. If all his household were afraid of him, Harry was not of his household. Let them see that being the alien and the prisoner gave him a stature greater and not less than theirs. He looked steadily back into the hollow dark eyes that studied him unsmiling across the circle, and wiped his hands slowly, flexing the tingling fingers ready for the hilt again, though the shock of that one harsh impact had not yet passed out of them.

"With your leave, my lord? I'm ready when he is."

Isambard had taken the tourney sword from Stury and gripped its hilt with a long, emaciated hand, pressing the rounded point into the ground and leaning his weight upon it in an experimental thrust.

"Not my length, but it will serve. If you're so ready and fain, Harry, you may give me the benefit of a few minutes' exercise."

So he won't have old Nicholas made a fool of, thought Harry, without surprise or any great resentment, and I'm to get a thrashing for it by another way. Well, let's take it further, since he offers me the first such meeting he's ever condescended to put in my way. He braced his sturdy feet squarely into the ground and lifted a bright, inimical stare to Isambard's face, a naked challenge that might well escape reading by any other present, but would surely speak clearly enough to him.

"But, my lord, there's nothing at issue between you and me; it was Master Stury who wanted satisfaction."

He felt all the young squires of Parfois shift and grin at that, understandably gratified at hearing him back out so hastily. Someone close at Isambard's elbow sniggered. Harry let them enjoy the taste of it, and never lowered his eyes. Isambard himself had neither moved nor smiled; he balanced the heavy sword and watched Harry across the runnels of splintered light, waiting without impatience. He knew there was more to come.

"But if you please to try me with unblunted swords, my lord, I'll gladly give you a bout as best I can."

They gasped at that, aghast at his insolence and bristling against him for the dignity of Parfois; marvelling, too, at his hardihood, and sparing him a grudging morsel of pity for his folly. His own heart contracted a little at the stark sound of it, but he kept a stony front and waited. Only Isambard gave no sign of having heard more than a current remark any one of them there present might have made. His long fingers, handling the clumsy hilt with absent delicacy, never started or tightened; the movement of his head as he looked up over the blade was smooth and slow, even the long, thoughtful stare he bent upon Harry's face gave nothing away to those who watched him so narrowly, and waited for him to crush the impudent boy or kill him, according as his humour led him.

Harry expected a curt refusal, and a part of his mind, honest in sensible physical fear, would have welcomed it. But the great eyes, burning tranquilly in their clear pits of polished bone, smiled at him faintly and held no anger or impatience. Not that that made it any safer to have meddled with him; he could kill just as well without either.

"Bring a pair of combat swords, Walter."

His voice was placid. No one dared so much as look consternation while he denied it. Langholme went without a word, tramping heavily into the armoury.

"No haste, Harry," said Isambard, seeing the boy reach for his discarded helm. "You're hardly breathed yet, take your time."

"You'll put on harness, my lord?" said Harry, quick to anticipate a slight and take offence at it.

"Oh, be content, I'll match you piece for piece." He turned over the pile of leather hauberks with a casual foot and, discarding them as short of his measure, strode after Langholme into the dim coolness of the armoury.

When he was out of earshot they let out their pent breath in a gust of hushed abuse and advice at Harry, those who had some liking for him cursing him roundly for a fool to tempt death so wantonly and urging him to back out even now, however abjectly, those who had none promising him with satisfaction more than he had bargained for, at least a humiliating lesson in swordsmanship, at worst a maiming. None of them thought of death. They took it for granted that Isambard wanted him alive, since he had kept him so for nearly two years when he might very well have ended him; and they were no less sure that, since death was no part of his plans for the boy, the boy himself could not invoke it. Isambard could play with him as he pleased, beat him into repentance of his presumption, let him a little blood, mark him for life if the fancy took him, and then let him go.

Harry shut his ears, hunched his shoulders against abuse and advice together, and waited dourly, scrubbing the sense back into his tingling hand. What did they know of the good reasons he had for being afraid of what he had done? They could not even recognize what had happened before their very eyes. Only he knew how far in earnest was this apparent and dangerous game, and so far from shrinking from it, he felt his bowels burn in him for desire. There was fear in him, too, the fear of falling short as well as the sane man's fear of death; but these he would not acknowledge, and before Isambard came back from the armoury they had burned out of his body, and left only the molten lust of hatred and pride in possession of him.

Langholme flattened the length of a tilting spear against the crowding breasts that hemmed the ground, and enlarged the clear, trodden space for them. They were both long in the reach, the boy by five or six inches taller than his father before him, though still short by some three or four of Isambard's commanding height, and his young flesh built upon lighter, slenderer bones. At least let him have room to give back, if my lord was bent on punishing. Langholme swung the spear, none too gently, and was not happy. Who could have foreseen this in a little play no rougher than usual?

"Yes, give us room," said Isambard, flicking round him from under the open visor of the exercise helm a sharp glance that moved them back more effectively than Walter's spear. "And take this trash from under our feet, Nick." He kicked aside the pile of leather and cloth hauberks, and watched them hurried away out of his sight. "Walter, you'll stand marshal for us. So, Harry, are you ready to guard your head?"

"To the first hit, my lord?" ventured Langholme hopefully, eyeing his master's face before the visor closed.

"As Harry will have it, I'm content." Shadow covered the brilliant eyes, and in the easy voice there was nothing to be read.

"To the mastery," said Harry, carefully holding back the word "death," that was like a secret between the two of them there, and not to be shown to any other.

It was on them now, no way out but one, and wide enough only
for one. Langholme dropped the truncheon of a lance for the onset,
and they moved in with a double, weaving, essaying swiftness, like
one man before a mirror. The ring of staring faces, the girdle of avid
eyes, went out like quenched lights, the taut murmur of voices that
dared not speak aloud lurched away into silence; and they were left
alone in the world, as in a sense they had always been alone in it,
confronting each other in arms, from the moment of their first
meeting, the boy with his long score to settle for his father's sake,
the man with his heavy toll of debts to be paid.

Watching the balanced motions of the long arm that probed his
defences, Harry rehearsed within his mind the heads of his hatred,
and steadied his heart against the hope of vengeance. You are he
who brought my father here, with his foster-brother Adam Boteler,
to be your master-mason and build you a great church. Did he fail
of giving you what you asked? Did he default in his service? You
know he did not! It was in the church I first met with you, I saw
you stare upon my father's work, and you knew its perfection. You
yourself have owned it to me. In what particular did he play you
false, then? How did he offend? He took a captured Welsh princeling,
a child of nine, out of your hands when you would have done him
to death at King John's orders, and sent him in charge of Adam back
to Prince Llewelyn his foster-father. That was all! Cheated King
John of Owen ap Ivor's little body, and you of a morsel of your
ghastly fealty that you loathed and yet would not forego. And came
back and delivered himself into your power, because he had sworn
not to forsake you until his master-work was finished. And finish
it he did, in chains, and when the last pile and hurdle of the scaffolding came down you brought him out before his own church to a
traitor's death, a fearful death. "That heart of yours," you said, "I'll
have living out of your body—" And so you would have done, but
that Madonna Benedetta whom you brought from Paris with you,
Madonna Benedetta whom you loved, went about secretly to find
him a better end, quick and clean, at the hands of her archer, John
the Fletcher. And even then, even then you could not let him be!
Nor her, because she loved him and saved him. You stripped her
living and him dead, and bound them fast and sent them down the
Severn in flood, to rot in each other's arms for ever, if John the

Fletcher had not drawn them ashore and given the one life and the other quiet burial at Strata Marcella. You can never have done, short of your devil's will. You picked up her traces again, with my poor little mother still feeble from bearing me, where Benedetta had hidden us, and hunted the three of us over the border into Gwynedd, to a refuge you never foresaw, to Prince Llewelyn's maenol and Prince Llewelyn's fostering.

And did you think I would not come back? Did you think you were clear of the last Talvace? That the story could end so?

Yet he had made the assay too soon, climbing the escarpment of sandstone at fifteen to hide himself in the church, until he could break into Parfois by stealth in search of his vengeance. And in the church they had met, and in the church he had done his best to kill, to kill at all costs, even if he himself must die to achieve it. He remembered that bitter struggle in the triforium, the desperate leap to take his enemy with him over the edge, thirty feet down to the flagstones below. He felt the gaunt hand twisting mercilessly in his collar, gripping cotte and shirt and flesh and all, dragging him back to fling him down against the wall, beneath the corbels his father had carved. He remembered, with a ferocity that brought the blood stinging now in his smitten cheek, three brisk, deliberate blows, from that same hard palm that gripped the hilt before him now, and sent the point flickering low to test his guard. He heard the cool voice say: "That's for despising your own life, fool." And then the cell below the tower, and the long captivity, the long baiting that was not over yet.

They had never fought but that once; never until this day had Isambard consented to meet him so again.

All the accumulated grudges of the years gathered into Harry's sword hand and flowed into the steel. If he squandered this hour there would be no second such hour for him. The enormous weight of the occasion made his arm tremble and ache for a moment, and then fused hand and weapon and arm into one intelligent lightning.

The swords touched and slid away, hissing, whirled and clanged again head-high, and parted again harmlessly. How often he had watched Isambard at sword-play, and seen the formidable face graver and stiller than at other times, measuring as it were another man's efforts, not his own. Now he glimpsed the eyes that held him fixed through the grille of the visor, and saw them smiling. This stroke he knew, he had seen it a hundred times and admired its cunning, studying in his own mind how to deal with it. Now he dealt, and his eye was sure and his arm competent. And the eyes confronting him burned to deep red, and laughed. They laughed still as Harry lunged and swung, following the parry closer than the echo of the steel, and his point grazed Isambard's shoulder as he leaped away from the stroke.

The ring of faces, dizzily reappearing for an instant out of the void that circled them, breathed amazement and wonder in a great, shivering sigh, and again vanished.

There was blood in Harry's mouth, he swallowed it and sickened; but he had only bitten his tongue in the stress of his lust. And he had lost the opportunity to follow up that unexpected success. Never wait to see the result of your stroke, drive in another one after it, and another, before he can believe in the first. He's old, sixty-eight, an old man, you can tire him out and wear him down until his hand sags or his foot falters. He knows you mean to do it. He consented. He said: "I am content." To the mastery, you said, but he heard the word you did not say, and he said: "I am content."

Isambard's long arm swung fast and hard at his head. He was late in parrying, but he reached it. The flat of the blade bruised his shoulder as he hurled the blow away from him. The stunned muscles shrieked, and he swallowed his heart and leaped back to draw one breath at least out of range. The spurt of panic burned out instantly into steely coldness. The flurry of blows that drove hard after him were put off as solidly as though a rock covered him, and he would not withdraw another step from his enemy. His eye was as quick as the old man's, his arm as steady, and surely he could outlast him. All he lacked was the long experience, the recession of battlefields shadowy behind him, the terrible wit that could bring new strokes from the very revulsion of the ones freshly parried, the invention that was never lost for a surprise. Watch and be ready, no other way. Remember all you have seen of him, these two years. And if he wavers for an instant, wrest the bout from him then, for it will never happen but once.

Even on that once he did not rely, and it was well, for Isambard did not release him for a moment from the intensity of his concentration. Hand and eye and light-ranging foot, he gave him the best that was in him; and the critical glance that directed the sword laughed and approved the mirrored intensity that glared back at him and clashed steel so imperturbably against steel, waiting with such ferocious patience for the single chance.

Sweat running on them both now, the arm muscles groaning at the weight and the exertion, the arched thighs straining, even the vaults of the braced feet a stretched articulation of pain; but neither of them would show any sign. The jarring shocks of sword against sword shivered through the nerves of shoulder and side, but still eye crossed eye warily, following every insinuating stroke without pause.

The ring of faces had swung back into vision, the murmur had grown feverish, almost fearful. Langholme shifted uneasily, stretched senses tingling, in agony whether to meddle or leave ill alone. At the edge of his consciousness Harry was aware of these things, but he had no attention to spare for them. It was Isambard who felt the disquiet at his back, and for one instant flashed a glance aside to warn them off from touching what they did not understand.

Harry caught the infinitesimal shift of the head, the momentary release from the eyes that fixed him. He was in like a fury, his sword flashing cross-wise, and lunging beneath the startled blade that leaped with recovering skill to beat him off. There was no parry left within Isambard's reach, fast as he was, he could do no more than leap back once and again before the onslaught to get arm-room to stand the boy away from him. And Harry pressed after, fierce on his advantage, driving them both by the weight of his attack into the ring of appalled spectators that broke and gave them place.

And suddenly he was down, Isambard was down! A long pace back, close to the wall now, and the trailing cord of a laced helm rolled under his foot, and he was down, on knee and hip along the beaten earth, the sword half-torn from his hand. He fell with the expert lightness of a cat, he gathered his lean legs under him with a cat's startling speed, but Harry's rush had flung the boy astride him before he could rise, and Harry's point was at his throat.

A moment they hung thus arrested, and the world froze round them into such a stillness and silence that they heard the creeping of the sweat in their eyebrows, and the tightening of their sinews as the boy gripped and braced his blade, and the man took fast hold of the ground and held still for the blow.

Then every held breath had broken in a gusty cry, and Langholme was lunging to come at them, with Nicholas Stury hot on his heels; but there was no need for them, the thing was over. Harry had swung away and walked back on tremulous legs to the extreme of the ground, and was waiting there with his point in the earth for his enemy to rise. A clamour of voices rushed to protest that the vantage was no vantage, that but for the cord my lord would not have fallen. A dozen arms were offered eagerly to help him to rise. As though he needed any help from them! He was on his feet before they could touch him, stamping the earth experimentally and putting off solicitude with contempt and impatience.

Young Thomas Blount, foremost as ever in courting favour, cried in his high, provocative voice: "You'd do better to keep him to hammer and punch, my lord. He even fights like a stone-mason."

Harry heard that, but distantly, and it added nothing considerable to the score he had marked up long ago against Thomas. It was doubtful if Isambard heard it at all. He stood with the recovered sword dangling from one hand, staring across the circle of stamped ground at the boy who waited with head stubbornly lowered.

"It was no vantage," said Langholme, in a voice that shook with the reverberations of an excitement already ebbing into unreality. Give them time, they'd come to think they had dreamed the point steady at their lord's throat, the tightening fingers and the tensed bodies. He'd overrun, and could not halt short of his fallen opponent, that was all.

"I've claimed none," said Harry shortly.

"Then, my lord, if you're content—"

Walter wanted it over: from the first he'd had no liking for it. He alone, perhaps, of all those watchful hangers-on, felt something of the tearing current that moved beneath the quiet surface, dragging those two antagonists, bound by hatred as close as lovers, headlong downstream and out of reach.

"Are you content, Harry?" said Isambard. The voice had no implications; he would not prompt him.

"My lord, neither of us has yet had the mastery."

Fool, fool, he thought, furious with his own quaking body, feeble now with bewilderment and reaction, you can hardly hold the hilt. What use is it to invite him to kill you? But he shut his teeth on the words, and stiffened his legs under him, and would not withdraw. He owed his enemy a death for a death, nobody should say he grudged him his due.

"As you will," said Isambard, and the shadow of a smile flared in his eyes for a moment, as he marked in the level of the stubborn voice the tremor that did not show in the braced legs. "Guard your head!"

Harry did his best. His body obeyed him, but with less conviction than he would have liked, as though it no longer believed in the bitterness of his intent. Three times he fought off the probing blade, late and anxiously, contending with the quivering of his own wrist no less than the hard certainty of his opponent's. Then he got his second wind, and trod the ground more vigorously. It should not be all for nothing. It must not. The old man was surely tiring. He failed to press home, his movements were slowing, he held off from too close an engagement.

Harry drew breath hard, and closed. Isambard gave ground by one measured pace, and the boy followed, encouraged, and putting aside a tentative stroke that felt for his left side, swung suddenly with all his weight. Isambard sprang in beneath the blade, locked hilt under hilt, and wrenched the boy off-balance across his braced thigh. There was no haste about the final execution. He stepped back coolly, swung a measured round blow at the blade as Harry lurched to keep his legs under him, and struck it dispassionately and with no wasted force out of the boy's hand. It clattered three yards away upon the ground, and the blade sang aloud like a broken bow-string.

For the second time a huge, concerted sigh shuddered away after the snapped tension. Content, this time, with the right ending. And young Thomas Blount laughed. High and clear and deliberate, a peal of laughter as nicely calculated as a girl's. It sent the echoes flying, and rang gallingly in Harry's ears as he tramped wearily across to pick up his sword from the ground. He lifted a closed and shuttered face; Thomas should get no satisfaction from him.

Isambard swung on his heel, the sword still in his hand.

"Ah, Thomas! You found this a poor showing?" Voice and movement had the suddenness of a whip-lash, but his face was amiable and smiling. "Then come and show him his errors. Come, give him a lesson in swordsmanship, it would please me to see you matched." He reversed the sword in his hand and held it out by the blade. "Harry'll not refuse to learn from a master."

Between the shoulders of the men-at-arms Harry saw Thomas's face fallen into pale consternation. He essayed a smile that sat badly askew upon his smooth features, and faded blankly when Isambard gave no sign of withdrawing the proffered hilt. All heads had turned; a good many of the men-at-arms were grinning. One should be very careful with laughter; it so easily shifts to the other side of one's face.

"My lord," protested Thomas, mustering what remained of his assurance, "he's in no condition to fight another bout. Look at him! It would be no fair match."

"He'll waive the point. Harry, have you yet the breath for another encounter?"

"Gladly, my lord!" said Harry, his face bright and grim.

"There, my bold heart, you hear that? Come, let me see you school him."

"My lord," said Thomas, backing away from the hilt with a nervous grin fixed on his pale face, "he must needs consent if you order. He can lose no glory by such a match, and I can get none. My lord, you would not ask me to fight a tired and bruised man?"

His eyes were uneasy, but his voice was bold in its indignant innocence. Thomas would always find a way to slide gracefully out of every situation that was not to his liking, and never yet had his master failed to laugh and let him make good his escape. Why should it be different this time?

"Well said, my noble Thomas, my pattern of chivalry. I could not ask you to do so rude an injury to your honour." He stood smiling a little, not kindly, and tossed the sword from hand to hand. "Then we'll see you matched at a more suitable time," he said, the smile twisting suddenly into an oblique and devilish grin. "Tomorrow, when Harry is as fresh as you, and you both have glory to gain or lose."

A moment he looked his most indulged page in the eye to drive home the threat, and then turned and held out the sword imperiously for Walter to take from him. "Remind me, Thomas," he said, and flung away towards the archway of the inner ward. The short bark of his laughter, hard and clear, was blown back to them over his shoulder.

His withdrawal had sent the blood back into Thomas's cheeks in a wave of relief, but that laugh ripened the rising wave into a crimson surge of mortification. The heavy breath that hissed round him as the tension broke resolved itself unmistakably into a quiet titter at his expense, and the broad grins of the men-at-arms bit like acid at his sore dignity.

"Ah, be easy, lad," said Langholme, shouldering the combat swords resignedly, "he won't hold you to it. You keep your mouth shut and keep out of his way tomorrow, and he'll be pleased to forget. He never meant to drive it to the issue."

More galling comfort never was uttered. Thomas bit at lips suddenly quivering with temper and spite, and looked round wildly at his grinning compeers. He had enjoyed a favourite's ascendancy among them, was he to let it slip out of his fingers now without a struggle? He struck out recklessly to reassert himself, before the urgent moment could escape him and leave him discredited for ever.

"And well he did not! He may lower himself to play with labourers and stone-hewers if he pleases, but it's not for him to ask it of others."

His voice was high and hard with rage; it carried to Harry's indifferent ears, and swung him round in a momentary hesitation whether to resent it. Did Thomas Blount matter enough, that a man should do him the honour of quarrelling with him? Sometimes Harry had suspected that not affection but tolerant disdain accounted for Isambard's attitude to Thomas, and the long rein on which he let him run. And what Isambard could shrug off from his consciousness, that Harry could let pass, too. Why should he dissipate on frivolities like Thomas the concentration of hatred that belonged only to his master? He turned on his heel dourly to tramp away.

"Stone-hewers, and rank even at their craft," said Thomas rashly, seeing the brown homespun back turned squarely on him, and misreading the signs. "Stone-butchers, like father like son!"

That brought Harry back, without haste but with head formidably lowered. Thomas did not give back before him. Langholme was there, and a dozen more of the elders, they would not let the affair come to anything.

"You were pleased to mention my father," said Harry civilly. "The exact matter I think I did not hear well. Be good enough to say it over again for me."

There were three yards of space between them, and Langholme already had a shoulder thrust forward warningly, and an eye commanding the master-of-arms to be ready on the other side. Thomas weighed chances, and made his bid.

"I called him a stone-butcher, like his son after him."

He had miscalculated the degree of protection to be expected from the elders. Langholme, fended off by a lunging elbow, reeled several yards across the exercise ground, and Thomas Blount was on his back in the dust with Harry on top of him. They rolled and snarled like fighting dogs, and before Nicholas Stury and a dozen more had got a grip on them and torn them bodily apart, Isambard was back among them like a thunder-cloud, red-eyed and stormy-browed.

"How's this? Will you be at each other's throats as soon as my back is turned? You were not so fain a moment since. Am I to have my wards turned into a schoolboys' brawling-ground? You, Walter, who began this? How did it fall out?"

Langholme told the tale fairly enough, and half a dozen voices joined in, retailing word for word what had passed.

"So that was the way of it," said Isambard grimly. "You must trust me, Thomas, there are men in the world who will not have their sires abused. I know well you have little love for yours."

"My lord, if I said what I thought too openly, is that cause for falling on me by surprise?"

"My lord," said Harry contemptuously, "he was staring me in the eye when I fell upon him. Where's the surprise there?"

"You may save your breath, both of you, you have need of it. This shall be fought out and finished here and now."

"With whatever weapons he pleases," grunted Harry scornfully.

"With what weapons *I* please," said Isambard, the deep fires burning tall in his eyes. "And I please you shall fight it out with none. I'll have no killing, and no mortal damage, but you may teach each other what lessons you can with your own good arms. Three falls, and I'll see fair play." He swept an imperious arm round the circle. "Stand back there, and give them place. And, Walter, set them on."

Against that voice and that face there was no possible appeal. Harry stripped off his cotte gleefully, and went to his place grinning. Thomas crept mute and reluctant to his, and shed his brocade with trembling hands. He was a year older than his opponent, and heavier, well matched with him in height and reach, but no wrestler. It took Harry no more than two minutes to down him heavily and pin him by the shoulders at Isambard's very feet.

With the first fall he forgot his own aches and exertions, with the second he outlived his anger. In the third bout he put Thomas down almost as gently as he would have dumped the youngest of his antagonists on his back at practice.

"For a stone-butcher," said Isambard critically, "that was very prettily done. Well, Thomas, you have what you would have. And I rede you both, let that be an ending."

Thomas picked himself up from the ground slowly, and slowly limped to reclaim his cotte. He was not greatly hurt, even the limp was largely for his own comfort and justification; he kept his eyes lowered from them all as he wiped the dust from his face.

A few of his fellows, some in obstinate allegiance and some in rough compassion, encircled him and made good-natured efforts to pass off his defeat with commonplaces, but he did not give them a word or a look. Only once did he look up, and that was when Isambard passed him without a glance and walked away into the inner ward; then indeed the dishevelled head lifted, the blue eyes flashed one long, half-veiled stare after the erect figure, and again were hooded. But Harry had caught the gleam beneath the large, fair eyelids, bleak and bitter as winter. This was no ending. For Thomas Blount's humiliation and loss of status no one would ever be forgiven, least of all the lord of Parfois.

Isambard came into the tracing-house at sundown, when the light lay level and long across the corner bench by the window, and lit small golden fires on every rounded brown knuckle on Harry's hands as he worked. The stone burned into a gold not so far different from that burnished skin, drawn so supply and closely over the bone, moving so rhythmically and faintly over the smoothly gloved joints. Golden hands and golden stone glowed in a single radiant focus of light, as though they had fused into one life. There was a hawk, with arched wings and stretched throat, prisoned within the stone, half-frantic to burst from its captivity; the patient hands laboured delicately at its liberation. Isambard came to his shoulder, and the boy paid him no heed. Not one light, loving stroke of the mallet on the punch rang a wry note or broke the easy rhythm.

The stone was a fragment of the last ashlars left after the church of Parfois had reached its wonderful and terrible completion, and its builder his strange and awful end. The boy handled it with love and respect, and infinite and uncharacteristic patience, for it had hardened with the years of exposure, and carving it now challenged all his half-tested powers. He smoothed a thumb along the braced pinion, and blew off fine dust that settled again in a thousand glittering points of light.

"Well?" said Isambard at his shoulder. "Were you content with your victory?"

"No, my lord." He exchanged his punch for a finer one, and began to hollow out the stretched feathers of the hawk's wing.

"Faith, you're hard to please. Why not? You did what you would with him."

"The bout favoured me. Thomas is too lofty to think wrestling a fit sport for a gentleman. And I could have beaten him with whatever weapons you might have allowed us."

Isambard laughed, pushing aside the litter of tools to make room for himself on the bench. "I take that to be a truthful word, if not a modest one."

"You should have given us blunted tourney swords. He prides himself on his swordsmanship."

"And you could still have beaten him black and blue? So you could, but he would have suffered all the more to satisfy your vanity. What kind of mercy is that on your enemy?" said Isambard, grinning.

Harry frowned down at his work and stood off for a moment to look at it more critically. He did not lift his eyes as he said abruptly: "You'd best be careful of him."

"Careful of him? Of Thomas?"

"If we had not an enemy in him before," said Harry seriously, "we have one now, you as well as I."

"That gives us at least one thing in common, then, if the only one."

He had taken up one of the fine chisels, and was playing with it absently, testing its edge with a lean brown thumb, but his eyes were steady and measuring upon Harry's face.

"Boy," he said abruptly, "let me understand you. As I read it, you came looking for me here, two years ago, to pay off a score you owed me for your father's death. And no fault of yours if you did not pay it at our first meeting. By God, you did your best. All through these two years you've been waiting and hoping for as good a chance again, now that you have your growth. Have I the right of it? Did I indeed bring Master Harry to his death? Did you truly come looking for me dagger in hand, there in his church? Have I had my pleasure all these months in keeping you at heel here, and tormenting you with glimpses of liberty? Did I play you all manner of tricks to get out of you the secret of his burial place?"

"And tore him out of it," said Harry, the mallet abruptly silent in his hand, "like a scavenging wolf as you are."

A cruel trick indeed Isambard had played on him that time, leading him to believe, when all persuasions and threats failed, that he had blurted out the secret in his sleep, and then setting Thomas on to him, Thomas with his candid, deceitful face and his hypocritical sympathy, to promise him escape and lead him out of Parfois by night. And he in his desperate anxiety had fallen headlong into the trap, and led them straight as a homing bird to the nameless grave under the walls of Strata Marcella. He remembered Isambard's smiling face in the moonlight, his fingers tracing the shape of the carved leaf in the stone, his assuaged voice saying: "Take him back, he's told me what I wanted to know."

"Ah, good! I begin to think you had clean forgotten. I see you have it as fresh in mind as the day it happened—when you swore to kill me for it. Do you remember?"

"I well remember," said the boy grimly, and set his hands again to his work, turning a shoulder on his questioner. Piercingly clear he heard his own voice crying: "There's no name vile enough, my lord, for creatures like you who vent their spite even on the dead."

"And have not changed your mind?" The tapping of the mallet spaced out the silence evenly. "Then why did you not kill me when you had the chance, like a sensible man?"

The rhythm lurched, faltered, was taken up again stubbornly.

"Do you think God is going to throw me on my knees at your feet every day? It was ungrateful to toss his gift back in his teeth. Why am I still alive? Tell me!"

"I could not take advantage of an old man," said Harry viciously.

"It will do you no good with me to try to offend. In the pursuit of knowledge I do not take offence easily. I *am* old. Say it over a hundred times to yourself, and still it will not make you my master with a sword, and you know it. Not yet! Why am I still here to plague you? I will know."

"It was mere chance that you fell," said Harry, goaded. "I would not have your life on those terms."

Isambard threw back his head in a short, harsh bark of laughter. "There's a true Talvace word, at least. That I believe. In his time he would not take favours from man nor God, and you're as like him in that as one oak is to another. And yet," he said, sharp as a lance and abruptly grave again, "that's not the whole truth, neither. What, would you hold your hand on a battlefield, because your enemy's girth broke?"

"We were not on a battlefield," said Harry, taking his hands from the stone with reluctance, for the light had dulled into dusk, and the gold was faded to dun. He put down his tools gently, as though too sharp a sound might have set the tranquil surface of the everyday world quaking, and let the demons of disruption through at him. Behind him the silence gathered intense and still.

"We were not?" said Isambard, low-voiced through the hush. "Where else have you and I been since the day we met, Harry? When you looked me in the eye and invited me to something more than play do you think I did not know it was a challenge to the death? God knows you had waited for it long enough. Why did you refuse it when it fell ripe into your hand?"

The fading of the day had veiled his face, he was a gaunt shadow against the clear pallor of the window. By the utter stillness of his body, by the level and muted voice. Harry knew that he had reached the thing he had come here to say.

"You need not hold your hand," he said deliberately, "from any fear of consequences. I have already given orders, and bound de Guichet and Walter by oath to see them respected, that if you should kill me in fair fight there shall be no revenges. You will be held to have won your liberty fairly."

Harry rolled down his sleeves in dogged composure, and fell to putting his tools away. "You should have told me that before," he said grimly.

"I'll give you another chance tomorrow."

The moment was past, the voice already lifting to astringent mockery; in a minute more he would be flinging words again in the old fashion, every one with a sting like a whip.

"Do you not want your freedom? With the princess of Aberffraw and David your prince-brother already bedded at the abbot's town house in Shrewsbury? Not more than two hours' ride away, Harry, and only this old body between you and their arms."

He had learned to keep his hands steady and his face mute, under whatsoever goadings; there were no sparks to be struck from him now by these means, even though his heart ached in him to think of the Princess Joan and David so close, and he helpless to go to them, or even send them a word of his love and loyalty. Did he not want his freedom! By day he could tire out his body and cloak up his mind well enough, but at night in his bed the anguish of his longing to be at liberty gripped him by the vitals and wrung him until he clenched his teeth in his forearm to solace himself with a more bearable pain.

He was seventeen, and had been mewed up here nearly two years; and the uneasy truce between England and Wales, the year's truce that bound Llewelyn's hands from reaching out to loose his foster-son, still held intact, for all the long memoranda of accusations filed by either side, and all the listed infringements, and bade fair to be extended for another year when the first was out. The envoys of King Henry and Prince Llewelyn were off-loading their pack-horses in their Shrewsbury lodgings at this very moment, and scanning their briefs ready for the meeting in Shrewsbury castle three days hence. Their business this time was merely to agree upon arrangements for the sitting of a papal court later in the year, to adjudicate upon the many allegations of border infringements. But agree they would, and come to the winter court bent on agreement, too, for King Henry had things on his mind that made it necessary to him that Wales should remain pacified, and the Prince of Aberffraw had his son's inheritance to secure in full, and must not put it in danger by a premature act of war. Yes, the truce would continue, and with it his captivity. Isambard saw to it that he was well-informed; he knew how little to expect from man.

But God, it seemed, had presented him Isambard's throat bared to his point, and he had refused the gift. And why? Did he even know? For fear of being hanged for it? He strained back to recapture the truth of that moment, but it did not seem to him that anything would have been changed, even if he had known what Isambard had just told him. And Isambard, whose every word and deed had a purpose behind it, was deploying before him still dearer enticements than merely his freedom. Only this old body between you and their arms! Harry looked for the oblique intent. He had been tempted to break faith; was he now being tempted to do murder?

"You may carry them my respectful duty and service," he said steadily, "when you go to the king's court tomorrow. I could not have a more punctilious messenger."

"For the price of a word you might carry your own message," said Isambard softly. "Give me your parole to return with me afterwards, and you shall go to Shrewsbury in my train."

"No, my lord. I give you no more paroles, now or ever. When the time and the means serve me to escape you, I shall go, and there'll be no word of mine tying my feet then."

"Harry, Harry, when will you learn to bend with the wind? How many times already have you essayed to leave me?"

"As I make the count, five. But there will be other such essays yet to come."

"And five times been brought back before ever you reached the rock outside the walls. And main glad you were, once at least, to be hoisted back to solid ground with all your bones unbroken. And how long is it now since you found foot-room even to begin on such another enterprise? With two archers at your heels at every step? Give up, Harry, there's no escape from Parfois for you. Take the chance to ride out at the gate when it's offered you."

"No," said Harry, rolling up the much-used parchments that carried his drawings. He had learned not to waste energy in shouting; the refusal was as absolute as death, but also as still.

Isambard sighed elaborately. "As you please. I cannot give if you will not take. But remember what I have told you. Next time, if you can bring me to a next time after the fright you've given me, strike home. No one in Parfois will slit your throat for slitting mine. There may well be some," he said, sliding from the bench and beating the stone-dust from his crimson cotte with a vigorous hand, "who would thank you for it."

He was turning towards the door when they both heard, hollow and deep, the thudding of hoofs on the timbers of the bridge, coming fast. The deep cleft in the sandstone, that severed the castle of Parfois on its cliff from the grassy headland where the great church stood, took the sound and sent it rolling in cavernous echoes between the walls of rock. As soon as the riders reached the cobbles under the archway of the gatehouse, the hoofbeats ceased to be audible; only the dying reverberations, like distant thunder, quaked away into stillness slowly and left a quivering on the air.

Isambard had halted, ears pricked. Riders at night and in haste were few at Parfois, but at such a time, when the court was trundling its ponderous way into Shrewsbury, this might mean no more than a visit from one or another of the nobility of the march, on his way to join the king. Harry had reared his head no less intently. From anything unwonted he could still hope.

Blown horses stamping in the outer ward, the creak of stirrup-leathers, boots tramping the cobbles, words passing urgent and low. Isambard's wild-beast senses caught the known voice first.

"Walter!" he said, head up, like a stag nosing aliens on the air. But it could not be. Why should Langholme ride back all this way, when he had but set out for Shrewsbury in the early afternoon, to make ready the town house in the Wyle for his lord's coming, and see his bed-linen aired and his plate burnished? And why, if for some unknown errand come he must, should he come riding hard, and with at least one stranger in his train? There was a voice Isambard did not recognize for a man of his own: hoarse and low, choked with the dust of riding and creaky with long fatigue.

He was at the door in three long strides, and came breast to breast with them on the threshold. Langholme knew where to look for his master at this hour.

"My lord," he said, gusty with haste, "there's news you should hear at once. I left all in train in Shrewsbury, and made bold to bring the messenger back with me." The man was at his elbow, grey in the face with weariness, hollow eyes fevered. Isambard looked upon him and knew him: a minor knight of the earl of Kent's following, and trustworthy. He had run errands more than once between de Burgh's three castles in Gwent and this outpost above the Severn on the borders of Wales. But then he had worn the red and green mascles of the justiciar's livery, and now he came cloaked and anonymous.

Isambard's deep eyes flamed redly. He caught the man by the arm and drew him within.

"Here, in here! And, Harry, do you close the door."

"Shall I go, my lord?" said Harry, springing to obey.

"No, stay. No need to cry the alarm too soon. Now speak out, man, quickly. Yes, before the boy you may, he's in my worst secrets already. What brings you north in such haste? And in this case?" The absent device cried aloud.

"My lord, the earl of Kent—no man who can shed his livery is wearing it today. Safer so! My Lord, he's down—he's out of grace and out of office. Six days ago, before the whole council, the king turned on him and accused him of monstrous acts, and put him from his side and from all authority. He's impeached for his very life. And Stephen Segrave who helped to bring him down is justiciar of England in his room."

So it was come. Hubert de Burgh, the great earl, the king's master, was fallen, down and out of office, and the ground shaky under many another foot. His Poitevin rivals had their day and their way. Peter des Roches, bishop of Winchester, no question, had been the prop at Henry's elbow that gave him the courage to turn on his best servant. Let de Burgh be what else he would—not even this cataclysm could make of him saint or martyr—yet he had certainly been the ablest, the most devoted, the most honest administrator in the land of England, and the one who best grasped what England was, and what she could be. In the past Isambard had forgiven him much for the sake of that quality in him, the vision of England that passed beyond the bounds of a feudal honour, and looked towards a nation, an indisseverable unity fenced within an impregnable sea.

And did not this flagged floor underfoot quiver a little upon the bedrock of Parfois?

"I came to warn you, my lord," said the messenger, coughing dust out of his lungs. "Look to yourself, for any who have held with him in the past may be in danger now. Look well to yourself!"

"Ay, so I will," said Isambard, and the oblique smile came and went upon his mouth like a sudden wry lightning. He stood for a moment with head reared and black brows drawn together, staring ruefully back upon a heyday that was gone, comet-like, into perpetual eclipse. "Sit down here, man, and tell me. I must hear all. And, Harry, do you go and fetch wine for him."

"Am I to bring it myself?" asked Harry doubtfully.

"Fool, do you think I want some ninny like Thomas? And make haste."

Why should he, on that brusque word, take to his heels and run to do Isambard's errand? He crossed the outer ward full gallop, his heart in a turmoil of excitement and confusion, caught up against his will into the troubled affairs of this England which his mind and upbringing insisted was no country of his, but to which his blood leaned irresistibly in an unwilling alliance. And because he was curious he ran back again with the wine hardly less precipitately, greedy even for the few words he had missed.

The three heads turned sharply as he entered the tracing-house, and turned back again, satisfied, at sight of him. Why should that give him so unmistakable a tremor of pleasure? They were none of his people, not one of them; why should he take pride in being trusted by his enemies? None the less, he poured and offered the wine with a conscious delight in his own quiet, adroit movements, that never broke the thread of the narration.

"—honour for honour, these last weeks, for every new grant to des Rivaulx the like to my master. And then they were all together, early last month, at my lord's manor of Burgh in Norfolk, and there at Bromholm priory the king pledged himself to maintain all his grants and charters to them all, my master no less than the Poitevins. By the most solemn oaths he bound himself, and his heirs after him, and took God for his surety."

"So he would," said Isambard grimly, "when most he purposes to undo both the oath and the man to whom he binds himself."

"But to all—he bound himself to all. Why should the earl have doubted him? We thought the danger was past, and the contention between them resolved. And even if he had foreseen this then, how could he have warded it off? What could he have done but run, and empty-handed at that? And the Lady Margaret, and his daughter? Would he ever have got them out of the king's hands? But hear what followed! Come the end of July there was to have been a great round table held, and London would have been full. But what does the king do but issue a letter prohibiting it, and ordering all those who purposed to attend it to make ready instead to escort him to Shrewsbury here for this meeting with the Welsh. All's been done in good haste, the safe-conducts issued for the Welsh princess and her train, all to empty London and turn men's eyes away from what else he intended, at least until it was done."

"And there was no want of a bishop ready to his hand, to preach against the sinfulness of tournaments, and prop up his decree," said Isambard, tramping the floor with long, light paces, bright and fierce in the gathering dark. "This came from Winchester's brain, not from the king's."

"True, my lord, he did speak against the round table, and before the king acted."

"Well, and having set his stage? Six days ago, you say, in council—Who first opened against the justiciar? Des Roches, or Rivaulx?"

"I was not there, my lord, but Gilbert Basset was, and I had it from him. The bishop of Winchester was at the king's elbow throughout, but the storm arose out of a seemingly clear sky, and it was the king himself who brewed it. He turned on my lord the earl in a burst of rage, like a frantic man, and God knows as though he verily believed what he said—"

"He does believe," said Isambard, wrenched into stillness in the middle of his furious walking by a violent spurt of laughter. "It's his secret. He can produce such a sacred rage at will, and believe in it as in the gospel. I've seen him do it to suit his purpose, over no more than the getting of a jewel he fancied."

"—and accused him of I know not what crimes and enormities, and called on any who willed to confirm, or had any complaints to urge against my lord, to speak out fearlessly. And speak they did, not des Roches and Rivaulx only, but many another. Why not? They had the signal, they knew how to please the king and get a foot on the ladder at the same time—over the earl's trampled face. He was the mounting-block for many an ambitious office-seeker that day, I tell you. And then the king declared him solemnly deprived of all his offices, and named Segrave justiciar in his stead."

"But in God's name, man, did he not speak out in his own defence?"

"The king would not hear him. Speak he did, swearing he was as true a man to his lord as any ever lived, and had done nothing to affront his duty or his conscience. But they shouted him down. And they say the king was loudest in the shouting."

"The divine outburst had him well into his stride then, and out of reach of fear. It must have cost des Roches a deal of cunning and persuasion to launch him, but once his sails were well filled he'd drive. Have I not seen it? What then? He has not dared clap him in hold? Not the Tower? Even in his holy exultation he would not dare!"

"No, my lord, he's yet at liberty, but for how long only God knows. King Henry ordered him from his presence and bade him hold himself at his disposal to answer the charges. But even so they could not let him rest. Within two days they were after him to demand an accounting of all treasury receipts and all his official holdings, back to the late king's time. The bear-pit they made of England then, and to demand an exact accounting!"

"He had a charter of quittance from King John, exempting him from any such accounting. That I know."

"He pleaded it, but my lord bishop of Winchester nudged the king's elbow again and prompted him that King John's death rendered his charter null and void. And the upshot of it is they've formulated a list of charges against him, and summoned him to appear before the council at Lambeth on the fourteenth of September coming, to answer them. And having so contrived his ruin, the king took up the court by the roots and dragged it with him here to Shrewsbury, out of the way of the Poitevins until they close the trap on him past escaping. What use to defend himself, when his judges are his accusers?"

"And where is he now? Is he free to move?"

"No, my lord, he's watched day and night, he can't stir abroad. But they let him retire to Merton priory by Wimbledon to prepare his answer, and while he's there he's safe at least from violence. The lady's at Bury St. Edmunds, and no one's troubled her there yet, thank God. It's my hope they'll scruple to touch the sister of the king of Scots."

"So that's how it stands! And des Rivaulx holds custody of the household accounts, with boundless authority, and the treasury filled with his friends. I tell you, this is to be a country run from the wardrobe unless we stir ourselves. I counted over the number of his county sheriffdoms lately, and made the tale twenty-one. We shall see the great offices of state withering away to fatten the privy chamber, and baronage and commons left without voices or rights. One pillar of the house is down, it seems, and no man to lift a hand to prop it. What, did no one speak for him? Was there not *one* to give them the lie?"

"Not one. Chester was not there, or he might have opened his great throat. He hates the earl, but with an honest hate. And he hates conspiracy and injustice even more. But he's old, and sick, they say. He was not there."

"And the charges?" said Isambard, halting abruptly before the drained messenger.

Harry stood watching with held breath, appalled by the calm, even the cheerfulness, of the leaning face; only devils, surely, can devour trouble and distress and smile over them thus serenely. The shock of the news, the reeling shock of seeing his England jarred shivering off her course, these were already accepted and mastered. Whatever he meant to do now to cover his own traces he would do with resolution and precision, nothing in agitation, nothing without thought. It had seemed to Harry sometimes that the lord of Parfois truly loved his England, yet here he assembled his powers to his own defence, and left her lying adrift to dangerous currents without a scruple.

"Let me know the charges, and then I have done, then I can deal. All the charges."

De Burgh's knight—no one had named him, perhaps no one remembered his name—propped his sagging eyelids and held his forehead, dredging out the last details.

"All his household were watched. I got away by night and joined myself to a company of the advance party for Shrewsbury, where I had friends to give me cover, and so I've ridden the news to three or four others who may be attainted like you, having been of his way of thinking. The charges—but there'll be more by now, for they're beating them out of the bushes like conies—they accuse him of writing to the duke of Austria, when the king was of a mind to marry his daughter, and putting him off the match so that the suit failed."

"God's life!" said Isambard, laughing through his teeth. "They must think we have all short memories. That suit foundered of its own weight, and the king was never better than lukewarm in it at that."

"And of hampering the king in his campaign for the recovery of Normandy."

"Ah, that's another matter. So we did, and well for him we did, or he'd have left his kingdom of England there, too. Go on!"

"Of seducing the Lady Margaret, when she was in his wardship in King John's day, and seeking to make his heirs kings of Scotland by marrying her."

"Faith, it's Alexander should complain of that, not Henry. Even if it were true! This will never hit, and they know it."

"But it adds one to the list, and every straw counts. Then there's a tale that he stole from the treasury a stone, one that makes its wearer invincible and puts him out of reach of wounds, and sent it privily to the prince of Aberffraw."

"Ah, that's ingenious—some soured soldier thought of that. A master-stroke to find an apology for Llewelyn's prowess, as well as an arrow to loose at Hubert."

"There are those who believe it, my lord. As they'll believe also the next count, that my lord of Kent sent letters to Prince Llewelyn condoning the execution of William de Breos, after he was taken with the Princess Joan."

At mention of that discovery, long past and half-healed in his memory but still quick in anguish at the first touch, Harry's flesh shrank and burned. It came so unexpectedly, he dreaded that Isambard might have seen him flinch. But the musing voice said only: "That he owned the prince's right I doubt not. I know none who denied it. But that he wrote such letters is a wild shot. Well, is that all?"

"Yet one more, my lord, but the most dangerous and the hardest to disprove. And it was the bishop of Winchester first laid it. That the earl has feathered his own nest these many years by dealing dishonestly with the treasury."

"Which of them that ever held office has not?" said Isambard with a curl of his lip. "And I won't deny the possibility even where Hubert's concerned. There's no blinking his inordinate appetite for castles. But on balance I take it to be likely he stole less than most, and gave better value for it. And that at least," he added reasonably, "can't be levelled at me. I've never handled treasury funds, I've held no office that could be plundered. Well, so we have it. And not one man among them to say a word in his defence!"

"My lord, the thing was sprung so suddenly, and most went with the tide. And then, there were many quick to pay off old grudges, never thinking what worse grievances they might come to carry against the Poitevins. It's my hope that some will take thought later, with cooler heads, and in time their doubts will speak out."

"I pray you may be right. I owe you thanks for bringing me word, friend. I might have ridden down into Shrewsbury tomorrow with no thought for the game before me, and been taken on the hip." He turned to Langholme, who waited with an anxious face, eyes straining upon his lord's darkened countenance. "See him well lodged and cared for, Walter. Go or stay, friend, at your desire, and choose what you need from my stable. I am in your debt. And, Walter, I have changed thoughts about my ride to Shrewsbury."

"You will not go, my lord?" said Langholme almost eagerly.

"But I will go, Walter, and with double the retinue I proposed, and thrice the splendour. But first house our guest, he has need of sleep. Then come to me, and let's see what provision is needful."

They departed, and a great quietness fell upon the two who were left alone in the tracing-house. Suddenly they saw how dark it had grown while their minds were on other things. Night folded the shapes of bench and tracing-tables and chests, and pale, mellow stone.

"My lord," said Harry, hollow and small with wariness and wonder, "what will you do?"

"Do, Harry? I will go down, attended like a prince, and myself attend on my king, as is my duty. And I will have dutiful speech with him," said the low, light voice out of the gathering dark, "whether he will or no, Harry, whether he will or no."

King Henry held audience before supper in the great guest chamber of Shrewsbury abbey, in a gilded chair set up on a dais draped with gold and red brocades and velvets, and against a backcloth of tapestries unrolled not two hours earlier from the pack-saddles of his unwieldy train. He was in high spirits, and even for him inordinately fine, with jewels in his ears and on his long, fastidious fingers. The nobility of the march bruised their loyal lips on his gold-set rubies, and trod delicately about the skirts of his glittering gown. The air still quivered faintly with the reverberations of a resounding fall; they breathed the dust from it, and held their breath. He felt the tension of awe that held them poised against him, and a sweet excitement filled him. It was done, it was truth, and no longer an aching wish, an unsatisfied appetite; they were the proof of it. He had made the great, the effortful beginning; the second step and the third would be easy, and who would dare try to halt him now?

He was twenty-five years old, and out of tutelage. The release of power ran in his blood like wine, and he felt a gust of triumphant hatred against the old men, with their experience and their assurance and their iron determination to cramp and fetter him from all action of his own. Old men, spent, cautious, slow to venture but absolute to instruct and hector him, and hem him about with prohibitions and warnings. He thought of the shedding of his shackles, and his heart leaped with angry joy, remembering the broken, bleak, foolish astonishment in the justiciar's ageing eyes. He could not believe that his world was shattered, that his fledgeling had taken flight, that his day was over. A long day, a golden day, gone down at last in a clap of thunder.

Thanks be to God, said the king devoutly in his heart, savouring the joy of his freedom, and to my sweet saint who stood by me and put the words of justice into my mouth. O blessed Saint Edward, sweet Confessor, this year on your day there shall be more new knights than ever before, and the clerks in my chapel shall chant the *"Christus vincit."* Only be with me still, and show me how to confound my enemies. Breathe in the faces of those who set themselves up against me, like the fiery wind of God, and let them be blown out of my path even as the earl of Kent, to their destruction. To their ruin!

Now my house shall be set in order, he thought, exulting, and I shall be the master in it. Not de Burgh with his stifling cage of law and custom and civil right, not these old men walled up in their feudal honours, not my turbulent barons of the march, but I the head and my household officers the instrument, and a sound order under us. O sweet Saint Edward, be with me and I shall show them the truth of kingship.

He closed his eyes momentarily upon the ecstasy of his heart's prayer, shutting out the gaudily-coloured throng that filled his audience chamber. He opened them again, smiling with the pleasure of his thoughts, upon a face like a death's-head, beautiful and dreadful, that advanced towards him between the ranks of his clerks and courtiers, and nightmare-like smiled upon him.

He called soundlessly upon his unfailing patron, and the dazzle of light that swam towards him and bore the terrible reminder ever closer dimmed at the saint's touch, and resolved itself into a surcoat stiff and glittering with gold thread, over a golden-brown cotte, covering a veritable human body and no shape of dreams. A lean body and tall, and erect as a larch, bearing aloft that formidable head that smiled faintly and grimly as it drew near and leaned over his hand. He had extended it to ward off a terror, but the gesture was easily turned to regal account as he surrendered his long, jewelled fingers for the kiss of the lord of Parfois.

An old man. Always old men; there was no easy escape from them, they pressed in on him wherever he turned. Ralf Isambard

of Mormesnil, Erington, Fleace and Parfois, and some fifty other
lordships and manors scattered over England. What did he want
with this resplendent attire, what right had he to that arrogant and
wonderful walk of his, with death looking out of his head through
the two deep, restless, insatiable eyes, that burned red in the heart
of their blackness? The great forehead, once as sheer as a cliff,
showed now the polished ivory of the skull within, the cheek-bones
stood gaunt from the fleshless face, and the iron jaw, clean-shaven
in the old Norman manner still, thrust pale against the drawn brown
skin. A death's-head. But who would have thought that the stark
lines of bones could be so beautiful?

"You are welcome to our court, my lord," said the king; but his
fingers shrank from the touch of the dry lips. They barely brushed
his rings and were away, as though they sensed his revulsion, and
willed indifferently to indulge him. He remembered with a kind of
rage that this was yet another of the elders from whom he had taken
advice too tamely all these years. On all matters appertaining to the
Welsh marches Isambard's word had run like a royal writ. Had he
not urged the removal of the de Breos wardship from Richard of
Cornwall, only last year, and its handing over to de Burgh? Henry
stiffened, remembering. He was ready to find treason in all old men.
All, perhaps, but the bishop of Winchester, who had helped him to
cut himself free from their leading strings at last.

"I am at your Grace's bidding and service at all times," said
Isambard, and straightened up from the sensitive, irresolute hand
to look into the pale, comely face, a little melancholy in repose, a
little petulant in speech. The short brown beard carefully curled as
always, the rich hair meticulously dressed and perfumed. He was of
no more than medium height, and slender, but give him his due, he
could pass for a king.

A pity, though, that his one drooping eyelid should give a look
of worldly cunning to a countenance and a creature so transparent.
An unchancy flibbertigibbet of a young man, always blowing hot or
ice-cold, with no happy mean, for ever with his head laid in your
bosom or his dagger in your back; and yet there was still a kind of
innocence that clung about him, like an outworn garment from his
childhood, not always very becoming to the grown man, but treacher-

ously disarming to those who might otherwise have been tempted to treat him like a man, and demand a man's measure from him.

"I trust your Grace had pleasant riding by the way," said Isambard amiably. His eyes, in ambush like momentarily peaceable wolves in their deep caverns, passed at leisure over the faces of the assembled court, and lingered longest on those nearest the king. "And sweet company," he said, and his voice was honey.

They must have left des Rivaulx in London, no doubt to keep close watch on the game in progress and stop every bolthole the quarry might try. And Winchester was too subtle to appear always at the king's elbow. But Brian de Lisle was there in his stead, to give weight and reverence as an old adherent of King John among the new, young, ambitious faces. De Craucombe, Henry's steward of the household, hovered close to the king's chair, Passelewe hung discreetly behind it, the royal clerk *par excellence*, the new man of affairs, propertyless as yet but already hungry, birthless but already quietly treading out about him the competence that should keep his descendants in coat-armour.

The old baronies were being silently dismembered to make new for such men as these. The great council of the land, if they did not stand to and defend its rights, would be left to moulder harmlessly, high and dry of the life-stream of government, while the diverted flood turned the mills of this little clique in the king's wardrobe, and every source of the king's revenue converged into their hands. Already des Rivaulx had the exchequer, as well as the purse of the household, and he who held the purse held the power. And the thing had been done so well, never a move against de Burgh until all was ready and the king primed and brought to the pitch of ecstasy necessary for action.

There were honest men there, too, in plenty, Isambard's peers and contemporaries. He turned to salute three or four of them, turned again to look round the room with a long, raking stare, and back to the king.

"But where is the earl of Kent?" he said, in a voice pitched to carry without over-emphasis to the farthest corner of the great room. "I did not see his livery in the courtyard."

The silence fell like a stone, crushing and cold. Heads turned almost stealthily in the hush. The bright assembly held its breath.

King Henry's face had paled with apprehension and shock, and the timid beginning of a defensive rage. He gripped the arms of his chair nervously, looked aside quickly at de Lisle for prompting, and as furiously wrenched his gaze back to Isambard's face, aware of the desperate need he had to lean for once on no one but himself.

"I cannot believe, my lord," he said, "that you are ignorant of what has passed concerning the earl of Kent."

"Why, certain rumours have come to my ears, but I paid them no heed. Unless I hear it from your Grace's own lips that you have so used your best and most faithful servant, I should be loath to believe it. It would not be the first time rumour has slandered my king. Shall I be quick to think your Grace unjust and ungrateful? And so ready a gull for the spites of place-seekers who grudge the best his eminence?"

After the white of consternation the red of mortification surged in the king's too eloquent face. He felt the hue of shame, and willed it with all his strength to become the hot red of anger, for shame he could not afford and must not acknowledge.

"I have in good earnest been gulled by place-seekers," he said, his voice thin and high, "and for all too long a time. But that is over, and I am awake to my error. The earl of Kent suffers no wrong from us. He has his due and no more. His due, did I say? He has a measure of mercy more than his due; he has his freedom yet, and a grant of time to answer his accusers."

"And is it your Grace who tells me so? Then am I to accept that what else was told me is true? The justiciar is put from his office? And charged with I know not what treasons?"

"He is, my lord, and justly. And justly!"

"And stripped of the honours your Grace lately heaped upon him? Those royal castles and manors you delighted to bestow, all snatched back from him? Is that true, too? And the office pledged him lifelong, by oath, so short a time ago?"

He saw the king's face blanch at that, and wondered for a moment if superstitious dread could get any foothold in that rich soil of self-persuasion; and for a moment he abated the hardness of his tone to give the seed time to grow.

"Your Grace, I stand as true a man to you as any in this land, against you I will no offence. But for your soul's sake, take care you yourself do not offend. You are being betrayed into a wrong which time to come will hold against you. Think better of it now, and take back what has been done, while there is still time."

He had been too generous, it seemed, to what was after all but the beginning of the holy rage. The burning pallor, white as pure flame, seared the colour even from the king's eyes and left them staring grey as glass. Better so, thought Isambard, warming into a strong, perverse content. I am too old to change now, I could not stomach this without the knife-edge and the drop below.

"My lord, do you defend him?" The king breathed thickly. "A felon who has robbed our treasury to provide himself, and that for many years? One who stood in our way when we willed to take back our province of Normandy? One who has been rather in the French king's service than in mine? The earl of Kent shall answer for all. Think better of it? Well I may think better of the clemency I have showed him, and consider to take back from him full payment where I might have pardoned him the half. He has done me greater wrong than plundering my revenues. He has plundered my reputation and my spirit, gaining ascendancy over me by sorcery. I have drunk with him, trusted him—Do you doubt me? You shall see the charge brought home, you shall see it proven on him."

So that was to be the excuse and the vindication of his long tolerance. Since someone must carry the burden of the king's changefulness and weakness, as well lay it all on one pair of shoulders. Sorcery! That blunt, practical, self-made man, that collector of castles, that tireless, devoted, grasping, generous administrator! And was there still more to come? It seemed they had indeed been busy beating the bushes for charges to lay against him.

"He has killed privily, with poison. Do you defend that? Old William of Salisbury he made away with thus, and Pembroke, too—and our good archbishop—"

What, even Grant in Italy? These were wilder and wilder flights, and Henry was whipping himself deliberately into a frenzy that might well give birth to still more fantastic images. Isambard stood before him and watched without passion how the young body jerked and writhed, as though tethered by the clinging hands to the arms of the chair. His patron, he thought, got his visions in quietness, as

simply as a child. This one sends his demon out to drag them down
to him unwilling.

"—besides the horrible impiety committed against Holy Church
in the person of those Italian priests it pleased us to advance to
livings here in our country. For it was he, and that's been shown,
who suborned this William Wither, this Yorkshire blasphemer, to
his acts of violence. And he who dealt so rigorously and cruelly after
those troubles in our city of London, and killed wantonly when he
might have shown mercy—"

"At the peril of your realm he might," said Isambard dryly, "but
in my view you have need to be glad, your Grace, that he had the
hardihood to deal as he dealt. And all that can possibly be urged
against him on that score your Grace has known since the event; it
is late to turn it against him now."

"It is never too late to do justice. The arm of law should be long
enough to reach through time, and so it shall prove. I will have the
full penalties loosed upon him. And there are others, I say there are
others, my lord, who will do well to consider their steps and put a
guard on their tongues."

The gentlemen of the retinue had drawn in a little about them,
stepping delicately, watching the king's face as the mirror of their
own conduct. Isambard looked round them calmly and without
haste, and saw in their closed visages the measure of the reserve de
Burgh had failed to estimate with any accuracy. Dislike would not
have shut their mouths so firmly from saying one word in his
defence. What sealed off their compassion from him was his alien
nature. He was not of them, and never had been. Their lands had
come to them by right, and been worn as easily as their clothes.
Their birth was such that they had no need to assert it. The earl of
Kent had come landless and ambitious, climbing into their hitherto
unviolated stronghold, anxious, assertive, jealous of ceremony, himself the first of the new men, and the loneliest. In their midst and
richer in establishment than they, he had never been accepted. They
neither envied nor acknowledged him; nor would they reach a hand
to him now that he was down. He was nothing to them. And to me?
thought Isambard, marvelling a little at being thus confronted with
his own impregnable fortress of birth and blood. In the name of
God, what is he to me?

"I am grateful, your Grace, for that word of warning, for so I read it. Nevertheless, will you hear me a word more? I have somewhat to say for the earl of Kent, before you come to judgement."

He waited for no permission; better to take what might otherwise be denied, and he was speaking now not for the king only. Before the half of it was said Henry was out of his chair, his face congested with so violent a flush of blood that Isambard spared one detached and measuring glance for the hilt of the royal dress-sword, and the elegant hand working in fury so close to it. There was no Ranulf of Chester here now to drag him from Henry's point at need, as once he had dragged his enemy de Burgh. That outburst of spleen at the unreadiness of the fleet Henry had meant to use to invade Normandy—the dearest ambition of his dreams—showed now as a prophetic glimpse of a deep and formidable hatred, not the childish tantrum they had thought it.

Who knows, thought Isambard, but I may die a royal death yet? And he swept aside the gilded folds of his surcoat with a disdainful hand, to show that he had not so much as an ornamental dagger in his belt.

"—and I charge your Grace, take thought how this will look to those who watch you closely from Europe, and what they will say of you where kings meet together. Do you think you can make them believe that the earl of Kent was ever less than loyal to you, them who have known his works as well as you, and understood them better? I tell you, he has held you firm in your place when none other could, and lent you his heart's blood many a time. If he has maintained himself, God witness he has also maintained you, and set you up ever more firmly in your kingdom, and you have good need to thank him and remember him in your prayers. He is a man, and faulty. But I think you, of all men, have no right to complain of him, for he has not spared himself in your service. And look you how this will be read. You lay yourself open to the charge that the king of England is without gratitude or humanity, if this is how he uses his friends. Unless," said Isambard, loud and grim over the rising scream he saw contorting the king's throat, "they say of you more charitably that you have not the wit to know who your friends are."

The hand on the sword-hilt was twisting and trembling. A velvet-

shod foot stamped impotently at the hollow dais, and the voice that
came out of the congested throat was husky and laboured with fury.

"My lord," whispered the king, gulping air, "I told you beware
lest you stir my memory too well. You, too, I remember—you,
too—in Normandy when I was hedged about from every venture
that might have won me back a lost kingdom. Kept fretting in
camp, and my men wasting their hearts and their harness in play—
inglorious, inglorious! Well I remember! You, you were hand in
glove with him then. You were his man always. Take heed that you
do not pay a like price for it."

"Under you," said Isambard, blunt and clear, "I have been nobody's man but my own since your father died. I have done as I
judged right, for you and for England, and if it marched often with
the judgement of the earl of Kent, do you marvel that I speak up
for his sound services now? Well for you that we made shift in
Normandy to keep you from any act that would have brought the
king of France into the field, or you would have left your kingdom
of England there, and likely your life with it. You would have your
folly, but at least we saw to it that it cost you no more than it need.
Be grateful!"

The scream came then, a blazing outcry almost void of words.
The king lunged forward with a contorted face, and Passelewe, leaning from behind his chair, caught him insinuatingly by the arm and
whispered in his ear. A flurry of voices murmured in agitation, a
few of the elders closed in about the throne, but the king waved
them furiously away. Isambard stood impassive, watching him with
the crooked smile dragging his long lips out of line.

"My lord Isambard—"

He trembled still, but he had his voice in control; those frenzies
of his knew always how far to go, and where to stop.

"My lord Isambard, you charge yourself with treason and think
no shame. And if I use towards you a mercy I could not show
towards the earl of Kent, take it thankfully and make no further
presumption upon my grace, for I shall not so withhold my justice
a second time. I will not have suspect traitors about me." His voice
was rising again, shrill as a woman's with injury. "You are dismissed, my lord. Go back to your castle of Parfois, and there remain
until I call you back to my presence. When I return to Shrewsbury

for the papal court I may send for you to attend on me. Till then, think in your retirement what words you have used to me, and marvel that you are left at liberty. Go!" he said, translated and exalted in his rage like a man invulnerable within his strongest castle. "Get out of my sight! Get to your hermitage!"

"At your pleasure, your Grace, to stay or go!"

Isambard swept him a deep bow, and withdrew from him half the length of the hall without turning his face away. They saw the oblique smile curl into something between disdain and honest amusement. The dark cheeks did not flush; the highlights over the jutting bones, the stark shadows beneath, were as fixed as stone. The skirts of his resplendent surcoat whirled about him in a coruscation of gold embroidery as he turned deliberately and walked to the door, between the silent ranks that parted to let him through. He did not look back; and his knights, who had waited upon him in watchful quietness all this time, fell in at his back and followed him from the king's presence. In the courtyard their grooms sprang to attend them, and the young squires held their stirrups and mounted after them, a princely company, orderly and proud and splendidly appointed. It was like the departure of an army.

The king heard them go, and shook with an anguish of detestation. How dared they, how dared they withdraw from his censure with the discipline and assurance of conquerors? How dared that man, that gilded *memento mori*, gather up the honours from between them with a sweep of his bony hand, and leave his lord here thus bereft and disparaged?

Isambard rode easily, the reins loose over his wrist, the smile still touching his mouth. They were out of sight of the wall of Shrewsbury, and pacing the broad grassy verge of the Roman road, when he suddenly put back his iron-grey head and laughed aloud. All this for de Burgh!

"God's wounds!" said Isambard to the green dusk that hung like a silver-sewn web over his head. "You would think I loved the man!"

Chapter Two

Parfois, Shrewsbury:
December 1232

*T*he snow came early but grudgingly that year, filming over the meadows by Severn so thinly that the dormant grasses showed through in pale and frosty green. Harry stood on the leaded roof of the King's Tower, huddled in his felt cloak against the biting wind, and looked down into the distant valley, from the crowded roofs of Pool, upstream, to the grey walls of Strata Marcella downstream. His abbreviated world went no farther; the murk of snow crept in and folded the hills from him, and all he could see of Wales was the cold shore glittering with frost, and the first darker heaving of the trees on the slope behind. The shallow by-channels of the river were frozen, and shone sullenly with a lambent light in their hollows; only the main stream, edged with ice, still flowed darkly down towards Breidden, rolling its sombre brown waters along the foot of the Long Mountain, far below the turrets of Parfois.

He looked long at the Welsh shore, and it seemed to him like the countryside of a dream, for ever beyond his reach. Under those grey abbey walls he had embraced his father's unviolated grave, and unwittingly betrayed it to violation. What had Isambard done with the poor, hunted bones? Ripped them limb-meal and sent them down the Severn again, to complete his thwarted vengeance? By that ford, pale beneath its broken brown water, he had crossed the river to ride after his foster-brother and prince, when Isambard had let him out on his long leash of temptation to his bounden duty in last year's war, and by the same ford he had returned according to his promise when the war was over and his freedom again forfeit. Now in the icy stillness of winter the desired land withdrew from him, hiding in leaden cloud, and he could hardly believe that he would ever set foot on its summer hills again. A mere ribbon of river between them, but he could not cross. The birds that came back at night to the warmer roosting-grounds of Parfois from their Welsh pastures made nothing of their incredible journey. He watched them come and go, and envied them their wings; and the unceasing ache of longing knotted itself a little more tightly into his vitals.

From this eyrie there was no way down for him without wings, not even into England, not even to the invisible assart below there in the woods, where Aelis waited for word of him, and no word ever came.

He owed so much to Aelis and her father. When he had run from Aber and come prowling about Parfois in search of his vengeance they had taken him in and given him house-room without question, thinking him some runaway from justice or from a hard master. Many a fugitive had passed through their hands; they had no fear of outlaws. Aelis had helped him in everything, fed him, mended his clothes, showed him the paths that scaled the cliffs below the castle. When he was known to be prisoner, she had sent word to Castell Coch, that the news might reach Llewelyn at Aber. And while he was with her, while there was time, he had not even been very kind to her! Thus from his eyrie he saw himself below, infinitely small, ungrateful and inadequate. Even when he was loosed out to his war, and slept that last night under her father's roof, he had used her like a child and told her but half the truth, saving the worse half for his return; and pride, conscience, whatever it was that drove him, had cheated him in the end, and left Aelis uncomforted.

So she did not even know, she did not even know that he was so near! She thought him free, and by this time must be sure he had forgotten her. Perhaps she had even ceased to care, and thought no more of him. His heart turned in him, furious to deny it, fighting off the pain, but the fear clung to him and would not be driven away. What better had he deserved of her?

"What, still bent on leaving me, Harry?" said Isambard, sweet and rueful at his shoulder. He could move more softly than a cat when he willed; but he could not startle Harry now, they had played this bitter game too often. There was his place, leaning at his favourite prisoner's back, whispering like a prompting devil in his ear. "Ah, but put off your flight until more clement weather. I should not like to have to hack you out of the Severn ice."

"Why not?" said Harry. "You cast my father into it, why stick at sending me after him?"

"I'm not done with you, Harry. You do not cease to please me. Not yet!" And that must be true, or he could easily have killed him, that day in the summer, instead of merely bludgeoning the sword out of his hand. "But should you not be looking rather towards England?" said Isambard, leaning his cloaked elbows on the weathered stone at Harry's side. "Prince David and his mother are in Shrewsbury again. In two days' time the papal commission meets at Saint Mary's. Would you not like to be there to see it?"

"Would not you, my lord? King Henry lies at Wenlock priory, so I've heard. Won't you put on your cloth of gold and go and attend on him?"

"Well struck, Harry!" said Isambard with a crow of laughter. "Lay about you and give as good as you get. I am as like to be called back to favour with my king as you are to be loosed to your prince. But I doubt you suffer from the banishment more than I."

"As yet, my lord, as yet."

Harry slid one curious glance along his shoulder at the hawk profile that gazed down so tranquilly into the river valley, and could find no tremor of regret or uneasiness anywhere in its fierce, fine lines. Was it true that he cared so little? That he felt neither shame nor fear in his disgrace?

Parfois had quaked to its rocky foundations when he rode in from Shrewsbury late at night in his banished splendour. Harry well remembered the running and whispering, the agitated speculations, the torches flaring, Langholme white and stunned into silence attending his lord to bed; and in the heart of the turmoil, brisk and calm and as if unaware of the storm he had raised, that barbaric golden figure stripping its rings and yawning, and calling the first neglectful servant sharply to heel, to demonstrate beyond question that nothing here was changed. His hand had been as heavy as formerly, but no heavier. No one paid for his disgrace, no one took advantage of it; he saw to that.

And gradually, the passing days easing the awe that gripped them all, the story of the king's audience had come out, as the knights who had attended him there opened their bewildered minds to those who had not seen. Wantonly, deliberately, he had invited his own fall, out of pride, out of spleen, out of that vendetta he had against life, that kept him always walking the edge of the precipice and defying death to come and take him. Or perhaps coolly, for a purpose, to frighten King Henry—they said he was easily frightened by men of authority—into reconsidering his courses, and relaxing a little the rigour of his grip on the earl of Kent.

If that was it, had he struck as far astray as it had seemed? De Burgh had fared ill enough, in all conscience, hounded, stripped, plucked out of sanctuary, driven from pillar to post, robbed, imprisoned, and shut up now under guard in exhausted retirement at Devizes. Was that failure? Or was it a success that he was still alive? They said the London mob had been loosed on him once by the king's order, and only old Ranulf of Chester had stood up and forced Henry to call off his pack. Five weeks later old Ranulf himself was dead; and de Burgh in his extremity, they said, had wept and prayed earnestly for his ancient enemy's soul. But how if Isambard had played the same part earlier, and stood off a more private death?

"Don't build too hopefully on my fall, Harry," counselled Isambard, grinning at him along a lean shoulder. "Oh, I doubt not he would like to move against me, but what he dare do he's done already and, as you see, it was feeble enough. I am no de Burgh, to be lopped like a tree. I have no manors of his gift to be snatched back from me whenever he loses his temper. I hold no royal castles, nor never coveted any; he cannot strip me of one furlong of land. My line is older than his, and all I have is mine by inheritance. Nor have I ever held or sought office, or handled royal monies, or the funds of the realm, either, which is the chief hold they have on poor, harried Hubert. I am unassailable. I have nothing he can take from me but his countenance, and that I can spare as willingly as he denies it."

"You have a life," said Harry.

"You are more likely by far to be the death of me, Harry, than ever King Henry is."

"You comfort me, my lord. Consider on that promise, and have some care for yourself." He hesitated a moment, hugging the folds of frieze more closely about him, but whether to shut out the icy wind or to shadow his face he did not know. The toe of his shoe kicked moodily at the stones of the merlon against which he leaned. "There are some," he blurted, "who are licking their lips."

"Because I have put myself into temporary eclipse? I doubt not. Do you think there was ever a man whose disgrace did not give comfort and pleasure to somebody? I am as well hated as any and better than most. That's no news to me."

Harry would willingly have left it at that, but it seemed his tongue had more to say. It came out of him grudgingly enough, but it came.

"Some close about you," he said, "turned very thoughtful after you came home from Shrewsbury. There's those in your household are none too stable in their allegiance. As soon as they're sure you've had your day they'll be off to meet the coming men."

Isambard looked up from his musing on the steel-grey river below. He was smiling.

"The coming men," he said, pondering the phrase, and the soft, contemplative note of his voice said plainly that he had understood. Those who most pretended indignant devotion to him were already casting speculative glances out of the corners of their eyes at the rising fortunes of des Rivaulx's new men, those competent clerks and functionaries of the household who had climbed into office with their leader. One of the closest at his elbow, so they said, was William Isambard, the old man's younger son, the same whose boyhood clothes had been refashioned for Harry to wear, when first he was a prisoner in Parfois. William had waited a long time for his inheritance. And the old man showed no disposition as yet to die, or even to grow senile; to be honest, it had not even dawned on him yet that he was old. The king's displeasure might be useful; it might even be fed with new fuel if it threatened to cool.

Was it a new thought to Isambard? There was no telling; he had

that formidable face of his in such control that no man could read
the mind behind it, unless he pleased to lay it open, and it was his
pleasure always to confuse and confound. Harry wished he had not
spoken. Why should he warn him? What was it to him if they
betrayed him?

"And who are they, these snakes in my bosom?" invited the soft
voice gently. "Name them, Harry, name them. I can be grateful,
like other men, when I see cause."

"No!" said Harry, jerking indignantly away from the too close
scrutiny of the illusionless eyes. "I'm not your spy."

"Child, child, not for your freedom? Their names, and you can
turn the key in the lock and let yourself out. The princess will feast
you in Shrewsbury tonight, and you'll ride home at David's side.
What more could I offer you?"

Sweet, unbearably sweet, the voice and the promise, and even the
close, caressing regard of the deep eyes, smiling at him so temptingly
and tenderly. Praise be to God, he knew the way of it now, he had
mastered it, he was not even shaken.

"You waste your time, my lord. You know you'll get no names
from me." Once he would have raged and hurled abuse, like stones
fending off an advancing enemy. For a moment he was consciously
proud of his growth. Something, at least, he owed to Isambard.
What use would there be in lesser tempters trying him, after this?

"No, Harry? Then listen if I am so far astray." And he named
them, one by one with terrible accuracy, down to Thomas Blount
who was no more than an afterthought, a trivial note at the end.
"And de Guichet, of course," said Isambard without bitterness, and
he laughed to see how the boy, who had accepted all with a stony
face, turned and gaped at him on hearing the name of the seneschal
of Parfois.

"Did you not have him in your list? Then you lacked the chief."
He stood up from the chilly stone and stretched himself. "I am too
old to learn caution at my age, Harry; I must play the cards as they
fall. But never think I am in error about the love men bear me. I
have lived with them a long time; I can read passably well by now."

"I see you need no help from me," said the boy, smarting. "Neither with your master nor your servants."

"My master? Ah, King Henry! To be plain with you, child,

though I am his man, whether he believes it or no, he is no man's master, not even his own. His father, let him be what he would and as faulty as he would, was a man. This one is a reliquary of spites and prejudices. Even the virtues he has, even his piety and his charity, he uses as counters for bargaining with God."

Harry turned his head in quick alarm to look for his two guards, who would surely be lounging somewhere in the most sheltered corner above the staircase. "My lord, keep your voice down!"

"Ah, they're out of earshot, Harry. Why should they follow you out into this wind? They know you'll not jump to your death; you're absolute for life."

"My lord, no one will say as much of you. Think, have you not exposed yourself enough?" Harry shrank in amazement from the note of his own illogical anger. "You'd best not speak so of the king before everyone."

"Nor do I," said Isambard, smiling, and took him by the arm and turned him towards the dark hollow of the staircase where the archers waited, "Only to my enemies, Harry," he said softly into his ear. "A man's safe with his honest enemies. Do I not know you? You'd no more deliver me over to the king's justice than you'd exempt me from your own."

The splendid assembly gathered in Saint Mary's church on the sixth of December dispersed towards nightfall, and all the people of Shrewsbury jostled about the college close to see them go.

First the papal legates, grave gentlemen and reverend, swathed to the eyes in gowns and cloaks, for their Italian blood ran thin and chill in this inhospitable climate. Their liveried servants were more gorgeous than they, and made a stately procession, but for the caution and irregularity of their gait on the frozen cobbles of the close. Then the king with his retinue, and the crowded street rang with illustrious names as the horses paced by: Ralf Neville, bishop of Chichester and chancellor of England, Segrave, the new justiciar, de Lacy, earl of Lincoln and constable of Chester since old Ranulf's death. And that tall lord with the open face and the austere smile was Richard, earl marshal, the new earl of Pembroke, more than a year established now in his unexpected honour. He was the second of five fine brothers, and had never looked to inherit, but the eldest had died childless, and Richard, long settled on his French estates, had been called home in haste to fill his place. More foreigner than Englishman as he might be, it was already being rumoured about the court that he was no lover of King Henry's Poitevin officers, and had a good English respect for the established order and custom of the realm, which these bade fair to dismember.

Baron and earl and functionary, bishop and prelate, knight banneret and knight simple, the noble cavalcade swept down the Wyle, young King Henry in the midst in his glory and dignity, of which he was always tender and aware.

There had not been so many great personages in Shrewsbury since the days of King John, from whom the town had extorted so many useful charters and liberties in return for its cash and loyalty. Flourishing business followed the crown; the burghesses of the borough shouted their acclaims very contentedly, stamping their cold feet on the frozen, rutted ground and breathing fanfares of silver vapour into the sparkling air. Even the Welsh, when they came, got no black looks, only the same craning curiosity. Many a time they had terrorised the borders, and once within living memory ravaged Frankwell and occupied the town; but where was the sense of looking on them as enemies, when hardly a native-born family in the borough was without kin on the western side of Severn? Boundaries were recognised and jealously guarded by kings, but common folk could not carry on their daily business without crossing them freely, and leaving their footprints impartially on either side, and now and again their accidental children, into the bargain.

The Welsh came afoot, for the abbot's town house, where they were lodged, was but a short walk from the king's free chapel of Saint Mary's. The princess of Aberffraw and lady of Snowdon, Llewelyn's consort and King John's daughter, swept out of the close on her son's arm, out of the shadow of the squat sandstone tower into the torchlit gateway, and there paused for a moment to catch up her long skirt and drape it over her arm. A tall, grave woman, vigorous of movement and calm of face. She walked with assurance, unsmiling, untroubled, and there was no telling from her countenance whether she was carrying triumph or disaster back to her husband in Aber. She had lived all her life exposed to the torchlight and the craning stares, holding her own in a world of statesmen and princes for Llewelyn's sake; she knew how to contain and protect both her mind and her heart. And yet hardly more than a year ago, as every man in England and Wales knew, she had laid in her husband's prison for faithlessness, and her lover de Breos had hanged on the salt marshes of Aber, a dear price to pay for any woman, even a princess.

They stretched their necks to view her as she passed, and thought her hardly worth the risk: her hair greying under the gold circlet, her cheeks pale and her eyes sombre. She would never see forty again. And he so young and gallant! What had he seen in her, that they could not see?

Joan sustained the burden of their eyes, and felt nothing now of the anguish of her first re-entry into the light. When she was on Llewelyn's business she was Llewelyn; her voice took on the authority of his voice, the words she chose were the words he would have chosen, even in her gestures she caught the ardour and magnificence of his large and generous movements. While he had no occasion for timidity or shame, she could not be put out of countenance. She had risen before the legates at the chancel steps and spoken for more than an hour in bold and reasoned terms, detailing without heat the many infringements of the border, the many infractions of the terms of truce, with which Llewelyn charged his English neighbours. And she had sat with an unmoved face to listen to the counter-charges, and been the first to urge concessions and a new good will upon both parties, offering redress where it might be adjudged due from Wales, and claiming it with formal courtesy where it was due from England. Could any man among them have done better? Llewelyn was in her blood and in her spirit, an eagle from the crags of Snowdon looking through her face from his nest within her mind.

On her right hand walked her son, David, Llewelyn's heir acknowledged; tall and slender and fair like his mother, and grave almost to sadness like her, but with a quick, flashing smile, rare and brief, that was his father's gift. On her left, the older man must be Ednyfed Fychan, Llewelyn's chief agent and confidant for many years. And the thickset, dark young man who followed hard on their heels, reported the more knowing among the crowd, was Prince David's foster-brother, Owen ap Ivor ap Madoc, no mean princeling himself in the cantrefs of Arfon and Ardudwy.

They paced the frozen ruts of the street, the sergeants clearing a way for them; they came and passed, their retinue of dark, stocky, wild tribal princelings behind them. At the corner of the Wyle the watching crowd was shaken by a convulsion that suddenly cast out a slight, cloaked figure into their path; one of the sergeants stretched his staff to block the way, but she darted round him, quick as a squirrel, and had Owen ap Ivor by the arm before anyone could thrust between.

"Master, wait! Master Owen!"

He looked down, startled, into a bright oval face, rosy with cold in the frame of the brown hood. Blue eyes, fringed with long, childish lashes, stared up imploringly into his. "Master Owen, you remember me, Aelis?"

The sergeant had her by the arm, and would have hustled her away, but Owen held her by the wrist and put him off with a reassuring hand.

"Let her be, she does no harm. Let her speak."

The momentary flurry of movement had reached Joan's ears, she turned to look back.

"What is it? If the child would ask something of us, let her not be denied."

The day had gone well for Wales, they owed alms to whoever sued for them. She came back with her long, impetuous step, and looked gravely into the girl's face. A young creature, not more than sixteen, her slight body shrouded and shapeless within the coarse cloak all the country people wore. She was frightened now, she tried to draw back, but Owen held her, his arm about her shoulders for fear she should slip out of his grasp and be off into the crowd.

"Madam, this is that child I told you of, she that sent us word once of one we'd lost."

It was only habit to hold back names from his tongue. Who in this self-confident border borough would have heard of Harry Talvace?

"Shall I bid her to the house?" he said quickly, seeing the bright flame of understanding flare in Joan's face.

"Yes, do so. Yes, come, child, follow us to our lodgings, and you shall have your asking, whatever it may be."

The creature was wild as a forest doe, and might run from her if

Owen relaxed his hold. Joan turned and went on her way with a hastened step, to leave them alone together. Owen she knew and would trust; and if her wanting was sharp enough, she would come in search of it. The fierce and innocent face moved her; it was quick with desire, and so agonizingly young. She would come! Even if he loosed her now, even if she cowered and hid like a deer in the covert, yet she would come.

"Follow us home," said Owen quickly into the tangle of corn-coloured hair that burst in soft strands from under the rough hood. "In the courtyard I'll wait for you; come to me there."

She gave him one wild, wary glance of her great eyes, and her mouth shaped a silent assent. Then she darted back from him and was lost among the throng; but when he looked back at the gate of the abbot's house he saw her slipping silently along the wall after them, shadowy and quick and shy, like a city cat hunting by dusk. She was close on the heels of the youngest pages as they entered the courtyard, and her step so light that no one heard and challenged her. The gate closed after her. She turned at that, and it seemed that she would have clawed her way out again in a panic if she could, but by then it was too late.

He ran and caught her by the shoulder, holding her hard when she would have drawn back from him. "Aelis, why? This is foolishness. You knew me, you called me. Come in to us, come and say what you have to say. What have I done to frighten you?"

"I didn't know," she said incoherently. "I never thought you'd be so close to the lady. All I meant was a word alone with you; I never wanted this." But her body had softened and calmed between his hands, and she went unresisting where he led her.

"Are you afraid of the princess? No need. Even if she were not kindness born, she owes you kindness, as we all do."

"I'm not afraid," said Aelis with indignation, and thrust him off stiffly and walked before him into the hall.

The torches were burning already, hissing and resin scented in their sconces on the walls. The log fire in the hearth cast leaping lights and shadows over the smoky brown panelling, and over the princess as she put off her cloak and held out a cold foot to the blaze. Two or three of her women were about her, busy with unlacing her shoes and bringing her her house gown, but when she heard the latch of the door, and saw the girl quivering, curious and shy on the threshold, she put them off with an uplifted hand and sent them away.

"Madam," said Owen, when the door had closed after their rustling skirts, "this is Aelis, Robert's daughter, who first sent us word last year, when Harry was lost, that he was carried prisoner into Parfois. She and her father had him in their care some weeks, not knowing who he was, and were good to him. And but for her we should not have learned so soon what had befallen him."

Aelis bent her knee and averted her eyes, casting quick glances from under her long gold lashes first at the lady, and then at the young prince, who had come forward out of the shadows and stood behind his mother's chair. They were richly but sombrely dressed; they wore jewels and velvets and brocades, for they came from a ceremonious occasion of state, where splendour was a formidable weapon in every party's armoury. Aelis was a little afraid that Owen had made her sound like a beggar come to be rewarded, and the lady might strip off one of her rings and pay her off for her services accordingly. Not that she would not have liked to hold that shining red stone in her hand and put it on her finger; but not as quittance for her share in Harry Talvace.

But Joan said only: "Then we are deep in your debt, Aelis. And it seems to me we may in some sort be able to repay, for you had something to ask of us. Ask it now, and if it's in our gift you shall have it."

"I only wanted to ask Master Owen," said Aelis, slipping back the rusty folds of her cloak upon her shoulders, "if he could give me word of Harry."

Word of him for word of him: that was a fair and dignified exchange.

"When he got free from Parfois," she said, warming now into ardour and anxiety, "he came to our cottage for his horse, and slept the dark hours with us, and promised to come back when he could. And since then I've had no word of him. I came here to Shrewsbury thinking he might come in attendance on your lordship, and I might at least see him and be sure he was well. Maybe speak with him," she said, and flushed suddenly and angrily at having exposed her need and her longing before them. "Not that he owes me anything, or that I have anything to ask of him, except only to know that all's well with him. But when he didn't come, and I saw Master Owen pass so close, I made bold to call to him, only to ask for news."

She saw the look they exchanged, and wondered at the shadow that passed from eye to eye; and she held her breath for fear that there was none but bad news to tell. In a year and a half how much could happen! And she with no way of knowing whether he lived or died.

"And you did not know, then?" said Owen wonderingly. "He was with you, and told you nothing?"

Joan saw the young face chill with apprehension, and the great eyes, bluer than speedwells, widen and darken in a terror she could well comprehend. Fear for oneself can be mastered, there comes a time when it is pointless; but for fear for another dearer than oneself there's no cure, however gallant the spirit, however lofty the mind.

"He's alive," she said, reaching for the largest and readiest comfort she could find in words, "and please God he's well. And if he did not keep his promise yet, it's because the time's not yet come, and not because he's forsworn. I never knew him break his word, child, and he'll not begin now."

She saw the soft, rich colour flood the girl's smooth cheeks again, and the smiling light of joy quicken in the assuaged eyes, and shrank from what more there was to tell; but she had begun it, and she would not leave it to Owen to add the bad to the good.

"He should have told you the truth," she said, "about his freedom. It was no more than conditional, until the war should end. And when it ended he was pledged to go back into captivity. He'd given his word. And he kept it."

Aelis lifted her head, staring from great eyes that did not know whether to be grateful or grieved. The cloak slipped from her shoulders unnoticed, and left her standing slender and still in her rough, dun-coloured gown of homespun, her hair disordered by the heavy hood and falling out of its coils. The uncurling strands had a dark-gold lustre, clothing her with a splendour of her own.

"He's back in Parfois!" she said in a bitter whisper, and let out her breath in a long sigh.

"A year ago and more."

"He should have come to me when he returned," said Aelis faintly in her pain. "He could have trusted me."

"Surely he trusted you, child. He did not come to us at Aber, either, before he went back. When he was newly let out and came running to you, I doubt it seemed to him he had all the time in the world. Only when his parole fell due did he come to see to what hard terms he had bound himself. To return to his prison as soon as peace was made, that was the pledge he'd given. And he held to it, to every word and scruple of it. Even you were a mile out of his way, I doubt, and his honour was too proud and too sore to bend and take you in. It's how men treat us," said Joan with a wry smile. "If we would have them at all we must take them as they are."

The girl stood mute, quivering a little, unaware how eloquent her eyes were. Back in Parfois, they lamented, prisoner again and nothing gained for all this year of waiting. And so near, and I felt nothing, and so wretched, and I sometimes blaming him. But he hadn't forgotten, they exulted. If he didn't come it was because he could not.

"Madam, what can we do?" she said appealingly.

"Little enough, except wait and hope." At sixteen there could be nothing harder to do; at sixteen there is so little time. "Go back to Parfois," said Joan gently, "and keep watch as best you can on all that happens there. If there is anything strange, anything we should know, send word to the castellan at Castell Coch, as you did once before, and we shall hear of it. And believe that Harry has not forgotten his word to you. He'll keep it when he can."

She looked at the bright face, the vulnerable mouth, the radiant eyes, at the beginning of beauty not yet awakened, and her heart ached for the tyranny of time, of which she, having relinquished youth, had enough and to spare. No, she thought, he will not have forgotten!

"And this place, this assart of yours by the Severn, it is a long way from here. How did you come?"

"I walked." She smiled a little at that. What other way did they suppose poor people had of getting about?

"Alone?" said Owen. "Or is your father here in the town with you?"

"How could we both leave the cow and the hens? No, I came alone. I'm not afraid," she said. "Footpads pay no heed to people like me; what have I got they could covet?"

"You must not go back alone. Owen, have Madoc make ready a horse for her, and send two safe men to bring her home. And David, bid Margaret prepare supper for her before she goes."

They went upon their errands obediently, and the two women, left together in the warm room pulsating with firelight and torch-light, looked long and covertly at each other, and said no word for a while.

"And do you love him so much?" said Joan at length, sharp and sudden across the silence.

"I want nothing from him," said Aelis haughtily, "but what he freely wills to give me."

"That I believe. But that is not what I asked you."

In the shadow of the dark-gold hair the blue eyes lifted fiercely to her face. "Yes," said Aelis, "I love him."

The legates departed, the brilliant assembly of nobles and bishops and princes began to disperse, and Shrewsbury's winter heyday was over. They parted in amity and good order. The king had already approved and ratified the agreement reached before the court, ear-nestly affirming the good will to peace of both parties, and setting up an arbitration commission to adjust all the issues which might arise between them. Both sides had bound themselves to accept whatever rulings the commission might make, and agreed without difficulty to the names put forward; and the legates had solemnly handed over their powers to the bench thus filled, and set out for London, leaving their blessing upon the continued peace.

Would Henry have been so amenable if his mind had not been on other matters? Wales was almost invisible to him now, he saw only what he and his new order meant to make of England. He had never room for more than one passion at a time.

Having thus taken every advantage of his preoccupation, and doubtless thanked God for it, the Welsh party left the abbot's town house, and took the winter road for Aber.

Harry worked late at his bench that day, and would not leave it to go in for his supper even after the light failed. The hall would be full, the torches there too revealing, and he was not ready yet to show his face. However he might cover his hurts from sight, that did not keep them from aching.

They had been so near to him, and it might as well have been the width of the world. He sat curled on his dark bench in the cold, fingering his unfinished work desperately to fill his mind and give his courage ground, but he could not get the princess out of his eyes. He saw her now always as he had last seen her, in Llewelyn's chair, frowning over Llewelyn's dispatches, so changed and still for the lost year, grey and ageing and in need of every creature who loved her. Now she would be riding away from him mile by mile with David and Owen beside her, lighting down somewhere to spend the night, perhaps at Valle Crucis, and tomorrow setting out on another day's journey, dragging out the stretched cords of his heart with her. They were going home to his mother, to the great prince who had been one more father to him, and to Adam, who had supplied Master Harry's place lovingly and patiently ever since his son came into the world. And he must lie here kicking his heels and fretting his heart out; and no end to it, never a sign that it might some day end. The peace was sacred, and David's inheritance must not be imperilled. And here was he, the price of it, suddenly in tears of frustration and misery and loneliness, and scrubbing his cheeks angrily with a coarse sleeve to wipe the shame hurriedly away. He must have his hour in the dark, even if it cost him his supper. He could not face them yet.

So it happened that he was still crouched among his tools, and stroking the half-cut stone for comfort, when the rolling, distant thunder of hoofs crossing the bridge from the plateau of the great church brought his head up alertly and froze his sad senses into instant attention. Apart from the guard there would be few people abroad in the outer ward at this hour. He mustered enough curiosity to slide down from his bench and feel his way out of the dark tracing-house to see who these riders might be. The court was still in Shrewsbury abbey. More than one pair of ears in Parfois would be stretched anxiously for any sign of Isambard's being taken back into favour. If this was a summons from the king there would be some scurrying to get back into the old alignment.

Half a dozen riders were dismounting by the stable-yard; he saw them fitfully by torchlight, and as silhouettes against the faint glitter of frost on the thin snow. Well-muffled, well-mounted men, with large voices and confident gait; they could well be from court. The grooms were running to take their horses, and two or three pages to hold their stirrups; and the officer of the guard was being exceedingly respectful and attentive to their leader, who had lighted down and was stamping his chilled feet. Harry drew near, his ears pricked for names, since he could not hope to recognize faces; but in the issue it was the stranger's face that identified him.

A tall, well-made man, this visitor, with a rich beard and lavish clothes. For all the beard, for all the flickering light and darkness that showed him only by glimpses, there was likeness enough to put a name to him. He carried more flesh, he had not the malice or the glitter or the beauty; nevertheless, at sight he owned his sire.

So this was William Isambard, whose clothes Harry had worn; the younger son, the courtier, the new man, des Rivaulx's man. Careful though he might be to go with the running tide, it seemed his blood was thick enough to bring him visiting to the father who could not go to him.

And then one of the torches flared, with a hissing of resinous wood, and cast a stronger light for a full minute upon the visitor's face. Hot eyes, quick and resolute, looked round upon Parfois in a sweeping stare, weighing and measuring and assessing the very harness and mounting-blocks of the stable-yard. He was smiling, the kind of smile which is not meant to be shared. The few steps he took across the cobbles had the large assurance of a proprietor.

And suddenly de Guichet was coming to meet him out of the archway of the inner ward. What was he doing out of hall at this hour? No one had run with a message yet, no one had called him. The seneschal should have been close at his lord's side.

Close at his lord's side! And perhaps he was. He came hastening with lavish surprise, his bow was no more obsequious than was reasonable to his master's son; but his voice, loud and clear in the first astonished greeting, fell very readily into a confidential undertone as they drew together. It was nothing, only a pricking of the thumbs, a tremor of the imagination; and yet it bit into Harry's mind like acid, and left a mark there was no erasing. No commitment yet, it was too soon; nothing, only a small, cautious reconnaissance, to make sure how the land lay. But very surely this was no embassage from the king; William was here on William's own business.

Suddenly Harry thought of Isambard at his high table in the crowded hall, of the thousand or so knights and squires and retainers and men-at-arms of his household gathered below him, of the inescapable light that would show them every motion, every change in his face. He claimed to care nothing for his banishment, did he, to set no store by the hope of his recall to the king's favour? They should see, they should see whether he cared! They should see his hopes raised, if secretly he cherished hopes, and see them dashed; and if he came unscathed through that test let him devise what punishment he would for Harry in return.

Harry ran, his heart beating up hot and vengeful into his throat, and slid through the shadowy archway ahead of them, and came first to the steps of the great hall. The din and the smoke and the warmth came out to meet him. He edged between the hurrying scullions and began to thread his way in haste towards the high table.

He could very well have gone round and whispered his message into Isambard's ear, but that was not what he wanted. He came to the steps of the dais and mounted them boldly, taking his stand at the end of the high table, where he could command a view of the hall and leave Isambard exposed to the eyes of every man present.

"My lord—!"

He waited a moment for the expectant hush; he wanted them all to hear, not merely the knights, but the last pot-boy at the end of the room.

"My lord, there are messengers come from Shrewsbury to wait on you, from the court."

There was so little time, he could hope for no more than two minutes before they made their entry and shattered the grand illusion. But two minutes was enough. The babel of voices, stilled to hear him, broke out again on a lower, warier note, wondering, excited, waiting for the proof. Isambard's lounging body did not stiffen in his chair, his hands did not tighten on the tapestried arms; only his eyes widened a little and his eyebrows rose, and he sat looking speculatively at Harry across the loaded table, not as though he disbelieved, rather as though he wondered at the reason behind the announcement. If he was glad and relieved, if he felt any small, thankful surge of triumph and exultation, he dissembled them uncommonly well. He kept, you would have said, an open mind, and waited the event with a certain amount of illusionless interest, but without any great concern.

No, it was not he who rose to the bait. If Harry had wanted a revelation, he had it. He looked round the high table in one wild glance, and saw how many faces closed like shuttered windows, how many pairs of eyes, flaring for one instant into uneasiness and consternation, glazed over next moment in the sealed countenances, and cloaked up the motions of the minds within. In haste and disquiet they made their reassessments, and composed their faces woodenly to cover the agony. All the waverers eased their coats on their shoulders, ready to turn them again according to the way the wind blew. Harry stood dumb with dismay to see how many they were.

"Well, bid them in," said Isambard, and the dryness of his voice brought the blood to the messenger's cheeks. "They are welcome."

"They are here, my lord."

It was done now; he could not undo it if he would. He stepped aside into the hangings of the dais as de Guichet came in by the high door, bright and dutiful as became the bearer of tidings, with William Isambard at his back.

Every eye in the room flashed to them, and settled upon the newcomer. A vast sigh shuddered through the air and quaked into absolute silence, as William walked to meet his father, bowed above the extended hand, and kissed the fleshless cheek. The two faces leaned together a moment, and their likeness and their violent differences shocked Harry like a blow. It was done so tenderly, with such filial devotion. He heard the affectionate greeting, the air between was so still.

"My dear lord and father, I grieve to see you unhappy."

"Do you see me so, William?" said Isambard with his crooked grin. "I had thought I looked in very fair spirits. You, I see, are in good heart enough. Do you stay with us for a while, now that you are here?"

"I would I might, but the king leaves Shrewsbury tomorrow, and I must ride back in good time. I have no leave of absence for more than a few hours."

"I could spare you the half of mine. I have leave of absence without limit. Sit down with me here, then, while you have licence, and let me hear your news." He made room for his son on his right hand, and the pages ran to cover for him and pour the wine. Across the table Isambard lifted his sardonic glance to Harry Talvace, frozen and mute against the wall.

"Go to your place, Harry," he said mildly. "You did your errand well. I could hardly have bettered it myself."

That was praise he could well have done without, but he could not complain that he had not earned it. He went on trembling legs, burningly aware of de Guichet's eyes boring into his back. The seneschal could not well ask his lord which errand, but he could reason and connect sharply enough. Maybe he was wondering now on whose side this lonely alien was playing, and whether the mocking intimacy Isambard affected with him did not cover his private employment as a spy about the castle wards. Harry felt the complications of intrigue sticking to his fingers, and the sensation outraged him, as though he had found himself physically soiled by some filth he could not wipe off. And even when he had taken his seat at a lower table among the young gentlemen-at-arms of birth comparable with his own, he was not delivered from having to hear the voices from the dais. It seemed that Isambard was bent on pitching the tone of the conversation so high and clear that it should carry a fair way down the hall and reach hundreds of witnesses; and in the presence of the noble and unexpected guest the young men of the retinue hushed their own talk into whispers, so that he had no defence from hearing.

"And how did you leave his Grace?" asked Isambard serenely, tilting his wine-cup to catch the captive ruby in the light of the candles on the table. "Is he content with his prolonged truce?"

"Very well content, and in excellent spirits. He goes to keep Christmas at Worcester."

"And you with him, William?"

"I have that honour. As an officer of his household now—"

"Ah, yes, I had not forgotten. But put *my* household out of its pain, man: he did not send you to call me back to court?"

"Alas, no, Father, not yet. Give him time, and he'll cool. His Grace was cruelly hurt by your censure, but I know it came from your loyal heart, and your concern for him. Only wait, and he'll forgive. I shall be there at his right hand to see that you're not forgotten."

"Ah, that I never doubted," said Isambard, smiling like a happy devil. "And you will be my advocate and speak for me, will you not, my son? For the honesty of my intent and the unquestionable faithfulness of my attachment to him?"

"You know I will, my lord. Assiduously."

"Assiduously!" He uttered it slowly, rolling it on his tongue as if it had a flavour stronger and more to his taste than the wine. "I marvel, William, that he spared you to me even for an hour, you whom he values so highly. Let me see, is it three sheriffdoms you hold now, or four? I have forgotten."

"Four, my lord."

"And his Grace has been pleased to confer another manor upon you for your services, so I heard."

"Yes, my lord—Burhythe, in Suffolk. I have not seen it yet. When the court moves south I must ride over and view it."

"On my word, I'm glad one of us is in the ascendant. I never doubted your vigour and efficiency. If you stand my friend how can I fail to speed in the end?"

"In good earnest, Father, I've done my best, but the time is not ripe yet. He's very bitter against de Burgh, as I for one can well understand. Bide here and wait and trust me, and I won't fail you."

"I call that more than generous in you," said Isambard, "seeing you do not hold with me over the issue of the earl of Kent."

Was it deliberate or merely habit in him, that he still insisted on using the old style and title, now ripped from the fallen statesman's name?

"I do not. But I know the honesty with which you hold your views, and I know you are the king's true man, and that's enough."

"And how was it with the earl of Kent when you left London? What was the news of him?"

Twice in a row could not be accident; this was perversity. He was declaring his contempt for the judgement and his continued respect for the victim, publicly and provocatively.

William told more than he was asked, and elaborated the whole sorry tale so willingly that Harry could not but read something of a threat and a warning into the narration. Why else should he dwell on the malice and viciousness of the long persecution, that shrieked out the king's meanness of spirit even while the narrator found excuses for his venom? No man had ever been more mercilessly hounded than de Burgh. By the time he should have appeared before the king's council at Lambeth in September they had amassed so long and gross a farrago of charges against him, and so many were pressing for his blood, that it was no wonder he feared for his life to come.

And then to tear him out of sanctuary and, when the bishops in holy indignation forced his restoration to the altar, to lay siege to him there for the forty days' respite needed before he could be declared outlaw, to deny access even to his priest, to forbid the very servants who took his food to speak a word to him, to have his personal seal ceremoniously destroyed and his prayer-book taken away from him, and at the end of the forty days triumphantly and righteously to withdraw food and attendants from him, so that he must needs surrender himself or starve. Was that the behaviour of a king, or of a vindictive child sick with his own spleen? The Tower must have seemed like a gentle hermitage after such usage.

All the same, Henry had not killed him. Why not? Because Isambard first and Ranulf of Chester afterwards had spoken for too large and formidable a body of opinion to be quite ignored? At least when Hubert came before the commission of earls and the justiciar at Cornhill the issue had been pressed less vigorously than might have been expected, considering what had gone before. Surely sick to the heart of the whole business of living and struggling by then, de Burgh, it seemed, had refused steadily to submit to a judgement or make a defence, and simply thrown himself on the king's mercy, to use as he would. The lands of his inheritance or purchase had been left to him, but all those held of the crown stripped from him with his earldom; and the four earls of the commission, Richard of Pembroke, Lacy of Lincoln, Richard of Cornwall and the earl of Surrey, held the broken man in protective custody at Devizes. Held him, thought Harry, watching William Isambard's face as he deployed the wretched details of the long harrying, more gently far than the king would have wished could he have had his way.

"I take it very kindly, dear son," said Isambard, spreading his velvet sleeves at ease over the board, "that you go to such pains to acquaint me with every circumstance. I take the warning as it is meant. I am a tamed man, William, I grow old."

The glow of his secret amusement had ripped ten years from him, or else the wine was flowing more freely than usual up there at the high table; and the wolf had never roved more happily at liberty than now in his mildly smiling eyes.

"It is my fixed intent to do it at leisure and in liberty," he said with gentle emphasis, and pledged his son with an infinitely private parody of the affection and deference William was lavishing on him.

Rather ill-matched at first sight, those two; but by the time he had watched them to the end of the long supper Harry was not so sure the son favoured the father as little as he had thought. His was a different subtlety, yet he was subtle. In his way he went as directly and dauntingly for what he wanted as the old man had always done, and would tread down whoever stood in his way with as little compunction. But his wants were comprehensible things, land, office, money, power, and therefore his ways could be guessed at with some accuracy; and he would not care that they were known provided they could not be blocked. He must know that his father was laughing at him now, and it mattered to him not at all, and certainly would not deter him from his purpose. But who knew what the old wolf wanted, and who could guess by what devious ways he pursued his ends? Land, status, money, power, all had fallen early into his hands. These were not what tormented him, and it was not for these he tormented others.

"I am sorry from my heart," said William when he rose at last from the table, "that I cannot offer you better comfort, or stay with you longer. I ride with the advance party tomorrow, to make all ready for the king. But when next I visit you I pray it may be with better news." He seemed to hesitate for a moment, and lowered his voice a little when he proceeded, but so little that those at the knights' tables and some below could not choose but hear. "If you wish to have some message carried, I'll gladly be your courier."

Harry heard that, and his senses tightened in silent resistance, as though by straining his flesh he could cry a warning. But Isambard, rising and stretching lazily beside his son, and by some two or three inches the taller of the two, let the invitation rebound stonily from his eroded cliff of a forehead, and smiled.

"Why, since you are so kind, you may carry my respectful greetings and service—to the king."

They went out together, and the irony of their going was almost more than Harry could bear. For William offered his arm tenderly to his hard, athletic sire, and the old man in pure mischief took it, and leaned heavily upon it all the way out into the inner ward, and across the frosty parclose to the archway and the stable-yard.

For the life of him Harry did not know why he followed. It was nothing to him which of them destroyed the other, he wished all their house under the sod; and yet he was drawn after them wretchedly, raging at himself but still following, with pricked ears and anxious heart, to see the party from Shrewsbury mount and ride. He saw William Isambard stoop to the old man's hand, and then, rising, lean to his gaunt cheek once again with the deferential kiss of a loving and faithful son.

The stab of prophetic anguish pinned Harry to the wall, and set him writhing in the shadows where he stood. He dug his nails into the stones, suddenly overwhelmed with shame, as though he had seen and abetted a terrible twilight betrayal. Smoke of torches and murmur of voices, and one coming all affection and loyalty, with a kiss and an acknowledgement.

They were gone. The bridge creaked before them and thundered distantly under them, and for a few minutes crisp, frosty echoes of hoofbeats clanged hollowly back from the plateau of the church, before the cavalcade swept away into silence down the ramp to the lower guard.

Isambard, straightening with a cat's fluid grace from his parody of an old man's careful walk, shrugged off his attendants and stalked back alone through the dark archway. He all but flattened Harry into the wall, and stretched an arm good-humouredly enough to steady him on his legs again.

"What, Harry, have you not been busy enough for one night?"

There was no displeasure in his voice, only the faint, distant echo of laughter, though he was not laughing now. He held him a moment between his hands, peering narrowly through the frosty starlight that showed them to each other silvery and strange, more transparent than by day.

"Never look so shamefaced, child," he said, clapping him hard on the shoulder. "What have you to hang your head about? It was I bred him, not you."

He had gone but a couple of steps more when he halted abruptly and looked back. He was himself again, his eyes quick with demons, his mouth wry.

"The dispensations of God are always just," he said. "We get the sons we deserve."

Chapter Three

Aber, Strata Marcella:
August 1233

*A*bove the last dry-stone sheepfold, above the russet flanks of the heather, where the tussocky upland grass bleached in the sun mile upon rolling mile, there was an old wooden calvary under a penthouse-roof of shingles, and beside it the two anchorite huts: Saint Clydog's, of withies and daub, on the left, a beehive with a lancet doorway facing east, and on the right the stone cell of the holy woman of Aber, with a carved lintel and an arched window to southward. All round from sky to sky there was nothing to see but the seeding grasses and the grazing sheep, and in the occasional hollow the clustering, low bushes above the coney-runs. But in the still of the August day the sound of the sea came floating on the hushed air, the long, slow heave and fall of the rising tide along the salt marshes of Aber, far below and out of sight; and sometimes in the evening they could hear, infinitely faint and far, all the little bells ringing in all the little oratories on Ynys Lanog of the saints, across the silver strait.

Saint Clydog and the holy woman were under the direct protection of Prince Llewelyn, and could have commanded whatever comforts they would from him, but they never asked for anything. What he sent up to them by his regular monthly messenger he sent of his own will, before they could so much as feel want; and much of it they gave again, to the birds and the small, shy beasts of the hills, and the rare travellers who passed by on the upland pathways. The saint had all but forgotten that he had a body, and took thought only to give it what would keep it from crying out on him from hunger, and disturbing his prayers. And the woman, who had once been broad and bold and sturdy as a tower, had fined away these last years into pure, steely flame, wearing away her flesh from within and without. Her eyes were full and calm, and fixed always a little beyond the rim of what other men could see. They had a deep, clear colour like purple irises, that the full light of noon paled to lustrous grey. The country people said that Saint Clydog saw into the future, but what Madonna Benedetta saw nobody knew, except that it was not in this world. And yet the rest of her face was not made for repose, not for a life withdrawn and a blessed death. It had such breadth and challenge in its bones, such a curled, bright, reso- lute flower of a mouth. The queens in the old stories had such faces, and the great sorrows of them, and their loves, came to mind in beholding Benedetta, and put a new awe and a new meaning into the name they had for her; for great sorrow and great love are awful and holy.

Of the past she never spoke. In the solitude and silence of the hills there was no need, and among the herdsmen who brought milk and eggs to her door there was no curiosity. She had been there for sixteen years, and might have been there always, like the heather on Moel Wnion or the outcrop rocks above the brook, so unquestion- ingly did they accept her. If she had drifted from Italy to France with a Parisian merchant grown fat on the pickings of the Crusades, from France to England in the loftier company of the lord of Parfois, and from England to Wales as a fugitive at last from that same formidable lover, what was that to them? Why ask whence the seed had blown that rooted and flowered to stillness and holiness among their native grasses?

There were things they did know concerning her. She had brought with her in her flight a lady, a servant and a child, and placed them all under Prince Llewelyn's powerful protection. The lady had married the prince's English mason, who was foster-brother to her first husband, so they said, and had long been close and kind with her; and her son had grown up well fathered by craftsman and monarch alike, and well loved and more than a little over-indulged by his princely foster-brothers. But a good boy for all that. There had been the devil to pay when he ran away from his privileged place at Aber on some mad quest after his father's murderer; the cloud of his loss still hung upon the court, and rescue still delayed.

But the holy woman of Aber, though she had taken no vows, kept her place constant as the crown of the mountain in her fixed station, abiding by her silent bargain with God, never looked reproach, never uttered complaint, never gave house-room to desire. Only when the boy's mother paid her rare visits, bringing back the old world in her fresh, fierce voice and brilliant, grieving eyes, did the blood quicken in Benedetta's cheeks to the stirring of God knew what memories.

She sat in the grass of the hollow hillside above the huts, with Gilleis beside her, watching the men cut fresh withies in the fold of the brook below. Adam Boteler, master-mason to the prince, was big and comely and fair, and at this distance there was no telling which of his thick locks were flaxen and which were white. Gilleis, as often as her eyes chanced to rest upon him, softened and smiled secretly, heavy with the weight of her tenderness. Second husbands find a place of their own in generous hearts, where they have room and to spare without ever infringing the rights of the first. And in any case, the two had been all but inseparable, when both were living, and lain in the same bed long before they had ever set eyes on Gilleis Otley. It was a question whether she always knew which of them she held in her arms, or made any distinction between them.

"Adam misses him as sorely as I do," said Gilleis. "Would ever you think that I could almost hope for a war? I never wished ill to any poor creature, English or Welsh, but now it shames me to feel my blood quicken when I hear of these disorders in the south, and of the earl of Pembroke collecting his malcontents together in Gwent. How else are we ever to get Harry back? The prince made a vow to go and fetch him in arms, but while there's truce how can he move?"

"And how will civil war in England help him?" said Benedetta, looking up over the embroidery she held in her lap. "He cannot take sides for earl or king unless someone first offers offence to his territories."

"Ah, but here are Pembroke's holdings so tangled into Wales that the king can hardly move against him without infringing land that's Welsh. That's cause enough to bring us in, if once these brawls turn into warfare. And let his hands be once loosed, and the prince will keep his word. That I know! But oh, Benedetta, it curdles my blood to find myself wishing for it. There are other women have sons, as dear to them as mine to me; how can I wish them sorrow to bring mine home?"

"God forbid," said Benedetta, "that ever I should preach patience to any man. But God may have other ways of bringing him home."

"What other ways? He'll take no ransom for him, he'll neither give nor sell. 'How can I put a price on a Talvace?' he says. Philip told us how he smiled as he said it. My child's growing a man," said Gilleis, grieving, "and I have not seen him for two years."

It was nearer four since Benedetta had seen him, but that she kept unsaid. What use was there in measuring love by days and months? One hour, one night, could contain so much of it that even if no second such miracle came before death, life would still have been filled to the brim.

"Ah, but I remember he did not visit you at all, that time," said Gilleis, reaching a remorseful hand to touch her sleeve. "He meant to, but then he pressed his promise so hard it would not bear any indulgence. The proud wretch! The poor lamb! 'If it were anyone else,' he said, 'but to that man not one scruple, not one farthing short of my debts.' "

"I know," said Benedetta, very still. "I had the prince to be his messenger to me. I know!"

" 'There is no price he has at his command,' says Isambard when Rhys went to him on the prince's errand, that last time, 'no price in money or aught else I would take for Harry Talvace. I'll name none and I'll consider none he may name, not in land, nor falcons, nor flesh.' And to think how he delights in using him! Oh, Benedetta, when he told me how he came there to him in his cell, and took away food and drink and light from him one by one, how he had him dragged to the rack—"

"But he never used it," said Benedetta suddenly and strangely, and raised the clear grey glance of her eyes to the rim of the grass-land, where the hawks wheeled in great, languid circles.

"—and always tempting and trying him, to get out of him where Harry was laid, until he tricked him into betraying the place. And then to tear my dear out of his grave . . . And to think the man who used the father so has the son in his hands, and can't be forced to give him up."

"Tell me," said Benedetta abruptly, folding her hands on her work, "what Harry told you of his captivity. Tell me the whole of it. The prince brought his message faithfully and delivered it well, but these things he never told me. I'm hungry for every crumb of him; give me to eat."

Gilleis drew close and poured out the long, strange story. The boy had stamped his own smouldering distrust and hatred into his mother's mind and found a ready soil there. Every test and tempta-tion imposed on him she recounted. All had been done in malice and mockery, all, even that astonishing act of releasing him to his prince's side for the duration of the bitter war of two years ago. He had surely willed him to break parole and never come back. To demoralise the boy would be to have the better of his race and his blood, and to destroy sire and son together at last.

"And where's it to end?" lamented Gilleis. "If he cannot break him to dishonour, how much longer will he keep his hands from worse? If he had not sent such a message back to Rhys I should have been afraid for Harry's very life, and even with his pledge to keep the child safe, how can I be content he'll do him no injury? I know he never yet broke faith, if he had no other virtures, but there's a first time for every recreant—"

"But he did so swear? To keep him safe?"

" 'Come when you will,' he said, 'fetch him away if you can. Till then I'll hold him safe for you.' But how can we know he'll keep his oath?"

"It would be late to change," said Benedetta, and turned again to her work. Her hands were steady, but her eyes looked far away, and into a sudden brightness that dazzled and blinded them.

The men were coming up from the brook, John the Fletcher shouldering the cut withies, Adam swinging the brushing-hooks. Every year there were repairs to be made to Saint Clydog's modest cell, but he would not have them build him a hut of stone. He, too, was too old for changes. Benedetta turned her head and looked along the hillside to where he sat nursing his beads and revolving his interminable thoughts, hardly more than a tussock of bleached grass himself in the tangled head of Moel Wnion. He looked as if he had been there since the beginning of time; and he would be there still when she was gone. Had he not told her so once, when the inner sight opened within him, and a voice cried out of him in the night and brought her running?

Llewelyn's messenger was re-saddling the horses, below at the cross. Adam came and dropped into the grass beside the women, sunburned and gentle and flushed with the work.

"We'd best be moving soon, lass. The sun's dropping lower. If you've had your women's talk out?" He knew what the subject would be, it had them all by the heart; they were bled pale from living with it. He slipped his arm round his wife's shoulders and drew her close; she leaned to him gladly and gratefully, but he felt the ache in her for the boy whose place he could not supply.

"Women's talk, is it?" said Benedetta. "We were on matters of state. I hear the earl marshal has withdrawn himself from the king's council, and taken a great number of other lords with him, out of discontent with the new order. Is it true there's even some fighting in the south?"

"Why, since de Burgh fell, and in such fashion," said Adam, "there's no man in England trusts the law to keep him from a like fate. If it could happen to Kent it can happen to Pembroke; small blame to him for placing himself out of the king's reach. Since he made himself the voice for all those who dared not speak out against the Poitevins themselves, the king may well be planning to clap him in hold and beat up charges against him as busily as he did with the other. They could lean on custom and feudal law once to preserve them from summary usage, but custom and law are being thrust out of court now. If the charters are to count for nothing, then a man must preserve his rights himself as best he can."

"But how did this dissension grow into violence? It seems they've gone past complaining, if the king has summoned the host to assemble at Gloucester, as Gilleis tells me. That looks like war in good earnest. What does he mean to do with his host from Gloucester?"

"Take it into Ireland, so they're saying, and strike at Marshall through his lands in Leinster. There was some talk that de Burgh's nephew there might be disaffected, too, for his uncle's sake, but there's no love lost between Marshall and de Burgh over there, and it seems likely Richard de Burgh will hold with the king. So Henry may find work for his muster nearer home, after all. The whole flare-up came from a small spark, but it's well ablaze now. And the issue's not so small, neither, if there's to be any law left. There was a manor belonging to Gilbert Basset of Wycombe that the king wanted to give to one of his own servants, and he disseised Basset of it without any proper process. 'By the king's will' is law enough, nowadays. Richard Marshall stood up for Basset, and before you could turn he was being warned Henry meant to seize and ruin him when next he came to attend the great council. So he never came. It might not be true, but there's de Burgh to show the way it's done, and even an earl has only one life to lose. He took himself into Pembroke, and mustered his confederacy after him. And now the king's going to all lengths to have extra watch kept everywhere, and calling in hostages from the barons of the march, like his father before him. And what with Basset having served once as constable at Devizes, and knowing the castle too well for comfort, there's an alarm that he means to take Hubert de Burgh out of captivity and have him away to join the earl marshal's allies in Wales. The king has his own guards in Devizes now, and I doubt the poor wretch will find his bed grow harder again, even if they leave him out of irons. They say the bishop of Winchester is busy persuading the king to make him Hubert's gaoler. Some say he's even urging his execution. I doubt the one would be as effective as the other. They ran to him for help when the mob was after Hubert, that first time. The bishop reproved them for interrupting his prayers, and closed the door on them."

"What if the king marches on the earl marshal's Welsh lands, what then? What will the prince do?"

Adam shook his head. "If he can forbear, I think he'd liefer. This government has never threatened him, and the peace, if it can hold, serves his turn well. But if the king breaks it, and the prince is pressed hard to take sides, he'll surely side with the earl marshal."

"Then the matter of Harry may solve itself," said Benedetta, "for surely Isambard will hold with the king. He has always been the king's true man, even when his heart and his judgement went the opposite way. John went far to sicken him, but he held by John to the death, and if John's son calls him on his fealty, he'll come in arms. He'll be on his way to Gloucester now."

"He would," said Adam ruefully, "if the king had summoned him. But with things the way they were there, I stake my head that's one place where the writ won't be served." He saw the pale, bright face quicken with wonder, and the grey eyes flare wide. "Did you not know he's out of grace? The king has forbidden him his presence and ordered him to remain at Parfois until he sees fit to recall him. A year ago, about this time, it befell. And no one ever thought to tell you?"

It was not so surprising, after all. They rode up here but two or three times a year, and there were other things to talk about when they came. Isambard had cost them grief enough in the old days to banish his name for ever between them, if young Harry had not renewed the ancient pain and called him back into their minds only too nearly and dearly.

Benedetta arose from the grass, gathering her thoughts like mustering armies behind the deep grey of her eyes.

"How did he come to this case?"

"As we heard it, it was just after de Burgh's fall, when King Henry came to Shrewsbury. Isambard went down in his state, and told the king in open audience he did very foully and ungratefully, and the earl of Kent was a loyal servant to him, not deserving of such usage. Gave it to him in his teeth, and would not abate one word for the king's anger."

"That rings true," said Benedetta, frowning back into her own memories. "That he would, and all the more for threatening. And he's down, is he? Disgraced and banished the court?"

"Till the king recalls him. But there are those who think he never will. And sure I am," said Adam, as they went three abreast down the hill to the waiting horses, "he'll hardly call him to the muster against Earl Richard, if he reckons him to be of de Burgh's party, for what with their common enmity against the Poitevins, though God knows it's almost all they have in common, Pembroke's party and de Burgh's are being lumped together as one. No, Isambard will sleep undisturbed in Parfois. The king daren't call on him to fulfil his dues, and daren't move against him."

"And Harry'll still lie and rot under close guard," said Gilleis bitterly. She heard Benedetta draw breath upon a stab of pain, and turned remorsefully to embrace her. "Ah, it's wicked in me to complain, when you love him, too, and miss him as I do. All his best years taken from us! Who will help him to his manhood there? Who'll delight in him and measure the strides he makes? And forgive him his mistakes, and love him for what he does well?"

"God will," said Benedetta, staring great-eyed against the far pallor of the sky, "if there's none other. And God can provide him another if he chooses."

All night she lay awake, and the dead came into her bed and lay with her. She held him in her arms, and he was both father and son, and doubly dear. She smoothed her cheek against his head, covering him with her cloak of crimson hair, silvered over now with the dust of time; and the turmoil within her and the calm without fought out the long hours of the dark with words that had no voice but silence. My heart, my love, my little one, my sweet friend. Is it time? Has the world a use for me, after all? Has the child a use for me? Has God a use for me? Have I been keeping faith with him all this time that I lay here still, or have I been breaking faith? My soul, my darling, what must I do? Once I kneeled to him, kissed his feet, prayed him for your life, and was denied. There was no price I had to offer him that could buy you back, no way but to take you by force, and so I took you. But how if I am richer now? How if I can offer him a ransom for the child that even he will not refuse? And how if I pray him this once more, and how if I am heard? Will you lend me your countenance and approval, or will you turn from me? My love, my heart, I am in darkness. Light me! I know no other lantern but you.

She had held him but once in life like this, on the night before he died. It had taken so little prompting to induce the old chaplain to remind his lord how it had always been his custom to allow condemned men their chosen indulgence before they died, and Isambard in open hall had pledged himself to grant anything short of liberty. Still she could see that stricken, dreadful mask with which he had received the trembling answer: "My lord, he asks—May God forgive him!—he asks for Madonna Benedetta to be his bedfellow." He had pledged himself and he could not withdraw; and smiling, smiling she had gone from him, slowly, careful that he should know how she gloried in his anguish and impotence. "It touches your honour. What am I beside the sacredness of your word?"

Eye to eye with him now above her darling's sleep, she stood him off unsmiling. When did I ever deceive you until then? I told you from the first, when you would have me come with you to Parfois, that my love was given once for all, though he that had it neither loved nor desired me, nor ever would. But still you would have me, all that was left of me, even on those terms. And I came, and I kept my bargain with you. "Until death or he call me from you," I said, "or you discard me." And death and Harry called me from you with one voice, and then you thought you understood all. Fool, could you but have heard the first word I had for him when he reached his hands to me! "She's safe, she's well, she sends you her heart's love." Could you but have seen in what manner of fellowship we passed that night, the only night ever I had my love in my arms! How I talked to him of Gilleis and of his child that would be born, and promised him that he should not be broken, that death was in God's gift, not in yours.

Then, as now, Harry had slept while she watched out the hours, loving and sinless; and in the morning she had kissed him awake to make himself fine for death. What did Gilleis know, or Adam, or any other living creature, of that inexpressible union? But God knew, and God could rip time apart and give the hour back to her, to hold her heart steady while she found her way. Where were the slender, nimble bones now, the intrepid hands, the swart, stubborn face? Ravished from the secret grave, tumbled, perhaps, down the Severn a second time to end that vengeance, as Adam bitterly believed. Yet not lost; even this lesser part of him God might yet restore her.

When the first softening of the darkness came before dawn she rose from her sleepless bed and went up to the crest of the hill, where the wind was waking and the moan of the sea came up to her, the heave and fall of the incoming tide, like great sighs from a long-remembered grief, grown still and tranquil at last after great anguish. She loosed her long hair about her, and paced out the remaining hours of the night like a questing hound in the colourless grass, silent and intent and charged, waiting for the sign. And in the dawn she came down from the hill, with a calm upon her like the finished stone, which is shaped and perfected and must not be touched again, for awe of its absolute integrity.

John the Fletcher, squat and bowed and brown as an oak, was rolling up his bedding from across her threshold. She had stepped over him in the night and he had never stirred, and for that he was angry with himself and her. What was the use of a watchdog, if she could evade his guard so easily?

"So you're there, are you?" he said gruffly, stepping out of the doorway to let her go by. "What ailed you to go gallivanting about in the night? If you wanted aught you should have sent me on your errand. What else am I for?"

"For comfort and company to me, and much more besides. I wanted nothing but air and quiet, and what was there to harm me there on the hill?"

"And no shoes on your feet against the chill of the dew," he said crossly, and brought the thonged leather shoes and made her put them on, warming her feet in his calloused palms before he shut their whiteness up from sight. "Do you want to be laid sick, and only me for nurse?"

"I could well do worse, John."

He had nursed her once, long ago, how tenderly and constantly, drawing her back half-unwilling from the door-sill of death. She remembered the hard hands cradling her head, and wiping away the apprentice tears of this second birth. And a pitcher of milk warm from the cow, she remembered that, and a countrywoman with dark gold hair and gentle eyes; dead now, so they said, having first stamped a child in her own true image. Benedetta felt the old years gathering about her like close acquaintances, unchanged and unforgotten. This new day in which she moved was all the days of her life, like the instant of death in a heart at peace.

"But I have an errand for you now," she said, putting out her hand and touching his grey, bushy hair as he latched her shoes.

"There's a letter I must write and send. Will you ride with it, when you've broken your fast?"

"I never yet knew you to remember everything you had to tell Mistress Boteler when she came up," he said tolerantly. "I suppose there's threads you should have asked for, and had so much else to say you never called it to mind. Yes, I'll ride. You write your letter."

"It's not to Gilleis this time, John, it's a longer ride I had in mind for you. But leave me write it first, and I'll tell you."

He gave her a long, sharp look for that, but asked her nothing more then. There was nothing she could ask of him he would not give her, even his silence and absence if she willed it so. He left her alone with the newly-pointed pen he kept fine for her, and a cleaned parchment from the chest, and she wrote with deliberation, pondering the words. By the time she had finished, and sealed the roll closely and carefully, he was waiting for her with milk and new bread, and honey from the heather bees. He had three hives in a sheltered place in a hollow below, and nursed his swarms through the winter lovingly so that Benedetta should not want for sweets.

"Am I to saddle up now? I see you've done your writing."

"You'll need food with you," she said, coming gently to the heart of it. "And money for your lodging on the way. I told you it's a long ride."

He was stiffening already with doubt and wariness. "Where is it you'd have me go?"

"To Parfois, John, to my lord Isambard."

It was out. She saw the knotty hands shut into fists at his sides, and the gleam of old remembrance spring like flame in his sharp eyes. He had forgotten nothing and forgiven nothing. Whoever forgave, John never would. Once his life had been wantonly threatened, and she had retrieved it, but it was not that he saw, sharp and clear after years, at the mention of Isambard's name. He saw the Severn in turgid brown flood below the Long Mountain, and the dead man and the living woman, bound together breast to naked breast, rolled under in the deep currents and dragged down towards Breidden, wound in the streaming weed of her long red hair.

"Have you no errand I can do for you in hell?" he said. "There's cleaner company there."

"But Harry's in Parfois, John," she said mildly. "Will you go?"

"Ah, I thought that was what you had in your mind. You know well I'll go wherever you send me, but not gladly, not there," said John grimly. "For you'll get nothing for your pleading. Wait and let the prince fetch him away with the sword. I'd liefer not see you stoop to beg and be refused."

"But how if I am not refused? What right have I, John, to hold back from trying, when it may be he'll give me the boy, for all you say?"

"Others have asked. Others have pleaded and offered ransom, and I know not what, and never a word back but mockery. Why should you submit yourself to the same usage?"

"Why should I spare myself the same usage? Who am I, that I should go free? Ah, John," she said in a sudden soft cry, "bear with me. I do only what I must."

"I'll go," he said resignedly. At worst she would not have to see Ralf Isambard's triumph. If he could bring her back nothing but a refusal, at least he could spare her the cruellest of it. "God he knows I'd rather cut his throat than speak him fair, but what you bid me do I'll do, and God spare you from any pain of my giving. Let me have your letter then. What am I to do when I get to Parfois?'

"Tell them at the lower guard that you ask admittance to my lord Isambard, with a message from Benedetta Foscari. And to prove that you do truly come from me," she said, "you will take him this."

She stripped the ring from the little finger of her left hand. Often she had wondered why she had kept it, that single opal in its circlet of gold. It was the only thing he had left on her, when he stripped her and had her flung into the river, so small a thing neither she nor he had thought of it, or she would surely have tossed it at his feet. He had given it to her in Paris, before ever they crossed the sea together on their way to Parfois, he with his heart set on her, she with hers full of Harry Talvace.

"He'll know that," she said, "past doubting."

He took it in his brown, horny palm, and held it gingerly, as though it might burn him, or break in his grasp.

"And if he have me killed on sight?" he said reasonably.

"If he receives you as a messenger he'll not harm you. For good or evil, he was always punctilious. Once he lets you in your life will be sacred. He'd kill anyone who touched you or offered you offence."

"And if I speed?" he said.

"Then give him my letter and bring me back his reply, whether he write it or speak it. And God go with you, John, and prosper my intent."

"Amen!" growled John, but without much faith.

When he had made his preparations, she followed him out and watched him buckle on saddlebags and cloak. Saint Clydog beneath the crucifix never turned his ancient head, but she felt that he knew already what was afoot, and would speak his mind about it when it suited him.

"John—!" She held him by the stirrup-leather when he would have drawn away. "You're not angry with me?"

He looked down at her, and through the bushy beard she saw the smile tremulous on his mouth for love of her.

"Never be angry with me," she said like a child. "If I had not you, what should I do?"

"God love you!" said John, shaken, and his hand pushed back her hood and stroked clumsily over the mane of her hair. "My little lass!" he said, and pulled away from her and set spurs to his horse down the hill.

When the prior of Strata Marcella came back from Prime, somewhat after seven in the morning, it was to find one of the hospitaller's assistants waiting anxiously at the door of his chamber, to ask audience for an importunate guest.

"He slept here the night, Father, and had nothing further then to ask of us. But this morning he came to me and begged that you would see him on a grave matter. He says there's life and death in it."

"What manner of man is he?" asked the prior, frowning.

"A manservant, Father, and trusty. We have provided him a roof before. He is servant of that lady who brought the body of Master Talvace to rest here. They call him John the Fletcher."

"Bid him come," said the prior. For what touched the affairs of Madonna Benedetta, however she chose to hide herself from sight and memory in a cranny of the north Welsh hills, touched Llewelyn's great princedom and was knotted close with his generous patronage of the Cistercian order on this side of Severn. He could not afford to turn away any man of hers.

John the Fletcher came into the cool, stony cell, and went on his knees to kiss the prior's hand. The thin fingers blessed him.

"My son, you have something to ask of me. I am listening."

John got to his feet, square and knotty and brown like the bole of a tree, a growth out of the soil of Flintshire. He held Benedetta's letter before him in both hands, his fingers tight on the coil of parchment.

"Father, this is a story I must tell my own way, for I need your help, and I need that you should know the whole of it. Three days ago my mistress wrote this letter, and bade me take it, with her ring to be my warrant, to Ralf Isambard of Parfois, and there to deliver it into his own hands, and bring back his answer. Father, it is well known to you that this man holds prisoner young Harry Talvace, who is foster-son to Prince Llewelyn, and dear, more than dear, to my mistress. It was she brought him safe out of England when he was but a child new-born, and his mother with him. I know, for I was her man on that journey as I've been her man ever since, and shall be as long as I live. Father, what was I to think when she sent me with a letter to Isambard?"

The prior pondered for a moment what seemed to him a plain question, and hardly likely to account for the darkness in the weathered face before him.

"I suppose that Madonna Benedetta desired to make her own plea for the release of the boy, trusting to move a heart that once set a high value on any wish of hers. I suppose that she hoped to win him where others with ransoms had failed."

"And that seems to you a reasonable hope, Father?"

"It is not *likely*. But it is not unreasonable. There is nothing to be lost by the attempt."

"Then I am justified so far," said John grimly, "for so I thought also, and I took the letter and rode, thinking no ill though I expected little good. Sure I was she would be refused, and in some cruel fashion as the devil lent him wit, who has always lent him more than enough. And yet there was still the small corner of hope that he might be moved. All these years he's had no word of her, I doubt he knows certainly whether she's living or dead. To hold her ring in his hand again, suddenly, without warning, I thought it might shake even a stone. Yet consider, Father, how he used her before. What, give her what she wanted, he who cast her living into Severn there and sent her down with Master Harry bound in her arms, to rot with him unburied? No! Rather if he knew of a thing she still wanted, of a thing she would plead for, it would be joy to him to use it for her hurt and shame. Why did I ever trust her? Why did I believe it? Yet she never lied to me. Take the letter, she said, and bring me the answer. It was I who took the text as read, and never asked her what I was carrying."

"It was your duty so to do," said the prior sternly. "It is still your duty."

"My duty as a servant. But I am a man, too. I was a man first. I do my duty by her, being her servant, as well as I may. But I love her, being a man, more than my life or my duty. She covered me with her cloak and kept me man alive—man, not servant! Shall I let her go to her death to keep my own record virgin?"

"You have read the letter!" said the prior, rising in indignation.

"Father, if I could read I should have no need of you. I am not asking you to tell me what to do." He came a step closer, holding the parchment before him. "Father, in the night I dreamed of her. I was by the Severn in flood, brown and full and fast it was, and the timbers of the stage creaking and straining in the run of it. Many a night I've seen it in my sleep, but never so clear. And like that day, she came down the current pale and naked, with a man in her arms, and like that day I went in and drew them ashore. But this time the man stood up from between my hands as I unbound him, and went from us alive and hale, and I saw it was the young one, the boy she wills to set free. And this time she lay in my arms, and I breathed my breath into her mouth, and warmed her in my bosom, and she never moved again. I held her on my heart dead, Father. And when I woke I knew it was God sent me the dream, and it was her death I was carrying, under her own seal."

The hoarse voice had stilled and stilled to a husky whisper; the words came slowly, too laden with his dread and faith for passion to find any room in them. At the end of it he lifted his shaggy head and looked the prior in the face, advancing the rolled parchment on his hands like an offering.

"Father, read it to me. I must know what she does, that I may know what I am to do."

The prior drew back a step in haste to avoid the touch. "I cannot violate your lady's seal, man. What is it you are asking me to do?"

"There is no need. I have parted the seal. I can mend it again. A fine knife and a candle-flame is all I need."

"You have opened it? What treason is this towards your mistress? What have you done?"

He knew that he cast his breath into the wind; as well ask a tree knotted into the roots of the mountains to suffer a sense of guilt for growing after its urgent and laborious nature. And who was he, in the face of such an intensity of love and fear, to herd all issues into the compartments of social usage? It was the unlettered man who had the eloquence now; it might be he who saw the truth plainest.

"I have done what I must. I would not ask it of you. For what I've done I'll answer to God in the day of judgement, and if he wills to damn my soul for it I'll never murmur, so long as hers stays in her dear body until God please to come to her quietly and take it to himself. Should I come to you, Father, with anything that made me ashamed? What do I matter? What's honour to me? My honour is to keep her from harm and from grief. I have no other; I want none."

The prior had half-stretched out his hand towards the letter, only to hesitate and draw back again.

"Father, read it to me. I could have gone to one of your novices with it, but I came to you because I want the blessing of God on my unfaithfulness that I see as faithfulness. I have not concealed anything. I want no forgiveness. Only tell me what she has written to him."

"In the name of God," said the prior, and laid hold of it strongly and unrolled it between his hands.

The silence was long and heavy, weighted with the unbearable burden of the man's waiting, agonised eyes. By the silence he knew all but the words she had used, and knowing her as he knew her, he could guess even at those. Nevertheless, the prior began to read, in a low and level voice:

"To the most noble and puissant Ralf Isambard, lord of Mormesnil, Erington, Fleace and Parfois, these:

"My lord, you are in possession of the person of Harry Talvace, son of that Harry Talvace whom doubtless you remember all the better for having the print of him constantly before you. I am in possession of the body and life of Benedetta Foscari, sometime well known to you. As to the body, it is not now so rare a property that I should think it of any great value to you. As to the life, if you do set any value on it, as once you gave me dear cause to suppose you did, it is still intact to be disposed of at my will. If you are pleased to consider the exchange of your prisoner for mine, I will close with you on those terms. And on the exchange I place no conditions, except that all debts and grudges whatsoever you may hold against Harry Talvace shall be held to be perpetually discharged, and he set at liberty, with horse and habit and all that is his. Of my person and my life, if you accept them, you may dispose as you please. Send me back your word, aye or no, and if it be aye, I will come at once to Parfois.

"In the hope and expectation, therefore, that I shall shortly see you face to face, I spare to use many compliments, adding to these only the prayer that your lordship may live long enough and be of a gentle enough mind to open your gates to me again after many years.

"By the hand of my beloved and trusted John the Fletcher, this tenth day of August, 1233.

"Benedetta Foscari."

The thread ran on unbroken to the end, though the low voice thinned with realisation at "As to the life," and when he reached the "beloved and trusted" John put up his gnarled hands helplessly in an aimless gesture of hurt and longing, and twisted his fingers in his beard. When it was done, and the silence had lasted a moment unbroken, the sounds of the world came in faintly, the chanting of the first mass, a scattered bawling of sheep from the river meadows, a shrill arguing of birds.

"Did I not tell you?" said John thickly, through the knotted anguish in his throat. "She is giving her life away, to one that used her as he used her, giving herself back to him to be stripped and shamed and drowned again, to get the boy free. Ah, mistress, was it right to use me so! Was it fair?"

"God sort all!" said the prior in a shaken whisper, and the parchment trembled in his hands. "You will not deliver the letter? Such a bargain must not be made."

"God sort all, but under him I'll do what I can." He held out his hand, stonily calm now that he knew the worst of it. For a moment his heart had drawn him to turn his horse and ride back in anger and horror, to confront her and reproach her for using him so ill. But that was already past. There were other ways of dealing, now that he knew. "Give it back to me, Father. You've done your part, and I thank you. The rest is for me to do."

"But you will not deliver it?" The prior watched him roll it up carefully, handling with bitter delicacy the slit seal he had yet to repair.

To that he answered nothing, only hid the letter in the breast of his cotte, and drew back with soft, sidelong steps towards the door. His eyes were bright and hard over the pain; he had no more need of anyone here.

"Pray for us, Father," he said from the doorway. "Pray for us all, that we come out of this without scathe."

Chapter Four

Parfois: *August* 1233

*I*sambard came down from the crest of the Long Mountain refreshed and in good humour after his ride, his iron-grey hair uncovered to the sun and the wind, half a dozen of the young gentlemen of his retinue cantering gaily at his back. At the foot of the rising road that climbed the ramp to Parfois the chestnut horse, eased and happy and in no hurry to go back to his stall, dropped into a gentle amble; and Isambard loosed the rein low on his neck and let him have his way. They were in high content with each other; it galled Harry, no doubt, to see his Barbarossa go so blithely under his enemy, but he contrived to contain his chagrin, and even to utter an occasional formal word of thanks for the beast's excellent condition and the care that had been taken of him. Stiff-lipped and stiff-necked, but roundly and steadily, as became a man, and looking his captor straight in the eye as he paid his disagreeable dues.

They came to the place where the track narrowed and the trees closed in, hiding the rocky drop on the left side, the rising slope of broken grass on the right. The one completed tower of the lower guard came into sight, and the piled building materials stacked about it, undressed stone, timbers, laths, scaffolding, cords and hurdles and the glaring white of lime, lining the path for twenty yards down the ramp. The second of the old towers had already been pulled down, and the rubble and stone of its falling waited to be cleared away. The foundation plan of the new one which was to replace it was staked out with thin white cords opposite its finished fellow. They had had to cut down to the bedrock to make a firm enough base for such a weight so near the edge of the steep slope. The light of mid-morning danced and glared from the stripped, pale sandstone.

Isambard remembered another site cleared and pegged out for building, and beside the great open scar the first cartloads of stone from the distant quarry in Bryn, fresh from their voyage up the Severn, dove-grey with overtones of gold, with all that splendour of beauty sealed-up and safe within it, all those shapes of worship and wonder. He never saw dressed stone lying ready but he thought of the great leaves uncurling in Master Harry's church, upholding on their taut, triumphant fronds the vault of heaven and all the world to come.

"My lord," said young Thomas Blount, assiduous at his elbow, "here's the warden watching for you. I think there's some messenger come; that horse is surely none of ours. It looks like a mountain pony."

Isambard withdrew his eyes from the inward vision that beckoned him so often since the boy's coming, and looked ahead to see the guard at the tower holding a shaggy cob, brown and short and powerful, and in the act of alighting from it a brown, short, powerful man, even a little like his beast in the thickness of his bristly, greying beard and curly hair. Bright, alert eyes, narrowed against the sun, stared at him from under bushy brows. A stab of recollection pierced and eluded him; he could not recall that this stocky countryman had or could have anything to do with him, and yet the prick at his heart set him staring back into the past, and would not be discounted.

"My lord," said the warden, respectful at his stirrup, "here's a fellow says he comes with a letter for you from one you used to know well. But he'll give no name, and he'll hand over the letter to no one but you. He says he has a token will satisfy you. Will you be pleased to speak with him?"

Isambard walked the chestnut horse slowly forward, and looked down long and thoughtfully at the man who stood before him waiting without reverence or speech. The narrowed eyes stared back at him impenetrably, and gave no sign.

"Do I not know you, fellow?"

"That's not for me to say, my lord. But I know you," said John the Fletcher.

The voice did its part. Twin flames kindled in Isambard's eyes and burned up into red. There was no recognition yet, only the knowledge that time had turned, and sent the past to meet him at his own gate. He freed his right foot from the stirrup, and in a rush of dutiful zeal Thomas was down from the saddle and holding the other one for him as he dismounted. He was even more devoted in his services of late, always present, always ready, always near, so near that hardly a word escaped his pricked ears if he had his way.

Isambard brushed him off with a quick frown, never taking his eyes from the messenger's lined face.

"Were you not my man once?"

"Body and soul, my lord. More yours than the horse you're riding."

That brought a more perceptible smile. Isambard let his lean fingers caress the chestnut's burnished neck, but his eyes went on searching behind the surly face and the opaque stare for the lost image. He was a long step nearer; the fellow knew Harry Talvace's horse, and did not fear to declare his knowledge.

"You say you have a token I shall know. Let me see it."

John reached into his breast and brought out the ring. The small gold circlet, so small that even she had had to wear it on her little finger, rocked gently in the seamed hand, and the heavy opal took the light and devoured it, burning into a sullen, blue-veiled glow.

Isambard had put out his hand to take it up before he saw it clearly enough for recognition, and the shiver that passed through the extended fingers and checked them on the air was visible to them all, and sent a convulsion of wonder and wariness through them no less. All eyes flashed from the token to Isambard's face, dreading his lightnings and sharp with anxiety to avoid them in time. He was always incalculable, and here they were lost. He hung in such a stillness that they did not know what might blaze out of it. They held their breath, shifting uneasily in the agony of waiting, and he was no more aware of them than he was of the breeze that ruffled his hair. Even his face was still as death, but without the tranquillity of death, still with the potentialities of pain and rage and love and hatred quick in the charged lines of it, and only God knew what in ambush under the great arched eyelids.

"Do you know your own gifts again, my lord?" said John the Fletcher.

Yes, he knew them now, both gifts, the ring and the man. Eighteen years is a long time; it lowers a man's stature, hobbles his gait, whitens his hair, corrodes his face, but leaves him still that look in the eye that spells his hatred plain, and that acid in the heart that burns through into the tongue.

Isambard looked back into a well of memories. This was the fellow she had snatched from the dog's jaws and asked of him in Paris, the same who vanished with her into Wales at the end of it, and helped her to get Gilleis and the child safe to Llewelyn's care. And he it was who had loosed the shot that robbed the Gascon executioner of his prey. Strange how the images came back, those that mattered least springing to life most readily and clearly, with every line and colour restored. The Gascon he could recall now perfectly, a thin, elegant fellow who looked like a well-born prelate, and prided himself on knowing how to disembowel a man and still leave him a voice to lament. The very warders who had kept Master Harry in his last captivity had left their images not far beneath the surface of memory, ready to quicken at a touch. Only she withdrew herself, shadowy and remote. He knew every line of her, yet the eyes of his mind peered and strained after her in vain; she would not show herself.

The arrested hand continued its broken gesture, took up the ring and held it delicately.

"I am satisfied," he said, and his voice was low and mild.

"Then give me audience in private to deliver my lady's letter."

"You may follow us up to the church."

Not into the wards, not yet. Harry Talvace might be abroad at this hour, at exercise with the youngsters, or out in the sun before the tracing-house with his tools and his stone. Whatever this trespasser from the past might be bringing, it would be folly to let the boy see him too soon.

"Let him come after us," said Isambard to the warden, and turned to remount Barbarossa; and there was Thomas in devoted haste at the stirrup, his fresh blue eyes, that could muster so blankly innocent a stare, still a little too bright with the curiosity the unknown lady of the ring had roused in him. Let him look sidelong under his lashes as attentively as he would, he'd get no more now; his lord's face was closed and calm. He had broken the tension with finger and thumb as he took up the ring, and flicked the shards of the incident away from him with authority; none the less, Thomas saw him stow away the ring in the breast of his cotte, and found a certain interest in the manner in which he did it.

They trotted up the ramp, and out on to the grassy plateau where the church stood; and there Isambard dismissed his companions.

The sun was high, the shadows raven and thin beneath the crenellated wall of Parfois, the roofs that seemed dull black under cloud were now glowing copper. In the church, when Isambard thrust open the wicket in the great west door and led the way into the porch, the direct rays of the sun lay almost vertically through the windows, and spilled jewels down the walls beneath; and all the great inverted ship of the nave, to the remotest boss at the end of the roof-rib, was full of reflected light. The air quivered with it, like the last almost soundless echo of a note of music. Radiance and space seemed to lift their steps from the stones and set them afloat towards the vault.

"Give me her letter," said Isambard.

He took the roll and broke the seal without hesitation, and John breathed again, the first leap already safely passed. He watched the dark face for a moment, until the rainbow light beyond the motionless head shimmered with the intensity of his stare, and the haggard's profile stark against it grew black by contrast.

Isambard had read but a few lines when he swung abruptly on his heel and walked with the parchment the length of the nave. There he stood with his back turned, and read to the end in silence, and even then remained still for a long time. There was no sound at all, only the trembling of the living light, that seemed to sing although it was voiceless. Once John heard the heavy iron latch of the wicket relax and shift in its socket, as though the door had been moved by the touch of a hand or the weight of a leaning body; but it was a sound so small that he would not have heard it at all but for the intense hush within, and he paid no heed to it then, and forgot it afterwards.

Even if Isambard had not known the hand so well, the broad, bold hand as resolute as a man's, the very wording would have been enough to call her back to him. The unendurable memories crowded in after her; her face burned clear to him at last, wide-set eyes and noble bones, the passionate and adventurous mouth, the great cloak of dark-red hair. Eighteen years! What had time made of her now?

He turned and came back, his long, soft tread quiet on the stones. No triumph in his face, no shame, no grief, nothing; only the faint curl of the long lips, and the windows of the hollow eyes shuttered.

"Say to your lady that her offer is accepted. Say to her: Yes, come."

"That's all your answer, my lord?"

"She'll need no more. And in exchange for her token, take her this." It was the ruby from his own finger, so seldom disturbed from its place that he had some ado to get it over the knuckle, and it left a pale band about the lean brown flesh when he had succeeded in removing it. "She'll know it," he said, looking down at his hand with a dark smile. "She'll need no more words."

"My lord, since you accept her terms—"

His head came up sharply at that, fire looked out of his eyes again for a moment. "You know the content, do you?"

"She trusted me," said John, abrupt and harsh, twisting the knife in his own wound.

"Aye, so she might. I remember she had good reason. Well?"

"Since you accept her terms, I am bold to ask you a favour she did not ask for herself. You know you can trust her word as she trusts yours. If you mean to give her the boy, give him now. Let him come back with me, and give her the joy of seeing him alive and well before she yields herself up to you in this place."

"No," said Isambard at once. "That I can't do."

"You know well she'll keep her bargain."

"I do know it. But the boy is another matter. Do you think he would let such a bargain stand, between her and me, and he with no say in it? You would find he would have the last and the loudest say," said Isambard dryly. "I know him. He has but to set eyes on you here, and to be told: Go, go with him, you're free. Do you think he would not know who had bought him out of hold? And do you think he'd ever rest until he knew on what terms?"

John stood open-mouthed, knocked out of words. It was no more than the truth, and he should have known it for himself. There would be no getting Harry safe out of Parfois that way. If this failed, all failed, and he was left without excuse or recourse but to let her surrender herself or to lie to her and leave Harry undelivered. If once he could have got the boy away to Llewelyn's care he had trusted to the prince's power to prevent Benedetta from keeping so bad a bargain. There would have been argument enough and accusations of bad faith. What did that matter? It was he, and he only, who could be condemned as the faith-breaker, equally treacherous to them all; and the rest would have been compounded somehow by ransom, by arbitration, by reference to the truce commission, by any means short of giving up the recovered fosterling. He had foreseen every difficulty but this simplest difficulty of all. Harry would never suffer it.

"He's but a boy," he said, arguing strenuously against his own heart. "He need not be told the truth, however hard he may question."

"And do you think, fool, you would ever get him over the bridge until he had an answer that satisfied him? Or stir him a step afterwards? He would not budge. No, he stays here until she comes to set him free. Go, deliver my answer to her."

The audience was over; no king could have made it more royally clear.

"Will you enter Parfois and refresh yourself and your beast before you ride?" he asked. "I could not bid you in until Harry was put well out of your way, but he'll be safe out of sight before now."

"I ate my last at your table many years gone, my lord. I want no roof of yours over me, and no bread of yours in my mouth."

"As you will," said Isambard with a shrug and a sigh. "Then I forbear from offering you other rewards I see you would cast back in my teeth. And my thanks, I fear, you will regard too lightly to make them worth tendering. Nevertheless, I thank you."

It was over. There was no more to be gained here. John withdrew from him into the shadow of the porch, and left the lord of Parfois standing tall and still and black in the nave of his church with the singing air bright about him, a carillon of colours tremulous as sunlit water, or the vibration of wings in flight. The figure in the midst might have been of stone. The same head in stone held up the voussoirs of the doorway beside him as he emerged into the warmth of the noonday meadow. Of the two images the one Master Harry had made was the more eloquent; and even after eighteen years of weathering it was questionable if it could match the man within for hardness.

Fifty yards away in the meadow Thomas Blount strolled with an arm over the saddle of the grazing cob, his girlish face as serene and blank as the summer sky.

Aelis flew to meet him as he came in through the little gate of the paddock. She had been milking, and had her skirt kilted up to her knees, and her hair coiled on her head to be out of her way.

"Did you see him? Is he well?" She caught at the cob's bridle and led him towards the undercroft; better not to show him in the open field or about the clearing, for fear somebody should see and recognise him. Travellers were few along their riverside path, but Parfois was near and perilous.

John shook his head glumly. "No, not a glimpse. Leave me go in to your father, lass, I must talk to him. No, I got nothing. He isn't let out of the wards, and I wasn't let in. Or not until they'd smoothed him away out of reach somewhere."

"But you did talk of him? John," she said, clutching at his arm, "it's true he's alive, isn't it? That's something we can cling to?"

Was he even sure of that? Could a man be sure of anything he had not seen and touched and heard with his own good senses? But he soothed her quickly: "He's alive. And well, too, by all accounts."

"But you could not get him free," she said with conviction, and bit fiercely on what could hardly be called a disappointment, since she had expected little else.

"No, we've still to wait a little while, my lass."

What could he tell her? He did not even know himself what was to be done next. The one thing certain was that he would not go back to Benedetta at Aber and deliver the ring and the message, and let her keep her terms. Whatever happened, she should never fall into Isambard's hands again. He could go back and lie to her, tell her her offer had been refused, but that would be to leave Harry unransomed and uncomforted still. And besides, he found himself afraid of facing her with the lie. She had known him so long that he was crystal to her; she might see the falsehood rising black and alien in his throat, and reject it as he uttered it. She might even see from the hang-dog look of him that he had betrayed her, violated her letter and done everything counter to her will. A life without her trust was no life. He could not go back to her empty-handed. If there was another way he must find it. If he prayed for it, would God hear prayers from one so lost in treasons and disloyalties? He might hear the girl, might even speak through her. She at least was clean of all stain.

"But what happened?" she persisted, blue eyes brilliant in her roused and resolute face. "What did they say to you?"

"Come in to your father, girl, and I'll tell you."

They stabled the cob, and went in to Robert in the house, and John told them the whole of it.

"You'll not go back with that for a word," said Robert.

"I'd die first. There's no one else but the handful of us here knows she's even tried to buy him. I would have turned back and told her what I'd done, and refused her errand, if I had not thought I might win him to let the boy go on trust. She would have wanted to pay the score when she knew, but I meant to make sure the prince had the ordering of it before then. But I was the world's fool to think it could be done so. He was right: Harry would never have let any of us take his load from him. Even if I'd tricked him into coming home with me, he'd have been off back as soon as he heard the truth. And I doubt now whether the prince would have stood in his way. I doubt he'd have kissed him and sent him off with his blessing. So we're back where we were before. I've played her false," he said bitterly, "that's the only change. And for nothing! For nothing gained!"

"What will you do?" asked Robert, low-voiced.

"Do I know? If God would but nudge my elbow and show me a way. There must be one, if we could but find it."

The girl sat crouched on the floor with her chin in her palms and her eyes flaring wide, and who could tell what she was thinking? Maybe she would have sold Madonna Benedetta ten times over to

win Harry out of captivity. Maybe she had the contempt of most
women for the fooleries of honour, that would yield up a man's life
for a scruple, and compel an obstinate boy to return to durance
voluntarily rather than enjoy his freedom and accept the slur of
faith-breaking with it. But she had taken the boy to her heart, and
his values and his virtues with him, and more than likely his faults,
too. No, she would never blame him. She accepted that he had done
what he must. Her mind was moving upon other paths.

"If the old lord died," she said suddenly, "we should have no
need to trouble any more."

She did not know what she had said. The silence, that was like
the silence after a thunderclap to John, had no terrible significance
for her. She went wistfully along the same path.

"No one else there would care to keep him; your prince could
buy him out of prison with no more sweat than a little bargaining.
It's the old man keeps him just to plague him. If the son had the
disposing of him, you'd see he'd let him go lightly enough. He never
knew Master Harry, and he knows nothing of Harry, either. What's
a Talvace to him? He'd sell him gladly, for the sake of good will."

She lifted her head and looked up at John with wide eyes innocent
of any dark intent, seeing no distortion in the reflected understanding which stared back at her.

"You told us the king wants no more enemies; he has enough.
And the king's new men have no call to go looking for any, now so
many lords are up in arms against them. The lord Isambard's son
is one of the king's men. He stands to lose much if his enemies gain
allies in Wales. He'd *give* Harry to Prince Llewelyn, to keep him
content and this border quiet."

Out of the mouths of maids and little children the oracles come.
He sat with face half-turned away from her, to hide the unbearable
spark of hope and intent that burned up behind his eyes and made
a core of molten heat in his mind. She was right; she had put her
finger on the only pathway, and pointed where it led. William
Isambard held office now, was hand in glove with des Rivaulx, and
close, close in his counsels; he stood to fall with the Poitevins if they
fell. He had favour and power and place to lose. If he inherited here,
his interest would be to keep the prince of Aberffraw from entering
into the earl marshal's confederacy, and so greatly strengthening

des Rivaulx's enemies. Llewelyn would only have to ask, and he would get his foster-son back unharmed. At a price or as a gift, what did it matter? William would be glad to find he had such a gift in his power to make, and if he put a price on him for form's sake it would be a nominal one, the better to engage Llewelyn's gratitude and stay his hand from any inimical action.

From all accounts there was no love lost between father and son, either. William had waited a long time for his inheritance. He might be only too happy if the old man could be hurried out of the world.

"That's very like," said Robert ruefully, "but he won't die just for our asking. He owes a death to a good many folks, besides the death he owes to God. But I doubt we must wait for it to come in its own good time."

But need they? Need they? These hands had loosed the shaft that took Master Harry out of the world before the hangman could touch him. They had said in the villages that it was God who took him, and the arrow had come from somewhere far higher than the top of the church tower. Might not God have another use yet for the same hands and the same skill? It would take him a few days to make ready, to work out place and time. And Robert and Aelis must know nothing. What need was there for them to be involved? If the thing went well, the secret was safer with one than with three; and if it went awry, better only one should suffer the consequences.

And he had been alone with him in the church that day, and had not recognised the opportunity when it leaned to his hand. The erect back turned, the attendants all dismissed, the way open to him to leave after the act; and yet the dagger in his belt had not started and loosened to summon his hand, or pricked the blind flesh that stood inert and let the hour go by. It would never again be so easy to do the deed and withdraw alive. What did that matter? He had relinquished his claim on life, if she needed his death.

"Ah, I know," said Aelis, sighing. "It's mortal sin even to think of such things. I was just seeing, all in a moment, how simple everything would be if he died."

He was waiting for another utterance that would light his way, but God spoke no more by her. The burden came down upon his own shoulders, and he let it lie, knowing it was not more than he could bear. Mortal sin, she said, to think of it. Much worse to do it.

He had let go the charge of his own life, he sent his own soul after it, not in defiance, but in resignation and humility. Well that one man should be damned, if that was God's price for setting Benedetta's heart at rest.

"You'll bide over the night?" said Robert gently, seeing him withdrawn and lost so far within the always solitary reaches of his mind.

"Gratefully, Robert, gratefully. But tomorrow I must ride." He did not say where, he did not say it would not be far, and Robert asked him nothing. They were of one mind. It was well not to know.

He was three days about his preparations. The bow he borrowed from the armoury of Castell Coch, and used Owen ap Ivor's name to get it, though the manservant of the holy woman of Aber had good enough credit wherever the prince's writ ran. He made use of the butts there, also, to loosen the cords of his ageing arms, and get his eye in at a target, for he had had little practice of late with a long-bow. To justify the loan and the earnestness of his trials he told some tale of a contest and a wager against an Englishman in Shrewsbury who fancied his arm, and they would have given him anything he asked, and their ready and varied advice into the bargain, to down an Englishman. John had been so long on their side of the border that they had forgotten his birth; almost he had forgotten it himself.

The skill came back readily into his hands, and the power into his shoulders. His eye had never lost its keenness and judgement. When he was satisfied with his weapon he recrossed Severn by the ford at Pool, hid bow and shafts in a copse of bushes close beneath the steep escarpment of the ramp to Parfois, and pastured his cob on a long line in a clearing nearer the river. He kept away from Robert's usual pathways, and avoided the places where he knew his snares would be. Once or twice during those two days he caught glimpses of him slipping unobtrusively through the trees, and once he saw Aelis in the dawn taking night-lines out of the river. By then he did not miss them; his sense of loneliness was so deeply accepted that it seemed to be his natural and eternal condition, and it was as if he did not look to see the silence broken again. He went back no more to the companionable butts of Castell Coch; he was not drawn to the assart above the mill. Beyond the act he contemplated there was nothing. If he survived it he would be coming as a stranger into a strange world, with everything to learn again, even speech.

The first night in the woods under the mountain he slept rolled in his cloak in the bushes. After that he did not sleep at all. He spent the hours of daylight watching the approaches to Parfois, and searching for the best and most commanding spot he could find from which to cover the lower guard. He could go no higher except by climbing, and he had not the native-born Welshman's agility or head for heights, and wanted, besides, to remain where he had at least a reasonable chance of retreating rapidly after the thing was done. He had no will to throw his life away; if it must be offered, let it be offered as something of value, and prized accordingly. God should not be able to complain that his creature had despised his gift.

Twice a day Isambard rode, at least while the summer weather invited. Sometimes he went in company, with his young men about him in a riot of colours, and his falconers in attendance, to hawk across the open heath by the old earth fort. Sometimes he rode almost alone, Langholme keeping his distance behind him, and perhaps two favoured youngsters suffered to take exercise with him provided they did not intrude on his solitary mood. Once John was in a fair way to draw on him as he rode so, upright and sombre and alone, but held his hand because the distance was too great for certainty. On the third day he would be in his chosen station, and there would be no haste about loosing the shaft, and no fear of a miss or a mere flesh-wound.

The trees clustered close and thickly at the edge of the ramp below the lower guard, on the valley side where the foundation of the new tower was scored deep through turf and soil to the rock. Piled stone for building, and the old masonry and rubble waiting to be carted away, made a ragged rampart between the road and the downward slope. A man could drop from one of the trees there and go running and leaping from bush to bush down the raw slope towards the river, while his pursuers were climbing over the barrier of stone to be after him, and ploughing through the lesser hazards of cords and timber and hurdles. And the greater of the trees commanded a clear view of the space between the towers, and the road beyond, down which all riders from Parfois must approach and pass. It was full summer, the screen of leafage thick enough to hide an army. John chose an elm that spread its branches clear across the road, overhanging the pale grey stacks of stone. There was room enough in the crotch for him to sit out the night in very fair comfort, and with the first light of dawn he shifted outward to the branches, and found himself a firm station facing the descending ramp.

The early evening would have given him better prospects of shaking off pursuit in the woods and by the river; but the morning ride offered him the better light for what he had to do. Yesterday they had stayed a while to watch the masons, while Isambard conferred with his master of the works. It could have been done then, if John had been better placed, but he had been on the ground, among bushes that marred his view and his aim, and would have betrayed him by their rustling before he could draw. This time there should be no such wasted moment. If God offered, John was ready to take.

The light grew and brightened; the labourers came, and the masons, and the guard yawned in the sun and watched them matching and measuring. Two or three young journeymen sat by the roadside dressing stone, spattering the pale grass of August with glittering grey chips of granite, fine as frost. A creaking cart came up the slope and unloaded butt after butt of fresh, unslaked lime, tipped out in a grey-white mountain beside the road. Master Edmund came down from the castle with his clerk at his back when the sun was already climbing, and stood by to see the laying of the first courses of stone on the stripped rock. The daily business of Parfois went forward briskly, and the watcher in the elm waited without impatience. On so fine a morning Isambard could not fail to ride.

It was past eight when he came, late for him; but at last the shimmer of bright colours quaked through the trees and hung among the branches like flowers, as the morning cavalcade poured down the path from the plateau of the church. The soft thudding of hoofs quivered along the ground; today he went handsomely attended, with half a dozen knights at his back, besides the squires and the pages and the gentlemen-at-arms, ambitious younger sons of knightly families getting their training for a hard life in which only the fittest would survive, and the weak would be elbowed aside and trampled underfoot. They took their strenuous apprenticeship lightly and gaily enough, perfected their courtly skills and their ability in arms, and hoped to be advanced to a manor somewhere in return for their services.

They had not yet begun to desert their lord, it seemed; his position was held to be unassailable, and the king's present troubles had made even the waverers draw in their horns again and reflect on Isambard's prospects of regaining his ascendancy. If de Burgh could fall so suddenly and resoundingly, so could Winchester in his turn when the wind changed. There was no telling yet which way this present contention would go. Tomorrow Isambard might be up again, or the Poitevins might have the better of the struggle, and he go down finally and utterly with the broken men. But for the moment the place-seekers and land-hungry were holding their hands. If ever he fell beyond recovery, the signs would show early. The landless knights would be the first to go, the younger sons with a career to make the second. And Langholme, it might well be, the last. Why should a man feel loyalty to one far out of reach of love?

The man in the elm tree steadied his knee cautiously against the branch on which it rested, and reached over his shoulder for a shaft, never taking his eyes from the lofty head that rode so high and easily above the lean, black-clad shoulders of the lord of Parfois. The summer glow was on him, burnishing all the sharp edges of bone into bronze and gold. He looked no more than fifty. The chestnut he had between his knees was Harry Talvace's Barbarossa. For the last time, thought John, moving softly among the leaves that they might not stir.

Softly he fitted the shaft to the string, and softly drew it back a little, and waited. The point nosed gently between the leaves, and reached hungrily towards Isambard's breast, there where the black cloth cotte was opened and the white shirt loosed over the heart.

There was no haste. The cavalcade came winding its way down at a dancing walk. He had still time to count the heads of the young and agile who would have to be reckoned with in flight, and to offer thanks that they came without hounds. He circled experimentally with the elbow of his drawing arm, and there was space and freedom enough for all the movement he would need.

Nearer now. Langholme was at his lord's heels, several of the younger men jostling to left and right, but no one rode close beside him. At the head of every cortège he would always be alone. Gay with voices and glowing with colours his court followed him down to the tower of the lower guard; and there he halted to speak with Master Edmund and walk his horse the length of the newly-begun foundation. He dismounted, and tossed Barbarossa's bridle to Langholme. That was well, that made him a better target, if the workmen would keep from standing too near him; and the awe in which they held him moved with him like an invisible wall, thrusting them back before him, so that but for Master Edmund he stood alone.

Some of his retinue had dismounted, too, used to his halts and guessing at the length of this one. That would hamper the movements of those still mounted, at least for a moment. But there were a few archers among the company. He must do it now, quickly, while the ranks were still closing at leisure, before they were fully assembled beside the tower. The range was short and certain, the light perfect. If only the old man would stand aside!

Master Edmund, eager and proud, darted from his lord's side at that moment, pacing out the shape of the proposed outer wall, and marked its thickness with a stamp of his foot. Isambard stood alone, his head turned to follow the old man's movements, his uncovered breast fronting the pathway, bared to the shaft that strained to his flesh like a living thing.

"Christ aid!" whispered John from dry lips, and with all the weight and passion and skill of his body he drew the bow.

It was the force of his hatred that undid him. Under the ultimate strain of his thrusting knee the branch cracked and gave, and the sped shaft, splitting the radiant air with a whining cry, lurched downward out of true. The group below heard the vibration, felt it in their flesh and looked up aghast, before ever the shaft struck and sang, quivering, in the earth at Isambard's feet. Not six inches from his long stirrup-shoe it bristled and quaked, whining still with an angry sound. He had jerked round and stood staring, for once slow to react to danger. How far must his mind have been from this place and these affairs of every day, to keep him there entranced and exposed, open to assault.

John had recovered his balance with a convulsive heave, reeling back against the main crotch of the tree from the downward lurch which had all but displaced him. His hand was at his shoulder, plucking out the second arrow in frantic haste, when the archers found him by the threshing of the branches.

A boy's voice shrilled: "There! In the elm!"

Langholme had leaped to catch his lord by the arm, and drag him into cover. They were locked immovably together for a moment, and John hung in agony on his bow-string, willing them to part. His fingers were tightening on the shaft, gripping for the steady pull, foot braced, knee braced, when the archers below drew and loosed. There was not a second between the shots, but it was John who was late. He could have transfixed the pair of them where they stood clasped and inseparable, but what had Langholme ever done to him or his?

The burning bolt took him in the breast in an explosion of shock and pain, driving him backwards with a rending of leaves. There was air rushing past his face, stopping his breath, and, at the end of an instant that seemed a year long, a burst of pain and terror and darkness that enveloped him body and spirit like a gust of flame.

They saw him fall, and gasped aloud, shuddering to the awful, shattering sound of his bones smashing on the stacked stone. Turning in mid-air, he struck the barrier of granite with a sickening shock, and was flung off like a jointless doll into the heap of lime.

Isambard stood stricken into stillness and silence, staring uncomprehendingly from wide, blank eyes. But those about him tore their feet from the grass and ran, baying like hounds, upon the spot where the intruder had fallen. Before Isambard could drag himself back to the scene they were on their victim with stones, staves, swords, whatever they had that could maim and bludgeon and kill.

He heard the dreadful, wordless crying, and thrust Langholme off with a sweep of his long arm. The flames rekindled, surging in his stunned eyes. He ran, shouting aloud at the last pitch of his voice, raging, slashing at the nearest with his short riding-whip to drive them off.

"Let be! Off, I say, off! Let him alone!"

Those who were not too far gone in frenzy to hear and understand fell back from him dismayed, dropping their weapons and shrinking out of his reach. He hurled himself between, swinging the whip about him like a flail, calling them off ferociously, like hounds at fault, until they gave before him and ran, cowering, and so let him through to the broken thing that heaved and jerked and moaned in the smoking lime.

Blood steamed and boiled about it, and heat struck him in the face as he leaned and stared. The bronze mask hung motionless for a moment, the eyes fixed and veiled. At his feet the torn remnant of a man writhed and stiffened in spasmodic contortions, half hacked to pieces, and out of it came a low, continuous, lamentable sound. It had still two eyes unmarked in the ruin of a face, light blue eyes, bright to frenzy, that fixed upon Isambard's countenance in an intolerable stare, and knew him, and were known.

The designers of slow death could not have done worse to him, and yet the eyes lived, with a tenacious, burning intelligence that would keep him chained for interminable hours yet to this nightmare of pain.

Isambard set hand to the dagger at his belt, and dropped smoothly and surely as a hawk for the stretched and palpitating throat.

The last convulsion of passion shook the dying man, the last blaze of defiance heaved him from the ground. Clawing on either side his maimed body, he filled both hands with lime and flung it into the plunging, haggard's face. Too late Isambard threw up his arm. The charge took him heavily, filling and searing eyes and nostrils and lips. Blindly, gasping, he fell and rolled upon John the Fletcher's floundering body. Running feet shook the ground; he felt hands reaching out to him, and even in that extreme bellowed at them, spitting out scalding foam and corroding pain:

"Stand back! Let us alone!"

It seemed his voice still had authority. Blind, his mouth burning, his eyes a furnace of agony, he lay panting over his enemy, jerking his head from side to side to shake off pain that clung to him and clawed him; and yet they obeyed him. They hung over him in an appalled circle, but they kept their distance, afraid to trespass where he had forbidden it.

Close in his ear shallow, rustling breath strained and laboured, and a dreadful, desolate, animal sound that made his flesh shrink with terror that it might be coming from his own mouth. He shut his teeth upon the furnace within, and still the keening tore at his senses. He felt towards it with his left hand, touched cloth, climbed a heaving shoulder to a crushed breast, blood hot under his palm. The cords of the old throat were taut, the battered head strained back. He laid his fingers along the jerking flesh, and the dagger slid in between them quick and cleanly.

A rush of blood gushed over his hands. The awful lament broke upon a bubbling cough, and sighed into silence. The broken body ceased to heave under him, quivered faintly for a long minute, and then relaxed and lay blessedly still.

Isambard took his hands from the dagger, and rolled away from his kill with his arms clenched hard over his face. He came to his knees, and still the hush and stillness about him held. They were afraid even to go to him until he commanded, and he could not unclench his teeth for fear of howling aloud. He could see nothing through the rush of water in his eyes, that boiled as it flowed, and ran scalding through his closed eyelids and down the hollows of his golden mask. He dragged one arm down from his eyes and dug his nails into the hard flesh of his breast inside the open bosom of his shirt, to provide himself with an easier pain, and croaked through his teeth:

"My eyes—water—My eyes burn—"

They stirred then, and a horrified murmur broke like bees in swarm; some ran, some cried to others up the slope to ride for Master Hilliard the physician. From a confusion of sounds he found none of any comfort, and groped round him with a lame hand, turning up his contorted face with tight-shut, streaming eyes and strained lips to the light.

"Walter—!"

"Here, my lord!" Langholme was on his knees beside him with a rush, his arms supporting him.

"Help me rise, Walter. Get me home—out of their sight." The burned lips whispered clumsily and slowly, but the words were clear. He gripped his squire's steadying arm and set one foot to ground, and drove himself upright.

"Rest here, my lord, wait—lie in the shade till Master Hilliard comes. You cannot go. We'll bring a litter." Langholme's teeth were chattering with shock and distress.

"No, get me home. I am not sick, I can ride. Bring me to Barbarossa, and mount me. I will go. I will not be a spectacle here. . . ."

Trembling and appalled, Langholme brought him on his arm the few yards to where the horse grazed quietly, calmed now after the brief turmoil. Isambard walked like a drunken man, the pain twisting his head ceaselessly after the ease that was nowhere to be found, and the coolness that turned to fire as it touched. The bony fingers gripped ever tighter in Langholme's arm, until he could not choose but wince at the pressure; then they released him quickly and lay almost lightly on his sleeve, but he felt them rigid, like a dead man's.

"I am hurting you, Walter. Forgive me!"

"No," he said, shaking, "no!" and wished the grip back again. "Here's the bridle, my lord." The groping left hand reached for it, gathered it steadily, pressed hard knuckles into the glossy neck for an instant in a laboured caress. "And here the stirrup. Your foot . . . so." He was up; he gripped with muscular knees and drew the first longer, steadier breath.

"Give me a kerchief, Walter. And stay by me!"

He held the kerchief to his eyes as they went, his head down, like a mourning woman, and halfway up the ramp. Langholme, anxious and attentive at his elbow, saw that his lord's teeth were locked tightly in the folds of linen, and the bone of his jaw stood pale and rigid from the brown flesh.

The young men of the retinue, shocked into silence, drew aside from the path to let them pass, and fell in close behind them subdued and orderly, their only speech agitated whispers. Falconers and pages and knights and grooms filed after them across the plateau of the church, and over the bridge into Parfois. They brought him in procession through the wards to his own apartments in the Lady's Tower, the physician running before, de Guichet coming in solicitous haste to embrace his lord and all but carry him up the stone staircase.

The door closed and shut the crowd out from him. They could bubble and marvel and shout as much as they would now, and exult if they would; he was out of their reach. He could uncover his marred face, and let go the iron grip he must keep on something or someone in order to be silent. He could groan and curse and do whatever he would, except weep; if he wept, the brine of his eyes would burn like boiling pitch.

He let them bed him, and bathe away the blood and dust with water, and the lime with milk. He could not eat, but they made him take raw eggs to ease his burning mouth and throat. They closed to the shutters to protect him from the light. He lay on his pillows and surrendered all care for himself, turning submissively under the physician's hands and obedient to every order. All his own energies were engaged with containing and coming to terms with his pain, for it would not be a short acquaintance; that he knew. There was but one thing that needed his attention besides, and that could wait for an hour at least, until they had had their will of him and left him alone.

They even discussed him across his great bed, the old leech and de Guichet, as though he were asleep or dead, or a child, or a beast that was sick. His swollen lips smiled a little at that, and never grudged the pain.

"Is he gravely burned, Master Hilliard? Will he be marked?"

Did it matter? That old mask had had a long day, it could live out the evening without beauty.

"Very little, I think, very little. He's strong, he has no fever. He'll do well if he'll only be ruled and lie quiet. The eyes, of course—" Do him justice, he did hesitate there, and sink his voice a little when he resumed. "The eyes are a more serious matter. We cannot tell as yet. We must hope."

The eyes are a more serious matter! To a man who uses them as one weapon of his authority, much more serious.

From beneath the steeped linen that covered his mouth he said: "Leave me now, I should like to rest. But let Walter stay."

"He shall, my lord, he shall. Someone must be with you, to keep these cloths moistened with milk. Master Langholme, bathe my lord's eyes and see the pads kept damp over them, and send for me at once if there's any show of fever."

He was gone; they were all gone but Langholme, hushed and still beside the bed. Quietness and pain wrapped him, and he lay and let them possess him, ungrudging. What was done was done; no one could take him back to the beginning of the day and let him have the living of it over again. He must make what he could of what remained.

"Walter!"

"Here, my lord."

"Walter, I have work for you more testing than moistening my

dressings with milk. That poor wretch below there—him I killed—
he brought me a letter a few days gone, and I gave him my answer
to take back again, but it seems he thought to win a more acceptable
trophy than I sent by him. Somewhere about him you'll find my
ring, the ruby. Will you go deliver it in his stead?"

"My lord, whatever you bid me," said Langholme earnestly.

"To a lady you may remember. To Madonna Benedetta Foscari.
I killed her, but she would not die, Walter. She's turned Welsh-
woman, and hidden herself, I judge, somewhere not far from
Llewelyn's maenol at Aber. More's the pity, I never asked him
where she lived or what she did, but if you ask for her round Aber
I think you'll find her."

"And what am I to say to her with the ring, my lord?"

"Say to her that I say: Yes, come, your offer is accepted." The
words brought him a certain evening content; it was time that it
should be ended, he could not keep the borrowed joy for ever. "Only
that. She will know. And tell her what befell her servant. Tell it
truly, and she will understand. She knows him better than I, and I
know him now well enough. God rest him!"

"He tried to kill you," said Langholme, sombre and wondering.

"I owed him that twice over. What he has given me may be part
payment of my debts, who knows? Only tell her."

Langholme hesitated, loathe to leave the bedside. "Am I to ride
now, my lord?"

"Now, Walter. Send up one of the pages to me if you will, but
bid him stay outside the door. If I want him I can call."

He heard the reluctant footsteps turn to the door, and called him
back for a moment: "And, Walter . . . when you have taken back
the ring from him . . . . see his body cared for. Tell de Guichet he is
to have proper burial."

Harry had barely crossed from the stables to the tracing house and
moved his work into the sun when he heard them riding in, so
numerous a company that they could hardly be other than the
hawking party returning. He peered out for a moment to see them
pass on their way to the stables and the mews, astonished that they
should have come back so soon. Isambard, whatever he might be,
was not capricious. But he was in time to see only a handful of the

young men, riding in rather subdued order, and unusually circum-spectly, but with nothing about them to indicate disaster. He turned back to his work, but could not settle to it for the thought of Barba-rossa cheated of his outing; and presently he laid down his chisel sullenly but resignedly, and went back to the stables, at least to groom and pet his favourite, and if possible to beg another rider for him. He was as well with Isambard as any, no blinking it, and went under him joyfully; but someone else would do at a pinch. There must be errands to be done out of Parfois, at some time during the day, and Walter would lend an understanding ear to his request.

The stable-yard was full of returned riders, and some were silent and pale and some feverishly voluble, and all out of their usual selves. Harry stood at a loss, staring from one group to another.

"What is it? What's happened?"

Three or four turned and began telling him together, so variously that he was little wiser, but much shaken.

"What, my lord shot at? From a tree? And *hurt*?" There could be no other reason for this return, Isambard would never turn back merely for a stray shaft loosed at his life. Harry looked round wildly for Barbarossa. "And his horse? *My* horse!"

Barbarossa was there, pawing discontentedly outside his stall in the hold of a groom. Harry took the glowing head to his heart, and breathed again; not a scratch, nor a stain of sweat on him. He turned a doubtful face.

"There was no damage? My lord was not hit?"

"Not by the arrow, no. The fellow who shot at him was brought down, though, and what was left of him *he* finished with his own hands. But he got a fistful of lime in his eyes, doing it. We brought him home streaming like a widow at a funeral, and they've closed the shutters on him and fetched in his physician."

"Is he bad?" asked Harry uncertainly.

"Who's to know yet? Bad enough to quieten him for a while."

"And the man who loosed at him is dead, you say? Who was he?"

That none of them knew. There were plenty of desperate fellows about the borders who had grudges enough against Isambard, who could tell which of them had staked his life on so crazy a throw?

"But dead—dead is one way of saying it! If you'd seen him!

Some of the archers got to him in a hurry, till *he* whipped them off and cut the poor devil's throat. He wouldn't have them touch their master's meat!"

"And he's taken to his bed?"

That knocked him hard, it was so unlikely. When had Isambard ever spared himself or entertained so much as the thought of sickness and weakness? Harry groomed his darling, and thought of it over and over, and listened to the confusion of whispers and rumours and comments that buzzed round him, with a curious trouble in his heart.

There was no Isambard in hall at dinner, and no de Guichet or Langholme, either. Harry went looking for someone who might know the truth of it and be willing to tell it. Walter was still with Isambard in his bedchamber. Harry sat down at the foot of the staircase and waited, and presently de Guichet and the physician came down from the sick man's room with sombre faces and hushed voices, and went away across the inner ward. He did not ask them for news; they were no friends of his. But in a little while he heard footsteps descending, and looked up to see Langholme coming down towards him.

He scrambled up and confronted him in haste. "Walter, how is it with him? I heard from some of the others what happened. Is he bad?"

"Bad enough," said Walter shortly. "Burned and in pain. But he's still his own master and ours, for all that, and I'm on his errand, so don't keep me."

He would not stay, but Harry ran after him and walked beside him, questioning still. "The man who shot at him—Walter, who was he? Roger said a Welshman by his bow and his clothes. Was he a Welshman?" Langholme halted abruptly, seeing the anxiety in the blue-green eyes; the boy had it in his mind and on his heart that this death somehow lay at his door.

"Welsh he may be, but he's no concern of yours, as far as I can see. He came as a messenger to my lord from a lady, and was to have taken a message back again. But for some reason best known to himself he chose rather to stay and attempt my lord's life. There were old grudges. No fault of yours," he said kindly enough. "Go and chip your stone, boy, and let be. He's alive, and will be, even if it's no joy just now.''

Harry kept his place, clinging to the arm that would have put him gently by. There were too many echoes here that struck true in his heart—a Welshman, a lady, old grudges. ''What lady?'' he said. ''You know, Walter, you must tell me.''

''One that you probably know well enough, but I tell you this is nothing to do with your case. It's old history, before you were born.''

''Walter, what lady? I must know her name.''

''Madonna Benedetta, if you must know.''

The colour ebbed from Harry's face and left him pale as the wall. He took his hand from Langholme's arm to feel at his own blanched cheek, and stood staring with wide, sick, green eyes.

''Madonna Benedetta,'' he said in a whisper. ''John the Fletcher! Oh God, Oh God, *John*! And he killed him—he cut his throat—''

Langholme turned and took him by the arms, holding him before him. There was no leaving him like this. If he had every detail he might make sense of it, and come to his own senses.

''He killed him, yes. Dear God, boy, listen to me. I saw it. He was blind and burned, with his eyes and his mouth full of lime, and he felt his way to his throat and killed him. Did they never tell you? He'd fallen from a tree on the piled stone—if he had a whole bone in him it was wonder—and the men-at-arms had run at him, besides, with stones and staves and whatever they found to hand. He beat them off from him to keep the man alive, if you ask me what I think, but it was gone long past that by the time he got to him. And he killed him. I tell you, I saw it. It was more like a mercy to a broken-backed beast, and one he valued at that, than the dispatching of an enemy. And do you know what was his last charge to me now? See his body cared for, he says. Tell de Guichet he's to have proper buriel. And I'm off to do it.''

He plucked his hands from him, and went about the first of his errands; and Harry, trembling and amazed, refuged in his corner of the deserted tracing-house and was seen no more that afternoon. But when he came out it was to march straight to the Lady's Tower, and ask with humility and some constraint if Isambard would be pleased to receive him.

* * *

The bedchamber was a room he had never seen before, large and rich, hung with tapestries and summer branches that gave a green, warm scent of the woods to it. The scent of sickness was there, too, acrid and faint and daunting; and the man in the great bed lay so still beneath the single linen cover that he might almost have been composed ready for his coffin. The wonderful head stared at the ceiling from two round white eyes of linen that steamed faintly. The cloth that covered his mouth had been removed, and the mis-shapen lips, swollen and scarlet, were fast closed on any utterance. Harry watched the great bony breast rise and fall, and shook to the shallow irregularities and broken rhythm of pain.

He did not know why he had come at all, he had nothing to say; the coming was everything, but it seemed to him now an incomprehensible folly that it should be expected to speak for itself. He closed the door behind him very softly, though the man in the bed was not asleep; and slowly, on dragging feet, he approached the bedside.

"Is it you indeed, Harry?" said Isambard, fumbling out the words through stiff lips. "This is an honour I never looked for."

"You did not come to me or send for me, my lord," said Harry, in self-defence playing the prisoner still, "so I came to you."

"Ah, you thought I should want my daily report on you?" Even thus distorted, the voice kept the honeyed sweetness he could use when he would, caressing and tormenting; and even on the marred lips the half-smile could still play its shadowy game. "And did the day go well without me, Harry?"

"My lord," he said hardily, "I think it did not go well *with* you."

He had not meant to keep that tone; it was so deeply engrained a habit with them now that it was hard to leave it, and the dismaying words came out of themselves, before he was aware. But he would not soften them now they were sped. He watched the deepening of the shadows in the hollow cheeks, the brief contortion of the mouth that told him Isambard was smiling.

"The more reason it should go well with my best enemy."

He remembered then that the boy must have known Benedetta's man from his childhood, closely enough to have some affection for him. "But that it served another even worse than me," he said with compunction, "and he a friend of yours. Have they told you?"

The small, constrained voice out of the darkness above him said: "Yes." The face he could see clearly in his mind's eye, wary and grave, even a little sullen and ungracious, solemn eyes lowered to the pillowed head of his enemy brought low. No joy in them, but somewhere a shadow of baffled doubt that there should have been joy. He was still enough of a child for that, though the child was passing.

"And told you who he was? But that I think they could not, for none of them knew it. It was Benedetta's man, that archer of hers she had from me. I have forgotten his name—"

"John the Fletcher," said Harry in a very low voice.

"Ah, John was it?" He drew breath painfully, and raised himself a little upon his pillows. "I see you do know." Silence between them a moment. "Did they tell you also that I killed him?"

The careful voice, articulating so laboriously, probed its way through to the heart. It was as though that death and loss had lodged somewhere in the borders of Harry's consciousness until now, known but not yet fully realized, and Isambard had suddenly reached into the middle of his being and laid his affirmation there. He opened his lips to answer and could not, he was so full of tears, and must carry himself with aching care for fear they spilled over.

"Faith, I am sorry, child," said Isambard.

"And I, my lord."

It was hard to breathe, harder to speak, and worst was the dread in him that the man in the bed could follow every vibration of the struggle that convulsed him. His head was turned a little on the pillow, to bring the shrouded eyes to bear on his visitor, as though he strained after another kind of sight. Wanting one sense, he still saw too far into other men for comfort, and without eyes he could still out-stare his opponents.

"That he missed his aim, Harry?"

In answer to that, nothing. The young mouth drawn down a little now, no doubt, dourly and forbiddingly, the eyes withdrawn to fix on something harmless and insensate that could not stare back at him. The skin rugs, the gilded chair, the Norman ancestors in the tapestry, with their conical helms and long hauberks. Isambard had felt the green glance leave him, but not to go far. He was learning already how to orientate himself by the slight movements other men made; even the light rustling of a sleeve had meaning.

"I'm thirsty, Harry. There's a pitcher there on the chest. Give me a drink."

And so he did; quietly and neatly, like a well-trained page, he poured milk, and came and raised Isambard in one arm, while with the other hand he held the cup to his lips. For a moment the lord of Parfois lay against his enemy's shoulder, and felt under his cheek the strong, eager beating of the boy's heart, that hated him so faithfully and well but would not pay him less than his due.

"I thank you, Harry, that was kindly done."

The supporting arm lowered him carefully to his pillow again as soon as he made to go, and withdrew from him without any intimation of relief or loathing. The eyes, those eyes whose changeable mid-sea colouring was belied by their aggressive steadiness, had come back to him; he felt them taking in with awe and wonder the details of his disfigurement, and the obliterating pads of linen like death-pennies on his eyes.

"True," he said thoughtfully, "I should have been the one who died, if we all had our deserts. The comfort of the wicked is that in this world we so seldom do. But I am sorry you have lost a friend. I would have spared him to you if I could."

Would the boy stoop to ask what he must be longing to know? He had come a long way since the first inquisition in a cell below the Warden's Tower, when he had shut his frightened, obstinate young mouth and presented a stony front of silence; but he had come by his own stubborn ways, and he was not so greatly changed. Growth, after all, is not so much a matter of change as of ripening, and what alters most is the degree of clarity with which we see one another. Had I, thought Isambard, to lose my eyes in order to see him so clearly? He will not ask.

And he did not ask. John the Fletcher had come with a message from Benedetta, and the lord of Parfois had given him a reply to take back to her. But John had not taken it, and John was dead. That was all he knew. He had no means of knowing whether the message had to do with him or no, or what was to happen now; for the moment that was put aside. He had come here upon another errand; his trouble was that for the life of him he could not determine exactly what it was or how to set about it. All he knew was that it had brought him here, and more than half-unwilling, at that, and that he could spare no energy for anything else until he had fulfilled what it required of him.

"I am sorry, my lord," said the low, dogged voice, picking its way none too graciously, "that you have met with this misfortune. I am very sorry you are in pain."

It cost him a deal of discomfort to get it out, but he did it; and by the great sigh he heaved, his heart was eased of an uncommon load when he was rid of it.

Isambard lay quiet, smiling his mangled smile into the timbers of the ceiling, where the dusk was beginning to gather. His long, emaciated hand, half-open on the sheet beside him, held the unexpected offering very gently, like a bird that had come to him of its own grace and could not with honour be caged, or held a moment longer than it chose to rest in his palm. But neither need he move or speak too soon, and frighten it away. He was still so long that the boy grew restive, and stole closer to discover if he had fallen asleep.

"Harry!" said the voice from the bed at length, very quietly.

"My lord?"

"Bathe my eyes before you go."

Harry brought the small bowl of milk and herbal infusions from the chest, and with fearful fingers, holding his breath, lifted the pads from Isambard's eyes. The sight of the swollen lids, red-rimmed and raw, made him draw in his breath sharply, grieved for the ruin of what had surely been beauty. That, too, Isambard understood.

"Ah, that will mend," he said, and lay submissive beneath the boy's careful ministrations. His touch was light and shy, and his steady, earnest breathing fanned Isambard's cheek as he bent close. At the end of it Isambard opened his eyes fully for the first time, and looked up into his face.

A pale blur, with vaguely discernible features, and an undefined shining of great eyes. No more than that. And then the light hurt and warned him, and he lay back and let his lids close upon that glimpse of his charmed bird. No dove, certainly, more a young gerfalcon, and a wild one at that. It was not to be expected that it would return to him often, or remain with him long. But if he refrained from closing his hand it might at least leave with him the last frond or two of its eyas-down when it soared.

Chapter Five

Parfois: *September* 1233

*H*e came out of his fever on the fourth night with senses clear and cold, his mind like a new sword, his body so weak that when he tried to lift his hand from the bed it would not obey him. There was light in the room, a candle burning. He saw it only as a pale, diffused aureole about a white point, summoning shadows, separating them dark from pale; but he saw it. Shapes so vague as to be no solider than cloud yet served to identify for him the corners of his own bedchamber. Someone was asleep and snoring on a wooden chair beside the bed. It seemed death had no use for him yet. He turned back to the world without regret, but without illusions. It would be no easy world henceforth for him.

Men were moving shadows, things were fixed shadows. And sometimes the two became confused, and he found that shapes which had clustered so still between him and the light could move and disperse when he showed he was aware of them. He knew then that it behoved him to nurse and value the senses he had left, for he was going to need them; and he thanked God, with a gambler's satisfaction, that his hearing was sharp as a wildcat's even without any cultivation on his part, and could be polished to even rarer brilliance now that he knew the need. There were tendencies in the moving shadows that cried a warning plainly enough; hesitations to move at command, that silent clustering together in his presence, and that palpable attention of their eyes in unrelenting attendance on him. Everything had acquired an extreme significance, every aspect of human behaviour could enlighten him if he courted his opportunities.

The voices, of course, the voices were still grave, concerned, prompt, obsequious; they knew he still had his ears. But on the second day after his return to reason he began to observe that the page who was left to wait on him made no great haste to jump to his orders. His lord called for water, for he was still plagued with an inordinate thirst; and the boy, secure that his name would not be required of him and his face was a blur that might have belonged to any of the youngsters about the household, came in his own good time, and served indifferently and inattentively. Isambard let it go then, well aware that he could barely lift a hand, much less lay the boy flat as he deserved. But he made acute note of the cocky young voice, and knew he could pick it out again from a dozen not so far different. Give him six or seven days of convalescence, and the patience to bide his time, and the score should be paid, for the sake of all who might fall into the same error.

They let Harry in to him that afternoon. The head on the pillows was raised alertly at the sound of his step, the face turned towards him pricked and aware, like a pointing hound.

"Harry!" said Isambard with satisfaction, not questioning, confirming his own excellent intuition. "Child, you come very timely," he said, when they were alone and the door shut. "Come here to me and lend me an arm to get out of this bed, for I'm sick to death of it."

"My lord," said Harry, appalled, and lending the arm rather to hold him where he was than to help him out of it, "you'll kill yourself. Only two days since you were still in fever."

"Ah! Have you asked after me, then, while I've been out of my wits?"

Harry had, daily, and daily been denied entry to the sickroom, until this day when Isambard's recovered senses and strongly asserted will made it politic to avoid the appearance of keeping him under too strait a guard. If he wanted the boy, let him have him.

"You cannot stand," said Harry sternly, forbearing from answering the question. "You should lie quiet for a week or more before you put foot to ground."

"But I cannot afford a week, Harry. In a week I shall be allowed to stand and go, with even Hilliard's blessing, and there will be a hundred pairs of eyes watching to see how poor a show I make of it. I intend they shall have good reason to think again. Can you be secret?" He laughed at the stiff silence that answered him. "Then who better for my purpose? Give me a little of your patience and obstinacy—I know you have more than enough of that—and I shall be ready and able to run before they know I can walk."

He braced one hand into the mattress, and clung to Harry's arm with the other, and swung his legs out of the bed. As long as Harry had known him he had carried no flesh but the hard, spare muscle and sinew that clothed his long bones so magnificently; now fever had wasted the half of that from him, and pitted neck and shoulders and trunk with blue hollows. But he had lived a rigorous, athlete's life, and the frame of strength and agility and grace was still there, ready and willing to make the assay.

"My body never yet was my master," he said, wrapping his gown about him on the edge of the bed. "Let's see if I can still make it do my bidding, before I begin on the bodies of others."

The boy was standing back doubtfully, watching him. Now that the fires in his eyes had cooled, and the burns about his lips had fined down and dried into flat, brownish scars, he was not so greatly changed. The same brown stains flecked his forehead and cheekbones, but in the bronze of his skin they were not offensive. Only the ravaged eyes, still inflamed and red about the rims and dulled and darkened within, the high lids distorted by swollen tissue, defaced his old splendour. The oblique smile came haltingly on a slightly misshapen mouth. The hands that fumbled at his gown were a hawk's talons without the dexterity, for he was still very weak and moved with the calculated deliberation of one who knows his own feebleness.

He had caught the quality of Harry's fixed silence. He looked up quickly, and the tilt of his head challenged.

"Are you pitying me, boy?" The voice still had a core of steel.

"No, my lord. Do you know of any reason why I should?"

"I know of every reason why you should not," said Isambard

grimly. "Let me but see the light of pity in your eye and, by God, I'll take a whip to you, as mannish as you are."

"When you can lift one," said Harry tartly, bent on wiping out the word "pity" from between them. "You'd have trouble holding one at this moment. Do you want me to be your prop, or don't you?"

He lent his arm and his shoulder as they were needed, and flatly refused both when he thought they had driven the worn body to exhaustion. The first day it was no more than the assay of standing, and walking a few unsteady steps about the bed; but day by day Isambard drove his resigned frame to more strenuous efforts, until he was prowling the length and breadth of the room like a caged tiger. By the time Master Hilliard ceremoniously allowed him to rise from his bed he was ready to daunt them all by the manner of his return.

They had expected a wavering invalid to be half-led, half-carried into the sun, and propped in his cushioned chair, there to lie as helpless a prisoner as in his fever-bed, at the mercy of the arms that waited upon him. Isambard had himself carefully and elegantly dressed, and came forth from his room in his old splendour, treading the uneven timbered floor with confidence, and descending the stair-case without leaning or stumbling. When Master Hilliard protested that he was mad to venture so far, Isambard laughed in his face. Who was to know that he saw only a blur of darkness against a steadily dimming light? It was impossible to tell from the appearance of his eyes whether he could see or no; by his movements they judged that he could. Even the young squire who went before and lent him a shoulder seemed to be used rather as a decoration than a prop.

He chose out at leisure the neglectful page to attend him to the mews and kennels, crooking a finger imperiously to summon him from among a dozen of his fellows; and who was to know that he had selected him by his voice alone, locating by means of a quick and accurate ear one shadow among shadows? The boy allowed himself to wonder, and half in bravado and half in the complacent conviction that he could not be detected, fell a pace behind in their walk to the kennels, and amused his following friends with a rapid parody of his lord's large and arrogant gait. Isambard heard the infinitesimal ripple of suppressed laughter that followed him, and tracked it contentedly to its source. He was round like a greyhound, and by sheer good fortune took the youngster neatly enough by the forearm he flung up in alarm to protect his head; his hair would have done just as well. A twist brought him to his knees, bleating now like a scared lamb.

"You are very forward to entertain us, my friend," said Isambard, smiling down at him grimly. "You shall be given all possible scope. Let's hear if you can also sing." And he delivered him to be whipped on the spot, and stood by to ensure that his order was carried out.

After that the pages were markedly more prompt and respectful, and there was need for only one more demonstration to restore the quality of the hush that had always accompanied him about his castle wards. When one of the kennel-masters mishandled a deer-hound bitch, and answered sullenly on being called to account for it, Isambard took the occasion as it offered, and laid him flat with a blow of his bony fist that slit the man's cheek open. He struck as the fellow muttered, using the voice to guide the blow into a face he could barely see, and the effort he put into it all but dropped him over his victim. But these secrets he managed to preserve to himself alone, and not until he had returned in good order to his bedchamber and closed the door on them all did he acknowledge at last the failing of his flesh. He lay on the bed staring into the growing darkness that had nothing to do with the ending of the September day.

It was all very well striking out about him thus publicly once or twice, with a madman's luck, to demonstrate that he was still to be reckoned with. But how much time could he buy by these means? He dared not appear in hall, he could not eat with them, or ride, or ever again engage in sword-play, without betraying that he could no longer see anything more precise than light and shadow. All the more difficult of the small operations the human body performs daily without thought, such nothings as pouring wine or sealing a letter, he must keep out of sight behind his closed door, until such time as he could evolve some arduous technique for dissembling his disability as he performed them; and no matter how ingeniously he planned, no matter how assiduously he schooled ears and fingers to do duty for his ruined eyes, sooner or later some detail must betray him. He could hope for nothing else. The time was coming when even light and darkness would be one; he knew that by infallible signs.

I shall be a blind old man, he thought, standing eye to eye with himself in the darkness on which he could still conjure pictures and colours from within, now all from without failed him. A blind, clumsy old man, fumbling his food and spilling his wine. I shall give orders, and they'll say yes to me very civilly for a time, but do nothing, secure that I cannot pursue them. And in a while they'll no longer trouble to answer or heed me. Today I've staved off certainty; they've drawn in their horns for a while. How long? A week? I doubt it.

Not long enough, then, for Benedetta to come to him and depart again with the gift he kept for her. He had refused to face that certainty until now, but he could fend it off no longer. It was time to set about clearing the ground about him, so that he might bring down no more people with him in his fall. What kind of protection would a blind man be to either the boy or the woman? Get them all away, all those who could be used to influence him, all those whom he could be used to harm. In the last battlefield let there be no cover anywhere to allow the enemy to approach undetected. Walter, when he returned from his errand, must be sent on another, a longer, one that would keep him well clear of the clash to come. Harry must go, and Benedetta must never come. These things settled, the innocent put out of reach, the liabilities disposed of, he could set to work to fortify his position and delight in his last warfare.

"What are they saying of me now?" he asked, when Harry came in to see him that night.

"They say your friend the devil had lent you a new pair of legs and two more eyes," said Harry, not without a certain note of grudging admiration.

"Do they so? Good! I'm glad I did not take my life in my hands on the staircase for nothing. But I doubt we're all going to find it a short-term loan."

"And they do not say," said Harry deliberately, "but I know, that de Guichet sent off a courier with a letter yesterday, to the king's camp at Usk."

There was so equivocal a note in his voice at this that Isambard drew himself sharply to attention, and controlled whatever reaction he might have shown to the news. The boy would have to be handled carefully. Already the straight stare of his eyes had grown uncomfortably close and searching.

"Ah, so you know that, do you? And how did you come to be let into the secret?"

He let his thin hands lie open and easy on the arms of his great chair, to have their tranquillity seen. It was not so difficult, after all, to deceive the outer world, for a time at least, by means of one carefully planned sortie; but Harry had paced him about the room here day after day, and had better opportunities to use his eyes and his wits.

"I came late from the tracing-house, and went to the stables in the dark to have a moment with Barbarossa before sleeping. Young Clifford was there saddling up, and that was queer enough at that hour, you'll allow. He had one strap of his saddle-roll broken, and he was in haste, so he borrowed one of mine. He said he'd return it as soon as he came back from Usk. And since he can hardly be going with a message to the earl of Pembroke inside Usk castle, his business must be with the king's host laying siege to it. He ran off to collect his dispatch, and thought no more of me. I waited to see him come again, and it was de Guichet who sped him from the doorway of the Warden's Tower. I saw him make a parchment secure in the breast of his cotte before he mounted. In the dark," said Harry sombrely, "it wasn't hard to lie close. I know Parfois very well by now."

"You take a deal of interest in this letter," said Isambard, placidly smiling. "Shall I recite you the content?"

"No need, I can do it myself. Not word for word, but as near as makes no matter. 'If you should be of a mind for it,' it says, 'the game is running well. The old wolf we held off from hunting has come by an injury, and is no more to be feared—being blind—' "

He broke off there, seeing the lean fingers clench and the starting bones of the face pale from bronze to pallid gold.

"Did you think I did not know?" he said, low-voiced and quivering. "There was one night you all but put your hand into one of the candles, if I had not snatched it away, and you never knew. You can practise on them outside, knowing every stone of the wards as you do, but beware of letting any get too close to you. And even so, what will you do when you have your body in health again, and no excuse left to keep a boy under your hand to lean on, to count you down the stairs and show you by his own movements where you must turn?"

"Faith, child!" said Isambard, relaxing with a sigh, "I have been wondering the same thing myself."

All things combined to confirm him in his conviction. It was time, and more than time, to set his house in order. He sat back in the gilded chair, gathering his faculties calmly, as a provident general marshals his troops for a critical field.

"It's true, then?" said Harry, confounded. "You cannot see at all?" In spite of his certainty he had almost hoped for a flat denial, even for some proof that he was mistaken.

"Between night and day I see a shade of difference." Even that, if he had said all, grew daily less discernible. He put it by with a movement of his hand, turning his mind to what was left. Blind or seeing, he must dispose as best he might and fight out the day. If de Guichet had sent word to William yesterday, today he might well have suffered some doubts of his wisdom; but would he on that account call the messenger back? It was not likely. The throw was made, and could not be withdrawn; they would stand to it, and watch him warily until the answer came. De Guichet would always be safe enough, never having committed himself publicly. As the mastery went, so would he go.

"You spoke of Usk," said Isambard, frowning over his thoughts as though his long-sighted eyes still served him. "Pembroke had it garrisoned and provisioned. You say the king has attacked there?"

Both sides had hitherto held off from irrevocable action, Henry probably from timidity and incompetence, the earl marshal out of his strong reluctance to put to the issue of battle what he held to be rather a matter for reform. No man had ever less ambition to be a rebel and a leader of rebels, but the times and his own sense of right had thrust him into it, and he would not deny.

"By what I hear, the king made up his mind to take Usk, by way of a demonstration, to bring the earl to heel. Before he laid siege to the castle he denounced his feudal obligations to the earl and all his confederates, and Pembroke has renounced his homage to King Henry in return, and so have Basset and Siward and all the rest."

"Then this is no mere matter of punishing a rebellious vassal," said Isambard, "or taking an outlaw. It's war, open and honourable, between man and man. The king has disarmed himself of his own best weapon, but I see he could hardly take the first action without cutting the link. And Pembroke held off with such patience. Henry could always hesitate and change course, but he never knew how to sit and wait."

"But he's had no success at Usk, or so they're saying. We heard today that he's thought better of the attempt, and sent envoys to the earl, suggesting a way to an honourable peace. If the earl will formally surrender Usk to him he's promised to restore it within fifteen days, and to give him safe conduct to come back to the council at the next meeting, where he shall have a proper examination of all his grievances, and reform where reform's due."

"Ah, that's my Henry!" said Isambard with a short crow of laughter. "He would promise the world, if God would but save him his face. But when his face feels its dignity secure, the earl had better have a good lawyer to bind the pledges, and a hand on his hilt into the bargain. And has Richard taken him at his word?"

"My lord, we've heard no more."

"He will. He can do no other, feeling as he feels. He may doubt the king's honesty, but he cannot let the offer go by. Now Henry could close this without discredit, and disarm his enemies, if he would but keep to terms. But I'd wager my soul that when fifteen days are come and gone he'll say no word about handing Pembroke his castle back. As for reform, we shall hear no more of that. You could never give him a penny out of magnanimity but he would jump to it you were a fool or afraid, and grasp at the whole mark. He's had his knuckles rapped more than once for it, but he never learns. And Richard Marshall," said Isambard reflectively, "is neither a fool nor afraid. Well, so it stands, does it? Within a month the whole march will be in on the king's side, and Wales cannot stay out. It will be a race for which first sets light to the heather. And a border castle cannot be left in suspect hands when the march is burning."

He smiled, the old, wolfish smile, pricking up his head to the scent of the blown smoke, and his ears to the sounds of battle; but he shut his teeth upon the rest of his thoughts.

A border castle in an advanced position, such as Parfois, must be in the hands of a trusted castellan at such a time. War is war, and old established right must give way to need. In the king's name, in England's name, in the name of William's long hunger, blind Ralf Isambard, near his dotage and already compromised by his championship of Hubert de Burgh, that hapless prisoner in Devizes, might plausibly be displaced from authority and held in protective custody in his son's charge, and that without reproach to the best and most magnanimous of monarchs. Cautiously, of course. His honour was widely scattered, and discretion was necessary, for fear some garrisons of his elsewhere might feel it their duty to question his retirement. They might even ask that he be produced alive, which would do the royal credit no good, even if the demand could still be complied with. Scandal would be avoided if possible. But the exigencies of war cover a multitude of irregularities.

Did he believe that the king would lend himself to such a piece of business? A difficult question. The king would be very careful not to know of any proceedings which might actually be looked upon as criminal. His hands would cover his eyes from seeing evil, but it would be reasonable to assume that he would be peering through his fingers. If the worst came to the worst he could produce a revelation of treasons plotted against him, and a holy and righteous rage to prove that he was the injured party. Who could determine how much of what went on in that curious mind was self-deception?

"Harry? Are you still there?" It was so quiet in the bedchamber that for a moment he thought himself alone.

"Here, my lord."

First things first. Let William lean to des Rivaulx's ear, and des Rivaulx to the king's, and let them compound among them as they would; the next move here in Parfois was plain. He should have recognized it long since, on the day of John the Fletcher's death; he should never have sent Walter with the ring, after the way had been closed to him once with so marked and forbidding a sign. But his heart had refused to acknowledge what his mind must have known, even then, only too well, that he could not hope and must not seek ever to see Benedetta again.

"Harry, you have long desired to go home."

The distrustful silence hung between them like a curtain, but blind eyes are not hampered by obstructions. He saw the young face quicken and lift, eyes watching him hungrily, alert for the trick behind the words.

"And so you shall," he said with deliberation. "You will make ready tonight. Put together your things—the tools also if you will, such of them as you can easily carry—and tomorrow morning I will see to it that the gate is opened to you." Horse and habit and all that is his, Benedetta had said. All that is his, and more than he came with.

"Go?" said Harry in a stunned whisper, somewhere on the distant side of the room.

"Go, child. You heard me very well. You know that I mean what I say. Go and prepare yourself, and never fear that I have any trick to play on you this time. No one will drag you back. You're free."

There was silence for a long moment. He felt the leap and surge of the fierce young heart towards liberty, heard the frantic clapping of the half-extended wings for an instant, before they were hushed and stroked and muted back into stillness. The struggle that convulsed the boy, flesh and spirit, vibrated through Isambard's own body and left him shaken and amazed.

Blunt and loud: "I won't go!" said Harry.

Fulfilled and joyful, what did he need now with eyes? What did he need with more years of life? They could give him nothing better or stranger than this. *Nunc dimittis*, he thought, lying mute in his sweet amazement and smiling into the dark. Lord, now lettest thou thy servant depart. In peace? I doubt it, he owned, and smiled still. What had he ever had to do with peace? But in enlargement and content.

So he, too, had felt the gathering insecurity, and feared it not for himself, but for the old, blind man suddenly vulnerable among fair-weather friends, who would turn on him as soon as the wind changed. How could a man abandon even his enemy in such a case? But how could he say as much to his enemy?

"I won't go," repeated Harry, challenging the silence.

Not his most attractive voice, rather surly and stubborn, and unreasonably furious, like a child's utterance when he feels he has been driven into a false position by unfair means, and is discharging all the weight of his own self-reproach and pain upon his elders. A voice that must have earned him many a box on the ears in his childhood. But gently now, to the man, and not the child. The voice was a recoil and a defence; behind it the man could be reached, for the words were his, and the indignant heart from which they had risen was his. He would listen to reason. There was no need to fear a final refusal; was it too dear an indulgence to hold this one in his hands for a moment before he let it go from him?

"Yes, Harry, you'll go. Not at my command, but because you must. There are reasons enough."

The boy had expected and dreaded astonishment and questions, and been ready to counter them with what might have been insolence but for its complications of bewilderment and distress. To be understood without the need for words was more vexing, in a way, than to be pressed for explanations. No one likes to be read like a book. Nevertheless, he heaved a great breath of relief at not having to account for his change of heart, he who had fought tooth and nail for the freedom he was now refusing.

"You have no choice, Harry," said Isambard gently. "There is something I have not told you. If you refuse to go, Madonna Benedetta will come here to Parfois to surrender herself in your place. If I cannot be sure of affording you protection any longer, how can I guarantee her protection?"

That brought the boy across the room in a rush of light steps, to crouch beside the arm of the chair and catch at the lean, long hand. "Madonna Benedetta? Coming here? But how—What compact was this? And not a word to me! Never a word! Was *this* the message John brought you?" He was quivering with anger and dismay. "How dared you? You had no right . . . no right . . . !"

"Neither had she, but she did it. She offered her own person in exchange for you, and I accepted the offer. Your John, God rest him, thought to get you out of my hands by a different way and make the bargain void, and it might have been well if he had succeeded, but he did not, and we must live with what we have. After he was dead I sent Walter in his place to take my ring and my pledge to her, never thinking how soon I might have cause to wish both back again. I doubt he's thought it best to avoid Aber, and had to waste some time hunting for her, but by this he has surely done his errand. And if you do not go and halt her on the way, she will come to

Parfois to be your ransom. And just at a time when I can no longer be sure of my power to hold her safe." He closed his fingers with careful respect upon the boy's smooth, vital hand. "And that's why you must go, since I cannot. You must ride and intercept her on the way, tell her both you and she are free of all debts and commitments to me, and take her safely home."

"You could send someone else," said Harry, distracted and trembling.

"No one else, not even the elders who knew her once, can be so sure as you of knowing her now. No one else can present her in his own person with the prize she's coming to purchase. And for the rest—consider my household, Harry. With Walter already out of it, whom would you trust with such an errand? No, you cannot evade your duty; it's you must go."

Harry's head went down in a revulsion of helpless bewilderment, his forehead on the clasped hands, while he searched his heart wildly, in agony to single out what he ought to do from what he wanted to do. Out of hiding his muffled voice blurted desperately:

"But how can I leave you?"

No question now of dignity and reticence, and no sense of having compromised or lost them. Naked and simple the words came, and he said them, and was eased.

"You can because you must. And if you want a more selfish reason from me, because I can get along, saving your lordship's presence, better without you than with you. Walter will be here soon to supply a pair of eyes and an honest tongue for my use, and what more could you do if you stayed? The greatest aid you can furnish me is to take Benedetta out of danger. Never fear for me," he said, himself marvelling at the serenity of his voice, "I am an old campaigner; I can hold my own here on my own ground. Go and make all ready, and tomorrow, as soon as you've broken your fast, come here to me. I'll put you on your way myself."

It was necessary. Who knew if the thought might not strike de Guichet that the boy had better be retained, that he might some day be a useful bargaining counter?

"Well, will you go?"

The smooth forehead stirred on his hand, the troubled face came up to him slowly; he felt the long, anxious stare of the sea-green

eyes searching him through and through, and knew that he had won
his way. He would go because he must. It was not necessary to find
comfort for him; life would soon do that.

"I'll go," said Harry.

They came to the gatehouse together as the long, level shafts of the
dawn threaded it and felt their golden way into the outer ward.
Isambard's left hand gestured, and the guards who had looked
askance at the prisoner fell back obediently and let them pass.

They stepped on to the timbers of the bridge, and Barbarossa's
hoofs sent their hollow echo reverberating along the rocky cleft
below. Before them on its high plateau of grassland, fringed with
trees along the edges of the escarpments on either side, the church
of Parfois soared like a golden lance. The singing light fingered its
way into every course of masonry framing the deep doorway and
the great east window, and set the taut lines of the tower quivering
like the strings of a harp.

Here, thought Isambard in his darkness, *he* came forth, that day.
She had him by the hand, she loosed his fingers then and fell behind
him. Something she cried into his ear as he looked up. I saw his face
clearly, I can see it still, amazed and enchanted by the thing he had
made. And then he fell. Here, just here, he fell, and she caught him
in her arms and sank to the ground with him, and held him on her
heart as he died. It took such a little time for him to die, hardly long
enough for her to kiss him on the mouth. When we took him from
her he was far out of our reach. We stripped him by the river. Naked
and brown, he was like one of the country boys along Severnside
who learn to swim as they learn to walk. Slender and wiry and
young. And dead.

"My lord," said Master Harry's son, watching the lofty hawk's
face beside him, and feeling the lean hand grip tighter about his
arm, "is anything the matter?"

"Nothing, Harry. I was remembering something past. Old men
do." His voice was still sardonic when he chose to describe himself
as old; after all its batterings his body could not believe that it had
lost its youth.

There was a matter still between them of a death, and the ravishing of a grave. He thought they might yet come to speech

about it, and if he would not have welcomed the reckoning at this last moment, he would not have shrunk from it. But Harry walked beside him and was silent, matching his easy, young-man's stride to the deliberate and careful steps of his companion, and nursing him away from any broken ground or stony places. Barbarossa sniffed the morning air and danced for joy.

Close to the tower now, close to the pale scar of the foundation, enclosed in its rising wall. They heard the voices of the masons, the scraping of shovels in mortar, the chink of hammers and chisels on stone. There were many people there, others of the household besides the workmen and the guard. De Guichet was there, talking to Master Edmund; Isambard heard his voice among the many voices, and smiled. He was waiting for one arriving rather than for a departure.

"When you meet her, be sure you say to her that there are no debts remaining. You know which way she is likely to come?"

"There's but one good and direct way from Aber, my lord."

"Good! Then I can leave her safely in your hands. Are we yet at the guard point?"

"Fifty yards more, my lord."

"Take me through, Harry, before you mount. I would have you off my boundary. What do you see in their faces?"

"I think they are still in awe of you. They go on with what they are doing, but with their eyes on us. The guards have moved back to leave your way open."

He was still princely; he could still command dread. And they were still not sure, not quite sure, how the wind might veer.

"That's well. Are we through now?"

"Yes, my lord."

"Then here we say our farewells."

They halted, strangely irresolute now. Barbarossa pulled impatiently at Harry's wrist, wild to be off. He turned a moment to chide and soothe him.

"They are all watching us. Some have stopped work. I think it is only that they wonder."

"Let them wonder. You mount and ride, and lose no time. God speed, and commend me to Madonna Benedetta."

Harry turned to mount, and could not; looked over his shoulder and turned back, feeling his heart in him torn in two.

"My lord, I'm loath—"

"Arrogant imp," said Isambard, "do you think no one can make shift without you? Be off, I don't need you."

The still splendid figure, alert, fastidiously shaven, carefully and richly dressed, had borne witness in every movement to the continued competence of his vision, until this last moment of leave-taking. Suddenly he wavered, made an abrupt step forward, and raised a hesitant hand, groping towards his parting prisoner in a blind and helpless gesture; and Harry, forgetting everything but that fumbling hand feeling for his face, caught it in his and guided it to his cheek. Its fellow came gently, of its own accord, and held him. The beautiful head stooped a little, the hawk face inclined, the hard, scarred lips saluted his cheek very lightly.

Silently, trembling, he submitted to the kiss of kinship; and when he was released he reached impulsively and returned it, with a child's fervour and clumsiness.

"God be with you, my lord."

Nothing more, not a word. Explanation was out of his reach, justification he did not need, understanding was somewhere within him, heart-deep, part of him now whether he would or no, and not to be questioned. He set his foot in the stirrup and mounted. Barbarossa stamped the ground gladly and stretched towards the valley in an unchecked canter, and the wind of their going, sharp with the morning coolness, stung where Isambard's kiss had rested.

They were gone. It was over. And now he could set his mind to what remained to be done, and fear, in the sense that he understood fear, was finished with. The game of life and death had still to be played, but the stakes were within his control now, and mattered no more than a game should matter. He stood listening until the soft thudding of the hoofs in the grassy ground had ebbed away into the valley. Then he turned, and took a step back towards the towers of the lower guard, and suddenly he was alone, without light or landmarks, in a featureless landscape of nightmare.

He listened for the hammers, but the hammers had stopped; for the voices, but the voices were silent. Uphill he must go; but he felt carefully about him with a stretched toe, and could not determine how the slope lay. He had lost his guide, and made no provision to

replace him; but there was surely more in this silence than their
covert interest in his movements and caprices. The quality of their
stares crowded and burdened him. Sweat broke in his palms. What
had he done? Something revealing, something irrevocable, that betrayed the weakness of his position. For they knew he was helpless.
They knew he was blind.

Then he understood. Every eye had been on him when he lifted
his hand tentatively towards Harry's face. But for that he might
have kept up his deception even now, called to Master Edmund,
made some pretext to get him to his side so that he might make use
of him on the first stage of the return journey, and borrow a man
from him for the rest. It was too late now; they knew. There would
be no more pretending. Harry had taken the hand as it reached sadly
astray, and laid it to his cheek. Did I not say, he thought ruefully,
that he'd be the death of me yet?

So now he had the choice of fumbling his way back dangerously
and ludicrously alone, or commanding help openly, and accepting
their knowledge and his own loss. He was aware of many watchers,
none moved, many gratified, not one anxious to help him. Even
when he called peremptorily for a shoulder to lean on, the stillness
and the silence held. He knew his loneliness.

"Master Edmund! Where is Master Edmund? Bid him here to
me, some of you. Move!"

Slowly, grudgingly, they stirred. Only one creature, somewhere
there in the foundations of the tower, dropped something out of
his arm with a flat wooden clap against the stone of the rising wall,
and came in a shamed run to take him by the arm. Something
new was revealed to him in the touch. Never in his life until now
had he been a target for compassion. It needed some adjustment
to welcome it, even in his situation, yet he did it in the measure
of the first step they took together. Whoever this fellow might be,
he had a right to his enlarging impulse; only a mean heart could
grudge it to him.

"Here, my lord, this way." The hand turned him and put him on
the smoothest of the roadway. "Lean on me. Is it back to your
apartments you would go?"

A kind voice, young but not very young, and one that would
have been timorous in addressing the lord of Parfois in any other

circumstances. The careful steps that attended Isambard's long strides were those of a small man, the arm on which he leaned his hand was thin. The eyes that were only just being born in him drew him a picture from these contacts, of a young fellow of about thirty-four or five, somewhat below medium height, and of modest and gentle appearance and mild attainments. Not a mason, the muscular development was not there, the fingers had not that kind of dexterity that went with tools. The sleeve was rough home-spun, but the wrist was smooth.

"Friend," said Isambard, using new forms of address in new situations, and tasting the lessons of his old age as sharply and acutely as those of his youth, "I think I should know you. Have you been in my service long?"

"Nearly twenty years, my lord. Take care here, the ground is stony."

"You are one of those engaged on the tower, are you not? As I think, a clerk."

"Yes, my lord."

Twenty years a clerk about the building-works of Parfois made him but a boy when Master Harry Talvace fell to the arrow of God and of John the Fletcher. Here, on this spot, where the morning sun lay bright along the open grassland before the bridge. There had been a boy then in the tracing-house, one who ran faithfully and adoringly at his heels, cleaned parchments for him, dwelt on his every word and stroke like a worshipper, and wept himself half-blind at his fall. The small, transmitted lightning of Master Harry's passionate kindness quivered, muted, in the hand that guided Master Harry's destroyer back to his refuge.

"I know you now," said Isambard. "Your name, as I recall, is Simon. You were his clerk."

"I was, my lord."

How was it that he knew, without the need for thought or question, who "he" must be? He answered readily, with no note of wonder at the length of this cast. Harry is as alive to him as to me, thought Isambard, astonished, and as timeless.

"We are at the bridge, my lord. Step a little high."

Master Edmund had done nothing to advance him. He was jealous always of those Harry most relied on, Isambard reflected. And he had brief thoughts, as they crossed the outer ward, of repairing that minor injustice; till he recalled at his own door, with honesty and certainty, that his favour was hardly likely to advance any man again, unless it was into an early grave.

From the leads of the tower roof, in the old days, he had been able to see the blue hills of central Wales rearing to westward, across the wide green valley laced with silver; and Pool upstream, and Strata Marcella down, had balanced each other in the sunlight, grey stone against grey stone. Even in his blindness something of the enlargement of freedom came to him there. The air blew clean across from the lofty peat-bogs and the shallow heron-pools in the uplands, and brought scents of heather and withering autumn grass, its seeds ripened and shed.

Somewhere beyond those dim, remembered shapes of heath and cloud Benedetta and Harry rode homeward now together without haste. Walter on his return journey had not encountered Harry, for Walter had come by way of Shrewsbury, to gather the latest news of King Henry's devious proceedings at Usk; but surely by now the woman and the boy must be nearing Aber. His heart was delivered of them.

"She took the ring from me," Walter had faithfully reported what he did not understand, "and I think she was glad, until I told her what befell her man. She was quiet a long time, but she did not weep or rail. She said that she took that guilt upon her, that she should have opened her heart to him. And she said that there would be a time to talk of it."

Nothing more. The rest she had kept for her coming, when she had made, as she said, provision for the old man who dwelt beside her; and now he would never hear it. There might have been a time to talk of all things that lay unfinished between them, but now there never would, never in this dear world.

So much the better. She was safe, she had her darling again; and as for him, the house of his mind was swept clean and the fortress of his loneliness well provided. Walter was dismissed to Fleace, on the pretext that his master meant to follow him there shortly; and Simon the clerk was gone with him, recommended to service under Humphrey Paunton's mason at work on the new hall there. One more innocent from under his feet, clear of the stray shots that cared little where they fell. Parfois in the days to come would be no place for gentle creatures who took pity on their enemies grown old and blind, and led them by the hand out of harm's way.

He turned from his dark contemplation of Wales when the wind grew chill. The upper reaches of the tower staircase were narrow and worn; one of the pages usually led him up there, and waited within call until he chose to come down. But on this evening of late September he called, and no page came.

He waited and called again, less patiently. He listened, and there was no young foot stirring, no voice answering; but there were other sounds, rising with a slow, spiral splendour out of the wards below. A ceremonious clashing of hoofs in procession, a murmur of voices quick with excitement and eagerness; all distant, all belonging to the lower world, and filtered through the golden acres of air. Some company riding in. The young men still rode, still hawked and hunted; every day the outer ward and the stable-yard were busy with riders. But this had a different sound, alien and bright.

He waited to see if they would bring him word, but no word came. He was neither surprised nor dismayed, for he had expected nothing. And after a while, satisfied that his attendant had deserted him to run and stare with the rest of the household in the outer ward, he felt his way along the merlons to the doorway, and began to descend alone. Step by step, with due caution on the tapering treads, it took him a long time to negotiate the upper flights. It did not matter. He had plenty of time.

Between the thick walls he was closed in from the world, and there was no sound but the sounds of his own body, his feet treading slowly and carefully from worn stair to stair, his long, even breathing, the steady, strong beat of his heart thudding at the cage of his bony breast. At every arrow-slit in the turns of the well a current of cool, sweet air blew over him, and at every brief landing the darkness seemed heavier. He no longer saw either shapes or shades; all was one darkness.

He reached the level of his own apartments, and stood for a moment by the stair-head, listening with reared head and stretched ears. No movement within the tower, no voices. From without, heard more faintly here, a certain hum and bustle that had still a note of excitement in it. But somewhere here, close to him, he felt rather than heard the even rise and fall of breathing. Not his own: that rhythm he knew intimately by now. Somewhere in a room aside from him, but with the door open between. And so still. And by its very evenness and quietness, whoever breathed and waited there was aware of him.

He felt his way along the wall, and reached across to the doorway of his own great chamber. The door stood half open; he had closed it with his own hand when he left it, an hour earlier. He pushed it fully open and went in, without concealment and striding easily, for here he knew every knot in the timbers, and every irregularity in the oak of the floorboards. At leisure he took his stand in the centre of the room, and turned his imperious face, that quenched lantern of splendid bone, slowly to left and right, and fastened after a moment on the direction in which he felt the palpable presence. There he fixed and held, utterly calm and sure of himself, and faintly smiling.

Someone was sitting in his great chair, an act of usurpation that marked, at least, the end of a pretence. His smile deepened at that. He took his time about considering identities. A large, self-confident breath, a sense of bulk, someone broad-set and well-fleshed; but uneasy under the blind stare, for he stirred a little in the cushions, and then, in a movement which startled Isambard into astonished laughter, got to his feet. He thought he had him then; taking his lord's chair in the first place and quitting it now chimed so well with his nature, and were so revealing.

"De Guichet?" he said, disappointed and disdainful.

"No," said a voice out of the darkness before him, soft, smiling and deliberate, "not de Guichet."

"Ah, is it you? Fair, sweet son," said Isambard in a large sigh of understanding and fulfilment, "what has kept you so long? I've been looking for you these ten days."

Chapter Six

Aber: *October* 1233

Saint Clydog came out of the long dream unwillingly, to a grey sky hanging low over Moel Wnion and a distant, desolate crying of the sea, an empty hut, a quenched hearth, an unpeopled heart, and an agitated young man crouched before him in the deep grass, holding his knees in big, supple, golden-brown hands and staring up into his face with great urgent eyes that he had seen somewhere before, in another countenance. A desperate voice battered insistently at his reluctant senses with a name, coaxing, pleading, bullying, cajoling, dragging him back to a world he desired to know no longer. He tried to shut up his ears and seal his spirit, but the hands held him cruelly, and the voice like the hilt of a dagger pounded at the closed doors, and would not leave him to his quietness.

"Where is Madonna Benedetta? Listen to me! Help me! I must find her. Where is Madonna Benedetta?"

The old man opened his eyes fully, and with infinite pain dragged himself back into the fragile confines of his body, that little cage in which the great bird fluttered feebly with cramped wings and bursting heart. He remembered this face: this was the boy who had beckoned her away.

778

"She is gone," he said, shrinking in the grip of the young hands that did not know how strong they were.

"I *see*, I *know* she is gone." The coarse blanket was folded on the narrow brychan, the fire-stone was cold, the arched window to southward stared blind. "When did she go? How is it I have not met her along the way?"

Harry knelt in the grass, holding the saint's aged knees in his palms, staring up into the face that was no more than a drift of draggled grey down from a hedgerow of thistles, lit by two remote and dim blue eyes.

"Dear saint, help me! I must find her, I have a message to deliver."

"She is gone to Parfois," said Saint Clydog, the old voice suddenly clear and aware. "There was a squire who came and brought her an answer to her message. She begged me a boy to care for me and keep me, and then she went from me on her journey."

"To Parfois? But I've come from Parfois. At every grange and hospice on the way I've inquired for her, and never any news. She has not passed that road. I thought to find her still here." He leaned and took the frail little hands that lay light as moths in the old man's lap. "Did she ride alone? Surely she took some escort with her from Aber? The prince would never let her—"

He halted there, sure as soon as he posed the question that no one could have known better than Benedetta what the prince would and would not let her do. To have her come down out of her chosen solitude would be like having the sun turn back towards dawn from the zenith. Her every move would have been questioned earnestly.

"She did not go near Aber," he said, loudly and bitterly, enraged with his own stupidity. "Oh, sweet saint, tell me quickly, which way did she go? Who attended her?"

In Aber they could not even be aware yet that she was strayed from her place.

"She went down by the hill road into Bangor," said Saint Clydog, staring above the boy's head as though he saw her now taking that lonely path over the shoulder of the mountain. "She asked Bishop Martin for a boy to attend on me, and for a horse and a mounted manservant for herself, to bring her as far as Parfois. And I did not see her again. Only the boy came up to me. He's there below now at the brook, fishing. A good boy, but young and strange. I was used to John the Fletcher," he said wistfully.

"Then she took the road straight from Bangor?" It would mean that from Dolgynwal on she would be travelling by the same road on which he had made such haste. If she had been a day earlier, or he a day later, they would surely have met. "When did she leave here?" he questioned, shaking fiercely at the rough brown sleeve. "How many days since?"

"Three days—or was it four? It rained when she was gone. Two days were rainy, and then the sun came for a little while, and that was yesterday. Four days ago."

"And your boy—when did he come?"

"Towards nightfall, on the day after she left me. A good boy. Quiet," said Saint Clydog, dropping the feeble tears of old age down his tangled beard unawares. "There's no peace where there are women. They must be for ever coming and going. I always knew she would not live out her life here."

Harry was up out of the grass like a rising bird. Give her one night's rest in Bangor before she rode, and she could be only three days advanced on the journey. Past Dolgynwal by now, surely, while he rode up here in his ignorance still watching for her on the direct road. She could still be overtaken. He turned to reach for Barbarossa's bridle, and then, remembering his manners, plunged as impulsively back again to plump to his knees before the saint and ask his blessing.

"Sir, pray for me! That I find her in time!"

The wrinkled hand touched his head, and rested a moment like a dry leaf caught in the tangle of his hair.

"In God's time, or in yours?" said Saint Clydog sadly.

He rode down the steep cleft of the valley beside the stream, and the great enclosed shape of the prince's maenol came into sight below him, backed into the fissure of the hills and commanding the narrow strip of marshland and meadow above the sands. The long, dark line of the encircling wall and rampart folded hall and stables and living quarters, kitchen and kennels and mews, the low tower of the royal apartments on its broad undercroft, and the timber keep on its towering motte. Outside the wall the village sprawled, clinging to shelter, and the little river bound the maenol in a silver ribbon before it flowed down through the level marshes to the sea. His heart leaped and clamoured in his breast, frantic to be there.

He could have turned Barbarossa, and ridden straight back along the way he had come; but he had taken thought in time that he needed help with this hunt, and more men on fresher horses would have a better chance of success. The first thing he must do, before he rode again, was to pour out the whole story into Llewelyn's ears. He need fear no long explanations there, no checks of sheer incomprehension; his foster-father's quick senses leaped into under-standing as naturally as trees lean to the light. He need only cry out what was needful, and questions could wait for an ampler time.

Past the mill the road opened out and grew less steep, and he spurred eagerly, and came at a canter into the postern gate. The offered challenge fell away from him before a cry of recognition and joy. He leaned to reach a hand to old friends as he rode by them, and to gasp out his haste. The dark gateway in the tall timber wall gulped him and gave him back to the light of day within, as he reined to a standstill in the courtyard before the hall.

A woman at the well knew him, and dropped her pitcher to run and cry the news. Men came running, men he had wrestled and climbed and played with from childhood, surrounding him, hoisting him bodily out of the saddle, crying questions, fondling him, passing him boisterously from hand to hand. He fought them off, panting.

"The prince—first I must speak with the prince. I must! Don't keep me!" Somewhere in his heart a frantic child, in tears of excite-ment and joy, was howling rather for his mother, but that must wait.

He had set off at a run for the steps of the hall, but they lifted voices and hands to turn him towards Llewelyn's private apartments, and ran on his heels to bring him there with acclaim, until he outran them on the wings of his eagerness and burst in at the door of the prince's tower alone. Up the great staircase in four striding leaps, like a deer-hound, and the heavy door of the private audience-room was hurled back to the wall before his rush, and he was in Llewelyn's presence.

The three men at the table, heads close and faces grave and intent, looked up as one man, startled and wary. The stranger's hand went to his hilt with formidable rapidity but admirable smoothness. Ednyfed Fychan came to his feet, frowning, and opened his lips to challenge the unmannerly intruder. Llewelyn, who sat with his back to the door, turned a scowl of impatience and displeasure; but the next moment the blaze of knowledge flamed in his face. He let out a great bellow of: "Harry!" The chair, whirled aside to give him passage, span jarring back against the wall. He leaped to meet the boy's impetuous rush, arms spread to take him to his heart.

Harry ran and flung himself at the prince's feet, and caught the great right hand down to his breast, kissing it fervently, laying his forehead for an instant against Llewelyn's knees before he was caught by the arms and hoisted exuberantly to his feet.

"Harry, is it you? Is it you indeed?"

Long arms strained him to a broad, brocaded breast; he felt the massive, impetuous beat of the prince's heart pulse through his body, shaking him to the marrow of his bones. Bearded lips kissed his cheek and his brow, and he was held off to be devoured by far-sighted black eyes blazing with laughter and delight. A hard palm under his unshaven chin turned up his face to be read and re-read.

"Stand to be seen, boy, give me my fill. Why, you're taller by inches than Owen, I'll swear, and pressing David close." He was round upon the seneschal with shining eyes. "Run, Ednyfed, send for my lady, have her bring Gilleis with her—tell them Harry's come home safe and sound. And David, and Owen—and Adam Boteler if he's to be found. Hurry!" And upon the stranger, who had withdrawn courteously into the shadows, and stood watching them with a slight, grave, uncomprehending smile:

"You'll pardon us; it's not every day I regain a son. This is my foster-child, Harry Talvace, who has been prisoner this long time to Ralf Isambard at Parfois. It's nearly two years since we've set eyes on him, and never a word or a sign that we could hope to see him burst in like this—as loud and unruly as ever," said Llewelyn, and thumped Harry heartily on the back. "Make your reverence, boy, to Alan Delahaye. He is come to us as envoy from the earl of Pembroke."

Harry made his bow and his excuses, still further excited and confused by this mention of the earl marshal. What could Pembroke want to discuss with the prince of Aberffraw but the issue of peace and war?

"I beg you'll forgive so rude an interruption, sir. I would not have ventured to burst in unbidden, but there's a matter that can't wait. My Lord, may I speak?"

"You may, you must," said Llewelyn. "I'm waiting to hear. How is it we have you again? Are you free in very truth this time? Have you broken out of hold?"

"From Parfois," said Delahaye dryly, "I think he'd be the first."

"I did not break out." Seven times in all he had made the attempt, there was nothing any Englishman could teach him about the impregnability of Parfois. "He set me free. But—"

"What, are there still buts? What has he devised this time to your hurt? If this wind holds, it's I shall be paying off the account with him."

"My lord, it's not as you suppose. But I'm charged with an errand I could not do yet, and until it's done I'm not free. Madonna Benedetta—she's gone from her place, and I must find her."

"Madonna Benedetta, gone from her place? What's this? An errand? *His* errand," said Llewelyn, falling upon the word like a hawk upon its prey. "And to her!" He drew the boy with him back to his chair, set him on a footstool at his feet, and kept fast hold of him by the hands. "Tell me!"

Harry took breath and poured out the whole of it short and bare into his lap. The prince's great, vital hands held him, and never started or tightened.

Before the tale was done the prince's message had brought them all running to confirm with their own eyes that Harry was back among them, to touch him for proof and hold fast after touching. Gilleis came flying with skirts kilted up like a wild girl, and flung herself upon him in a rush of happy, incredulous tears. He opened his arms to her without pausing in his tale, and Llewelyn surrendered him without relaxing for a moment the intensity of his attention. Gilleis knelt beside her son, kissed his breathless mouth once between the tumbling words, and kept her arms fast about him to the end. Owen came, glowing with the news, and David, flushed and bright with joy. Adam Boteler came, and leaned to kiss his stepson gently on the head. The princess came, and the boy, distracted, would have risen and knelt to her, but she reached a hand to quiet him and hold him where he was, and touched for present salutation the preoccupied lips that brushed a kiss upon her fingertips between the syllables of Benedetta's name.

"I was at fault; I made too great haste, and thought too little. If I'd taken the road more easily I should surely have met her on the way. You see I must go back, I can't rest till I've found her and brought her home. Oh, Mother, you'll give me leave for a few days more—"

Gilleis closed his lips with her palm and hushed him. She knew already, by the height and the breadth of him, and the golden-brown down of his chin and the deep voice, and by the look of his eyes even when he smiled at her thus through dazed tears, shaken to the heart by the warmth of his welcome home, that she must give him leave lifelong if she wanted to keep him now. The years she had lost there was no replacing. Even the years restored might all too soon be forfeit to another woman, but let that be faced when it came. He was free, he was his own man, and for her heart's quiet no less than for his, Benedetta must be regained.

"Child, do you think there's anything I could grudge her? Go with my blessing. If I could outride you after her, I would."

"But let me go in your place," offered Owen, seeing the weariness not far behind the brilliance of Harry's eyes. "You've taken no rest. Have you slept at all since you left Parfois?"

"Let him be," said Llewelyn briskly, wise in his young men, "this charge is his, not yours. Do you go with David, and choose him six good men who know the holy woman, and mount them well. Best send two by way of Bangor, Hal, to follow her traces the road she went, and take four over the hill track with you to meet the road at Dolgynwal. If you get word she's passed there, well and good. But if not, let two ride ahead fast with you, and two turn back to meet their fellows from Bangor, till they do hear certain news of her. You shall have my writ to take whatever mounts or men or aids you need as far as the border. There, go make your choice from the stables, and what else you need or want before you go, never spare to ask or take. God helping, we'll not lose Benedetta."

* * *

"A good lad," said Llewelyn, still gazing thoughtfully after them when the door was shut between. "Take him faults and all, as good a lad as ever stepped."

"One of the king's best allies on your borders," said Delahaye from his place in the shadows, "has troubles enough of his own, it seems. If you do choose to move south and lift the weight from the earl's flank, my lord, you need not fear Parfois, that's clear."

"Fear of Parfois would not trouble me. I have a vow registered in heaven concerning Parfois, in God's and my good time to take and destroy it for the sake of Talvace—the father and the son. And I see nothing here to loose me from that oath. Let the son be freed, yet the sire's dead, and his grave dishonoured. And yet—blinded!" he said, and shook his head over it, frowning. "I would have had him with all his powers at their best."

"You need not disturb him unless you choose. It's enough for us," said Delahaye, "that he should be out of the reckoning, and it seems this poor wretch who was killed has taken care of that. The earl would rather have you pin down Brecon for him while he keeps his hands free to clear the valley of the Usk. But should you choose indeed to pursue your vow, coming in upon our side at least gives you the opportunity."

"You do not believe," said Llewelyn, "that it can be done?"

His eyes kindled golden, like a hawk's, his head pricked up loftily to stare with joy upon the sweet temptation of the almost impossible. But he put it by, shaking the lure out of his vision. There were other considerations. If he went to war for the last time—surely the last time, for the latest years of his life must be given all to consolidating the kingdom he had carved out for his son—it would be for graver reasons than the satisfying of a boyish lust in his own heart. Something might yet be won and added to David's inheritance, his position as neighbour to England established yet more firmly, his native right more unmistakably demonstrated. The English had a marked liking and value for precedents and points of law and custom; it was for that tradition that Pembroke was fighting, whatever the personal wrongs that had launched this unexpected war. For that and for a standard of integrity in the relationships between men and government, so firmly fixed and well respected that it should be impossible for a weathercock king to disregard it.

And there lay the final and compelling reason for saying yes to Pembroke's proposal of alliance, beyond all the reasons of interest: Pembroke was in the right and Henry was in the wrong. Whatever the minor rights and wrongs of who struck first or who suffered deprivation first, seeing the whole great quarrel large, Pembroke was in the right.

"God disposes, my lord," said Delahaye, smiling. "I would not say there is any fortress that *cannot* be taken."

Llewelyn had moved so far from the impregnability of Parfois that it cost him an effort and a little wonder to get back to it.

"I doubt it will never be put to the issue," he said, a shade regretful still. "Please God, Harry will bring back Madonna Benedetta safe and well, and I shall have no stake within the wall there, to draw me to the assay. God who disposes must dispose of me and my vow, if I do not keep it. An archer with a handful of quicklime can be as effective as an angel with a flaming sword, I doubt." He turned resolutely from this unprofitable harrowing. "This warning that reached the earl on his way south to the council, and turned him back into Gwent—do you hold it certain it was true? Would the king have impeached him? He had given him guarantees, so recent that no one can have forgotten them."

"He gave de Burgh guarantees, an oath sealed on the relic of Bromholm, not a month before he felled him like a tree. And whoever sent the warning spoke no more than the truth about the king's intentions at Usk. The appointed time is well past, and he has made no move to give the castle back. That, too, he guaranteed. A good earnest for all his other promises."

"I grant you. And Usk," said Llewelyn with a glittering smile, "for all the king could not take it, is not impregnable."

"By this, I think, Turbeville is out of it, and the earl has his own again. He wearied of waiting for Henry to keep his word. But the true measure of the rottenness of the king's credit," said Delahaye fiercely, "is that such a warning could be received by any honourable man and not *dis*believed. It may not in every case be true, but in no case dare a man discount it, for all too evidently it *could* be true. To what has the crown come, if this must be said of it?"

A man is not necessarily a better advocate because he believes passionately in the cause he must argue; but his faith or his close alliance with Richard Marshall had lent Delahaye a conviction that rang more gratefully than eloquence in Llewelyn's ears. There was another test he could set beside the first, and the contrast was marked. If Pembroke had made him a promise, without the sanction of the rood of Bromholm or any other relic, he would have rested absolutely secure in its fulfilment. If one had come riding after him with a warning that Pembroke meant to betray him in Pembroke's own house, he would have laughed and ridden on without a qualm. The test of any man's honesty is whether you are willing to stake your life on it. Who would do that on King Henry's?

There was still time to reconsider. If he held with them he held with them to the end; no separate terms, no separate peace. How if the entire march came in with its full weight on the king's side? How if he brought in more and more foreign mercenaries like the Count de Guisnes and his Flemings? Des Rivaulx had seen to it that all the streams of revenue were channelled securely into his hands; as long as he lasted Henry could afford to buy troops abroad. He was well financed, he was making a strong bid for an established rule of his own, free of the council and loosed from custom and tradition. And he would deal with his enemies without mercy if he did prevail.

The time to think of the end was now, before he began. Not his own life and his own fortunes at stake now, but David's princedom, the dream of Wales. If he held with them now he held with them to the end, and prevailed or foundered with them. So be it! And now, he thought, smiling and content with his cast, let us give our minds to the details, and see to it that we prevail, and not founder.

"It will take me a little time to get my army into the field," he said deliberately, "but not so long as it will take Henry to bring in the lords of the march. By the end of the month I can be ready to cover your lord's flank from all assault from Shropshire and Herefordshire, without laying my own lands open." He spread his hands upon the table, pushing back his chair, happy and committed and at the edge of action.

"You may tell the earl of Pembroke my answer is: Yes. Before October is out I will declare for him, and take Gwynedd to war."

"My lord," said Delahaye, burning up like a furze fire, "I was sure of you."

It remained only to ensure that they should command success. Llewelyn stared into the coming weeks, brilliant-eyed, measuring the musters of Corbett and Lacy and FitzAlan on his borders. But not Parfois. Parfois held, if Harry had the tale right—and Harry was shrewd enough, and had had every opportunity to assess the possibilities for himself—the seeds of its own civil war. If Ralf Isambard held his own, Henry would never call him into service, for Henry, an ill judge of men, did not trust him. If he let his governance slip through his fingers. . . .

"Blinded!" said Llewelyn, brought up short again upon the inconceivable image of darkness. "God knows at the worst I never wished him that!"

The small, chill wind of the evening over the shoulder of Moel Wnion brought with it into the grassy hollow the salt breath and the melancholy crying of the ebbing tide along Lavan sands. Far across the strait all the little bells of all the oratories on Ynys Lanog of the saints made a tiny, stammering chime, the faint recollection of a long-past dream of bells.

Saint Clydog was in the very doorway when he heard them, and for a moment he stayed with his foot across the threshold, uncertain whether they were calling him forward or back. They had a sweetness like the first intimation of bliss, but very far away; they had a sadness like the last convulsion of remembered sorrow. He peered forward into a darkness pulsing with the promise of light, but his eyes had still too much earth in them, and he could not see into the brightness beyond. He looked over his shoulder into the twilit hollow, but his vision was hazy already with the as yet unrealised image of light, and the shapes of the world withdrew from him.

But after all, there was no longer any reason to stay. The shapes of the world were the shapes of emptiness and loss. No light in the stone hut, no foot on the door-sill, no voice at dawn. No more to be said here, no more to be done, no more truant boys for whom he must wait. No need, no need to have waited for Harry.

The sea mourned, the gathering night shivered, cold and loneliness and sorrow stood silent at his back. And the angel that attended his sleeping and his waking drew him on through the doorway, reassuring him gently that the woman would not be far behind him. He looked back no more towards the desolation where she had been. He went on, deaf to the voices that entreated him to return, untouched by the hands that clung to him, free of all the prayers, troubled no more by the burden of gifts and vigils and visions. He entered at the doorway of the dark, stepping over the door-sill of his yet unmade grave, and time closed behind him so softly that no one ever knew the moment when the latch slid into place.

His boy, coming up from the hut an hour later to lead him to bed, found only the little huddle of bird-bones discarded in the grass.

Chapter Seven

Parfois: *October to November* 1233

At Dolgynwal they picked up her tracks, and held them strongly for a great part of the way, riding hard and drawing lavishly on Llewelyn's writ for remounts wherever their beasts laboured and there were fresh horses to be had. At Meifod she was but a matter of hours ahead, and Harry took heart to believe he would overtake her after all. Why had she pressed so? He would not have believed a woman could have kept her lead of him across Wales, and he riding night and day without sleep but what he snatched on the wing. His heart accused him that she made such haste for his sake, and he drove himself the harder.

And then, at Strata Marcella, they found no word of her. Could they have overridden her somewhere between, while she rested in some cottage? Two of his six Harry sent questing back, to make casts right and left from the road; two he ordered ahead with all speed to make straight for the ramp of Parfois and keep close watch there on all who approached the lower guard; and he himself with the remaining two turned south for Castell Coch beyond Pool, in case she had chosen the southern rather than the northern ford for her crossing of Severn. Wild with self-accusations, hugging to himself the blame for her speed and ardour and devotion as well as his own tardiness, Harry came into Castell Coch at the drop of night, reeling in the saddle; and yes, she had been there, but no, she was there no longer. She would not sleep the night over, she rode again in the late evening, not long before sunset, barely an hour past.

Harry turned his horse and rode for the ford of Pool. Severn was hardly higher than its summer level yet, they splashed through it and threaded the silver pools in the water-meadows beyond; and as soon as the ground was firm under their feet Harry was spurring into a gallop again. Up the green road from the river to the shoulder of the Long Mountain, and uphill again on the ramp, and one of his own men started out of the trees and waved him to a halt.

For all their haste they had come late. She was ahead of them still, and inside Parfois.

"Fair, sweet son," said Isambard, sighing, "you waste your time and mine. Not that I complain of that. My time's long enough, in all conscience, I can spare you a few hours and no grudges. But if you hope to get what you want out of me, you won't do it by these means. I told you from the first, I'll give you nothing—what you want from me you must take. Asking won't do it. Think, my heart, if I signed and sealed your delivery I should be depriving myself of these daily consolations, your sweet company, your filial solicitude. Even on one unchanging subject, I love to hear your voice."

"There are more ways than one of asking a question. As you may yet find, my beloved father. Your grandsire provided a very handsome array of persuasions, there under the Warden's Tower, and I may yet be put to the necessity of using them."

"I think not. If you had dared you would have used them long ago. Not that they would have gained you anything, that I promise you. No, if you have spared to break my bones or flay my flesh off them, it's for the same reason that you've not thrust me into some hole to dwindle into a foul and noisome old man, or set to to starve me into reason. It's because you may at any moment have to produce me before the world, whole and sound and not past recognition. If Paunton or d'Enville or some other of my castellans doesn't force you to show me, some travelling envoy of King Henry well may. And the one would be as awkward for you as the other, if I were not kept utterly presentable every hour of every day."

"You do well to threaten me with King Henry," said William, grinning. "It's well seen which of us two has his favour. I have his authority to hold and garrison Parfois for him against the Welsh, in spite of your head. Does that look as if he'll stir for you?"

"Not for me, William, not for me—but for himself he'll stir in no uncertain fashion, you'll find. Oh, I grant you Henry would hardly be displeased if you rough-handled me a little. But he would certainly be *embarrassed* if you were put to the necessity of producing me on a hurdle because a few of my bones were out of joint. He's committed to you, William, since he's accredited you his castellan here. Better not commit him to too much, or too irrevocably." He smoothed long fingers round his well-shaven jaw and yawned, and sat smiling aggravatingly towards his son's chair. "Drag him into murder when he's only expressly authorised robbery, and you'll see what a tiger the lamb can be in his own defence. You still don't know him as I do, William. He'll hound you to the day of your death if you compromise him."

"That might not be necessary. There are ways of accounting for injuries. A fall—blind men do sometimes venture alone and fall," the smiling voice mused, encouraged.

The echoes in this small, bare upper room of the tower were still unfamiliar to Isambard's ears, after the ampler air down below, in the apartments he had for so long made his own. It was like William to possess himself of those particular rooms, out of all the many he could have chosen, but it was not all vanity or spite, either. They commanded this solitary stair, and the well-guarded chamber above. No one had access here but William's leave.

"And dislocate wrists and ankles, or crush a few fingers on the way? No, you're no such fool. A whisper of scandal would be enough, and the king would take his arm from you and leave you to pay the score alone. And you know it. Besides, that is not what you want. You want title and right, so clear that no one can point at you. The king can give you command of my castle, in the name of England's safety, but title to my honour he cannot give you. While I live only I can give you that. Only I!" he said with finality and content, and laughed to hear the violent rustling of silk as William wrenched himself out of his chair and began to pace the room. The blind face followed his prowlings, amused and mischievous. "And I will not," said Isambard.

"Will you not, my beloved father? I swear you shall yet. And be thankful to do it. You shall sign and seal away your rights to me, living, ware, knowing well what you do. I offered you easy terms, honourable retirement to Erington or Mormesnil or wherever you would, a proper household and all that you could need. I take that back." The pacing feet halted abruptly. A hand caught at the old man's wrist and shook it fiercely. He felt his son's heavy shadow leaning over him. "Now you shall sign your goods and gear and lands and men over to me on my terms, and do what living you may afterwards on my bounty. I'll have your seal and your hand on the deed, no matter what it may cost you in torment or me in trouble. You hear me?"

But he knew he would not. To threaten was easy, but there was too much truth by half in what the old man had said. Henry might wish him dead, but for his own protection would surely turn and rend whoever killed him; Henry might relish the idea of putting to a little salutary pain the man who had rated him publicly before his court, but he would be the first to exclaim in horror over the deed and set the hounds on the doer if ever the facts came to light. How else could he ward off the shame and danger of being implicated? There had never been any relying on him if the day went awry, and there would be none now.

Isambard put off the displeasing grip from him with a strong turn of his wrist, and wiped the touch of the hand from his flesh.

"I hear the boast," he said disdainfully. "Now let me see you make it good if you can. Here I am. Force me!"

How many days now had he been defying the same threat? He had lost count of time in his darkness, and the servants who scrupulously dressed and groomed and shaved him, and provided him with food and drink and all his needs, had their orders not to give anything that need not be given. A word of news, a message from anyone without, a weapon—these he had never asked for, knowing they would not be granted. When had he ever begged favours of any man? He could hold his own here as he was, naked of friends. Better so. Whatever they practised must be practised upon him. So the deadlock held fast. He could not prevent William from establishing dominion over Parfois, William could not get from him the concession that would give his forcible dispossession the sanction of right. He had signed nothing, sealed nothing. In the keep of his own solitary spirit he held Parfois still.

Someone was at the door, the light double knock de Guichet used. Isambard was the first to hear it, and sat with held breath to trap and decipher the sounds that alone communicated with his darkened being now. They could not know how acutely trained his ear was becoming, or they would have taken even their whispers out of the room.

"My lord, Blount says he has news for you, something important—"

"Not now. Let him wait."

"My lord, it bears on—" That was never ended, unless the significant silence ended it. A glance thrown in his direction, a brow lifting. He braced his fingers along the arms of his chair, nerves at stretch. It bears on me; it bears on this issue between us. By what forgotten postern were they attempting entry now?

The door closed, and they were outside it. He was out of his chair like a cat, and across the room, left hand spread to confirm where the table stood and guide him safely past it, right hand flattened before him to find the panels of the door. He laid his ear to the wood, and listened, but they had taken the precaution of moving well away from his prison, and all he heard was the slight stir of his guard shifting his weight from foot to foot resignedly outside the door. He strained his senses beyond, catching at any sound, any word. There was a murmur at no great distance, but too low to have meaning, until suddenly William's voice rose from monotone, loud in anger:

"Fool, what do you know of it? You were hardly born. You could do your worst and he'd laugh. In God's name, what worse could you do than he did himself?"

And Thomas—always Thomas, busy Thomas, ambitious Thomas! Thank God at least for his high, girl's voice, that grew shrill in fright or indignation, and carried so much more clearly than de Guichet's deep tones. Thomas was both frightened and indignant now, and piping like a scared and ruffled bird.

"My lord, I tell you I was there, I saw his face." Hopeful, too, and vehement, certain of himself whoever doubted him. "If that was hate—" He was overridden then, and hushed, but he cried a moment later: "At least put it to the test!" And a silence, and a stillness, that needed no interpreting. Put it to the test—whatever it might be, why not? Whatever it might be, they had nothing else.

They were coming back. The guard laid hand to the latch of the door, fingered the heavy key, and that was warning enough. Isambard felt his way back to his chair, and composed himself with a care that was partly for his own conviction as well as theirs. Nobody knew better than he how much the tensions of the body could betray.

He was ready when they came. The click of the wooden latch, the massy, low creak of the heavy door swinging, footsteps entering. How many? All three by the varying treads he counted. Young Thomas had his reward, he was suffered to creep in here on his new master's heels to feast his eyes on the impotence of the old one. That was a large grace, but if his snare proved effective, whatever it might be, there was no alternative to trusting him hereafter; and if not, well, no doubt he could be intimidated or disposed of. It would pay William not to underestimate Thomas, thought Isambard, and smiled a little grimly, remembering Harry's warning. To his enemy, dear God! All the doctors of all the schools might find matter for a lifetime's disputation, trying to discover how the very ground of a man's warfare can revolve under his feet and leave him keeping his enemy's back against the whole world; but Harry went where his confident heart drove him, and did what it urged him to do, and his wisdom, like his simplicity, was far out of the philosophers' reach. Isambard fingered a spot in the hollow of his lean right cheek, and was slow to realize how the quality of his smile had changed. It did not matter. With the windows of the eyes shuttered there are not so many ways left, and none so dangerous, by which a man can betray himself.

"We wasted our time, it seems, arguing ways and means," said William's voice, softened, calculated, smiling. Do him justice, if he was unsure of his weapon he gave no sign of it; he moved in leisurely and easy, like a master. "There's a guest arrived will alter your mind for you without any effort on my part. Your guest, my dear father. Do you not remember inviting her? A certain lady who once knew you too well for her comfort, and thought it better to refuge in Wales. Ah, I see you do remember!"

He saw nothing, for there was nothing to see. Not a muscle of the bronze mask had moved until Isambard allowed his arched, arrogant brows to signal polite question and nothing more.

"It's not like you, William, to talk in riddles. Come to the meat, and let me at least stand on the same ground with you. I expect no guest. I invited none."

"My lord," said Thomas eagerly, "it was in the church, and every word I overheard. He sent word for her to come in place of Harry Talvace, and the ring passed as his token to her. He must have sent it by another messenger after her man was killed."

By another messenger! So they did not know, and he was so far blessed and justified in knowing it was not from Walter they had this cast. Busy Thomas in the porch there, with his ear at the door, storing up every crumb that might some day be used to choke his beloved lord. That accounted for their information, and eased his heart into the hope that information was all they had. Given a sharp eye to detect what the sight of her ring and the mention of her name had meant to him, this trick was simple enough. "I tell you I was there, I saw his face. If that was hate—" And William, who had occasionally sat sulking at the same table with Benedetta, and grudged her his father's gifts, William who knew how it had ended: "Fool, what do you know? You were hardly born. What worse could you do than he did himself?"

He acknowledged that thrust for truth, but he breathed again. Almost certainly this was a trick. He need not give an inch. There was no guest arrived. How could there be? Harry had met her by the way, and taken her safely home.

"She brought you your token again," said William, smooth as honey, and took his father's hand and opened it on his knee. Something small and hard was dropped into the palm, and involuntarily his fingers closed upon it, and with a burning convulsion of agony knew it. The facets of the ruby bit deep, like fangs. How? Walter had delivered it; how had it come here again? Was there ever a way but the one way he could not bear to consider? And if she was here, how best manipulate that ambivalent relationship of love and hate so that they should think their calculations mistaken and their lever ineffective?

"Ah, that!" he said, hands under control again now, turning the ring thoughtfully in his palm and threading it back upon his finger. "I'd forgotten. Small revenges have not much weight now. The score I had against her was hardly worth settling, after all. I turned Harry loose in the end without any ransom. What message did she send with this? Her forgiveness? As I remember her, she would always have the last word."

He laughed. It was not difficult, the blank, wary hush seemed to him so ludicrous, and their revulsions of doubt made so marked a heaviness upon the air. The ring would not go easily over his knuckle; he turned it indifferently, and drawing it off again, span it gently into the middle of the table.

"My joints are old and swollen, and by reversion it's yours in the end. I brought it from Acre in the Crusade—the stone is good. Wear it if it fits. Or give it to Thomas for his wages, if you think his tale worth it, but for my part I think he'd be overpaid."

They stared upon him all three, narrowly, doubtfully and long, even Thomas shaken.

"Fool," said William, turning a black stare upon the boy, "did I not tell you this would never move him?"

"My lord, he's lying." The girlish voice rose high with apprehension; it was not rubies he could expect if his invention proved useless now. "I saw his face, I heard his voice then, I *know* he'd sweat for her. Whatever happened between them once, whatever she did to him or he to her, she has him by the heart still."

"It can still be put to the trial," said de Guichet, low and rapidly, for his master's ear alone, but Isambard caught the words, all the more terrible because they were not meant for him, and by that token must be true. No question, then, but she was here and in their hands? Or had that whisper been meant to be overheard? Was that too great a subtlety to be attributed to de Guichet?

"True," said William, calmed, "we can easily put your indifference to the proof, my dear father. If you can't be marked, there's no such ban on touching her. How if we have you down with us to the cellars of the Warden's Tower, and teach the lady how to ask you for your signature and seal? Then we might discover in what regard you do hold her."

"I had thought you knew," said Isambard, sighing and yawning. "Many curious things have been said of me, but never, I think, that I had the habit of tossing my friends into the Severn."

"Then if you're still of the same mind we might pass an hour or two very pleasantly for you. You have not your eyes, it's true, but you'll hear well enough, we'll see to that. And we'll keep the deed at hand," said William tenderly, "in case you're moved to sign it of your own good will, out of charity even towards a woman you hate."

And he would do it? Why not, wanting his way as he wanted it? She was in his hands, he could make use of her, and in the turmoil of civil war who was ever to question the act close enough to bring it home to him? Perhaps by now he even knew he would not have to proceed far.

Isambard sat silent for a moment, revolving behind his calm, closed face the courses open to him; and it seemed to him that his outer defences were already lost from the moment that Benedetta entered at the gates. Could he buy more than a precarious safety for her even by surrendering his barony? He doubted it. If they found her effective, all the more surely they would not let her go as long as they needed a hold upon him; and as long as they held her he could be made to do anything they wished. They did not yet know that, but he knew it, it was one of the facts with which he had to deal. He smiled, acknowledging it. Give him yet a small measure more of life, and he might learn to go with his heart as impetuously as Harry, and question it and reason about it as little.

Two things only he could do. First, satisfy himself beyond doubt that they had her in their power; and second, give what was necessary to protect her if he could not deliver her. Give his honour into his son's hands, signed and sealed. Promise them his own submission and good behaviour as long as they used her well and gave him earnest of it.

"I do not believe," he said deliberately, "that Madonna Benedetta is here at all. If she is, confront me with her."

"Ah, no! Not that, my dear father. I have too high a respect for your wit to let you within speaking distance of her."

"Dear God, you have enough curbs on me, I should have thought. What could I do by speaking with her?"

"That I never quite know, and there's the rub with you. With your leave, I'll take no risks of any secrets passing under my nose. And forgive the crudity, but to show her to you from a window is hardly possible now."

"Then bring me where I can hear you speak with her, and I'll be content with that."

"Why not?" said de Guichet, after a moment of considering silence. "She's down in the great chamber below. Let us bring him to the head of the stairway, and he'll hear her voice plain enough, and she'll be none the wiser. Go down and greet her, and leave the door open between. Let him have his proof."

They brought in his guards to pin him by the arms before he so much as rose from his chair, they had still such a wary respect for his strength and cunning. He went docilely where they led him, stepping hesitantly down the spiral stone stair, feeling with anxious toes for the wider part of the treads, leaning on his warders; it was well to appear more, not less, helpless than he really was. Thomas tripped lightly ahead of him, elated now and sure of his reward.

By the stone balustrade at the head of the lower flight, outside the door of what had once been his own bedchamber, they halted their prisoner, and one of the guards with indifferent kindness took his groping hands and guided them to the rail. He heard William descend the last steps without haste, heard the door of the great room below open. In his memory he saw the faded tapestries within drinking and dulling the light from the narrow loopholes, and the heavy, carved chairs tall and spectral in the shadowy corners. And standing in the middle of the room, facing the doorway, waiting for the man she would not see, Benedetta.

In that moment he saw her clearly, splendidly large and generous of movement and regal in stillness, with breadth and valour in everything she did or thought or said, a woman, a tower, a world.

"Madam," said William's voice below him, echoing faintly hollow from within the lofty room, "you are most welcome back to Parfois."

She said: "I thank you," and it was enough. Her voice, unmistakable even after so long of absence, not changed, not dimmed at all. "I came at your father's wish. I did not think to see you here. Is he still so sick?"

"Not dangerously," said William, surely with a smile not far behind his eyes, if she had known how to read it. "Did his courier tell you what befell him? He has lost the sight of his eyes."

"He told me it might well be so," she said, low-voiced. "May I not see him?"

"Not yet, I regret. He is not well enough yet to be visited, and I am here as the king's castellan in his place. But I will have an apartment made ready for you, and if you will be patient and wait a little while, he will surely mend."

A moment of silence; no irresolution in it, only thought. Then the clear voice said with deliberation: "Yet he was master of himself, and sent me a plain message. And that was the day this injury was done him."

"He has been in fever since then," said William, a shade too quickly and easily. "As soon as he is fit you shall see him, and welcome."

"And you are come from his bedside now?" she said, so softly, so dryly, that there was no mistaking the irony. "I am glad he has so devoted a son to take his burdens from him."

She did not trust, she did not believe. She had forgotten nothing and lost nothing, she could still look through a man and leave him naked to his own self-knowledge. "He made a bargain with me," she said. "I hope you will honour it for him. He promised me that if I would come to Parfois to take his place, he would release Harry Talvace. Ask him, he will tell you. Ask him, and send the boy home."

Isambard's hands tightened on the stone. So she did not know. Somewhere along the way Harry and she had passed unknown, by what accident or chance he could not guess, and she who had come to set the boy free found even his captor captive. What must her anxiety be now for the child she had carried in her arms, new-born, to deliver to Llewelyn at Shrewsbury all those years ago? And he would not tell her! He would keep that, too, in store, in the armoury of his invisible weapons, for use later at need.

"That we can surely discuss tomorrow. You are tired now, and a day or two more is nothing lost. Tomorrow we may be able to talk to my father about the boy."

"Harry is well?" she said, sharp and fierce with dread.

"He is very well."

"May I see him?"

"Later, when you have rested."

And was she to be content with that, sleep on that, ask and ask day after day and still be held off and tormented with perhaps, and later, and tomorrow, until evasions added up to certainty of harm? One thing at least could be saved for her, her peace of mind and heart over the child. Isambard calculated instants and words, and the length of time it would take to shift a hand from his arm to his mouth. How many words had he for the phrasing of what might be his last communication with her? He might be adding to her danger by a shade, but what was lost there could be regained when he conceded his seal and consented to strip himself bare; and in the meantime she could sleep serenely, and thank God that Harry was out of the battle.

He leaned over the stone balustrade, and suddenly flung his arms wide, thrusting his guards off-balance; and in a great voice he cried down the well of the staircase:

"Harry's safe. I sent him—"

So far, and one of the clutching hands found his mouth. He wrenched aside and freed his lips again for a moment.

"—sent him to meet—"

No more then. They dragged him back by both arms, a hard forearm in a cloth sleeve was clamped over his mouth. De Guichet had him by the hair, wrenching his head back. He heard Benedetta cry: "Ralf!" and knew that at least she had heard him. He heard running footsteps below, the slam of the door closing. Then he was down on his back on the flagstones, and they were on top of him, and with what breath he had left he was laughing, even with his mouth choked with a fold of his own surcoat. Someone struck him in the face, so puny and spiteful a blow that he thought it must have come from Thomas, and hardly even grudged him his morsel of satisfaction.

They dragged him bodily back up the staircase, and they were not gentle. They flung him down in his own chair, and shut the door, trembling, on him and on themselves, cursing him low-voiced and viciously.

He wiped a trickle of blood from the corner of his mouth, and shook his surcoat into order. By the time he had his breath mastered enough for speech William was in at the door and stooping over him. The air shook and grew hot with his rage, but he kept it in. All he said, in the suppressed, breathy voice of extreme forbearance, was: "Do you think that was wise?"

"Not wise," owned Isambard, still fingering blood away from his lip, "but at least honest. I'm ready to study wisdom now if you make it worth my while. Where have you lodged her?"

"Where you'll hear no more of her," said William, breathing hard.

"Ah, but I shall. Or you'll get nothing from me. This much I'll promise you, not to try to speak to her or call her attention again, if you for your part will put me in the way of assuring myself, now and then, that she's alive and well and not molested. Bring me where I can hear her speak but once a week, and that's enough for me."

"And is it you who can afford to lay down terms?"

"I think," he said, "I can. If I am to give over to you my title in all I have, then I must have somewhat in exchange from you, and your oath to keep it."

He heard his son draw deep, satisfied breath, sure now of the mastery, sure of the value of his hostage. "Is not my word enough for you?" he said, with hypocritical indignation.

"Fair, sweet son," said Isambard gently, "no. I would not stake a dog's life on your word, since you ask me. I must have it on oath that you will use Madonna Benedetta well, keep her as she should be kept, and give her a measure of freedom—ah, content you, it can stop short of the place where I am, have I not promised you to let her alone?" He did not even ask for her liberation; he knew it would not, could not be granted, not yet, not until his abdication of his rights was published and accepted, perhaps not until he was safely, demonstrably, respectably dead.

"Swear to what I shall ask of you concerning her," he said deliberately, "and you may bring on your deed when you will. I'll sign it, and deliver you my great seal."

* * *

Harry would have ridden in after her, but for the hollow doubt that opened in his heart like a wound, and held him back to wait for morning. If all was as he had left it within there, there was nothing to prevent him from following her and bringing her away with him; but he knew, by the desperation of his own ride after her, that he did not believe he would find the order in Parfois unchanged.

He lay curled under the bushes in his cloak through the dark hours, sleeping for a few minutes now and then, starting awake again to harrow over old ground yet once more, and reproach himself for every moment lost on that ride; and at first light he roused himself to climb up through the bushes and reconnoitre the lower guard. The men there were strangers to him; even their officer he had never seen before, he who had lived the greater part of four years of his life in the castle, and learned to know every man in the garrison. He kept watch all the morning through, and it was past noon when he saw the bright cortège weaving its way merrily down between the trees, and dropped into thicker cover to see them go by.

Three falconers, two of them known to him but the third a stranger, knights and squires and pages, faces he knew now, the court of Parfois dancing attendance on its lord, and in very ceremonious state indeed. In their midst, the stem and centre of their brightness, rode the man he had last seen by torchlight, mounting in the outer ward after kissing his father a dutiful farewell.

Large and confident in proprietorship, arching his neck in swinging stares about his domain and smiling to see its excellence, William Isambard rode out to hawk on the crest of the Long Mountain. And at his elbow Thomas Blount cantered assiduous and devoted, feeding his master with smiles and sallies. Thomas, who never expanded his leaves but to the rising sun. In their glory, the one and the other of them, men in possession.

So there was no rushing back into Parfois, to make, if his fears were justified, one more hostage, one more sword to be held at the old man's throat. That would not help or deliver Madonna Benedetta; it would simply deprive her of one ally who might yet be of use to her if he kept his freedom of action. There was no salve to his conscience in an empty and contemptible heroism, which would only serve to place in greater danger the very people he desired to protect.

Had William put his father from his place? Or was he moving cautiously, content as yet to be his father's proxy, now the old man could no longer be active about his own affairs? He rode out attended like a conqueror, but the hangers-on would be courting him as their effective lord in either case. Dared he proceed so far and so fast as to depose his father? What Harry needed first was certainty. If he could not go in and out and listen to the whispers inside Parfois, there were those who could. There were men in the villages who had kinsfolk in the castle; and if he did not know where to find them and how to reach their confidence, he knew those who did.

He sent his men back to Castell Coch, there to rest and wait for him, and went alone along the riverside path he remembered so well. With the small green paddock barely in sight between the trees, and the faint smell of wood-smoke from the hearth just tickling his nostrils, he halted and stood silent on the path; for Aelis was there in the yard, raking out the ashes of the fire from under her clay oven at the end of baking.

Such a weight of fondness gathered about his heart at sight of her that he felt himself braced and magnified to carry it, a man endowed and burdened with the world. Her hair, heavy gold, hung over her shoulder in a thick braid. She had grown tall and slender, and the shape of her, as she stooped to her task with long, smooth, faintly weary movements, was the shape of a woman, daunting and wonderful. Her face, pensively inclined, had a mysterious air of sadness. At once humbly and vaingloriously he added that to the load of his own guilt. What comfort and joy had she ever had of him? He had brought her nothing but trouble and pain and labour since the day she and her father had first taken him in.

He wanted to call to her, and he was afraid and ashamed, for some reason he himself could not understand, to disturb the delicate concentration with which she was working. As though he expected her to turn to him at the first word, as though she must drop whatever she was doing, and run to wait on his concerns. He knew he was about to pour out the sum of his trouble and tiredness into her lap for comfort, when he would rather have been bringing her

some better gift, something to please her, something to shed reflected light upon her, and not exact attentions for him. He came
always demanding, even if he was too proud or too small-hearted
to do it openly; and there was such a thirst and hunger in him to
give to her.

She heard a twig snap beneath the horse's tread, and rose and
stood tall and ready before the gate, head reared, eyes wide, fronting
the gap in the trees where the rider must appear. The horse was
from Meifod, and unknown to her; she waited, intent and still, to
get a closer view of the man. Green light and greener shadow between the leaves veiled him from her recognition a moment, and
then she knew. By what motion of his tired body in the saddle, by
what tilt of his head or trick of his carriage, who knows? He was
still a dappled shadow-man on a pied horse, thirty yards away from
her along the narrow ride; but she knew.

She let fall the forgotten scraper out of her hand, she seemed to
stretch her head upward for a moment and grow taller, as though
she would strain free of the tall grass of time that had hidden him
from her. Then such a blaze of silent joy flamed in her face that he
could not believe he was the source of it, and looked beyond himself
for some better cause implied in him, her sisterly kindness pitying
the prisoner and radiant at his release, her selfless pleasure in his
bettered fortunes. No one, not even his mother, had looked at him
like that, or hung so still and rapt in joy, a joy that must be for him,
since it could not be of him. Why should anyone be so purely glad
of Harry Talvace?

As always when he was at his sorest and haughtiest, praise undid
him. The magnificat of her eyes delighting in him cut the ground
from under his feet, and set him trembling in a passion of humility.
He tumbled from the saddle, clumsy with haste and weariness, and
ran and dropped at her feet like a shot bird. She had sprung to meet
him, but he dropped through her arms, catching at the slight brown
hands and drawing them down against his cheek, pressing her open
palms to his forehead and eyelids.

"Oh, Aelis! Oh, Aelis!" he said, his voice no more than a quick,
fluttering warmth in the palm of her hand.

"Harry, is it you? Is it truth this time? Are you free?"

She took her hands from him only to stroke and fondle him in a

rapture of tenderness, putting back the tangle of brown hair from
his forehead with a maternal gesture of the hand that had been an
urchin's so short a while ago.

"Not yet. Not quite free. There's something I had to do, and I've
failed badly, and there's all to put right—"

"But you need not go back?" She lifted his face to her by the chin
to look into his eyes, her voice quick and jealous in alarm. "Are you
only loosed to go running off to the war, like that last time? Oh,
why did you never tell me, that time? I waited and waited, and never
a word. You wouldn't do that to me again? You'd tell me, if you
had to go back into Parfois?"

"I'd tell you. I would tell you. It's not like that. I'm loosed, but
I'm not free." He had so much of his own to tell that the sense of
what she had just told him penetrated his senses but slowly, and the
sting came with a sudden shock of excitement and ardour, hoisting
him from his knees with a leap. "Running off to the war, you said?
Is it come, then? Is it war already?"

"So they were saying at Castell Coch this noon. The miller was
across with flour, and he brought back word. They're saying your
prince has declared for the earl marshal, and taken his muster south
to Builth. Is it true, do you think? Could it be true?"

"Yes," he said, momentarily caught away from her, staring over
her head eagerly into the uncertainties of the future. If the prince
was in the field, then his foster-son had an army at his back. "Yes,
it could well be true," he said, quivering, and caught too late the
still, woman's sadness in her eyes, already steeled to new waiting
without complaint. The princess had given her fair warning. If we
want them at all we must take them as they are.

"You'd best come in," she said with determination, "and tell me
now what it is you're at. Father's away at Forden, but he'll be home
in an hour or so, and happy to see you whole and free again. Can
you bide overnight at least? And if there's anything you need from
us before you go—"

"Ah, no!" he said, suddenly flooded with the molten weight of
his tenderness, as though his heart had burst. "I'll not leave you
yet. Not yet! I need your help to know what I must know, but more
than that I need from you, my dove, my dear."

He took her face between his hands and turned it up to him softly, and between his palms she began to flush and tremble. He kissed over the soft curve of her cheek from brow to chin, kissed her grave eyelids closed, smoothed with his lips the golden arches of her brows.

"If I must go again, it's only to come back the sooner. However far I must go, however far, I'll surely come back. I love—" he said, whispering his way down her cheek, and having arrived thus inarticulate at her mouth, fastened there like a famishing man, and tasting her tears, closed astonished lids upon his own.

At the light touch on his shoulder he started out of a dream of pursuit and loss, instantly wide-awake like a hound, ears pricked and nostrils quivering to the scent of a stranger in the room; his hand was at his dagger hilt and a knee braced under him to rise before Aelis could close her fingers round his wrist and soothe him into stillness.

"Hush, now! Here's no harm. But there's news for you."

The light of a candle-end glimmered by the hearth, and cast wavering shadows among the smoky beams of the ceiling. Robert was up and making fast the door softly on the thick darkness of a murky November midnight; and in a huddle of rugs over the slow fire damped down for the night a man lay steaming and shivering, one naked arm stretched out from his coverings to the cup Aelis held to him. His teeth chattered against the rim as he drank. Beard and hair drooped lank and wet. The rags he had stripped off oozed a slow pool of water in the rough boards of the floor. Wild eyes looked up at Harry across the rim of the cup, ready with hostility, sharp with fear.

"Be easy," said Robert, low and quickly to them both, "there's none here but friends."

"What is it? What happened?"

"He's from Leighton. He came down the river, like your father once, but alive. One of three taken in Isambard's private chase last evening, and won free before they could get him into hold, but they broke an arm for him before he took to the river. Here, lend me an arm of yours to hold him while I set the bone."

Harry went down on his knees and raised the chilled body to lie in his lap. It was not the first such injury Robert had handled, and not by many a one the first runaway he had hidden and put across the Severn by night.

"One of his foresters struck at me with his staff when I ran," said the fugitive, through teeth clamped fast to stop their chattering. "But for that I'd have been across the river without the need of a boat. I could make no headway across the current with only one arm to steady me. All I could do was go down fast with it, and crawl ashore when I was out of their reach and sight."

"They'll be hunting him," said Harry, and lifted a flaring green stare of alarm to Robert's face.

"No, they think me drowned. I lay low in the bushes until I heard them draw off." It was near to frost outside; he might well have got his death that way in escaping the river.

"Safe enough here for a day," said Robert, large hands busy and gentle at the distorted forearm, as brown and sinewy as his own. "Hold fast now! And Aelis, the linen band here."

She had been tearing and rolling it in the edge of the candlelight; she came to Harry's side and held the roll ready. Faintly they heard the bone grate. The huddled body jerked once in Harry's arms, as the man turned his head and clenched his teeth in the fold of the rug that wrapped him; but in a moment the grip relaxed again, and he bore the rest of it without stir or murmur.

"Tomorrow night we'll put you over into Wales," said Robert, making firm the first smooth turn of the linen about the cased forearm. "He's had his belly-full of the lordship of Parfois, Harry. Ask him, he knows. It was strangers, not Shropshire men, who took them with the venison."

"Strangers?" repeated Harry sharply, and leaped ahead into understanding. "William's men!"

"William's men, and laying claim to be the foresters of Parfois. And ready to stand to it, too."

"They brought us into Leighton," said the poacher, his head rolling back wearily into Harry's shoulder, "and Wilfrid's wife came running with the rest and saw us, and had the good wit to run for the reeve. And he came and argued for us, that they had no right to clap us into Parfois's prison when they had no authority from the old lord. The chase is his, he says, not his son's, and without we see his order and seal to back you, we'll not let you take them. We'll send to the justice, he says, and if any man wills to charge them he must do it according to law. And the village was standing by watching all, four to every man of theirs, so they had need to mind how they handled it. They claimed the lord William had the king's authority as castellan of Parfois, but old Harald, God bless him, wouldn't have it make any difference; he said only the lord of the honour could have us taken into private custody. Then they laid claim to that right, too, saying the lord Ralf had ceded his honour to his son. And Harald said bluntly he'd never believe it unless he had the proof of it under the old lord's signature and seal. Till then, he said, he'd hold us, and deliver us when there was due warrant shown. He could do no more: we had the two beasts we'd taken slung on poles between us when they caught us, there was no denying them. It took a bold man to go as far as he went, but of late we've been left in peace in the woods, and we took in measure, and spared to tempt our luck too hard, and he fairly believed this was no more than a presumption by the son's men, taking vantage of the father's infirmity. And hold us he did, and they went off threatening.''

''But they came again,'' said Harry with certainty, shifting a little to give the injured man more ease. His eyes flashed to where Aelis stood, and found her watching him with a face wary and regretful. She knew the ending already.

''In the late evening, and de Guichet the seneschal with them. And brought a parchment with him, and would have Harald read it out to all the village. And then they took us, and nobody could prevent without turning it into a hanging matter, and God knows we never wanted that. But I thought on the cells under Parfois, and how a man could rot there, and I cut and ran when we passed through the copse, and would have got over the river well enough but for this chance blow.''

''Then your reeve had his proof? He can read? He read the parchment himself, you say?'' Why was he clutching at even the last doubt, when he already knew, in his heart, both the end and the means? They had seen her value, then, and turned her to calculated use. How else could they have extorted concessions from Isambard? Had they threatened his own safety he would have laughed in their faces.

"That he can, and better than many a clerk. If he could have found a grain of justification for it he'd have had somebody ride to the justice. No, there's no gainsaying this. He read it aloud as he was told, with de Guichet standing over him, and showed the hand and the seal for all to recognise. It was no lie. The old wolf's done what I never thought he'd do, crippled or no—delivered over all his lands to his son—freely, he wrote, of his own will and desire. Signed everything he has over to the lord William with his own hand, and put his great seal to it, and lain down somewhere in a warm corner of his hall like an old, blind hound, to die."

Chapter Eight

Brecon, Aber, Parfois:
Early December 1233

At Builth he had thought to find Llewelyn, but the prince had moved south, and was laying siege to the castle and town of Brecon, and penning close within its walls the great garrison the king had looked to use as reserves for his harried companies. The border stood to arms, but as yet hung in a sultry and uneasy stillness. But already Basset and Siward had swooped upon Devizes to pluck de Burgh out of hold, and spirited him across the Severn estuary to the earl marshal's castle of Striguil, while Earl Richard himself blazed like a bush-fire through Gwent. Abergavenny had fallen to him, and Newport and Monmouth; he had raided the king's camp in the chilly dawn of a November day, and driven him headlong out of Grosmont. John of Monmouth was hard put to it to remuster the royal armies, and had them standing off now warily while the earl marshal consolidated his gains and reprovisioned his castles. And the winter had come down early on the hills, but could not quench the fire.

Over Mynydd Eppynt the snow lay thinly, a lace veil over the mountain's faded, wintry hair; but the falls were not yet deep enough nor the wind bleak enough to drive Harry into the valley ways. He took the upland road at the best speed he could make; and

before twilight he saw from the crest overhanging the Usk the dull
glow of fires and the hanging pall of smoke above the town of
Brecon.

Smoke wreathed the black, gnawed shape of the castle, stark
against the palpitating gleam of fires burning out in the town below.
Smoke clung like a gauze scarf, faintly rippling in the wind, about
the thick grey tower and fortress walls of the priory church. Harry's
eyes travelled the long, lofty line of its great roof, and found it
whole, and was glad, and then half-ashamed of his pleasure in the
survival of stone when he looked beyond at the reeking ruins of the
homes of men. All that the people of Brecon had built up again since
the last destruction lay blackened and razed now by the soiled wintry
waters of the river, a desolation, de-peopled but for the dead. Huddled and cramped within the castle wards, the survivors hoarded
their food and water, and waited for the relief King Henry's Flemish
mercenaries must surely be bringing from Gloucester. But day after
day they kept watch from the walls, and never a sign of the banners
or the lances bright above the snowy hills.

In the sullen dusk the fires glowed and faded, smouldered and
spat into spasmodic bursts of flame as the fallen timbers settled.
And on the hill-slopes above the bank of Honddu, drawn tight
round the stubborn castle, the contravallation and circumvallation of
Llewelyn's camp stood black against the snow, and the gaunt dark
shapes of mangon and trebuchet still battered fitfully at the scarred
walls. No need to press the assault too closely, he had them sealed
in from all help, and the countryside scoured clean of provisions;
and he believed no more than they now did in the king's will to
relieve them. He could hold them immobilised at his pleasure without loss of men, while Earl Richard swept his way through the
valleys of Usk and Wye, and carried all before him.

The riders from Builth were sharply challenged at the borders of
the camp, for they came at a gallop with their cloaks drawn up about
their chins and capuchons low over their brows against the thin,
driving snow. Harry slid from the saddle, stiff with weariness, and
asked after the prince; and on that the sentry knew him and hailed
him gladly, and he was passed eagerly from friend to friend through
the circling single street of this circumscribed town, congested with
stores and arms and cattle and horses, to Llewelyn's pavilion.

From the murk and the gathering dark he stumbled into a close, pungent warmth, and from the low, rug-strewn brychan both his foster-brothers shouted his name and rose to close with him gladly. He put them off almost roughly, though his eyes acknowledged and warmed to them. He threw himself on his knees at Llewelyn's feet, and kissed the hand that reached to lift him.

"Harry, you're welcome to my heart! You've kept us waiting long for your news."

Harry lifted a travel-stained face; from heavy lids swollen and bruised with wakefulness the green eyes stared appalled, suddenly confronted with the impossibility of communicating what he himself had experienced without understanding. Llewelyn caught the confused light of bewilderment and despair and appeal, and leaned and kissed him heartily.

"How have you fared?"

The constriction of helplessness that had settled like frost on Harry's tongue melted, and the words came bursting out of him without concealment or calculation.

"My lord, badly. I've let her slip through my hands. My lord, we made what haste we could, but Madonna Benedetta kept her lead of us. She's in Parfois, for all we could do." That had the unpleasant ring of self-excuse, and he had no will to soften his own guilt by the least shade. "I am to blame," he said, fending off sympathy fiercely.

"The rate you set out from Aber," said David warmly, "if she outrode you she must have ridden like a lover to his wedding."

"I did press hard," owned Harry, shaking. "I thought I did. We missed her by no more than an hour, but we missed her, and what I did may have been well meant, but it was not enough. And that's not the worst. I would have gone in openly and asked for her, and he would have let me bring her away with me, but the time for that was gone by, too. They were strangers at the lower guard when we came there. We drew off and kept watch on the gates, and in the morning we saw William Isambard riding out with his falconers and his knights about him, like a prince. All those who most fawned on the father have turned to court the son. We saw it, and had the taste then of what had happened, but we could not be sure. I waited to have it all before I brought you word."

He had wanted to heal with his own energy and devotion what he conceived he had done amiss, to recover single-handed what he had lost. He's ridden his beasts almost to foundering, and taken no rests himself along the way, thought Llewelyn. Whoever comforts him, for all that, he'll fight off like an enemy.

"We sent men into the villages, but they knew no more than we did, and were waiting and wondering like us. I thought to get word by a fellow Aelis found for me, who goes in and out carting away rubble from the old tower. I bade him find out Langholme with a message, but he brought back word Langholme was gone, sent away somewhere on his lord's errand and never returned. Walter would never have left him willingly. And if he sent him away, I well know why. He would not have one of us near who might be made to suffer for his sake. If he still had his way there, he would have sent Madonna Benedetta home again out of Parfois, with an escort to bear her company and keep her safe on the road. I knew in my heart then that all was wrong within there. But then came this man by night, a poacher taken with two comrades in the act, in Isambard's own chase. And then we had certainty."

He drew breath to tell the whole of that tale, and cut it short enough.

"It was the reeve himself who read it out to them, and he knew both the seal and the hand. The king's writ making him castellan would never have served. But this was Isambard's own act and deed. And Madonna Benedetta is the instrument they've used to get their will of him! It's for her protection he's sealed away his honour to his son, and while William holds her he can make his father do whatever he will."

"This is a very strange showing," said Owen, frowning dubiously over the puzzle. "Saving your presence, Harry, you've changed your tune. I thought he proposed harm to her himself. So we all thought. The old scores were never settled. From all we knew of him and all we heard from you, she had no need to expect better of him than another humiliation and death. Granted he relented of his worst intent, since he sent you off to meet her and turn her back. But do you tell us now he's beggared himself to keep her from harm?'

"Only God knows, my lord," said Harry passionately, clinging with wild green eyes to Llewelyn's face, "if ever he willed to do her hurt, when he took her at her word and bade her come. But *I* know he would die now to keep her safe from hurt at William's hands. And if William does not know it yet, it will go hard but he'll learn it soon, and make ill use of it, too. Beggared himself for her—yes, so I swear he has. And I dread he's a close-guarded prisoner for her. And if there's aught more they want of him, they'll make use of her again to bring him to heel."

"If he's signed away his all," said David reasonably, "what more is there to be pressed out of him? What are the family quarrels of the Isambards to us? It seems to me we might very well deal directly with this new lord of Parfois, and strike a bargain with him for Madonna Benedetta. He can spare her now; she's served her turn. Why should he want to keep her longer?"

"No!" Harry held his aching head between his hands, for it was so heavy now with the warmth and the fumes of the low brazier that he could scarcely carry it upright. "If we sent to ransom her he'd wonder and fear how much we knew of his dealings already, and how much she might be able to tell. Do you think he'd hesitate to do murder, if he thought his treason was to come out?"

"Ah, you're dreaming, lad!" David flung an arm round his shoulders and shook him rallyingly. "Whatever he feared from her telling, he'd fear far more to do her to death after the prince of Aberffraw had claimed her for his own. He'd never dare touch her."

"Not her! *Him!*" Harry threw off the affectionate arm furiously. "How long do you think *he* would live," he cried, quaking with anger and distress and despair, "if they had cause to fear too close questioning over him? A move from us, a visitor due from the king, an old friend passing out of turn and asking to see him, any one might be his death. I'm feared, I'm feared it will be soon! There are those in other castles of his who won't believe too easily in his giving up his honour. Signature, seal and all, they'll want his word for it face to face that he gave it of his own free will. While he's alive there'll be no peace for William. And it wants but a worn tread on a stair—a blind man's not so hard to kill."

They stared upon him great-eyed with astonishment, the hurtful words of wonder and doubt ready on their lips. They loved him, and meant him no hurt, but what did they know of Parfois? What did they know of the long, strange, testing companionship, that had shaped and sharpened and whetted him without his knowledge, and brought him about in his own tracks to confront once again, as if for the first time, his ancient enemy? How could he hope for understanding, he who understood nothing of what had befallen him? He went where his heart drove him, and trusted it to know its way. What else could he do?

"The boy's right!" said Llewelyn roundly, head reared, eyes beginning to shine with the reflected light from action contemplated. He reached a hand to clap Harry about the shoulders and draw him close to his side. "At the first move from us touching their hostage, Isambard's life would not be worth an hour's purchase. But I can do better than that. William Isambard holds that march for the king, does he? Let's prove his fitness for his command."

The two young men were gazing at him with as much consternation and as little comprehension as was in the looks they turned upon Harry; and Harry himself had lifted heavy eyes to search his face with scarcely less bewilderment, but with a reviving gleam of hope and ardour that warmed his heart.

"Owen, go and find Madoc. Bid him come to me in half an hour, and bring his captains, for tomorrow I'll have him move from Brecon. I think we have held this garrison penned long enough; they have work to do here will keep them from under Earl Richard's feet a few weeks yet. There's one way at least, the only one, I can approach Parfois now and not be suspect, and that's in arms."

He turned his glittering glance upon his son, met his wondering eyes, and smiled. "David, go with him. Leave us a little while alone."

They went, faithfully and readily, but they did not understand. They recognised and welcomed his intent, but the reasoning that moved him to it was beyond their grasp.

"Never trouble for them," said Llewelyn, when they were gone. "What you don't tell they'll come to know in God's good time. They're young yet, they look for reason and order in all things. But they love you too well to question. Lean on them, whatever your need, and they'll not let you fall."

"My lord," said the boy, trembling, "I know it."

But what was he to say of the prince, who spanned the gulf of incomprehension at one stride, and took the very burden of wondering and agonising from him? He slid to the ground beside Llewelyn's chair, and laid his head with a great, shuddering sigh of gratitude upon the prince's knees, clinging to him in silence; and after a moment dry sobs began to quake through him, softly and without distress.

Llewelyn smoothed a hand over the shock of brown hair, and held him so. "I know! I know! What you did was not enough, but neither could I have done better. No man can go through his life without some day falling short. You must learn to live with yourself failures and all. As princes do. As I do." The bowed head made a brief, violent motion of denial, and he soothed and held it between his long palms gently, smiling a little ruefully into his own memories.

"As *he* does," said Llewelyn softly, and stirred to the long, answering sigh of deliverance and peace. "Do you think he would find any fault with you for failing?"

There was never any need to tell him anything, with that way he had of leaping into the heart of whatever creature he loved, and feeling in his own spirit the surges and stresses that contested the sealed being of his tongue-tied child. And yet once that clairvoyance of love had failed him, and cost them all a year of desolation. Harry, too, remembered.

"If you've read it aright, Harry, *she* will be safe enough. If they still need her as a hostage for his quiescence, they'll take very good care of her. And even if she's served her turn, they have nothing to gain by harming her, and no reason to wish her harm. And for him—I tell you this, Harry, if no one leaps too soon to question William's title and right or meddle with his secrets, then he'll be very loathe to put his father out of the world yet. You need not fear that mishap on the stairs. It would come far too abruptly on the publishing of the deed, and raise doubts in too many minds. King Henry has no use for compromised men about him, there'd be neither office nor countenance for William once the world began to whisper against him. No, he'll rather let some weeks or months go by, if he safely can. That he desires this death I don't deny. Like you, I see it plain. But with a measure of discretion, for fear he should bring on himself the very notice he desires to avoid. And not yet! Not yet!"

"My lord!" said Harry, clinging to him fervently as to a rock in a stormy sea. "Everything I see so changed. He never hurt me, nor let others. Nor broke his word to me." His voice came muffled and dazed out of the folds of the prince's gown, proffering glimpses of the truth as his groping fingers found them. "He struck de Guichet once. For me. When I would have despaired, he forbade me. When I was down, he pricked me up again. And yet—and yet he—"

"And yet he ripped your father out of his grave," said Llewelyn, laying before him gently the thing he could not say.

Abruptly, briefly and passionately the boy wept. It was the one thing he could not see changed, and the one thing he could not bear.

"Child, child," said Llewelyn, soothing him with rough, warm caresses as he would have fondled a much-loved hound, "do you think you're the only one groping? We're all in the dark together. Wait until God please to clear the sky. You can, you have time."

"Oh, my lord, I'm so astray! I understand nothing!"

"Let it bide, Harry, let it bide. You have time. But time is what William shall not have. For we'll be under his walls before he dreams, and he shall have more to think about than his stolen inheritance. We'll not ask for our holy woman again; we'll not offer a price, we'll give them no warning that we know or care aught about my lord Isambard, you and I. We'll go in arms and take castle and prisoners and usurper and all. And you with your own hands, Harry, shall give back to Isambard first his liberty and, after, all that is his. Will that content you?"

Wonderful, inscrutable, appropriate, he thought, looking down at the young, heavy head upon his knees, are the dispensations of God. To this has he brought down our revenges, Harry, yours and mine. I vowed to take and destroy Parfois for your sake, and so, by God, I may, but not as I looked to encompass it when the vow was made. And how many promises have you not made in your heart to that young father of yours to have Isambard's life for his? Never thinking how strangely you would be moved to dispose of it when at last you held it in your hands, giving it back thus freely, and with it a morsel of your own heart turned traitor. Traitor as the world's usage measures, but I think you have as good a guide in your breast as any the world can provide you. Neither do I question. God knows what he is about.

Harry had made no answer, unless it was due answer that his

clinging hands slipped down gently into the skirts of Llewelyn's gown, and his body softened and sighed eloquently against Llewelyn's knees. Vindicated, reassured, accepted, abetted, he had let himself fall unresisting into the arms of the prodigious sleep that had been waiting and reaching for him ever since he rode from Parfois. He confided utterly. He was content.

Llewelyn leaned and gathered the boy into his arms, as roughly and affectionately as long ago he would have hoisted the child worn-out with play and plumped him down in his bed, secure that nothing short of a thunderclap could awaken him. "The length of you, boy!" he said, hefting him bodily from the ground and tumbling him on the brychan. "Could you not bear to let him outdo you even in inches?"

Harry stretched out with a vast sigh of pure pleasure, and burrowed his cheek into the rugs. The distant warmth of the voice reached him, and he drew it down with him, smiling, into the bottomless well of his sleep; in a moment he put up an arm to cover his face from the light, and shuddered once from head to foot, and then was blissfully still.

"You may well!" said Llewelyn, pulling the covers over him. "There was never one of my own led me the dances you have. God knows, child," he said, looking down with a shadowed smile upon the long, rapturous heave and fall of Harry's sleeping breath, "whether we can save him for you. But in the name of God we'll try."

He sat down beside the bed to ponder the enterprise laid so confidingly in his hands. Man proposes, man performs; but God turns the very ground on which he stands, and leads him to a consummation he never foresaw. He rides to destroy his enemy, and arrives to deliver him. Well, so be it. God knows what he is about.

And for the practical problems, they were not in dispute. The assault of Parfois, captains and engineers would say with one voice, is an impossibility. Good, thought Llewelyn, roused and restless, brooding above the sprawled limbs and eased, trusting face of the boy, that's agreed. Now let's see how best to set about it.

"There!" said Gilleis between laughter and exasperation, appealing to the princess over her son's shoulder. "What did I tell you? He brings me my son back for an hour, only to take away my husband as well. What are we to do with these men?''

"More to the point," said Joan with her rueful smile, "what are we to do without them? We lack them more often than we have them. You and I, Gilleis, will pack up and ride after them to Castell Coch for Christmas. If we keep it here it's plain we shall keep it alone."

"If it were not for Benedetta," vowed Gilleis, "I would not lend you Adam. He's a master-mason, not a soldier. But for her—if you asked me for the blood out of my veins, what could I do but bare my arm for the knife? Oh, Harry, if you could but remember that ride we made together into Shrewsbury, when you were no more than two or three weeks old. She in Robert's clothes, and you asleep in her arms as sound as in your own bed, you trusted her so—and well you might. Oh, Harry," she said, drawing him to her heart again, "bring her off safely!"

Having him again, even thus changed and grown, so much more his own, so much less hers, she had shaken off years of her age, and glowed and flushed like a wild girl, her great black eyes radiant. He felt himself her elder, and loved her the more for it.

"Mother, we'll do what we can. The prince says she'll surely be safe in Parfois for a while, and trust me, he's moving fast to her rescue. The vanguard were away in the night, before ever I awoke. Madoc and his men will be over Severn by now, above and below Parfois, and the prince with his main army has abandoned Brecon to join them."

He saw again the shell of the razed town smoking, the battered walls of the castle stained and reeking. The Welsh must have had more than half of their force on the march before the garrison realised that their long ordeal was over, and ventured to put forth cautious foraging parties into the ashes of the town. And little enough they would find there, and little enough in the countryside for miles around. There would be no pursuit from Brecon, no recovering sortie to harry the rear-guard. The defenders would have just enough strength left to hunt their food, but none to spare for their enemies.

"What men can do we'll do," he said. "And we need Adam for our engineer. It was the prince thought of it, and sent me here to fetch him. He knows rock, and he knows Parfois, says the prince, and what there is to be known about quarrying he knows as well as any man. If we can't get up there to them, he says, we'll bring them down to us, castle and all. Men who wanted building-stone, he says, have brought down mountainsides before now, and turned bigger crags than Parfois into caverns, and why should not we do as much for Madonna Benedetta? So you see, Mother, you can't grudge him to us. Four years, says the prince to me, you've surely been trying your best to gnaw your way out; if there's a weak place from within you'll lay your finger on it, and if there's a means of probing it from without, Adam will show us the way. Put your heads together on your ride, he says, and cross Severn with a handful of ideas ready, or I'll put you to slaving in the camp kitchens, he says, as no use for better.''

"And rightly, too," said Gilleis warmly, hugging him to a heart bursting with pride and pain and happiness. "There, of course he'll come for her, with all his heart he'll come. Run and find your father and tell him, child, he's up at the sheepfolds.''

Harry embraced her briefly and was off like a greyhound.

"Father, foster-brother," said Gilleis, looking after him fondly as the door swung crashing to. "Dear God, I hardly know which of them I'm talking to nowadays!''

They crossed Severn by the ford at Pool, in the bitter frost of a dark dawn. From the early snow and the first thaw the water was high, and had covered every hollow of the low meadows, and later frost, night after night hardening and day after day scarcely yielding even at noon, had turned every pool into sheet-ice. The main course of the river was treacherous black fringe ice for some yards on either bank, and ran brown and dark and turgid in the centre, bringing down broken floes with it from the hills to make their passage hazardous. In midstream the horses lost their footing and had to swim, and getting them back on to the shore was dangerous work, for the ice crumbled under them wherever they tried it, and left them floundering against the jagged edges, breast-high to a barrier of knives. Harry had to dismount precariously on to the black surface and prospect for a sheltered place where a spit of land jutted into the flood; and there they coaxed their labouring beasts on to shallower and sounder ice that brought them slithering and snorting to the bank at last.

Barbarossa allowed himself to be led, quivering, along the tongue of solid land, and was all but safe in the deep, snowy grass when he shied violently at a gleam of colour that slashed at his eyes out of the water. Harry had much ado to quiet him and get him past it, and no leisure to wonder or stare until that was done. But when they looked to see what had startled him they drew breath almost as sharply as the frightened beast.

Under the ice the crimson gold of Isambard's livery shone from a dinted shield, and a face stared up at them with wide-open eyes, long, greying hair tangled over a broken brow. What light there was in that early hour lay burning in the colours, and found points of brightness in the shoulder of a chain-mail hauberk. They beheld the first of Parfois's dead; and looking about them now with eyes alerted for the signs, they traced the running course of the brief battle at the ford.

Here a helmet, there a broken sword, frozen into the shallows of Severn. Drifted close under the bank where the currents had dug out a deep pool, four more bodies, all English; if there had been Welsh dead, the Welsh had carried them away for burial, but these lay untended. An unstrung bow, half-buried in snow, tripped them as they stepped into the long grass. Broken arrows, a bloody shred of a white surcoat, stiff as steel, the stains bleached to a faded rose-colour. Last, in the edge of the forest, contorted among bushes, a thick, muscular body arched over the stump of a sword as he had crawled and frozen and died; they turned him face-to-the-light, and he turned all of one piece like a stone grotesque for a gargoyle, and showed them the bushy beard and hard countenance of old Nicholas Stury, the master-of-arms.

Harry looked long at him, and a small gaping emptiness of dismay opened within his heart and began to ache like a wound. This was nothing new; he had seen dead men before, even some of his own killing, and never wasted overmuch thought on them. Why should the sight of a known face trouble him now as soon as he stepped on to English ground? A man for whom he had had no love or even liking, a surly old bully who had enjoyed battering his more timid pupils at exercise, and taken it sourly against the grain if anyone bested him: what need was there to weep for Stury? And yet they had brushed shoulders daily in the orderly routine of Parfois for a matter of nearly four years, and had some part, however grudgingly, in each other's life; and a man whose comings and goings you have shared for so long is flesh to you, and blood, and quirks and moods and all, closer than a stranger whether you will or no. Harry signed the stone-cold forehead with a cross, and turned to the path and left him so.

"One that you knew?" said Adam from the saddle, watching the boy's fixed face and sombre eyes.

"Yes," said Harry shortly, and offered nothing more.

"Was he good to you?" asked Adam, assaying a guess wide of the mark.

"No. Nor to any other that ever I noticed. But he was alive, and doubtless he liked living no less than the kindly men do—in his own fashion." He put old Nicholas by with a shrug, and mounted and crossed the ribbon of meadow towards the woods. There would be more of them, no question; he had better get used to the thought.

The murk of cloud hung so low and thick that now they were on the English shore they could not see the Welsh, and the shape of the Long Mountain over them was only a purple-black gloom of trees receding into mist. But now their pricked nostrils quivered to the heavy stench that hung over the forest, and they knew that half at least of the obscurity that clouded the world was not mist, but smoke. Iron frost could keep the corpses from stinking, but could not quiet the acrid fumes of fire. Under the fresh snow they began to tread charred brushwood, and the trees stood here and there as mere blackened stumps with the broken remnants of branches. The underbrush was burned away in many places, thorn and bramble and bracken and all, and the beasts had fled the desolation. Only a few birds, returning, hopped and pecked in the snow, the first creatures to take fright, the first to take heart, the frailest and the most resilient of the forest's children.

They passed a burned cottage, the stumps of the walls standing stark out of the snow; and huddled close to it, powdered over by the last fall, the cottager lay with the broken shaft of a Welsh arrow upright in his back. That gave them fair warning what to expect when they came to the hamlet below Leighton: a wilderness of

blackened shells of houses, empty byres, a dead dog or two, and one
luckless villager who had stood to and defended his winter store
instead of taking to his heels. The rest were either huddled inside
Parfois before the invaders, or fled into the distant reaches of the
forest with the beasts, to live or starve as best they could. Every
grain of corn, every cow, every fowl, had been swept up to swell the
commissariat of Llewelyn's camp; and the first outpost of the Welsh
army challenged them here, and gave them word of the prince.

He had drawn up his engines of war and the main body of his
army to feign a frontal attack upon the ramp of Parfois, and keep
the garrison in a heat of dread for their lower guard, while his
mountaineers prospected the rock on which the castle itself stood.
Contravallation and circumvallation had been drawn tightly round
the single approach, and there in the siege town they would find the
prince's headquarters; but all round Parfois from river back to river
again was strung the loose, mobile line of Welsh strong-points,
sealing the castle off from the world. No one could get in to them,
nor could they break out; if they had twenty posterns to bring them
like conies out of the sandstone, they would still find themselves
with the strangling cord of enemy troops, and have to fight their
way through.

"We've not left a pig or a chicken or a handful of corn that could
help to feed them," said the sentry, grinning. "They never had time
to shift their stores, we were on them too fast. If we can't dig them
out we can starve them out."

"And the people? What's become of them?" asked Harry, staring
upon the naked ruins that had once been homes.

"They ran, most of them. Some into the castle, to make more
mouths to feed, some into the woods. And some crossed us, like
fools, and we had to kill them."

What better could he have expected? This was war, and it was he
who had launched it. Efficient war, war with a deadly purpose, no
longer a game of strategy. He had leaped gladly to welcome it when
the prince proposed this assault in arms, seeing in it the fulfilment
of his own obligations and the deliverance of his own soul. But it
was these who had to pay for it. He had seen Cardigan surrender,
he had seen Brecon burn, but there he had come lightly and gone
lightly, playing the game as it came, and only occasionally troubled

at heart by the revelation of life and death; he had come and gone a child and a stranger. Here he was a man and a neighbour, and every death bereaved him in his new manhood.

He stared appalled at the ravished granaries and plundered byres. Here in these villages, Adam had once told him, his father had helped to bring in the harvest when too many of the menfolk were pressed for King John's levies; he had argued the rights of these same cottagers and franklins and villeins sturdily against their lord, felt for their wrongs, sealed into stone for ever his affirmation of their humanity. The son came now to empty the barns and slaughter the cattle, and pin the farmer to his own door-sill with steel. And he could not withdraw. He was committed, he above all: all this coil had arisen for his sake.

"And those in the forest?" he asked, his heart sickening within him for fear. She would be safe, surely! Surely? If David forgot, David who had seen her but once, Owen would see to it that she and her father came unscathed out of it, and bring them to a place of shelter as he had promised. Yet he could not avoid the burden by laying it on Owen. The responsibility was his; he should have foreseen what war and siege must mean, the assarts in ruins, the forest in flames.

"Gone to some holes best known to themselves," said the sentry, heaving a careless shoulder. "There were some living wild that would burrow with the foxes rather than run to Parfois for cover, and some that likely would have run there if they could, but never had the chance. We were over the river before they knew. We got their beasts, they had no time to move them. If they lived as light as us they'd be quicker on the wing."

Harry wheeled Barbarossa and was off again in an agony of dread; and when Adam without question stretched to match his pace, he turned to search his face with one wild glance, and found little wonder there, and much compunction.

"I should have warned you," said Adam, as they checked where the path grew steep.

"I should have known. How else could Parfois be sealed and taken? Oh, Adam," he said, "I begin to know that I was born English."

"No help for it now, lad," said Adam with grim gentleness. "We go through with it." He thought in his heart, are you come to that already? Well, Harry would love you the more for it. "There's Benedetta to win," he said, and shut his mouth in time upon Isambard's name.

"I don't forget. It's I began this, and I'll see it to its end."

He wanted to ease his heart by speaking of Aelis, but he could not, even to Adam who knew her, who had slept in Robert's house and broken bread of her baking. His mouth dried up with fear on the shape of her name, and he spurred uphill towards the casual, muffled thunder of the trebuchets. Where they wanted cover they had left the trees alone, and only the daylong ponderous duel between mangon and arblast had spattered the branches with shot and littered the snow with splintered boughs. Harry and Adam were in the outer lines before they knew, and the palisades rose about them and drew them into the narrow siege town, swarming with men and beasts; and there was Owen hailing them gladly from a lean-to under the wall.

Harry came plunging from the saddle to meet him. He heard not a word of what Owen began to say to him.

"Where's Aelis?" he demanded, as blunt as a blow.

"God knows, Harry!" said Owen honestly, the brightness of welcome struck from his face. "And God knows I'm sorry to have no better an answer to make. It fell out not as we'd planned, and I missed my chance. I've had men out searching—"

"But you should have made provision," shouted Harry, shaking him furiously between his hands. "You promised! Could I be with the vanguard as well as on my way to Aber? I thought you would ride for her the minute you crossed Severn. I thought you'd have her and her father safe in Castell Coch before you loosed your men. Dear God, what have you let them do?"

"But I was not with the vanguard, either, no more than you were. Could I know how it would fall out? They had orders to wait and cover the ford until I overtook them there, but by pure chance they ran full tilt into a company of troops from Parfois, on the Welsh bank after a runaway villein, and bore them back through the water in a running fight. With the secret out, what could Madoc do but drive hard ashore and set to work? When I came through the ford next day the forest was burning and the villages were black."

"And you did not stir for her," panted Harry. "You let her be hunted into the earth like a vixen—you never thought of her—"

He took his hands from his foster-brother to knot them in anguish and unbelief, they burned with such a dismaying lust to batter hard at Owen's anxious face. Owen caught the clenched and welded fists to him indignantly, and flung an arm about the boy and held him still.

"God's truth, Harry, I did think of her, and ride for her, too, the minute I had grace to go. But it was done by then. The cottage was ash, and the cow was slaughtered—What would you have? They had to work fast, and what was there to set Robert's assart apart from all the rest?"

That truth went into Harry like a wound; for indeed how was his loss and grief different from any other man's? The wife of that dead cottager below there had as good a right to her sorrow as he to his. For every death someone suffered this very fury of protest and pain that convulsed him now.

"And they were gone? And did you even look for them?"

"What do you think I am, Hal? For two days and more I had men out searching, and the assart is watched still in case they come back. There were traces, we tried to follow them—"

"They didn't go into Parfois? But they wouldn't, they knew—"

"No, into the forest. Both, I swear it, Hal, I saw the tracks. But there was fresh snow that night, and they were covered deep, and we lost them. Sooth, I'm sorry! I'd give this hand to get them safe back."

"What good's that?" said Harry roughly, and put him off with stiff movements to arm's length, and so got free of him. He stood back from them, his face grey like the soiled snow. "Where is the prince? I must get leave of him. I must go to her."

"Go to her? Dear God, boy, where will you go? They may well be in Shrewsbury by now."

Did he believe it? Harry did not. The Welsh were on both flanks of the Long Mountain, and who would venture to try and thread their lines now, once having tasted the fire?

"Where is the prince?" he repeated fiercely; and hard on the answer he turned, spinning on his heel, and lunged away from them.

"Wait, I'll come with you," cried Owen, shaken and grieving.

"Let him be," said Adam. "Do you think I would not go? He'll have neither you nor me."

"No!" He turned to wave them back furiously. "I want no one; I'll go alone."

There was no time to soften that rejection, let them think what they would. Hunted and bereft and afraid, Aelis would never show herself now but to him, and the more surely if he came empty-handed and alone. He ran from them, and burst breathless and tense into Llewelyn's presence, and bent the knee to him, the words he needed ready on his lips, and pared to the bone.

"My lord, I've done my errand, Adam is here. And here I deliver you my lady's letters. And now, my lord, give me leave yet to go and look for Robert and Aelis, who housed and helped me when I was lone here. They've taken to the woods from us, and their home's burned. Give me leave till I find and bring them to shelter, as they sheltered me."

He lifted his head, and looked into the bright falcon's eyes that stared upon him unastonished, ware and wise from the heart; to one out of reach of surprise there was nothing that could not be said.

"My lord, this is no light prayer," said Harry, desperately grave. "From my soul I love her, and I mean to make her my wife."

The fence of the paddock was down, the garden a waste of snow, the assart deserted. Of the little house only the charred and blackened crucks leaned like broken teeth. Owen's two watchmen had split Aelis's clay oven apart to make a hearth, and were feeding their fire with the remains of her chicken-coops.

"Day and night, watch and watch about here." they grumbled, "and never a sign of life. We're wasting our time here. They won't come back."

So Harry thought, too, while these two remained. "Get back to your fellows," he said, "and leave the place solitary."

"That's more than my skin's worth," objected the elder of the two, eyeing him sharply, "if Owen ap Ivor comes to hear of it. He gave us plain orders to stay and keep watch here."

"No matter for that. Go and report to him that Talvace released you from that order, and I'll be your warrant he'll find no fault with you. And dout your fire before you go, and take away all with you. If there's anyone to see, let them know the watch is withdrawn."

On that assurance they doused the glow in the shattered oven, nothing loath, and took their remaining stores and made off cheerfully back towards their camp; and Harry was left to the desolation where Aelis had been.

No use calling her now, she would not come. If she lived, if she still lurked somewhere in these violated woods, she would have to be hunted and taken like a wild creature. The first time, he thought in the anguish of his heart, they waited without fear when the Welshmen came, knowing it must be I who brought them, and thinking no harm; and the steel was out and the arrow fitted and the torch at the roof before they knew what was happening to them. Maybe she saw her cow driven off, and the first chicken's neck wrung, before she could believe in fear. Maybe Robert roared at them to let be, and stood in their way; maybe he was bleeding when he ran for his life at last. And she—No, why should they come near us again willingly, after such a treason? Not even to me! Least of all to me, if she did not love me, poor Aelis! I am the cause of this. God forgive me, and help me to make amends.

And where would they run, schooled at last to terror? Not towards the ridge of the Long Mountain, for there lay Parfois, and there they would be trapped between the devil and the deep. These particular fugitives had as good reason to fight shy of Parfois as to run from the Welsh. Not along the used pathways that clung to the level ground below the ridge, for there mounted men could go freely, and they would soon be ridden down. No, towards the river they must have gone, to lie clear of both armies in the precarious fringe of land that neither coveted. There at least they might hope to make their way round the whole terrible contention, if it cost them days and nights of labour to do it, or at the ford at Buttington they might make shift to cross the river and find shelter in Strata Marcella, where the good brothers would not ask a destitute man his parentage before they took him in.

The thick woodland along the riverside, where no paths were, had escaped the fire. He left Barbarossa tethered, and took to the underbrush, and with fearful patience hunted her downstream along the shore. Twice he saw bodies lying tangled in the frozen weed where they had drifted, and walled in with the thickening ice, and clawed his way down to them with his heart in his throat; but they were none of his, and he breathed again and pressed doggedly on. He would not go back without her.

The mill had not escaped them: it was emptied and stripped and fired, and the miller lay hacked and dead in his own frozen pool. But they had not waited to see the destruction completed, and a contrary wind had spared the undercroft and left it a whole roof. Harry searched the ruins eagerly, for this was the first shelter that had offered; but nothing living stirred in the wreckage, and across yards of black ice the boat lay motionless, islanded and helpless in the grip of the frost.

He searched hour after hour while the day slipped by him without consciousness of hunger or thirst or cold or weariness; downstream to Buttington and beyond, until his own heart warned him he had spent that hope, and must needs turn and look elsewhere. Nevertheless, on the way upstream he kept to the river fringes as before, sure of his reasoning; even in panic and confusion Robert would know what he did, and keep to the riverside, where alone they might hope to escape pursuit and avoid chance encounters. Chilled in body and spirit, still he held obstinately to his hunting. And in the last of the light, with the murky winter dusk heavy on his eyes, he came again within sight of the mill, and that from a tongue of land downstream and thickly wooded, where the fire had not reached, and he himself could move unseen.

He halted and froze there, staring. From the boat a slight dark figure crept out over the ice towards the mill. Stooped and limping she went, like a sick child, like a cripple, she so straight and wild and light; but he knew her by the instant convulsion of pain that rent his heart and dragged the desperate tears to his eyes, and by the joy beyond the agony, that started him whispering thanks and vows to God silently within his trembling lips.

She lived, she moved, he would take her and tame her again however she fought, hold her in his hands from escaping him, fold her in his arms tightly from doing herself an injury in her terror, until the touch of him moved and melted her even against her will, and she listened to him and grew quiet, too weary to fear any more, too spent to fight any more; until his words and his caresses touched her understanding and stroked her erected feathers to rest, and her heart and her body knew him and turned to him. Even against her will!

He stole forward with aching care through the trees, lost her before she came to land, hurried with dread scalding his heels, and found her again as she climbed from the ice to the shore. Step by wincing step he closed in upon her, in fear of the snapping of a twig or the stirring of a branch that could betray him. He came to the sagging fence that hemmed the small garden of the mill.

Why had he not examined that plot as carefully as the mill itself on his way downstream? He could not have missed the strange signs of human occupation then, and he would have known she was there, hiding from him, hiding from every terrible touch of man, who had done to her such infamous things. She thought herself alone now in the shelter of the dropping night, and she had crept from her place of refuge to continue her work. Shaking and half-blind, he saw that she had brought a mattock from the miller's store, and was trying to break the iron ground with it. How long had she laboured at it already, to have hollowed out that pitiful, shallow trench that showed black in the smooth undulations of the snow?

She had rags of sacking bound round her feet and hands, and only the tatters of a sack about her shoulders over her coarse gown; she must have run without even a cloak. Her long hair hung tangled on her neck, coiled carelessly out of her way. Her face he could not see, partly for the dusk and partly for the shadow of her hair. He stole from cover at her back, climbed over the wooden pales, and closed like a hunting cat.

For all his caution, she heard him. She sprang round and away from him, sudden and silent, and heaved up the mattock to strike at his head. He caught the flare of wild eyes, enormous in a pinched and pallid face, and could not tell if she knew him, or if she had any senses left in her to recall him. The face was rigid and blank, a broken fragment of the ice from the river, the eyes blue flames of fear and horror. He leaped in beneath the blow, and the stock of the mattock bruised and numbed his shoulder. The fingers that grasped at her closed on the hem of the sacking cloak, and she wrenched

herself away from him and left it in his hand, and, flinging down
her weapon, ran from him madly like a wounded deer towards the
shelter of the trees.

He was after her instantly, and even desperation could not help
her to outrun him. At the garden pale he caught her by a fistful of
her gown and her hair, and at the lamentable cry she gave the breath
knotted and sobbed in his throat in an answering whimper of pain,
but he could not and would not let her go. She turned and sank her
teeth into his wrist, and down they came together into the snow.
She fell with hardly more substance than a leaf, so slight and light
under him, her struggling arms so thin, that all his being flooded
with an inconsolable torrent of grief and horror and shame. But
there was no help for it; he lay upon her with all his weight, pinning
her down until she tired, struggling with her until he held her
helpless, only her poor head weaving in agony from side to side to
evade even his glance, as though that, too, had power to hurt and
kill.

He eased his grip of her a little, feeling her body grow still under
him, and in a flash she had freed one arm, and her nails tore furrows
down his cheek. He caught and pinned her wrist and let his weight
lie on her, not daring to risk so much again. Even his head he laid
hard against hers, cheek to cheek, his brow upon the snow, to hold
her still. She heaved and panted in long, quivering breaths, and
the feel of her thinness and coldness and hate passed into him in
convulsions of desire and anguish, until the ache of his body after
her was almost more than he could bear.

"Aelis! Aelis!"

He had hardly voice to speak her name, but he whispered it
brokenly over and over into her ear. There was no tremor of knowledge, no softening, no acknowledgement in the rigid body under
him. Yet she knew what he did not, that he was weeping, in great
gulping sobs that shattered the syllables of her name. Through the
thin chink of her human astonishment wonder came in, and pity
hesitated on its heels, shy to follow. The quality of her stillness
changed. When he dared to lift his head and look at her again the
great eyes, fixed and dilated with shock, held a small, awakening
flame of doubt and thought that heartened him to believe the mind
and the soul were still alive in her.

"Aelis, don't you know me? Harry? Don't fight me, don't run. I came to find you, to take you with me. Aelis, my love, my little heart, don't be afraid of me—"

Not yet. It meant nothing to her yet but a faint and not unpleasant sound that for once did not threaten her. There would be a long time to wait before she came back to him, but at least she had cast the first glance over her shoulder.

He took one hand from her at last, still with terrible caution, unloosed the chain of his cloak and dropped it over her. Shifting his weight carefully, he snatched her up in one arm before she was aware, pinning both her arms above the elbow, and rolled the cloak round her, twisting the folds close so that she could not fight him. She started and struggled in returning panic, but that effort was soon spent. The sensation of warmth reached and confounded her; for the first time she felt that there might be kindness in the hands that wrapped her, and the arms that held her prisoner.

He had her now, she was helpless. He raised her into his arms, and carried her into the undercroft of the mill. There were the remains of a bolt of dry hay in the corner; he sat down with her there and made a nest for her, and hushed and soothed her; but he did not cease to hold her fast in his arms, for fear she should break from him and escape him again.

"I came as soon as I could, as soon as I knew. No one will hurt you now. I'll take care of you. I'll take you away to a safe place. I'll take you to my mother—"

Over and over he told her all his heart, over and over he stroked and gentled her. She softened a little in his arms, the frozen pallor of her face eased. He laid his lips to her forehead, and she trembled and turned her eyes upon him in wonder and longing, remembering caresses. Then he kissed her slowly and gently, brow and cheek and throat, and at last her mouth; and it awoke under his touch, and stirred and quickened to him, fastening hungrily with a great sigh.

His body was quiet enough now, heavy and selfless with tenderness; he could wait his time. He held her fast until the exhaustion of wonder went over her like a wave of the sea, and she fell asleep in his arms. After that he waited a long time, until he could be sure she would not lightly awake, and then he laid her down and lapped her close in the hay, and went out noiselessly from the hut. The door was broken-hinged but heavy; he barred it upon her, and knew that she could not move it. There were things he had to do.

First he crept out over the ice, the rising moon showing him where the boat lay. An old canvas was stretched over the thwarts, a fold of it turned back as she had left it. And he found what he had known in his heart he would find. Robert was there, stiff and stark where he had died, his wounds in breast and arm crusted through the bandages she had torn from her shift. Her cloak was here, too, tenderly laid over her father's body. Half-naked to the bitter cold, she had set herself to the long labour of hacking out a grave for her dead in the frozen earth. That at least he could spare her. Robert had a son now, too late to help him living, but at least in time to bury him, dead.

Harry knelt on the ice and said a prayer for the departed soul; and suddenly the burden of his responsibilities and the load of his guilt overwhelmed him for a moment, and a burst of tears shook him as the wind shakes an aspen tree. But it was brief enough, and left him whole and calm. He rose and went back to the shore, and made his way as fast as he could to the place where he had left Barbarossa tethered. He brought him, eager and uneasy and indignant, back to the mill, and into the shelter where Aelis still slept. There was bread and meat and wine in his saddle-bags, and the horse's great body would be their fire against the cold of the night.

She lay as he had left her. He put his hands upon her, there being now no light by which to see her; and she did not stir. But when he loosed the folds of the cloak and crept in beside her and wrapped it closely round them both, she stretched and sighed; and as he took her in his arms and drew her close to share his warmth with her, she turned to him confidingly in her sleep, and nestled against his heart.

All night he lay wakeful and held her in his arms. And in the morning she opened her bruised eyes, washed by sleep to the clean, virgin blue of cornflowers, and said: "Harry!" doubtfully and wistfully, as though she had dreamed of him.

"I'm here," he said, taut and tremulous with hope, and kissed her on the cheek, the gentle, reassuring kiss he would have offered to a child.

She threw her arms about his neck suddenly, and strained him to her with all her strength. The barrier of loneliness that had held back her tears broke, and the torrent of her grief spent itself gratefully on his breast.

He fed and nursed her, kindled fires to warm her, held her in his arms by night, and by day hollowed out for bitter penance Robert's iron grave. By the second evening, when he had made a sledge of boughs and drawn the swathed body ashore over the ice for burial, she rose and came out to him of her own will, her face pale and sombre but wonderfully calm, and helped him to lay her father in his grave. She prayed with him, and her grief was a human grief, and bearable, and her tears came softly, not for an inconceivable horror, but for a comprehensible sorrow, no longer past healing.

On the third day they left the mill, and crossed the ford at Pool. There was no difficulty now; from shore to shore the river was frozen over. Harry muffled Barbarossa's hoofs in bindings of rag, and led him across without danger.

They came into the gates of Castell Coch about noon, and there were other travellers arrived but a quarter of an hour before them, and busy unloading in the courtyard. Harry saw the bright bla-zonings of Gwynedd, counted the array of grooms and squires and chamberlains, and knew that the princess had kept her word and come early to the borders, to keep Christmas close to her lord. He was eased and glad, for now he could confide Aelis to the safest of all safe-keeping; but he was constrained and uneasy, too, for some new and quite unexpected instinct quickened in him at a touch, warning him that it is not so simple to tell your mother that you have become a man and a lover without giving her warning or asking her leave.

Gilleis, coming out from the princess's apartment to see Joan's personal baggage carried in, halted on the steps of the hall at sight of the chestnut horse pacing in with his double burden. She forgot her errand, forgot the annoyances of travel and the relief of arrival. All she saw was that sturdy, well-set young man, a stranger with sombre, resolute eyes, and a stubble three days old and yellow as ducklings on his chin, holding the slender girl before him in his arms as though she were a chalice of gold from which he feared to spill one drop of nectar. She watched him dismount, taking his arm so softly and reluctantly from about the swathed figure, and her exasperation flared at seeing him ride without a cloak in such weather, and chilled with more than foreboding as she realised that indeed he had had a cloak, but the girl was wearing it. And pale and thin and soiled as she was, she wore it like the purple, and leaned to Harry, as he raised his arms to lift her down, with the naked, confiding worship kings seldom inspire. For that Gilleis warmed to her, even in her pain.

Her time was come upon her too soon. He was not yet nineteen, and for four years she had lacked him, and now to lose him to gold hair and a wild and innocent face, and eyes like cornflowers in an unreaped field!

He set the girl on her feet with delicate care, as though the earth might bruise her. He gave his bridle to a groom, and turned towards the hall with his arm clasped close about his companion's shoulders. And then he saw his mother standing, and knew that he was seen.

Gilleis marshalled her powers and her love, and went down to meet and embrace him.

"Mother," he said, "I'm thankful you're come. Here's one I should be glad to confide to your care, one who befriended me, and is orphaned through me. This is Aelis, Robert's daughter, of whom you've heard tell from me. We're newly come from burying her father."

He took her in his arm again, for she had hung back from intruding upon their greeting; he brought her forward with a high colour and a grave face.

"Mother, this is my bride I'm bringing to you. Take her and keep her safe for me till I come. But for you and me she has no one and nothing in the world now."

His voice was careful and proud and even, but Gilleis saw the child who was gone look out of his eyes for a moment, between defiance and appeal, before the young man fronted her again with his high, imperious stare. God bless the boy, she thought, saved by the irresistible laughter that moved her always at the ingenuous solemnities of men, does he think I had ambitions to match him with some little Welsh princess with a couple of cantrefs in her pocket? Or did God teach him the cunning to come at me this way, knowing I could never give him up with a good grace but to some poor creature who had nothing besides? If it must come, what's left me to do but embrace it? Better give him freely than have him wrested from me.

She looked at the girl, and saw the dark rings under her eyes, the pallor of her cold cheeks, the poverty of her dress. So young and so lonely, without possessions, without kin, who could grudge her that close clasp of hands by which she clung to the world, and hope, and the promise of happiness?

"And where should you take her," said Gilleis roundly, "if not to me?" And she took Aelis from him, took her to her heart and kissed her warmly. "Child, you're dearly welcome. God knows I'm sorry for your loss, but I'm glad of my own gain." God record the lie to me for merit and not for sin, she thought, and teach me to make truth of it. "Come in with me," she said. "Come in from the cold, both of you, and warm yourselves at the fire, for you look perished with this frost. Come in to the princess and tell her your news; she'll be happy for you."

He said no to that, already light with relief and straining back anxiously towards his duty. But her reward was with her, for he hugged and kissed her again with the exuberance of joy, over his trouble and riding smoothly now. Like all the men, she thought, a sunny soul when you get your way; and she laughed at herself and him, and the old delight was still fresh and untarnished. What had ailed him to doubt, or her to fear? Had his father asked any man's leave when he chose her to wife? And had she forgotten the boldness of her own courses, when she set her heart on Harry Talvace of all men, and so staked her life that it should win her him or lose her all?

"I can't stay, Mother, I must go back, there's work waiting for me. I know Parfois from within; they need me there. Only take care of her, and I'm happy. And love her, Mother," he said in a pleading whisper into her ear, "for *I* love her dearly."

"And who should take better care of her than her mother?" said Gilleis, hugging him back with good will. "And who should love her more? There, then, if you must go you can be easy about us here. We shall do very pleasantly together, pulling you to pieces till you come again. There are things I can teach her about you! There, child, be off if you must. Kiss her and trust her to me."

He kissed her, and took his cloak and went, content for his women-folk and off like an arrow to the burrowers under Parfois, busy probing the rock for every fault and fissure where heat or frost or iron could bite.

They looked after him in a brief and perilous silence, and when he was gone they looked at each other for the first time narrowly and deeply.

"Madam," said Aelis, measuring what might well prove to be a formidable opponent, "I will be obedient to you, and grateful, and learn of you how best to serve him. But I tell you now, I will not give him up."

Who would have thought at first glance that she had so high a heart in her? Gilleis studied her long and thoughtfully, saw beyond the pallor of cold and privation and grief the resolution and compo-sure of the clear face, the deep spark in the eyes that looked back at her so straightly, marked how the flower of a mouth nevertheless fashioned and finished every word, and cut it free with the cleanness of a sword. She knew what she had said, and what she had said she meant; the challenge was there to be accepted or let lie, *she* would not change. She gave honest warning, without bitterness or malice; but if she had to fight for him, she would give no quarter.

"For I think," said Aelis with deliberation, blue eyes as bright and daunting as swords, "I am not what you would have chosen for him."

"Girl," said Gilleis with a sudden blazing smile, "as God sees me, I begin to think you *are!*"

Chapter Nine

Parfois: *December* 1233

*I*n the night, in the deceptive silence of the motionless frost, Parfois lay as still and untouched as the very stars overhead. It was bright in the great hall, even pinched as they were now for candles; and sparing as they had to be with food and ale and wine for their swollen garrison, yet they did well enough. On the roof of the Lady's Tower William Isambard paced out his nightly vigil, watching the glimmerings of fires distant under the mountain, the tiny links of the chain that bound him close within his own guard, and yet left him in such apparent peace. The very waiting was heavy to bear; three times he had tried to lift it by well-armed sorties in strength, but the burden of his losses had taught him to forbear such costly relief. He kept his lower guard by main force, the battered tower there reinforced by a hurried three-fold barrier reared from Master Edmund's building-stone, and manned by half the garrison. If the ramp was taken they could bring up their engines to the plateau of the church, and assault the castle itself at close quarters; but as long as it held Parfois was impregnable, its capture an impossibility. And here he beheld it beneath him, intact and orderly and quiet, inviolate, inviolable.

Down under their feet, like conies, like moles, the Welsh pecked tirelessly at the rock on which their fortress stood, gnawing it inch-meal away from under them. But where was the sense in that? What could they hope to do like that? As well set out to drain the river with ladles.

It maddened him when the old master-mason insisted daily on reporting his perpetual obsession, or when de Guichet, following him here at night, thought fit to refer to the same derisory activity. Did it matter that they broke their fool teeth chipping away the earth? Every man knew the Welsh could climb, every man acknowledged they could scale the cliff and thread the gully that severed the rock of Parfois from the rock of the church. What then? They could get no engines up there, there were no practicable posts even for their archers; and even if they could have climbed to the very foot of the wall itself, they could bring up no ladders to it. Let them burrow!

"My lord, Master Edmund says he still hears them. Under the gate-towers, but most clearly under the outer armoury and the tracing-house. He swears they are mining there under us."

"Let them! What good can it do them? The one bolt-hole that could have been dangerous we've stopped with stones, and the doors within are guarded. If my fool father had not made use of it for his tricks we need not have sacrificed even that; they'd never have found it from without if the boy had not known it already. And there are no more such posterns."

"No, my lord. But there are crevices and shallow caves. And the prince of Aberffraw has his masons, too, who know how to quarry rock as well as Master Edmund does."

"And do you think they can tunnel a way into Parfois? In how many years? Let them burrow! Pick them off when you can, and leave troubling me with them."

There were archers stationed perpetually on top of the gate-towers and the walk between them, and on every gallery of the wall on that side. Occasionally an incautious clansman showed himself clear of the cliff, and paid for it, but of late they had learned to lie close, and the overhang gave them generous shelter. Once at least, when the Welsh had brought up by night a larger party than usual, and were detected, the defenders had tipped oil down into the gully and thrown torches after it, and lit a flare that drove several men screaming in flames from cover, to be executed at leisure by the bowmen on the wall. But they were quick to learn. They hugged the cliff now, and came singly and in silence, and perhaps they had enlarged their holes enough to lie clear of the range of fire. But what of it? Let them grope busily in the dark until they grew as blind as the old man himself. What harm could they do there?

"As you will, my lord. We do what can be done. The boy, my lord, is also a mason, you'll recall; he learned under Master Edmund—"

"Leave that, I said. Is there more to tell?"

"Not new, my lord. The old lord, your father, has asked again if he may walk in the inner ward, mornings. I said I would ask you. He's sickly with being mewed up so long, after the life he's lived. You might think well to let him out to the air now and then." The brief, meaning look he lifted to William's face added: "—if you still want to keep him."

That brought an assuaged smile. It was an acknowledgement of the reversal if that demon of arrogance had been brought to ask favours.

"Let him, then, so he's watched carefully. No one is likely to mind him now. No need to attend him, if he wills to walk let him do it as best he may, but watch that he keeps to the inner ward. The woman's safe in the outer ward, she cannot come to him. Does she ever ask for him?"

"No, my lord, she asks for nothing."

She asked for nothing. She seemed not to be a prisoner; she moved through her days in quietness, perception and thought, untroubled in the centre of the stillness at the heart of the whirlwind. Sometimes they almost feared her. The wide-set eyes took in with so daunting a tranquillity and so precise an intelligence the detail of other people's madness, while she moved immune. If death came for her, she would examine it with as large a calm, and go with it as readily. The holy woman of Aber, the Venetian courtesan, the adventuress who had come back to Parfois as a prize of war from the Crusades—she had seen and experienced so much that she was out of reach of astonishment. She was of small relevance now. With this warfare on his hands he would have been glad to be rid of her if he could, but she was there, and no help for it; and she might yet be needed, she was the only goad that could move the old man if he turned obstinate again.

"See he keeps from her."

"He will, my lord, he pledged it."

"Do you see to it, I said. I trust neither him nor her. With whom does she spend her time?"

With no one. Or with everyone. She would return words readily, yet she had no need of any man's company.

"Sometimes with the women, or the musicians. She plays and sings; they say, well. And the fellow from Reichenau, rogue as he may be, he has some learning—she talks of books with him."

That was one more guest they would willingly have done without, the spoiled monk with his glib tongue and his knowing eyes, who had come south from Chester with his pack and his stories, to peddle a dubious fragment of the rood of Saint Peter to the old man. Ralf Isambard had been known in his day as a collector of such relics, and a witty tongue could get board and largesse out of him even if the merchandise was suspect. Straight from the Holy Land, the fellow said, fresh from shipboard and still pale from sickness after a winter crossing from France. And to Parfois he came, and in Parfois he was penned perforce now until the Welsh should withdraw; and mightily he complained of his ill luck, in falling unawares into such a wasp's nest the minute he set foot in England after years.

"I could never abide these scholarly women. The devil made them. But my father's taste was always for the devil's creations, for all his crusading piety." He swung abruptly towards the tower stair. "What's that? Who comes? Did I not tell you to keep them from me at this hour?"

"My lord, they know your wishes, there's not one would dare—"

The footsteps on the stone treads, mounting at speed, echoed hollowly out of the dark doorway.

"—without good need," said de Guichet, and went in haste to meet the intruder.

One of the chamberlains came bursting breathlessly out of the narrow shaft of the stairs, stumbled at the lintel, and made haste to humble himself before William's frowning face.

"My lord, pardon! This is too urgent to keep. The well—the great well, the one in the outer ward—"

"Fool, do I need telling where my wells are? What of it? What's amiss?"

There were two wells within the walls, one, the older and for some years inadequate to their needs, in the deepest heart of the inner ward, the second and newer in the outer ward, not far from the gate-towers; and on this richer supply the garrison chiefly depended.

"My lord, it's dry!"

"Dry? Fool, how can it run dry? When did it even sink before?" Purpling, William gripped the man by the shoulder and swung him round to the light of the half-moon. "Are you drunk, to run with such a folly? Who told you this?"

"My lord, the scullions who went to draw water there brought the word to the master-butler, and he to me. But I did not take it on trust, I went to put it to the test myself. My lord, it's all too true. We lowered and lowered and got nothing, and never touched water until we touched rock alongside. There's but a puddle at the bottom of the shaft. Come and see, my lord, you'll find it as I've said."

But his lord had already dropped him and swooped through the doorway like a plunging hawk, and was descending the stairs in great circling leaps.

The blind man in his sealed and guarded room heard the clamour go by, and turned his head with ears pricked to catch the few words that flew within earshot as they passed. He was quick to connect as to hear; sometimes his perception made even his guards afraid. He had but to catch the word "well" and the hubbub and agitation in the voices, and he knew. In his darkness he could reason at leisure, without the need to run and confirm. He thought of that ponderous household of more than a thousand souls, the measure of their cups suddenly dwindled to thimbles, the length of their resistance shrunken to the depth of the inner well. There had been trouble enough even in peaceful dry summers until they sank the second well.

Who was it had shrugged off the industrious burrowings of the Welshmen so lightly and contemptuously, calling them conies and moles? His bellowings rang loud and frantic now as he cursed them. What could they do, indeed! They had shown him what they could do. They could plot with exact care the position of the well; they had those among them who knew it to a yard. They could send their patient craftsmen up into the gully, and set them to work under the shelter of the overhanging gate-towers, quarrying away at the rock, prising with steel crows at every fault and every fissure that led them inwards towards the shaft, until they hammered their way through, and the first thin spurt of water told them they had tapped the spring. Easy work then to enlarge the leak until it could drain the lifeblood of Parfois, and send it trickling away in a new stream down the gully, to fall in a series of silver strings over the cliff, and make its way to the brook and the river below.

Doubtless when daylight came they would be able to see for themselves, from the gate-towers, Severn's new tributary threading the rocks below them, far out of reach of their thirst. The flow might even be strong enough to keep it from freezing for a night or two, until the first pressure was spent and only the steady feed of the spring remained.

"Well done, Harry!" said Isambard, laughing into the dark. "From one mole to another, well burrowed!"

It was three days after the piercing of the well when the renegade monk of Reichenau, pressed into service carrying timber to repair the barricades at the lower guard, fell twice under his load, and complained of pain and sickness. They pricked him to his feet again at lance-point, sure that he was play-acting to escape from his labours, for he shunned work as the devil shuns holy water. But when at last the party returned across the bridge into Parfois, he reached the rim of the empty well and leaned there hunched over fearful cramps, and in a moment he straightened up and fell on his face, stiffly as a log falls, and rebounded and rolled like a log, his mouth open and running spittle into the frozen snow.

A page, young and innocent enough to feel pity, ran to tend him, but one of the men-at-arms caught the boy back by the arm.

"Let be! Don't touch him! Who knows what ails him?"

Others who had hesitated stepped hurriedly back at that, staring uneasily upon the fallen man, who stirred feebly and groaned, the breath heavy and loud between his parted lips. He spread his arms, and those nearest shrank from him. A faint stain of blood marked the snow beside his mouth.

Madonna Benedetta came out from the doorway of the Warden's Tower, crossed the ward with her long, vehement step, and went on her knees beside the sick man. To her no one said: "Let be!" No one reached to hold her back. Prisoner as she was, her actions were her own.

"Paulinus!"

He had the name of one of the sweetest singers of the antique world, though she thought he had bestowed it upon himself and not got it from his parents in baptism. And indeed he had a certain graceless sweetness still about him, for all his rogueries, and a touch of the true freshet in his voice sometimes that clearly caught even himself unawares. She touched his shoulder, and he turned and opened his eyes. Within the circlet of his sometime tonsure the hair grew greyer and thinner, an old man's ragged hair. His face bore the marks of his life; if he had run from his cloister and turned *vagus*, the world had battered him enough for it.

"Paulinus, what is it? Where's your hurt?"

He rolled his head against her sleeve, and could not speak.

"Some of you help me with him," she said, looking round upon the starers with authority. "We must get him to his bed."

They gazed at her warily, and with small, furtive movements inched not forward but back. One said: "Do we know what ails him? Best leave him alone. You may be the next, mistress." And they shifted and murmured uneasily.

There was nothing to be got from them, and if he lay here in the frost he would surely die; she had no time to wonder or persuade. She lifted him sturdily, her hands beneath his armpits, and stooping, drew his arm round her neck and held him about the body.

"Can you rise? Lean on me, and try. It's not so far, and I'll help you. You mustn't stay here."

He did his best. Labouring he came to his knees, and got one foot under him. His face was dark, as though the blood thickened purple beneath the skin. He groaned and wrenched at his throat and breast, dragging open his gown as if he could not breathe; and plainly they saw then how his flesh was mottled with crimson stains. Over his chest and climbing his neck the angry blotches erupted and swelled, and he clawed at them and drew blood.

The crowd reeled backwards, and broke into a confusion of cries and warnings. She had not realised until then how many they were, all round her, all staring upon her, and others gathering on the run from every quarter, until de Guichet himself came striding to see what this excitement could be. He was thrusting his way through towards them when first somebody whispered:

"Plague!"

It was a spark to tinder; it flared in an instant, and was taken up on all sides in a mad outcry, hardly a word now, only a bellowing of beasts. De Guichet broke through upon them roaring, and recoiled faster than he came at sight of the mottled body and marred face. Hands clutched at him, protesting and imploring.

"Plague! He's brought the plague from overseas. God pity us all, plague's among us!"

"This is not plague," cried Benedetta stoutly, keeping her hold of Paulinus as he swayed at her side. "Plague I know, plague I've seen, and this is none. Let me get him within, and ask your own physician."

They screamed no to that. Bad enough he should be even within the walls, but he must not be lodged among them like a whole man.

"Nor her, neither," shrilled one of the women. "She's held him, she's handled him, she's as foul as he. God help us all if she's let run loose among us."

"Put them out," voices began to cry, shrill and hard, scarcely human in their terror. "Out of Parfois! We won't have them within the walls. Drive them out!"

"This is not plague," Benedetta cried into the wind. "His death will be on you if you cast him out. He'll die of cold, not of plague, and God will require his life of you."

They shouted her down. She saw all round her a fantastic dance of terrified faces, she was battered by the shrieking of frenzied voices. The sick man's head lolled on her shoulder. She held him upright, standing off his frightened enemies with her broad brow and blazing eyes; but she saw death walking towards him, and the shadow touched herself no less than him. She turned her head quickly, searching for one face, one, that kept its wits and its human-

ity, and offered her an ally to whom she might appeal; but the
demon of panic, more contagious than plague, had stricken them all
into the grotesque anonymity of masks.

"My lord," said de Guichet's voice behind her, shaking and appalled, "plague—we're harbouring plague among us."

She turned, and saw William Isambard. Doubtless he had heard
the turmoil and come in anger to know the reason, with raised voice
and noise enough, if there had not been too hideous a clamour
already for him to make himself heard. When he struck out about
him with his fists, after his ready fashion, then they knew who
roared at their backs, and broke apart and gave him place; and so
brought him headlong to the front, face to face with Paulinus and
still ignorant of what waited for him. She turned in time to see him
recoil with a leap that sent the nearest babblers reeling. She saw his
face in the instant of recognition, stricken white and motionless in
its grimace of displeasure, the eyes fallen blank as glass, empty
lanterns until fear found a colour and a spark to kindle them again.

At that she smiled, and he saw the smile. She, with her arm about
the pestilence and death's hand heavy on her shoulder, still had
heart to laugh at him. Anger came back to habit with his fear. But
what did it matter? He had no power at all, he went where he must,
where circumstances thrust him. There was no help in him.

"How came this? How long has he been so?"

"God knows, my lord! He must have brought the contagion with
him from shipboard. Only now he fell, and we saw—"

They crowded close about their master, those who dared clutching
at his sleeves in demand and entreaty.

"My lord, save us! Cast them out before they poison us all!"

"My lord, for mercy's sake!"

"Look at her! His mark's on her now, no one can make her clean
again. Drive them both out quickly—drive out the plague from
among us, or we're all lost like her."

"My lord," said de Guichet, quaking, "what's to be done with
them? If this is indeed plague—"

They clamoured that it was, that it would flare through Parfois,
shut in as it was and short of water and food, like a flame through
dry grass, and make of the castle a graveyard. William bellowed for
silence, and shut the nearest bleating mouth with his fist.

"Hold your fool tongues! Do you suppose I want pestilence in my house? Have I less to lose than you? Whether this is plague or no, I dare not harbour it. We'll have them out of here in short order."

"The man will die," said Benedetta, "if you put him out in the cold. In God's name give him at least a shelter where I can tend him. A hut outside the walls, where we cannot breathe contagion on you, anything, so he has a roof over him."

"He shall have a roof over him, and space enough," said William, and the cold, frightened eyes that had learned to hate her when she laughed took some comfort now when she stooped to beg, even though she did it as one having rights. "De Guichet, take them and shut them into the church. Fasten the doors on them. All the doors. Nail up the lower windows, make them secure."

"Yes, my lord."

"On your head be it if they break out. Get them hence, get them out of the wards, I care not how. You have men enough."

He drew back thankfully, his eyes still on the woman and her groaning burden. She saw him shudder with the same dread and revulsion that had made monsters of the men of Parfois, men no worse than most of their kind when they were not mortally afraid. He drew his furred gown about him and put a fastidious distance between himself and the contagion of misery, but he did not leave the scene, he waited apart to see his orders carried out. He had not only a life to lose like any other man, but a garrison at war to safeguard and preserve, and his castle and his lordship depended on keeping them not only from disease but also from the panic fear of disease. In her heart she did not blame him overmuch; and though she had opened her lips to entreat him once again she did not do it. For the baying of the pack he would not have heard; but if he had heard he would not have heeded.

"Hold up, my heart," she said into the ear of the rogue monk, and braced her shoulder under his, "for the good name of all scholars."

His eyes rolled wide and stared upon her, and the sharp mind was still there, raging within the failing body. The contortion of his mouth she knew for a wry smile, the kind fortune had chiefly drawn from him all his life long, and very fitting for a salute to his death.

"Where you go, I go, too," she said. "Even a cold welcome's warmer, shared."

Why should the unwilled cruelty of fear blaze so readily into the hot frenzy of hatred? The men-at-arms had run for lances, and for all their terror came almost with glee, levelling the steel. Benedetta turned about to put her body between them and the sick man, baring her teeth at the foremost like a hound on guard.

"Are you men? Keep off! Touch him, and by God I'll breathe plague down your throats though I must claw my way up your lances to reach you. Spit me, and you must shift my carcass with your own hands, plague and all. Let us alone and we'll quit your company as fast as we can. Use your goads on us and I'll make you bury us."

For all their din they heard that, and wavered. The lances hovered, even touched her breast. She gave back not at all, she even leaned a little forward, as best she might for the weight that hung upon her shoulder, and pressed her body to the points, staring the too eager herdsmen in the face with wide and blazing eyes; and the steel shrank from her touch, and left her ungrazed. Him they would have pricked along, had he been alone, for by no other means could they have driven him out of their gates. And if he had died on the way they would have transfixed him and dropped man and lances into the gully to breed among the Welshmen. But she was a different matter. With her aid he might make shift to walk to his tomb, and spare them the need of touching him even at a lance's length. And there was no denying she had shocked them into second thoughts about driving her too far. Who could tell? She might be holy, after all, as the Welsh held her. The lightning of God might do her bidding. They brandished their weapons all round her as she addressed herself to the melancholy journey out of Parfois, but they held off from drawing blood, however they howled and threatened.

Paulinus moved with dragging feet at her side, heaving harsh breaths that rattled in his throat. As best he might, he walked; and when he was forced to halt for a moment, she wound both arms about him and held him upright against her breast, eyes flaring warnings over his shoulder, until he was ready to drag himself yet a few yards towards his death. Slow and lame and bitter was the journey, with the hunt for ever snapping at their heels and the din of frantic voices shrill and cruel in their ears. All Parfois ran shrieking after them, followed them streaming across the drawbridge, hemmed them into the narrow path that led straight to the church. Even the men from the guard-posts that ringed the plateau left their stations and came panting with excitement, to stare and question and add their voices to the babel.

So they brought them to the west door, and drove them within. She turned then to look from face to face, and with quiet eyes and still voice she said: "For charity give us at least food and water."

Water? They had but one inadequate well now to keep a thousand souls alive, why waste a drop on two already condemned to death? Food? Who knew how long they might have to hold out yet? They could spare nothing.

The door swung to and closed upon her face. All round Master Harry's church the men of Parfois seethed, making fast doors. They ran with timbers and nails and hammers, sealing the world within from the world without, closing the tomb.

Young Thomas Blount came back from the entombment and leaned to his lord's ear in the shelter of the merlons on the wall.

"My lord," he said, soft and content and fat with his own cleverness, "it's done. They're penned so fast they'll never break out."

"That's well," said William, and for all he kept his eyes on the deceptive stillness below in the river valley, he listened yet. There was more news than that in the voice.

"And, my lord—" The boy's fair head leaned closer to whisper: "—they're three, not two, within there."

William turned his head then for a moment, to cast one steel-bright glance into the gleeful face. The archers manning the wall moved at no great distance; he eyed them thoughtfully and questioned from motionless lips: "The third?"

"My lord, when the alarm began the old blind man was at his exercise. Those who were watching the archway forgot him and ran with the rest, and he heard and followed. I saw him hanging on the edge of the crowd, he'd know who it was we had at the end of the lances, and where they were bound. I did not see him or think of him again till we were circling the church. I was first round to the south door, and I saw what no other saw." Smiling, sure of his ground, he dropped the words softly into the waiting ear that inclined to him. "He's gone to her. I saw him enter. He's sealed up in the church with the plague-carriers."

A moment of silence, while William's bearded face kept its stony calm; then a sharp gleam of interest and gratification showed for an instant in his eyes. Low-voiced, he asked:

"You are sure?"

"Sure, my lord."

"And no one else marked him?"

"No one, my lord. They had no eyes for anything but the business they were about."

No one. No one but clever Thomas, who had such sharp eyes, and knew so well how to make use of what they saw to ingratiate himself with his master.

"And you've said no word to any but me?"

"No, my lord, I swear it."

"No need, boy, no need. Your word is enough. So this is private between us two. And we've seen nothing—eh, Thomas?"

"Nothing, my lord. When they venture at last to come and confess they've lost their charge I shall be trembling with them."

"That's my own Thomas! I shan't forget your devotion."

"My lord, I serve as I can."

"And you shall not lack your reward. Come to me tonight, to the tower, and you shall have present earnest of my favour. Come privately and early, before de Guichet reports to me. I would not have him made privy to what you and I know."

"Trust me, my lord! Two who have seen nothing is better reckoning than three.

And there went a happy man, secure in his duty well done and his lord's gratitude well earned. What better could one wish him than to keep that high content of heart to his life's end?

The hand that pointed down towards the Welsh fires in the valley, the same hand that had bestowed the lavish gift on him only a few moments since, scooped suddenly along the rim of the embrasure between the merlons, where the white of the latest fall lay thick, and flew to clamp like steel over his face, filling mouth and nostrils with frozen snow. The arm that had leaned so flatteringly upon his shoulders dropped to grip him about the thighs and heave him from his feet. He had no time even to claw at the stone as he was hoisted over it. He fell without so much as a cry, choking on startling coldness. He fell with the words of commendation and affection still quick in his ears.

William leaned over and looked down into the dark, faintly silvered with starlight before the rise of the moon. He stroked his sleeves into order, and listened for the impact below, but it was long in coming and dull and muffled when it came; he doubted if it would reach any other ears. He smoothed out at leisure the long tracks of his fingers in the snow, modelling the edge to its old sharp ridge, filed by the wind. The Lady's Tower stood sheer above the cliff; only the Welsh, far below there where the cover of bushes and trees began, were likely to stumble on the remains of Thomas Blount, and wonder how he had been ushered out of the world. A pity about the clasp, he need not have been so over-generous. Some tribesman would be swaggering with gold fasteners to his tattered cloak within the week.

A pity, but no matter. And now let any other charge me that I knew and connived at my father's self-murder. I am clean. The obstinate old fool refused to die an open, blameless death becoming his age; this was his own choice. Who am I to cross my father's wishes? Am I his seneschal, that I should break in on his devotions? Am I his confessor, that I should stand between him and his mistress? Did I give any orders concerning him, except to enlarge his liberty? Was I there when he hid himself in the church? All Parfois knows I was not. I have seen nothing, I know nothing.

And one, Thomas, one is better than two.

He was pacing the leads of the tower, heavy and pre-occupied and alone as was his blameless habit at this hour, when de Guichet came up to make his nightly report.

Benedetta came in from the west porch dragging wearily, cramped with the ache of half-carrying the dying man; but when she stepped within and the praying hands of the nave arched over her she was drawn erect, and opened her lips and drank her fill of the inexhaustible radiance of the air within that space.

Beneath the altar the singing children on the great stone frontal filled their sturdy young lungs, and lifted to the light rapt, delightful faces and earnest, bawling mouths round as rosy apples. Above them the great lancets soared like launched arrows. The length of the nave the fluted pillars burgeoned into the wonderful, coiling, clustering, living leaves, the leaves of the holy tree, the tree of hope, the tree of affirmation, the tree of love. Out of their quivering tension of energy the ribs of the roof sprang, arched to contain the great charged space that was the shape of beauty and prayer; and at the roof-rib they met, and the glowing bosses that bound them were like notes of music, cries of joy, the inaudible sound of the warmth of hands clasping.

The hammers had ceased their wood-pecking chorus at the outer doors, the grave-diggers were gone; softer sounds could come in to her now, a hungry calling of birds, cold and plaintive, a snatch of drunken song from one of the outposts along the escarpment, the slow, hesitant steps of a man, leather feeling its way upon stone.

She raised her head intently then, for that sound was close and strange, and before her, not behind. Paulinus could not have passed her, she would have known; nor did she believe that he would ever walk thus steadily and firmly again. But there was no other man; there could be none. She waited, and the steps resumed, halted again, waited as with breath held to match her waiting.

And then she saw him. He had come from the south porch, and stood so matched with one of the slender, springing uprights of the rood-screen that until he stirred she could not find him. Tall, lean to emaciation, sombre in browns, gold at his belt and his breast, the ageless body still erect as a larch, the head still wonderful, shapely, proud. Not even age could spoil those immortal shapes of bone, or deface the immaculate fit of the cap of iron-grey hair over the lofty skull. The face, fleshless and still, quested upon the air blindly, straining after her. It had a terrible and admirable patience, that sat strangely in its humility and simplicity upon those arrogant and splendid features. He was not marred, but for the darkening of the deep eyes, torches burned out and blackened to charcoal under the high bronze brow.

"My lord?"

The vault took her low voice and filled every corner with it, as though the stone spoke.

He turned his blind, searching stare instantly upon her. She saw the face full; she saw the quenched eyes find her, she saw the long lips smile.

"My lady!" He loosed his hold upon the screen, and with reared head and intent face came towards her; but still at some little distance he halted and waited again of courtesy, lest he should seem to lay claim to her, who had no claim now upon anything in the world that was not given out of charity.

"My lord, what are you doing here?"

"My lady, listening to your voice and praising God. And, as I think, dying."

The same voice, the old voice, but of its own will it had relinquished command and turned within, to the argument of the soul. Not in penitence: she had seen penitents, and this was none. But the breaking of age he accepted for experience and profit with as sincere a passion as the making of youth, and that which was strange and new to him, even humiliation and death, he took and examined with whole-hearted curiosity, and never drew back. Penitents recoil; he went forward, and what he let fall by the way was sloughed because he outgrew it, and not because he repented of it.

"Praise be to God, you cannot send me away. Touch me," he said, smiling, "breathe on me, give me your contagion."

"Why have you thrown your life away?" she said, sharp with protest and reproach. "Were not two of us enough?"

"I have not thrown it away. I'll keep it as best I may, as long as I may. I have only laid it where God may take it if he will; and if he spare, I'll take it up gladly and carry it yet a mile or two more. Will you not take my hand, Benedetta?"

At the sound of her name in his mouth she started, as if someone long absent had called her; and she laid her hand in his because she could not leave it lying thus patient and empty in air. But at the closing of his long, lean fingers she achieved again the visitation of peace.

He had chosen to die with her; that she knew. And blind though he might be, this at least he had done with open eyes. No man would bring them food or water now, no one would open the doors to them. Parfois could not be starved out fast enough to save them, nor did she believe it could yet be taken by storm. And what she knew, he knew better, for he was Parfois, the blood and the life of it, whoever had wrested it from him.

"This is the only place," he said, "large enough to contain me upright, and provide me breath enough to fill my body. Don't grudge me this escape, I've been in strait keeping long enough. Moreover, you have a sick man to care for, and good need of one like me, who carries his own plagues and fears no other. Where have you left him?"

"In the porch. I could not get him farther. I came to see what provision I could make for him."

"We have a world," said Isambard, turning his blind gaze at large about his last barony. "We have the house of the archangels, and the forests of heaven. Chapels enough to choose from for his death-bed and your bower, privacy at need, and a place of meeting, the most beautiful in England. Praise God, in my day I made good endowments, whether for piety or pride God best knows, but we have the benefit of it now. There's a chest full of vestments and altar-cloths and draperies. Come, take what you need for his bed, and choose where you'll have it laid, and I'll carry him there. Is it plague?" He loosed her hand, he moved before her with assurance in his own best kingdom, and looked back with a crooked smile when she was slow to answer. "To God and me it's all one. I do but ask."

"I think," she said, following him, "he brought some fluctuating fever with him from the east, and has some aggravation of it now from a poison in his food. But it's enough. For I think he will die."

"So shall we all, bond and free," said Isambard. "There's nothing there for grieving. But at least let him die covered and warm. It will be bitter cold here by night."

He brought her to the great, carved chest that held the trappings of the altar, with the assurance of one who knew every worn place in every stone about this church of his. He lifted the lid, and turned the eternal questioning of his blind face upon her.

"Take what you will."

She did not hesitate to fill her arms. "He's plagued by thirst. He was groaning for water."

"We have water," he said instantly. "There's water in the stoups, at least the walls keep out the frost. Better, we have wine. There's wine in the sacristy. Pity indeed we have no food. But if he'll die the more gently drunk than sober, in God's name, why not? I think the mercy of heaven would not hold it against him that his last act of contrition was a little thick on the tongue. Come, see where you'll have him laid, and I'll bring him there. I lack nothing but eyes. Hands I have, make use of them how you will."

And so she did, moving side by side with him in dreamlike simplicity about the business of living and dying. Together they piled a broad bed of tapestries and brocades and embroideries in the small chantry chapel to southward of the high altar, walled round every way from draughts, where their shared warmth could at least temper the bitter cold. Together they carried Paulinus of Reichenau and laid him there, and wrapped him in such velvets as had never before touched that worn and venturesome skin of his. Together they took chalices of wine and candles from the sacristy, and bore them to their sanctuary against the falling night. He fumbled flint and steel doggedly in his hands, but she took them from him, and herself blew upon the spark that caught the tinder, and fanned it into a small, quick flame. It went to her heart that he should think of light for them, he who had no further need of light.

"There's a cresset-stone in the choir yonder, and another within the west door, but I doubt if there's oil beyond what's left in them. They keep the oil outside. The smaller I could bring here into the corner. It would give warmth as well as light."

He brought it, dragging it after him upon a length of velvet, for fear it should scratch or crack Master Harry's tiles. It had thirteen cups, and was carved between them with a deep-cut tracery of vine-leaves.

"His making," said Isambard, smoothing his fingertips gently along the coiling stems, "like all here. All we have is twice-borrowed, once from God, like our lives from the beginning, and once from him. Shall we light it? Lend me your eyes, I am not to be trusted with fire."

"If this is all we have," she said practically, "we might do well to spare it for a worse time. We shall be here long enough."

He turned his questing face a little, as though he looked upon the sick man, who lay open-eyed and shivering and mute in his princely wrappings. The rattle of his breath and the burning of his flesh spoke eloquently even to one without eyes.

"We shall. But his time, as I think, is short. Keep it, then, until his need is at its sharpest." He measured the oil in the shallow round cups with a fastidious fingertip, and wiped away the smoky smear upon scarlet and gold embroideries. "There's little enough we can do for him, but we can spare him a death in the dark." He smiled, feeling her sharp and rueful glance upon him. "*I* shall not need it, that's true enough. What's darkness to me? I habit with darkness, I have no fear of it. I have no fear, Benedetta," he said, soft-voiced and still, "of anything except that I may yet awaken in some other place, without you, and know that this was something I dreamed in my captivity."

"It is no dream," she said, her voice shaken and low. "I am here, and you I know by sight and touch to be very man. And I think we shall not be divided now, for good or ill, as long as we live."

"You comfort me," he said.

Where were they now, the years that had set them apart body and mind and spirit, the tensions and the terrors, the spites and the revenges? Where were they gone, the irrevocable memories of wrong and grief, the love unpaid, the injuries unrequited? They moved in tranquillity about the furnishing of their last household and the cherishing of their last guest, and felt no need to speak of the past; mutually forgiven, if this was forgiveness that looked back now and felt no sting, with nothing asked or answered, nothing atoned for.

They were far beyond any such needs, spent into quietness, all hatreds and distresses burned out. And all loves, too? God knew! Love has so many faces.

Paulinus of Reichenau lay for two days and two nights in high fever, while the flesh steamed and pared away from his shaking bones, and the two who nursed him watched over him without pause and held him swathed in his covers. On the third day the fever ebbed before the near approach of death, and he opened his eyes wonderingly upon the strange paradise of his cell. The slender stone pillars of the chapel arched above him into a vault like a double star. He was wrapped in velvets and silks, purple and gold and rich blue like colours for a king. Candles burned beside him on tall candlesticks of iron, and in the corner the cresset-stone sent up its thirteen small,

straight flames out of the last inch of oil. The faint smell of smoke
touched nostrils that knew nothing of the stench of his own sweat
and sickness, and set them quivering. On one side the woman sat
cradling his hand in hers. On the other an unknown man with the
lofty and far-looking face of death gazed down at him with hooded
eyes that had no radiance; but the austere countenance was calm
and did not threaten. Nevertheless, he was afraid.

He whispered his need, and the woman leaned to listen close, for
his voice was no more than a thread, frayed almost away to silence.

"A priest—I'm heavy with this load."

"Here's no priest," said Benedetta, "only God. Speak to me, and
never fear. He has sharper ears than mine."

With all the strength of his clinging to her hand, it seemed to her
she nursed only the claw of a dead bird. Close to the final silence he
found a voice that had more substance than his dwindling body.

"I have not been a great sinner—only a persevering one—I studied hard to improve."

He saw her smile, and was appeased. However sorry a creature
man may be, he should think shame to think shame of what his
maker made. Himself to the end, he made his wry confession word
by word as his strength served, and drew it out long.

"Even this rood of mine—a fake, but a good fake—my own work.
To tell truth, it was a morsel of a wine-cask from Angers. My
lord Isambard—would never have known the difference. All these
lordlings are fools—"

The man who stood brooding beside him put back his head and
laughed aloud, like a boon companion over a tavern tale, like a
pleased child at the fall of a pompous knight into the kennel on a
muddy day. If death could laugh like that, what was there to fear?
Startled and warmed, Paulinus essayed to echo the laugh, and choked
on it feebly. She lifted him, and he died on her arm, as easily as
snuffing out the last candle.

"He's gone," she said, and she was glad, for he was not made for
hard dying.

They said the prayers for him together; and then with one of the
giant iron candle-spikes for a crow Isambard opened the two-year-
old grave of old Father Hubert in the choir, and there beside the

chaplain of Parfois they laid the renegade monk and peddler of relics, and there buried him.

"I doubt if the old man would relish the company," said Isambard, straightening flushed and breathless from the lowering of the stone, "but if he will not give him a night's shelter in his house he's no Christian. God rest him! To die laughing is no bad death!"

And then they were alone.

"What is it?" asked Benedetta, waking in the night to the long, low rumbling echoes of rock shifting and falling.

"Nothing to fright us. Only the Welsh moles gnawing away the foundations from under Parfois." He drew the covers up more closely round her, and stroked back the coils of heavy hair from her thin and fallen cheek. "Many more such bites, and they'll bring down the walls. The weight of the gate-towers could well be their downfall. And there the gully is shallowest. If the gate-house falls, the wall is breached and they have a ladder to reach it by."

"What if they bring down towers and rock on themselves?" she whispered, aghast.

"For shame, my heart! Can you not trust Adam Boteler to know his business? How many years did he quarry stone for me in Bryn, and did you ever hear of his losing a man that way?"

She turned her mind back with wonder and effort to the stresses convulsing the outer world, where armies clashed and princes still contended. "Can they speed so? Is it possible to take Parfois this way?"

"Rankly impossible. But so it was to breach and drain the well, and they did it. Who knows if they will confound prophecy a second time?" The faintly-drawn breath that warmed his throat was even and calm, her body tranquil in his arms, but for fear she should fall back into the torment of hope he said with careful gentleness: "It cannot come in time to deliver us, my heart. We must not trust in it."

"I am content," she said. "I look for no deliverance."

Did she even desire it now? She looked into her heart, and could find there no desires at all, except, perhaps, the impossible longing to see the boy again. Yet they had tried to deliver themselves, day after day, as creatures in duty bound to live if they could, she the eyes and he the hands probing every cranny of their prison; but every door was sealed and every lower window securely barred, and there was no way out. The search had helped them during the worst days, when they were still strong and hunger was at its sharpest, courteously to conceal from each other the gnawings of the wolves within. The pack had drawn off now, sated, leaving behind the dullest of aches, and a languor that told them their days were beginning to draw in. By night they lay clenched fast in each other's arms, with the mutual chaste kindness of their bodies staying each other between the hours of shallow and dream-filled sleep.

"Forgive me," said Isambard, "for bringing you to this. God knows you owed me no second death."

"I came of my own will," she said. "There is nothing to forgive. It was I asked you to open your doors to me again, you did but grant my asking. More than my asking! I never ventured to suppose I should be taken back even into your bed."

The wry mouth pressed against her hair shook for a moment with a tremor of laughter, as brief as it was silent. "Ah, Benedetta! Ah, Benedetta! I never dared to hope you would come. Girl, I meant to give him to you freely. I would have brought him, all unsuspecting, to meet you at the gate. You need not even have crossed my threshold, unless you pleased to do me so much honour of your own grace."

"I do believe it. All the same, I think I should have come in. And delivered you the price I offered for him, whether you would or no."

"Because you are of the boy's mind, and would not be beholden to me?" he asked ruefully. "Or because I was old and threatened and blind, and you pitied me?"

"Pitied you? No, I was never so far out in my reckoning as that. Rather because I was ageing and secure and barren without you. And because I had it in my heart that it was time, and that you were come to the same crossroad where I stood. I could not get it out of my mind that there was still something you and I had to set about doing together, before the tale of our days was made up. I did not know it was dying. But liefer with you than with any," she said, speaking her mind with the old large and resolute generosity.

She had always a princely way with words. He would have borrowed that for his tombstone, he thought, if there had been a mason by to cut it for him. Liefer with you than with any! Living, dying, my best and dearest, in heaven or hell or where you will, liefer with you than with any!

"Benedetta!"

"My lord?"

"Hear me a word or two, here in the night, and be as blind to me while I speak as I am to you. I have yet somewhat on my heart."

"I am listening," she said. "I am blind."

"You have never asked me," said Isambard, his voice level and low beside her in the dark, "what I did with him when I snatched him out of his grave."

She lay still, her breath held for an instant; it came so suddenly and softly upon her, like the drawing of a curtain from between her and the light. Thus she had lain, roused and wakeful, with Harry in her arms, and death waiting its hour without impatience at the door. Time had completed another immeasurable circle, and restored the lost balance of love.

"I know what you did with him," she said simply. "He is where he should be. He is here with us, under the altar."

A deep sigh ebbed out of him; the clasp of his hands softened. He did not ask how she knew. In this marvellous eloquence of silence and stillness where was the need? At every breath they drew in knowledge and reassurance until all questions fell away like shadows from the brightness.

"I opened the tomb alone," he said after a long, charmed while of quietness, "with these hands. It was to have been mine, but I ceded it to him as having the better right. With one of his own iron crows I raised the stone, and mighty surprised I was to see how much thought and engineering must go to the act if one man takes it on himself alone. In these arms I lifted him down to his true place, and gave him cloth of gold to lie in, and covered him to his rest."

She felt the passion that quickened in the stillness of his long hands, as though in this moment they embraced not her wasted and withering flesh, but Harry's young, slender, stubborn bones.

"I know it was your wish," said Isambard with bitter compunction, "that the hands of love should some day lay him there. For that at least forgive me."

"No need," said Benedetta. "I am content."

His fingertips moved softly over her face, lingering on her lips. "You are smiling," he said, marvelling.

"Would you rather I wept?" she said. "I could weep."

"Ah, no! When did I ever see you weep? You laughed when you struck me down and went to him. You laughed when you were dragged to your death for him."

"I wept when they dragged me back to life."

"It may well be. Life without him was no such wonderful matter. God knows, girl, whether I more grudged you to him or him to you. Since he died I never could take pleasure in any man's death. I never shed blood but it was his blood, never hanged even the meanest felon but it was Harry's neck they roped. I never came to the point of distraining on a tenant or flogging a villein but I heard him outarguing me, and drew in my hand. If I forgot how his face looked, it confronted me endlessly here, and if I forgot the pleasure and excitement he had in other men, I saw it again in the stones of this house, and there was no escape from it. He has been a contagion in my blood, he who could not leave hewing and carving even when he was dead. Many a time have I cursed him for it and struggled to be rid of him, but I never could.

"And I knew I had destroyed him. And for all I could feel no guilt, I knew I had robbed the world and maimed myself. Against his life taken I had nothing to set but my own. And if it was forfeit I willed to pay it, but I had no clarity in me to judge, and no heart to surrender cravenly what might not be due, even though I had no joy in it. But as I might I offered it where God might take it at will, and never shut my hand on it to snatch it back. And time and again he let it lie. And this is strange, Benedetta, that as often as I offered it to be taken I valued and wanted it the more. Dead, Harry taught me how to love life, and I learned hard. The dearer it grew to me, the greater agony it cost me, still to expose it, but I would not withdraw. So it may be I have paid, take it all in all, somewhat of my debts."

In the momentary silence the fabric of the church and the rock beneath it quivered to another slow, rumbling fall, and they held their breath and listened until it was spent.

"Benedetta!" he felt with searching fingers along her cheek as the tremor stilled, and touched eyelids still fast closed; but the lashes were wet. "Ah, my heart, not for me! Why?"

"Go on," she said, her voice no more than a breath caught and held gently in the palm of his hand. "You had yet more to say to me."

"To you or to God. But God knows it all before I speak. And now I see that there is little enough of me you do not know." Nevertheless he resumed softly, with long pauses, as though the crowding memories caught him away even from her into wonder and forgetfulness.

"And then the boy came. Here in this place he appeared before me suddenly, the mould and pattern of his sire. I could not let him go. I had to find out if the same mettle was there, if I was living this agony to no purpose, if God was fooling me. I never struck him but once, when he willed to throw his own life away so he could take mine—and he fifteen years old, and all this dear world his for the taking, and to value it so little! But in his heart I think he was glad even to take my blows, and know by the sting he was well alive. I never had to teach him so again, but in my fashion I used him hard. Sometimes I rapped him harder than I knew, but always he rang true. I knocked him, and he knocked me as best he could, but never could I tame him. And at the end of it the wheel came round full, for like his father before him he staked his own liberty and life to stand by a threatened child that was nothing to him. And this time— oh, Benedetta, conceive it!—this time I was the child! I gave him his liberty, I bade him go. And he would not! Out of care for me, out of fear for me, because I was blind and open to my enemies, he would not leave me."

The long night was passing, the first faint glimmer of shape and proportion gathered and grew over their heads. Before there was vision there was form, the enlargement of peace, the impress of tranquillity. In a while the tension of the vaulting would spring into their consciousness; she would see it, and he through his hands and his body and his blood would feel and remember what she saw, and share her delight. The detail would come later, the light carving it afresh with every dawn.

"Now I have lived a miracle, I know how softly and naturally they come forth upon the world. I was Harry's against my will, and Harry is mine against his will. Not a small part of what he knows I have taught him. What he is, in part I have made him. I am in his blood as his father has been in mine. And please God, to as faithful an ending. For of all the good I have to bequeath, God be my witness, I have made him the heir. And only God knows," said Isambard, smiling in his assuaged repose of joy, "how I have prized and loved him."

She opened her eyes upon the noon light, and reflected sunshine quivering in the vault of the nave. The angels in the bosses cried aloud to God, arching their golden wings.

She lay in the soiled wealth of brocades and silks, her face a wisp of whiteness drawn over staring cheek-bones, and a great, rapt shining of eyes, her body a little armful of bones, the skeleton shining through the skin. The heaven of light leaned to her, tremulous as gossamer, durable as stone. No, more lasting than that, long as memory, durable as love.

For the achievement was not in the stone, though the stone had burst into flower under his hands. If the shell that holds this shape of splendour were broken and lost, she said in her heart, marvelling, yet this miracle would be here for ever, because he once conceived it and made it live. As the soul outwears the body, his work will outwear the stone. Eyes that have once seen it see all things differently thereafter, having learned the measure of wholeness. And what we have learned we surely transmit to others, and what we have received of revelation somehow we give again, in a perpetual laying on of hands. Shatter this church, and still in some secret measure Harry will have changed the world.

Most marvellous of all it was, to her audacious spirit, to see that perfection is not the end of energy, nor peace the end of venturing. Both are beginnings, and not of stagnation or weariness, but of some inconceivable ardour of passion that draws out the powers to their highest, and lengthens the longings of the heart beyond the last limitation of knowledge. They acknowledge no limitation; they are prolonged to infinity; time has no meaning for them, now is forever, here is everywhere. Go nowhere, make no more effort, wait, here all things come to you, enter into you, are one with you.

Her mind lay clear and still like a pool of mountain water in her wasted and enfeebled body, reflecting the vibrant changes of the light. Often she dreamed of water since the stoups had run dry, for all their austere husbandry, and left them only a dwindling drop of wine to keep off thirst. She moved now only when she must; she slept often, and dreamed much. She knew the brevity of her powers, and hoarded them for the efforts that must be made. The effort of re-coiling and pinning her great burden of hair exhausted her, speech hung heavy as lead, her garments had the weight of the world. She refuged in stillness, and her spirit lay open to wonder. Wait, go nowhere, here all things come to you and are one with you.

She put out a shrunken hand and felt for Isambard beside her, her eyes still dazzled with the heaven of ecstatic light that drew her upwards into the vault. No quick, careful hand came to meet her touch. She looked round then, the contours of earthly things shaking into clarity again about her, the tracery of the chantry, the cresset-stone, long ago darkened, the sultry, rich colourings of the bed, here in shadow. Isambard was gone from beside her. How long had she lacked him? For time she had no memory; she knew only that this must be the height of the day, but of what day only God knew.

She lay listening, and there were sounds that quickened a chord somewhere in her heart, and touched some instant recollection of solemnity and pity. The grating of metal against stone, a long, heaving breath that halted on intense silence, a gusty panting that ebbed in a groan of effort and relief. A pause, and again the probing and prising under the stone, and this time by an inch it slid from its place, she heard stone and stone engage. She understood then. He had left her sleeping, and gone to open a grave for her.

He cannot, alone, she thought, dismayed, and caught at the slender, springing pillars of the chantry to drag herself upright. He'll break bones and heart, and die.

Clasping and embracing her way from pillar to pillar, she brought herself out of the chapel into the choir, and instinctively turned her eyes to the spot where old Father Hubert's tomb sheltered his unexpected guest from Reichenau. Where else should he look for a resting-place for her? The stone was hardly settled yet, and could be turned back against the solid wood of the stalls without overmuch risk of breakage. But the corner was empty and still, the stone undisturbed. Higher, towards the altar, inch by inch another stone was levered carefully from its place. She heard the deep gasps of effort fetched up from a labouring heart, the long pauses between, while he gathered his body for one more assault. And without sight, his fingers painfully and patiently and perilously serving him for eyes! Her own eyes filled and dazzled for him, she who never wept. She groped her way towards him, holding by the stalls, and at the steps of the presbytery her meagre tears dried and left her vision clear, and she saw him.

The brief, chill sunlight, bright and hard as ice, poured through the lancets of the east window and spilled jewels upon the paving of the floor. In the cascade of green and gold and scarlet Isambard lay face-down over his improvised tools, heaving exhausted breaths into his body. He had broken two of the heavy candle-spikes, and torn and rasped his own fingers to the already starting bone; but he had done what he had set out to do.

Under the high altar, under the great frontal with its singing children, the centre stone was levered aside upon its fellows, and the shimmering stars and lozenges of light fell glittering like winter flowers into the stone-lined pit of Harry Talvace's grave.

Her body failed her at the steps, and brought her to her knees; and on her knees she dragged herself to his side across the bright waste. For the pounding of blood in his ears he did not hear her come; he lay panting, his spread hand dangling a drop of blood over the rim of the tomb, his brow against the stone. Only when she laid her hand on him did he raise his head and show her the bright, fierce ruin of his beauty, the faded, ambiguous mask of devil and angel yellow as brass, the quenched eyes mute under their lofty, fleshless lids, all the petrified splendour of death, yet with life and passion blazing through it to the end.

"And will you send me back," she said, touching his dusty brow with feeble fingers like the stems of withered flowers, "to be his bedfellow again?"

"Where else?" he said. "Where else should I lay you? If you go before, make my peace—make my peace!"

He laid his head in her lap and wound his skeleton arms about her, and so lay still. She cradled the rough grey crown of hair in her hands, and over his shoulders she looked into the grave. It was not so deep, she saw the stone lining bone-dry in the withering cold, and the sheen of the cloth of gold almost untarnished. She saw the slender little bones outlined in that glowing shroud, the quiet head that showed through its princely veil the soft, muted form of a sleeping face. She thought of the cell beneath Parfois, and the dark, dear head heavy on her breast all the night through.

She took Isambard's head between her wasted hands and lifted his face to her, and kissed him on the brow.

"You wanted his heart once," she said. "Put in your hand and take it. He would not grudge it to you now."

Chapter Ten

Parfois: *December* 1233 *to January* 1234

*F*or three days the fire burned in the rock beneath Parfois. They heard from the walk between the gate-towers, in the quiet of the night, the busy, muffled crackling of brushwood and branches, and the rushing and roaring of wind as the flames devoured the air; and by day, though these sounds were buried and lost beneath the ordinary commotion of life under siege, they had other signs to keep the prodigy in mind. For on the first morning, before the dawn had even a flush of colour to brighten it, one of the guard had run bellowing to his officer that smoke was belching from the empty well-shaft, that hell was boiling beneath Parfois, and the day of judgement upon them. They burst in upon William Isambard with the same wild story, and he cursed them for fools, but he ran to see. Adam's chimney fumed to the leaden sky, spitting hot air aloft in a column of blackness, and the crackling of flaming thorn from deep within the rock terrified them with threats of demons. By night there was a faint glow over the shaft, to redouble their uneasiness. Argue and reason as he might, William could not reassure his garrison that these were natural portents; and when he had shut himself in his own bedchamber with his thoughts he himself found small comfort there.

The sharp, withering wind in the funnel of the ravine served Llewelyn well, and kept the fire ablaze at intense heat longer than Adam had dared to hope. On the second night Parfois shook to the sudden, rumbling falls in the heart of the rock. Only then did they begin to understand what was happening to their stronghold. The earth under their feet quaked. In dread they moved about their labours on the threatened ground, trying to keep their very weight from falling too heavily, lowering their voices for fear the shock of a cry might set the walls tumbling. Smoke rolled along the gully and hid the valley from them. The frozen brook flowed again, but daily now it changed its course as the gradual landslips settled, and nightly the frost climbed again to silence a few more feet of water, as the fire burned down and the rock cooled.

On the fourth night the frost came into its own, gripping with ferocity where the fire had already ravaged. It was the twenty-second of December, and the hardest night of the winter. Towards morning all Parfois leaped from its bed in terror to the grinding roar of rock and masonry collapsing together, as the cliff-face split like thunder beneath the gatehouse, and the western tower, the foundations ripped away from under it, burst from base to roof, and crashed forty feet into the gully. The eastern tower still stood, the bridge lurching drunkenly from one chain; but the walls had sagged out of true, and cracked in jagged lightning slashes, and beneath them the smoking dust of the fall parted on the wind to disclose great slabs of rock hanging precariously, ready to shift at a touch.

William drew out the survivors, and beat and cursed his shocked garrison to work rigging a new bridge, reinforcing the lower guard, and manning the breach with every creature they had who could bear arms, feverishly expectant that Llewelyn would press his assault while they were in confusion. But whatever the temptations, Adam knew better than that, and Llewelyn was wise enough to be schooled in a business which was new to him. The rock was hardly cold yet; there would be fresh falls before the day was out, and to set men to scaling that quaking, choking mass before it had had at least a day to settle was to invite their deaths. So William had his day's grace, and time to think over the impregnability of his Parfois.

He gnawed his knuckles on his tower, feeling the lofty mass

vibrate beneath him still. It was time to admit the doubt that had never been real until now. The wall was breached, the well pierced, his garrison shaken to the heart. He stared into a morrow as bleak as the frozen valley below. If Parfois should hold he might yet carry all with him, secure his honour in the teeth of Humphrey Paunton's distrust—what was his error there, what had made the old fool at Fleace bristle and demand sureties?—discover the third body in the plague-church with loud and convincing innocence and grief, bury him publicly and honourably, and have the king's blessing still, and the king's protecting shadow to justify him. With Henry's commission instructing him, with England's borders to lose or save, that dispossession could hardly be questioned. And how could he know, when the old dotard slipped his collar and vanished during the alarm, where he had chosen to hide himself? How could he seek him beyond the walls of Parfois, when he was close beset here, with a tight Welsh cordon drawn round him? Had he not believed him fallen from the rock in his blindness, and grieved for him as dead? He had taken enough pains to establish the image of his filial anxiety. Could he have known that he was in the church? No one could accuse him, he had seen to that. No, if Parfois held, if he remained profitable to the king and kept his castle, all things would march yet.

But here he was, brought up newly and coldly against the knowledge that Parfois could fall.

And then? If Llewelyn captured Parfois, if Llewelyn opened the sealed church, what then? He would raise such an outcry over the body of Ralf Isambard that no counter-eloquence would ever be able quite to silence the first scream of parricide. The nice presentation of the case William had ready at his finger-ends would be shattered from the beginning, his cause lost before ever it was heard. The very suspicion would be enough to undo him. The old man had known well enough what he was talking about when he had said that Henry would take away his arm and leave his servant to pay the score alone at the first breath of scandal. There would be no future for the man at whom the prince of Aberffraw had flung the accusation of parricide. He heard his father's voice still, infuriatingly confident and amused, saying: "He'll hound you to the day of your death if you compromise him."

The resolution hardened within him that the bodies in the church must never be found, never at least in their own recognizable shapes. Could he have the doors unsealed and the dead secretly buried? No, the garrison would break if he added the renewed dread of plague to the terrors they already suffered.

But since the Welsh had made use of fire, why should he not borrow from them, and credit them with the invention? There was woodwork enough within the church; in this frost it should blaze no less merrily than Llewelyn's underground furnace. There was oil in store there close beside it, oil for the cressets and the lamps. The wind was westerly and keen. Two or three men, chosen for their thick heads, could do the work for him well enough from the western windows, without entering, and believe they were purging the last threat of plague. And let Llewelyn make what he would of the charred, unrecognisable bones.

Before dawn on Christmas Eve Llewelyn's camp, roused and in arms in readiness for the assault, looked up at maimed Parfois to see a new, tall tongue of flame soar on the wind, and unfurl into a long, streaming banner fringed with smoke. They straightened and stared; Llewelyn came out from his pavilion in haste at the alarm, and Harry, half-armed, ran with a cry of desolation and fury to clutch at Adam's arm.

"The church! Adam, they've fired the church!"

Like a torch, like a beacon, Master Harry's noble tower sprang upon the murky dawn, filled with angry light, and from its highest windows the wavering banneroles of flame streamed westwards upon a veering wind like long red-gold hair.

On that Christmas Eve they took Parfois.

The three-pronged attack had been planned with precision, but it was put into action some hours before the time intended, and in fierce haste. Llewelyn with something less than one-third of his total forces developed at last the frontal attack so long expected, and with no preliminary dawn battering by his engines of war the ranks of his knights drove hard at the tower and barricades of the lower guard. David with his companies had climbed into the mouth of the gully from the east during the hours of darkness, and turned loose his best archers to find for themselves niches in the rock from which they could command the jagged breach in the wall above, and pick off any defenders who exposed themselves there; for the greatest danger to the assault party would be the insecurity of their ground, the shifting mass that could all too easily be set rolling again by one boulder thrust over the edge. The rest of David's men lay close in what cover they could find, ready to press home a second wave of attack as soon as their comrades from the west had made the ascent. These, the main body of the assault, held off until the alarm on the ramp had drawn reinforcements tumbling in haste over the improvised bridge to fend off Llewelyn's repeated and damaging charges, and the clamour from among the trees had reached the steady, savage music of a pitched battle. Then Owen loosed them, and they broke cover and swarmed upwards into the gully of torn and tumbled rock.

Harry was the first to reach the treacherous fringes of the fall, and he set foot on the shifting rubble of rock without hesitation, and pressed on against the steep slope towards the breach in the wall. The defenders above were chary of approaching the edge of the fall too closely for fear of its rottenness, and from their more withdrawn stations their marksmanship was none too accurate. He was in greater danger from the quaking ladder of rock he climbed than from the enemy above. Twice he set foot on a hold that gave under him and brought him down, and once he started a terrifying slide, and would have gone down with it to grind his bones in the jostling rocks below if someone labouring close at his elbow had not snatched him aside and clung over him grimly by head and hands and splayed feet until the dust subsided and the quaking surface stilled.

"Gently, now, gently!" said Adam's voice in his ear. "Keep your father's son alive, boy, and let the church wait."

He wondered then, with the corner of his mind he could spare for the exercise, what Adam was doing there so opportunely at his elbow, Adam who was engineer rather than soldier, and had no business to be storming the breach with the men-at-arms. But he had no time for more than a quick glance and a breathless word, and then he was up and climbing again like a squirrel.

If de Guichet's men in the ward above them had not feared to venture close to the rim they might, with some losses to themselves, have stood off greater numbers than Owen brought against them, for they had but to start the nearest stones rolling, and they could have swept the Welshmen down like pebbles in a torrent. But their spirits were shaken and low, the hard earth of the outer ward was ripped apart by cracks that widened perceptibly at every shock, and they had but to set foot on this crazed surface to feel it quake beneath them. Not until Harry and the foremost of his fellows were groping for foot-and hand-holds to clamber over the crumbling rim did the defenders discard one terror under pressure from a greater, and the boldest leaped to slash at the spread hands and undefended heads that heaved over the edge into their vision, and prise loose the boulders and blocks of masonry that hung balanced on the edge of the fall.

They had left it late. The archers below, who had been waiting for them with fevered restraint, loosed gladly at every target that stood clear, and it was a rolling body, not a stone, that started the first slide. Harry missed his footing and slid a yard or two on his face, lunged upward again to see one of the blocks of hewn stone from the gate-tower rocking above him, and glimpsed de Guichet himself leaning with braced shoulder to dislodge it. For an instant they stared upon each other eye to eye through the grilles of their closed visors, and death hesitated between them. Then one of David's archers loosed without haste from a niche in the opposite wall of the gully, and de Guichet dropped and lay embracing his missile, one slack hand dangling. A little dust trickled from the pressure of his wrist and ran harmlessly down the slope like a puff of wind. The stone swung gently, and kept its place.

Harry breathed ease after his instant of honest terror, and scrambled aside to give the obstacle a wide berth, shouting a warning to those below. They had not all been so fortunate: he heard the clatter and roar of rocks descending, away to his right, and prayed for David's men.

He was up now, he was over the edge in a flurry of running dust. Thick as fog it hung everywhere on the air of the bright morning, dust and smoke and the stench of burning. The fire had split the rock, the frost was pulverising it. The taste of sandstone was in his throat as he launched himself across the few yards of shattered ground and into the ranks of Parfois. Close on his heels, as his sword engaged, the men of Gwynedd came pouring, to keep his flanks and lend their weight to his, to drive forward clear of the dangerous ground, guarding at their backs an arena where their fellows might arrive without danger.

Once the firm ground was won, Parfois was won. After that it was but a matter of fighting forward until resistance broke, and of never giving back a step before the desperate rallies that sought to sweep them over the edge.

David's men came after, and more easily and carefully, being delivered now from the most immediate peril. The archers in the gully changed ground, and plunged across the ravine to seek cover on the inward side, whence they could rake the plateau of the church, or at least pick off anyone foolish enough to expose himself near the edge. The defenders upon the walls and the towers were hampered by the close engagement in the ward below them, where friend and foe hung locked inextricably together, and arrows might strike the one as indifferently as the other. Before noon it was grown into a matter of sheer weight against weight. Buckler to buckler, breast to breast, the Welsh thrust their way outward from the breach like ripples spreading over a pond from a tossed pebble. They held the outer ward, and could take their time about clearing the towers. The archway to the inner ward was blocked against them stubbornly for a while, until they broke their way into the Warden's Tower and, swarming out along the wall, set their archers to raking the ground within from every angle. They drove in the gate, and they were through.

They parted company then, secure of their holding, and Owen pressed forward to clear the inner ward, while David detached half his force to turn back over the bridge, and take in the rear the companies that were still resisting Llewelyn's advance. But that battle had already broken out of the trees to the open ground of the plateau, and it needed only the alarm of David's coming to end it. The remnant of Parfois broke and ran, or dropped their weapons and surrendered themselves to any enemy who would hold his hand long enough to accept them. The castle was lost, no late heroism could retrieve it now.

Harry was through the archway into the inner ward among the first, and driving hand to hand towards the Lady's Tower. Swept into the arms of the enemy, they fought across the ward in a confused mass, locked so close that they shortened their swords and used their arms like wrestlers. The confused blazonings of Parfois, the colours of knighthood and the dun of men-at-arms, danced before Harry's dazzled eyes. He thrust off strongly from the mailed shoulder that was flung against his breast, and made room before him for his blade; and the man he had thrust away caught the flash of the steel and swung instinctively, head-down, to lunge beneath the stroke. His visor and a long strip of his mail gorget were ripped away; there was blood smearing his cheek. Harry stared into the face of William Isambard.

They bristled like dogs, and in an instant they were at each other like dogs. Harry lost sight of the turmoil around him, his vision drawing in to the single struggle. They were but two left in the world and none other by, only objects that hemmed and cramped their field, frustrating the man's longer reach and hampering the boy's more passionate speed and lightness.

This was a formidable swordsman, and no play, but deadly earnest; why had his heart failed in him for a moment, and let in the swinging blade so close to his hip? The build of his opponent, the long movements, the balance of the strokes that stood him off, all knocked at his senses with a familiarity that was like physical pain. This rapid recoil he knew, and the darting stroke that came out of it so unexpectedly, and the lightning lunge beneath the half-successful parry. But he knew the answers to them also. They had learned from the same master; they would see who had been the more apt and devoted pupil.

That early slash that had caused him one instant of wavering for the father's sake had drawn blood for the son. The sleeve of his banded mail hauberk had exposed his stretched wrist, and his glove was full of blood, his hilt slippery. Faces swam at him for a moment out of the press, bodies closed and hampered him, struggling movements impeded his sword arm. He shook off all, and clung with fixed, fierce eyes and darting, weaving point to his opponent. And when he felt the congestion of struggle reel away from his back he gave place by one rapid step, like one daunted or tiring. His enemy followed close, a blazing glance taking fire from the omen. Harry thrust tentatively for William's left side, and William beat off the stroke and swung suddenly with all his weight.

Harry sprang in beneath the blow, locked hilt under hilt to hold off the blade from his face, and wrenched sword and man onward together over his braced thigh. No time here, no space for the measured swing with which Isambard had once disarmed him. Instead he flung himself with all his strength upon his reeling enemy and brought him to the ground among the stamping feet, and with the weight of his body held down the arm that had not relinquished the sword. His own blade he had dropped to free his hands. His dagger was out before William could heave him off, the point pricked beneath the ear from which the covering mail was ripped away.

"Where are they?" he panted furiously. "What have you done with them? Where is Madonna Benedetta?"

A knee heaved beneath him, driving at his belly, but the weight of William's own harness hampered him. Harry leaned on the steel hard enough to feel the flesh shrink from it.

"Where is she? And your father? Speak, or I'll kill you! If you've harmed them—"

Through his teeth William spat: "Find them!" and hissed and moaned at the thrust of the knife-point. It bit and held; the close green glare of the eyes never wavered.

"By God, I will know! You *shall* tell me! *Where?*"

"In the church!"

The words were prised in a snarling moan from drawn-back lips tight with rage and hate. Folly, folly to have admitted to any knowledge at all! And why the truth? But the boy had death in his voice and eyes, he meant killing or knowing, and the flesh cries to live.

"The church!" said Harry, jerking upright on a horrified breath, and saw flames start again before his eyes. He let go of the stretched throat, he took his weight from the still able and treacherous arms, forgetting everything but the dread that drove him. He set foot to ground and was up in one spring, turning from his prisoner without another word or thought for him, turning to tear his way out of the press and run for the glowing shell of his father's church.

A hand lunged and took him about the ankle, bringing him down heavily and knocking the breath out of him. He rolled instinctively upon the dagger, keeping it out of reach with his own body until he could free his arm. He let the vengeful hands find his throat rather than let the dagger go, and half-blind, half-choked, he felt with clawing fingers for William's neck, and struck beneath the angle of the jaw, driving the steel home deep. Not consciously aiming to kill now, or even to wound, only to break free by the most certain way, and go to find his own.

Blood gushed streaming over his hand and arm, the body locked with his jerked and heaved in one immense convulsion, and the hands that gripped his throat relaxed and fell away harmlessly, twitching on the ground. Still gasping, still with darkened eyes, he tore himself free and battered his way loose from the press, and ran wildly through the archway into the outer ward. There arms caught at him and held him, and for a moment he fought to break away, until he knew Adam's voice and raised great, frantic eyes to stare into his face.

"The church! They're in the church!"

"They? Who?" said Adam, springing to meet the word.

"Benedetta—and Isambard—I made him tell me—"

Then they were running together, and Harry was weeping, and did not know it, and would not have cared if he had known. Llewelyn's companies were just crossing the bridge into Parfois, gradually and cautiously for fear of putting too great a strain upon the timbers. Harry ran headlong across in the teeth of the careful riders, and caught at the prince's rein.

"My lord, my lord, he's killed them—the church—They were in the church—"

He could not speak for the labouring of his bruised throat. It was Adam who cried the news in a fashion they could understand. Llewelyn was out of the saddle with a spring, and shouting his orders before the words were off Adam's lips; and with swords and axes, with whatever tools they could find, they rushed to hack away the barricades that sealed the doors of the church.

The fire had died down while they fought, the veering wind turning back the flames to westward. The windows of the nave were out, threads of lead from the cames streaked the stonework, smoke blackened it; within, the charred remnants of beams still glowed. There the heat beat them back when they had the door stripped and essayed to enter, but they saw sky yawning at them where a part of the vault had fallen. The tower was a cooling shell, windowless, roofless. The fire must have reached the choir before its impetus slackened as the wind changed. But when they circled the smoking hulk to the east end they saw the great lancets of the altar window intact, the stonework almost unstained; and the small door of the sacristy was whole and unmarked.

"Open here," said Llewelyn, and Harry was the first to drive a chisel under the timbers and begin to prise out the long nails. Streaked with grime and stone-dust and blood he wrenched away the last obstacle, and finding the door locked and the key absent, went to work on it with an axe until he burst the lock and was flung forward into the sacristy.

The roof of the presbytery was blackened, and the air still quivered with heat, but not beyond what they could bear. They stripped off their helms and entered, hushed and fearful. Faint fronds of smoke coiled in the vault, and the smell of burning rolled over them from the choir, where the charred stalls were still outlined with a few glowing embers of the heat that had devoured them. But the flagged surface of the presbytery floor let them walk its stones unscorched, and the altar with its angelic choir stood immaculate and beautiful. Beneath it the yawning rectangle of darkness drew their eyes. In wonder and dread they approached, and fearfully they looked into the open grave.

In the bottom of the well of stone Benedetta lay upon velvet, her long hair like quenched fire about her head, a gold-embroidered altar-cloth over her like a coverlet. Her hands were thin and tranquil upon the bright, coiling flowers, her face was a shape of ivory skin drawn taut over the pure pattern of its gallant bones. Someone had carefully closed and weighted the great arched eyelids and composed with love and reverence the emaciated body. Her they knew, every man among them; they knew her even though she was no more than the half of the woman they had known.

But the golden shape that lay beside her, that had been lifted and moved to make room for her, who knew that? Man or woman? So slight, no taller than she, and she had not been tall. So long dead, for on the cloth of gold was traced faintly the fragile shape of the bones within. Buried with so much honour, like a prince or a cardinal, but with something humble and strange at his feet—a mason's mallet, a chisel, a fine punch, the common tools of the craft.

And black athwart their brightness, sudden and terrible as a descending angel, a long, dark shape plunged head-down between the two, his brow pressed into the crook of a golden arm, his wide sleeves spread like wings over the honoured sleepers. Long arms embraced them, binding all three together. On the gaunt fingers that folded them even in death with such an intensity of passion, the rings hung slack, dangling between swollen joints. Too weak to climb out of the grave when his work was done, thus he had fallen and thus he had died. The hands still agonised, clasping those two whom he had buried; but against the cleft heart in the golden shroud the old, proud head rested as gently as in sleep.

Not fire nor frost nor summer nor winter would ever again have any power to trouble those three, or set them at enmity.

The boy stood motionless and mute at the foot of the grave, his lashes low on his cheeks, staring in wonder and dread at the measure of his loss and the magnitude of his gain. He was still for so long that they began to fear for him, but no one ventured to touch him. Under the grime of dust and sweat and tears his pallor was extreme, but so was the calm that had come upon him. When he looked up it was to meet the prince's grave, considerate eyes, bent upon him from a courteous distance.

"You have close kin here," said Llewelyn gently. "Closer to you than to any."

"Yes," said Harry in a whisper. Was he speaking of one only, or of two of them? Or of all? For he had always been quick to follow the wanderings of his children's hearts, even when they themselves were lost.

"It is for you to order all things here as you would have them. We will so dispose as you see fit."

The young head came up quickly then to devour the prince's face in a hungry green stare. He opened his lips to answer, and fell trembling.

"My lord, with respect—there's one in Castell Coch has a better right. I would have her see," he said, low-voiced, "what we have seen."

"That's well thought of, and like a dutiful son. Adam," said Llewelyn, "ride to Castell Coch and ask Mistress Gilleis if she will come to us here. Tell her there's a matter on which we wait to hear her pleasure. Say that by the grace of God we have found Master Harry's body.''

Gilleis came before the light was gone, pale and silent by Adam's side.

The chaos of the battle yet lingered below Parfois, the dead lay where they had fallen; but the prince was in William Isambard's lavish apartments by then, and William was in the chapel, on a trestle before the altar, washed and cleansed of the blood Harry had let him, with the death-pennies on his eyes. Gilleis passed by the battered tower of the lower guard without a glance, and picked her way through the litter of cast and broken harness and cast and broken bodies on the ramp. She saw nothing of all this. Her eyes looked inward, looked back. In life or in death, Harry's face had never been so clear to her as it was now. The old hates, the old loves rose in her bitterly like contending tides.

On the plateau Llewelyn was waiting, and young Harry came to her stirrup to lift her down. The sea-green eyes, the grave embrace went to her heart like wounds; since he had got that fierce, earnest, man's face on him there was no question whose son he was, body and spirit. He kissed her hand, and then her cheek, and brought her on his arm into the shell of the church of Parfois; and Adam fell back and let them go first and alone.

At the grave-side even Harry disengaged himself and stood apart from her. She looked into the stone pit, and drew breath deeply once as though she checked what might have been a cry; and then for a long time she was silent and still and pale, her eyes lowered to the two bright shapes, and the spread arms that covered them like a cross.

She saw the torchlight quiver upon the golden shroud, as though the dear bones it wrapped stirred for a moment to the recollection of life, and would have risen to her. She saw the lean dark arm embracing his body, and the hand, the same hand that had swathed him in his royal winding-sheet, seemed to close its wasted fingers more jealously and tenderly upon his arm. All the agony, all the hate and the loving, the wrongs and the revenges, came down softly into this little space at the end.

She looked up at last, and across the open grave she saw her son's face, pale with passion, watching her. A long stride nearer the fullness of his inheritance than yesterday, and wanting something of her, and willing himself not to let his longing show in his eyes, for fear she should give for his sake what for her own she would have denied. Oh, Harry, she thought, show me what I am to do! I'm torn so many ways. But he would not. This she must resolve alone.

Nevertheless, the possessive pain that clamoured behind her still face fell shamed to silence as she gazed at him. The true impress, the single legacy, and hers, to give if not to keep. She had but to give him freely, and she could not lose or want for him. And was she, then, so poor that she could not give a little sleeping-space in Harry's ground to these who had good need of rest?

Must there still be banishment, and dividing, and ravishing of graves?

"Cover them over!" said Gilleis, and saw the warm flush of joy quicken in Harry's cheek, and the wild gratitude of love in his eyes. "Cover them over. Let them rest."

At the last moment, when the men of the rear-guard were stamping their chilled feet in the snow at the head of the ramp, and David was calling impatiently back to him from the bridge, he took his foot from the stirrup again and turned back to the tracing-house.

Half the ground of the outer ward was crazed with cracks now, and daily the small, unregarded crumbs of sandstone slid away softly into the ravine. It was high time to be gone. Another yard of the curtain wall had slithered away in the night; come the spring, Parfois would be given over to the crows.

High time to leave, and they were the last to go. The women had set off on their journey back to Aber on the fourth day of Christmas, with Adam to bear them company on the way, and the baggage trains of booty from Parfois trailing after them half a mile along the snow. Harry had ridden as far as the ford with them, to see them safe across, and kissed Aelis before them all at parting, to seal his rights in her. To tell the truth, he stood in some jealous awe of her now, she had grown so dangerously aware of her womanhood since she put up her hair beneath a wimple and took to wearing his mother's gowns. They were close and confident, those two, they tended to catch each other's eye and smile over him when they thought he was not attending—or, more daunting by far, when they knew very well he was. He would have to mind his interests with them, or they would compound together to have the whip hand of him.

Two days after the departure of the princess and her retinue, the disarmed garrison had marched out of Parfois, with what they stood in, their personal goods, and a sparing allowance of stores. The best of their horses and hawks and hounds, and all their military gear, were forfeit to the conquerors, but they were happy enough to be allowed to take their lives and their freedom in their hands, and pledge their word to stand no more in arms against Llewelyn. Some had gone to Fleace, with courteous letters from the prince of Aberffraw to Humphrey Paunton, acquainting him with the manner of the death and burial of his lord, so that in due course the news might be laid in proper form before King Henry. Some had set out for Erington, on the border of Herefordshire. Isambard's wide and scattered honour fell now to his elder son Gilles, in Normandy, if the king saw fit to grant his title, but after the trouble Richard Marshall had cost him he would be chary of admitting another Norman-bred magnate and vassal of the king of France to such a position of power in England. Let them fight it out how they would, Ralf Isambard slept no less soundly.

And yet a great line was passing here, and he, Harry Talvace, had lopped the last branch from that formidable tree. The pomp of the world seemed empty and ephemeral enough in depopulated Parfois after the garrison was gone.

And after the vanquished, the victors. They left on the eve of the New Year, the prince and all his captains, hot towards Breidden in arms, leaving David to bring the rear-guard after. The whole border lay open to them for plunder, for on the day after Christmas the earl marshal had beaten John of Monmouth out and out in a pitched battle, close to the town from which he took his name, and there was no royal army active in the field now to stand between the king's enemies and the king's quaking subjects along the march.

"Leave the lad Herefordshire," Llewelyn had said largely when the dispatches reached him, "he's earned it. We'll go north and east and have the heart out of Shropshire. Rising nineteen years since Benedetta came galloping after me to the gates of Shrewsbury, Harry, and brought me you for my pains. I have a fancy to knock at their doors again, even if it cost me another such penance."

And he had ridden blithely but purposefully to his reiving; and God help the villagers under the Breidden, and the uneasy burghers of Shrewsbury, for war was a killing thing. It had killed Parfois. Even if Gilles came, even if he essayed to rebuild this shattered fortress, the venture could not prosper. The rock was riven and the heart was still. The man was dead who had been the spirit of Parfois, dead and buried beneath the altar of his own church with his love and his love's love, with his dark deeds and his bright; that book let God decipher, none other had the right. His arch-enemy had had masses said over him, and his most irreconcilable prisoner had prayed passionately peace to his soul.

And now they were going, the last companies, David's clansmen eager and fierce after their prey, David himself not loath, for he had a border to consolidate, and to force acknowledgement of it with terror now was to hold it the more firmly hereafter. The last hoof-beats had left the hollow-ringing field of the bridge, and hushed in the snow of the plateau. Only Harry Talvace still lingered, the last to leave the shaken ground of his four-year captivity.

The silence fell about him like a muffling cloak, curtaining him from the world. The early, angry light of a January morning, shot with slanting red gleams of sun from beneath hanging cloud, edged the merlons of the wall with scarlet. The door of the Warden's Tower, the ports of armoury and mews and stables, stood open upon emptiness. No one moving, no voice where there had been so many voices, not even a dog left to bring life back to mind; only he, Harry Talvace, crossing the seamed and rotting ground softly, with breath hushed in awe of the silence, pushing open the dragging door of the tracing-house across a cracked, uneven floor, standing on the threshold of the forsaken room and staring round him upon the long tracing-tables where Master Harry had pieced out his ambitious plans, and the bench where he had marshalled punches and chisels to hand and sketched out his ideas in stone. The fruit of his labour they had defaced with fire, but they could not destroy it.

Harry stood and gazed, and the room was full of echoes, quick and piercing in his heart: "Not his match! Have you not the heart in you to be anything but best? How many are his match?" And how significantly now, how poignantly: "The dispensations of God are always just. We get the sons we deserve." Why had he so often failed to hear or understand the things that were said to him?

Recollection drew for him the outline of the erect and fleshless shoulders, the poised head, the shadowed, oblique smile against the window, and quickened the voice again to the old tormenting sweetness. Here he had first been offered his father's tools, and the fragmentary stones he had left behind him at his untimely death. Here he had been schooled hard to work ungoaded under provocation, and learned even that lesson at last. And if the work he had done could not match, would never match, his father's achievement, had he not the heart in him to be anything but best? They should see that he had, that he knew how to serve humbly and faithfully where he deserved.

Looking back now in amazement at those four years he could not feel that he had been unhappy; and that was strange enough, after all his agonizing. But stranger far it was to look calmly upon the long fretting and scheming and struggling after liberty, and be unable now to recapture the sense of having been a prisoner.

He crossed the room silently to the bench he had been allowed to use as his own; and there in the corner, thrust back against the wall, was the sketch Master Harry had made in stone for the last head he ever set in the triforium of the church of Parfois. Harry had taken it to be a final self-portrait: But Isambard had known better: "This is no signature at the end, but a prophecy at the beginning. Do you not know yourself?"

He had not known himself, but he had believed; then, even then, with his will or against his will, he had trusted Isambard to know truth and tell him truth. He did not know himself even now, the head still daunted, bewildered, excited him with its promise and its clarity; but still he believed. There was yet some way to go, but he had set his feet on the road to that identity, and he would reach it all in good time.

Strangely wonderful he had thought himself, fondling the planes of that young head, strangely wonderful, and a terrible responsibility. He closed his hands upon it again, and the same passionate pride and humility gathered molten about his heart.

He took the large cloth in which Master Edmund had been wont to roll his parchments, and wrapped the head in it hastily, sure that David would be losing patience by now and sending someone back for him. The bundle was small but heavy; they'd think him mad for loading Barbarossa with twenty extra pounds, when they had some hard riding to do. No matter, he would not leave it here.

He cast one last quick glance about the room, knowing he might never see it again, and then he went out with his precious prize under his arm, and drew the door to after him; and there was Owen just lighting down beside Barbarossa, and tossing the reins on his horse's neck.

"The devil, Harry, what ails you to be mooning here still? What were you at? David's off without us."

"We'll overtake him," said Harry, stowing his unwieldy bundle hastily away in the saddle-bag, where it hung heavily and clumsily, and Barbarossa shifted indignantly at the heft of it. "I just thought of something I'd liefer not leave here."

"Stir then, man, and let's be after them. We'll be well out of here," said Owen, eyes roving the derelict stones that sagged towards the ravine. "Come the thaw, half this headland will crumble away. I'd sooner not be too close to Parfois then."

Harry mounted and spurred for the narrow timbers of the bridge, delivered now of his need to look back. The past was resolved, the future he had swinging at his saddle-bow. As soon as they were off the bridge and trotting across the plateau towards the trees Owen drew alongside, and leaned to prod curiously at the bundle.

"What is it you've got there?" He clapped a hand to the bag and exclaimed at the weight, punched it and cursed tenderly over his bruised fist. "Dear heaven, what have you loaded the poor beast with? Stone? What can you want with such a lump? There's stone everywhere, must you carry it with you on the march?"

"It's a design of my father's," said Harry placatingly, giving the husk and keeping the heart of his own counsel. "I thought some day I might manage to copy it."

Epilogue

Parfois: *July* 1234

*A*fter six months he rode that way again.

They were retracing their steps from the great meeting at Myddle, from the signing of the triumphant peace that had crowned Llewelyn's achievement and set the seal on his life-work. Richard Marshall's war was lost and won, and his brief, splendid and tempestuous life, strange for a man who had desired only order and justice, had ended in the hour of his victory. A greater prelate than Winchester, and a better, had put Winchester from power; a sounder order than even the efficient des Rivaulx could impose had dispensed with des Rivaulx's expert services. England, by and large, had its dour and sensible will; and Wales had the confirmation of all its conquests, peace within its borders, respect without. No wonder David took his retinue home to Aber in high spirits.

They rode by way of Knockin. From Parfois to the very walls of Shrewsbury they had burned and killed and plundered, and nowhere with greater slaughter than here, about the ditches of this battered castle. That had happened in January; and now in July half the fields lay untilled for want of men to do the work, and the women laboured desolately into the dark to raise a little food for their children.

Meeting the eyes of the widows of Knockin, Harry was not proud of himself. Well, he had learned hard, perhaps, but he had learned thoroughly; he knew now what it was in him to do.

A whole chapter of a chronicle had been written in the march since that January campaign. So well had it run, so securely had they established themselves as masters of the border, that Earl Richard had felt his position in Wales to be safe, and taken himself off to Ireland, to retrieve the castles the king's men had purloined from him in Leinster. He had left Hubert de Burgh with Basset and Siward in command at Striguil, and sailed for Leinster early in February. And that same month Edmund of Abingdon, treasurer of Salisbury, had received the royal confirmation of his election to the vacant archbishopric of Canterbury, and attended the great council.

What did Henry think now of his new saint? Had he given him his voice willingly, or sullenly and grudgingly for want of the courage to resist? For Edmund Rich had begun his primacy, before ever he was installed, by leading the bishops in a demand for the dismissal of Henry's hated ministers and a return to the rule of law and charter. Henry had wriggled and quibbled and pleaded for time; but they had carried their point in principle, and sent the bishops of Lichfield and Rochester to the border at once, to sound out Llewelyn with a view to conciliation and peace. They had found no difficulty there: he was willing and ready, since it seemed the chief point at issue was as good as conceded. After the necessary to-ing and fro-ing over terms they had agreed upon a truce at the end of March, and arranged to meet and effect a permanent settlement on the second of May.

Armed with such a tactical success, fortified by this manifest forbearance and good will on the part of a prince who might very well have exploited his advantage by holding out for steeper terms, Archbishop Edmund had come to the April council with all the bishops of the province of Canterbury solidly at his back, but for the lone wolf Winchester whom they were bent on pulling down. Henry could no longer protect his favourites without risking injury to himself, and he never went so far or so fast that he could not stop short of that. Rumour said he had taken Winchester and des Rivaulx and Segrave into monastic retirement with him for a while after the February council, sure sign, by token of his usage of de Burgh, that they could look for nothing good from him once it became advisable in his own interest to abandon them. However that might be, he had announced their dismissal when the bishops pressed him, and promised reform, a return to the constitution, all that was demanded of him. Not knowing then, for no one in England yet knew, that his enemy was already on his death-bed.

For Earl Richard had allowed himself to be persuaded to a meeting with the king's men on the meads of Kildare on the first day of April, and somehow, no one knew how or by what hand, he had been set upon with swords and fatally wounded. Treachery, some said, and involving the highest. Others put it down to a flare of temper when the argument ran high, for Richard would have his castles back, and there were those who had no mind to let go what they had taken. However it was, Richard Marshall was carried from the Curragh to a bed he never left again, and after two weeks he was dead. Dead with victory and reform and honour in his grasp, that fine, high-minded man who had never willed to make war on his king.

The news had come like a thunderclap in England, shaking men to the hearts, and not least King Henry himself. Had he truly lent his countenance secretly to the earl's murder? Or had des Roches and his close companions taken the act upon themselves, and brought the suspicion of complicity unjustly upon the king? Whatever the truth of it, he had made frantic haste to cover and deliver himself by turning like a tiger upon his ministers. Until then it had seemed that they might be allowed to withdraw without undue disgrace, but now for a time they tasted what they had visited upon de Burgh, hunted from place to place, denounced and proscribed, until the bishops who had brought about their downfall stood between them and their sovereign frantic with his own righteousness, and lent them a hand to rise. Commissions sat to hear complaints against them, investigators searched out every detail of their conduct in office, and checked every penny they had handled. De Burgh had his revenge.

Howbeit, the earl marshal was dead. And Llewelyn, when he heard the news, had declined to proceed with the May meeting. He was gone who should have been the negotiator for the English confederacy; until all his adherents should receive satisfactory terms of peace Llewelyn would accept none. And the protection he ex-

tended to them in this act had been effective enough to hasten a
general conciliation. May had seen Gilbert, the new earl marshal,
granted safe-conducts for himself and his brothers, for de Burgh and
Basset and Siward and all the other confederates, to come to the
council at Gloucester under the archbishop's protection and seek the
king's grace. Pardoned, their outlawry declared illegal, their lands
restored, themselves admitted again to favour, some even to office,
they had good cause to be thankful for so formidable and faithful
an ally as the prince of Aberffraw.

"He would have laughed himself sore," said Harry suddenly,
concluding aloud the sequence of thought he had been following in
silence, "could he have seen how it all ended."

"He?" said David absently, and flashed an inquiring glance at his
young foster-brother, only to snatch it back again in haste as he
recollected who "he" must be. "What, with de Burgh admitted to
the council again, and Winchester and des Rivaulx down where they
kicked de Burgh? And the prince my father riding to the rescue of
his oldest enemy, and keeping his vow to take and destroy his Parfois
none the less—yes, a man might find a kind of laughter there, I
suppose, if he had the heart. And I always heard he was de Burgh's
man."

"He had the heart," said Harry roundly. "And he was his own
man, and no other's."

"But the cream of the joke," said Owen, "is that if this French
Isambard you speak of does come to claim his English honour,
Parfois is one castle he must do without. By the terms of the
agreement he can't rebuild."

And that was true: Parfois had its death-wound from them. The
agreement Llewelyn had signed at Myddle, with the archbishop
himself in attendance, had as its ground adherence to the state of
things at the outbreak of Earl Richard's war. Every party kept what
he had in his possession then, however recently conquered; Builth
and Cardigan remained in the hold of the princes of Gwynedd, and
that was no mean gain. But no new castles were to be built, no
ruined ones restored. Good-bye, Parfois! And most appropriate,
perhaps, that it should not outlive Ralf Isambard.

For two years only that truce was sealed; but by consent it could
be renewed year by year thereafter; and who would venture to try

and take Builth or Cardigan from between the paws of the lion now? Llewelyn had shown England once for all who was master along the march as long as he lived, and done all man could to ensure that David should be regarded with the same awe and respect thereafter. Under the castle of Myddle, among the bright pavilions spread on the summer meads, they had seen the apotheosis of Gwynedd, and surely, surely, the true conception of a princedom of Wales. It remained only to bring it safely to birth, and that was for the statesmen, not the soldiers.

"My lord—" said Harry, clearing his throat gruffly upon the declaration he had been nursing ever since they left Myddle; and flushed and hesitated at the stilted sound of this address, when there was no one within earshot but the three of them.

"My lord!" David mocked him gaily and gently. He was happy in the summer and the fair weather, and their triumphant achievement, and even in his ceremonial finery, and the pleasure of riding light, without the cumbrous casings of steel. He was in no mood to be grave, but with all his heart he could be kind.

"I've had it on my mind," said Harry, his solemnity unshaken, "to speak to you about my future, now that we have peace and, God willing, hope to have it for years to come. Your inheritance is secure now. If ever you should need to call me to you again, you know I'll come with all my heart. But while you're not in need, I ask you to let me from your side to my own craft."

He could not say outright the thing that most troubled him, the dismay he felt at the price even of this victory, the burned villages, the scattered corpses, the slaughtered cattle, the fields unploughed that should have been golden, the earth desolate that should have been yielding generously. Born English and raised Welsh, his heart and mind fought on both sides. How could he shed Welsh blood or English, and not feel himself bleed? But there was more to it even than that. The denial of life, the frustration of fruitfulness, affronted the deepest instinct in him. He could not be a breaker, it was against his bent.

"Your own craft?" said David, astonished and laughing. "The times I've heard Adam trying to drive you to your tools, when you were a lad in Aber, and you slipping away the minute his back was turned to run to the tilting. And as apt as you were at it, too! What's come to you suddenly?"

"It's not so sudden. That was long ago, and I've been working with Isambard's master-mason in Parfois since then. And I've seen my father's work. That's enough to set a man off after him. I could not ask to leave you while this war was on our hands. But I've seen now what I want. A career in arms is very well," said Harry sturdily, "but I can't find my satisfaction this way. I'm a stonemason, like my father before me, and that's what I mean to be. If you'll give me your good word?"

"My good word you have, whatever you choose to do, Hal, surely you know it. And Adam will be happy to have you broken to harness at last. And yet it's a pity," said David regretfully. "You quit yourself so well at Parfois. You should have heard how the prince commended you when you were not by. Have you told him what you intend?"

"Yes, my lord, before we rode. He said I must broach it to you. And he said I should do whatever I must for my heart's content, and so long as I did it with my might I had his blessing. But you're my prince and my brother, and I'd fain have yours, too."

"Could I refuse it to you?" said David heartily. "You do as your heart needs, and never fret. Good swordsmanship's never wasted, even on a stonemason."

"Then hear me one more request." He had paled a little with the intensity of his desire. "May I ride south, where the roads meet, and go down to Parfois? I'll not linger, I promise you. I want only to see it this once more. Before you reach Oswestry I'll be with you again."

Owen opened his lips to offer to go with him, and closed them again with the offer still unmade. He knew when Harry willed to be alone. So at the crossroads at Knockin they parted, Harry riding south towards Breidden, and his brothers north towards Oswestry, with their retinue behind them. The mason rode unattended, and that was fitting, too. Adam had said long ago that it was time he faced his own estate.

This was the countryside they had torn to pieces on their way to Shrewsbury, and the wreckage still stood stark to challenge him

wherever he turned his eyes. In the villages they had crept back to
the ruin of their homes, those who survived, they had even built
themselves brush hovels to tide them through the kinder summer,
and were building hard at better shelters against the winter to come.
So much destruction, so much suffering, so much waste, all affronts
to the passion of affirmation he felt within him, the urge he had
towards life, and joy, and creation, and fulfilment. Let there be no
more such campaigns! Let them keep these houses, and reclaim these
wasted fields! Let them get new sons, and win the derelict earth to
bear again! The doggedness with which they had taken up the
threads of living was itself a reassurance. They were men, they could
not be downed so easily.

He crossed the river at Buttington, a summer river now green
with weed, white with floating crowfoot, smiling and drowsy. He
came along the riverside path by the mill, he passed the ruined assart,
the cords of his memory knotting into a momentary congestion of
pain. He rode beneath the cliff of Parfois, and there on a sudden the
path was stopped. Rock and masonry together blocked his way. He
took to the woods close beside the water, and made his way laboriously round the obstacle, the lie of the land still hiding the heights
from him. Only when he reached the green slopes beneath the path
that climbed to the ramp could he look up for the crenellated crests
of wall and tower against the sky, and see the light filtering through
the ravine that separated castle from church.

His heart turned and cried in him, torn between grief and exaltation, so sudden and violent was the vision he had of the passing of
the world's power and glory. The mighty of the march were fallen
indeed. The ravine showed no lance of light transfixing its shadowy
spaces; the sudden thaws and rotting snows of February had crumbled away the misused rock from under the wall until the shattered
ground could no longer hold up the vast weight it bore, and yard by
yard, stone by stone, the curtain wall had cracked and slid and heeled
away, silting down into the ravine to fill up the shallower place
beneath the bridge, and gradually spreading to shed fringes of rubble
and rock from either end down the cliffs below. The bridge had slid
with the rest, but only to settle harmlessly, uselessly, a few feet
below its old level. A man could walk up the ramp now and cross
into Parfois without need of bridges. Into what was left of Parfois!

And the destruction could not end there, for between the subsiding bulk above and the overburdened foundations below the rock would have no rest. The balance and tension that held up all had been disrupted, and the ruin they had begun could not be halted. Time and weather would fret stone from stone, seeds would settle among the lurching staircases and cracking floors, and grow to saplings, bursting the walls apart. Young oaks would grow and root in Isambard's great chamber, and ravens nest in the jagged bones of the King's Tower. Fifty years, and Parfois would be no more than a name clinging to a desolation, a levelled place where once there had been a great rock and a great house.

The Warden's Tower was down, and had flung its huge head clean across the gully in dying, and buried its stone forehead deep in the grassy level of the plateau. The tracing-house was down, with all that had clung close to this southern expanse of the curtain wall. The constant shocks had even shaken away the edges of the plateau, there were torn-out trees lying among the rubble below. For the thick summer leafage on those that remained he could not see even the tower of the church from where he stood. In dread and awe, with the silence and the desolation closing cold about his heart, he turned Barbarossa and began to mount the path.

At the sharp bend where the ramp began he saw, and for a moment could not persuade his doubting brain that he had really seen, the cart-tracks driven deep into the soft grass of summer. Why should there be traffic of carts here now, with no hungry household to feed and supply? Someone cutting and carrying away wood? He saw no great sign of timber's having been carried; there were usually axe-chips or dust to be found where the reivers had been. Brushings for firing? In the middle of summer? No one could be so forward and provident in these bereaved villages, where every surviving man's labour was claimed over and over for the mere necessities of the day. Yet the ruts in the bruised grass climbed with him. They were not new, they had worn through the turf in places and bared the soil and the stone. Carts heavily laden; and he guessed now with what merchandise. It was not wind and weather and frost and thaw only that had helped to bring down the walls of Parfois.

The solitary tower of the lower guard, battered to the ground during the siege, lay in a litter of rubble and mortar in the grass grown tall and seeding whitely beside the path. Very slight, those few scattered piles of stone, to be the remains of such a massive strongpoint. The outline of the new tower was lost in the growth of brambles and vetches. The worked stone of the barricades, dressed for building, had vanished clean.

He came to the crest of the ramp, where the trees fell away, and halted with breath caught hard in his throat to stop a cry. The Warden's Tower had flung its hard skull far in dying. The gutted tower of the church had received that impact at its roots, and fallen westward upon the vault of the nave, crushing it. The shaft of gold, the stem of the holy tree, was broken. All that tapering, soaring subtlety of beauty, fluted with quivering tensions of light and shadow, withdrawing stage by stage in charmed proportion and drawing the eyes and the heart after it—all lost, all defaced for ever, past recovery now. The great vault fallen with the tower, the west window, with its harp-strings of deep moulding in which the light played such threnodies, standing stark over a chaos of shattered stone.

He dropped from the saddle in frantic haste, as though hands dreamed for a moment that rescue was possible. He clambered through the beautiful ecstatic arches of the nave, touching and fondling and near to weeping, but that the dismay that opened within his heart was like a well of darkness, too deep and awful for tears. He flung himself on his knees at the foot of Master Harry's grave, above which the vault of the presbytery still soared undamaged, and the nine several images of Owen in childhood still inclined their seraphic heads over their psalters and instruments, and sang and played to the glory of God.

But to what end? To what end, if this was all? The prayer he had begun died in his throat, sticking fast to choking.

It takes, then, so short a time for castles and churches to fall to ruin, once men have withdrawn from them. How much of his father's master-work had the carts carried away already? If his eyes had been open he would have seen the manifest traces. Castle and church together they were helping to bring down, and steadily pilfering stone from both. Every village within ten miles must be privy to the quiet dismemberment. Everything they had had they had lost in the winter campaign, burned and razed and slaughtered; and here for the carting was a vast supply of ready-cut stone to their hands, to build new homes, sheep-folds, yards, byres, barns, all that they needed. When they had used what lay on the ground, they would bring down the rest after it. With no Isambard in Parfois, who was to restrain them? It would take time to complete the undoing, but given ten years, or twenty, they would have erased all. All dissipated, all lost, all his father's work, passed clean out of mind as though it had never been. Is creation no more durable than destruction, after all? Is this the end, not only of the breakers, but of the makers, too? Then to what end is any effort or any passion?

He came back to Barbarossa with a set and stony face, bleak as winter in the rich, soft sunlight. He mounted and turned from the church of Parfois with averted face, and rode down the ramp without looking back. Did it alter the value of the work, that men destroyed it? Was it less valid because it was unrecognised and misused? But was there *nothing* remaining? Not one echo after such music?

He had no wish to return by the same way, to see again the desolation above him against the sky. He turned instead towards Leighton, to cross the river by the ford at Pool, and take the road north for Oswestry after his brothers.

Now that he was ready to see them, his eyes began to pick out everywhere the stolen bones of Parfois. Threading the village, he saw them built, massy and incongruous, into the rising walls of new cottages. Master Harry's stone from the quarry in Bryn was unmistakable with the sun on it, waking the soft gold that slept within the clear, warm grey. Here and there he caught that gleam, and the jealous ache in his heart gnawed afresh at every reminder; until at the end of the village he was suddenly brought up short by a small shock of wonder, and stood at gaze, his resolute despair for the first time a little shaken.

The smith of Leighton had crowned the yard-posts of his toft with two small capitals; the crudely-built but not ill-proportioned pillars burst at the top into twin clusters of radiant, living leaves, the same that had held up the vault of Isambard's chantry chapel. And was it after all so absolute a violation? If he had not seen in them something that took him by the heart, would he have carted them all this way and gone to the labour to set them up there, where they had no function but to delight?

He rode on, slowly and thoughtfully, questioning his own heart no less than their actions. The byre-wall of the farm beyond was crested with the moulded stones of the string-courses from the tower; and there at the gate they had set up a segment of a clustered pillar to seal the end of the wall. Wasted? Desecrated? Lost? What Parfois had lost someone humbler had found.

Harry's heart revived, mistrustfully yet, and against his will; his love was sore in him, and he grudged them their scattered morsels of what should have been whole and all men's, and was hot against them for the disintegration with which, however unwittingly and under whatever pressure, they had leagued themselves. The poor ravished stones shone in the sun, golden as fallen ears of grain. He came down towards the river bank still at odds with his own doubt, though the youth in him ached with its willingness to be comforted.

The beds of osiers, just beginning to redden, flushed along the edge of the river below the ford. There was a tumble-down hut there where a weaver plied his craft; white, peeled wands lay piled to hand in the grass, and the frame of a coracle was pegged down to the ground beside them, half the light shell of basketry already filled in. Through the doorless opening half-turned away from the river he could see the stacked osiers within, and five or six long, narrow eel-grigs shining with newness; but the sound that pricked his ears came strangely from such a workshop.

Busy and absorbed and content, the steady tap-tapping of metal and stone. What need had they of hammers in an osier-weaver's hut? They prided themselves on securing whatever must be secured with withies. For pure curiosity, and because that diligent pecking caught so intimately at his own tender memory, Harry lighted down from Barbarossa's back, and slipped soundlessly into the hut.

A lean, wild boy, not more than eleven or twelve years old, was bending engrossed over something he had propped upon a rough wooden block in the light from the vacant window. His shock-head was stooped over it lovingly; for the neglected coracle he cared not at all.

When Harry's foot stirred the osiers the boy gave a whimper of fright, and span round with an arm thrown up to protect his head. The hand had a flat, heavy pebble in it; its fellow grasped a long iron nail.

"Easy, easy!–" said Harry mildly. "I'm neither the devil nor your master, I mean you no harm."

A pinched brown face peered up at him distrustfully from under the fell of dark hair. The child was used to blows, and expected them from every quarter, but his sharp eyes had more than fear in them, a desperate and devoted bravery. He kept his wiry little body between Harry and whatever it was he cherished there in his private place; and he kept his hold on the strange objects which were clearly not meant to serve him as weapons.

"What have you there?" said Harry, roused and curious.

"It's mine." The boy spread his arms defensively, a spark kindling in his dark eyes. "I brought it here myself. It's not stealing. If they can take them, why shouldn't I?"

Harry put down a hand and moved him gently aside by the shoulder; and at the touch a brighter boldness eased the boy's face, and he stood calmly, no longer trying to hide his treasure. Those he had need to fight shy of had another way of handling him. He resented being watched and interrupted, but he had nothing to fear, and if he made no show of concern the interloper would go away the sooner.

A block of Master Harry's yellow stone—with those puny arms, how had the child ever conveyed it here?—stood upon the uneven stump of a tree. The others had spent their fondness on carved stones, this child on one yet to be carved. Stone and nail were for mallet and punch. Who had even taught him the manner of tool he needed, or how to set about the shaping of such an intractable material? The small, grimy hands made the best of their clumsy instruments, held them with conviction and passion. And propped on the stacked osiers beneath which, most likely, he hid all these things from his elders and natural enemies, was a broken fragment of one of the corbels from the south aisle, a curving branch, a countryman's sly head, the muzzle of a braced hound pointing game.

He had begun by copying it, crudely but vividly; and then on the tilt of the poacher's cautious face the sculptor's ambitious hand had itched, his imagination had taken fire. The man who had crouched still burst out of the bushes, the hound leaped. Botched, clumsy but alive, they broke cover to course the quarry, and there was glee in them, and devilment, even though they had the scrawled drawing of a child. With a stone and a nail, dear heaven! And no one belonging to him, likely, no one within a mile of him, who would not clout him for it and toss the rubbish into the river if they caught him at it. But he had found something he would not easily let go. His fierce face spoke for him, his charged eyes and purposeful hand. He had discovered a well of fire within himself, he would not let it be quenched.

"Who showed you," said Harry, "how to do this?"

"Nobody. I tried. I looked at that one, and tried."

"And had you seen such before?"

"Not like these! Have you been there? There are faces there! Alive, like my mother. I never saw such. I couldn't take them, but I found this in the grass under the wall, and hid it. Would you think there could be trees, and animals, and men in the stone?"

"There can be anything in the stone," said Harry. "All the creatures of God. Who knows it better than you? Two of them you've loosed there that never had life before."

"I wanted to make such things myself," said the boy. "I'll make more yet," he said, "and better," and set his dour young face like stone.

"If you want it enough, you'll make them. Creatures as alive as your mother, and churches like that great church." And, by God, thought Harry, drinking deeply of a well-spring of revelation and gratitude and joy, he well might, he has the passion in him, and he has a true eye and a daring hand. "God prosper the work to you," he said, and turned back into the sunshine with a lightening heart.

The child watched him mount and ride, burning eyes remotely gratified but still aloof and self-sufficient. Had Harry carried any tools about him, he would have given them to him gladly, but he was in his finery and had nothing to give, and indeed this single and possessed heart needed nothing from him, not even encouragement. Where he was going, there he would go, and nothing would halt him or turn him back. A torch lit from one spark of that communicable fire scattered now so widely, a green shoot from the fallen scarlet seed of Master Harry's blood and life and passion, the indestructible seed with which all this countryside was sown.

And he only the first fruits of the harvest.

Harry tightened his knees upon Barbarossa's glossy barrel, and